MAYHEM IN GREECE

In *Mayhem in Greece* Dennis Wheatley's readers will share in a new adventure of love and espionage set in modern Greece. Original as ever, Mr. Wheatley has produced a new type of hero in Robbie Grenn, a young man who, owing to an injury when young, has never even been to school. Espionage would hardly seem to be his métier, yet to prove that he is as good as other men Robbie takes up the challenge that lands him in peril of his life many times. Interwoven with his adventure is the story of his relationship with the lovely Stephanie, the first girl with whom the chronically shy young man has ever had more than a passing acquaintance. As this is a Wheatley book we need hardly add that the suspense is acute and the dénouement remarkable.

Mr. Wheatley, with his flair for blending the exciting and the informative, has embodied in his narrative some stories from Greek mythology told in an off-beat manner which presents the gods and heroes as human characters involved in tragedies and comedies as grim or humorously bawdy as any put upon the Restoration stage.

BY DENNIS WHEATLEY

NOVELS

The Launching of Roger Brook
The Shadow of Tyburn Tree
The Rising Storm
The Man Who Killed the King
The Dark Secret of Josephine
The Rape of Venice
The Sultan's Daughter

The Scarlet Impostor
Faked Passports
The Black Baroness
V for Vengeance
Come into My Parlour
Traitors' Gate

The Prisoner in the Mask
Vendetta in Spain
The Second Seal
Three Inquisitive People
The Forbidden Territory
The Devil Rides Out
The Golden Spaniard
Strange Conflict
Codeword—Golden Fleece

The Quest of Julian Day
The Sword of Fate
Bill for the Use of a Body

Black August
Contraband

To the Devil—a Daughter
The Satanist

The Eunuch of Stamboul
The Secret War
The Fabulous Valley
Sixty Days to Live
Such Power is Dangerous
Uncharted Seas
The Man Who Missed the War
The Haunting of Toby Jugg
Star of Ill-Omen
They Found Atlantis
The Island Where Time Stands Still
The Ka of Gifford Hillary
Curtain of Fear
Mayhem in Greece

They Used Dark Forces

SHORT STORIES

Mediterranean Nights
Gunmen, Gallants and Ghosts

HISTORICAL

Old Rowley
(*A Private Life of Charles II*)
Red Eagle
(*A Story of the Russian Revolution*)

AUTOBIOGRAPHICAL

Stranger than Fiction
(*War Papers for the Joint Planning Staff*)
Saturdays with Bricks

IN PREPARATION

Dangerous Inheritance

DENNIS WHEATLEY

Mayhem in Greece

ARROW BOOKS

ARROW BOOKS LTD
178–202 Great Portland Street, London, W.1

 AN IMPRINT OF THE HUTCHINSON GROUP

London Melbourne Sydney
Auckland Bombay Toronto
Johannesburg New York

First published by
Hutchinson & Co. (*Publishers*) Ltd. 1962
Arrow edition 1964
This edition 1965

*Made and printed in Great Britain
by The Anchor Press, Ltd.,
Tiptree, Essex*

For

HELEN

A long overdue 'thank you' for securing me my first review in the Sunday Times, *and for many years of friendship.*

And for my good friend,

JOHN

AUTHOR'S NOTE

This story could not be set in any country other
than Greece, and that the principal character should
be related to the British Ambassador there was
essential to it. In consequence, I had to invent
Sir Finsterhorn Grenn. I wish it to be clearly
understood that this character has no resemblance
to any British Ambassador to Greece, past or
present, or to any other member of Her Majesty's
Foreign Service, and is entirely fictitious. So, too, is
Mr. Havelka and all the other characters who, as
Czech or Greek officials, play a part in this story.

Contents

1	Portrait of a Hero (?)	11
2	The Budding Author	28
3	Unorthodox Behaviour	43
4	'When First we Practise to Deceive'	52
5	Hero Number One	66
6	The Amateur Cracksman	82
7	A Dreadful Half-hour	106
8	'Stop Thief! Stop Thief!'	121
9	Midnight Conference	131
10	Who Knows What is Round the Corner?	143
11	Enter the Lady	169
12	Making Hay while the Sun Shines	184
13	You Have Been Warned	202
14	Of Hades and a Double Bed	225
15	The Villa Dione	241
16	The Biter Bit	252
17	Of Troy and a Submarine	272
18	The Amateur Photographer	294
19	A Bolt from the Blue	313
20	No Holds Barred	334
21	Twelve Hours to Live	348

CONTENTS

22 Wanted for Murder 369

23 On the Run 387

24 The Persistent American 413

25 A Trap is Set 431

26 The Show-down 465

Epilogue 504

1

Portrait of a Hero (?)

HAD Robbie Grenn been a normal young man it is reasonable to assume that, instead of sitting in the sunshine outside a restaurant overlooking the blue waters of the Aegean, he would have been doing a job in an office or have become an officer in one of the fighting Services. Moreover, he would not have been able to understand a conversation in Czech he overheard there, which led to pain and grief for a number of people and sudden death for several others.

But Robbie was not quite normal. He was what is termed 'a late developer'; although it was the private opinion of his uncle, Sir Finsterhorn Grenn, the British Ambassador in Athens, with whom he had been living for the past year, that 'poor Robbie's brain will never develop sufficiently for him to be of much use in the world'.

The root of the trouble was that, at the age of six, Robbie and his parents had been victims of an air crash. Both his parents had been killed, and the head injuries he had sustained had at first caused his life to be despaired of. Being a strong, healthy child, he had pulled through, but the set-back had been so serious that he had had to learn to talk, and even walk, again.

His uncle felt very strongly that Robbie might still have caught up had it not been for the two women who took charge of him. They were his elderly, utterly devoted nurse, and his mother's sister, Aunt Emily, who had brought him up at her home in Cheltenham. For several years after the accident,

Nanny Fisher had not taken a single day off. She had waited on him hand and foot, refusing to allow him to do the simplest things for himself, from fear that the least strain might prove too much for him. Aunt Emily had, from time to time, urged that Robbie was now well enough to look after himself; but she was a much weaker character than Nanny Fisher, so her protests had been over-ruled.

It had been out of the question to send him to kindergarten, and even when he had entered his teens the two women shrank from sending him to school. He was a most lovable little boy, but mentally far behind his age, and his movements were still ill-co-ordinated; so they could not bear the thought of him becoming the butt of other children. First governesses and then tutors had been engaged to educate him privately but, apart from teaching him to read, write and do simple sums, they found great difficulty in instilling much knowledge into him. This was not altogether because his brain was slow, but because years of coddling by Nanny Fisher had ingrained in him a chronic laziness. He could not be made to concentrate upon his lessons.

On the other hand, he could concentrate perfectly well when it called for no effort on his own part. He loved being read to, particularly fairy stories and, later, romantic legends such as those about the Knights of the Round Table, the great French champion Bayard, and the mythical heroes of ancient Greece. He loved music also—although only the popular kind, for he had never been introduced to any other—but he would sit for hours playing his gramophone, and needed to hear a tune only once to be able to hum it.

It was from the latter gift that there arose the only accomplishment he possessed. One day, when he was buying records, he included among his purchases, owing to the fascination that chivalry had for him, one in French, because it was a selection from the *Lays of the Troubadours*. No doubt his ear for music explained the speed with which he picked up the phrases. Two days later, to Aunt Emily's astonishment, she came upon him singing the songs from memory, with an impeccable accent.

That night, on her knees beside her bed, she gave fervent thanks to God for having solved a problem that had long worried her in secret. Robbie was an only child, and had inherited from his father a quite considerable sum which, on being handed over by his trustees when he was twenty-one, would provide him with a very adequate income. But Aunt Emily was one of those spinster ladies for whom the spread of Socialist ideas held a constant nagging menace. As a kindly and charitable soul, she was glad to see poorer people benefit from the Welfare State. But it was she and her kind who were paying for it. The nationalisation of the railways had robbed her of an appreciable part of her own income, and such horrible bogies as Local Government Compulsory Purchase Orders, further Rent Restriction Acts and the possibility of a Capital Levy caused her sleepless nights at times.

Such matters for dread might not be just round the corner, but she felt there was good cause to fear that, sooner or later, another Socialist Government might well bring in measures which would deprive her poor, helpless Robbie of most of his money. However, a man who could speak several languages could always make a living. Next day she bought him a set of English-French phrase records, and persuaded him to start learning French. He took to it like a duck to water.

Robbie was then seventeen and he was delighted with his new achievement. More records were bought and he became so intrigued that he agreed to have language tutors. Within a year he could talk French and German fluently. But Aunt Emily was not content with that. She held the optimistic belief that before many years had passed the West and the East would settle their differences and the Iron Curtain be lifted. Then trade with the countries behind it would increase enormously. Few English people had even a smattering of their languages, so a man who could speak them well would be assured of a highly-paid job.

Being by no means a fool, Robbie willingly accepted his aunt's idea. He still stubbornly refused to study mathematics, grammar, geography and other subjects he found dull, but devoted several hours a day to learning languages, and later reading books in them. By the time he was twenty-one, he had mastered Polish, Czech and Hungarian, and was doing well in Spanish and Italian. Moreover, although his general education remained extremely sketchy, he had subconsciously absorbed, from the books he read, a considerable amount of knowledge about European countries, their literature, music and art.

Soon after he came of age Aunt Emily fell ill and, seven months later, to his terrible distress, died of cancer. His only close remaining relative was his father's brother, Sir Finsterhorn Grenn, who had just been appointed British Ambassador to Athens. For some weeks after his aunt's death Robbie had been completely broken up; so, on the assumption that he was still incapable of looking after himself, Sir Finsterhorn had, a shade reluctantly, mooted the idea that Robbie should accompany him and his wife to Greece.

Lady Grenn had also, at first, been far from enthusiastic about this idea, as she feared that to have a young man who was not quite normal as a permanent guest at the Embassy would prove a constant embarrassment. But Robbie had seized so eagerly on the tentative suggestion that they had felt compelled to make it a definite invitation and, after he had spent a few days in their company, Lady Grenn had found her fears groundless.

He was very shy and a little awkward in his movements, appearing even more so on account of his size; for the underdevelopment of his brain seemed to have been compensated for by physical growth. He was well over six feet tall, stronglimbed and enormously broad-shouldered. From under Aunt Emily's protective wing he had seen so little of the world that at first he found it difficult to talk to strangers, but once drawn out he could be interesting and infectiously enthusiastic about his own subjects. He had, too, one asset that more than compensated for his simple mind: he radiated honesty, kindness and willingness to do anything within his limited powers to help others. In consequence, Lady Grenn soon grew very fond of him, and he of her, although she could never, for him, take the place of his beloved Aunt Emily.

His year in Greece had greatly broadened his horizon, as well as adding yet another language to his repertoire. He had also become capable of going about on his own, buying his own clothes and doing many things that he had never attempted to do while in England. Although he had never been abroad before, on his arrival he had not felt like a stranger. So many of his hours had been spent reading and re-reading the Greek myths and legends that he felt that he had returned to a land that he already knew well. Indeed, with his highly romantic nature, sometimes he almost persuaded himself that he had caught a glimpse of one of Zeus's giant limbs among the clouds, or of a satyr darting behind an ancient olive tree in some woodland glade.

Only one thing marred his complete happiness: Sir Finster-horn's insistence that he should take up some form of work. Anxious to please his uncle, he had allowed himself to be initiated into various simple jobs about the Embassy, but in none of them had he given satisfaction. He had never been trained to follow a routine and found keeping set hours intolerable. Moreover, as he had no interest in these tasks, his mind wandered while doing them, so he proved more bother than he was worth. Since coming to Greece, he had taken to alternating his reading about mythical heroes with luridly-covered paper-backs of the gangster-sex variety. That he should quite often lie on a mattress in the garden reading such trash, or simply dreaming the hours away, intensely irritated the hard-working Ambassador, and caused him every few weeks to return to the charge. But Robbie could be neither coaxed nor bullied into sticking to anything for more than a few days and, as he had ample money of his own, there were no means of forcing him to do so.

Yet his uncle's periodic upbraidings greatly distressed him, and at length he had been inspired by an idea which he hoped would put a stop to them. To the astonishment of everyone present at the time, he had announced his intention of writing a book. It was to be about the gods, goddesses and heroes of ancient Greece. Regarding him as quite incapable of producing such a work, his hearers were, at first, completely non-plussed; but they refrained from saying that the subject had already been done to death. Then, rather than hurt his feelings, they hastily began to encourage him to undertake this project.

So there was Robbie, now twenty-three years of age—a big, burly young man with a slight stoop and a rather round face, the most outstanding feature of which was a pair of big brown eyes that looked as if, at any moment, they might light up with a kindly smile—sitting, on a fine morning in mid-March, at a table near the edge of the yacht harbour at Piraeus, the great port of Athens.

This harbour, known as Toyrcolimano, consisted of a small, nearly landlocked bay protected by tall cliffs. Upon one of them an ancient castle had been replaced by the Royal Greek Yacht Club, and down in the harbour a hundred or more yachts, ranging from eighteen-footers to millionaires' sea-going vessels, lay at anchor. Below the cliffs, in a semi-circle, were ranged half a dozen or more restaurants, and across the road each enjoyed a section of the wharf on which to set out tables shaded by colourful umbrellas.

Unlike the great commercial harbour that lay a mile away on the far side of the city, Toyrcolimano looked out on to the Gulf of Athens. To the south-west, through the forest of yacht masts, rose the misty outline of the island of Aegina, and the most easterly promontory of the Peloponnesus. To the south, the Gulf stretched away, so deep a blue that it recalled Homer's phrase, 'the wine dark sea'. In that direction, it was broken only by the grey bulk of an aircraft carrier and half a dozen warships attendant on her.

It was with the intention of going aboard the carrier that Robbie had that morning come by bus from Athens. The previous evening, as the Fleet was in for a few days, the Ambassador had given a cocktail party for its officers. As such official receptions were a regular feature of life at the Embassy, Robbie was no longer nervous at them. In fact, he had by then been trained by Lady Grenn to look out for guests who were standing alone, introduce himself and help to see that they enjoyed themselves. As no one of any importance ever took much notice of him, he had a fellow-feeling for others who looked ill at ease, and took pleasure in making them feel at home. On this occasion he had done the honours for a young lieufenant named MacLean and, before they parted, MacLean had invited him to lunch the following day in the wardroom of the carrier.

When he accepted, MacLean had simply said: 'That's fine. Then if you'll be at the jetty at half past twelve, I'll come off in a launch and pick you up; then I'll take you for a run round the Fleet before we go aboard for lunch.'

Robbie had assumed that MacLean meant the jetty at the Yacht Club end of Toyrcolimano Bay, as on previous visits he had seen naval officers landing there. He arrived there only five minutes late, but there was no sign of MacLean. Glad that he had not kept his new friend waiting, he sat down and dreamily watched the traffic plying back and forth from the warships. A few pinnaces put in at the jetty, and twenty minutes passed, but there was still no sign of MacLean. Seeing that it was now nearly one o'clock, he enquired of a petty officer for the lieutenant, to be told to his dismay that only senior officers were privileged to land at the Yacht Club jetty. Junior officers, ratings, liberty boats and stores were all landed or taken off at the main harbour on the far side of the headland.

To have got there and found the right steps in the huge port would have taken at least half an hour and by then, Robbie felt, MacLean would have decided that something had prevented his keeping the appointment, and have returned to the carrier. Very disappointed at having literally 'missed the boat', he made his way to one of the restaurants and ordered lunch for himself.

As is customary in all but the smarter restaurants in Greece, he went straight to the kitchen to see what was to be had. The restaurants at Toyrcolimano specialize in fish and have little else to offer, apart from cheese and fruit as a second course; but he was shown a fine array of mullet, lobsters, octopus and fresh sardines. Having selected a large lobster, he went out to a table on the wharf and, to while away the twenty minutes while his lunch was being cooked, ordered an *ouzo*.

As it was a day in mid-week, and the tourist season had not yet started, few of the tables were occupied; but the old men who earned a precarious living selling roast peanuts or the favourite Greek sweet, sticky nougat, were, as usual, meandering hopefully from table to table. From one of them he bought a bag of peanuts to munch with his drink, then he began casually to scan the people who were already lunching in his vicinity.

At the table just in front of him there were two men. One was in profile to him; he was dark-haired, tallish, wiry-looking, about thirty-five; had lean, sunken cheeks, a hard jaw and a hair-line moustache. The other, who had his back to Robbie, was older, fatter, broad-shouldered and bald, but for a fringe of brown hair round the sides and back of his head.

That bald head rang a vague bell in Robbie's mind, then he realized that the two men were talking in Czech. At that the penny dropped. Robbie had not actually met him, but the man had been pointed out to him at one of the many Embassy cocktail parties as the First Secretary at the Czechoslovak Legation.

No noise of traffic or street vendors calling their wares penetrated to the secluded bay beneath the cliffs. The silence was broken only by the gentle lapping of water against the sides of the yachts as they lay at their moorings, and the occasional clatter of a knife or fork; so the voices of the two men, although low, came quite clearly to Robbie. Had they been speaking Greek, he would probably have ignored them, and have lapsed into one of his frequent, happy day-dreams. But it was over a year now since he had practised his Czech, so he deliberately listened to their conversation, just to see how well he could follow it.

With considerable pleasure, he soon found that he could understand what they were saying without the least difficulty. They were talking about tobacco and oil. Neither was a subject in which he took any interest so, at the time, when it emerged that the Czech Government had just purchased the Greek tobacco crop and, as part of the deal, acquired rights to prospect for oil in Greece, that meant nothing to him.

In due course his lobster arrived. When he was half-way through it, the two men paid their bill and got up to go. As the elder, bald-headed man turned round, seeing him face to face confirmed Robbie's belief that he was the First Secretary of the Czechoslovak Legation. Neither of them gave him more than a bare glance as they passed his table, and as he went on with his lunch his mind turned to matters more interesting to him.

He began, not for the first time, to speculate on why

Aphrodite, the Venus of the Greeks, the loveliest of all the goddesses, should have chosen for a husband the lame, ill-featured, soot-begrimed Hephaestus, the blacksmith of the gods, who spent eternity labouring at a forge.

Since his middle teens, Robbie had suffered the pangs of love for a succession of young lovelies, mostly a little older than himself; but he had never even kissed a girl, let alone had an affaire with one. On the few occasions when the opportunity had offered, he had felt terribly tempted to take the hand of his divinity-of-the-time-being and blurt out his feelings for her; but he had been too shy to tell her quietly that he loved her, and had feared that if once he touched her the overwhelming desire to seize and devour her with kisses would prove too much for him. Tongue-tied, and blushing furiously at his thoughts, he had let those few chances slip, and had sublimated his passion into endless day-dreams in which, as a knight in shining armour, he had rescued these fair and mysterious creatures from dragons, ogres, witches and an infinite variety of more down-to-earth perils.

As he thought about Aphrodite and her ugly, crippled husband, he recalled reading somewhere that the gods and goddesses of the Greek Pantheon were no more than larger-than-life human beings, conjured up by the imagination of a simple people, and that the acts with which they were credited portrayed the normal tendencies inherent in men and women. If that were so, it argued that sometimes the loveliest girls could fall in love with men whom other people considered lacking in attraction. Conscious as he was that, although everybody seemed to like him, it was largely due to pity because they really regarded him as a good-natured but awkward, useless fool, Robbie thought that perhaps, after all, one day the gods would make up to him for all he lacked by causing some beautiful girl to prefer him to all her other suitors, however amusing, distinguished and sought-after they might be.

Having nothing to do and all day in which to do it, he decided to spend the afternoon wandering about the Piraeus; so when he had finished his lunch he climbed the steep steps up to the corniche road and caught a bus that took him across the peninsula and down through the city. On its far side lay the two great basins, crowded with ships of all kinds and descriptions. For a while he strolled about the wharves, then went to the market, as the activities there had always fascinated him.

The market consisted of a warren of narrow alleys and broader arcades covering such a big area that it was almost a town in itself. As it was now the siesta hour, there was little going on, although most of the shops were still open, their owners dozing behind stalls but ready enough to do business should a potential customer appear.

The goods on sale presented a curious blend of East and West that was typical of modern Greece. Facing the harbour was a line of a dozen shoe shops, and most prominent among all their displays were ladies' shoes of the latest fashion. Hard by them was a group of sweet-makers, offering Turkish delight, almond paste and nougat of a dozen flavours, exactly similar to the sweetmeats being sold in the bazaars of Cairo and Baghdad. There was a score of wireless shops crammed with television sets, and as many others which dealt in hand-embroidered costumes of the richest hues, made after patterns hundreds of years old. On the slabs of the fish shops, in addition to the more usual type of fish, were great piles of sea-urchins, baby squids and, here and there, a fearsome-looking spiky monster of the deep. Prominent in the butchers' shops hung long lines of legs of baby lamb, for the pasture in Greece is so poor that farmers cannot afford to rear many lambs to sheep, so are compelled to slaughter them while still in their infancy. For the visitor from Western Europe they provide a special delight, since they are as tender as chicken and, when cooked with herbs, much more delicious. Many of the shops sold only plastic gadgets for the most modern kitchens, while others carried on the ancient trade of scent distillers, tempting the women with big glass jars of lemon-verbena, gardenia, stephanotis and attar-of-roses.

While Robbie, his broad shoulders a little stooped, wended his way between the long lines of stalls, he was surrounded by a little group of children, who pestered him continually with shrill cries for largesse. Most people would have found them an annoyance and sought to drive them away, but he was used to being followed by such urchins, and many of them were so pretty that he always thought of them as cherubs. It was typical of his good nature that, in his left trouser pocket, he always carried a store of drachma copper coins, to toss from time to time, with a wide-mouthed grin, to these importunate little devils.

Soon after four o'clock he decided to return to Athens, so caught a local bus that would take him back to the other side of the Piraeus. At the terminal there he took one of the bigger buses that plied between the port and the capital. When it had covered a quarter of a mile along the coast road it passed the great oil refinery that had recently been erected as a part of the N.A.T.O. programme to supply the Fleets of the Western Powers.

The sight of it brought back to him the conversation he had overheard at lunch, and raised several questions in his mind. The oil for it was, he had always assumed, brought from the Middle East by the tankers that were frequently lying off it. He had certainly never heard that there were any oil wells in Greece. Yet if oil deposits were lying under Greece why had they never been tapped and exploited?

The multi-millionaire Aristotle Onassis was a Greek. He controlled the greatest tanker fleet in the world, so he should know more about oil than most people. Moreover, he was a patriot. Recently, regardless whether he made or lost money, he had financed Greece's Olympic Airways, improving their efficiency and comfort to a degree that would enable them to compete with the best airlines in Europe, and this solely with the object of bringing more visitors to Greece so that more money should be spent in his fascinating but impoverished country. Since he had done that, why should he not have used some of his millions to open up for Greece a great natural source of wealth—the oil that the two Czechs had conveyed the impression that they believed to be there for the getting?

The bus rattled on through the ten kilometres of built-up area that separated Athens from the sea. Long ago it had been a broad corridor, enclosed by two long walls. In the fifth century B.C. Sparta had been the great land power in Greece, and Athens' only hope of survival lay in keeping open her communications with her powerful fleet which still held the seas. The great Athenian Themistocles had decreed the building and garrisoning of these thirteen miles of walls and so, by bringing the Piraeus within the fortification of the capital, saved his city.

A few centuries later the conquering Romans had destroyed those walls, so that only a few vestiges of them now remained, and the strip of territory had gradually become a backyard of the city, dotted with suburban villas, rows of shops, garages, plots of land for sale and modern churches. Whenever the bus passed a church several of the passengers in it crossed themselves, as great numbers of Greeks are still deeply religious. But Robbie hardly noticed them or the uninspiring buildings that lined both sides of the road. His mind was slowly revolving the question of why Mr. Onassis should have neglected to exploit the oil resources of his own country, and he could find no answer to it.

As Robbie entered the Embassy, Euan Wettering was crossing its spacious hall. He was another permanent guest there, and a nephew of Lady Grenn, so he and Robbie were cousins by marriage. He was a few years older than Robbie, and two young men could hardly have differed more in both physique and character. Euan was small and frail-looking, but he made up for his lack of inches by an aggressive, even bumptious, manner. He was extremely clever, having achieved a double First at Cambridge, and he had taken up archaeology as a profession. On learning of Sir Finsterhorn's appointment, he had promptly wangled a post with the British School of Archaeology in Athens, feeling confident that his aunt would invite him to make his home in the Embassy. Having established himself there, he took every advantage of the prestige it gave him and used it freely to entertain his friends, thereby saving his own money. Secretly he envied Robbie both his fine physique and his fortune, but scarcely bothered to hide the fact that he despised him as a half-wit.

'Euan!' Robbie called, as his cousin made for the stairs. 'Just a moment, please.'

'Well; what is it?' Euan replied impatiently.

'Tell me something. Have you ever found any traces of oil during your archaeological digs?'

'Good lord, no! I only wish we had. We're always kept disgracefully short of funds, and to strike a gusher would be a godsend.'

'Do you think there's any chance of doing so?'

'No. There's not the least likelihood of finding oil anywhere in Greece. But I must rush or I'll be late for the Swanson's cocktail party.' Turning away, Euan ran swiftly up the stairs.

Three hours later they met again at dinner. Lady Grenn had recently left for England to be with her elderly mother who was about to undergo a serious operation, and it so happened that this was one of the comparatively rare nights when Sir Finsterhorn was neither entertaining nor dining out, so the party consisted only of him and the two young men.

The Ambassador was a tall, thin man with a prominent forehead from which the hair had receded, and a grey moustache that drooped at the ends. He was reputed to be extremely shrewd and had a very courteous manner, but he had no hobbies, few intimates and, as far as Robbie knew, had never been known to unbend. His father had been a famous mountaineer, and had met his mother while she was on holiday in Switzerland. His name was an Anglicized version of Finsteraahorn, and was given him in memory of his father's having proposed on the lower slopes of that mountain.

Dinner ran its normal course, with Euan Wettering and the Ambassador talking of events and their acquaintances, while Robbie made a silent third. That was not because either of the others had any intention of being rude to him, and when there were dinner parties at which the conversation was general, he always made a minor contribution to it; but early in his stay, it had been found that his knowledge of the matters usually discussed when they were dining *en famille* was so sketchy that it was a waste of time to ask his opinion, so he had become quite used to being ignored.

It was not until the dessert had been put on the table that Euan suddenly addressed him.

'What's this bee you've got in your bonnet, Robbie, about there being oil in Greece?'

Robbie looked up with a start. 'Oh—er—well, it isn't my idea exactly, but the Czechs seem to think there is.'

'The Czechs?' repeated Sir Finsterhorn, with a sharp glance from under his shaggy eyebrows.

With a nod, Robbie proceeded to give an account of the conversation he had overheard that day while lunching at Toyrcolimano.

'Oh, come! ' exclaimed Euan when he had done. 'You don't expect us to believe that, do you? I bet you made it up.'

'I'm not given to making up stories,' Robbie protested mildly.

'Yes, you are. Lounging about all day as you do, your head gets full of nonsense. All these stories you are digging up about the gods and heroes for your book are only myths, yet you look on them as though they had really happened in some distant past. And now it seems you've started day-dreaming about oil and the Czechs.'

'No, honestly, Euan, I really did hear those chaps talking, just as I've said.'

'Do you mean to tell me that you understand Czech well enough to have taken in all they said?'

Attacked on his one accomplishment, Robbie bridled at last and retorted: 'You may be cleverer than I am in lots of ways, but even your Greek is lousy and——'

Euan opened his mouth to snap at him, but the Ambassador raised a hand, silencing them both, and said:

'We are all aware of your talents as a linguist, Robbie. On that account I find it all the more regrettable that you don't avail yourself of them to secure some suitable employment, instead of idling about and wasting your time trying to write a book. I don't wish to be unkind but, for all of us who know you, there is no escaping the fact that you are quite incapable of producing a work of literature.'

With a frown, Robbie looked down at his plate and muttered: 'I like doing it, sir; and I don't care what anyone says, I'm going to finish it. Anyway, Euan asked me about this business of the oil and the Czechs and what I have told him is the truth. He can believe it or not, as he likes.'

'Then we'll accept your word for that,' Sir Finsterhorn said more mildly, 'and I'd like you to describe those two men to me again.'

When Robbie had complied, the Ambassador nodded. 'I don't know who the tall, dark man would be, but you are right about the other being the Czech First Secretary. His name is Alois Nejedly. Are you quite sure that he said that his Government had purchased the Greek tobacco crop?'

'Quite certain, sir. He referred to it more than once.'

The Ambassador frowned. 'It's strange that I've heard no rumour about that.'

'If it's true, the Greeks must be cock-a-hoop,' put in Euan.

'Why should they be, about selling it to the Czechs rather than to anyone else?' Robbie enquired.

His uncle gave him a pitying look. 'My dear boy, surely you know that a considerable percentage of the Greek peasantry depends almost entirely on tobacco-growing for its living. If their Government cannot dispose of the crop for these people at a fair price, they would starve. To sell has become more difficult year by year, ever since the First World War, when so many people took to smoking Virginia cigarettes and the so-called "Turkish" went out of fashion.'

Euan nodded. 'But why in the world should the Czechs want to buy Macedonian leaf when all the Iron Curtain countries are supplied by Russia from the tobacco plantations in the Crimea?'

'Surely that's obvious.' Robbie looked across at him brightly. 'It must be because the Greeks included in the deal the right to prospect for oil.'

'But there is no oil in Greece,' the Ambassador and Euan shot at him almost simultaneously.

'Then there must be something else behind it,' said Robbie with simple logic.

Sir Finsterhorn gave him a slightly supercilious look. 'Since that is your opinion, perhaps you can suggest what?'

Robbie returned a blank stare. 'I haven't an idea, sir. How could I have?'

'It was you who overheard this conversation. If you are right in your assumption, during this talk they might have dropped some hint.'

'No, sir, I'm afraid I can't recall anything that might help. You see, at the time I took it for granted that they were discus-

sing a straightforward deal. It was only later that I became
a bit puzzled. It struck me as queer that if oil were to be had in
Greece Mr. Onassis should not have bothered to develop it.
And now you both say there isn't any. That being the case,
the whole thing looks pretty fishy to me, but I expect in a few
days you will have found out what they're up to.'

'How do you propose that I should set about it?'

'Well—er—isn't that what the Secret Service is for?'

Euan gave a sudden, sharp laugh. 'The Secret Service!
D'you think they've nothing better to do than to investigate
wildly improbable yarns brought in by nit-wits like you?'

'Oh, Euan! Why are you so beastly?' Robbie protested.
'After all, if there is something sinister behind this business,
it ought to be investigated.'

Sir Finsterhorn coughed. 'Of course, Robbie; of course.
But Euan is right about our Intelligence people being kept
pretty busy with one thing and another; and in this matter I
cannot feel that there is sufficient justification for calling them
in. You must remember that there is no basis of probability
for such a deal having taken place, and no supporting evidence
of any kind for your story. It may quite well be that since these
men were talking in a foreign language you put a completely
wrong interpretation on what they said.'

'I did not, Uncle! I did not!' Robbie insisted. 'I didn't miss
a word, and I couldn't be more certain about what they said.'
Suddenly a bold, utterly revolutionary idea entered his mind.
'I know,' he went on swiftly. 'If you don't want to call the
Secret Service people in, why shouldn't I have a cut at it? You
are always badgering me to do a job, and this is one I'd like.
I understand Czech and can talk it fairly fluently. Let me try
my hand at finding out about this business for you.'

The other two stared at him in astonishment. For a moment
there was dead silence at the table. Then Euan said with a
grin, 'Well, this should beat any comic strip ever printed. Just
think of it! Our Robbie, gun in hand, chasing his tail in circles
while imagining himself to be Bulldog Drummond.'

Sir Finsterhorn shook his head. 'Really, Robbie, you
should try to keep that romantic imagination of yours within
bounds. The very idea of a young man who, at the age of

twenty-three, is still incapable of qualifying for his G.C.E. undertaking such a mission is fantastic. You wouldn't even know how to make a start. Forget it, my dear boy, and stick to that little book you are writing. If it proves reasonably readable I'll have a few hundred copies privately printed for you and we can send them out as presents to the children of our friends next Christmas.'

By his offer to get Robbie's book published the Ambassador had intended to soften his previous low rating of his nephew's intelligence. But from beginning to end his words were like whiplashes on the big, awkward young man sitting beside him.

Thrusting back his chair, Robbie stood up and, without a word, almost ran from the room. Outside in the hall he could no longer hold back the tears that had started to his big, brown eyes. Weeping as though his heart would break, he lurched from side to side up the stairs, muttering fiercely:

'They think I'm a moron. But I'm not. I'll show them! I'll show them!'

2

The Budding Author

LADY GRENN had arranged for Robbie a pleasant bed-sitting room on the third floor, where he could read and, if so inclined, work without being disturbed. On reaching it, he flung himself on to his bed and, for some ten minutes, wept bitterly.

In spite of all he had been told about the aircraft crash in which he had so narrowly escaped death, and the effect of the injuries inflicted on himself as a result of it, he had never fully accepted the fact that he differed from other people. All his life, until quite recently, he had been hedged about with love and, even during the past year, everyone he had met, with the one exception of Euan, had appeared to like him and had treated him as a normal person.

Yet his uncle had spurned with contempt his offer to try to find out for him what lay at the bottom of the Czech deal with the Greek Government. Still worse, he had, without even seeing it, stigmatized the book upon which Robbie had been working so laboriously for the past two months as being at best fit only for children.

Gradually, the sobs that shook Robbie's big frame grew more infrequent. When they had ceased altogether he dried his eyes, sat up and went over to his desk. From it he took his manuscript. So far he had filled one thick exercise book and nearly half another with his large, round, childish writing. Feeling now an urgent need to reassure himself about the quality of his work, he switched on the desk light and began to re-read the first chapter, which went as follows:

CHAPTER I

ZEUS AND HIS FAMILY

The beginning of things seems to be a bit confused, but I suppose that's hardly to be wondered at as there could have been no one there to set down exactly what did happen.

Anyhow, the first divinities we have any record of are Uranus, the Sky, and his wife Gaea, the Earth. Between them they had an enormous brood of most horrible children. Among them were the six boy and six girl Titans, the three Cyclopes who each had only one eye in the middle of his forehead, and three Monsters each of whom had one hundred arms and fifty heads.

Uranus was not at all happy about the sort of children his wife had produced. In fact, he disliked them so much that he shut them all up in a huge cave. Naturally their mother, Gaea, was pretty upset about that, and she made up her mind to get even with him. She managed to smuggle her youngest Titan son, Cronos, out of the cave, armed him with a sickle and set him on his father. Cronos must have caught his papa napping, as he inflicted a terrible wound on him, I suppose the worst that can be inflicted on a man. History does not relate if it actually killed him. Perhaps nothing could, as he was a god. If so, it must have been jolly hard on him, because afterwards there was no longer any point in his going to bed with a girl, and the gods were tremendously keen on that sort of thing.

All we know is that Uranus' blood gushed out and formed lots more monsters, which showed that he was just as much to blame for the horrid brood Gaea had produced as she was. Anyhow, we hear no more of him, and Cronos became top god in his place.

Cronos married his sister, Rhea, who afterwards became known as the Mother of the Gods, because it was she who gave birth to the Royal Family of Olympus. But for quite a time, it didn't look as though she were going to get any pleasure out of her children. Cronos proved an even more unpleasant person than his father. I suppose he was afraid that, when his sons grew up, one for them might spoil his fun for life, just as he had his poor papa's. Anyway, every time Rhea gave birth to a baby, he grabbed and swallowed it.

One after the other, he pushed three girl children, Hestia, Demeter and Hera, down his mighty throat, then two boys, Hades and Poseidon. By that time, Rhea was getting pretty fed up, so when she was about to have her sixth child she consulted her mother, Gaea, who said: 'You go and have your baby in Crete, ducks, and between us we'll pull a fast one over your old man,' or words to that effect. Rhea went off to Crete and had Zeus in a cave, then Gaea took the infant and had him brought up in secret by two nymphs on Mount Ida. Meanwhile, Rhea had hurried back to her hubby and presented him with a big stone wrapped in swaddling clothes. The great mutt swallowed it, believing it to be her baby. In due course Zeus reached manhood and dethroned his horrible father, then he gave him something very nasty to drink, which caused him to sick up the five children he had swallowed.

Having become top god, Zeus was very touchy about his rights, and he never thought twice before chucking a thunderbolt at anyone who upset him. But he was a much pleasanter character than either his father or grandfather, and really rather easy-going. When appealed to by the others, his judgments were usually just, although he didn't like being bothered by such matters, because his mind was always occupied with thinking up the quickest way to seduce either a goddess or some lovely mortal maiden. In fact, he doesn't seem to have taken much interest in anything else.

His first act was one of clemency, and it cost him dear. He released his uncles, the Titans, from their prison, but instead of being grateful they ganged up against him and supported their brother, Cronos, in an attempt to regain the throne. There followed a ten-year war and Rhea's children might have got the worst of it if Zeus had not also released from prison the three Cyclopes and the three Monsters, who took his side. Even then it must have been one hell of a battle. Zeus with his brothers, sisters and friends occupied Mount Olympus, in the north-east of Greece, and the Titans Mount Othrys, a hundred miles further south. For weapons they used great rocks and even small mountains, hurling them through the air at one another. But the Monsters, each with a hundred hands, must have made awfully useful allies in that sort of war; so in the end Zeus won and drove all the Titans down to Tartarus, the lowest region of the Underworld.

After the defeat of the Titans, another rebellion broke out, and this time Olympus was attacked by a race of half-human half-reptile Giants. They had sprung up from the blood that had dripped from Grandpa Uranus when Cronos had mutilated him, so they were creatures of earth but absolutely enormous. Their leader Typhon had huge serpents wriggling out from every part of his body, and all the gods except Zeus were scared stiff at the sight of him. In fact they ran as far as Egypt. But Hercules came to their help and between them they succeeded in killing off these horrid monsters except for Typhon, and him Zeus imprisoned under the red-hot cauldron of a volcano in Sicily named Mount Etna.

After that there was peace on Mount Olympus and the gods were able to settle down to a jolly life of drinking nectar and making love.

Zeus behaved very decently to his brothers. To Hades, who is much better known by his Roman name of Pluto—and so dear reader I shall call him that—he gave the Kingdom of the Underworld. It was called Hades after him, and although in modern times that word has more or less taken on the same meaning as Hell, only a part of it, Tartarus, was the sort of Hell that until quite recently millions of unfortunate Christians were brought up to be terrified of.

The greater part of Hades was a dark gloomy region to which people were carried by Thanatos, as Pluto's henchman, Death, was called, when they died. Once inside it their bodies became shades, most of whom wandered about there quite pointlessly and rather miserably for a very long time. All the same, it was regarded as very important to get into Hades, and to do so a dead person had to be ferried across an underground river called the Styx by a boatman named Charon.

If the body had not been provided with a piece of money to give him, its ghost had to remain this side of the river in a more miserable state than ever.

The reason people were so anxious to get into Hades was because it did mean that, sooner or later, they would be able to return to earth in another body. There was also a sporting chance that they might be allowed to spend their time of waiting in a special part of the Underworld called the Elysian Fields, which was lit up and a sort of glorified Country Club. But only the ghosts of the best people, and those who had put up a jolly good show during their lives, were allowed to potter about in there.

On the other hand, if the gods took a dim view of you, your body might be pitched down the chute to Tartarus, and there suffer the most appalling tortures, some of which I will tell you about later on.

To his other brother Poseidon, the Neptune of the Romans, Zeus gave dominion over the oceans, seas, lakes and rivers. He was also known as the Earth-shaker and, if the number of earthquakes that occur in Greece and the Aegean are anything to go by, he is still very active.

For himself, Zeus kept Heaven and Earth. That is why he was afterwards always known as King of Gods and Men. But to each of his sisters he also gave special powers.

The eldest, Hestia, he made goddess of the family hearth. She was a pleasant woman but very stand-offish. In fact it seems that she had a thing against men. She couldn't even be induced to marry, and turned down both Apollo and Poseidon. It is probably because she was such a prude that we don't hear much about her, but later on she came into her own. The Romans worshipped her as Vesta and made all their most beautiful debs into Vestal Virgins to tend the sacred fires in her temple.

Demeter figured much more prominently in people's minds, because she was given the job of looking after agriculture. In those days nearly everyone was dependent on the crops they could raise so naturally there were a great many temples to her, and on her feast days everyone queued up to pay homage to her.

Hera, Zeus's youngest sister, he took as his wife, or I should say principal wife. He made her Queen of Heaven but he had several other wives, among them Demeter, and, in addition, he tricked any number of young women into providing him with a night or two of fun during his frequent visits to his earthly Kingdom.

His first wife was Metis, the personification of Wisdom, but his Grandma, Gaea, put him wise to it that if he had a son by her he would bump him off. So, improving on his father's idea, as soon as he had put her in the family way he swallowed her, baby and all.

Next he married his aunt, Themis, one of the lady Titans. She was a very good sort and did him proud by producing as his children not only Law, Justice and Peace, but also the Seasons and the Fates. About this time, as a side line, he spent nine nights with her sister, Mnemosyne, who gave birth to the nine Muses.

Why he should have made Hera, instead of Themis, Queen of Heaven, history does not relate. I suppose the answer is that Hera was darned good-looking and that was her price. Anyhow, although he is supposed to have acquired unlimited wisdom by swallowing Metis, he certainly did not show it by making Hera his Queen. She was the patroness of marriage and conjugal fidelity, and as Zeus was one hundred per cent sold on free love she naturally made his life hell.

As he was always giving her cause for jealousy one can't altogether blame her for behaving like a shrew to him, but she was not content with that. She showed the most extraordinary cunning and vindictiveness in bringing misery to his girl friends, who really weren't to blame; and personally I don't think being virtuous oneself justifies anyone in making lots of other people desperately unhappy.

At one time Hera got so mad with Zeus that she conspired against him with Poseidon, Apollo and Athene, and they managed to tie him up. But the Monster Briareus came to his rescue. Themis evidently bore no grudge against Hera for supplanting her. She even acted as Hera's dresser on State occasions and provided her with beauty aids and wise counsel.

In addition she was Mistress of Ceremonies at the Olympian Court and in the role of 'universal aunt' was beloved by all.

Ares, or Mars as the Romans called him, was the only child who owed his birth to both Zeus and Hera, but perhaps that is to be accounted for by the Royal couple's strained relations. As they were always quarrelling, it seems logical that Ares should become the god of War. He was ill-tempered, sullen, brutal, stupid and altogether a most unattractive type. None of his family had any time for him at all and one day his father said to him: 'Of all my children I dislike you most. You take after your Mother and enjoy nothing but bickering. For two pins I'd kick you off the Mount'—or words to that effect. Surprisingly enough, too, he was not even a great champion in combat. He had several cracks at Athene, because she set herself up as a sort of female Minister of Defence for the cities in which she was worshipped; but she always got the better of him, and Hercules and one or two other Heroes gave him quite a beating up.

Two of Zeus's other children who played a very prominent part in the lives of gods and men were the twins, Apollo and Artemis. Their mother, Leto, was the beautiful daughter of a Titan, and when it got around that Zeus had made her preg. Hera became hopping mad. She threatened any country that sheltered Leto with every sort of calamity, so the poor girl traipsed all round the eastern Med. begging to be taken in, until Poseidon took pity on her and provided her with a floating island on which to have her babies. Later he anchored it to the sea-bottom; it was called Delos and became, after Delphi, Apollo's most famous shrine, because he was born there.

Finding the equivalent of a bed in a maternity ward was by no means the end of Leto's troubles. When her time came she could not do her stuff because that bitch Hera had forbidden Ilithyia, the goddess of Childbirth, to leave Olympus. All the other gods and goddesses hurried to Delos with fruit, flowers and sympathy, but their standing around holding hands didn't do any good. For nine days and nights Leto suffered intolerable agony. Then kind auntie Themis came to the rescue and, somehow, got Ilithyia down from Olympus to Delos.

Even then Hera would not let up, and sent Python to

destroy Leto and her twins. Fortunately for all concerned Themis had brought some ambrosia and nectar along in her mother's-bag and she fed it to the new-born Apollo. Instantly he leapt from his swaddling clothes a full-grown man and chased the huge serpent to Delphi, where he slew it and set up a temple to himself. It was in connection with this event that the High Priestess who afterwards prophesied there was known as the Pythoness.

Apollo was the best-looking and most popular of all the gods. He was the Lord of Light, and Helios, who drove the chariot of the Sun, was only one of his henchmen. He caused the crops to ripen, protected the flocks and herds, and was the first god to go in for healing. He was the inventor of music and, as patron of the arts, was attended by the nine Muses. In addition he was willing to tell people's fortunes at his Oracles. So you can see what a useful god he was to be on the right side of.

Artemis, known to the Romans as Diana the huntress, was a decidedly hearty type. Like her twin brother she shed light, but Selene, the Moon goddess, acted as stand-in for her. This enabled her to spend most of her time in the woods, where she went about dressed in a kilt and attended by a bevy of hockey-playing types known as the Pleiades. She was a fanatical prude and so strongly disapproved of parlour games that, when the great hunter Orion made a pass at her, she shot him with one of her deadly arrows. An unfortunate chap called Actaeon fared even worse. One hot day when he was out seeing what he could get for the pot, he happened to come upon her just as she had slipped off her kilt to take a dip in a pool. Before he could even take his eyes off her she had turned him into a stag and had him torn to pieces by his own hounds. She had no mercy either on her sport-loving hoydens, if any of them allowed themselves to be picked up and taken behind the bushes. To have bumped them off just because they had had a little fun seems to me very unfair because, however chaste you may be yourself, it's not right to be beastly to other people who feel differently.

Hermes, the Roman Mercury, was the son of Zeus by Maia, the eldest of Artemis's troop of huntresses. I bet the goddess was furious with her papa for having done the dirty on one of her muscular virgins, but evidently she couldn't do anything to prevent it. Zeus made this son the Messenger of the Gods, so he wore winged sandals and wings in his tin hat, just as you often see his picture on postage stamps. As he got around a lot, that naturally led to his becoming the god of Travel. In those days there were no Hellenic cruises on which people went just for pleasure; travel meant going places on business, so Hermes was also the patron of Commerce. That, of course, included cattle, as in ancient times herds largely represented wealth. But he was a bit of a bad hat, and the very day he was born he took to stealing. His first exploit was to drive off fifty heifers from a pedigree herd of which Apollo was in charge, and when accused of the theft he refused to come clean. Luckily for him, while on this raid he had found a tortoise and turned its shell into a lyre. Apollo was so pleased with this new musical instrument that he forgave his baby brother and even gave him a magic wand to play with. Hermes became a very active glib-tongued young rogue. He was the patron of thieves, athletes and inventors, and himself invented the alphabet. He had a sense of humour, too, and was always playing tricks on his relations. At various times he stole Poseidon's trident, Artemis's arrows and Aphrodite's girdle. But he must have had a lot of charm, for they always forgave him and he became the pet of the family.

Dionysus was Zeus's son by Semele, a daughter of King Cadmus. He was the god of Wine and went about crowned with a wreath of ivy and laurel and with bunches of grapes dangling from his ears. He was frightfully keen on letting people know what a jolly good drink wine is, so he became his own representative and travelled all over the place giving vine roots to anyone he could induce to plant them. He even went as far as India, and brought back with him a team of tigers to draw his chariot. Apart from his sales campaign he didn't do much except preside over revels as a rather cynical host. Like Artemis he had a number of constant companions. The chief of these was Silenus, who had been his tutor. This old fellow followed him round rolling from side to side on the back of a donkey, because he was always tight, but he was incredibly wise and could foretell the future. The rest of Dionysus's set consisted of goat-footed Satyrs and a crowd of lecherous women known as Bacchantes. They all gave the glad hand to anyone who was ready to join in their fun but could turn very nasty to people who refused. Anyone like St. Paul would have got very short shrift from them. They danced in a drunken frenzy round spoil-sports like him, then tore them in pieces.

Pallas Athene was another virgin goddess and an extremely powerful one. The gentle reader will recall that Zeus swallowed his first wife Metis when she was already with child. Evidently he could not digest them because one day he got a most frightful headache. Apparently Metis's baby had gestated, or whatever you call it, and gone to his head. To relieve the pain Hephaestus took what seems to me rather a drastic measure; he crowned the old boy with an axe. However, it did the trick. Out of his split skull sprang Pallas Athene fully grown and fully armed. She was very keen on arts and crafts and everything to do with women in the home. But her most important role was as a protectress of cities into which she had introduced order, law and justice, and, having been conceived by Metis, she was much the wisest of the goddesses.

Hera was even more annoyed with Zeus for having a child off his own bat, than by his seducing all sorts of not too unwilling pretty strumpets; so she decided to see what she could do by herself.

Hephaestus was the result of her effort, but she bungled things badly. He was born lame in both legs and such an ugly little bag of bones that in a savage rage she threw the poor mite out of heaven. A Sea Nymph, named Thetis, rescued him and brought him up in her grotto, where he taught himself to make all sorts of lovely and ingenious toys. Then, wishing to get a bit of his own back on his mama, he sent her a beautiful golden throne. Hera was delighted, but it was the original of those Renaissance contraptions on which chaps like the Borgias used to invite their guests to sit before cutting their throats. The moment Hera sat on it the arms flipped across her and there she was, caught like a bird in a snare. All the other Immortals had a go at freeing her but none of them could, so Hephaestus had to be sent for. His price for pressing the secret spring that would let his mama out was that one of the prettiest goddesses should consent to become his wife. That being agreed upon, mother and son decided to let bygones be bygones and he was made Blacksmith to the gods with the Cyclopes as his assistants and a forge in Mount Etna. It was he who supplied Zeus with thunderbolts and forged arms and armour of all kinds for his family, as well as building palaces for them, will see mod. cons. and lots of gadgets. Very ungratefully, I think, owing to his limp, his ugliness and his begrimed appearance, the others used him as their butt, and whenever he visited Olympus they made dirty cracks at him. Nevertheless, it was Aphrodite, the loveliest goddess of them all, who agreed to become his wife.

Aphrodite was unique among the heavenly brood because she had not even one physical parent—that is unless you can count the bits that Cronos cut off his father Uranus. These were cast into the sea not far from Cyprus, and they acted like a ton of dynamite. A huge water-spout leapt up and for miles around the sea was churned into foam. From this foam Aphrodite sprang to life, already grown up and endowed with breathtaking beauty. She was one of those languorous types, with so much S.A. that no man could resist her, and being the hottest ever of hot-mommas she couldn't keep her hands off the men either. She even took to having parties with that oaf Ares when he winked a bloodshot eye at her, but Hephaestus got to hear of it and played a neat trick on them. One afternoon when he was hard at it in his forge, Ares came lumbering into Aphrodite's boudoir, gave the V sign and said: 'What about it?' She smiled back and replied: 'O.K. by me.' So they both took their clothes off, went over to her couch and lay down on it. But the cunning Hephaestus had fashioned a net so fine that it was invisible, yet so strong that it could not be broken, and fixed it up above his wife's couch. Under the pressure of their combined weight a spring beneath the couch released the net which fell round it, trapping them. After they had had their fun they dozed for a bit, until it was time for Ares to make himself scarce. Then they both nearly threw a fit because they found they were in a cage.

Now it's a funny thing, but the Immortals were really a very modest lot and, except when making love, were ashamed to be seen with their clothes even a little disarranged, let alone with no clothes on at all. Hephaestus came home from work, saw that his trick had worked, then brought everyone he could find on Olympus to come and have a look at the guilty couple. At the sight of them both starko and red with shame trapped on the couch, all the other Immortals laughed themselves nearly sick, and afterwards Aphrodite and Ares could hardly hold up their heads for months. Still it didn't cure Aphrodite from being unfaithful, because she was made that way. But for the future she took handsome mortals as her lovers, and any number of lucky chaps spent nights with her that must have left them wondering in the morning what had hit them.

With Zeus in the Chair, the gods and goddesses I have described, except for those who did not dwell on Olympus, were the Twelve who formed the Great Council of the Gods. But there were many other Immortals, and I will mention a few of the better-known ones before closing this chapter.

Prometheus was a cousin of Zeus. It was he who made Man, by modelling a piece of clay into a body, copied from those of the gods, but of course very much smaller, then giving it life. He was so pleased with his toy that to help it support itself on earth he stole for it from Olympus the invaluable gift of Fire. As Fire was considered sacred, when Zeus heard of this sacrilege he blew his top. He had the wretched Prometheus chained to a rock in the Caucasus and sentenced him to have his liver picked out by an eagle every day for thirty thousand years. For the old man to be so vindictive he must have been terribly put out, but perhaps this happened on a day when he had been chasing a pretty nymph and she had changed herself into a hedgehog, or something, just as he got at her. Anyhow, he was so peeved about the whole affair that, to cancel out Prometheus's gift, he had Hephaestus make Woman, and sent her down to bring every sort of trouble to Man.

Pandora was the name given to her, and Zeus's children, feeling that their papa had been an awful meanie, rallied round to soften up her impact. Aphrodite gave her beauty, Apollo taught her how to sing, Hermes instructed her in artfulness and so on. But Zeus still had a card up his sleeve. He gave her a beautiful box and told her not to open it. Of course, the cunning old so-and-so knew jolly well that she would not be able to resist the temptation to look inside, and sure enough she did. Out flew plague, jealousy, deceit and all the vices and ills that afflict mankind.

Atlas was another of Zeus's cousins. He sided with Cronos in the war against Olympus, and as a punishment Zeus condemned him to hold earth and sky apart for ever with his mighty shoulders.

Asclepius was a son of Apollo. To him his father delegated the power of healing. This Doctor god got so good at it that he went too far and began to restore the dead to life. Zeus took that as a frightful piece of cheek, so consigned him to oblivion, but not before he had had time to pass on his knowledge to his daughter Hygeia, and the many temples to him scattered all over Greece show how jolly grateful everybody was for what he'd done for them.

Orpheus was another of Apollo's sons, and was trained by his father to become a great musician. He had most rotten luck in a love affair, but I'll tell you about that later.

Cupid was Aphrodite's son. He usually took the form of a laughing cherub, and it was his job to make people fall in love. Anyone wounded by one of his arrows did so with the next person he or she set eyes on. He must have had a very busy time of it, but he had a lot of fun arousing passions that often led to most comical situations.

Pan was the son of Hermes who, for some strange reason, in order to enjoy Pan's mother, turned himself into a goat. This resulted in Pan being born with the legs of a goat and little horns sticking out of his curly head. Although this was obviously Hermes's fault, he was so ashamed of his son that the boy was never allowed to join in the jollifications up on Olympus, but was left to fend for himself in the woods. Compared to most of the other members of the Royal Family, Pan was at first very small fry, but later he made a name for himself that was to continue to ring a bell many centuries after those of most of his relations had come to mean nothing to the majority of people. As half-goat, half-man, he could give even his old grandfather points in chasing likely lasses round the bushes.

and as he attached himself to Dionysus there was nothing any-one could tell him about drunken orgies. It was no doubt because of that, and the fact that he became a great Master of Magic, which accounts for the Christians later regarding him as the embodiment of Evil, or even the Devil in person.

Of course there were minor gods and goddesses of all sorts, and other Immortals like the Furies and the Fates who at times made things very uncomfortable for people. We shall come across most of them when I tell you about the extraordinary adventures of the Heroes, as I hope to do later on. Anyhow, gentle reader, what I have written so far should give you a good background to the Royal Family that between them ran ancient Greece.

* * * * *

As Robbie laid his exercise book down, his brown eyes shone, no longer with tears but with happiness. Reading that first chapter had restored his belief in himself. As there were not many long words in it, he thought it was probably not very high-class English; but he felt that he had made up for that quite a bit by using some very impressive Americanisms picked up from the gangster paper-backs he had been reading in recent months. In any case, the pictures of the characters he wished to describe were perfectly clear to him, and, being so fascinated by them himself, he felt confident that other people would find what he had written interesting. Therefore, it was going to be a good book; and as neither his uncle nor Euan had yet read any of it, they had no right to say otherwise.

But it would be many weeks, at least, before he could finish it and enjoy the triumph of showing it to them. In the mean-time he must continue to smart under their disparagement of his capabilities, unless—yes, unless he could prove them wrong.

Already, as he had run sobbing upstairs, his distress had engendered in him a desperately wild idea. But now it did not seem so very wild. If he was capable of writing a readable book, why should he not also become a successful secret agent? If he could find out what lay behind the Czechs' deal with the Greeks, what a triumph that would be. His time was his own, he had ample money and he could talk both languages. What investigator could ask for more—except the brains to use them? That was the crux, and if he succeeded he would have proved himself once and for all. It was a challenge, like those he had so often read about. He made up his mind to accept it.

3

Unorthodox Behaviour

WHEN Robbie awoke next morning, the resolution he had made the previous night came swiftly into his mind. Having pondered it for a while, he began to realize that it was one thing to decide to ferret out the secrets of a foreign Power and quite another for anyone like himself to think of a way to set about it. Yet, uncultivated as his brain was in many respects, its very simplicity led to its working logically.

He would have been prepared to bet a pound to a penny that he had interpreted correctly the conversation between the two Czechs, but there was always the outside chance that he had misunderstood a part of it. Therefore, the first thing he must do was to confirm that the Czechs had actually bought the Greek tobacco crop. If they had, arrangements for its delivery must soon cause the news to become public, so it could not be regarded by the Greek Government as a very closely kept secret. Obviously then, to start off with, he could put the question to somebody who was in a position to know.

While he breakfasted downstairs, almost in silence, with Sir Finsterhorn and Euan Wettering, he got quite a lot of amusement from imagining the expressions their faces would take on if he announced how he intended to occupy himself that morning; but he knew from experience that neither of them would ask him his plans for the day and, if either of them did, he could for once reply evasively.

Breakfast over, he went to the office of his uncle's secretary and looked up the name of the Greek Minister for Commerce.

It was Mr. D. Nassopoulos. Noting the address of the Ministry, Robbie collected his hat and sallied forth on the first stage of his secret mission.

At the Ministry he asked to see the Minister. As he had no appointment, he would have been turned away but for a gentle persistence that was part of his character. That got him as far as the Minister's secretary, a severe-looking woman with crisp, iron-grey hair. With her, the name of Grenn rang a bell, and she asked if he was related to the British Ambassador. He told her that he was Sir Finsterhorn's nephew, but refused to give her any indication of the business upon which he had come. She said that her Chief had a very busy morning; but another of Robbie's long suits was patience, and he replied that he was quite willing to wait there until the afternoon. The result of his evident determination to remain until he obtained an interview with the Minister was that, twenty minutes later, he was shown in to him.

Mr. Nassopoulos proved to be a middle-aged man with slightly wavy black hair parted in the centre, a broad forehead and a narrow jaw. He was wearing glasses with thick, tortoise-shell rims, a black jacket and pin-striped trousers that could be seen through the kneehole of his big desk. As Robbie entered the room, the Minister politely stood up, flashed two rows of white teeth at him, extended his hand, and said:

'Mr. Grenn, a pleasure to see you. I hope His Excellency, your uncle, is well. Please to sit down and tell me to what I am owing the pleasure of this visit.'

Robbie took the proffered hand, sat down, made his acknowledgement in Greek, and continued in that language. 'I came, sir, to enquire into the possibility of buying the Greek tobacco crop.'

A momentary flicker in the Minister's eyes showed his sur-prise. After a very brief silence to collect his thoughts, he replied in Greek, 'This is the first I have heard that the British Government might be interested. I wish very much that we had been informed of this before, because my Government would have been very happy to enter into negotiations with yours on this matter. But, unfortunately, it is too late. This year's crop has already been sold to another country.'

Robbie gave him an amiable nod. 'Yes, I thought it had; but I wanted to make certain. I gather that most years you have some difficulty in getting a decent price for it, so please accept my congratulations on having unloaded it on the Czechs. As they can get plenty of tobacco from Russia quite cheaply, they must have been very keen to get this concession you have granted them to prospect here for oil.'

Nassopoulos's eyes opened wide and his voice held a distinct trace of annoyance, as he said: 'Mr. Grenn. We are all aware that, in diplomatic circles, transactions have a way of leaking out; but so far no official announcement has been made about this deal. Therefore, you surely must be aware that it is against protocol for you to pay me an official visit for the purpose of discussing it.'

'I suppose it is, sir,' Robbie replied, not quite knowing what the Minister meant by 'protocol'. Then he went on innocently: 'This isn't exactly an official visit. I came to see you because I understand that there is no oil in Greece, and I want to find out what is behind the deal.'

The Minister drew in a sharp breath and his dark eyebrows came down in a heavy frown. He was both angry and puzzled. Could it be that this big, round-faced young man was making fun of him? Surely not. Even if this were an unofficial visit, the British Ambassador would come down like a ton of bricks on his nephew if he were informed that he had made a mockery of a member of the Greek Government. Yet this bland enquiry into a negotiation still officially secret was a flagrant impertinence. All the same, perhaps it would be wiser not to regard it openly in that light. The British were still a power to be reckoned with. At times, they could be extremely arrogant, and it did not pay to cross them when they were in that mood. If he gave the young man a piece of his mind and threw him out his uncle might call him over the coals in private, but make an issue of the matter and demand an apology. That could do him, Nassopoulos, no good whether they got their apology or not. Better then to pretend that the young man's question was not a matter for justifiable resentment. After a moment he smiled and said:

'Mr. Grenn, please let me assure you, and kindly assure

His Excellency your uncle, that there is no ulterior motive behind this transaction. We wish to sell our tobacco crop at a fair price and the Czechs are prepared to pay it. Not because they particularly want our tobacco, but because the Iron Curtain countries now wish to develop better relations with Greece. That is the simple truth. As for our concession granting them rights to prospect for oil that, I imagine, is to serve as one of those myths with which many governments find it necessary to entertain their peoples in these days. We are convinced that there is no oil here, but the Czechs appear to believe there is; and, no doubt, the concession will be announced in their House of Representatives to justify their having paid a somewhat higher price for our tobacco than they would have had to pay for tobacco from the Crimea.'

Robbie's broad smile lit up his round face. 'I see, sir. Yes, that explains everything. Well, thanks a lot for having seen me and told me this.' He slowly came to his feet and added: 'I know you're busy, so I won't bother you further.'

Nassopoulos also stood up. His white teeth flashed and he extended his hand. 'It is a pleasure to have met you, Mr. Grenn. Please convey my compliments to His Excellency.'

Five minutes later Robbie was wending his way between the stalls of the flower sellers, as he crossed Klafthmonos Square, the centre of Athens' best shopping district. It was too early in the year for the great heat that affects the Greek capital during the summer months, but was a pleasant sunny day, warm enough for few people to be wearing overcoats. Being in no hurry, as he entered the upper part of Stadium Street, he paused to look in the windows of Athens' Fortnum and Mason. Among the de-luxe groceries displayed there reposed a large, toy pig as an advertisement for a brand of bacon. It was sitting up on its haunches and a mechanical device made its head turn slowly from side to side while its blue, china eyes rolled in their sockets, giving it an expression of gluttonous delight. Robbie adored it and often stood exchanging happy grins with it for several minutes.

Tearing himself away, he crossed the road and entered a big pâtisserie. The cake and sweet shops of Athens are perhaps rivalled only by those in Paris. Their windows are filled with every form of confection, from elaborate iced creations to an amazing variety of pastries and boxes of chocolates of all shapes and sizes. There are, too, at least six such shops to the square mile for every one in the West End of London. Chocolates made of every kind of nut and toffee, or filled with liqueurs, nougat and sugared almonds are their speciality, but they have much less choice to offer in soft chocolates and sweets made with cream, because of the permanent shortage of butter and fats in Greece.

Robbie was, therefore, surprised to see that a special display had been made of some boxes of large, vari-coloured fondants. He bought half a kilo and remarked on their being a new line, upon which the girl behind the counter told him that they had only just come in and were from Czechoslovakia.

That sent his mind back to his recent interview. With a gullibility that was a natural corollary to his own transparent honesty, he had accepted Mr. Nassopoulos' statement at its face value. By the time he had descended in the lift from the Minister's office, he had been laughing at himself for ever having imagined that there was something sinister behind the tobacco crop deal, and his own absurd idea that he might bring off a great coup if he took on the role of a secret agent. Now, his chance discovery that the Greeks were importing sweets from Czechoslovakia made it look as if the two countries had entered into a much wider bargain; in fact, it must be so, because Greece was much too poor a country to import anything without a *quid pro quo*, with the exception of essentials for her industries.

On the face of it, such a pact held no sinister meaning for the Western Powers, which made it seem odd to Robbie that Nassopoulos had not told him frankly about it. Of course, when making their offer for the tobacco crop, the Czechs, knowing there was no oil to be had in Greece, might quite well have insisted on the Greeks agreeing, in addition to that concession, to take some of their exports in part payment for the crop. Yet, if they were getting fair value in this way, why should they also have wanted the concession to prospect for oil?

Nassopoulos had given as their reason a wish to have something to show that would justify their paying a bigger price than was necessary for several million pounds' worth of tobacco. The Greeks had probably thought that strange, but they would have been the last people to raise any question about it, because it cost them nothing to give the concession, and their one anxiety must have been to dispose of their crop on satisfactory terms. Yet it was strange.

The Governments of democracies like Britain had to mind their ps and qs. If they used their people's money to buy in a bad market without some adequate justification, the papers created a stink about it, and several real bungles of that kind might lead to the Party in power being thrown out at the next election. But in the Iron Curtain countries matters were very different. The only thing their Governments had to watch out for was to retain the approval of 'Big Brother' in Moscow. The people had no say whatever in Communist-run countries. The Party bosses ran the show as they saw fit, and did not have to provide excuses for anything they chose to do with their nation's money.

All the way back, up the broad Vasilissis Sofias to Loukianou Street, on the corner of which stood the British Embassy, Robbie pondered this problem, but could find no answer to it.

At lunch there were half a dozen people, so he had to make polite conversation and postpone further thought about his problem until the guests had gone. Afterwards he went up to his room and tried to work at his book, but the right words would not come. That had happened on previous occasions and he had a sovereign remedy for it—an hour spent up on the Acropolis among the ancient temples never failed to bring him fresh inspiration.

He had no car of his own, neither had he ever attempted to drive one, for he had been told in his late teens that, owing to his slow responses, he would prove a danger to himself and others. Having walked down the broad boulevard, he picked up a taxi opposite the Royal Palace and, within ten minutes, was approaching the scene of Greece's greatest glory.

Like a big, oval island, the Acropolis stood out above the roofs of the city. Except for the steep slope at its south-west point that gave access to the almost level plateau on which stood its temples, its five-hundred-foot-high cliffs rose sheer on all sides. On national holidays and during the tourist season, it was floodlit at night by dozens of batteries, each consisting of a score of searchlights that played not only on its temples but also on its cliffs. Seen like that, the natural grandeur of its site crowned by the highest art of man, made it appear a city of palaces high up in the night sky, and a worthy dwelling for the gods. But even by day, seen from any angle, it was tremendously impressive.

Robbie's taxi took him along below its southern face, into which, during Greco-Roman times, had been built the Theatre of Dionysus, the long portico of Eumenes and the Odeon of Herodes Atticus. Turning north, it carried him half-way up the slope that had been made into a delightful park. For the remainder of the steep ascent he had to walk, but soon he had reached the Sacred Way and was climbing the broken stones that formed the staircase to the mighty Propylaea.

At the top of the giant staircase he paused to look back. On his left he now had the Temple of Victory, on his right the Column of Agrippa, above which had once towered the hundred-foot-high statue of Pallas Athene. Before him was spread the panorama of what had been the heart of the early city-state—the Areopagus, or Hill of Mars. There the Great Council had sat, to try such famous men as Socrates. Beyond it lay the stony hillside, with its gaping cells, in one of which Socrates had been imprisoned, and the Pnyx, a long slab of rock from which world-renowned orators had declaimed to assemblies of the people before they voted on the laws that were to govern the first democracy.

These nearer objects caught the eye against the backdrop of a splendid panorama. To the north-west the summits of the Aigaleos range were outlined against an azure sky, to the west lay Piraeus and the Isle of Salamis, to the south-west there sparkled the blue waters of the Gulf of Athens, and to the west rose the mountain of Hymettus, famous for its honey.

Turning, Robbie made his way toward the centre of the plateau. To his right front now lay the Parthenon. For over two thousand one hundred years it had retained, except for its looted interior, its pristine glory; but in 1687, when the vandal Turks were besieged on the Acropolis, they had used it as a powder magazine. A shell had blown up the magazine, shattering the greater part of the wonderful reliefs depicting the procession of the Panathenaea festival; but even so defaced, its rows of marble columns and perfect proportions made it a thing to marvel at.

Robbie knew every metope and corner of it, but he was not going there today. Instead, he inclined half left towards the Erechtheum, the second largest temple on the Acropolis, that had supporting its west portico the row of tall marble female figures called Caryatides. Instead of advancing so far, he stopped short in front of the south face of the temple. Some yards in front of it a solitary olive tree, the only tree of any kind on the Acropolis, was growing out of a square, stone trough.

It is related that, on the founding of Athens, Poseidon and Athene both wished to become the patron of the city. A Council of the gods was called, and Zeus decreed that the honour should go to whichever of the rivals produced a gift which would prove the more useful to men. The Sea King struck the earth with his trident and out sprang a horse. Athene produced an olive tree, and this symbol of peace and plenty was adjudged the more valuable gift; so she became the protectress of Athens.

As olive trees live for many hundreds of years, it is just possible that the quite slender tree now growing on the Acropolis may be an offshoot from the root of the first tree planted there in Athene's honour. However unlikely that may be, Robbie had never speculated on the question. It was enough for him that the tree was the symbol of the great goddess.

Although it was still early in the season, quite a number of tourists were rambling among the fallen monoliths scattered over the great plateau, and three conducted tours, including one of school-children, were making the round of the temples. For some minutes, Robbie had to wait until no one was near enough to notice what he was doing. Then he quickly pulled a small medicine bottle from his trouser pocket. Before leaving the Embassy, he had paid a visit to the dining room and filled it with his uncle's port. Now he quickly poured the contents of the bottle, as a libation to the goddess, at the root of her tree.

Shutting his eyes, he remained standing there, waiting for

counsel. But not, as had been the case on previous occasions, for inspiration as to how to proceed with his book. It was with that intent that he had started out, but he had since decided that he would not be able to go on with his book until he had freed his mind from the thoughts that had been agitating it for the past twenty-four hours.

Silently now, he prayed to the goddess either to assure him that he would be wasting his time in pursuing further the matter of the Greco-Czech agreement, or that it would be worth his while to do so.

A gentle breeze rustled the leaves of the olive tree, but to Robbie, through these rustlings, a quiet voice spoke.

'Strange mortal, who in these times has been granted the wisdom to understand that the gods can never die, and still have power to aid those who call upon them at their shrines. For the sake of my country and for yours, you must take up this quest, and whate'er befall, pursue it to the bitter end.'

4

'When First we Practise to Deceive'

THE gentle rustling of the leaves was suddenly drowned by a strident voice. Robbie felt sure that the goddess had been going on to whisper counsel to him, but he caught no further word. A conducted tour composed of Germans was approaching, and their fat guide was reeling off facts and figures for them in a monotonous bellow, as they advanced from round the south-east side of the Erechtheum.

Robbie was furious at the interruption, but there was nothing he could do about it; so, to get away from the crop-headed Herren and well-upholstered Frauen, who were now surrounding him like an incoming tide, he broke through the group and clambered up the steep steps in front of the main entrance to the temple.

Standing between the twenty-foot-high Ionic columns of the portico, he could look down over the nearby north wall of the Acropolis. Far below him lay the principal ruins of the ancient city: the great open area of the Agora where, in the narrow streets between a dozen temples, the Athenians had held their markets; the Theseum; the Library of Hadrian and the Tower of the Winds. But he looked down on them with unseeing eyes. For the moment, he could think of only one thing: he was now irrevocably committed.

As soon as the group of Germans moved on, he hastened back to the Sacred Olive Tree. Again he stood before it, with closed eyes, and prayed for guidance. Again the leaves rustled in the gentle breeze, but this time their rustling formed no pattern of whispered words. In vain he strained his ears, and reluctantly accepted that the goddess could no longer be there only when he heard footsteps close behind him and a voice with an American accent saying:

'Could you tell us, please, what this little tree would be doing here?'

It was a tall young man with three cameras slung about him, and a very pretty girl leaning on his arm. Robbie had little doubt that they were honeymooners, and he gladly told them about Athene's tree. He knew the Acropolis as well as any professional guide, and could talk much more interestingly about its ruins. At any other time, he would have offered to take them round, but he was still too overcome by the thought that one of the greatest of the Immortals had actually spoken to him to give his mind to anything else. Politely excusing himself, he hurried towards the north-east extremity of the plateau.

There, on the highest point of its slope, a large circular platform had been constructed, with a waist-high wall round it, from which the cliff dropped sheer. Above it, from a flagstaff, floated the flag of Greece, and this spot was known as the Belvedere for it gave the finest view of all from the Acropolis. To the north, the countless houses of the modern city stretched into the misty distance in the valley between Mount Poilikon and Mount Pendelikon. Nearer, one could pick out the principal buildings of the fashionable quarter; the Royal Palace facing on to Constitution Square; Venizelou Street with its fine university buildings; and the main boulevard, Stadium Street, running parallel to it. Beyond them, nearly two miles away, but still within the city, Mount Lycabettus, shaped like a sugar-loaf and nearly twice the height of the Acropolis, towered up, the sun glinting on the roofs of the monastery that crowned its summit. To the west lay the National Park, and across the river the modern Stadium, both, in the extraordinarily clear atmosphere that is peculiar to Greece, looking so close that one could have thrown stones into them.

The Belvedere was a favourite haunt of Robbie's to laze and dream, but now he was thinking hard of a way in which to set about the mission that the goddess had imposed upon him. He decided that it was most unlikely that he would get any more out of Nassopoulos, even if the Minister were aware, which seemed doubtful, of the Czechs' secret intentions. That left only the Czechs themselves as a source of information.

To pay a visit to the Czech Legation and ask someone there would obviously be a waste of time. That being so, the only course that remained seemed to be to think of some way to worm himself into their confidence.

It struck him then that perhaps, after all, the Czechs might have real grounds for believing that they could strike oil in Greece. Science, the world over, had advanced by leaps and bounds during the past ten years. Russia often used her satellites as cover for her own activities, and no one could deny that the Russian scientists, as far as anyone in the world, had recently penetrated the secrets of Nature. Perhaps some of them had devised an entirely new method of detecting various types of geological formation and, all unsuspected by the Greeks, oil did lie below their rugged mountains.

Spurred to sudden activity by this idea, Robbie left the Belvedere, walked as swiftly as he could across the uneven, pitted stones that formed the surface of the Acropolis, hurried down the slope and took one of the taxis that were always waiting in the car park for a fare. Jumping in, he told the driver to take him back into the city and stop at the nearest telephone kiosk.

From the kiosk he rang up the office of the United Kingdom Petroleum Company, and asked for Mr. Luke Beecham, the Company's chief representative in Greece. Beecham's work often entailed meetings with the Commercial Attaché, and he frequently paid visits to the Embassy, both on business and as a guest. He was a bachelor in his early forties, so was much older than Robbie, but he was a charming and kindly man and had often gone out of his way to be pleasant to the Ambassador's shy and somewhat ungainly nephew, to whom most people of any standing were inclined to speak only politely, then ignore. He had, too, several times asked Robbie to small parties at his flat, and had taken pains to draw him out.

In consequence, Robbie felt that Luke Beecham was a man whom he could trust, and that in the present matter it was a lucky break for him that the only man he really looked on as a friend should happen to be an expert on oil. In fact, he thought it might even be an indication that Athene meant to help him in his quest.

Beecham was still in his office and, when he came on the line, Robbie asked if he was free that evening. The reply was what he had feared, as Luke was an extremely popular person; he was going for cocktails to the Greek Chief of Staff and afterward giving dinner to an American couple at the Athénée Palace. However, his dinner date was not till nine o'clock and, at Robbie's pressing, he agreed to leave the cocktail party early so as to get to the hotel at half past eight.

Well before the time of his appointment, Robbie turned out of Stadium Street and walked through the big, glass swing-doors of Athens' most modern de-luxe hotel. Crossing the lofty hall, he went into the bar, sat down at a table and ordered himself a fresh orange juice with soda and laced with brandy. Ten minutes later, Luke, tall, fair, slim and unmistakably English in a Savile Row suit, joined him there.

When he had told the waiter to bring Luke a double dry Martini, Robbie said in a low voice: 'The matter I want to talk to you about is frightfully confidential, but I know I can trust you, and——'

'One minute,' Luke interrupted, giving a quick look round the bar. It was narrow and not very long, and there were only four other people in it; so if any of them had had a mind to listen, they could easily have overheard what was being said at Robbie's table.

Luke beckoned the waiter and told him to take their drinks up to the balcony, then he said: 'We'll go upstairs. There will be fewer people there.'

On the broad balcony that overlooked the hall, two middle-aged ladies were consuming Turkish coffee and a large dish of cream cakes. No other table was occupied, and when the waiter had set their drinks down on one, Luke turned to Robbie with a smile and said:

'Now, young man, go ahead. Let's hear what the trouble is that you've got yourself into.'

Robbie gave him a surprised glance. 'Oh, I'm in no trouble. I wanted to talk to you about oil. There isn't any in Greece, is there?'

'No; at least, not in quantities that it would pay to exploit commercially. For the sake of our poor old hard-up Greek friends I only wish there were.'

'That's what everyone says. But how about it being there all the time, only up to now no one's hit on the right way of discovering it?'

Luke frowned. 'I don't get you, Robbie. It simply is not there to discover.'

'You, and most other people, think so. I quite understand that. But you might be wrong. I mean, the Russian boffins are a pretty brainy lot. Look at the way they've photographed the back of the moon, and sent people up in rockets. Perhaps with radar, or something of that sort, they've found a way to look right down deep into the earth and get to know through different coloured rays about what sort of things are miles below its surface.'

'Well, anything is possible these days,' Luke admitted, 'and perhaps in a few years' time something of the kind may be invented. But I'd bet my last hundred drachmas that no country has anything like that yet. You see, new scientific processes hardly ever become working propositions within a short time of their first being thought up. Years of research and experiment have to go into them before they become operational. And in all the most advanced countries there are back-room boys working on more or less parallel lines, so one way and another all of them have a pretty shrewd idea about the things their rivals are trying to achieve. It follows that, if the Russians had perfected a device for doing as you suggest, it's as good as certain that I should have heard something about it. Even if they had, there are any number of places in which they could try it out with better prospects of making a strike than in

Greece. No, Robbie, it's not on. But tell me, what's put this extraordinary idea into your head?'

'A conversation I overheard yesterday, while I was lunching out at Toyrcolimano,' Robbie replied; then he told Luke the whole story up to his interview with Mr. Nassopoulos that morning.

Luke gave him a surprised grin. 'By jove, you have got a nerve. Talk about rushing in where angels fear to tread. I wonder he didn't have you thrown downstairs.'

'Why should he?' Robbie asked defensively. 'I only went to his office and asked him a civil question. Anyhow, he didn't.'

'No, and the reason why he didn't is because you are the nephew of the British Ambassador. You had better not let your uncle know what you've been up to, though. He would be hopping mad if he heard how you had taken the bull by the horns like this, or indeed if he knew you had taken any action at all in what is a strictly diplomatic affair.'

'Do you really think so? I've told you how he turned down my suggestion that I should try to find out what lies behind this business, but I took it that that was because he didn't consider me up to the job.'

On that Luke tactfully refrained from comment. Catching the eye of a waiter who was coming down the broad stairs from the big lounge on the first floor, he told the man to bring them another round of drinks. Then, after a moment's thought, he said:

'Anyway, I believe you're right that there is something fishy about this deal. From the Greeks' point of view, if the Czechs are mugs enough to ask for something that has no apparent value, they would be mugs themselves not to throw it into the package and accept the Czechs' explanation for wanting it, without enquiring further into the matter. But the Czechs' explanation does not hold water. None of these Communist Governments gives a damn for what the masses think of their administration. Most of the time, they don't even tell their people what they are up to. And if they did it wouldn't influence the elections, because they are a farce anyway.'

Robbie nodded eagerly. 'That's just how I see it. And whatever game the Czechs are playing we can be certain that it is not with the object of doing the Western Powers any good; so I mean to try and find out what it is.'

'I see.' Luke took a pull at his second dry Martini which the waiter had just set down in front of him, then shot a swift, sideways glance at his young companion, and asked: 'Are you going to tell Sir Finsterhorn about this project of yours?'

'No! Oh no!' Robbie exclaimed. 'This is my show, and until I've pulled it off I don't want him to know anything about it. You won't tell on me, Luke, will you?'

'Of course not, Robbie. I wouldn't dream of it. But you're taking on a pretty tough proposition. How do you intend to set about it?'

'Well; as I see it, the Czechs themselves are the only people who hold the answer to the riddle. I thought that somehow I might get into the Czech Legation.'

'What!' Luke sat up with a jerk. 'Play at being Gregory Sallust and burgle the place? God forbid! Any papers referring to this thing are certain to be in a safe, and you are no cracksman. Besides, if you were caught you would land yourself in most frightful trouble. No, Robbie; no.'

Robbie smiled. 'No, I'm afraid I'm not up to that sort of thing. What I thought was that I might get a job there.'

'A job! My dear chap, you wouldn't stand an earthly. Why in the world should they take you on?'

'I don't see why they shouldn't. Embassies and Legations often employ staff who are not their own nationals.'

'That's true,' Luke admitted after a moment; 'and I remember your telling me that you speak several Central European languages fluently. Well, perhaps they might, although I think it very unlikely. Anyway, I wish you luck.'

It was close on nine o'clock, so Robbie stood up. 'I had better be going now. Thanks for your good wishes and for letting me talk to you. You won't tell a soul about what I'm going to try to do, will you?'

Luke came to his feet and gave him a kindly pat on the shoulder. 'Certainly not, Robbie. I'm as close as an oyster about any secret that is entrusted to me. Let me know how you get on and, if there is any help that I can give you, don't hesitate to ask for it.'

Next morning at ten o'clock Robbie presented himself at the Czech Legation in Sekeri Street and adopted the same tactics as he had at the Greek Ministry of Commerce. He gave his name, asked to see the Minister, Mr. Havelka, and stated that, having no appointment, he was perfectly willing to await the Minister's convenience by sitting in the reception hall all day if need be.

On his name being sent upstairs, it rang a bell, as before, with the Minister's secretary. An enquiry came down if he were, in fact, a relative of the British Ambassador, and on his saying that he was Sir Finsterhorn's nephew he was told that the Minister would see him shortly. A quarter of an hour later he was taken up to the Minister's room.

Mr. Havelka proved to be a small, dark, bearded man, with piercing black eyes. He waved Robbie to a chair and, in halting English, asked the purpose of his visit.

Robbie replied in Czech that he was looking for a job, and it had occurred to him that there might be one going in the Czech Legation.

To attain his present position, Mr. Havelka had had to cultivate a poker face, but even he blinked at the idea of a nephew of the British Ambassador calmly asking to be taken on to his staff.

Instinctively, his head went down a little and his shoulders up, lest this strange animal should suddenly spring at him. Swiftly but cautiously his eyes ran over Robbie. Concluding that his visitor was neither mad nor dangerous, he stalled for time by asking: 'What qualifications have you?'

Robbie reeled off the languages he spoke. Havelka's brain was working like a dynamo. It was used to that. There had been times when, had it failed to do so, he would have found himself being marched off with the barrel of a pistol pressed hard into his back. He suspected a trap, but for once he was in a situation to which he had not got a clue. To gain further time in which to think, he pulled open a drawer in his desk, shuffled through some papers in it, and produced a document printed in Polish. Handing it to Robbie, he said: 'Please translate that into Czech.'

The document was about the exchange between the two countries of university students for vacation courses. The subject held no interest for Robbie, but he found that he was able to render quite a passable translation of it. While he slowly uttered the sentences, Havelka's quick, bird-like eyes continued to flicker over him.

The Czech was thinking: 'He must be an agent. No, he can't be. Even the British would not have the impudence to send one of their spies here openly to ask for a post. Perhaps he thinks himself a Communist. But if he is the Ambassador's nephew, that is hardly likely. Yet he might be. It has been reported that our propaganda is having excellent results among young people in England. The poor fools march now in their thousands to demand the banning of the bomb. If he is one of those, we could make good use of him. But how am I to know? Whatever I do, that swine Janos will say that I did wrong. If I send the fellow about his business, I shall be told that I missed a chance; if I take him on, Janos will rail at me for having endangered our security. How I wish that I could consult with Janos on occasions such as this. But no; he refuses all responsibility, maintains his role as butler all day and hands round the *slivovitz* with a sly smirk, then comes up here at night to pick holes in my day's work.'

When Robbie had finished the translation, the Minister said: 'Mr. Grenn, you are a nephew of the British Ambassador, so obviously of the capitalist class and, presumably, not a friend of Communism. What reason can you possibly have for seeking a position with us, which could carry only a very modest salary?'

This was the big fence, and Robbie knew it. For his years, he was remarkable in that he had never told a lie, or at least not more than a minor prevarication. Brought up and cared for solely by two adoring women, he had never had any cause to. Not until quite recently had he felt any urge to break away from his well-ordered life. He had never been forbidden to do anything except over-exert himself, he had never given way to any unbridled desire, he had never known the dread of being found out, or had any special secrets to keep. But after he had left Luke Beecham the previous evening, he had realized that he would never get anywhere with the Czechs unless he was prepared to lie to them.

It was more the strangeness of having to do so, rather than any definite moral scruple, that made him reluctant to abandon his habit of replying frankly to any question put to him. Yet he realized that he must and, recalling a story that Sir Finsterhorn was fond of telling about Sir Winston Churchill fortified him in his determination.

The story was to the effect that, during the war, the Prime Minister was asked to approve a scheme which, by deceiving our enemies, would bring pain and grief to them. Naturally, he expressed himself in favour of it and, as it required co-ordination at the highest levels, he enthusiastically took charge of it himself.

The plan required that certain false information should be disseminated on the Continent, by means of broadcasts. Of these there were two kinds: those issued in numerous foreign languages by certain Intelligence departments, and those in English which were the normal News Bulletins of the B.B.C. The first had a basis of truth, but at times included lies deliberately calculated to mystify and mislead the enemy; on the other hand, it had definitely been laid down in a directive to the B.B.C. that its News Bulletins, on which the captive peoples of Europe had come to rely so greatly, should tell the truth, and nothing but the truth.

A high executive of the Broadcasting Services was ordered to attend a midnight War Cabinet meeting. With graphic gestures, the great Prime Minister outlined the plan, and told the visitor what was required of him.

Perhaps someone on the P.M.'s staff had blundered and had produced the wrong man. At all events, as the visitor listened to the forceful phrases directed at him, he grew paler and paler. At length he burst out:

'But, sir! To do as you suggest would be entirely contrary to our established policy. You cannot possibly ask me to tell lies like this.'

For a moment the Prime Minister stared in amazement at the poor wretch. Then he turned to those about him and cried in ringing tones: 'What is this? Am I confronted with a man who refuses to lie in the service of his country? Take him away! Take him away! Never let me see his face again.'

Sir Finsterhorn always concluded this story by saying that it was, no doubt, apocryphal, but Robbie had a passionate admiration for Sir Winston and liked to think that it was true. In any case, it had registered deeply in his slow mind a conviction that to lie on behalf of one's country was a matter for praise rather than blame. In consequence, he now set about doing so in no uncertain manner.

Having thought out carefully beforehand what he should say, he told Mr. Havelka that he had quarrelled with his uncle on political grounds and that, on learning of his leanings towards Communism, Sir Finsterhorn had thrown him out of the house. He added that he had a little money, but not much; so must quickly find a job to support himself. As his only asset was a thorough knowledge of Central European languages, he was hoping to find employment and congenial companionship in the Legation of one of the Communist countries.

By this time, the Minister had convinced himself that there was little to be feared from Robbie. Honesty radiated from him, and he was obviously a simple type of not very high intelligence. But he could speak Czech fluently, so should be capable of performing some not very exacting job of work. It struck Havelka, too, that it might even be counted as a feather in his cap to have, as he would put it to his superiors, suborned the nephew of the British Ambassador and be making use of him.

Pulling thoughtfully at his little beard, he said: 'I sympathize with your situation, Mr. Grenn. To be deprived of a comfortable home on account of your political opinions is certainly hard. Yes, I would like to help you. Return here at ten o'clock on Monday morning. By then I think I will have found some employment for you.'

Two minutes later Mr. Havelka was striving not to wince as his hand was pressed in an iron grip by a beaming Robbie. Lightheartedly, Robbie ran downstairs and went out into the street.

It was another pleasant day; so he crossed the road, and went into the park. Even in spring the flowers there were indifferent, and during summer it was an arid waste; but as it was only a few hundred yards from the British Embassy Robbie often went for a stroll there in the morning.

He had just reached the big pavilion near the centre of the park when a sudden thought struck him. When telling the lies he had concocted to Havelka he had said that his uncle had thrown him out of the house. What if the Czechs discovered that was not true? They would then certainly believe him to be a spy, and his very successful morning's work would have been entirely wasted. Still worse, in future, as far as the Czechs were concerned, he would be a marked man; so what hope would he then have of succeeding in the task he had set himself?

As swiftly as the deflating of a pricked balloon, the elation he was feeling drained away from him. With his hands in his trouser pockets, with downcast head, he strolled on until he reached the southern end of the park. Crossing the road, he entered the grass enclosure that contains the remains of the vast Olympieion. Sitting down on a fragment of one of the mighty fallen pillars of the Temple, he strove to think things out.

After half an hour he decided that there was only one thing for it. He must leave the Embassy and go to live in an hotel.

That day Sir Finsterhorn was giving a lunch party, and it was after three o'clock before the last of his guests had departed. The moment he had courteously bowed them away he made for his sanctum. Robbie followed him, paused in the doorway, and said:

'I'd like to speak to you for a moment, Uncle. May I come in?'

The Ambassador had just sat down at his desk, and he looked up with a slight frown. That morning he had received a despatch from the Foreign Secretary concerning some rather delicate negotiations, and he was anxious to get to work on it without delay; but he said with his habitual politeness:

'This isn't a good time, Robbie. But if it will take only a moment go ahead.'

'I wanted to let you know, Uncle, that I've got a job.'

'Really!' Sir Finsterhorn's long face lit up with one of his rather rare but charming smiles. 'Well, I'm delighted, Robbie. Yes, delighted. What sort of a job is it?'

'Translating documents. At least, I expect that's what they'll want me to do.' Robbie took a deep breath then blurted out: 'Anyway, it's at the Czech Legation.'

The Ambassador suddenly became completely still. 'What's that you say?' he demanded, after a moment. 'The Czech Legation. If this is a joke, Robbie, I regard it as in the worst of taste. You cannot be speaking seriously.'

Robbie swallowed hard. 'Yes, sir, I am. I saw Mr. Havelka this morning; and he's promised to give me a job, starting on Monday.'

Sir Finsterhorn came slowly to his feet. 'Havelka took you on personally? I can't believe it. What possible reason could you have given to induce him to do so?'

'Well—er—it was my knowing the Central European languages. Making use of them is about the only way I could earn money. And . . . and, after all, Uncle, for months past you have been urging me to get a job.'

'I have indeed. You were utterly spoiled by your aunt and that old nurse of yours. Years ago, you should have been sent to a place where you could have been trained in some work suited to your limited abilities. That you are now twenty-three and still idling your life away is perfectly scandalous. But that you should be employed by the Czech Legation is unthinkable. You surely must know that, as long as the Cold War continues, those people must be regarded as our enemies. In fact, I am completely at a loss to understand Havelka's taking you on. That is, if you gave him your right name.'

'Oh, yes. I told him who I was and—and, to tell the truth, sir, I had to spin him a yarn that I had quarrelled with you over politics. I led him to believe that I was pro-Communist. It's really *that* I wanted to tell you. You see, to make the story stick I'll have to leave the Embassy and go to live in an hotel.'

The Ambassador's blue eyes sparkled angrily. 'And so you shall, my boy,' he snapped after a moment. 'I see the whole thing now. Havelka jumped at the chance of making a fool of me. For the British Ambassador's nephew to take service with the Czechs will make me the laughing-stock of Athens. When your aunt died you were incapable of looking after yourself. My wife and I gave you a home and this is how you have repaid us. But in this past year you have learnt enough to stand on your own feet. Very well, then. Pack your bags and don't let me see you here again.'

5

Hero Number One

TEN minutes later Robbie, near to tears, sat hunched up in the armchair in his bed-sitting room. For a while he was so completely shattered that he could not co-ordinate his thoughts. He had been prepared for his uncle to show marked disapproval when he admitted that he was posing as a pro-Communist, but had hoped that the fact that he had at last actually got himself a job would placate him. It had not occurred to him for one moment that, because he was to be employed by the Czechs, Sir Finsterhorn would be sufficiently enraged to cast him off and forbid him the Embassy. To attempt to spy on the Czechs while retaining his sheet anchor was one thing; to be thrust out into the world and on his own for the first time was a very different matter.

For a while he contemplated abandoning his plans and returning to England. Aunt Emily had left him her pleasant house at Cheltenham, together with its contents. Sir Finsterhorn had wanted him to sell it; but it was the only home he had known, and he did not need the money. Moreover, old Nanny Fisher, now nearly seventy, was still alive, and he could not bear the thought of her being put out at her age to make a new home for herself. Therefore he had dug in his toes against even letting the house, and had arranged for her to receive a sufficient sum to maintain it for him and to keep on their cook.

But Athene's words to him, conveyed through the rustling of the leaves on her sacred tree, were still fresh in his mind. She had charged him to go through with his quest to the bitter end, whatever might befall, and a command from the goddess was not to be ignored lightly.

He considered the possibility that he had only imagined hearing her voice. Had he heard it in a dream, he could have accepted that, but he had been wide-awake, and had deliberately sought her counsel. Further thought convinced him, too, that the harsh treatment meted out to him by his uncle was typical of the unexpected misfortunes which heroes of ancient times always met with on their quests.

The inhabitants of Olympus had been a jealous lot, and perpetually quarrelling with one another. For one of them to take a mortal under his or her protection was quite enough for one of the others to set about inflicting pain and grief upon him and hamper him at every turn. It might be that or, perhaps, Robbie thought, he might unwittingly have offended some member of the Olympian family.

They were all incurable busybodies. Apart from intriguing among themselves and making love, their principal sport had been to come down to earth and mingle with mortals; but not in their beautiful trimmings. They assumed disguises as crippled beggars or wrinkled old women clad in filthy rags. One of their favourite games was to ask for a night's lodging or a free ride on a ferry, and woe betide the unfortunate person who refused their request; he was lucky if he was not blinded there and then or turned into a lizard. It could be argued that these judgments on the spot were a far more effective way of inducing the ancient Greeks to be charitable to the poor and humble than the threats of hell and damnation in some uncertain future which were thundered forth centuries later by Christian fanatics. All the same, Robbie felt, these totally unexpected actions by the gods must have been extremely worrying for their worshippers.

Reluctantly, he concluded that, by appealing to Athene, he had laid himself open to becoming a plaything of the Immortals; so he must henceforth take the rough with the smooth, and rely on her to see him through.

As he had brought out from England nearly all his personal possessions he felt that he could hardly be expected to remove all of them that afternoon. He put his immediate requirements into a big suitcase, leaving the rest to be sent after him by arrangement when he had found permanent quarters for himself. Carrying the suitcase downstairs, he went out of the back of the house and crossed the garden.

The Embassy and its precincts occupied the whole block, the large garage at the far end of the garden opening on to Ploutarchou Street, on the opposite side of which was a big block of modern flats. In one of them lived Luke Beecham; so Robbie entered the block and asked for him.

It was a Friday, and to Robbie's dismay the porter told him that Mr. Beecham had just left in his car to spend the week-end with friends who had a seaside villa at Lavrion. This was a sad blow as, although Robbie had made many acquaintances in Athens, there were few that he could call friends, and no one other than Luke to whom he could confide his present trouble.

Still carrying his heavy bag, which, owing to his great strength, caused him little effort, he turned into the main boulevard and walked along it, debating what next to do. To get a room at an hotel was the obvious answer. Had he had the least experience in leading a double life he would have looked for some modest place suited to the role he was playing, but that never occurred to him. Most of the visitors who were invited to lunch or to dine at the Embassy stayed at the Grande Bretagne; so, without further thought, he went to it.

Unlike most more modern hotels, the Grande Bretagne had no shops facing the street occupying a large part of its ground floor level; instead, there were spacious lounges, two restaurants, a ballroom and cocktail bar large enough to have held one hundred people. Yet an air of quiet dignity prevailed and rarely more than a handful of visitors was to be seen sitting about, because so many of its patrons were rich enough to afford private suites.

The money left to Robbie by his parents had been well invested during his minority, so for the past two years he had been in receipt of a very handsome income. Up to the present, even with keeping open the house at Cheltenham, he had found no use for more than a third of it, so he had no hesitation in taking a small suite, as a sitting room of his own would enable him to work undisturbed on his book in the evenings. He would have preferred one that looked out on to the trees and fountains in Constitution Square, which always reminded him of Trafalgar Square in London. Constitution Square was also on a slope and, at its upper end, it was dominated by the Royal Palace, a building somewhat resembling the National Gallery. However, he felt that would be too much of an extravagance, so contented himself with a suite at the back, facing the backs of other buildings.

Having unpacked, he decided to take his mind off his worries by going to a film, and at the Orpheus Cinema saw Alec Guinness and Noël Coward in *Our Man in Havana*. He had chosen the film solely on the names of its stars, so it struck him as something more than a coincidence that it should turn out to be about the Secret Service. During the show its clever satire caused him to laugh uproariously, but the fact that its bewildered hero came out all right in the end gave him the more sober thought that perhaps Athene had deliberately sent him to see the film in order to cheer him up.

That idea braced him up for the remainder of the evening, but Saturday and Sunday dragged terribly, and during them he suffered from bouts of acute depression. Two visits to the Acropolis failed to bring him even a ray of comfort, and he found it impossible to concentrate sufficiently to work on his book. By Sunday evening, he was doubting his ability even to hold for long his job with the Czechs, let alone succeed in finding out their secret intentions. After dinner, up in his sitting room, he sat miserably, twisting his big fingers together, again sorely tempted to throw in his hand and either return to England or go back to the Embassy and grovel before his uncle. To distract his mind from such unhappy thoughts, he decided to make another attempt to write a few paragraphs of his book. As he took the manuscript from a drawer and laid it on the desk, it fell open of its own accord at Chapter IV. Instinctively he began to read what he had written:

THE HEROES

(NO. 1 HERCULES)

Hercules did so many heroic deeds that I think he is entitled to first place among the Heroes, but he had a sad life and was a very unlucky man. When I say he had bad luck, I really mean that he was constantly pursued by the vindictiveness of that old bitch Hera.

He was a son of Zeus by Alcmene, the wife of Amphitryon, King of Tiryns, which in ancient times was the port of Mycenae. As usual, the Father of the Gods did not let on who he was when he slept with this lady. He simply took the form of her husband and got into bed with her. I suppose he was much better at that sort of thing than King Amphitryon. Anyway, she rumbled him and he was so cock-a-hoop from the good time she had given him that, when he got back to Olympus, he decreed that the next male to be born in Amphitryon's family should be lord over all Greece.

At that, of course, Hera guessed what he had been up to, and flew into a frightful rage. As a first move, she caused poor Alcmene's labour to be prolonged until Hercules's cousin, Eurystheus, was born before him. As Zeus could not go back on his word, Eurystheus became top chap and Hercules his vassal.

Now that the cat was out of the bag, Alcmene did not dare to nurse her own child, so tried to fox Hera by putting her baby out into a field, hoping that his Immortal papa would see to it that someone took care of him. It so happened that Hera and Athene were taking a stroll that way and, seeing the infant, Hera picked it up. At times, apparently, the Immortals were shockingly dense, as Hera had no idea whose the baby was, and put it to her breast. Hercules was already a lusty chap, and he pulled so violently at her that she plucked him off and, in a pet, threw him back on to the ground. Athene, being much more decent, took charge of him and gave him to his own mother to bring up as a foundling.

Hera pretty soon tumbled to the true state of things and,

angrier than ever at being had for a mug, sent two snakes to kill Hercules in his cradle. His mother was asleep, and his nurse too petrified by fright to do anything about this; but Hercules woke up, roared with laughter and strangled both the snakes before they could do him any harm.

Woken by the din he made, Alcmene came running in and, amazed at her infant's extraordinary performance, fetched her husband to have a look at the dead snakes. King Amphitryon was so impressed that he sent for Tiresias, a famous blind seer, to tell the babe's fortune. Old Tiresias predicted that Hercules would become no end of a big shot, so Amphitryon had him educated by the very best teachers of all kinds and descriptions.

When he had grown up, the gods put him through a test. They caused him to meet two very attractive girls. One was named Pleasure and the other Duty. Pleasure was a most luscious blonde and offered to sleep with him right away. She also promised him a long life of ease and plenty with lots more blondes thrown in. Duty was a much more modest type and, like Sir Winston Churchill, offered him only blood, toil, tears and sweat. For some reason I can't possibly explain, he chose Duty, and he got exactly what she had promised him.

However, by choosing to follow Duty, he soon became the most famous champion in all Greece. Most of the gods felt that he had done the right thing, so they decided to help him all they could. Athene lent him a suit of armour from her temple. Hermes gave him a magic sword that could cut through anything. Hephaestus made him a special shield, and Apollo gave him some of his arrows. Equipped with these aids, he fairly racketed round Greece, slaying all sorts of monsters. Anyone who had a hydra-headed Griffon ravaging his garden had only to call in Hercules, and he put paid to the beast in no time at all.

Thebes was a city that he took special interest in, because Amphitryon, who had behaved to him as a father, had had to give up his own kingdom and had settled there. On hearing that Thebes was being attacked, Hercules sped to its assistance. Amphitryon was killed in the fray, but Hercules led the defenders to victory, and Creon, the King of Thebes, gave him his daughter Megara in marriage as a reward.

It looked as if he would now be able to settle down, and enjoy family life; but Hera had not forgotten about him, and this time she played him a most scurvy trick. She inflicted him with madness, so that he threw his own children on the fire and drove his horrified wife out of the house. When the poor chap came to himself and realized what he had done he was absolutely shattered. For a time he wandered round quite distraught while endeavouring to secure pardon from the gods.

They granted it to him. But I think the gentle reader will agree that, considering he didn't know what he was doing at the time, they treated him pretty scurvily. They had the Oracle at Delphi declare that as a penance he must do any ten jobs that his cousin, Eurystheus, ordered him to.

Nearly all these jobs entailed his having to slay some ferocious beast that was terrifying people for miles around, or stealing for Eurystheus something of value that was guarded by some other horrifying monster. His 'labours', as they were called, were as follows:

No. 1 To slay the Nemean lion.
No. 2 To slay the nine-headed snake, Hydra.
No. 3 To capture the golden-antlered stag, Cerynitis.
No. 4 To slay the Erymanthian boar.
No. 5 To clean the stables of King Augeias in a single day.
No. 6 To slay a flock of birds of prey called Stymphalides.
No. 7 To slay a mad Minoan bull.
No. 8 To capture the savage horses of Diomedes.
No. 9 To secure the girdle of Hippolyte, Queen of the Amazons.
No. 10 To steal a herd of red cattle from the giant Geryon.

These labours took him all over Greece, to Crete, to Asia and to Africa, and kept him hard at it for several years. Most of the monsters he had to tackle could not be harmed by ordinary weapons, so he had to rely mainly on cunning or his enormous strength.

In the case of the Nemean lion, he tore up a tree which he used as a club to strike it down, then strangled it with his bare hands. Afterwards he skinned it and used its skin as a cloak.

This is why he is often pictured dressed that way and holding a club.

With the Amazon Queen he was lucky. The Amazons were an Asiatic race of warrior women and not at all the sort of girls one would care to run into when taking a walk through the woods. They burned away their right breasts so as not to be hindered by their natural shape when bending a bow, and killed all their male children as soon as they were born. As they had been doing that for generations it is a bit of a mystery how they ever got in the family way. But perhaps they made the men captives they took from other races oblige before killing them off. Anyhow, Queen Hippolyte took such a good view of Hercules that she willingly gave him her girdle. Unfortunately Hera got to hear about this. She took the form of an Amazon herself and stirred all the other tough babies up against their visitor, so Hercules had to fight his way out of their country after all.

Diomedes, whose mares Hercules was sent to steal, must have been a horrible fellow. He fed these savage beasts on human flesh. But Hercules settled his hash. Quite literally in fact. He killed him, cut him up and gave him to his own mares to eat before driving them off.

Even given Hercules's strength and courage anyone might have despaired at the job of cleaning out King Augeias's stables in a single day. The King kept three thousand cattle and had not had a spadeful of their droppings taken away for thirty years, so you can imagine what mountains of dung there must have been. But our clever Hero succeeded in his task by diverting the course of two rivers, the torrents of which washed the stables clean.

Having pulled off this remarkable feat made it all the harder when his mean cousin Eurystheus insisted that this labour could not count as one of the ten, because King Augeias had offered Hercules a reward if he could do it. Even the fact that the King went back on his promise afterwards made no difference. In addition, Eurystheus ruled that the slaying of the Hydra should not count either, because Hercules had the help of his nephew who, as Hercules cut off the monster's heads, seared the bleeding necks with a flaming torch so that new heads could not grow out of them. In consequence the unfortunate Hercules had to take on two more labours.

No. 11 was to fetch three golden apples from the Garden of the Hesperides. This was the most difficult task yet, as no one even knew where the garden was. For ages Hercules wandered around trying to find out, until some nymphs tipped him off to go and ask the Old Man of the Sea. He caught this slippery customer and kept him bound in his own seaweed till he disclosed that the Garden was on an island in the Western Ocean, and that Prometheus would tell our Hero how to get there. Prometheus was still chained to a rock in the Caucasus, having his liver pecked out every day by an eagle. Hercules shot the eagle and rescued him. Naturally, Prometheus was jolly grateful and he suggested that, as Atlas was the father of the four Hesperides maidens, Hercules might persuade him to go and get the apples for him.

Hercules thanked him for the idea and crossed the Med. to Egypt. The Pharaoh there was accustomed once a year to sacrifice a stranger to his gods, and on seeing Hercules he thought he looked just the goods for the job. But it proved the Pharaoh's unlucky day. Hercules kept mum, allowed himself to be bound and led into the temple; then he snapped his bonds, gave a big horse-laugh and sacrificed the Pharaoh on his own altar.

After killing the odd giant in Libya, Hercules went on to Morocco where by this time Atlas had become frightfully tired of holding the world up on the back of his neck. Actually, I've never quite understood how he did this; unless he was upside down. But I can only tell you what the chronicles say he was doing. Anyhow, when Hercules offered to hold up the world for him if he would go and get the apples, he jumped at the chance of handing over his burden. He then went off to get the apples; but he must have been a bit soft in the head to bother about that as, when he came back with them, he said that he had no intention of taking the world on his shoulders again. That put Hercules in a very nasty spot, as he looked like being stuck with the world for good. However, he said to Atlas: 'All right, old chap, but just hold it for a moment, will you, so that I can bind some cords round my head to ease the pressure,' or words to that effect. Being a stupid great oaf, Atlas fell into the trap. As soon as he'd taken the world back Hercules roared with laughter and went off with the golden apples.

No. 12 was the most terrible labour of all. That beastly man Eurystheus ordered Hercules to go down into Hades and bring back its guardian, Cerberus, the three-headed hound of hell with fangs that dripped poison. Hercules had himself purified at Eleusis, then Hermes took him to Cape Tainarom, the southernmost point of Greece, where there was a cave leading down into the Underworld.

Most people would have been scared stiff at the thought of entering Hades, but he does not seem to have minded a bit and barged in as if he owned the place. Coming upon an old friend chained to a rock he released him, then he killed one of King Pluto's bulls so that by lapping up its blood some of the poor ghosts down there could get a taste of life. When the herdsman tried to interfere, Hercules seized him and would have crushed his ribs in if Queen Persephone had not come on the scene in time and begged him to let the poor chap go.

Soon afterwards he found himself face to face with Pluto, the dread lord of this grim domain; but far from getting cold feet he fitted an arrow to his bow and shot the King of Hades in the shoulder. God though Pluto was, he roared with rage and pain; yet so impressed was he with the courage of Hercules that he told him that he could take Cerberus away provided he used no weapon. Our hero then seized the terrible mastiff by the throat, threw it over his shoulder and carried it off in triumph.

When he cast the monster at Eurystheus's feet, his horrid cousin was so terrified that he freed him from all further obligation on condition that he returned Cerberus to his kennel.

Anyone would have thought that after completing his twelve labours Hercules would have been only too happy to settle down to a quiet life. But not a bit of it; he continued to roam the world doing mighty deeds as the champion of mankind against every sort of horror. He sailed with the Argonauts in search of the Golden Fleece, and had many other adventures too numerous to recount. During them the good Athene always sought to aid and protect him, but Hera's malice continued unabated.

He fell in love with a young woman named Iole, the daughter of King Eurytus, and by triumphing over the King in an archery contest won the right to marry her. But her papa got the wind up that Hercules would treat her as he had his first wife, so as a get-out accused him of having stolen some cattle. Iole's brother, Iphitus, had become frightfully pally with Hercules and set out with him to try to run the real thief to earth. Hoping to spot the stolen herd, they climbed a high tower and while they were up there that hateful Hera caused Hercules to go mad again. Not knowing what he did, he picked up his friend and threw him from the tower-top to die smashed to pieces a hundred feet below.

When Hercules got his wits back he was most terribly upset, and for months on end hiked from one temple to another, seeking pardon for his act; but no high-priest would give it, and the Pythoness at Delphi refused even to listen to him. By then he was so fed up that he snatched from under her the sacred tripod on which she sat to prophesy and made off with it.

When Apollo heard about this he became absolutely livid with rage. Hurtling down from Olympus, he demanded his property back. Hercules refused to give the tripod up unless he was pardoned for Iphitus's death, upon which the beautiful god and the stalwart hero came to blows. Zeus had to be fetched—no doubt from demonstrating the facts of life to some pretty popsie. Having separated the combatants he decreed that Hercules should be cleansed if he sold himself into slavery for three years and gave the money he got for this to Iphitus's children.

Hermes then led Hercules into Asia, where he let himself be sold for three talents to Omphale, Queen of Lydia. The sight of his mighty limbs soon gave this lady ideas, and she decided that she could find a much better use for him than chasing monsters and cattle thieves. Perhaps, too, Hercules had at last become a bit bored by that sort of thing. Anyhow, he let Omphale take his lion skin and club away from him and dress him up in silks and satins as though he were a court Eunuch, which he certainly was not. To please the Queen he even took up knitting socks and jumpers for himself; so his three years as a slave were passed in ease and luxury, and he might have fared far worse. But at the end of them he suddenly felt a revulsion for that sort of life and rather ungratefully walked out on Omphale without so much as a 'thank you', to seek fresh deeds of daring-do.

While in Hades, he had been given a message by the shade of Meleager for his beautiful sister Deianira, the daughter of King Oineus. Now, somewhat belatedly, our Hero went to Calydon and, having delivered the message to Deianira, fell in love with her. As the gentle reader may guess, he did not win her without a struggle; but he triumphed over his rival, a river god named Achelous, and carried Deianira off as his wife.

He then spent some time going round to even up the score with the numerous kings who from time to time during his long career had done him dirt. Among them was King Eurytus, the father of his former love Iole; and having killed the king, he made her into a slave girl.

Knowing what chaps usually did with slave girls, when Deianira heard about this she naturally refused to believe that Iole's job was simply to mix Hercules's drinks or wash his undies, and her jealousy led her to take a step that ended in the most ghastly tragedy.

Soon after she and Hercules were married they had had to cross a river that was in flood. The Centaur Nessus was standing on the bank offering to carry wayfarers across on his broad back. Hercules scorned his offer and swam the river, but he let Nessus carry Deianira over. The Centaur gave her one look and decided that she was just his dish, so on reaching the far bank he attempted to take her by force.

Hercules heard her shout: 'Help, Hercie, help! This big bum's trying to do you-know-what to me,' or words to that effect; and being a marvellous marksman Hercules shot the lecherous Centaur from a distance with an arrow that he had dipped in the poisoned blood of the Hydra. Nessus, writhing in his death agony, determined to get his own back on his slayer, so he gasped out to Deianira: 'Dip a shirt in my blood, sweetie. If ever you get a hunch that your old man's going off the rails persuade him to wear it. It'll act as a charm. He'll take a run-out powder on the other dame and come back with a present for you.'

Now that Deianira was having kittens about Hercules being up to no good with his old flame Iole, she sent it to him with a message that it was the very latest thing in gents' shirting and she thought he would look fine in it. All unsuspecting, Hercules put it on when about to do his 'thank you' sacrifice to the gods for having helped him put paid to King Eurytus. But the blood of Nessus had been envenomed from the poisoned arrow, and as soon as the shirt became warmed through by the sacrificial fire before which Hercules was standing it began to burn him. Next moment agonizing pains shot through all his limbs. In vain he tried to tear the terrible garment off. It stuck to his skin and became a white-hot shroud that caused his blood to boil.

Realizing that there could be no escape from death, he tore down the nearest trees and stacked them up into a funeral pyre. Then he flung himself upon it and persuaded his armour-bearer, Philoctetes, to light it beneath him. His last words were: 'Hera, thou art avenged. Give me a stepmother's gift of death.'

So perished the greatest of the Heroes. There came a terrible storm of thunder and lightning, during which Pallas Athene descended in her chariot and bore the immortal part of Hercules up to Olympus. By then even Hera's hatred of him had burnt itself out. She welcomed him among the gods and gave him for wife her daughter Hebe, the spirit of Eternal Youth.

*   *   *   *   *

When Robbie finished reading, his large brown eyes were glistening, and he was almost in tears. 'Poor, poor Hercules!' he thought. 'What a terrible time he had. His life had been one long series of combats with powerful beasts and hideous reptiles. All his love affairs had gone wrong, the Kings he had performed great deeds for had cheated him out of his rewards and he had spent the best years of his life doing penance for crimes committed while he was not responsible for his actions.

Then, to cap it all, he had died in agony. Still, after all, he had come out all right in the end. Athene had seen to it that he should be given a place for all eternity on Olympus, and no man could have asked more than to have for his own the lovely Hebe who would remain for ever young and gay.'

This last thought put a different complexion on the matter and cheered Robbie considerably. He needed no telling that he had neither the strength, the courage nor the quick wits of Hercules; but as against that, he did not expect to have to fight any fire-breathing dragons, and he did have one thing in common with the Hero—namely, the same patron. Whatever trials and tribulations might beset his path, he felt confident that Athene would arrange matters so that he, too, came out all right in the end.

Next morning, hardly able to contain his excitement, he was at the Czech Legation well before ten o'clock. Confidently announcing that he had an appointment with Mr. Havelka, he sent his name up. When a reply came down that the Minister would not be able to see him for some time, that did not in the least damp his spirits. It did not even occur to him that Havelka had not actually promised him a job and might not have found one for him. He sat down opposite a large portrait of the President of the Czechoslovakian Republic, and just let his thoughts drift.

Three-quarters of an hour later, a middle-aged man with hair cut *en brosse*, a blue jowl and a small paunch, who looked as though he ought to be wearing a Gestapo uniform and carrying a gun, entered the hall, halted in front of Robbie, gave a jerky bow and said: 'Cepicka.'

'Oh—er—yes.' Robbie quickly stood up. 'My name is Grenn. How d'you do?'

'Mistair Grenn,' nodded the other, then went on in Czech: 'Pan Havelka tells me you speak our language. He regrets not to receive you, but he has a great deal of work. He asks that you place yourself in my hands. Come with me, please.'

'By all means,' smiled Robbie, turning instinctively toward the stairs. It was only as Mr. Cepicka turned in the opposite direction, towards the door to the street, that Robbie noticed that he was carrying a hat. When he reached the door, he put on the hat, with the remark: 'It is not far, so we will walk.'

Much puzzled, Robbie caught him up and strode along beside him. Sekeri Street debouched on to the broad Leoforos Vasilissis Sofias Boulevard, on which the British Embassy lay, but was nearer the centre of the city. Twice Robbie attempted to start a conversation with his companion, but the gorilla-like Mr. Cepicka replied only in monosyllables. Having covered a few hundred yards, they reached Constitution Square. Maintaining a stolid silence, Cepicka walked purposefully across it and entered a turning just off Karageorgi Street. A little way along it, he turned into an alley that broadened out into a small courtyard. In the centre grew a gnarled olive tree; at the sides there were two small private houses, a shop that sold bales of coarse silk, and a travel agency. Cepicka marched into the latter and said abruptly to a tall, thin young man behind the counter: 'Comrade Krajcir. He is expecting me.'

'Yes, Comrade Cepicka,' replied the young man quickly, with a nervous smile. 'Please come this way.'

He ushered them into an inner office. There, behind a desk, a plump man of about forty was sitting. He had very black hair that grew low on his forehead, dark eyes under bushy brows, a rather round face and a dimpled chin. He stood up and shook hands solemnly with Cepicka, who said: 'I bring you the young man about whom the Comrade Minister spoke to you on the telephone.' Then he turned to Robbie and added:

'This is Comrade Marak Krajcir. He is in charge here and will provide for you the employment that you asked Pan Havelka to find for you.'

Comrade Krajcir smiled, displaying a gold tooth at the left side of his upper jaw, and held out his hand to Robbie. Taking it in a firm grip, Robbie bowed over it, murmured his own name, and said how happy he was to know Mr. Krajcir.

The blue-jowled, unsmiling Comrade Cepicka announced that, having executed the orders he had been given, he would leave them and, with a curt nod, made his exit.

The more amiable Krajcir invited Robbie to sit down, asked him if he was willing to start work right away and, on receiving a reply in the affirmative, informed him of the office hours he would be expected to keep. He then proposed a wage that was little more than a pittance, but added that a handsome commission would be given on all business brought to the agency.

It was barely ten minutes since Robbie had left the Czech Legation, and all this had happened so quickly that his slow mind had not yet taken in its full significance; so, ever eager to please, he agreed enthusiastically.

Only after having been introduced to the other members of the staff, and finding himself rubber-stamping a thick pile of travel folders, did it fully come home to him that he had been had for a mug.

Mr. Havelka happened at about that time to give a thought to Robbie, and he smiled in his little black beard. He felt that in this matter he had good reason to congratulate himself on having eaten his cake and kept it, too. He could take kudos from his superiors for having caused the British Ambassador to lose face by taking his nephew into his employment, yet he had placed Robbie as a stooge in the Czech Travel Agency, where he could not possibly find out any secrets.

That was what Mr. Havelka thought and, had he had only Robbie to deal with, he would have been right. Understandably, he had not taken Pallas Athene into his calculations and, as she was on Robbie's side, before Mr. Havelka was very much older he found, to his fury and alarm, that he had been entirely wrong.

6

The Amateur Cracksman

THAT night Robbie again seriously contemplated throwing in his hand. He had thought himself such a clever fellow to have talked Havelka into promising to find him a job, and it had never for a moment occurred to him that the job would not be in the Legation. But he now saw that, even if Havelka had believed his assertion that he had Communist sympathies, the Minister would never have been fool enough to give the nephew of the British Ambassador any employment which might enable him to secure knowledge of secret transactions.

In vain he racked his brains for some other line of approach by which he might ferret out the truth about the Czecho-Greek oil-tobacco deal. He could think of none. Yet, having had such high hopes of achieving, for the first time in his life, something worth while by his own initiative, to admit defeat after less than a week of endeavour would mean a humiliation almost beyond bearing.

After much cogitation, he decided that he could at least put off swallowing that final bitter pill as long as he continued to work at the Travel Agency, and that, while there, it was just possible that a new way of trying to achieve his object might occur to him; so next morning at eight o'clock, he duly reported for duty.

Comrade Krajcir's staff consisted of a Mrs. Sebesta, a grey-haired woman of uncertain age, with a determined chin and an ugly wart on her left cheek, who acted both as Krajcir's No. 2 and his secretary; a tall, young man with thin, receding fair hair, named Rudolph Pucik; and Ludmilla Duris, a brunette in her early twenties with a good figure, who would have been decidedly pretty had not her brown eyes been small and close-set. The last two took turns in answering enquiries at the counter and, when not so engaged, in sorting folders and addressing envelopes.

The plump, black-haired Krajcir made few demands on Robbie. He was easy-going by nature, and handled all the important business of the agency himself, so his appearances in the outer office were infrequent. The previous day he had handed Robbie over to Pani Sebesta and it was she who played the part of task-mistress to the juniors. She was eagle-eyed and revoltingly efficient, never for a moment failing to find jobs for her underlings. It was obvious that the lanky Rudolph and the attractively curved Ludmilla both cordially disliked her. To Robbie they gave an eager welcome, being quick to realize that, since he knew nothing whatever about the travel business, he would be given all the most dreary jobs that they had had to do previously. And that was what happened.

That no attempt was made to initiate him into the mysteries of time-tables, ship-sailings and conducted tours was rather a relief than otherwise, as he knew that he would have had con- siderable difficulty in mastering such things; but he found being made into a 'dog's-body' far from pleasant, and he soon became terribly bored with sorting endless stacks of folders into sets, stamping piles of envelopes and standing at the duplicating machine running off lists of hotels and their tariffs.

While employed on these jobs, he covertly kept an eye on all the customers who came to the agency, and listened to their conversation with his colleagues. Very few of them were people of substance seeking accommodation in good hotels or expen- sive travel outside Greece. Once or twice a day men, some of whom looked rather seedy, came in, asked for Krajcir and, evidently being known at the office, were shown straight in to him. But the great majority were men and women on holiday from Czechoslovakia. They were all good Communists who, as a reward for showing an enthusiastic Party spirit, had been nominated by their bosses for a fortnight's cruise in the eastern Mediterranean, and were in Athens only for a couple of nights.

Far from being customers wanting to hire cars or private guides, they had barely enough money to buy themselves a drink, and came in only to collect folders, with pictures of the places to which they had been, to take home with them.

After working in the agency for a few days, Robbie began to wonder how, with such a clientele, it could possibly pay its way. The answer, he decided, was that it didn't and must be run as part of a propaganda programme. But, listen as he did with commendable patience, not one word did he hear exchanged between the members of the staff, or between them and anyone who came to the agency, that had any connexion with oil or tobacco.

Unaccustomed as he was to being ordered about, and loathing as he did routine tasks, by the end of the week Robbie was thoroughly fed up and felt that he could not stick it a day longer. On the Friday, when Krajcir doled out to him his meagre pay, he actually had it on the tip of his tongue to give notice, but at that moment a telephone call came through for the manager; so Robbie had to leave his room and, on second thoughts, he decided to put off taking the irrevocable step till after the week-end.

His reason for postponing the issue was his suddenly remembering that Luke Beecham would be back in Athens next day. On the previous Monday evening, after his first day at the agency, Robbie had called at Luke's flat to tell him about his job, only to learn that, after spending the week-end in the villa that belonged to friends and looked out on Lavrion's sunny beach, Luke had left for one of his periodic spells at his Company's office in Salonika and would not be returning till Saturday. Although Robbie was now convinced that he was wasting his time at the agency, he still felt considerable qualms about abandoning his quest altogether and possibly incurring the anger of Pallas Athene. During the week, no other idea for continuing it in a new direction had come to him, but there was just a chance that Luke might produce one; so, when eight o'clock came, he said good night to his colleagues as usual, and walked round the corner to the Grande Bretagne.

The long siesta break, from midday until four in the after-noon, observed in most offices in Athens, had to be made

up by a four-hour working session morning and evening.
Robbie, being unaccustomed to such lengthy days of activity,
had found in the past week that, after dining, he had been too
tired to go to the last house at any of the cinemas. But after
going early to bed on the first two nights his mind, having
nothing new to think about, had once more become largely
occupied with his book. In consequence, on Wednesday and
Thursday evenings, instead of going straight to bed, he had got
into a dressing gown and had worked for an hour or two on a
new chapter. It was the story of another of the Heroes, and by
eleven o'clock on this Friday night, he finished it. Laying down
his pen with a sigh of satisfaction, he sat back and read over
what he had written:

THE HEROES

(NO. 2 PERSEUS)

Once upon a time, there was a King of Argos named Acrisius. Like most of the ancient Greeks he was terribly keen
about having his fortune told, so he consulted an Oracle.
Afterwards he wished he hadn't, because he was told that he
would die by the hand of his grandson. This worried him a
lot; but he had only one child, an unmarried daughter named
Danaë, and he thought he might manage to cheat Fate by
locking her up so that no man could get at her, because then
he wouldn't have any grandchildren.

So determined was he to keep Danaë a virgin that he was
not content to put her in an ordinary prison, in case some stalwart youth came along with a pick-axe and hacked a way to
her through the wall. For the job, he built a tower of brass
and shut the poor girl up in that. But the one thing he could
not do was to turn Danaë from a most lovely girl into an unattractive frump, and it was that which led to his going to all
this trouble for nothing.

Zeus happened to come coasting along on a cloud with
nothing much to do, and looking down he saw Danaë. The
gentle reader will guess what happened then. In the twinkling
of an eye the old rip had turned himself into a shower of gold

and streaked down through the top of the brass tower. From her attitude to life later it seems that Danaë thoroughly enjoyed what happened after that. Anyhow, the next time her father visited her he found to his dismay that she was in the family way, and too far gone for him to do anything about it.

The child to whom she gave birth was Perseus. When King Acrisius learned that she had had a boy he was so scared for himself that he thought of killing the child, but he just could not get up enough courage to have such blood-guilt on his hands. As the next best bet for yet avoiding the Fate decreed for him, he had the mother and her infant put in a wooden chest and the chest thrown into the sea, hoping that they would both drown or be dashed to pieces on a rocky shore.

Whatever one may think of Zeus's morals, he always did his best to look after girls who had given him a good time; so he got in touch with his brother Poseidon and asked him to do the necessary. The Sea King obliged by stilling the wind and waves and gently pushed the chest ashore on the island of Seriphos in the Aegean.

There Danaë and her infant were found by a fisherman named Dictys. He was a good man and took them to his house, where he brought Perseus up as his own child. As Perseus grew up he so greatly outshone in strength, agility and beauty all the other youngsters on the island that it became pretty clear to everyone that he must be the son of a god, and they willingly made him their leader.

But trouble was brewing. Dictys had a brother named Polydectes, who was chief of the island, and after a while he began to make passes at the beautiful Danaë. She proved very smell-face about this, and said that having had Zeus for a lover she was not prepared to play those sorts of games with any mere mortal. Perseus was very devoted to his mother and by then old enough to defend her. He said in no uncertain manner that if Polydectes laid a finger on her he'd sock him for six.

Feeling that he would stand a better chance with Danaë if he could get this tiresome young man out of the way, Polydectes ordered Perseus to go and slay a terrible monster called Medusa. Why Perseus, having defied Polydectes over the question of his mother, should have felt compelled to obey this order is by no means clear. But apparently Athene had been sending him dreams in which he saw himself as the equivalent in those days of a film star. Convinced that he could count on the backing of the goddess, he would have been a pretty poor fish if he hadn't been tempted to go off and do something spectacular, so as to be fêted and admired by all. Anyhow, he seems to have persuaded himself that his mother was quite capable of taking care of herself during his absence, and declared himself willing to go and put paid to Medusa.

When the news of this reached Olympus the gods became a bit worried, as they feared he might be biting off more than he could chew. Medusa was one of the three Gorgon sisters and the only one who was mortal, but she packed a weapon not much less deadly than an atom bomb. When young she had been rude to Athene, so the goddess had turned her hair into vipers and made her face so horrible that whoever she looked at was instantly turned to stone.

Athene, now scared that one of her protégés might be done in by her own handiwork, came hurrying down to Perseus to warn him to be jolly careful how he tackled this terrible foe. She told him that he would be as dead as a fried haddock if he even met Medusa's glance, and lent him her own shield which was so brightly polished that it could be used as a mirror and he would be able to see his enemy in it while his back was turned to her. Then some of the other gods rallied round. Hermes gave him his crooked sword that could cut through the thickest armour, and tied on his feet his own winged sandals that would enable him to fly over land and sea. Pluto sent him from the Underworld a magic helmet that made its wearer invisible and, finally, Athene provided him with a goat-skin bag in which to put Medusa's head when he had cut it off, because even in death it could instantly strike dead anyone who saw it.

It's a funny thing, but after providing Perseus with all this lease-lend help his immortal friends could not tell him where to find Medusa. They could only suggest that he should go and wring the information out of the Graeae, three half-sisters of the Gorgons who lived in the far-distant frozen north.

Having asked Athene to keep a protecting eye on his

Mama, Perseus set off without further delay. Hermes' sandals enabled him to fly like a jet-bomber to his destination and Pluto's helmet made him invisible. He came down in a region of eternal snows and icy mountains on the shores of the Hyperborean Sea.

There, crouching in a huddle, which is hardly to be wondered at seeing how cold it must have been, he found the three Grey Sisters. Their long white hair was frozen stiff with icicles and they were so old that they must have been pretty well past everything. I mean, when three people are reduced, as they were, to sharing one eye and one tooth between them, they can't be fit for much, can they?

Wearing the helmet that made him invisible, Perseus came creeping up on those poor old girls and, while they were bickering over who should have the eye to see the person whose footsteps they could hear crackling the icy ground, he snatched it from them.

At that, one gathers, their language became unprintable, but Perseus just danced around them making rude noises and told them that unless they told him where the Gorgons lived he'd take their tooth as well, then they wouldn't be able to munch whatever it was they did munch to keep the life in their skinny old bodies. Seeing that it was all up they came clean and gave him the address he wanted.

Having given them back their eye, he was off like a thermo-nuclear rocket out of the icy mists, heading south into the brilliant sunshine.

The gentle reader will appreciate that it is not exactly easy to figure out where places mentioned by the ancients are on the maps in use today, so I must be forgiven for not being able to tell you where the island was in which the Gorgons lived. But it was definitely in the tropics and as far as I can make out off the coast of Africa.

When Perseus arrived above it the three sisters were lying asleep in the middle of what must have looked like a cemetery, for all over the place there were statues of people and animals; though really, of course, they had once been alive and Medusa's glance had turned them to stone.

Medusa was lying between the other two and in one quick

look Perseus saw that she was a most repulsive creature. Her great body was covered in horny scales, her hair was a mass of writhing serpents, she had wings of brass and her hands and feet were terrible claws. Anxious to get the job done before she should wake up he wasted no time but held Athene's mirror-shield above his head¯ and focused her face in it. Whether he had practised such a tricky stroke before, history does not relate, but he struck backward over his shoulder with Hermes' crooked sword and in one mighty slash severed her head from her body. Then, fumbling behind him, he pushed the head into the goatskin bag that Athene had given him for this purpose. Cock-a-hoop at having pulled this fast one on her so easily he leapt skyward with a shout of triumph.

That was a silly thing to do, because it woke her horrible sisters. When they saw Medusa's headless corpse they nearly burst themselves with rage. Clashing their brass wings and screaming with fury they came hurtling after our hero. His goose would have been cooked in no time if he hadn't been able to clap on the helmet that Pluto had sent him, which made him invisible. That enabled him to give them the slip and turning north he sped over a vast desert that was probably the Sahara.

While he flew on, drops of Medusa's blood trickled out of the goatskin bag. As they fell on the sand below they turned into snakes and scorpions. That is why there are so many of these poisonous reptiles in Africa. However, he seems to have got a bit off his course, for instead of landing back in Greece he came down in Morocco.

By then he was pretty tired, and one can't wonder. Seeing old Atlas kneeling there supporting the world on his shoulders, and knowing that he owned the Garden of the Hesperides, Perseus asked if he might rest there for a while. But Atlas got the idea that he intended to pinch some of his golden apples, and refused him permission.

As the Greeks were very hot on observing the laws of hospitality towards strangers, Perseus decided to teach the giant a lesson. He uncovered Medusa's head, which still had the power to turn to stone anyone who looked at it, and showed it to Atlas. Before you could say 'Jack Robinson' the mighty giant had become a mountain. Personally I think that was a bit overdoing it, but that is what happened, and if you go to Morocco today you can see him with snow on his head and forests sprouting out of his chest and shoulders.

By then Perseus was either lost or thought he would like to fly round for a while before returning to his home on Seriphos. Anyway he shot off eastward, crossed the Nile and sped down the Red Sea. The south-western coast was then part of Nubia, as the ancients called Abyssinia, and, glancing down, Perseus chanced to see a great black rock sticking up some way from the shore with a girl chained to it. Naturally he went down to investigate and he found her to be an eyeful. Seeing the country they were in one would have expected her to be a coal-black negress, but not a bit of it. She was a lovely golden brown, and an absolute smasher, but tears were running from her lovely eyes and she was obviously needing to be rescued.

When he asked her how she came to be there she didn't answer, but shut her eyes and blushed crimson. The poor girl's trouble was that she had no clothes on and she felt too embarrassed to talk to a strange young man while naked. Being a well-brought-up chap, Perseus realized what was biting her and put his hat on, then asked his question again.

Now that he was invisible, the girl perked up. She said her name was Andromeda and that she was the only daughter of Cepheus, the King of those parts. Apparently her mother, Cassiope, had been silly enough to boast that she, Andromeda, was more beautiful than Poseidon's daughters, the Nereids. They had been very peeved when they heard this and persuaded their father to send a terrible sea monster to ravage King Cepheus's coast and gobble up all his fisher folk.

Much upset by this, the King had gone off to Libya and consulted the Oracle of Ammon there as to how he could protect his people. The Oracle had told him that the monster could be got rid of only by sacrificing his daughter to it. One need hardly add that the King and Queen did not like this idea one little bit; but after a while their people had forced them to take this terrible course, so poor Andromeda had been chained to the rock and was waiting for the monster to come and eat her.

She had only just finished telling Perseus this when she let out a terrible shriek, for at that very moment she had spotted the monster as it bobbed up from the depths some way behind him.

'Fear naught!' cried Perseus, or words to that effect, and in a trice he had freed Andromeda by cutting through her chains with Hermes' sword. Turning, he then sprang into the air and rushed upon the monster.

No doubt the gentle reader here expects me to describe a terrible combat, but if the truth be told it was a walkover. For all its foaming jaws and huge swishing tail the giant whale, or whatever it was, did not stand an earthly. Like a tennis ball endowed with perpetual motion, Perseus simply bounced up and down driving his sword into the poor brute's back every time he descended, till the sea was red with its blood and it turned stomach up showing that it was a goner.

When he had done his stuff a mighty cheer broke out. Andromeda's parents and half the population of the country-side had assembled near the shore to see the end of her. The scream she had given on spotting the monster had brought them running to the edge of the cliff, and now they came swarming down it to acclaim our Hero.

As soon as Andromeda had been got ashore and wrapped up in a blanket Perseus told her parents that he wanted to marry her. Just in case they should be against her taking a husband who was not out of the top drawer he added quickly that they would find him in their version of Debrett as a son of Zeus. On hearing this, the King was so delighted that he said Perseus could have the girl and the whole kingdom too if he liked; so everything seemed set fair for the two young people getting to know one another better.

However, it soon transpired that there was a fly in the oint-ment. Apparently King Cepheus had temporarily forgotten that Andromeda was already engaged to a chap called Phineus. When Phineus heard what was on he became very shirty, and he completely spoilt the wedding feast by turning up at it and demanding his promised bride.

They couldn't very well hustle him out, because they were dressed in their Sunday best whereas he had arrived armed to the teeth and backed by a crowd of armed retainers. What is more, as he was the equivalent of a member of the local Hunt, a lot of the wedding guests took his side against Perseus, who was a stranger.

Perseus, being the sort of chap he was, naturally defied Phineus and refused to give up his girl. For answer Phineus chucked his spear at him. That started a free-for-all, and for a few minutes it looked as if Perseus and the King's friends, who stuck by him, were going to get the worst of it. But Perseus had taken Medusa's head along with him to his wedding. It must have been a bit high by that time, but I suppose he didn't want to let it out of his sight. Anyhow, with a shout of 'All of you who are on my side shut your eyes,' he pulled the head out of its bag and showed it to the company.

That was that as far as Phineus and his pals were concerned. But it must have been rather a gloomy wedding afterwards, with a crowd of gentry who had just been turned to stone looking on.

Now that Perseus was married he wanted to go home; but Andromeda could not fly, so he had to build a ship to take her. When they reached Seriphos he learned that Polydectes had never let up from chasing his mother—not his own mother, of course, but Danaë—round the gooseberry bushes. In fact his behaviour had been so caddish that poor Danaë had found it necessary to take sanctuary in Athene's temple.

Straight away Perseus strode up to the castle to give this old wolf-whistler a piece of his mind. But Polydectes got in first. He was very rude to Perseus about his mother not having been married to his father, then he taunted him with coming home with his tail between his legs and no Medusa's head.

'That's what you think,' said Perseus, and promptly pulled the head out of the bag. This put paid to Polydectes and no doubt he was removed to decorate the local park. Perseus then made the good Dictys chief of the island and went off to tell his mother, I mean his own mother not Dictys', that she need no longer be afraid to leave the temple.

Apparently she had never let on to him that he was the grandson of the King of Argos, but she told him now; so he decided to go and pay his respects to his grandfather. But before setting out he returned to the gods the wonderful things with which they had equipped him, and he made a present of Medusa's head to Athene. She set the head in the middle of her shield, and you can see it there in most of the statues of her.

Someone tipped King Acrisius off that his grandson was on the way to see him and, recalling the prophecy, the old chap properly got the wind up. Rather than remain in Argos and face Perseus, he fled north to Larissa in Thessaly. When Perseus heard about this he followed him with the intention of assuring him that he bore him no ill-will about his treatment of his mother—oh, bother, I don't mean his own mother but Perseus' mother—and only wanted to say 'Hello!'

When Perseus arrived in Larissa, the King of that place was holding one of those sessions of Public Games which with the Greeks took the place of our Test matches and Cup Finals. As anyone could join in and our Hero rather fancied himself as an athlete he entered his name for all the events. My gentle reader will not be surprised to learn that he took all the prizes one after the other, but when it came to throwing the quoit Fate took a hand. Not only did his quoit go further than those of any of the other competitors, but a gust of wind gave it a sudden lift, carrying it right into the Royal Box. As a V.I.P. guest his grandpop had naturally been given a seat there. It hit the wicked old man slap on the head, killing him outright, and thus the prophecy was fulfilled.

Perseus was very upset about this and, even when he had had himself purified, he still didn't feel happy about taking over the kingdom of Argos, owing to his having come into it by killing his grandfather. In consequence he swapped it with a neighbour of his for the kingdom of Tiryns. There he built the great city of Mycenae, of which I shall have a lot to tell you later.

By his beautiful Andromeda he had lots of children and they lived happily ever after. The gods were so pleased about this that when they died they were granted immortality, and as bright stars given a place side by side in the heavens.

*   *   *   *   *

Having finished reading his chapter and put the manuscript away, Robbie went to bed in a more cheerful frame of mind than he had enjoyed for some time. He was pleased with his work and now looking forward to an end to the drudgery he had to endure at the Travel Agency. With his usual optimism and faith in people cleverer than himself, he was by now convinced that Luke would think of some new line of investigation which he could pursue, so that, without suffering the humiliation of having abandoned his quest, he could give Krajcir notice on Monday.

The Greeks being a hardworking people, comparatively few of the shops in Athens close for a half-day, and those that do shut on Wednesdays; so that, although next day was a Saturday, the agency was open for its usual hours. In the morning business was slack, but it became brisker when the office re-opened at four o'clock, as another Czechoslovakian cruise ship had docked that day at the Piraeus.

At about half past five a small crowd of these tourists-on-a-shoestring were collecting folders and enquiring how, with their very limited funds, they could see something of the night-life of Athens—a diversion not included in their Government-subsidized itinerary. Pani Sebesta had gone out to see a printer about some new stationery that was required, Rudolph and Ludmilla were fully occupied at the counter answering enquiries and Robbie was seated at a small table in the background, engaged in a chore that he had been given of cleaning Pani Sebesta's typewriter.

The bell on the door jangled again, and Robbie glanced up to see a tall, tanned, well-dressed man come in. With an impatient frown at the backs of the little crowd of tourists, the newcomer thrust his way through them and, seeing that both Rudolph and Ludmilla were engaged, called across to Robbie:

'Hi, you! Is Comrade Krajcir in?'

As the man spoke, Robbie's mouth fell open. He had at that moment recognized the lean, sunken cheeks, hard jaw, and black hair-line moustache of this impatient customer. It was he who had been discussing the tobacco-oil deal over lunch with the Czech First Secretary at Toyrcolimano ten days previously, and so a prime cause for the upheaval in Robbie's life that had since occurred.

'What . . . what name shall I give, sir?' he stammered.

'Barak,' replied the other. 'Comrade Václav Barak. He knows me; so if he's disengaged, I'll go straight in.'

'I'll just see, sir,' countered Robbie diplomatically, although he knew that Krajcir had no one with him. Stepping over to the door of the manager's office, he opened it a few inches and announced the visitor. Krajcir gave a quick nod, so he walked back to the counter, opened a low gate in it, and showed Mr. Barak in.

Breathless with excitement, Robbie sat down again at his table. Here was the break for which he had been praying. Barak must know all about the secret negotiations. But how could his visit be used to get hold of that knowledge?

Laboriously, Robbie's mind revolved the question. Perhaps he could follow Barak when he left, and find out where he lived? That would be a good start. How could he do that, though? Krajcir always saw his visitors out personally. To push past him and calmly walk off after the man to whom he had just said good-bye would be hardly possible. Krajcir would call him back and demand to know where he was going, Barak would hear them, look round and, having seen Robbie leave the agency in spite of Krajcir's protests, would soon realize that he was being followed. He would then turn upon Robbie and demand an explanation.

How about leaving the office now and lying in wait for Barak out in the street? That would mean questions from Ludmilla and Rudolph, but he could ignore them. However, a snag to that quickly presented itself. At about three o'clock, it had come on to rain so he had returned to the office in a macintosh. The agency's premises were modest and, having been constructed out of a part of the old courtyard, were also awkward. The only place available for the staff to keep their hats and coats was a small closet, to reach which they had to pass through Krajcir's office. In the circumstances, although it was still raining, and quite hard too, that would not have deterred most men from going out without a macintosh. But all his life Robbie had been trained for his own protection to follow habits. Being unused to thinking for himself, it never occurred to him that he would take little harm from going out unprotected into the rain, and what possible excuse could he make to Krajcir for going through his office, then emerging from the closet wearing or carrying his mac?

Agitated and frustrated, he sat on, staring at Mrs. Sebesta's typewriter. Here was a real chance thrown in his way, a perfect lead to solving the riddle which had become a nagging obsession with him; yet it seemed there was no way in which he could take advantage of it. He would have given even half a year's income to hear what Krajcir and Barak were saying to one another in the private office. The door to it was at his elbow and so ill-fitting that there was a gap of nearly an inch between the bottom and the floor, but the harsh voices of the tourists chattering on the far side of the counter created a background of noise sufficient to drown the murmur of the two voices that Robbie was straining his ears to hear.

It was then that Pallas Athene intervened to undo Mr. Havelka. Or at least Robbie interpreted the little thing that happened as evidence of her divine guidance. Through the open window fluttered a single leaf. For a moment, it hovered uncertainly on the floor, then the outer door opened to admit two more tourists. The sudden draught drove the leaf through the narrow gap below Krajcir's door into his office. Had it not been a special leaf it would have conveyed no message to Robbie, but it was a special leaf. Only one tree grew in the courtyard: the old gnarled olive, Athene's sacred tree. Indisputably, he thought, the leaf was her messenger, and had given him the lead to how to act.

He must follow it. Go in to Krajcir. But how could he? What possible excuse could he give for butting in when his boss was conferring with a visitor? Next moment, he had it.

Standing up, he gave one quick tap on Krajcir's door and, without waiting for permission to go in, pushed it open. At that moment, Barak was speaking and Robbie clearly heard the last words of his sentence. '. . . Rhodes and the other islands there is no special urgency, but for the groups at Patras and Corinth you must fix up accommodation right away.'

Krajcir looked up at Robbie with a frown. Hastily Robbie

muttered: 'I'm sorry, sir. I left some letters in my mac that I want to take to the post. D'you mind if I get them?'

'No; but be quick about it,' replied Krajcir sharply.

As Robbie went into the closet, pulling the door partly shut behind him, he heard Krajcir say. 'The *Bratislava* is not due to dock till the 31st, that's Monday week; so we've plenty of time. By Wednesday, I should be able to let you have full particulars of the arrangements I have made for the first three or four groups, and I'll have dealt with the others by the end of the week.'

Inside the closet Robbie was hastily fishing about in his pockets. From them, he unearthed a sheet of paper on which he had made some notes for his book, the last letter he had received from old Nanny Fisher and the bill for his week's stay at the Grande Bretagne, which he had received that morning. Not daring to linger there longer, he folded these together with the letter on top and, clutching them in the hand which would be farther from Krajcir as he passed his desk, quickly re-crossed the private office, closing its door to the outer office softly behind him.

A few minutes later, the two Czechs emerged from it and, without either of them giving a glance at Robbie, Krajcir saw Barak out into the courtyard.

To all appearances, Robbie had resumed his cleaning of Mrs. Sebesta's typewriter. Actually he was doing no more than dab at it automatically with the worn toothbrush he had been given for the job, while he endeavoured to assess the fruits of his first successful piece of espionage.

The *Bratislava* was obviously a Czechoslovakian ship, and due to make her first call at a Greek port on Monday the 31st. It seemed reasonable to assume that she was carrying as passengers a considerable number of Czechs who were to be distributed in groups about Greece and the islands. Anyhow, it appeared fairly certain that her first call was to be Patras, and that the intention was for two groups to be landed there, one of which would go on to Corinth. Although Robbie had no evidence on which to base his assumption, he felt no doubt at all that, as it was Barak who was initiating these arrangements, the groups were composed of technicians, and that they were being sent to Greece for some nefarious purpose, on the pretext of prospecting for oil.

Ludmilla happened to glance in Robbie's direction at that moment, and saw that he was smiling to himself. He had good reason to do so. Now that he had this definite lead to follow, he need have no further hesitation about giving in his notice to Krajcir. He was no longer even dependent on Luke's providing an idea which would enable him to continue his quest in some new direction. If he liked he could, without a qualm, walk out of the agency there and then, and simply not come back. But he decided that that would be an unnecessary rudeness to people who had treated him, if not with kindness, at least with politeness; and that, anyway, it would be foolish to sever his connection with Krajcir and the others so churlishly when there was nothing to be gained by so doing.

Some ten minutes later, Mrs. Sebesta returned from the printers; so now that Robbie was once more under her slave-driver's eye, he had to put considerably more energy into his attentions to her typewriter, but his mind continued to speculate excitedly on what he had learned owing to Barak's visit. After a while, it occurred to him that, as Krajcir had been instructed to find accommodation for these groups of Czechs, he must now have in his office a complete list of the numbers in each group and the places at which they intended to prospect for oil—or whatever it was they meant to set about under that cover. To leave the agency without securing that, or at least getting a sight of it, would surely be wanton neglect in exploiting to the full the chance he had been given. But how could he set about it?

Every evening at about half past six, it was Krajcir's custom to go out for about twenty minutes. He always remarked casually on leaving that he was going round the corner to 'consult with his associates'; but they all knew that he was simply slipping out to drink an *ouzo* at a nearby café, where he could be found if urgently needed.

His absence would offer a chance to get a look at the papers on his desk but, even as Robbie thought of it, he discarded the idea. It was most unlikely that Pani Sebesta would leave the agency again before closing time, and what possible excuse could he give for going into Krajcir's office? Certainly none that would justify his remaining there long enough to go through the Manager's papers, and any attempt to do so without such an excuse would almost certainly result in the Sebesta woman coming in to see what he was up to, and catching him red-handed.

For another half-hour he wrestled with his problem, then a daring thought came to him. Why should he not return after the office was closed, and break into it? The courtyard formed a cul-de-sac, so he would run no risk of being seen by passers-by, and after dark no one except the handful of people who lived there came in or out of it; so during the five or ten minutes it would take him to force an entry, the odds were all against anyone coming on the scene.

The idea filled him with renewed excitement, but when he began to consider the practical details, his ardour became a little damped. The outer door of the office not only had a mortice lock, but was further secured by a padlock. During his year in Greece, apart from picking up that language he had given no time to adding others to his repertoire and, having had endless free hours to fill, he had got through a considerable number of books. So many of these having been gangster thrillers, he needed no telling that professional burglars always went to work with jemmies, blow-torches, electric drills or sticks of gelignite. To obtain any of these aids to crime at such short notice was obviously out of the question, and that ruled out any hope of his forcing the door.

That left only the windows; but again he would have no means of forcing one, and to break a pane might easily attract the attention of someone in the houses on the opposite side of the courtyard. Perhaps, though, before leaving, he could manage to fix one of them so that it was not properly locked. The fact that his colleagues would remain at work in the outer office until closing time, when he himself would have to leave, ruled out any possibility of tampering with any of the three windows there; so it would have to be the one in Krajcir's private sanctum.

By this time he had finished cleaning the typewriter, and his taskmistress had put him on to stamping a pile of circulars.

When he was half-way through them, Krajcir came out and, with his usual announcement about 'having a word with his associates', went off for his aperitif. After stamping the remainder of the pile, Robbie gave a loud sniff, and muttered to old Pani Sebesta: 'Left my handkerchief in my mac; just going to get it.'

As he stepped into Krajcir's office, she gave him only a glance. Shutting the door behind him, he stepped quickly across to the open window. It was not a large one, so the catch that secured it could be reached from outside by stretching an arm through any of its panes, had one of them been missing. On the inner sill, partly hiding the lowest row of panes, stood a line of thick reference books.

Having already thought out what he meant to do, Robbie wasted no time but swiftly removed two of the reference books from the left end of the row. He then picked up a paper-weight from Krajcir's desk and gave the left corner pane a sharp tap with it. Nothing happened. His hand was trembling and beads of sweat had broken out on his forehead, but he nerved himself to give the pane another, harder, tap. That did it. The pane cracked but, to his relief, did not fall out. It was starred into four large and two small irregular triangles. Letting out his breath with a little gasp, he hastily put back the paper-weight and replaced the reference books. They hid all but two of the cracks in the upper part of the pane, and he felt that he would be very unlucky if, in the hour before closing time, Krajcir noticed them. He had been away barely two minutes when he returned to the outer office, violently blowing his nose.

For that last hour he remained on tenterhooks, but nothing out of the ordinary happened. At eight o'clock, the usual good-nights were said and the agency was locked up till Monday. A quarter of an hour later, hardly conscious of what he ate, he was having his dinner at the Grande Bretagne. During it, his mind was busily speculating on the best time at which to make his attempt. The classic choice seemed to be in the small hours of the morning, but against that was the fact that the streets would be almost empty; so it was much more likely that, if a policeman happened to spot anyone slipping into a cul-de-sac, he would come along to investigate. On the other hand, the majority of Athenians were very averse to going to bed early. At any time up till one o'clock, someone living in the cul-de-sac might come home from a party, the last house at one of the cinemas, or even from sitting talking with friends in a café.

While pondering this dilemma, it suddenly struck Robbie that the present was the perfect hour. There would still be plenty of people in the streets, but the inhabitants of the court-yard would either have already gone out or be occupied at home, eating their dinners. Pushing aside his compôte of man-darines, he hurried from the restaurant.

The rain had stopped and it was a warm evening so, with-out bothering to get a hat or coat, he walked quickly round to the agency. The courtyard was deserted. There were lights in the ground-floor windows of one of the houses and in several of the upper windows round the well, but all of them had their curtains drawn. After a quick look round, he went to the window of Krajcir's office. It lay at right angles to the agency's other three windows, as it was round a corner; so, while getting in through it, he could not be seen by anyone approaching from the street. For an illegal entry, things could not have been more propitious. Then, just as he was about to stretch out his hand to the broken pane, he was brought up short by a shattering thought. In his hurry, he had forgotten to collect his torch.

To switch on the light when he got into Krajcir's office would be asking for trouble. Any of the neighbours, see-ing a light there at that unusual hour, would be certain to become suspicious, see him through the window and, if they noticed that the door was still padlocked, send for the police. Yet without a light, how was he to read the papers he hoped to find in Krajcir's desk?

He had on him a pocket lighter. As long as he held it on, it would serve for him to read by; but he was hoping to copy down any particulars, so that he would not have to trust to memory, and he could not very well do that with only one hand. For a moment he stood there, a prey to awful indecision. Then he decided that, without a torch, it would take him three times as long to do the job, and that even then he might bungle it. Turning, he left the courtyard, at something between a walk and a run.

Once out in the street, he did run most of the way to the Grande Bretagne and back. To go up in the lift there and get his torch took him only three minutes, so he was away altogether for not much more than ten. The church clocks had not yet chimed nine and, to his immense relief, the situation in the courtyard had not changed. It was still deserted, and the curtains remained drawn across the lighted windows.

Panting, and trembling a little, he again stepped up to the window of Krajcir's office. With his forefinger he prodded the smallest triangle of glass in the cracked pane. It fell inward, making only a tiny tinkle. Now that he could use a thumb and finger, it was easy to wriggle the other pieces until they became free, and one by one he laid them silently on the ground. As he pushed his arm through the now empty space, three of the big reference books on the shelf inside fell to the floor with a muffled thump. A moment later, his upthrust fingers found the catch and pressed it back. Withdrawing his arm, he tried to lever up the lower section of the window. To his dismay, it would not budge. He had overlooked the fact that it was only the upper section that was opened every day; the lower one had probably not been opened for years. It was stuck fast.

Almost crying with frustration, he stepped back and stared at it. To have to abandon his venture now would be the most bitter pill. But perhaps he could get in through the top half of the window. He was quite tall enough to get a good grip on it when it was lowered, but it had one row of panes less than the lower section, so that, even when opened to its fullest extent, it would be a tight squeeze to get his big chest and shoulders through. In any case, there was no alternative to going in head first, so how, without risking a nasty injury, could he get down to the floor? Then, say he got stuck? The thought that he might be found there hours later, with his head and arms inside and his feet still kicking outside, was an appalling one. It would mean, too, that when he was rescued, he would be ignominiously marched off to the police station. He dared not risk it.

With a little sob of despair, he turned away and stumbled

round the corner. A sudden gust of wind came down the passage from the street, and he heard a light rustle. Looking up, he found himself facing the gnarled olive tree. Instantly and without question, he accepted the sound as Athene rebuking him for his cowardice.

Turning, he strode back to the window, thrust his arm in, pulled down the upper part and took a firm grip of it with both hands. One spring and his head and shoulders were through the gap. With an awkward push, he wriggled his chest over the sash. Next moment, his arms were flailing helplessly and his hands clutching empty air. There was nothing for it now but to go on wriggling until the bulk of his body was through. The weight of it brought up his feet with a sudden jerk. With difficulty he suppressed a cry of fear, and came down with a hideous crash on the floor.

By twisting as he fell, he managed to save his head, but from the sudden pain that shot through his left thumb and shoulder, he feared he had broken the one and dislocated the other. With a groan, he picked himself up. Although his thumb and shoulder continued to hurt considerably, he found that he could still move both freely; so he concluded that neither had sustained serious damage.

As soon as he had got his breath back, he shut the window and replaced the fallen reference books on the sill. Taking out his torch, he pressed the switch, praying that the bulb had not been broken by his fall. It had not, and a bright beam from it clove the almost total darkness. As chance would have it, the beam was aimed directly on Krajcir's safe. Robbie groaned again. What a fool he had been. He had forgotten all about the safe and, naturally, Krajcir would have locked up in it such important documents as those referring to the secret project in which the Czechs were engaged. As he could not possibly open the safe, he had taken this big risk and had hurt himself badly all for nothing.

Half-heartedly, he turned the torch on to Krajcir's desk. It offered no consolation, as there was not even a pad with scribbled notes on it. He pulled open the centre drawer. Inside, there was a blue folder containing only a few sheets of paper. One glance at the top one, and Robbie's full mouth suddenly broke into a rapturous smile. Here, after all, was the very thing he was after. Evidently, Krajcir could not be in the full confidence of his Legation. He could not have realized the importance of keeping secret the reservations Barak had instructed him to make, otherwise he would have locked up the folder.

Sitting down in Krajcir's swivel chair, Robbie laid his torch on the desk, and masked its light so that no more than a glow from it could be seen through the window. Taking a piece of letter paper from the rack and one of the pencils from a nearby holder, he began to copy, in his laborious hand, the particulars listed on the papers in the folder.

At a glance, he saw that in every case a house was to be rented that would accommodate eleven people; but sometimes accommodation in hotels was also required, although for two nights only, and in each of these places on different dates, beginning at Patras on March 31st and ending at Lesbos on April 12th. The bookings at hotels suggested that in some places the houses were not easily accessible from the ports. Where hotel accommodation was required, it was to be, in every case, first class for three and third class for eight. All arrangements and accounts were to be settled by the agency. The places at which either houses or bookings were required were Patras, Corinth, Pirgos, Kalamai, Kithira, Heraklion in Crete, Rhodes, Kos, Samnos, Chios and Lesbos.

Robbie's geography, if decidedly sketchy about other parts of the world, was hard to fault on the ancient world, and he at once realized that these ports and islands formed a chain from western Greece right round the Peloponnesus and up the coast of Turkey. The fact that the hotel bookings, starting at Patras on March 31st, were for progressive dates, confirmed his idea that the *Bratislava* was making a trip right round Greece, dropping off groups of her passengers as she went.

He was only half-way through copying the list when he was startled by a sudden noise. It came from the outer office. There had been a faint clang of metal, then the sound of a door being slammed. It could only be the door to the street. Next moment, faint but clear, he heard Krajcir's voice: 'Everything's ready for you, so it won't take long.'

Robbie's hands suddenly became damp and beads of sweat burst out on his forehead. For some reason, Krajcir had come back to the office and had brought another person with him. There were two of them, and he was trapped there.

7

A Dreadful Half-hour

Rᴏʙʙɪᴇ's heart missed a beat. Saliva suddenly ran hot in his mouth. Here was a premature and ignominious end to his activities as a secret agent. In a matter of moments, Krajcir would find him there and telephone for the police. He would be handcuffed, like any thief, and hauled off to the station. What would happen then? He had taken nothing, but there could be no disputing that he had broken in. How else could he have got there? Besides, they would discover that a pane had been removed from the window. It would be assumed that he had intended to burgle the place. What defence could he possibly offer? None. He would be sent to prison, have to mix with crooks and bullies, perform degrading tasks, suffer acute discomfort, live on revolting food, perhaps for several months, and for ever afterward be branded as a gaol-bird.

Stimulated by the shock of imminent discovery, his normally slow brain was whirling like a teetotum. Those appalling thoughts raced through it in a matter of seconds. Next moment, the impulse to escape such a fate automatically took charge. Any attempt to get out through the window must obviously fail. Long before he could possibly get it open and wriggle through it again, Krajcir would be upon him, seize him by the legs and haul him back. But there was the clothes closet.

With one sweep of his big hand, he swept the papers on which he had been working back into the folder, then thrust it into the drawer of the desk. Turning, he took two long strides on tiptoe, opened the closet door, slipped inside and pulled it to behind him.

He was only just in time. The door of the office opened as that of the closet swung to and, had the light been on, Krajcir must have caught sight of its movement. From fear that the sound of the door shutting would give him away, Robbie had not closed it completely. Next moment, through the two-inch gap that remained, he saw the light flash on, and heard the man who was with Krajcir ask:

'Have you much for me this week?'

'About the usual,' Krajcir replied. 'But there is nothing from Rhodes.'

The other grunted. 'Our man there is in the Radar ship. Perhaps it has been moved or gone off on some exercise, so that he was prevented from getting ashore.'

'Hello!' Krajcir's voice came again with a note of surprise. 'What's this?'

His companion gave an abrupt laugh. 'A torch, and rather a nice one. But what about it?'

Robbie, still in a dither, was fighting to control his breathing. At the word 'torch', the sweat turned cold on his forehead. Of course; he had left his torch on Krajcir's desk. He had not even had time to switch it off. Had it not been partly masked, and its beam dimmed by the strong electric light above the desk, they must have noticed it before. Now that they had, it was a complete give-away. They could not fail to realize that they had disturbed an intruder, and that he must be hiding somewhere close at hand. Certain now that his discovery was imminent, he wrung his big hands in an agony of apprehension, as he listened to the ensuing conversation.

'But it's not mine,' Krajcir said in a puzzled voice.

'Then it must belong to one of your staff.'

'No, I'll swear it wasn't here when I left the office an hour ago. Besides, it's still switched on. Someone must have broken in.'

'The door was padlocked when we arrived and all the windows were closed, so no one could have.'

'But how can one account, then, for a lighted torch being left on my desk?'

'You probably switched it on yourself when you picked it up. Anyway it's obvious that the safe has not been tampered with, and nothing else seems to have been disturbed. You are simply imagining things. One of your staff must have left it there, and you failed to notice it before. That's all there is to it. Now let's get to work. I'm beginning to need my dinner.'

As Robbie breathed again, there came the clink of keys, then the sound of the heavy door of the safe being swung open. For a few minutes there was a rustling of papers, then Krajcir's companion asked:

'I take it you will have no difficulty in finding accommodation for Barak's people?'

'I don't think so. Had it been later in the season I might have, but the tourist rush is some weeks from its peak yet. Anyhow, it is only a matter of fixing up the various groups for a couple of nights until they can move on to the villas and farmhouses we are taking for them. That reminds me, though. I meant to put in the safe the particulars Barak gave me, but it slipped my memory.'

'They wouldn't convey anything to your staff. Anyone who saw them would only take them for ordinary tourist bookings.'

'That's true. Even I have not been let into what it's all about, and that's none of my business. But Barak did stress to me that I was to treat the matter as top secret, so I may as well pop them in the safe while it is open.'

There came the sound of a drawer being pulled out, then a swift exclamation from Krajcir. 'Devil take it! Somebody *has* been here.'

'Are you sure? Has someone been at your papers?' The other man's voice now held quick concern.

'Yes, look here. These are the notes I took from Barak, and someone has been making a copy of them. I know that round, childish hand. By God, I've got it! That's the writing of the Englishman.'

'What Englishman?'

'The young fellow that Comrade Minister Havelka sent me.'

'You mean the British Ambassador's nephew?'

'Yes. He's quite useless. In fact he's such a dreamer that I'm not quite sure that he's all there. But I was ordered to give him a job.'

Even gripped as he was in an agony of apprehension, Robbie winced. He might be a bit slow at some things, but that did not justify anyone branding him as an idiot. Yet perhaps he was. Who but an idiot would have got himself involved in this sort of thing? And what a mess he had made of it. Not only had he left his torch behind, but also the notes he had taken—and they were in his writing, so he had given himself away completely.

'He was enough "all there" to copy your papers,' snapped Krajcir's companion. 'No doubt he only acted the part of a half-wit in order to lull any suspicions you might have of him.'

As Robbie had never acted any part, and was quite incapable of being anything but his ordinary, simple self, this brought him no consolation. Feeling as though he had the Sword of Damocles suspended above his head, he held his breath while waiting to learn what would happen next.

'I was not warned that he might be a spy,' Krajcir retorted angrily. 'But why, having taken these notes, should he have left them here?'

'Perhaps our arrival disturbed him.'

'That's it! His torch, left on the desk still alight! You must be right. And he couldn't have got away. We should have seen or heard him.'

Robbie stiffened. Every muscle in his body became taut, like those of a condemned man awaiting immediate execution. Next moment, the blow fell. Two swift steps sounded outside the cupboard door, then it was wrenched open.

For a few seconds Krajcir glared at him, then he snarled: 'So, Mister Englishman; you are a spy, eh? How did you get in here?'

'I—er—well, if you must know, through the window,' Robbie admitted lamely.

'You are in the British Secret Service, yes?'

'No, oh no,' Robbie swiftly protested. 'I assure you, Pan Krajcir, that I'm not.'

'Do not lie to me. You broke in here not to steal but to spy. We have evidence of it.'

'Yes, I know: It was silly of me to leave my torch on your desk . . . and the notes I'd taken.'

Krajcir took a pace back, and said harshly: 'Come out of there. You will sit down at my desk and write a full confession.'

This was something for which Robbie had not bargained. To be convicted was one thing, to confess was quite another. If he denied the charge, quite a lot of people might believe that the Czechs had used the fact that a young Englishman had taken a job with them to fake a charge against him, so that they could make anti-British propaganda out of the case. But to confess would give people no option about what to think. It would never be believed that he had gone into this on his own. They would take it as certain that his uncle had been behind the whole business, and lay the blame at his door for whatever happened to his nephew. Sir Finsterhorn had inspired no great devotion in Robbie but, all the same, he was not quite so simple as to fail to see the implications in this choice. Steeped as he was in the traditions of chivalry, since he had got himself into this mess nothing would have induced him to allow blame for it to be attributed to anyone else.

Stepping out of the cupboard, he slowly shook his head. 'No, Pan Krajcir, I'm afraid I couldn't do that.'

With set mouth, the other man stared at him, then spoke. Whereas Krajcir's voice had been imbued with anger and impatience, this one's held quiet authority. Till now, he had remained concealed behind the cupboard door. On stepping past it, Robbie got his first sight of him. Instantly, he recognized the square, bald-headed figure that he had last seen with Barak at Toyrcolimano. It was the First Secretary, Nejedly. He said:

'You will do as you are told, or take the consequences.'

Robbie's mouth twisted into a nervous, unhappy smile. 'You mean, you will send for the police?'

'Yes. Were you in my country, I could have you shot for what you have done. Here matters are different, but at least punishment can be secured for law-breakers who have been caught red-handed, as you have. Still, I am not a hard man; so I give you a choice. If you sit down, write a confession that I shall dictate, and sign it, I will let you go. If you refuse, you will spend tomorrow in a cell, and on Monday find yourself sentenced to a term of imprisonment.'

It was an offer that might have tempted many people, but not a young dreamer of dreams who thought of Bayard, that *chevalier sans peur et sans reproche,* as a man of only yesterday.

'No, thanks,' Robbie replied. 'You want me to implicate my uncle, don't you? But he had nothing to do with this, and I'm not playing.' As an afterthought he added: 'I don't mean to let you have it all your own way, either. After all, I'm one of the staff here. I shall say that I left something and came back—er—came back hoping to find Pan Krajcir still working in his office. Then . . . well, then, he wasn't here but I found a window open and so got in to get it. Yes, and I'll say that Mr. Krajcir asked me to make a copy of those notes for him before I left.'

The bald-headed Nejedly gave him a smile of contempt. 'You poor fool. Is it likely that, in a N.A.T.O. country, we would charge you with espionage? Even if convicted, with the sympathy of the West in your favour you would get off with only a token sentence. No. If you elect to go to court, it will be on a charge of having broken into the place and burgled it.'

'But I have stolen nothing! '

'Oh yes, you have.' Nejedly produced his notecase. From it, he took a thousand drachma note and two five hundreds. Holding them up, he went on: 'Comrade Krajcir will mark these. He will say that for some time he has had reason to believe that you have been stealing small sums of money from the till. This afternoon he laid a trap for you, by letting you see him put these away inside his bank paying-in book, then leaving you alone for a few minutes in this room. After the office was closed, he asked me to come back with him to see if you had taken the bait. Evidently you had feared to do so before the office closed. But you had left a window unlatched, and come back for it. Thus we were lucky enough to catch you red-handed.'

Robbie's tanned face paled slightly. There seemed no way in which he could counter this tissue of lies or prove them false. He was learning fast that he was no match for men like Nejedly. Meanwhile, the First Secretary was going on:

'We shall add that you resisted us. Comrade Krajcir is a patriot. He will willingly give a little of his blood for his country. I, too, will sacrifice my shirt. I will tear it open, then give Pan Krajcir a tap on the nose. Just enough to make it bleed. Then we shall be able to charge you with robbery with violence, and ensure that you receive a good stiff sentence. Come now, is it to be like that, or will you sit down and write a confession?'

The word 'violence' begot an idea in Robbie's mind. He had never struck anyone in his life, but why should he not start now? The odds were two to one against him but, if he was going to be charged anyway with assaulting them, he might as well have the fun of doing it. Besides—sudden happy thought—if he hit them hard enough, there was just a chance that he might manage to escape before their shouts brought help.

Nejedly, bald, moonfaced, and with slit eyes that suggested he might have a dash of Tartar blood, was stockily built with powerful shoulders and long arms. He was standing about six feet from Robbie and between him and the door to the outer office. Krajcir, his gold tooth showing in a servile but none-too-happy grin at his superior's announcement that he should submit to having his nose punched in the service of his country, was standing on Robbie's right, and nearer to him. He was the elder and, Robbie decided, the less dangerous of the two, so the best plan seemed to be to try to put him out of action first. Drawing back his right fist, he swung it hard at the side of Krajcir's face.

Had Robbie ever been taught to box, his superior height and strength would have enabled him to make short work of the two Czechs, but he had never even had to put up his fists to defend himself in a school playground. Instead of the blow taking Krajcir under the side of the jaw and knocking him out, it landed on his cheek, merely jerking his head round and causing him to stagger back against the wall.

When Robbie struck out, Nejedly was holding a brief-case. Swiftly he set it down on Krajcir's desk and sailed in, not with his fists but with his feet. As he ran forward, his right foot shot out. It caught Robbie a frightful crack on the shin. He let out a yelp and lifted the injured leg in the air. With surprising agility for one with his figure, Nejedly jumped back a pace then kicked out with his left foot at Robbie's other leg.

Had that second savage kick landed, it would have brought Robbie down. But Krajcir, his cheek bright red from the blow he had been struck, had now rounded on his aggressor. As he lurched forward to strike Robbie, he cannoned into Nejedly. Both the kick and the blow failed to find their mark. That gave Robbie a moment's breathing space. With no plan, and only brute strength to aid him, he came lumbering forward, flailing his big fists indiscriminately at the two Czechs.

One blow caught Krajcir on the forehead. Momentarily dazed, he again fell back against the wall. Another blow landed on Nejedly's shoulder. It had such force behind it that it knocked him sideways, and he almost fell. For a moment, there was a clear space of several feet between them. Seizing his chance, Robbie made a dash for the door. He was half-way there when Nejedly recovered sufficiently to grab his wrist. At that instant, Robbie had one foot raised for his next stride. The sudden jerk on his wrist threw him off balance. His head thrown back and, clutching vainly at the air with his free hand, he heeled over sideways. Before he could recover, he cannoned into Nejedly and they both crashed to the ground. Robbie came down on top. As he fell his bent elbow, with all his weight behind it, came down on Nejedly's stomach, temporarily driving the breath out of his body.

With an agonized groan, the Czech doubled up and, for the space of a few heartbeats, Robbie had him at his mercy. A Commando-trained agent would have put him out of the game for good by giving him one hard sock under the jaw. But Robbie had imbibed the tradition that one never hits a man when he is down. Slightly horrified by the sight of the bulging eyes and gasping mouth in the moon-like face beneath him, he stared at it for those few vital heartbeats, then struggled to his knees.

By then, Krajcir had recovered his wits. With a shouted curse, he launched himself from behind Robbie and grabbed him round the neck. Taken by surprise, Robbie felt himself being jerked backwards with his legs twisted under him. Kicking his legs free, he grasped Krajcir's wrists and broke his grip. Robbie was now flat on his back with Krajcir behind him, still standing. The Czech could not use his hands; so he gave a swift, sideways kick that caught Robbie in the ribs.

Robbie choked out an 'Ouch!' of pain, and let go of Krajcir's wrists so suddenly that the latter staggered back. Nejedly was now sitting up, but still gasping for breath. Rolling over, Robbie lurched to his feet. Krajcir was between him and the door. As Robbie came at him, his eyes showed sudden fear. He ducked a windmill swipe from one of Robbie's fists, and avoided the other by closing with him.

For a few moments they swayed in a clinch, stamping to and fro on the floor and panting for breath. But Robbie was far the stronger. Shifting his grip he broke Krajcir's hold, then seized him round the wrist. With one great heave, he lifted the Czech right off his feet and hurled him from him. Krajcir's ankle twisted under him as his foot came down on the floor. With a squeal of pain he spun half round, then toppled sideways. As he fell, his head hit the edge of the closet door. With a moan, he subsided in an ungainly heap and lay whimpering there.

No time was given to Robbie to savour his victory. Nejedly was on his feet again, and had armed himself by snatching up a heavy, ebony ruler from Krajcir's desk. As Krajcir slumped to the floor, Nejedly hit Robbie a stunning crack on the back of the head with the ruler. Robbie's eyes bulged. Then, against a curtain of blackness, he saw flashing stars and whirling circles.

With a groan, he lurched round. Nejedly was coming at him again. His sight cleared only just in time for him to glimpse the ruler held high. It was about to smash down into his face. Instinctively, he lifted a hand to ward off the blow.

His hand caught Nejedly in the chest, halting the forward lunge of his shoulders. The jolt was sufficient to deflect his aim, and the ruler thudded down on Robbie's upper arm.

Again Robbie staggered back, but was brought up sharp by the edge of Krajcir's desk. The sudden impact below his buttocks nearly sent his legs flying outward from under him. As his head and shoulders went back, he thrust his right hand behind him for support. It landed on the semi-circular handle of Nejedly's heavy brief-case. Grasping it firmly he flung himself forward from the desk, drawing the brief-case after him in a wide, semi-circular sweep. More by luck than judgment, it struck Nejedly on the side of the head and sent him spinning. The ruler flew out of his hand and, with outflung arms, he measured his length on the floor.

Robbie did not wait to see if he had knocked him out. Having temporarily got the better of both of his enemies, he took a deep breath and dashed for the door. In an instant, he was through it. A moment later, he had wrenched open the outer door of the agency and was in the courtyard. Still half dazed by the blow Nejedly had struck him on the back of the head, and much too excited by his first fight to think of anything but getting away, he ran as fast as his legs would carry him down the passage, out into the street and, dodging at considerable risk between two cars, across the road.

An angry shout from the policeman on point duty brought him to his senses; but by then the danger of his being run down was past. It was only then, too, that he realized that he was still clutching Nejedly's brief-case. A glance back at the far pavement showed him that he was not being pursued and, at a quick walk, he made his way round to the Grande Bretagne.

Up in his suite, he took stock of his injuries. His head was still aching abominably and, on gingerly feeling the place where he had been hit, he found it sticky with blood. He wondered uneasily if his skull was split and he ought to call in a doctor, but that would have meant answering some very awkward questions. The wound did not seem to be bleeding much, so he decided to bathe it with cold water and leave it at that for the present. Now that he had stopped running and walking, his leg also began to pain him severely. Turning up his trouser leg, he found that Nejedly's kick had broken the skin over his shin bone; so there was blood there, too, and the flesh all round was already colouring up into a first-class bruise.

Old Nanny Fisher had taught him that cuts should always be washed clean with soap and water as soon as possible; so, stoically clenching his teeth against the pain, he scrubbed his leg ruthlessly, thoroughly washed his head, then bound a hand-kerchief round the one and made a towel into a turban for the other.

On his way from the bathroom through the narrow hall-way of his little suite, he picked up the brief-case which he had thrown down there and carried it into the sitting-room. It was not locked, so he fished all the papers out of it and put them in a pile on his desk. His rough handling of himself when cleansing his wounds now paid a dividend, as by contrast they were throbbing only mildly, and, as soon as he realized what the papers were, he became so excited that he forgot his pain altogether.

There were some two dozen documents in all. Each was in an envelope addressed to Krajcir and marked 'Private', and the postmarks on the envelopes showed that they had come from different parts of Greece. The majority were handwritten, but a few were typed. The greater part were in Czech, but several were in Greek, three in English and two in German. None of them was addressed to a person, and their only signa-ture was a number which differed in each case.

Inexperienced as Robbie was in such matters, after glancing through only a few it was plain to him that these were the reports of a network of secret agents. Except in particu-lars, they varied little. All of them were concerned with ship-ping, and principally naval shipping. From them could be built up a complete picture of the recent movements of every N.A.T.O. warship, American, British, Greek and Turkish, in the waters of the north-eastern Mediterranean. Movements of oil tankers and supply ships were also covered. Where war-ships had been in, or lying off, ports, estimates were given of the number of men given shore leave, the state of their morale, and such political opinions as the majority of them appeared to hold. In a few cases, the names were given of men who nursed grievances against their officers, or who there was reason to believe were secretly pro-Communist.

It was evident that, for some reason, the Czechs considered it safer to have these secret reports sent to their Travel Agency rather than their Legation, and that Nejedly collected them from Krajcir once a week.

Robbie was naturally delighted with his haul. Although it was only a side-product of the mission he had set himself, he felt that indirectly it might prove a great help to him. That none of the names and addresses of the writers of the reports was given obviously detracted greatly from their value but, even so, it seemed certain that they would be of considerable interest to N.A.T.O. Intelligence, if only as a means of informing it of this great network of spies which was being run by the Czechs, no doubt at the orders of their Russian masters.

Sir Finsterhorn and Euan Wettering had poured scorn on Robbie's proposal that he should become a secret agent. Now he saw a rosy picture of himself casually presenting the results of his first coup, and of their regarding him with awe and a new respect. Blissfully he envisaged his uncle patting him on the shoulder, encouraging him to go on with his mission, and promising him the official help that had previously been denied.

So pleased with himself was Robbie that, his pains by now reduced to no more than dull aches, and feeling a little peckish from having skimped his dinner, he decided to celebrate by treating himself to an epicure's supper. One of the discoveries he had made while living at the Embassy was caviare and, having no idea how costly it was, he always regretted that it was doled out there in quite small portions. Picking up the house telephone, he rang down for six portions to be sent up to him with plenty of hot toast, then he ordered a bottle of French champagne to wash it down.

Scooping up the collection of reports, he thrust them back into the brief-case and snapped it shut. Then he went into his bedroom to tidy himself up. He had been sitting in his shirt and pants, but the collar of the shirt had become dirty and creased as a result of his fight and the cuffs had got wet when he washed his hair. Now he changed it for a clean one of white silk and, as he felt in festive mood, he put on a dinner jacket and black trousers. But he kept the towel wrapped round his head in the form of a turban from fear that, if he removed it, that might start his scalp bleeding again.

Perhaps it was the rather rakish air that the turban gave him but, as he glanced at himself in the mirror, it suddenly struck him that he was quite a fine-looking fellow. Yet his next thought saddened him a little. Although he might appear a fine figure of a man to himself, it was clear that women did not find him in the least attractive, for not one of them—that is, of anywhere near his own age—had ever taken more than a passing interest in him.

Theoretically, he had nothing to learn about sex. Some years before, while on holiday with his Aunt Emily at Scarborough, he had gone into a second-hand bookshop and bought several books on mythology. Seeing that he was a young man with plenty of money, the bookseller had persuaded him to add to his purchases a two-volume edition of Forberg's *Manual of Classical Erotology* which had the English as well as the Latin texts. He had had only the vaguest idea what the word 'Erotology' meant, but the bookseller had assured him that Forberg was a great authority on the customs of the Ancients, and that he certainly ought to add a copy to his collection.

When he got back to his hotel, he was surprised to find that the 'customs' referred to were not, as he had expected, accounts of betrothals and marriage rituals, possibly embellished with stories of the love affairs of the Immortals, but dealt entirely with the physical relations between men and women. Leaving nothing whatever to the imagination, Forberg described in detail every conceivable way in which a couple might gratify their passions. Further, to Robbie's astonishment and disgust, it then disclosed to him that certain people were not content with making love in a natural manner, and gave descriptions of homosexual practices. Finally, it gave an account of orgies held by the Emperor Tiberius on Capri, in which numbers of the guests indulged in the most extraordinary gymnastics.

Robbie was, therefore, even better primed in the 'facts of life' than many young men of his age, although he had never found an opportunity of making use of his knowledge. That was not because he had not wanted to, and at times he was troubled by a strong urge to demonstrate his virility. But he had been hopelessly handicapped by his extreme shyness where girls were concerned, and had not the first idea how to start an *affaire*.

To those he met socially he would not have dreamed of even hinting at the provocative thoughts they sometimes aroused in him, and the younger ones soon found him too dull to bother with. Had he but known it, during the past year a few married women he had met while at the Embassy had seen in his stalwart figure the makings of a very satisfactory lover; but he had proved so gauche and tongue-tied that, after a while, they, too, had decided that he was too much of a bore to be worth seducing. There had remained the possibility of scraping acquaintance with some pretty piece strolling in the park or sitting on her own in a café, and he had often contemplated some such adventure but, at the last moment, his courage had always failed him.

Yet, all thoughts of sex apart, he enjoyed basking in the company of pretty girls, and secretly it tormented him that he could find so little to say to them that he had never succeeded in making a friend of one. Being so inept with them and never having been known to ask a girl to lunch or dine was one of the things with which Euan Wettering had freqently taunted him. The memory of Euan's jibes made him flush now, and he would have given a very great deal to have had a girl friend whom he could have rung up there and then and asked out to supper, instead of having to celebrate on his own.

He had only just finished dressing when the door-bell of his suite rang. The chambermaid who turned down his bed had a passkey, but the waiters were not allowed keys; so, assuming that the supper he had ordered had been brought up, he walked out into the narrow hall and opened the door.

There, within a foot of him stood Krajcir, and with him

was the taciturn, blue-jowled Comrade Cepicka who, the previous Monday, had piloted him from the Czech Legation to the Travel Agency. Cepicka, looking more than ever like an ex-Gestapo thug, was wearing a long cloak. Half-hidden by it, he held an automatic, and he was pointing it at Robbie's stomach.

8

'Stop Thief! Stop Thief!'

FOR once, Robbie's mind worked swiftly. Before either of the men had time to put a foot in the door, he slammed it in their faces. Turning, he dashed into his sitting room, slammed the door of that, too, and shot the bolt.

Panic-stricken, he gazed wildly round him. What was he to do? Cepicka, having pointed a gun at him, showed that they meant business. He ought to have realized that they would stop at nothing to get back Nejedly's brief-case. When he was taken on at the agency, he had been asked for his private address, and it had not occurred to him that it might be a wise precaution to conceal from Krajcir that he was living at the Grande Bretagne. He recalled Krajcir raising his eyebrows and remarking on the incongruity of a young man who was staying at the most expensive hotel in Athens applying for such a poorly paid post. By then, he was becoming used to lying to the Czechs so he had said that his uncle made him a generous allowance, but had threatened to cut it off unless he found himself a regular job.

The sound of a sharp crack put an abrupt end to his brief meditations. Angrily he upbraided himself for wasting even seconds recalling the past. What did the reason matter for their having been able to run him to earth so quickly? They were after him, and with a gun. The sound he had just heard could only mean that they had already forced the lock on the outer door. Cepicka looked the kind of man who was used to doing that sort of thing. No doubt he had come well prepared with a pocketful of implements. In another few moments, they would have forced their way into the sitting room.

There was only one thing for it. To telephone down to the office was no use. His enemies would have broken in long before help could reach him. Grabbing the brief-case, Robbie pulled wide the French window of the room, and ran out on to its narrow balcony. Alongside the balcony was an iron fire-escape. Throwing a leg over the balcony railing, he grasped a rung of the ladder with his free hand, then swung himself out on to it. The ladder led down to a courtyard in which goods were delivered at the back of the hotel. As Robbie's room was on the third floor, he had quite a long way to go, and the speed of his descent was considerably hampered by the brief-case.

When he was about two-thirds of the way down, he heard a shout from above. Looking up, he saw the foreshortened silhouettes of Krajcir and Cepicka framed in his lighted window. Both of them were leaning over the balcony rail, and Cepicka called down to him in a guttural voice:

'Stop! Stop! Stay where you are, or I shoot!'

Robbie's heart gave a lurch. As the courtyard, now a dozen feet below him, was pitch dark, his figure was so indistinct against it that only a lucky shot could have hit him. But he was unaware of that, and imagined himself as a target in a shooting gallery. He was, moreover, too inexperienced to realize that secret agents may threaten their enemies, but are not such fools as to shoot them—except if cornered themselves—in places where there is a high risk that the shot will be heard and they are very likely to be caught. The idea of a bullet smacking into the top of his head terrified him. Swiftly he decided that allowing himself to be shot was not going to prevent their getting back the brief-case; and that, while it was one thing to lie for one's country, it was quite another to die for it to no good purpose. Halting in his tracks, he called up hastily:

'All right! Don't shoot. I won't go any further.'

It was then that his enemies blundered. Instead of ordering him to bring the brief-case back up to his room, they climbed out on to the fire-escape to come down and get it.

Krajcir was nearer the ladder, so got on to it first. While he descended the first dozen rungs, Robbie watched him, motionless, his mind entirely occupied with the bitter thought of having to surrender his prize. Suddenly, as he stared upward, it came to him that he was no longer covered. Even if Cepicka, while clinging to the ladder with one hand, tried to shoot him with the other, he would find it impossible, because Krajcir's bulky body formed a barrier between them.

Robbie gave a quick glance over his shoulder. The courtyard was quite small, and there was not a gleam of light in it. He could only just make out the entrance to a narrow passage that led from it to the street. Deciding that he would be very unlucky if he failed to reach it before the others got to the bottom of the ladder, he went down another five rungs on tiptoe. That brought him to the bottom section of the ladder, an eight-foot length which, as a precaution against burglars, was held horizontal by weights so that it could not be mounted from below. As he stepped on it, the weights lifted and its lower end swung down, hitting the ground with a loud clang.

Krajcir and Cepicka both paused in their descent and shouted something at him. But he was now committed to his attempt. Still clutching the brief-case, he slithered down the last few feet, stumbled on reaching the ground, recovered and dashed headlong for the entrance to the passage.

It was about two hundred feet in length. As he shot out of it into the street, he took a swift look over his shoulder. The darkness hid all sign of movement, but he knew that his enemies were after him. He could hear their running feet pounding across the stones of the courtyard.

Cannoning into an old gentleman who upbraided him for his clumsiness, he darted across the empty road. A moment later, a stream of traffic, just released from the cross-section a hundred yards away, filled it and temporarily masked him from the sight of his pursuers. Turning left, he headed for Stadium Street, knowing that there would be plenty of people there, and hoping to elude his enemies by mingling with the crowd. His long, swift strides quickly brought him to the corner.

Dodging in and out of the throng of pedestrians, he made his way down the broad boulevard. It was much lighter there, so he could see the strollers' faces clearly while thrusting his way through the gaps between them. As he did so, he wondered why so many of them gave him looks of astonishment. Suddenly he caught sight of his reflection in a shop window and gave a gasp of dismay. His head was still wrapped in its turban of towelling. In combination with his dinner-jacket suit, it made him a ludicrous sight. A moment later, somewhere in his rear he heard shouts in Greek of:

'Stop thief! Stop thief!'

He did not for an instant doubt that those cries applied to him. That accursed turban, bobbing along among the crowd, had given him away. Krajcir or Cepicka must have spotted it, and were after him again. He broke into a run, knocking people right and left as the cry 'Stop thief!' was taken up by a dozen voices. One man tried to clutch him, but Robbie fended him off with a shove that sent him reeling into the gutter. As if by magic, the other men and girls coming in his direction stepped aside hastily to give him passage, rather than attempt to grapple with such an obviously desperate character.

Breathless, but still running like a champion, he reached the broad side-street opposite Klafthmonos Square, which links Stadium Street with Venizelou Street. At the junction a traffic policeman, his attention attracted by the shouting, blew his whistle. Robbie dived round the corner out of the policeman's view, and raced on. But now that the police were about to join the hunt against him, he felt that his chances of escape were hopeless. In spite of all the lucky breaks he had had, matters had come full cycle. He was back where he had been when threatened by Nejedly in the agency; about to be dragged off to the police station and charged with theft.

But to prove theft, evidence of theft had to be produced. Nejedly had intended to make a false statement and, with Krajcir as his witness, use marked banknotes for that purpose. Now it would not be money but the brief-case which he would be charged with stealing. If only he could get rid of that, there would be no evidence against him.

As though by a special dispensation of the gods at his patroness Athene's request, the idea had no sooner entered his head than he realized that he was passing a site on which a new building was going up. Steel scaffolding already framed three skeleton floors while, at street level, a hundred and fifty foot frontage was screened from the pavement only by a temporary arrangement of crossed poles. Short, broad Korai Street, into which he had wheeled, was comparatively deserted. In a matter of seconds, he had scrambled over one of the low barriers, and was plunging about amongst heaps of sand, loose stones and rubble.

His pursuers had seen him dash round the corner but, by the time they came opposite the new building, he was well inside it. In there, it was as dark as it had been in the courtyard. The lights in the street hardly penetrated the gloom, revealing only dimly a forest of square cement pillars that rose from a floor that had been only partly boarded over.

There was now shouting in the street outside. Hastily he sought a place in which he could conceal the brief-case. The dim cavern in which he crouched presented only stark, vaguely-sensed rectangles, with not a contour among them that might afford a hiding-place. Its only irregularity lay in the floor. In some places there were piles of boards, in others open sections where joists and the stretches of concrete between them still lay exposed. That left him no choice. Kneeling down, he thrust the brief-case as far as he could under one of the boarded-over areas, then unwound his towel-turban and pushed it between two other joists that had boards nailed down on them.

The shouting out in the street had made him fear that, at any moment, he would be discovered, but apparently no one had seen him jump the barrier, for the noise passed and gradually died down. While running he had felt no pain from his injured leg, but now, as he crouched behind one of the big, square pillars, still trying to regain his breath, it began to throb as though being hit rhythmically with a hammer.

In an attempt to divert his thoughts from it, he strove to think out his next move. On consideration, now that he could no longer be incriminated by possession of the brief-case, he saw no reason why he should not make his way back to the Grand Bretagne. He could tell the hall porter that thieves had broken into his room; that he had valuable jewels there, so feared another raid; and, in case Cepicka tried to pay him a second visit, arrange for a man to stand guard all night outside his suite. All the same, he thought it wise to continue to lie 'doggo' for a while, until anyone who had seen him being chased was well clear of the vicinity.

Accordingly he remained where he was, his eyes closed and striving to ignore the painful throbbing in his leg, for what he reckoned to be a good twenty minutes. Then, straightening himself up, he tiptoed across the firm part of the floor to the barrier, and peered out. People were passing only intermittently. Taking advantage of a moment when no one was near enough to notice him, he slipped out on to the pavement.

Turning right, he walked quickly up the slope toward Venizelou Street then, at the corner, turned right again along it. As he did so, a shout went up from the opposite corner. To judge time when in darkness and a state of great anxiety is very difficult, and he had not bothered to put on his wrist watch again after taking it off to wash his head. Instead of remaining in hiding for twenty minutes, he had been lost to his pursuers for less than ten.

They had known that he must have gone to earth somewhere near-by, and were still keeping a watch for him. He gave a startled glance in the direction from which the shout had come. Cepicka, Krajcir and a policeman were standing in a group on the corner. Although he had got rid of his tell-tale turban, they had spotted him. Both the Czechs were pointing in his direction. Once more he took to his heels.

For a moment, Fortune relented and favoured him. A stream of traffic cut off his enemies. That gave him a good, flying start. Again he plunged through the crowd, scattering people right and left. As he darted between them, he tried to console himself with the thought that if he were caught, they would not now be able to charge him with stealing the briefcase. But by the time he had covered a hundred yards, it struck him that Krajcir might still trump up against him a charge of having stolen money from the agency. As he thought of that, his worst fears were realized. He heard the shrilling of the policeman's whistle. And again the cry was raised: 'Stop thief! Stop thief!'

Desperately he raced on, dodging some groups of pedestrians and thrusting aside the few men who half-heartedly attempted to tackle him, as though all his life he had played rugger with enthusiasm. He was still heading for the Grande Bretagne, although he now had little idea what he was going to do should he succeed in reaching it. The hall porter would certainly not be able or willing to save him from arrest by the police; yet he continued his wild career towards the hotel, as though to get there was an end in itself.

The blocks between Stadium Street and Venizelou Street are separated by a number of side streets. In almost every case, as he crossed them, the lights favoured him by letting traffic through that temporarily checked his pursuers. But by the time he reached Gian Smats Street, the last he had to cross before reaching the hotel, a mob of fifty people, headed by the policeman, was close on his heels.

The traffic was now against him. Only some desperate measure could save him from immediate capture. A private car, with two suitcases on its roof, and a man and girl inside, must have run him down if he had attempted to cross the road at that moment. He waited ten seconds. The policeman stretched out a hand to seize him by the collar. At that very instant, he took a flying leap and grabbed the roof rack of the passing car.

It carried him round the corner and, as traffic in Greece takes the right-hand side of the road, in the direction in which he had been heading. The girl screamed and the man cursed him. The car had been moving at a good pace, but its driver applied his brakes and, after fifty yards, brought it to a halt. While being dragged by the car, Robbie's feet had been bumping along the ground. As it pulled up, he let go of the luggage rack, stumbled, regained his balance and ran round in front of it on to the pavement. Right in front of him now was the Grande Bretagne's side entrance, which led to the hotel's banqueting and ball rooms.

Robbie gave a swift glance to his right. Thirty yards away, the policeman was coming on full tilt. He had now been joined by another, and they headed an excited crowd of idlers who had taken up the chase. Well to the front, Robbie glimpsed Cepicka, his scowling face now bright red with his exertions. Robbie knew that he could not hope for protection from the management of the hotel, but his nine days' stay there had given him a thorough knowledge of its ground-floor geography. With the new lead he had gained, he thought there was a sporting chance that he would be able to elude his pursuers in its maze of rooms and passages and, perhaps, find a hiding place before they could catch up with him.

As he dived for the big, glass double doors, the hall porter on duty there was just coming out. They collided violently. Robbie was swung round so that he faced towards Constitution Square. Suddenly his glance lit on a familiar sight. His uncle's Rolls was standing a few yards in front of the car on to which he had leapt. Beside it, staring at him in amazement, stood his uncle's chauffeur, Tompkins.

Thrusting the hall porter aside, he sprinted toward the Rolls. Tompkins, an old soldier with all the prejudices against 'foreigners' and their police of a Briton of his class, sized up the situation instantly. His not to reason why, his boss' nephew was in trouble. In a brace of shakes, he had both doors of the car open, and had scrambled into the driver's seat. With a gasp, Robbie flung himself into the back and slammed the door behind him.

The clutch slid in, the big car slid forward. Robbie righted himself on the seat, leaned forward and cried huskily: 'Well done, Tompkins! Back to the Embassy, and for God's sake step on it.'

'O.K., Mr. Robbie,' came the unruffled reply. None of the servants at the Embassy ever called Robbie 'Mr. Grenn'. Perhaps it was his never-failing cheerfulness, simplicity and kindliness, but it never occurred to them to condemn the useless life he led, and they took a far better view of him than did his uncle.

Squirming round, Robbie looked out through the back window of the car. What he saw made him bite his lip. He was not out of the wood yet. The two policemen had commandeered the car on which he had taken such a risky lift, and it was giving chase. Behind it, Cepicka was just jumping into a taxi, and another car had made a quick turn out of the line of oncoming traffic, with the evident intention of joining in the hunt. If the Rolls was checked by traffic lights and those cars came up with it, he might still be cornered and arrested.

The Rolls had shot across the corner of Constitution Square and entered the broad Vasilissis Sofias Boulevard, so it was now a straight run and only a quarter of a mile to go. But a lorry emerged from one of the turnings opposite the Royal Palace, forcing Tompkins to slow down. Holding his breath, Robbie continued to stare out of the back window. The driver of the car carrying the policemen was crouched over the wheel, getting every ounce out of his engine. It raced up to within a few yards of the Rolls. Robbie could clearly see the face of the girl beside the driver. It was white and wide-eyed with excitement. One of the policemen was leaning out of the left rear window, yelling at them to halt.

Tompkins swerved the Rolls and it passed the tail of the lorry, missing it by inches. As they cleared it, he put his foot hard down on the accelerator and the great silver car leapt forward again. Now that they had left the centre of the city behind, there was little traffic. In less than a minute, they covered the few hundred yards that brought them to within a stone's throw of the Embassy.

'Not the front entrance,' called Robbie quickly. 'Round to the garage. We can drive straight in there.'

'Just as you wish, Mr. Robbie; though you've no need to worry. We're well ahead of them now,' Tompkins replied with a laugh.

The Rolls sped on, passed the little Byzantine church on the corner, turned into Ploutarchou Street and, turning again, ran smoothly up the slope leading to the garage. Robbie slipped out to open the gates. He was still pulling them wide when the two pursuing cars and the taxi drew up in the street. Their occupants all got out and formed a little cluster on the pavement. Scowling angrily, the two policemen demanded that Robbie go with them to the station. Cepicka, speaking atrocious Greek, joined in with threats and curses, while the people in the last car, who had joined the chase for fun, stood by, goggle-eyed, to witness the outcome of the matter.

Robbie only smiled and shook his head. He knew, and the police knew, that he was now technically on British soil. They dared not infringe diplomatic privilege by coming in and removing him forcibly.

Tompkins ran the car into the garage and Robbie helped him shut the gates. The little crowd outside was now getting back into its cars, but Robbie was no longer smiling. He had escaped by taking sanctuary in the Embassy but, if he put a foot outside it, he would again make himself liable to arrest. He dared not leave it. And how was he going to explain to his uncle his presence there?

9

Midnight Conference

WHEN they had shut the garage gates, Tompkins said with a smile: 'Seems you got yourself in a spot of trouble, Mr. Robbie.'

'Yes,' Robbie agreed; then he added after a brief pause: 'They . . . I think they mistook me for a pick-pocket.' Much as he hated having to lie to Tompkins, he could not possibly tell him the truth. A moment later, he remembered that he was wearing a dinner jacket which rendered most unlikely the explanation he had given, but Tompkins' only comment was:

'Well, we saw them off all right. Bit of luck for you, though, that I'd just dropped your uncle at the G.B.'

'Just dropped him!' Robbie echoed. 'I thought you must have taken some guests back to the hotel after a dinner party. Surely it's very late for him to have gone out?'

Tompkins looked at him in surprise. 'No later than usual for a reception, Mr. Robbie. The invites are mostly for nine-forty-five, and H.E. likes to show up round ten o'clock.'

Robbie had believed it to be at least midnight. So much had happened to him since he had, with the rest of the staff, left the agency at eight o'clock. It seemed impossible that all the nerve-racking experiences he had been through had been crammed into less than two hours; yet he could not doubt that Tompkins was right.

However, what Tompkins had told him held one ray of comfort. As his uncle was out at a reception, he could enter the house without fear of running into him. Having thanked the chauffeur warmly for rescuing him, he walked the length of the garden and entered the Embassy by a side door that led to the servants' quarters. In her sitting room he found the middle-aged lady of Anglo-Greek descent who acted as housekeeper.

A little hesitantly, he said: 'Good evening, Mrs. Gonis. I . . . er, expect you're a bit surprised to see me, but I didn't have a chance to let you know that I was coming back tonight. Could you get someone to make up the bed in my old room?'

She gave him a motherly smile. 'Oh, I've kept it made up, Mr. Robbie, hoping you'd be back any time. We were all of us quite worried about your going off like that on your own.'

'That's awfully nice of you.' He smiled back. 'Then I think I'll go up there right away.'

'Have you had your supper?' she enquired.

'No, as a matter of fact, I haven't,' he admitted. 'But I don't want to put you to a lot of trouble.'

'It will be no trouble at all. There's some of that *moussaka* you're so fond of in the larder. One of the girls can soon heat it up in a glass dish, and there's a big piece of the *cassata* in the fridge left over from dinner. I'll send them up on a tray with a carafe of wine to the little writing room, and you can have them on the table there.'

Robbie's worries had not impaired his appetite, and a quarter of an hour later he was tucking into the *moussaka*. It was his favourite Greek dish, a sort of shepherd's pie, but made with slices of aubergine between the layers of mince and on top, instead of potato, a thick crust of eggs and toasted cheese.

While waiting for his supper, he had been conning over the decidedly alarming situation in which he found himself. Although he had escaped arrest, he feared that that was very unlikely to be the end of the matter. It seemed certain that the Czechs would press the police to take action against him and that, if not tonight, certainly tomorrow, a police chief would turn up to demand some form of satisfaction from Sir Finsterhorn. His uncle would undoubtedly be furious and, being a stickler for justice, might even order him out of the Embassy, so that justice could take its course.

If only he had been able to retain the brief-case with those papers in it, he felt that things would have been very different. At least, he would have had that valuable prize to hand over as a set-off against any awkwardness that his escapade might cause between the Greek Government and the British Embassy. Unorthodox as his actions had been, his uncle could hardly have thrown him to the lions after he had pulled off a coup of which any real Secret Service agent might be proud. But he had had to abandon the brief-case, and he very much feared that his uncle might think that he had invented the whole story about it, in the hope that it might get him out of his mess.

By the time he was digging into the vanilla ice with its inner layer of chocolate and core of frozen cream, rich with bits of marron glacé, angelica and glacé cherries, his spirits had gone down to zero. He felt convinced that his uncle would sacrifice him to the accepted concept of an Ambassador's duty and insist on handing him over to the Greeks to stand his trial. Again awful visions of a bleak prison and its incredible discomforts harrowed his thoughts.

His immediate problem, he felt, was to decide on what he should say to his uncle next morning. Should he come clean and tell the whole, unvarnished truth, or should he seek refuge in another tissue of the lies that he was so unaccustomed to telling, protest his innocence and declare that he was the victim of a put-up job by the Czechs, designed to embarrass the British Ambassador?

The latter course seemed to offer a better chance of securing his uncle's protection; but would he believe him? And, in any case, that could not save him from his uncle's anger, because he could not have been made use of in that way had he not, against Sir Finsterhorn's strenuous opposition, taken a job with the Czechs. He wished most desperately that he had someone to whom he could turn for advice. It was then that his slow mind clicked, and he thought of Luke Beecham.

He could not have rung up Luke from the agency, but had meant to do so after it closed that evening. His hectic experiences since had put the matter right out of his mind, but there was no reason why he should not do so now. Leaving his *cassata* unfinished, he hurried across the hall to the secretary's deserted office, and called Luke's number.

As he feared might prove the case, Luke was not in, but his man answered. Mr. Beecham was out at a dinner party and, unless he went on anywhere, should be home before midnight. Robbie said that he wished to see Mr. Beecham on a matter of the utmost urgency. When he did get home, would he please come to the Embassy by way of the garage entrance, where Mr. Grenn would be waiting up for him till any hour. Realizing that the man would go to bed if his master did not arrive home within the next hour or so, Robbie asked him to write out the message and pin it to Mr. Beecham's pillow.

Returning to the little writing room at the back of the house, Robbie finished his *cassata* and drank up what remained of the carafe of Attika Demestika wine that Mrs. Gonis had sent up with his supper. By then, it was a little after eleven so, in case Luke might get home early, he went out into the garden.

It was a warm, cloudless night, with a myriad of stars shining brightly overhead. The sight of them made him think of the Immortals, after whom so many of the stars were named. Fervently, he prayed to his patroness, Athene, that Luke might not go on from his dinner party to the Coronet, the Flamingo, the Mocambo or one of the other Athenian night-clubs, as that would mean waiting for him until two or three in the morning.

Normally Robbie was not a heavy smoker, but as he paced up and down the parched lawn, keeping a watchful eye on the gate beside the garage, he lit cigarette after cigarette. At a quarter to twelve, he noticed the lights of the garage go on, and soon afterward heard the purr of the Rolls as Tompkins drove it off to bring home his master. Another ten minutes went by then, to his heartfelt relief, he saw beyond the iron grille of the side gate a dark figure, that caught the eye more readily owing to the starlight glinting on its white shirt front.

As he let in his visitor, Luke said: 'So you've returned to the fold, Robbie. Your having taken a job with the Czechs is the talk of Athens. I must say I give you full marks for having pulled it off; but a little bird told me that your uncle was so angry that he threw you out.'

'He didn't quite do that,' Robbie replied, leading the way

over to the summer house. 'To get the job, I had to pretend I was pro-Communist, and my staying on here wouldn't have fitted in. I meant to move out for a while, anyway, but when I told H.E. what was on, he got terribly shirty and told me that he wouldn't have me back.'

'One can hardly wonder. You have caused him a shocking loss of face. But, as you are back, I assume you've managed to patch things up with him.'

'No.' Robbie gave a heavy sigh as they sat down. 'I'm only here now because this evening I was chased by the police.'

'Good Lord! D'you mean you took sanctuary here, and your uncle doesn't know about it?'

'That's it. If I hadn't, I'd be spending the night in a prison cell.'

'My hat, Robbie! You have got yourself into a mess.'

'I know. I desperately need your advice. That's why I asked you to come over.'

Luke took out a cigar and said: 'All right. Tell me all.' Then he lit the cigar and sat back to listen.

It took Robbie a good ten minutes to give an account of all that had happened to him since last they had met, and he ended up: 'So you see, I've either got to come clean with my uncle and risk his handing me over to stand my trial, or swear I'm innocent and risk the Czechs and the police proving me to be a liar.'

For a moment Luke pulled thoughtfully on his cigar, then said: 'While you were being chased the first time, when you had the brief-case, do you think you were seen by anyone who knows you, and would talk about having seen you chased?'

'Not as far as I know. It's hardly likely. The chase could not have lasted more than a couple of minutes while I ran less than half the length of Stadium Street. But why do you ask?'

'Because, if that is so, the Czechs are going to find it devilish difficult to prove that you ever stole the brief-case.'

'The first policeman whose attention they attracted may have seen me holding it.'

'This happened after dark. In the uncertain light, he might have been mistaken. The fact that you had not got it when you emerged from the building site would throw doubt on his evidence.'

Robbie was hanging on Luke's words. 'Do you . . . do you really think, then, there's a chance that the Czechs may not bring a charge? There is the one they meant to trump up about my stealing money, too.'

'About that they haven't got a shred of evidence, so you can count it out. And I think the odds are against their bringing one about the brief-case unless they feel confident they can prove it. You see, it is already assumed in diplomatic circles that you've been ass enough to let them make propaganda out of you. If they do bring a case, it is certain to be thought that, having got you into their toils, this is a plot they have hatched to bring discredit on the British.'

'Then you think my fears about a police chief turning up here in the morning are groundless?'

'One can't say for certain; but there are times when one may save one's bacon by adopting a masterly policy of inactivity, and I'm inclined to think that this is one of them.'

Closing his eyes, Robbie gave a sigh of relief. 'What a marvellous chap you are, Luke. It would never have occurred to me that if I didn't tell my uncle, he might never know anything about it.'

'Of course, there's no guaranteeing that it won't somehow come out later,' Luke felt compelled to warn him.

Robbie nodded. 'That's true; and it makes it all the more rotten luck that I had to abandon the brief-case. If I still had it, I could have afforded to come clean and put myself in the clear once and for all. Being able to hand to my uncle that wad of secret papers would have justified what I've done.' Suddenly struck by an idea, he added: 'I say, though! If you think the police are not likely to grab me, I could go round to that building site tomorrow and collect the brief-case from the place where I hid it.'

Luke shook his head. 'No, Robbie, you mustn't do that. You would be crazy to leave the precincts of the Embassy during the next forty-eight hours. By then, if the Czechs have laid a charge, the police will have had to take some action, and you'll know about it in no uncertain manner from your uncle.

But you must give them a chance to come and ask him to hand you over. If they have not shown up by Tuesday, I think you will be able to count yourself in the clear. But if you go out before that, you might land right in the soup.'

'I see. In that case, I'll have to wait till later to collect the brief-case.'

Luke did not speak for a moment, then he said gently: 'If you do manage to retrieve it, Robbie, I don't think it would be a good idea to hand it over to H.E.'

'Why ever not? It would show that, for once, I've done something really worthwhile, and make him take quite a different view of me.'

'I know how you must feel about it, old chap. But I'm afraid you don't understand how careful people in your uncle's position have to be. It is an accepted thing that no diplomat should undertake any form of espionage while he is *en poste* abroad. That applies even to Naval, Military and Air Attachés. Of course, there is nothing against their reporting any developments they may be wily enough to worm out of their opposite numbers or obtain by other normal means, but snooping is definitely against the rules. After all, their job is to get on the best possible terms they can with the Government to which they are accredited, and they wouldn't get very far in that if they were constantly under suspicion of spying. Anyhow, that's the way it is, and as you are a member of the Ambassador's household, all that I've said applies, at least technically, to you.'

'But I haven't been spying on the Greeks,' Robbie protested, 'only on the Czechs. And that's quite different.'

'It's not, as far as this matter of principle is concerned. Any diplomat who was caught out using criminal means to secure the secrets of another would be automatically disgraced. So you see how terribly embarrassing it would be for H.E. if you made him privy to the fact that you stole some documents belonging to a foreign Government.'

Robbie's face fell. 'If that's the case, I'm glad you warned me. But if I can get hold of those papers again, it seems an awful waste to do nothing about them.'

After a moment, Luke said: 'As there is nothing to identify the agents that sent them in, I think you may be overestima-

ting their value, although, of course, our "I" people would certainly like to have the names of the crew members that are
mentioned as being pro-Communist.' Raising the hand that
held the cigar to emphasize his next words, he went on:

'Now this you must keep under your hat. And I mean that.
As it happens I know a chap to whom I could pass them on
with no questions asked about how I came by them. So if you
do escape exposure during these next few days, and later
manage to retrieve them, bring them along to me.'

'Oh, I say! That's wonderful!' Robbie's spirits soared
again. 'Even if they're only of small value, I'll feel then that
I haven't been through all this awful business for nothing.'

'Good. Now what do you intend to say to H.E. tomorrow?
I mean, about returning here without his permission.'

'I hadn't thought. Of course, I shall tell him that I've lost
my job with the Czechs, and I suppose I could throw myself
on his mercy.'

'You can if you've had enough of playing these Gregory
Sallust games; but otherwise it wouldn't be fair to him to ask
to be allowed to take up your quarters here again permanently.'

Robbie thought hard for a few moments, then he said: 'I'll
have to think about that. I may decide to chuck in my hand,
but I don't want to. There's a special reason why I feel that
I must go on until I've got to the bottom of this tobacco-oil
thing. And, although I had to leave behind the list I made of
the places where groups of Czechs are going to start prospecting, I can remember most of them; so I've got something
to go on.'

'Are you quite certain the accommodation Krajcir was
asked to book was not for batches of ordinary tourists?'

'Yes. Each group was divided into engineers and several
grades of technicians. I'd bet anything that they are up to some
game or other that won't do the Western Powers any good.'

Luke stood up. 'In that case, I'd be the last person to
dissuade you from finding out all you can. Anyhow, I'll be
keeping my fingers crossed for you these next few days. Should
the worst happen, and H.E. does let the police cart you off,
give me a ring, and I'll get you a decent lawyer. Now, I
think it's time for bed.'

As Robbie escorted his friend back to the side gate and let him out, he said again and again how grateful he was for his advice. Then, after a last good night, he re-crossed the garden and went up to his room. Suddenly, he felt very tired. In spite of the anxiety he still felt about the outcome of the animosity he had aroused in the Czechs, almost as soon as his head touched the pillow he fell sound asleep.

In the morning, knowing that his uncle disliked unpunctuality, he was first down in the breakfast room. Euan Wettering arrived a few minutes later, gave him a surprised stare and said:

'Well, who would have thought of seeing our young fellow-traveller. What's the latest news from Moscow?'

Robbie reddened. 'You know jolly well that I only pretended Communist sympathies to get a job. Uncle must have told you that.'

'He told me that you had suddenly got the bit between your teeth and nothing he could say would prevent your disgracing the family.'

'He has been at me often enough to get a job,' Robbie muttered sullenly. 'And I got about the only sort of job I could be any good at.'

Euan grinned. 'Am I to assume, then, that you have come back to tell us how successful you have been at it?'

At that moment, Sir Finsterhorn entered the room and Euan went on sarcastically: 'Look who's here, sir. The Kremlin's latest and most brilliant protégé. He has come back to tell us that he has just been appointed to lead the Glorious, Boneheaded, Thugminded Youth Movement of Czechoslovakia.'

'Shut up, Euan! Shut up!' Robbie burst out in desperation. 'Mind your own damned business.'

The expression on the Ambassador's face had shown no perceptible change. As he sat down at the table, he asked in a calm voice: 'When did you get back, Robbie?'

'Last night, sir,' Robbie told him. 'And please don't take any notice of the things Euan is saying. The truth is that I've got the sack, and I felt I ought to come back and tell you about it.'

'I don't mind betting one thing,' Euan chortled. 'You didn't get the sack for pinching the bottom of one of those plump-breasted workers' joys that the Iron Curtain countries send abroad as typists in their Legations. Did you sock your boss, or was it just laziness?'

'Euan!' Sir Finsterhorn intervened sharply. 'Why you should display so much malice toward Robbie, I have no idea. You will kindly refrain from baiting him. It will do us no harm to eat our breakfasts in silence. As for you, Robbie, I should like a few words with you in private afterwards.'

In the belief that the presence of a third party, even if antagonistic, tends to make matters easier during a dreaded interview, Robbie had hoped to get through his ordeal over breakfast. Now, Sir Finsterhorn's ban on speech condemned him to fifteen minutes' agonizing introspection and growing panic. At last the meal was finished, and he followed the Ambassador across the hall into his study.

Sitting down at his desk, Sir Finsterhorn put the tips of his fingers together, looked over them at Robbie and said only: 'Well?'

'I've not much to say, sir,' Robbie announced awkwardly. 'I didn't exactly get the sack. They put me into their Travel Agency, and I spent simply hours sorting folders and stamping envelopes. After a week of it, I was completely fed-up, and last night I had a row with the Manager, a chap named Krajcir. And I . . . well, I just decided to leave.'

'Does this mean that you are not going back; that you have broken with your Czech friends permanently?'

Robbie nodded violently. 'Oh yes, Uncle.' Then he added with unconscious candour: 'I'm sure they wouldn't give me another job, even if I asked for one.'

Sir Finsterhorn allowed his expression of severity to relax a trifle. 'You are, I trust, aware that this escapade of yours caused me grave embarrassment?'

'Yes, Uncle. I'm afraid it must have. I'm terribly sorry about that.'

'And I told you that if you took this job, I would not have you back at the Embassy?'

'I know. I realize now that I ought not to have gone against your wishes. But . . . well, I was terribly keen to prove myself.'

Again Sir Finsterhorn's face became a shade more amiable, and he said: 'I'm not blaming you for that, Robbie. Your upbringing has been so very different from that of a normal young man. It's only natural that you should suffer at times from a feeling of inferiority and wish to show people that they underestimate your capabilities. Even so, it is most unfortunate that you should have chosen to attempt to do so in a manner that has brought such discredit on yourself and embarrassment to all of us here at the Embassy. What have you in mind to do now?'

'Well, Uncle. I . . . I was hoping that you would forgive me and let me remain here . . .'

Robbie had been about to say 'for the next few days'. But Sir Finsterhorn cut in with a quick shake of his head. 'Forgive you, yes; but let you remain here, no. Your having proclaimed yourself a pro-Communist makes that impossible.'

Robbie caught his breath. His heart seemed to rise up into his throat and choke him. His dread of arrest and prison surged back, leaving him for the moment tongue-tied. Luke had said so very definitely that if he left the Embassy during the next forty-eight hours, and the Czechs demanded police action against him, his number would be up. If his uncle expelled him here and now, he might find the police waiting round the corner, on the chance that he would be fool enough to come out, and they would be able to pull him in without going to all the trouble involved in making representations through diplomatic channels. At last, he managed to stutter:

'Uncle . . . please! Can't you let me stay here for a day or two? I . . . I mean, it will take me quite a time to pack. Can't I stay here just till Monday night?'

Sir Finsterhorn suddenly smiled. 'My dear Robbie, there's no need to take what I said like that. I've no wish to hurry you unduly. Of course, you must have time to pack and make your arrangements. In my view, your best plan would be to return to England. At least you have shown us that you are perfectly capable of taking care of yourself; and if you can do that in Athens, you can certainly do so in Cheltenham. No doubt you could arrange matters so that you leave here by the end of the week.'

'Oh, thank you, Uncle; thank you,' Robbie murmured, almost overcome with relief. Then, seeing that the interview was over, he turned and quickly left the room.

He had won his reprieve, but he knew that he was still very far from being out of the wood. At any time that day or the next, the police or a representative of the Greek Foreign Office might come to see his uncle, and blow everything wide open. He could only pray that Luke was right and the Czechs would decide that they had not a strong enough case against him to press for action. But if Luke proved wrong, the line he had taken of concealing the truth would make his case worse than ever. He had burnt his boats, and with them any hope that his uncle would give him protection.

10

Who Knows
What is Round the Corner?

THAT Sunday proved the worst day that Robbie had ever spent in his life. It seemed interminable and, as though drawn by a magnet, he could not resist spending the greater part of it hovering in the vicinity of the hall. As his uncle's secretary was off duty, he used his room as a listening post, sitting in it with the door ajar and a book, on which he found it impossible to concentrate, on his lap. Every time the front-door bell rang, he jumped up and peered out, waiting with pounding heart to find out who the caller was.

So absorbed was his mind with the fear that it could be only a matter of time before he would have to face exposure, that it was not until after twelve o'clock that it occurred to him that he ought to do something about the belongings he had left at the Grande Bretagne. Glad of the chance to occupy himself with something that would temporarily take his thoughts off his nerve-racking vigil, he went in search of his uncle's valet, Loadham.

This lean, cadaverous individual also pressed Robbie's trousers and looked after his clothes. He took a gloomy pleasure in describing life in the great houses in which, when younger, he had served masters much more blue-blooded than Sir Finsterhorn, and Robbie was a good listener. Moreover, with his habitual generosity, Robbie gave Loadham a handsome tip every week; so their relations were distinctly cordial.

Having run Loadham to earth, he opened matters by giving him his usual weekly tip, although he had been away for the past week. He then asked him to go to the Grand Bretagne, pay his bill and collect his things. A little nervously, he added: 'I came back here last night because some thieves broke into my suite at the hotel. The management don't know that, so they may expect me to pay for the damage to the doors. If they do, don't mention the thieves; just pay up without argument. And . . . er, Loadham, I'd be awfully grateful if you didn't say anything about this to anybody.'

As Loadham took the blank cheque that Robbie had made out, he gave him a pained look that almost amounted to a reprimand. 'As though I should ever dream of such a thing, Mr. Robbie. None of my gentlemen has ever had to complain about my discretion.'

Satisfied that Loadham would not give him away, Robbie hastened back to the hall, fearful now that a bringer of explosive tidings might have appeared on the scene in his absence; but an anxious enquiry of the footman on duty reassured him. No one had called during the past half-hour.

Both Sir Finsterhorn and Euan were out for lunch, so he ate the meal in solitary state. Afterwards, knowing that his uncle would not be back for some hours, he determined to be firm with himself and spend the afternoon lying down in his room. Up there, he found that Loadham had accomplished his mission. The valet had put away all his clothes, but his other belongings were in their usual places and, with heartfelt thanks, he saw that his precious manuscript was on his desk.

After an hour of attempting to doze, he gave it up and went downstairs again. It had crossed his mind that, if the police did call while his uncle was out, at least he would know that he must expect the worst and be prepared for a second visit from them. It was not until after six that the awful tension from which he was suffering began to ease, as Greek officials would be certain to consider an Ambassador's convenience. It seemed unlikely, therefore, that they would put off seeking an interview until an hour when he might be entertaining people to drinks.

It happened, too, that Sir Finsterhorn had invited a number of people in for cocktails that evening, and afterwards he was giving a small, bachelor dinner party to introduce a newly arrived Military Attaché to his French, Italian and Turkish opposite numbers. So, from seven o'clock onwards, Robbie's apprehensions perforce nagged at him only intermittently; but by the time he got to bed, he was thoroughly worn out.

That nothing untoward had occurred on Sunday should have reduced his fears considerably. Yet soon after he woke, the horrid thought came to him that, the Greek Foreign Office being manned only by a skeleton staff on the Sabbath, the police were unlikely to have made the necessary contacts there on that day. Therefore, his period of maximum danger had yet to be faced.

Again, like an uneasy ghost, he haunted the hall and stair-case until several people had asked him what he was waiting for. Driven by this up to the first-floor landing, he hovered there for a while, cold shivers going down his spine at every ring of the front-door bell. A lunch party forced him to endeavour to behave normally from one o'clock until nearly three. Then, so that he might continue to keep his tormented watch on the hall, he adopted the expedient of pretending to go into the matter of his return to England. At intervals, he rang up in turn every travel agency, air line and shipping company he could think of, and made copious notes of flying times, sailings and fares. Somehow, he got through the after-noon and it was drink-time again. Euan was entertaining a party of American archaeologists on Sir Finsterhorn's liquor, and their talk meant little to Robbie; but he helped himself liberally to cocktails and stood about keeping an anxious eye on his uncle, in case one of the staff came in to say that some-one was asking for him.

By eight o'clock, Robbie was three parts tight, but the amount he had drunk had made him take a rosier view of things. He was at last beginning to believe that Luke must have been right, and that he need not have feared exposure after all.

Having just seen off two of his guests, Euan passed within a few paces of him and, noticing that his face was chalk-white, paused to ask: 'What's the matter, Robbie? You look as if you'd just seen a ghost.'

Robbie was feeling distinctly queasy. Gulping down the hot

saliva that was running in his mouth, he mumbled: 'Nothing. Well—nothing much. It's only that . . . that I'm not feeling very well.'

Euan shot a quick look at Sir Finsterhorn, then said with a kindness unusual in him: 'Your trouble, my lad, is that you've been knocking it back too hard, and if you make an ass of yourself at dinner, the Old Man will have your head off. Better go up to your room. I'll re-arrange the places at the dinner table and tell him that you've eaten something that has disagreed with you.'

'Thanks, Euan,' Robbie nodded. 'Jolly decent of you.' Then, with an uncertain smile, he straightened his shoulders and left what remained of the party.

Upstairs he was sick, had a bath and felt better. Flopping into bed, he at last relaxed, and the lingering fumes of the alcohol he had imbibed helped to dull his brain into sleep.

On the Tuesday morning, he came downstairs to breakfast with a ravenous appetite, but still not entirely easy in his mind. It had struck him that, instead of calling on his uncle, the Greek authorities might take up the matter of his criminal activities by sending the Ambassador a written memorandum. If they had done that, it would have been drafted only the day before, and so would arrive in that morning's post.

Once more on tenterhooks through breakfast and after it, he hung about in the vicinity of his uncle's study until a quarter past ten, fearing that at any moment the secretary might emerge with a dread summons for him. But when the secretary did appear, he gave Robbie a smiling nod, and by that time the morning's post must have been opened and dealt with. It was only then, after what seemed to him an unending nightmare of uncertainty, that he felt he might dare to think of the future.

During the past two days, he had found it utterly impossible. But now he had to make up his mind whether to return to England, as his uncle wished, or remain on in Greece. Whichever way he decided, he must now begin making arrangements in earnest, for he had to be out of the Embassy before the end of the week.

It was a lovely day, and he badly needed a change of

scene; so he rang up a garage from which he sometimes hired cars, and asked them to send one round. When it arrived, he told the man to drive him out to Sounion. There, he felt, on the headland between sea and sky, at the southernmost point of the peninsula of Attica, would be as good a place as any for him to think things out.

Within five minutes, the car had passed Hadrian's Arch and swung into the broad, straight boulevard that leads to the coast; but when they reached the Gulf, instead of turning right towards the Piraeus, it turned left and passed the Athens Airport at Phaleron. The road then followed the shore, twisting in and out along a score of charming bays in which blue seas broke on golden sands. Here and there, for some fifteen miles, there were clusters of villas, small hotels and cafés. These, later in the year, would be crowded with Athenian holiday-makers, but for the last thirty miles modern buildings were comparatively few and the rugged grandeur of the scene hardly differed from what it must have been in the days of the ancient Greeks.

It was a little after twelve o'clock when the car turned inland, ran up a steep, twisting road and deposited Robbie at the Tourist Pavilion below the headland. In front of it was an array of tables under gay umbrellas, but only one coachload of tourists was scattered among them enjoying iced drinks or an early lunch. In the kitchen of the restaurant, he found that a fisherman had just brought in a catch of *kalamarákia*, so he ordered a dish of the baby squids to be put aside for him and fried at a quarter past one. Then he set out to trudge up the last half mile to the temple of Poseidon, which crowns this lofty promontory.

The temple was built in the Great Age, under Pericles; it is made of pure white marble, and twelve of its original nineteen Doric columns are still standing. To either side of it, the coast falls away, so that it dominates the scene for many miles around. In the background, the green slopes of olive groves and vineyards merge into the brown of uncultivable land broken by stony outcrop, then rise to rocky heights, sharply outlined against a bright blue sky. To the east, south and west, the much darker blue of the sea again meets the sky, broken only here and there by a fleecy white cloud. Seen from whichever angle, the Temple presents one of the loveliest sights in all Greece.

But today Robbie had no eyes for its beauty. Walking past it to within a few yards of the edge of the cliff, he sat down there and, pulling a long stem of wild grass, began to nibble at it. Apart from a few tourists strolling round the ruin in his rear, the place was deserted, and the only sound was the ceaseless pounding of the surf on the rocks far below.

Although he had told Luke during their midnight talk that, if he escaped arrest, he wanted to continue with his self-imposed mission, he had been so scared during the past two days by the results of his initial efforts that he had almost decided to return to England. But now that harrowing episode appeared to be behind him, and he was once more greatly tempted to make use of the information he had secured.

The fact that it was a leaf from Athene's sacred tree blowing through the open window that had led to his coming by the list of places at which groups of Czechs were shortly to begin their operations seemed to him positive evidence that the goddess was keeping a watchful eye on him. Perhaps, indeed, it was she who had in some way influenced events so that he might remain free to carry on the quest with which she had charged him. If so, and he now abandoned it, he might well become the victim of her wrath. There was also the personal side of the matter. This was the one chance he had to prove himself as good as other men. If he rejected it, no other might come his way, and that would mean the acceptance for life of a shaming inferiority.

Before he had been sitting there for fifteen minutes, he had decided that he would stay in Greece.

The next question was how should he set about resuming his mission? Having 'cooked his goose' with the Czechs, it was clear that he could not hope to get anything more out of them by remaining in Athens. He must, then, go to some of the places where they were about to commence work, and endeavour to find out what they were up to.

This idea immediately appealed to him because, although he had been in Greece for a year, he had had no opportunity to see anything of the country except in the vicinity of Athens.

During the past summer, he had longed to visit some of the shrines such as Delphi and Olympia, made famous by his beloved gods. However, he had then still been too nervous of having to talk to the groups of strangers with whom he would have had to travel in the long-distance buses used for conducted tours. As he could not drive a car, he had been unable to make such trips on his own.

This last objection still held, if he meant to visit a chain of places some of which were several hundred miles apart, and yet remain mobile. The railway system in Greece made transit by it from one coast town to another extremely difficult and tedious. It then occurred to him that he could quite well afford to hire a car and driver. To conceal from the driver the true purpose of his journey, he could say that he was collecting information for his book. Some further thought produced an improvement on this idea. It would be greatly preferable to have an educated companion with him as driver, instead of an ordinary mechanic. Why should he not secure a secretary who would also act as chauffeur? When they broke their journey for a day or two, he could give the man some typing to do, and that would materially strengthen his cover as an author writing a book on the gods and their temples.

By the time he had walked back to the restaurant, he was so pleased with his plan that he treated himself to a half bottle of St. Helena—a white wine from Aechia that resembles a good quality hock and is one of the most expensive wines in Greece —to wash down the squids. Having rounded off his meal with a huge, sun-ripe orange, he sent for pencil and paper and set about drafting an advertisement.

After much sucking of the pencil and several false starts, he produced the following:

Young gentleman requires chauffeur who will also carry out light secretarial duties while driving him on tour of Peloponnesus. Good pay, all found. No interviews given. Write qualifications fully to Robert Grenn, British Embassy.

He had inserted the phrase *no interviews given* as an afterthought as he feared that, if a number of applicants queued up in the hall of the Embassy to see him, his uncle might be annoyed.

As there was no point in his getting back to Athens until the newspaper offices re-opened, he spent the next hour up on the headland again, thinking about his book; but soon after four, he was back in the capital, handing in his advertisement at the offices of *Kathimerini*, for insertion next day in the Personal Column.

Before returning to the Embassy, he walked down Korai Street with a view to making a swift reconnaissance of the building site in which he had hidden the brief-case, for he was contemplating a return there after dark that night to retrieve it. As he strolled past, the low barrier of crossed poles over which he had jumped proved no obstruction, now that it was daylight, to his seeing the whole of the ground floor. It seemed much larger than when he had crouched there in the dark. There were at least twenty of the square, concrete pillars, and it might have been near any one of a dozen of them that he had hidden the brief-case. Yet worse, since Saturday, the workmen had completed the boarding over of the floor, so, even had he known near which pillar to look, it would have meant bringing implements to lever up the planks before he could retrieve his prize. To attempt to pull up half the floor was obviously out of the question.

With a sigh, he reconciled himself to the permanent loss of the reports that had been near costing him so dear. As some consolation he recalled Luke's opinion that, since they contained no clues to the identity of the agents who had written them, they would probably not have proved of any great value to N.A.T.O. Intelligence.

Dismissing the matter from his mind, he spent a cheerful hour before dinner sorting out his things into those that could be got into two suitcases to go in the boot of a car, and the rest which he felt sure his uncle would allow him to leave at the Embassy until—as he would say—he could send for them.

While he was so employed, Loadham arrived on the scene and enquired the reason for this disturbance of drawers and cupboards. When Robbie told him, the cadaverous valet shook his head sadly over his young master's impending departure, but insisted that he should not pack for himself. He had only to put aside, for packing, the things he meant to take with him. Loadham would pack them when instructed to do so and, after Robbie's departure, take care of everything else.

This arrangement left Robbie nothing to do after dinner; so, his mind free of worry, he returned to his book, re-reading parts of it with a view to getting in the mood to start a new chapter next day. On looking through the chapter on Jason, he was far from satisfied with it; so on the Wednesday, instead of tackling a fresh subject, he re-wrote the chapter. And this is how it read when he finally laid down his pen that night:

THE HEROES

(NO. 3 JASON)

I'm not sure that I ought not to have headed this chapter THE ARGONAUTS, or even THE GOLDEN FLEECE, because both would be more likely to ring a bell in my kind reader's mind than just the name of Jason.

Anyhow, as I have now managed to wedge these romantic words into the first paragraph readers will have a pretty good idea what this chapter is about.

I have not yet told you about Chiron. He was an old, white-headed Centaur who lived in a cave up on Mount Pelion, which is not far from the coast in north-eastern Greece, and he was looked on by everyone as quite the top tutor of his day. He had the misfortune to die very painfully from having scratched himself with one of Hercules's poisoned arrows, but before that lots of Kings used to send their sons to be educated by him. In fact his cave seems to have been a sort of Eton of those days.

Of course they didn't use books, or not much, anyway, but he taught them all the sort of things that really matter, like being kind to old people, reverence for the gods and sticking to one's pals through thick and thin. Besides this he coached them in hunting, wrestling, dancing, mountain climbing and how to play the harp and sing, so he must have been quite an exceptional sort of Prof.

Jason spent most of his youth as one of Chiron's pupils, with a whole lot of other young Princes; although at the time he had no idea that he too came out of the top drawer. Actually his father, Aeson, should have been a King, but he had come unstuck through letting his kingdom be stolen from him by his wicked half-brother Pelias. This Pelias was a very unpleasant type as given half a chance he would have killed young Jason, so as to make certain he wouldn't be around to claim the kingdom when he grew up. That is why Aeson hurried little Jason off to live with old Chiron on Mount Pelion.

Jason soon grew as big as I am and he was very much quicker at doing things. He was a match for any of the others at throwing a spear or scaling a cliff, and he didn't mind swimming in icy torrents in mid-winter a bit. What is more, he had taken in all old Chiron had told him about never telling people what a fine fellow he was and showing a sort of polite indifference when dishes were put on the table that were his very favourite thing to eat. I hesitate to say so, but he seems to me to have been a bit of a prig.

At length the day came when Chiron decided that he had turned out a star pupil with no further edges to be rounded off, so he gave Jason the lowdown about his birth and how his father had been done down by Pelias.

Our Hero at once became as mad as a hatter. He would not delay a single day, but next morning set off down the mountain towards the coast where the kingdom lay that should have been his. After springing from rock to rock like a billy-goat for an hour or two, he got down to vineyards, orchards and fields of corn, but then he found himself facing a rushing river.

On its bank was sitting an old woman dressed in filthy rags and moaning to herself: 'Who will carry me across?'

You and I, dear reader, would have known the answer to that one, but Jason very nearly missed the boat. He looked at her as though she were something the cat had brought in; but, luckily for him, on second thoughts he remembered what Chiron had told him about acting as a good guy to anyone in trouble. Hiding his annoyance as best he could, he said: 'All right, mother, I'll take you over.'

No sooner had he spoken than she leapt upon his back and

flung her skinny arms round his neck. Far from happy, he waded into the river, slipping and stumbling and cutting his feet on hidden rocks. She clung to him like a limpet and seemed to weigh a ton, so he came near to drowning and had one hell of a time before he managed to stagger with her up the opposite bank.

As you will have guessed she then leapt lightly to the ground and dazzled the poor chap by turning into a female sheathed in silk and surrounded by a sort of full-length halo of incandescent light. It transpired that she was Hera, Zeus's official wife, and what follows is one of the few things I shall have to record to that horrid woman's credit. She told him that as he had proved himself to be a charitable type, he could call on her for help whenever he needed it. And in this case she was as good as her word—or at least now and then.

Feeling distinctly pleased with himself, Jason slogged on towards the city, the towers of which he could now see in the distance. However, his progress was slowed up quite a bit because while fording the river one of his sandals had been gripped by the mud which sucked it off his foot. But he was much too tough to let a little thing like that get him down, and in due course he reached the capital.

Now although Jason did not know it, some years before King Pelias had consulted an Oracle. It had told him that he would lose his kingdom to a stranger who came to him with one bare foot. So it will be readily understood that when Jason presented himself at Court and the King saw that he was wearing only one sandal he nearly threw a fit.

Pulling himself together, Pelias asked Jason who he was, whence he came and all that. Jason, who was either lacking in imagination or a V.C. type that does not count the odds, promptly replied: 'I am the son of Aeson, come to claim my rights. Get off that throne or it will be the worse for you.'

Why Pelias did not call out his Guard and have Jason done in there and then, history does not tell us. Perhaps the prophecy had scared him down to his button boots, so that his mind was not ticking over properly, or he may have had a thing against taking human life. Anyhow, instead of having Jason's throat cut, he invited him to dinner.

While they were all having a wash and brush up, the King seems to have got his wits back. He had several lovely daughters so he sent for them and said: 'Listen, girls. This fellow Jason whom I've asked to dine is a heel. If we're not darned careful he'll have us all out of here on our ears, and you will find yourselves earning a living on the streets. Fortunately he seems a brainless lout, and you are his cousins, so you've got to cozen him, understand? Don't spare the petting, and leave the rest to me,' or words to that effect.

After that you can imagine what happened during dinner. The girls clustered round 'Cousin Jason' as though they were bees and he was the honey pot. They flickered their eyelashes and opened their eyes to the widest extent exclaiming 'Oh!' when they in turn felt his biceps. And they took jolly good care that his glass was never empty. When they felt that they had softened him up enough they gave the wink to their papa, and he brought on the star turn from the local cabaret.

This character's act was a monologue accompanied by occasional twangs on a harp. He told the story of how a Prince and Princess named Phrixus and Helle were terribly persecuted by their cruel stepmother Queen Ino, until the gods took pity on them and sent them a Golden Ram, that was a kind of animal aircraft, in which to get away from her. They mounted on its back and it must have done pretty well a vertical take-off. Anyway the pace was too hot for poor Helle. When they were crossing the Dardanelles she got giddy, fell off and was drowned; hence the ancients' name for the place, the Hellespont.

The story went on to the effect that Phrixus managed to cling on until the beast had carried him right up the coast of the Euxine Sea and made a safe landing in a country called Colchis, which was probably a part of what we now know as Rumania. Far from being grateful to the Ram, Phrixus proceeded to sacrifice it to Zeus then skinned it and hung its Fleece up in a sacred grove near what was probably a mouth of the Danube.

Phrixus settled down quite happily among the Colchians, married Chalciope, the eldest daughter of their King, whose name was Aeetes, and died in the land of his adoption. But the story did not end there. Why the Kings of those days had to be always consulting Oracles, goodness knows, for they never seem to have done them any good. Anyway, King Aeetes consulted one and it told him that as long as he held on to the Golden Fleece he would be all right, but if once he let it be taken off him he would be a deader.

In the circumstances he did some pretty serious thinking. This resulted in his managing to get hold of—but don't ask me how—a huge fire-breathing serpent that never slept, as guardian of the tree to which the Golden Fleece had been nailed.

The harp-strummer then ended on a note of lament. For some reason undisclosed—since Phrixus had been perfectly happy in Colchis and never made any attempt to return with the Fleece to Greece—his ghost would never lie quiet until the Fleece was brought back to the country of his birth.

By this time Jason must have had a cuddlesome cousin on each of his knees and a third breathing hard down the back of his neck. He was, too, as tight as a tick, otherwise he would never have done what he did.

Staggering to his feet he cried: 'Poo' ole Phrixus! Poo' ole Phrixus! Can't let 'is ghost lie restless in t'grave. I go an' get Fleece. Jus' leave everythin' t'me!'

I've never tried to write like a drunk speaks before, so I can only hope the above will give my readers the right impression.

Seeing that this great big softie had fallen into his trap, the King led the cheering and the girls all patted Jason on the back. Then I suppose his newly found relations carried him up to bed.

Next morning he had the whale of a hangover and realized what an ass he had made of himself. He was very tempted to back out, and I can appreciate his feelings because I've recently had a somewhat similar experience, except that I wasn't tiddly when I let myself in for it. But old Chiron had taught him that if a chap pledges himself to do something he is in honour bound to go through with it. So Jason wrapped his head in a wet towel and set about making a plan.

Living in those parts at the time there was a really wizard shipwright named Argus. Jason got hold of him and had him build a ship out of pine trees cut from Mount Pelion. It was a fifty-oared galley, strong enough to resist any storm yet light enough to be carried overland by its crew. That shows you what a clever old buffer Argus must have been, and it's not surprising that they called the ship after him, the *Argo*.

As a matter of fact not quite all the credit for the light but unsinkable vessel can go to Argus. In the meantime Jason had paid a visit to Hera's Oracle at Dodona. There was a sacred grove there with a great oak tree in it through which she spoke to people. The goddess told him to lop a limb off her oak and have it carved into a figurehead for his ship, then if he got into difficulties he was to consult it and it would tell him what to do. She also asked Athene to inspire Argus with her wisdom while he was building the vessel, so you see he had the benefit of the goddess's know-how.

Next Jason ran a recruiting campaign, to persuade a lot of other hard-boiled types to come with him. The other Heroes didn't need much persuading because by that time getting the Fleece back had become a thing that had to be done for the honour of Greece. Hercules, Theseus, Orpheus, Castor and Pollux, Admetus, Peleus and lots of others rolled up, fifty in all, including old Argus, who insisted on taking an oar. In addition they took Lynceus as their pilot and Tiphys as their steersman. They would have liked to have Hercules for their captain, but as Jason had started all this Hercules insisted that he should have the job.

When all was set, cunning King Pelias and his girls waved them good-bye. How Jason's pretty cousins felt about him by this time we are not informed. If he was keen about petting parties they were probably a bit misty-eyed, but their papa must have been chuckling in his beard at the happy thought that he would never set eyes on his troublesome nephew again.

Putting out from the coast of Thessaly, the *Argo* crossed the Aegean and anchored off the island of Lemnos. Some little time before, the women of this island had got bored with their husbands and boy friends, so they had killed them all. Thinking it over later, they came to the conclusion that this had been a big mistake. My lady readers will therefore easily imagine how pleased they were when Jason put in with his crew of fifty-odd likely lads. These stalwarts were pretty quick to realize that the gods had given them a lucky break, so from the very first night a good time was had by all. Not having even seen a man for goodness knows how long, the Lemnos girls fairly let themselves rip and spared no pains at all to get the Argonauts thinking that Lemnos was just the place to settle down in for good. Even Jason seems to have liked the idea.

But crusty old Hercules had remained in the ship. As my readers will remember, when young he had chosen Duty instead of Pleasure. So after these jollifications had been going on for some time he came ashore and told his companions what he thought of them. It may be that by then the Argonauts were beginning to find life on an island entirely populated by women a bit exhausting. Anyhow, they admitted that they ought to be ashamed of themselves, and agreed to continue their voyage.

Having sailed up the Hellespont they entered the Propontis Sea, which we now call the Sea of Marmara. There they put in to a haven on its south coast and were kindly received by Cyzicus, the King of the Doliones. This young man was just about to get married and invited them to his wedding feast. Hercules, not being keen on that sort of thing, went off on his own, and it was as well he did. He found that while all the inhabitants of the place were celebrating, a race of giants had come down from the hills and were blocking up the mouth of the harbour with huge stones.

He gave the alarm and kept the giants off with his poisoned arrows until the other Argonauts came on the scene and managed to get their vessel to sea. But later that night a storm drove them back on to the coast. The Doliones, thinking they were enemy raiders, set upon them. In the fight that followed several of the Doliones were killed, among them young King Cyzicus. When daylight came, the mistake was discovered. Everyone was upset, but the Argonauts could only express their regrets and stay over to attend the funeral rites.

Farther along the same coast the Mysians welcomed and gave a party for them. But once again Hercules behaved like a boor and wouldn't join in the fun. However, this time he had something special to occupy him. He had recently broken his oar and he went off into the forest to look for a pine tree large enough to make an oar suitable to his immense strength.

I have never done any rowing myself, but I should have thought that having one oar much bigger than all the rest would have made things pretty tricky. Still, that's beside the point. With him he took Polyphemus, a pal of his, and a beautiful youth named Hylas, of whom he was very fond.

Having found a pine tree that he liked the look of, Hercules sent young Hylas to fetch some water for their frugal supper, then took off his coat to cut the tree down. Hylas found a lake and was kneeling down on its bank to fill whatever it was he had brought with him when a lot of pretty heads bobbed up nearby. These belonged to Water Nymphs who owned the place. After one look at Hylas these girls decided that they could have a lot of fun with such a good-looking chap if only they could keep him with them. So they pulled him in and he never came up again.

Polyphemus heard his shout and ran to get Hercules. Thinking their young friend had been carried off by robbers, they searched the woods all night and went on searching them for some days afterwards. Meanwhile the other Argonauts were getting a bit restive, because the wind was fair. At length, believing H. and Co. must all be dead, they sailed without them. However, before they had gone far a sea god called Glaucus surfaced near the vessel and said for them not to worry. Hercules was O.K. and before long he would have plenty of other things on his plate, so he wouldn't really mind very much not having been in on getting the Golden Fleece.

Their next call was on the King of the Bebrycians. He was not a nice person, as he was very strong and his fun was to insist that any stranger should box with him, then knock them out. In Pollux, who took him on, he caught a Tartar, for he got knocked out himself.

King Phineus, whose country they came to soon after, they found in very poor shape. He was blind and three horrid creatures called Harpies never ceased from tormenting him. They were enormous vultures with women's faces and every time the blind King tried to eat anything they either snatched it from him or made a nasty mess on it. Why he had not long since starved to death is a mystery, and I don't see either how he managed to govern his kingdom.

Fortunately several of the Argonauts were the sons of gods by good-looking girls, and two of them had been born with wings. So they flapped up into the air and sent the Harpies packing. Anxious to repay the people who had at last enabled him to eat a decent dinner, Phineus warned them that they were heading for two floating islands of icy rock called the Symplegades. These islands had a nasty habit of parting, then when a ship was sailing between them suddenly closing and crushing it to bits. Phineus tipped Jason off to take a dove aboard and let it fly between the islands first.

Jason took this advice and when they came to the icebergs, as that is what they must have been, he sent the dove through the channel. The two 'bergs came together with a clang and, believe it or not, nipped off the dove's tail feathers. But the shock made them bounce apart, and by rowing all out the Argonauts managed to get through just in time. Personally, instead of risking going between them I should have rowed round one of them, but none of our Heroes seems to have thought of that.

By this time they were well up in the cold Black Sea and there they had many other adventures, including being attacked by a flock of enormous birds called the Stymphalides. Their feathers were made of brass and they could shoot them off like javelins, so to be pulling at an oar beneath them can have been no fun at all. But half the Argonauts kept rowing while the other half banged their spears on their bronze shields, and the noise scared the birds off.

They were now drawing near to Colchis, but before going in for their attempt to make off with the Fleece, they anchored under the lee of an island some way off the coast. Here they had a stroke of luck, for they came upon four naked youths who had been shipwrecked there. These turned out to be the sons of Phrixus, so they were able to tell the Argonauts all about the court of King Aeetes and guide them to it.

Naturally these young men's mother, Chalciope, was delighted to see them again, and her much younger sister, Medea, instantly took a very good view of Jason. But King

Aeetes felt a bit uneasy at his house being filled with all these forceful-looking Argonauts, and after supper, when Jason told him what they had come for, he looked very glum indeed.

Jason related all the perils they had been through and claimed the Fleece as their reward. I am no lawyer, but it doesn't seem to me that even shooting Niagara Falls, climbing Mount Everest, going to the bottom of the sea in a bathysphere then being first man up in the stratosphere would entitle one to ask for the Crown Jewels. King Aeetes saw it as I do, but he made Jason a sporting offer.

He said: 'I've got a couple of brazen bulls that belch fire from their nostrils. You can have a shot at harnessing them and using them to plough a four-acre field. I'll then provide you with a satchel full of dragons' teeth to sow the field with. From each tooth there will spring up a fully armed warrior and you will have to take them on single-handed. If you can get through that programme between dawn and dusk I'll let you have a crack at my sleepless serpent that guards the Golden Fleece.'

Being a Hero, Jason said: 'Done!' and went back to his ship to get some shut-eye. But the two Princesses had got butterflies in the tummy about him. Chalciope was afraid that if Jason fell down on the job her papa would have all the rest of the Argonauts killed, and with them her sons for having brought them there. So she slipped on a dressing-gown and went along to Medea's room to ask her help.

Her reason for hoping that her younger sister might be able to put a fast one over their papa was because Medea was a very clever witch. As Medea already had ants in her pants about Jason, she needed no urging to play. Getting into whatever were the equivalent in those days of gumboots and a warmly lined macintosh, she sneaked out of the palace and went into the woods. There she gathered all sorts of herbs and, having brought them back to the kitchen, stewed them down, while muttering enchantments various, until their juices had become a paste. Putting a veil round her head, she then took the magic ointment she had made down to the *Argo*, which was moored in the river, and had Jason roused from his sleep. She told him that if he wished to come through next day's ordeal alive he must smear this stuff all over his body and his weapons, then nothing could harm him or break them.

Having guessed who she was and already having the same sort of yen for her that she had for him, he thought he could trust her. But when morning came, being a leery sort of cove, he smeared on the ointment then asked some of his pals to try their weapons on him.

This test having proved satisfactory, he went off quite cheerfully to face anything that was coming his way. When he reached the field he threw his spear, sword and helmet aside and stripped to the buff. But of course in those days the girls who were looking on were quite used to chaps doing that. When the brazen bulls were released from their underground stable, they came roaring up like a couple of camouflaged tanks equipped with flame throwers. But Jason just stood there letting them charge him and dash their horns against his unbreakable shield. Presumably he played them like a Spanish matador until he had taken some of the stuffing out of them. Then he chucked away his shield and put on a rodeo act, seizing the bulls by the horns and throwing them on their backs. How he managed to tackle both of them at once passes my comprehension, but he got them yoked up and goaded them into ploughing the four-acre field.

By then King Aeetes was beginning to look a bit green in the gills, but he gave Jason the bag of dragons' teeth and continued to hope that our Hero would bite the dust. No sooner had Jason sown the teeth than row upon row of fierce warriors sprang up from the furrows. It was now up to Jason to kill every one of them before the sun set, but in the middle of the night Medea had whispered to him a trick for getting rid of them that would save his breath.

Doing as she had told him, he picked up a great stone boulder and heaved it right into the middle of the host that was about to set upon him. It may be that these warriors had come to life too quickly to be more than half-baked. Anyhow, none of them seemed to have seen him hurl this great stone; they only realized that it had come down in the midst of them. Those nearest where it had landed accused one of the others of having thrown it. Soon a fight started among them and they were all at one another's throats. Jason just stood looking on while the furrows were filled with blood and the field became black with corpses. By the time the sun went down there was not a single one left and the ground had swallowed them all up again. It was just as simple as that.

Jason then said to the King: 'Now, old cock. How about handing over the Fleece?'

But Aeetes, having been told years before by the Oracle that if he ever parted with it his number would be up, was not prepared to commit what would have amounted to hara-kiri just to please Jason. So he stalled for time and said: 'We'll have a chat about that in the morning.'

Actually he had already decided that the best thing he could do was to collect several hundred of his warriors together during the night and have them wipe the Argonauts off the slate next day. That his plan failed was partly due to Medea's having gone so weak in the knees over Jason, and partly owing to Aeetes's meanness. Having tumbled to what was afoot, Medea hurried off to warn the boy friend; but he and his pals wouldn't have had much chance to act on her warning if Aeetes had had the foresight to put them up in his palace. Had he done that he would have had a good chance of having them all murdered in their beds, or anyhow of preventing them from getting back to their ship. As it was the old skinflint left them to rough it on their own in a camp down by the river.

When Medea arrived they were still at supper. She told Jason that her papa meant to double-cross him and that his only chance of not being turned into cat's meat was to pinch the Fleece there and then and sail off with it before dawn. While the Argonauts jumped to it to get their vessel ready for sea, Jason set off with Medea and her young brother Absyrtus, who had tagged along with her, to the sacred grove.

Young Absyrtus trembled like a jelly when he heard the hissing of the huge poison-breathing snake that guarded the Fleece. But tackling it was just Children's Hour stuff to Medea. She bedevilled it by singing a low witches' chant, then sprinkled some magic powder she had brought with her on its eyes. That sent it to sleep, so all Jason had to do was to step over its body and tear the Fleece down from the tree to which it had been nailed.

When they got back to the ship, Medea said: 'If my pop tumbles to it that it was I who put you up to this, I shall be for the high jump. So how about taking me with you?'

Chivalry apart, by then her hip-wriggling act had got Jason where she wanted him, so he replied: 'Gladly, oh Maiden, and wilt thou honour me by becoming my bride?' or words to that effect.

So they went aboard, taking young Absyrtus with them, and by first light the *Argo* was standing out to sea with the Golden Fleece nailed to the mast and all sail set.

I would not like to sully my gentle readers' ears with the sort of language King Aeetes must have used when he heard what had happened, but he was not the chap to take that sort of thing lying down. In no time at all he had manned his fleet and put to sea in pursuit, and some of his ships were so fast that it seemed certain that they would catch up with the *Argo*.

When the leading vessel got so close that Medea could see the face of her papa as he stood glowering in the prow, she decided on taking drastic action. She made the Argonauts kill her young brother, cut him in pieces and throw the bits overboard. As Aeetes felt bound to give his son proper burial he had to heave to in order to fish the bits out of the water, and while he was kept busy doing that the *Argo* managed to get away.

Although Medea had saved their bacon, Jason must have been a bit worried on discovering the sort of better-half he had taken to his bosom. The gods, too, thought that her killing her young brother in this way was a most unsporting thing to do, and they made the Argonauts pay for it in no uncertain manner.

Instead of letting the *Argo* have a nice trip back to Greece they gave her a very unpleasant passage. Time after time she was carried off her course by tempests and driven on to unknown shores. For months on end her wretched crew humped her over land and across mountains until they reached the Med. But there were more storms after they had re-launched her, and she was washed up in North Africa. There, for some reason, they had to carry her again over miles of desert under a blistering sun. This went on for years and years, so when at last they did manage to get home those among them who had set out as hardy youths had become middle-aged men. If I'd been one of them I must say I'd have been pretty fed up with Jason for having caused me to waste the best years of my life. Still, they had got the Fleece.

Old Pelias was still alive, and was pretty shattered at seeing them again after all this time, as he had long counted them dead. But he once again dug his toes in about giving up his kingdom to Jason. However, Medea soon thought of a way to put him on the spot.

She told him she had the secret of restoring youth and laid on a demonstration by boiling a ram in a cauldron into which she had put a lot of herbs. When she pulled the ram out it had turned into a nice little lamb. The King asked to be made young too; so they prepared another cauldron and put him in it. As my readers will have guessed, Medea didn't put the right herbs in with him so the old fool was boiled alive.

Jason thought it such a scurvy trick that he refused to inherit the kingdom through her wicked deed. Instead he took a run-out powder on her and set off on his travels again. While staying in Corinth he fell in love with the King's daughter, a girl called Glauce, and decided to take her as his second wife. When Medea heard about this she pretended not to mind and sent Glauce a present of a beautiful wedding dress, but actually she was hopping mad and had first sprayed the garment with a subtle poison. When poor Glauce put it on it stuck to her flesh and burnt her to death, just as the shirt of Nessus did Hercules.

Not content with having spoiled Jason's fun, Medea then murdered the three children she had had by him. Feeling that to be the limit, he made up his mind to do her in. But by her magic arts she summoned up a chariot drawn by dragons and got away in it. Having lost Glauce and his children, and then Medea giving him the slip, sent him absolutely berserk and he killed himself.

From the above it will be seen that Jason did not have at all a happy life. But that was largely his own fault for having failed to keep his eye on the ball, and letting Pelias make him tight in the first place. All things considered, too, I don't think he deserves to be looked on as one of the top Heroes. He wouldn't have got anywhere without Medea, would he?

* * * * *

Robbie felt that the ending to this chapter was still a little weak but, during his re-writing, he had improved it considerably; so, pleased with his day's work, he went happily to bed.

First thing on Thursday morning, he ran downstairs to collect his post and hurried back to his room with it. It consisted entirely of replies to his advertisement, and there was a great stack of them; many more than he had expected.

Having opened several, he soon saw the reason. The idea of carrying out light secretarial duties for a young gentleman, and at the same time making a motor tour of the Peloponnesus, clearly held a strong appeal for a lot of young women in Athens. Even a number who already had jobs were prepared to sacrifice them in Robbie's interest, and several enclosed photographs.

This took him by surprise for, when he had drafted his advertisement, the idea of employing a woman had never entered his thoughts. Had he been a more sophisticated young man, he might have decided from the first to have a woman drive him and, when picking the most attractive applicant from a number of pretty girls, all sorts of interesting possibilities might have crossed his mind.

But the prospect of having a young woman as his sole companion, perhaps for several weeks, scared Robbie stiff. All girls held a frightening, if attractive, mystery for him that he still lacked the courage to explore. He had wanted a man to whom he could talk, and experience told him that when left alone with an attractive woman he usually dried up within a quarter of an hour. To have to strive to find things to say to a girl, day after day, would prove positive torture. On looking through the photographs, too, another aspect of the matter struck him. Perhaps, while picnicking in some lonely spot, he might be overcome by one of those urges he sometimes felt and, as he saw it, there being little chance that the lady would be willing to respond to his caresses, a most shaming and miserable situation would ensue.

Reluctantly, he put aside all the letters from women applicants, and went more carefully through those from men. These formed barely a fifth of the pile, and were very disappointing. Nearly all of them admitted either that they could not take shorthand, or were 'a bit out of practice'. A few could not even type, but asserted that they would make quick learners. Most of them were garage hands. The only applicant whose letter was obviously that of a well-educated man, stated that he would greatly enjoy making such a tour but, owing to his arthritis, could not undertake to drive more than fifty miles a day. Not one came anywhere near fulfilling Robbie's requirement of a good driver, not too far removed from his own age, who would prove a pleasant companion. And, as he had to be out of the Embassy by the end of the week, he could not delay, even for twenty-four hours, in making his choice.

Turning back to the letters from women, he went through them again, and found one from a Mrs. Papayannis. She stated that she had been driving for thirty years without one acident, knew the Peloponnesus like the back of her hand from having been hunted all over it during the war while an officer in the Women's Resistance, could type at 80 and took shorthand at 150. She was out of a job at the moment only because her chief, a distinguished scientist for whom she had worked for the past nine years, had recently died.

It was clear that she must be in the neighbourhood of fifty, an educated woman, but a real old battle-axe. Robbie felt he would be able to talk to her without humiliating diffidence and be free of all temptation to attempt the sort of thing that might cause him bitter regret. Pushing aside the other letters, he put hers in his pocket and decided to take her on.

She had given him her telephone number in her letter, adding that she had an engagement for that morning; so, if he were interested, would he phone her in the afternoon?

After breakfast, he went round to the garage he patronized and got a quotation for hiring a medium-size car by the week. Next he went to his bank, obtained a letter of credit and drew out a considerable sum in cash; then went for a stroll round the old quarter of the city to the west of Constitution Square. Its narrow streets with groups of shops that sold nothing but buttons, or materials, or embroidery always intrigued him, and for the whole way along Eolou Street, at which the section ended, he could look up at his beloved Acropolis dominating the city.

He returned to the Embassy a little before one o'clock. As he entered the hall, the butler was holding the telephone receiver, and called out to him: 'There's a lady on the phone for you, Mr. Robbie. She has already rung up twice this morning, but you were out.'

'Who is she?' Robbie asked in surprise.

'It's a Miss Stephanopoulos,' the butler replied. 'She says that it's urgent and she must speak to you personally.' Then he turned back to the instrument and said into it in Greek: 'Hold on, Miss. Mr. Grenn has just come in.'

Having no option, Robbie took the instrument from him and said a shade suspiciously: 'This is Robert Grenn. What did you wish to speak to me about?'

'About your advertisement in the *Kathimerini*,' a soft, slightly breathless voice replied. 'It's the very thing I'm looking for, and I'm sure that I could do all you want perfectly.'

'No!' said Robbie hastily. 'No! The post is already filled.'

'But it can't be!' The voice rose in the suggestion of a pathetic wail. 'You can't have had any applications for it until this morning.'

'That's true,' he admitted. 'But I've settled on the person to whom I mean to give the job.'

'Then unsettle it. Oh please, please!' The imploring note sounded to Robbie as if the girl on the other end of the line was actually getting down on her knees. 'You see, I've been counting on this since yesterday, and I've burned my boats. I must have it. I simply must!'

'No, really,' Robbie protested. 'I'm terribly sorry, but the fact that you have been counting on it is nothing to do with me.'

'Oh, but it is! You'll be responsible now if the most terrible things happen to me. You can't really be such a brute. You

said in the advert. you were young, and so am I. You ought
to be able to see my point of view.'

'Hang it all, I don't even know what trouble you are in,'
Robbie cried desperately.

'That's soon remedied.' The voice dropped back again to
a breathless coo. 'I'm telephoning from Floca's. I'm much
fatter than I'd like to be, but people say I've got a pretty face.
I'm wearing an absurd bit of blue veiling as a hat. You see, it
matches my eyes. And a bunch of stephanotis. You'll find me
at a table just on the right at the bottom of the stairs. Come
round so that we can talk this over.'

'No! Really! No!' exclaimed Robbie. 'I couldn't possibly.'

'You must,' came the quick reply. 'I'm starving. And I've
already cut a date, counting on you to give me lunch.'

Next moment, the line went dead. In vain Robbie kept
shouting into the instrument: 'Hello! Hello! Are you there?'
Then, realizing the futility of further efforts, he hung up.

Frowning, he looked about him. That a girl should try to
foist herself on him like that was intolerable. The cheek of it.
What were her troubles to do with him, anyway? Give her
lunch and listen to some mess she had got herself into! Why
should he? Certainly not. She had no claim on him. He didn't
even know her. Let her stew in her own juice.

At that moment, Euan crossed the hall on his way to the
dining room. With a casual glance at Robbie, he said: 'What
are you standing there looking so scared about? Come on in
and have some lunch.'

'I'm not scared of anything,' Robbie muttered. Then something suddenly clicked in his brain and, picking up his hat, he
added with apparent casualness, 'but I'm not lunching in
today. I happen to be giving lunch to a very pretty girl at
Floca's.' Then, after one glance at Euan, he walked towards the
front door.

As he crossed the threshold, he thought: 'Goodness only
knows what I'm letting myself in for. But, by God, the sight
of Euan's face was worth it.'

11

Enter the Lady

INSTEAD of hailing a taxi, Robbie walked to Floca's. This famous café, the smartest in Athens, is at the Constitution Square end of Venizelou Street; so it was not far, and he needed a little time in which to think. The sudden eruption of a strange young woman into his plans had left him temporarily dazed, but within a few minutes he was feeling as angry as it was ever in his mild nature to be: angry with her for assuming that he had only to come to the meeting she had had the cheek to demand for her to make him do as she wished, and angry with himself for having become committed simply to score a cheap victory over Euan.

Then it struck him that he had not promised to meet her and, before Euan had spoken to him, he had not intended to meet her; so he still need not. As he had already reached the corner of Constitution Square, he halted in his tracks and pulled out his case to smoke a cigarette while considering this. His case was empty, but no one need look far in Athens for fresh supplies of cigarettes. A hundred or more kiosks are dotted about the broad pavements of the principal streets, and all appear to do a thriving trade in exactly similar stocks—newspapers, magazines, sweets, tobacco, souvenirs and second-hand paper-back books.

Having replenished his case, he lit up and drew hard on the cigarette. It was certain that, later in the day, Euan would quiz him about having taken a girl out to lunch. If he refused to say anything about it, Euan would jump to the conclusion that he had lied about having a 'date'. On the other hand, never having done such a thing, would his imagination enable him to talk as if he had? He feared it would not. In either case, the odds were that he would be found out and have laid himself open to Euan's scathing ridicule. Then, like it or not, he had to go through with it.

Two minutes later, he arrived outside Floca's. The de-luxe café had a long frontage with a row of tables outside and two entrances, one into a big sweet shop and another into a lofty room, holding another fifty or so tables. In the rear of the latter, a short flight of stairs led up through a balustrade to the restaurant, considered by Robbie, who was fond of good food, to be the best in Athens.

At this hour, nearly every table in the café was taken, but he had only to glance in the direction of the stairs to identify the girl. She was not looking his way; so he had a moment, as he approached, to study her without causing her embarrassment. Nine out of ten of the women in the café were brunettes, and the blondes were obviously foreigners. He had instinctively assumed that, being a Greek, she, too, would be a brunette, and she might have passed as one; but there were bronze lights in the mass of short curls on which was perched the little arrangement of blue veiling that passed for a hat. Her face was broad, with a strong chin that had a dimple in it. She had a short nose, a wide mouth and well-curved but rather thick eyebrows that were darker than her hair. Her skin was a golden brown, and such make-up as she was wearing was not sufficient to be obvious. Robbie knew little about women's clothes but, mingling as he did with wealthy women who came as guests to the Embassy, he realized instinctively that hers, though neat, were not expensive. It was only the hat and the big bunch of stephanotis pinned to her well-rounded bust that gave her the appearance of smartness.

When he was within a few feet of her table, she suddenly caught sight of him, said 'Mr. Grenn', smiled, stood up and held out her hand. As he smiled back and took her hand, he saw that she was shorter than he had expected. The mop of chestnut hair only just topped his shoulder. He saw too that, though she was sturdily built, all her curves were in the right places. She had turned up to him a pair of clear blue eyes that sparkled with vitality. Temporarily mesmerized by them, he quite forgot to let go her hand, until she gently withdrew it.

Suddenly embarrassed, and wishing to make amends for this gaffe, he blurted out: 'You said you were a fat girl, but I don't think so.'

She gave him a surprised stare, then burst out laughing. 'What a funny way to greet a new acquaintance.'

'I . . . I'm sorry,' he stammered. 'I didn't mean to be rude.'

'No, I'm sure you didn't. And it was nice to hear that you think that. All the same, I wish I could drop a kilo or two. I suppose if I gave up eating sweets I could, but I simply adore them.' After a rather awkward pause, she added: 'Shall we sit down?'

'Yes, let's,' he replied hastily. 'Er . . . what would you like to drink?'

'Nothing more for the moment, thanks. I've just had an orange squash.'

Robbie beckoned a passing waiter and ordered himself an *ouzo*, then he turned back to her. He had arrived determined to say at once that he had already engaged the 'battle-axe' but, recalling the desperation in her voice when she had telephoned him, he now dreaded to see tears start to those blue eyes, which were regarding him with such friendliness. Yet, strive as he would, he could think of no other way to open the conversation. Their silence lasted long enough for him to get quite hot under the collar before she broke it by saying:

'I don't know if you got my name over the telephone. It is Stephanie Stephanopoulos.'

He would have liked to say: 'It's as pretty as you are,' but didn't dare. Even so, it gave him a lead, and he asked: 'Are you related to the Foreign Minister?'

'Only distantly. He is a cousin of my father.' Her mouth suddenly assumed a hard line, then she went on: 'It is because of my father that I answered your advertisement. He is an absolute brute. He is treating me abominably.'

'Good Lord!' Robbie exclaimed, then, his chivalrous instincts aroused, his mouth tightened too. 'You don't mean . . . you can't mean that he actually beats you?'

She gave a sudden giggle. 'No, not quite that. Even the peasants here have given up using their belts on daughters of my age.'

'How old are you?' he asked impulsively, and next moment could have bitten out his tongue. But she only laughed.

'Really, Mr. Grenn! You are a forthright person. Still, if you want to know, I'm just turned twenty-four.'

'I . . . er, apologize for asking that. But in what way is your father brutal to you?'

As the waiter set down Robbie's *ouzo* on the table, she replied: 'For the past week, he has kept me locked up in an attic on bread and water.'

'No! Really! The swine! . . . Sorry! I didn't mean to be rude about your father, but . . .'

'Oh! but that's not the worst.' The blue eyes widened and looked straight into his. 'He has threatened that if I won't do what he wants me to, he will put me out on to the street. And I haven't got a room of my own. The only sort of job I could get would be as a hostess in a night-club, and you know what *that* means.'

Robbie could guess. Swiftly, he detached his glance from the blue eyes and, to hide his embarrassment, swallowed his *ouzo* in one gulp. He promptly choked.

Showing quick concern, Miss Stephanopoulos picked up the small glass of water that had been brought with his *ouzo* as a chaser, and pressed it on him.

With a nod of thanks, he took it and, when he had recovered, asked: 'But what is it your father wants you to do?'

'To marry a man I loathe the sight of. He's a cement manufacturer and as rich as Croesus. But he's twice my age, and positively repulsive—like a great, fat, greasy slug.'

Robbie knew that, although the emancipation of women in the Balkans had made enormous strides since the Second World War, they were still far from having gained the complete freedom that women enjoyed in the Western world and that, among the upper classes, many marriages were still arranged between parents, with scant reference to their daughters. With a shake of his head, he said: 'That's too bad.

If he's as awful as you say, I can quite understand your digging in your toes.'

'I knew you would.' Her face lit up with a radiant smile. 'And now, I'm terribly hungry, so please give me some lunch.'

'Of course.' He came quickly to his feet. 'If you have been on bread and water for a week, you must be starving.'

Her skirt was fairly short and, as he followed her up the little flight of stairs to the restaurant, he found himself staring at her legs. She would not have stood a hope of being taken on in a dancing chorus. They were much too short and sturdy. But, all the same, they were perfectly proportioned, with neat ankles and medium-small feet.

When the head waiter brought the menu, she chose Scampi Newberg, to be followed by a woodcock. As Robbie liked scampi and knew that in Greece at that season woodcock was excellent eating, he followed suit. But his prolonged glance at Miss Stephanopoulos's nylon-clad lower limbs had acted on him like a red light. He knew that he must not let this go any further; so, as they broke their caraway-seed-sprinkled rolls, he said:

'You say that if your father throws you out, you would have to become a night-club hostess. But, since you are qualified for a secretarial post, why shouldn't you get a job in an office?'

She made a little grimace. 'I trained at a secretarial college, but that is quite a while ago. And I've never had a job, so my shorthand would be too slow now for me to get a decently paid one. But I could soon work it up if you wanted me to, and my typing is quite good. I can see, too, that you are the sort of man who needs a lot of taking care of, and I should be very good at that.'

Robbie responded only with a slightly nervous smile as she went on: 'There's another thing. My father is certain to ask the help of the police to get me back, and it would be fairly easy for them to trace me if I were working in an office here. About the only hope of my keeping my freedom would be to go underground and take a job in a night spot down at the Piraeus. But, of course, for me to disappear into the wilds of the Peloponnesus with you would be the perfect thing. That's why——'

'D'you think your father has already put the police on to you?' Robbie interrupted to ask, a little anxiously.

'Oh no. He will be away on business until Monday, and he can't know yet that I've left home.'

'How did you manage that?'

'Mother gave way to my pleading. She's a darling, and although she hated letting me go off on my own, she realized that it was the only way to save me from terrible unhappiness. Unfortunately, she's too weak to stand up to father, but her parents were English, and she doesn't at all approve of girls being forced into marriage, like this, just because one of their father's beastly old friends has a lot of money or influence.'

From the first, they had been talking in Greek, and Robbie's Greek was nowhere near as perfect as most of his other languages because, instead of learning it from records and tutors, he had picked it up by conversing with people of all classes. It had, however, struck him that the accent of his charming companion was somewhat unusual, and he said:

'You are half English, then. Have you ever been to England?'

'Not since I was a small girl, so I don't remember much about it. But English was my first language, and I still speak it with mother when we are alone. My father and mother met some years before the war, when he was the representative in London of a Greek shipping line. It wasn't till it looked as though England was about to be invaded that he brought us back here to live; and, of course, he couldn't then foresee that Greece would be over-run a year later.'

At this, it crossed Robbie's mind that, as his Greek was by no means perfect, it would be a decided advantage to have a secretary who could speak English, as he could then explain to her the more unusual words in his manuscript. Battle-axe Papayannis might not, whereas this girl definitely . . . Sternly he put the thought from him, but only for it to be followed by another. He had entirely overlooked the fact that, if he had a secretary who did not understand English, she would find it next to impossible to type his manuscript at all.

Miss Stephanopoulos broke in on this disturbing thought by asking: 'When do you propose that we should leave Athens?'

Startled, he stammered: 'But . . . but I haven't said I'd take you. I can't, you know; really. I . . . I've as good as promised the job to someone else.'

'As good as!' she repeated angrily. 'That doesn't mean a thing. You *must* take me. You said you would before we came up to lunch. You can't go back on that now.'

'I said no such thing. I——'

'You did! You did!' Suddenly her voice changed to a high, pleading note. 'Oh please, please! You are my only hope of getting out of Athens. If you don't, any awful thing that happens to me will be your fault. You will have deliberately thrown me to the wolves. But rather than——'

'Hush!' Robbie implored her in a hoarse whisper. 'For goodness sake, keep your voice down. People at the other tables are staring at us.' But she ignored him and, tears of desperation welling up in her blue eyes, she hurried on:

'Rather than let that happen, I'll go down to the beach and swim out to sea and drown myself. And I thought you were so nice, so understanding. Mother has always told me that English gentlemen are the most chivalrous in the world. But that isn't true. You're just mean and horrid.'

Wittingly or unwittingly, she had hit Robbie on his soft spot. Like a pricked balloon, he caved in and said hastily: 'All right; all right. You've no need to cry. Please don't. People will think I've done something awful to you. Since you're in such a mess, I'll get you out of it.'

Like April sunshine after rain, her face lit up again. 'That's sweet of you. I knew you would the moment I saw you.'

'I hope your driving is better than your shorthand,' he said, a little glumly.

'Oh, I drive quite well; and I suppose over long distances we'll be taking it turn and turn about. What make of car have you?'

'I haven't a car. I'm hiring one from a garage. As a matter of fact, I don't know the first thing about cars so I can't even tell you what kind it was that I chose when I went there this morning.'

She regarded him in astonishment. 'Does that mean you can't even drive a car?'

He nodded. 'That's it. There will be no turn and turn about. The driving will be entirely up to you, and I'll not be able to give you any help if we have a breakdown, either. It's taking on quite a lot, and a girl like you must have some friends to whom she can turn when in trouble; so perhaps you would like to reconsider it.'

'Certainly not.' Her jaw hardened, and the momentary hope Robbie had had of escaping from this disturber of his peace flickered out. With another of her bewildering changes, she became extremely practical. 'I may not have a willowy figure, but I was given staying power as a compensation. I'll keep on driving you for as long as most men could. As for friends, of course I have friends; but none who could take me in and hide me for any length of time. It is true that I had a lunch date that I put off to meet you. But only with a girl who would have let me share her flat for a few nights, if I became absolutely desperate.'

'I see. How about money? What sort of salary do you want?'

She shrugged. 'Anything that suits you. Your advertisement said "all found", so all I'll need is a few pence to powder my nose. About this car, though. I think I ought to give it a trial run before we set off.'

'That's a good idea. When we've finished lunch, I'll give you a note to the garage telling them to let you take it out this afternoon.'

'Thanks. And when do we start?'

'Tomorrow morning, if that's all right with you.'

'The sooner the better, as far as I am concerned. That is, after I've had a chance to say good-bye to mother and collect my clothes.'

'Perhaps you'll bring the car round to the British Embassy in the morning, at about ten o'clock, then?'

'Yes, sir.' Her teeth flashed in a sudden smile. 'Am I to

call you that, or Mr. Grenn or . . . my handsome rescuer from an awful fate?'

No girl had ever before called Robbie handsome. He flushed to the ears, and stammered: 'Most . . . most people just call me Robbie. I . . : I'd like you to do that.'

'Robbie it shall be,' she cooed. 'And you must call me Stephanie.'

The rest of their lunch passed very pleasantly, and somehow it seemed quite natural to him that, before they left Floca's, he bought her a huge box of chocolates.

When she left him a few minutes later, he was, for a time, quite bemused. The absurd bow of blue veiling perched on the crisp chestnut curls had hardly bobbed out of sight among the crowd before he began to wonder whether the whole episode had not been one of his daydreams. It seemed almost impossible to believe that he had spent nearly two hours with a pretty girl and that, after the first ten minutes, his shyness had entirely left him. Of course, she had been looking to him to save her from a terrible situation, so the circumstances were exceptional. Even so, it seemed a miracle that he should have found his tongue to such a degree that he had kept her laughing happily through the greater part of a long meal.

For over half an hour, he wandered the streets aimlessly, savouring again snatches of their conversation and recalling the swiftly changing expressions of the golden-brown face, still so vivid in his memory. Then he gradually came down to earth and began to think about preparations for their departure. He was just about to turn back towards the Embassy, when it occurred to him that he had not yet had a chance to thank Luke Beecham for his sound advice, and that he also owed it to Luke to let him know of his new plan; so he made his way to the United Kingdom Petroleum Company's office.

It was just opening for the afternoon session, so he caught Luke coming in, and was taken straight up by him to his comfortable room on the first floor. As Luke closed the door behind them, he smiled and said: 'So all went well. I felt pretty sure it would; and if it hadn't, I'd very soon have heard about it.'

Robbie grinned back. 'Yes, your "Masterly Policy of Inactivity'' proved a winner. On the whole, too, H.E. behaved very decently. He said he couldn't let me stay on permanently at the Embassy, but gave me till the end of this week to pack up.'

Luke lit a cigar, perched himself on the corner of his desk, and said: 'I see. And where do you intend to go?'

Sitting down, and stretching out his long legs, Robbie divulged his plan for continuing his investigation, under cover of gathering information for his book, by making a tour of the places in which the Czech groups were soon to be stationed.

'But I thought you couldn't drive a car,' Luke remarked. 'Isn't that going to be an awful handicap?'

Robbie gave a happy laugh. 'I'm hiring a car and I advertised for a chauffeur-secretary. As a matter of fact, I've just come from giving lunch to the one I've settled on, and she's a jolly pretty girl.'

Luke's brows contracted slightly, and he asked: 'Is that wise, Robbie?'

'Why? What have you got against it?' Robbie countered defensively. 'She's driven several makes of car, and can type my manuscript. What's more, she will make a very pleasant companion.'

'I don't doubt that.' Luke's voice was a shade cynical. 'But have you thought that your going off into the blue like that might lead to quite a nasty scandal?'

'I don't see why it should. In the places to which we're going, it's unlikely that we shall run into anyone we know. Anyhow that didn't seem to bother her, and it certainly doesn't me.'

'I suppose you have taken up her references?'

Robbie did not feel that he ought to divulge Stephanie's private troubles, which would have put the matter of references, even if he had thought of it, out of the question; so he shook his head. 'No, I didn't think it necessary.'

'But, my young friend, it is,' Luke insisted. 'You are a rich and eligible bachelor. Surely you realize that by taking an attractive young woman off with you to stay in a series of hotels, you are laying yourself open to blackmail. This girl will only have to say that you seduced her on a promise of marriage, and you'll find that you have landed yourself in the hell of an expensive mess.'

This argument came home to Robbie with sudden force when he recalled the photographs of enticing-looking ladies he had received in the post that morning. But again he shook his head. 'No, really Luke, I'm sure you've no need to worry about that. This girl is related to the Greek Foreign Secretary, Stephanopoulos, and she's highly respectable. Besides, although she is a good-looker, she's got her feet firmly on the ground. She's not at all a "come-hither" girl, but the practical type. Even if I tried anything on her, which I don't intend to, I wouldn't mind betting that I'd get a box on the ear. We shall be good friends, that's all.'

Luke shrugged. 'I wouldn't like to risk it. Still, it seems that you have made up your mind, and it's your affair.'

After a moment, Robbie said: 'Look, there's an idea which occurred to me while I was on the way here. As I've told you, my cover for this job will be collecting information for my book. Fortunately, there are ancient temples and things scattered all over the Peloponnesus, but it may turn out that one of these groups will start to operate in a place quite a long way from anything of that sort. If so, I'll require another kind of cover, and since they are supposed to be prospecting for oil, I don't see why someone else shouldn't too. I wouldn't want any pay, of course, but I was wondering if I could carry some form of credentials from you that would enable me to make all sorts of enquiries as though I were an oil man.'

Luke was silent for a moment, then he shook his head. 'No, Robbie. I'm afraid I couldn't do that. The snag is that, although you have no official connections, you will be acting as a secret agent. That has already led you into taking illegal action, and may easily do so again. If you were caught and had a document on you accrediting you to my Company, we couldn't laugh that off. It would be said that United Kingdom Petroleum had abused its position here to cover espionage. If that happened, my chiefs in London might quite well give me the sack.'

Robbie's face showed his disappointment, but he said at

once: 'I hadn't thought of that. If I had, I'd never have dreamt of suggesting it.'

'Wait a minute.' Luke gave a wave with his cigar. 'I believe I see a way to handle this. I could give you some of our cards. They are engraved simply with the name of the Company, this address and telephone number, and underneath "represented by . . ." followed by a blank space in which any member of the staff sent out on some odd job can write his name. You could use those for your enquiries. If you were caught with some of them on you, we should still be in the clear. There would be nothing to show that you were employed by us. I should deny all knowledge of your activities, and say that you must have either managed somehow to pinch the cards or had had them printed yourself.'

'That's marvellous! ' exclaimed Robbie, jumping to his feet. 'Are you quite sure, though, that it couldn't possibly get you into trouble?'

'Quite certain. I'll give you a packet of cards before you go.'

For another ten minutes, they talked of Robbie's proposed programme; then, with Luke's good wishes for his success, and a packet of fifty cards in his pocket, he left the office.

With buoyant step he walked back to the Embassy, then cheerfully set to in earnest to sort out the things he intended to take with him. Yet, now and again, he felt a twinge of anxiety. He had still to break it to his uncle that, instead of returning to England, he intended to stay on in Greece, and he feared that Sir Finsterhorn might take that rather badly.

He had already learned that there were to be people coming both for drinks and a small dinner party at the Embassy that night, so he expected that he would have to bottle himself up for the whole evening before a chance came for him to get the unwelcome news off his chest. But he was spared that by a piece of luck.

When he came down to the big drawing room he found Euan there, and that, contrary to his custom, the Ambassador was also present, although there were still at least ten minutes to go before the first guests were due to arrive. Moreover

Robbie did not even have to open the subject, for Sir Finsterhorn said at once:

'What is this I hear, Robbie, of your having advertised in
yesterday's *Kathimerini* for a chauffeur-secretary?'

Normally, called to book as he felt sure he was about to be,
Robbie would have hesitated and floundered; but he was
amazed to find that since lunch he had acquired a new confidence in himself. Looking his uncle straight in the eye, he
replied:

'That's right, sir. I decided that it would be a pity to leave
Greece without seeing some of the most famous temples; so
I've hired a car and a chauffeur to take me on a tour of the
Peloponnesus.'

To his surprise, Sir Finsterhorn nodded quite amicably.
'That's a good idea. You should be able to pick up some useful
local colour for your book; er . . . that is, if you mean to go
on with it.'

'Oh yes. More than half of it is written now, and I hope
anyway to get the rest of it roughed out while I'm on this
trip.'

For some minutes they talked of the most important places
for him to visit and Euan, his professional interest as an
archaeologist aroused, for once showed no malice. He even
offered to get out a list of things at each place that should not
be missed and, when he learned that Robbie intended to leave
at ten o'clock next morning, promised to have it ready by then.

That evening, Robbie found himself quite exceptionally
loquacious. The hours passed quickly for him and, when he
went up to bed, he gave his mind over to happy dreams. But
he woke early, and was suddenly taken with a fit of the jitters.
All that had happened to him in the past eighteen hours seemed
too good to be true. Reconsidered in the light of early morning, could Stephanie's story really hold water? Surely, in these
days, parents did not still force girls of twenty-four into
marriages repugnant to them, and threaten to throw them on
the streets if they refused to obey? Perhaps the whole thing was
a cruel hoax and she had been laughing at him all the time.

But why should a strange young woman, who could not
possibly have anything against him, use her abilities as an

actress to make him look a fool? There could be a reason, though. Someone who had seen his advertisement, and knew what a simple-minded chap he was, might have put her up to it. It was possible that they had induced her to do it by offering her a big bet with long odds in her favour if she could afterwards say that she had landed the job.

Suddenly, he thought of Euan. It was strange that the previous evening Euan had not made a single reference to his taking a girl out to lunch. For once, he could not have been nicer, and surely that must have sinister implications? Euan knew so many people in Athens. It might well be that he knew Stephanie, and that it was he who had put her up to this. If so, and she failed to turn up, Euan would be on hand to witness the outcome of his joke, so that he could laugh with his friends afterwards while describing Robbie's bitter disappointment. That would be the final humiliation.

Miserable and worried almost silly, Robbie got up, did his final packing and went down to breakfast. Sir Finsterhorn was in a pleasant mood and Euan gave the impression of being in unusually high spirits; a fact that Robbie registered with a sinking feeling that it confirmed his worst fears. Yet it was now impossible for him not to go through with the drill to which he had committed himself.

After breakfast he took leave of his uncle, and thanked him with the best words he could find for having had him to stay at the Embassy for so long, adding that he would write his gratitude to Lady Grenn for all her kindness to him. He then made the round of the house to say good-bye to the staff, and was deeply touched by the regrets they expressed that he should be leaving.

At a quarter to ten, Loadham brought his suitcases down to the hall. Opening the front door, Robbie stood on the threshold, still desperately hoping, yet hardly daring to accept the possibility that Stephanie might drive up and carry him away. The next ten minutes were an agony. Then, at five to ten, his heart gave a bound. The car that he had selected—which he later learned was a Ford Zephyr—came hurtling into the semi-circular drive. With admirable precision the brakes were applied, bringing it to a halt opposite the door. Stephanie, now bareheaded and dressed in a neat tweed suit, was driving it.

With a glowing face, Robbie ran forward to greet her. Calling to Loadham to stow his bags in the boot, he walked quickly back into the hall to collect his raincoat. At that moment, Euan appeared. Thrusting a big envelope into Robbie's hand, he said:

'Don't go without this. It's the list of things you must not miss.' Then his glance lit on the car outside and in it the finely chiselled profile crowned by chestnut curls of the girl sitting at the wheel.

His mouth dropped open, and he swung round on Robbie. 'I say! So that's your chauffeuse-secretary! Well, I'll be damned! You secretive old devil. I'd never have thought in a thousand years that you would get hold of a peach like her to drive you round Greece.'

Robbie's smile was seraphic. This was unalloyed triumph. Yet he might well have hesitated to get into the Ford, could he have foreseen the end that the gods had decreed for it.

12

Making Hay
while the Sun Shines

Rᴏʙʙɪᴇ was still blissfully savouring the cloud of glory in which he had departed, when he was roused from it by Stephanie's asking: 'Do you want to get to Patras for lunch?'

On the previous day he had told her that the big port on the Ionian Sea was the first place at which he wished to make a stay. However, he had not even hinted at his real reason for this, and the *Bratislava*, with the groups of Czechs on board, was not due to dock there till Monday. So he replied: 'Oh no! I doubt if we could, anyway. It must be well over two hundred kilometres.'

'We could if I step on it,' she assured him. 'Your garage has done you jolly well with this car. She goes like a bird.'

'Splendid. I felt sure they would. The chaps there are always awfully nice to me. But there's no hurry about getting to Patras. I thought we would take it easy, and lunch at Corinth.'

Her next question was: 'What make of typewriter is yours?'

'Oh dear!' he exclaimed ruefully. 'I hadn't thought of that. I can't type, so I haven't got one.'

She slowed down the car. 'Well; I can't type your manuscript without a machine, can I? If you want me to, we had better get hold of one before we leave Athens. They are expensive things to buy, but I think I know a place where you could hire one.'

He agreed at once, so she turned the car in the direction of

Omonias Square—the Oxford Circus of Athens—and, in a street just off it, selected a portable with Roman lettering that seemed to have seen little service. As Robbie could now give no permanent address, he had to buy it outright; but he had plenty of money on him, and could obtain more at Patras. They then had to make a call at a stationer's, to buy typing paper, carbons and ribbons; so it was well past eleven o'clock before, having by-passed the Piraeus, they came out on to the famous coast road which, for over two thousand years, has been known as the 'Sacred Way'.

Soon they reached Daphni with its ancient convent among tall, candle-like cypress trees, and the little church with the gold mosaics that make it one of the great gems of Byzantine architecture. After another few kilometres, they had a splendid view on their left of the island of Salamis and the blue, almost landlocked bay that separated it from the mainland. Many centuries before, at some spot on the road they were now travelling, the mighty Persian King of Kings must have sat for a whole day, his confident hopes gradually turning to fear and despair, as he watched the much smaller Athenian Fleet destroying his mighty Armada—a victory that, by saving Greece from Asiatic domination, changed the whole history of the world.

The road then turned inland, and the seaward skyline was rendered hideous by clusters of tall chimneys, belching smoke from distilleries, cement works and soap factories. Robbie frowned at them in disgust and said: 'One would have thought there were plenty of other places on the coast where they could have built those horrors. To have chosen Eleusis for them is the all-time high in modern vandalism.'

'It was at Eleusis that the famous Mysteries used to be held, wasn't it?' Stephanie remarked. 'And this road is called the Sacred Way because it was along it that the great processions used to come. I wonder what really happened at the Mysteries? Someone told me once that it was only a ceremony at which, when they came of age, young people of the upper classes were let into the secret that all they had been taught about there being gods and goddesses was bunkum; but that they must continue to support the priesthood because a little religion was good for the masses.'

Robbie gave her a shocked glance. 'I'm sure you're not right about that. To the ancient Greeks of all classes, the gods were very real, otherwise they wouldn't have gone in such fear of them. For example, the Mysteries here were in honour of Demeter, and if they hadn't done their stuff at her festivals, they would have been frightened that their crops would fail. There was a time when she caused a most terrible famine, and they never forgot it. But being a Greek yourself, you must know all about that.'

'I suppose I ought to, but at the schools I went to they didn't give much time to ancient history. I'll have to mug it up a bit now, though, if I'm to understand the allusions to the characters in this book of yours that you were telling me about yesterday.'

'If you read all the chapters I've already written, before you start to do any typing, that would be a help,' Robbie suggested. 'But I haven't done the story of Demeter and Persephone yet. If you like, I'll tell it to you now.'

'Oh, please do,' Stephanie smiled. 'As a child I used to adore being read to and told stories.'

'Right-oh.' Robbie paused for a moment to collect his thoughts, then began: 'Well, I'd better start from the beginning. Demeter was one of the six children of Cronos and Rhea, so Poseidon, the King of the Sea; Pluto, the King of the Underworld; and Zeus, King of both Heaven and Earth, were her brothers.

'In those days, apart from the Royal Family the world was mainly inhabited by monsters, so you'll understand how it was that, to begin with, for marrying and, er . . . that sort of thing, these brothers and sisters had no one but one another.

'Demeter was very good-looking, and Poseidon got a crush on her. But she took the same sort of dim view of him that you do of your cement magnate, so one night she slipped out of Olympus and came down here to live in Arcadia. To make even more certain of escaping Poseidon's unwelcome attentions, she changed herself into a mare and joined a big herd. However, he was terribly keen on her, so he hunted for her all over the place and eventually he saw through her disguise. Then he turned himself into a stallion and . . . er . . .' Robbie suddenly reddened and came to an abrupt stop.

'Then they did what the bees and the birds do,' Stephanie helped him out, adding with a little titter: 'I am twenty-four, you know; so it's quite a time since I learnt about the facts of life.'

Robbie gave an awkward laugh. 'Thanks for being so frank. Otherwise, I'd have had an awful time trying to spare your blushes. You see, so much of that sort of thing went on among the gods and goddesses that if one cuts it out, their histories hardly make sense.

'To continue, then. As a result of the *affaire*, Demeter gave birth to a horse that could talk, and had men's feet instead of hooves on its right legs. She felt frightfully sick at the way she had been treated, so——'

'I bet she did. What girl wouldn't?'

'Ah! Yes, of course. Well, she made herself look like a Fury, and went to live on her own in a cave. Zeus was the youngest of the family, but had managed to become top-boy, and had given all his brothers and sisters jobs to do; so in fairness to the others, he couldn't let Demeter go on shirking. Down he came to her cave, and made her return with him to Olympus. By then she had become a lovely girl again, and suddenly he felt an urge . . . I mean, he, too, began to take a good view of her.'

'More bees and birds stuff?'

'That's it; but she was just as much against letting him as she had been with Poseidon, so he had to deceive her by turning himself into a bull.'

'Was she crazy about bulls, then?'

'I've no idea. But that's the way Zeus did the trick, and as a result Demeter had a daughter named Kore—although she is much better known by the name she took later, Persephone. I don't think I mentioned it, but Demeter had the most marvellous golden hair and her daughter, who took after her, was just as lovely. Although Demeter continued to associate with the Olympians, she was still a bit sulky with Zeus for having taken her against her will, and spent quite a lot of her time in Sicily. Then, just when Persephone had become a really smashing teenager, Eros played one of his mischievous tricks.'

'Eros was another name for Cupid, wasn't it?'

'Yes; and whoever he shot one of his arrows into fell in love with the next person they set eyes on. In this case he shot Pluto, and the King of the Underworld came up in a fiery chariot out of Mount Etna, roaring with rage. In a flash, he was half-way across the island and came down on the shore of a beautiful lake near the mountain stronghold of Enna. There, in a meadow, he saw young Persephone with her companions, making daisy chains. Snatching her up, he drove his pitchfork into the ground. It opened, and he carried Persephone straight down to the dark realm of Hades.'

Stephanie breathed a sigh. 'It seems that all sorts of exciting things happened to girls in those days.'

Robbie turned to stare at her. 'You wouldn't like to be carried off like that, would you?'

'It would depend on whether I liked the chap. There is something to be said for a tempestuous wooing. But I'm interrupting the story.'

'Well, naturally, Demeter was terribly upset at her daughter having disappeared, and fairly rushed about the world looking for her. At length the Sun God, Helios, let on to her that it was Pluto who had ravished Persephone.'

'What a lovely word. It's so descriptive. But go on.'

'He also told her that it was really Zeus's fault, because he had said he had nothing against Pluto's acquiring the young blonde to brighten up his gloomy kingdom. At that, Demeter got more up-stage than ever. She severed all connection with her family and said that mortals were much nicer; in future she would live among them.

'After wandering all over the place, she turned up at Eleusis, in the guise of an old woman dressed in rags. She spun the people there a yarn that she had been carried off by pirates, but, being too old to be much fun for them, they had put her ashore on the coast nearby. The King of Eleusis was a chap named Celeus, and his wife, Metaneira, had just had a baby.

Hearing that Demeter had been offering her services round the town as a nurse, they decided to take her on.

'In spite of her rags, they guessed from her bearing that she must be someone rather special, so they offered to treat her as one of the family. But she wouldn't eat or drink with them, and just stood staring at the ground, until one of the slave girls made a bawdy joke. That set her off laughing, and eased the situation a bit. The baby, Demophoön, was given to her to take care of.

'Instead of feeding the infant, she breathed on him, smeared his body with ambrosia, and at night put him in the fire, so that all that was mortal in him should be burnt away. The result was that he grew like a young god, but one night his mother happened to come into the nursery just as Demeter was piling red-hot coals on him. His mum threw a fit, and——'

'Saints preserve us! I don't wonder.'

'Neither do I. But Demeter was extremely peeved at having her project interfered with. In a rage, she told Metaneira that she had ruined everything, and that it would no longer be possible for her to make the boy an Immortal. Then she scared the pants off all those present by suddenly appearing to them in all her glory. While their knees were still knocking, she ordered them to build a big temple, and worship her in it; but, still in a huff, she said that she meant to resume her travels.

'However, before she left, she calmed down a bit and sent for the King's eldest son, Triptolemus. Out of gratitude for the years that his family had given her a home, she gave him some grains of corn and taught him to plough and sow. Previous to this, the Greeks had lived on milk, honey, vegetables and, when they could get them, meat and fish. She told Triptolemus that he must share this secret with people in other parts of the world; so he spent years making demonstration tours, even as far away as Sicily, Scythia and Asia Minor. It was owing to his efforts that bread became the main item in everyone's diet.

'As she had said she would, Demeter went off on her wanderings again, but after some years she returned to Eleusis. By then, her bitterness about losing Persephone had become so acute that she decided to stage a sit-down strike. The job Zeus had given her was to look after agriculture, and now she announced that she would take her misery out on mankind by not letting any crops grow at all.

'You can imagine how alarmed everyone became when February, March and April passed without a single blade of anything showing above ground. The gods became pretty worried, too. Zeus sent a messenger to tell her that she must stop this nonsense, or the whole human race would perish; but she ignored him. Then all the gods and goddesses came down one after the other, and pleaded with her to let up. But she said she couldn't care less if everyone starved to death. The only terms on which she would allow things to grow were that she should be given back her daughter.

'Zeus realized that he had no option but to climb down, so he sent Hermes down to Pluto to tell him that he must give up his young mistress. Pluto didn't feel that he could say "To hell with you" to his powerful younger brother; but he had enjoyed having Persephone to stay with him, and he thought up a cunning ruse for ensuring that she should not leave him for good. Before she left for the upper world, he persuaded her to eat a pomegranate with him.

'When Persephone got back to her mother's arms and they had wept over one another for a bit, Demeter said: "While you were with that awful man, you didn't eat anything with him, did you, dearest?"

' "Oh no, I didn't need to, Mummy," replied the ravished maiden. "But he wasn't quite as hateful as you seem to think, and he was very anxious that I shouldn't be hungry on my way home; so we had a glass of wine and a pomegranate together."

' "You bloody young fool!" ' Robbie stopped abruptly, and with a contrite glance at Stephanie, muttered: 'Sorry, but I was getting a bit carried away. Anyhow, that is more or less what Demeter must have said. Then she explained to her daughter that the pomegranate was Hera's fruit. To share one with a man was standard practice as a formality by which one publicly accepted him as one's husband.

'Pluto, of course, claimed the girl back as his legally wedded wife, but Demeter threatened to go on strike again; so Zeus had to arbitrate between them. He proposed that Persephone should spend one-third of the year underground with her husband and two-thirds of it above ground with her mother. To everyone's relief, not least the still starving inhabitants of the earth, the compromise was agreed to.

'So, from then onwards, every year at Eleusis a great feast was held in October, when the leaves started to fall off the trees, and Persephone had to return to Hades, with entreaties that she would not get to like the place and stay there for good. And in February another was held with tremendous rejoicings, when the buds sprouted and blades of this and that appeared, showing that she was on her way back and there would be crops and a harvest to keep the human race going for another year.'

Seeing that Robbie had concluded his narrative, Stephanie said: 'As you are so interested in these things, I suppose you have been to see the ruins of Eleusis?'

'Oh yes,' he assured her, 'and those at Corinth and Sounion and the battlefield of Marathon, too. I've been to all the interesting places that I could get to in a day, but this is my first chance to go further afield.'

By this time, they were actually on the isthmus of Corinth and approaching the canal that enables ships to pass from the Ionian to the Aegean Sea, and saves them a two hundred mile journey round the rocky capes of the Peloponnesus. When they came to the bridge, Stephanie stopped the car and they got out to look over the parapet. The cut is nearly four miles long, and in places over two hundred feet deep, so from that height the strip of water below looked no wider than a broad pavement.

'You wouldn't think it's as broad as the Suez Canal, would you?' Robbie remarked. 'Or that the ancients would not have been afraid to take on the colossal task of cutting it?'

'They didn't,' replied Stephanie promptly. 'It wasn't open till the 'nineties.'

'I know, but the Romans planned it. The Emperor Nero dug out the first spadeful of earth himself, with a golden spade, and Vespasian sent him six thousand Jewish captives from Judaea to work on it.'

'Shades of Hitler!'

'Yes, the poor Jews have had a pretty raw deal all through history. Anyhow, the Romans were not the boys to give up lightly anything they set their hands to. They shifted thousands of tons of soil. Later, modern engineers adopted their original plan; so I've no doubt the Romans would have completed it if the job hadn't had to be called off, owing to the great insurrection of Vindex.'

Ten minutes later, they pulled up in Corinth at the Ivy restaurant on the quay, and had welcome drinks, then lunched at a table outside from which they could admire the bay. After the meal, Stephanie suggested a walk round the town but Robbie shook his head.

'There's nothing to see here; only straight streets and second-rate shops. It was built barely a hundred years ago, after the old town up on the hill was destroyed by an earthquake. In fact not much of this one is even that old, as it was wrecked by another earthquake in 1928.'

As the great heats had not yet come, they decided to push on with the longer part of their journey, for which the road lay nearly the whole way along the south shore of the Gulf of Corinth. For a while they were almost silent, then Stephanie asked: 'Why have you selected Patras as our first stop? It's a rather dirty, modern port, and as far as I know there is nothing of archaeological interest within miles.'

For a moment Robbie was as completely floored as if someone had tripped him up without warning. It had never occurred to him that he should provide an explanation of his choice, to make his cover stick.

'Oh, well . . . you see . . .' he floundered. 'It's like this, er . . .' Then, suddenly, his visit to Luke's office came back to him, and he hurried on: 'This isn't altogether a pleasure trip. I am associated with a business firm, and they have given me a few odd jobs to do in various places.'

'What sort of business are you in?'

'Er . . . oil,' Robbie admitted, a shade reluctantly.

'Do you mean that you sell petrol to garages, and that sort of thing?'

'No, oh no. It's just that I have to show my company's flag here and there, and make a few enquiries. There's another reason for my going to Patras, though,' he added, memory having suddenly come to his aid. 'Just across the head of the gulf lie the ruins of Calydon and Pleuron, and I'd very much like to see them.'

'If we're going to cross the gulf, I take it, then, that our next stop will be Delphi?' she remarked.

He shot her an uneasy glance. Nothing would have delighted him more than to spend a few days at Delphi, but unfortunately it was many miles from any of the sites at which the Czechs were scheduled to operate; so he replied rather lamely: 'No, I hadn't planned to go to Delphi. You see, there are, er . . . lots more interesting places.'

Raising her dark eyebrows, she shot him a surprised glance. 'Really! I thought Delphi was the *pièce de résistance* of all the ancient sanctuaries. That's where the priestesses used to get dopey in a cellar on the fumes of herbs, and prophesy to people who put their ears to the ground. Surely you are going to write about that, and how people came from all over the place to consult the famous Oracle?'

'Yes; oh yes, of course,' he hastened to assure her. 'But as a matter of fact, I don't think the Oracle was quite all that it was cracked up to be. Most of the answers it gave were terribly ambiguous. You were left to interpret them for yourself, so that left the Pythoness who made them sitting pretty on the basis of "heads I win, tails you lose". For example, look what happened to Croesus. Being a greedy type, he thought it might be a good idea to make war on his neighbour, Cyrus the Persian, and sack some of his cities; but, wanting to make certain before he started anything that he would get the best of it, he sent an Ambassador with costly presents to Delphi to consult the Oracle. The reply came back that his war against Persia would overthrow a mighty Empire. And it did—his own great Kingdom of Lydia.'

'I should have asked for my money back,' commented the practical Stephanie. 'Anyhow, it's better to be born lucky than rich.'

'How right you are! Even before Croesus lost his kingdom, he found that out. He had a favourite son named Atys, and one night he dreamed that the beautiful youth would die of a wound from an iron weapon. He got into such a tizzy about this that he wouldn't allow Atys to remain in the Army, found

G

him a lovely wife to keep him busy at home, and even had all
the spears and axes in the Palace hidden away, so that Atys
shouldn't cut himself on one by accident. But it wasn't any
good. A savage boar began to give trouble to the people in the
Mysian hills; so they sent to the King for help to kill it. He
collected his bravest hunters and Atys begged to be allowed to
go along. Croesus said "No", but Atys argued that a boar's
tusks were not made of iron, and persuaded his old man to let
him go on the hunt. They found the boar, and made a circle
round it. Naturally, all these young bloods wanted the kudos
of being the first to wound it. They all rushed in, and Atys
was just a fraction quicker than the rest. The boar didn't get
him, but the spear of one of his pals did; and that was that.
Look at Midas, too.'

'He was even richer than Croesus, wasn't he?'

'Yes, he was the King of Phrygia and the richest man in
the world, but even that didn't satisfy his avarice. One morning, he was walking in his garden and he came across old
Silenus. He was a kind of cask on legs, and one of the god
Dionysus's boon companions. The previous night, they had had
quite a party, and Silenus had got so drunk that he had lost
the others; and there he was sleeping it off under a bush.

'Midas gave him an outsize "hair of the dog", crowned
him with a wreath of fresh roses, then took the old soak back
to his patron. Dionysus was so pleased with the kindness shown
his henchman that he offered to grant Midas anything he liked
to ask.

'Without a second thought, Midas asked that everything he
touched should turn to gold. And, of course, it did—fruit,
flowers, stones; anything he picked up on his way home. His
clothes had become gold, too; so before he had gone far, he was
getting pretty puffed. Seeing a mule in a field he thought he
would ride, but the moment he mounted it, the animal became
solid gold and couldn't budge. When he did reach home, things
went from bad to worse. The water in which he tried to wash
turned to golden ice. He kissed one of his children, and the
poor mite became a golden bambino; he struck a slave and
found he had made a golden statue. By this time, really worried,
he was getting hungry; but when he sat down to lunch, every

bit of food he put in his mouth turned to gold, so he had to spit it out again. Hoping against hope that the whole thing was a bad dream, he lay down on his luxurious couch, but the great pile of soft cushions turned instantly to golden rocks.

'At crack of dawn, with not a stitch on, he hurried back to Dionysus. The god laughed at him at first, but later took compassion on his pleading and told him that, if he bathed in the spring from which the river Pactolus rose, he could get rid of his golden touch. For days on end, willing to barter all his wealth for even a penny bun and a cup of ersatz coffee, he staggered round, hunting for the source of the river. At last he found it, plunged in, and came out able to eat and drink again.'

'What an awful story. How about his child and the slave? Was he able to turn them back again?' Stephanie suppressed a smile, and went on wickedly: 'You didn't mention his wife, but if they were fond of one another, that must have been very awkward, mustn't it?'

'You mean if . . . Well, there's no record about that.' Hurriedly, Robbie changed the subject. 'That golden touch business wasn't Midas's only bit of bad luck or, if you prefer, stupidity. One day, he was taking a stroll through the woods and he came upon Apollo and Pan. Apollo had always prided himself on being the absolute tops where music was concerned, but Pan said he could get better music out of his reed flute than Apollo could out of his lyre. To settle the matter, they held a contest there and then, and asked Midas to act as judge. Midas said he liked Pan's pipes better and Apollo was furious. He said Midas had no more sense of harmony than an ass, so for the rest of his life he should go about with asses' ears. Poor Midas went home, hiding his head in a cloak; and after that, he was so ashamed of his great, pointed, hairy ears that he kept them covered up. But he couldn't keep the secret from his barber; so everyone got to know about it, and he became the laughing-stock of his Court.'

'I think that was very unsporting of Apollo, since he had asked Midas to act as judge. I've always been under the impression, too, that Apollo was one of the kindest of the gods.'

'So he was, generally speaking. He bestowed all sorts of benefits on mankind, but he could turn awfully nasty if anyone upset him. Look at what happened to Marsyas. Athene is said to have been the first of the Olympian family to take up music, but the others laughed so much at the way she blew out her cheeks when playing the flute that she flung the instrument aside, with a curse on anyone who picked it up. Marsyas was unlucky enough to find it. He was a very ugly, ignorant Satyr. However, the flute, having touched Athene's lips, made the most lovely music, so he was chump enough to challenge Apollo. Of course he hadn't an earthly, and as a punishment for his impertinence, the god had him flayed alive.'

'All the same,' remarked Stephanie thoughtfully, 'from what I remember about the gods and goddesses, Apollo must have been much the most attractive to women. He represented the warmth of the Sun and is always portrayed as strong-limbed and handsome, and he was both clever and brave. He would certainly have been my choice.'

'Oh, he was brave enough,' Robbie conceded. 'There was the occasion when two monster giants piled Mount Pelion on Mount Ossa, because they had designs on two of the goddesses and hoped to get up into Olympus and abduct them. Apollo caught the raiders at it, and drove them off single-handed. And, of course, he did have a lot of successful love affairs, but the girls weren't so universally smitten with him as one might suppose.

'Coronis, the daughter of the King of Lepiths, was a case in point. She two-timed him with a chap named Ischys, and a crow let on to Apollo about it. He was so angry at her having preferred a mortal to himself that he not only struck her and her boy friend dead, but cursed the crow so that all crows have had black feathers ever since. Then there was a girl at Delphi named Castalia who disliked him so much that, rather than sleep with him, she drowned herself in a fountain. With the beautiful Daphne, too, he had no luck. He did his utmost to seduce her with presents and all that, but she flatly refused to play; so he tried to take her by force. He had actually got his arms round her, but she prayed for help to the Earth-Mother Gaea, who did a quick magic, and before Apollo knew what was happening he found himself clutching a laurel bush. He must have felt awfully sick.'

Stephanie hooted with laughter. 'I bet he was! I would give anything to have seen his face. Have you any more funny stories like that?'

'Well,' Robbie temporized. 'I don't know about funny, unless you have a practical-joke sense of humour. Of course, the ancient Greeks were pretty primitive. Just as schoolboys still get a big laugh out of seeing an old gent slip up on a piece of banana peel, I suppose your remote ancestors fairly split their sides at seeing someone they didn't much care about turned into a lizard or a toad.

'That sort of thing was liable to happen to quite nice people too, because lots of the trees and nearly every stream and lake were the home of some supernatural being, and it was terribly easy to damage their property without meaning to. Then out they popped, and did the most unpleasant things.

'Take Dryope, for example. All she did was to pick a bright flower from a bush for her little girl. Red sap started to run because, as it happened, the bush was really a wood-nymph taking a nap, and the sap was her blood. "I'll learn you to go about wounding bushes," yelled the nymph in a fury—or words to that effect. And next moment Dryope found herself sprouting twigs and leaves. She had only just time to gasp out a prayer that her child might be allowed to come and play near her, before she became a bush herself. Then there was the awful business of Erysichthon; but, of course, he brought that on himself.'

'What terrible fate befell him?'

'Well, it was a sort of Midas trouble in reverse. In a general way, the oak was sacred to Hera; but there was one giant oak in Thessaly that Demeter had made her special property, and a bunch of Dryads living in the neighbourhood adopted it as an evening rendezvous to play "chase me round the mulberry bush" with a gang of young Satyrs. For some reason—I suppose because he wanted to build a ship or a new barn—Erysichthon, who was King of those parts, decided to have this oak cut down.

'In vain, the locals implored him not to. He put his woodmen on the job and after tremendous efforts the giant oak was felled. The Dryads were fed to the teeth at their jive centre being ruined, so they rushed off and complained to the management. Demeter naturally resented Erysichthon's having wrecked her dance hall, and assured the girls that she would see him off. She sent one of her Oreads up to the far, ice-bound north, having told her messenger to bring back Famine. When this character, with a head like a skull and his ribs sticking out through parchment skin, put in an appearance, Demeter simply said: "Go and do your stuff on Erysichthon."

'After his hard day's work helping to cut down the oak, you can imagine that the King had put away a good-sized steak for his dinner; but while he was asleep, Famine breathed upon him and he woke up as hungry as a hunter.

'I imagine he had a terrific "brekker". Fried eggs, sausages and bacon, kidneys on toast, kedgeree and rounded off with a few slices of York ham and half a cold grouse. You know, the sort of breakfast our great-grandfathers used to have in Victorian times. But it wasn't much good. By lunch time, he was again ravenous.

'From then on, he never suffered a trace of indigestion but, on the other hand, he could never cram himself with enough to satisfy his hunger. His appetite was so enormous that he ate all day, till he had no flocks and herds left to slaughter. In due course, he had to sell his jewels and his palace in order to buy enough to eat.

'At last, driven from his kingdom by his creditors, he had only one asset left—a lovely daughter named Mestra. As he was still tormented by hunger night and day, he decided to sell her as a slave. Luckily for her and for him, it happened that she had played "slap and tickle" with the great god Poseidon. In gratitude for the fun they had had, the Sea King had given her the power to turn herself into anything she liked. So each time her papa sold her for the price of a few cuts off the joint, she promptly became a bee or a beetle or a butterfly and came back to him, so that he could put her up for auction afresh.

'But after a while, the chaps who were in the money and on the look-out for lovelies who would keep them warm at nights tumbled to this. They formed a ring, and when Mestra was put up, refused to bid for her. That left Erysichthon completely in the ditch, and as Demeter refused to pardon him he had to eat himself.'

'That's quite enough for today, thank you,' said Stephanie.

But by that time they had rounded the great bend in the gulf and were nearing Patras. After the Piraeus and Salonika, it is the largest port in Greece and, as such, mainly a modern, commercial city. Earthquakes in its neighbourhood are frequent, but although the town has escaped recent devastation, it contains few ancient buildings of interest. It had not even occurred to Robbie to book rooms, but Stephanie had looked up the hotels and, finding that the Cecil in St. Andrew Street headed the list, she suggested that they go to it.

After a few enquiries, they found the way there, and Robbie booked two single rooms, each with a private bathroom. Stephanie then said that, after her drive, she would like to rest; so it was agreed that they should meet at eight o'clock down in the dining room. Robbie, who had lately been missing his long sessions of day-dreaming lying on his bed or a chaise-longue in the Embassy garden, decided that he could pass an hour or two very happily doing nothing; so he, too, went up to his room and enjoyed a belated siesta.

For dinner, Stephanie had changed into a cocktail frock, and so alluring did Robbie find her that, several times during the meal, the thought came to him how wonderful it would be if only he were a god and could carry her off into the woods and ravish her. But he sternly put such disturbing ideas from him and instead tried to draw her out about the sort of life she had led.

His efforts met with little success. As far as he could gather, she had not moved in Athenian society or, at all events, not its higher strata that mingled with the Diplomatic Corps. Her mother, she said, had never been really happy living in Greece, and had not many close friends. There were a few families with whom they dined from time to time or joined up with for beach parties in the summer. Her father, of course, was absorbed in his commercial interests and had a separate set of wealthy men friends, with whom he frequently spent the evening. She said that she had never been allowed to go to a night club, but various boy friends took her to the cinema and to subscription dances, and she had had one really desperate love affair of which she preferred not to talk. She added only that for her it had ended unhappily, because her father had not considered the man good enough for her; so he had married someone else. Robbie forbore from pressing her further on the subject.

They enjoyed their dinner, and lingered over it till nearly ten o'clock. Then, after a liqueur in the lounge, they went up to bed. As Robbie undressed, he could not remember ever having had such a happy day.

Next morning, he had just finished his breakfast in bed when the house telephone rang. It was Stephanie and, after briefly wishing him good morning, she said: 'Look. I take it you will be occupied all the morning doing your business with the oil people you've come here to see. I had to pack in such a hurry that I left at home quite a number of things I need, so I want to go out and do some shopping. Would it be all right with you if we meet here about one o'clock for lunch?'

Robbie was completely nonplussed. He had no oil people he had to see, and he had been looking forward to a pleasant morning exploring the town with Stephanie, while other young men turned round to cast envious eyes at him for having such a charming companion. But he realized at once that, unless he played up to the role he had given himself, he could not expect her to continue to believe in it; so he said, a little lamely:

'Yes, I've got a few people I have to see. All right, then. By all means do your shopping. I'll be waiting for you here around one o'clock.'

Having taken his time bathing and dressing, he spent two rather boring hours mooching round the straight, arcaded streets and squares of the city. By half-past twelve, fed up with his aimless wandering, he turned back towards the Cecil. When he was within a hundred yards of it, a tall, thin man came out from the hotel entrance and, with rapid strides, approached him. With a sudden shock, he recognized the man as Václav Barak.

So unexpected was the encounter that Robbie instinctively lifted his right hand a few inches, on an impulse to raise his hat. Next moment, he was contemplating an abrupt about-turn as the only means of avoiding coming face to face with Barak. He need not have worried. When they had first come into contact at Toyrcolimano, Barak had not given Robbie even a glance and, when he had seen him again as a stooge at the Travel Agency, he had not bothered to take in his features.

The lean, dark Czech, with the black, hair-line moustache, strode past Robbie without appearing to notice him. But this encounter brought home one thing to Robbie, in no uncertain manner. However delightful he might find this new experience of basking in the smiles of a lovely girl like Stephanie, it was not for that he had come to Patras. He had much more important fish to fry, and it was quite time that he gave serious thought to them.

13

You Have Been Warned

For Robbie, running into Barak had been like receiving a pail of ice-cold water on the back after hours of blissful sunbathing. He had still not fully recovered from the shock by lunch time, and was so distrait that Stephanie asked him if he was feeling ill. He assured her that he was quite well, and took refuge in saying that a business meeting he had had that morning had been rather worrying.

During the past half hour, he had been upbraiding himself for not even having bothered to check up that the *Bratislava* was arriving at Patras on Monday. Instead of mooning about the streets while Stephanie did her shopping, he could have gone to the port to find out. Barak's presence in Patras suggested that he had come there to meet the ship. Now that Robbie's conscience had been aroused, he felt he ought to pay a visit to the docks to gather any information that he could; so, with considerable reluctance, he told Stephanie that he would have to make another business call after the siesta.

The port has three basins, linked by a broad promenade nearly a mile in length and protected by a long breakwater. Having no experience in making investigations, Robbie wasted some time enquiring of dockhands and numerous ships' officers, coming and going along the wharf, if they could tell him anything about the arrival of the *Bratislava*. None of them could, but one suggested that he should try the Port Authority, and there he eventually ran to earth a clerk who pointed out to him on a plan the berth that had been reserved for the Czech ship, and told him she was due in some time on Monday afternoon.

By the time he got back to the Cecil, it was well past six. As soon as he joined Stephanie in the lounge, she asked: 'How do you suggest that we spend the evening?'

'I hadn't really thought,' he smiled. 'What would you like to do? How about a cinema?'

She shook the crisp, chestnut curls. 'I'd much rather go dancing.'

'I . . .' he flushed slightly. 'I'm afraid I can't dance. I've never learned.'

Her dark eyebrows arched up into her smooth forehead. 'What an unusual person you are. Have you anything against dancing?'

'No; it's not that. It's just . . . just that I've spent my time doing other things; listening to music; learning languages and, more recently, doing a lot of reading.'

'Then it's quite time you did learn. As a matter of fact, I've made enquiries, and the hall-porter recommended a place called The Pigalle. It is a restaurant as well, of course; so we could have dinner there.'

Bewitched as he had already become by his delightful secretary, Robbie made no demur, although inwardly he felt considerable trepidation about attempting this new venture. An hour or so later, they took a taxi round to The Pigalle.

It had little resemblance to the famous Parisian establishment of that name. Few wealthy travellers visit Patras, or even tourists with holiday money to burn. Its patrons were local business men or ships' officers, the former with their wives or mistresses, and the latter being entertained by a number of not very glamorous dance hostesses. The lights were dim, the floor small and on two sides of the room there were a number of alcoves, to one of which, after a glance at Robbie's well-cut clothes, a head waiter led them.

The meal was passable although, as everywhere in Greece except in the very best hotels, rendered less appetizing by being served on near-cold plates. As against that, Robbie found the bottle of Achaia champagne that he had ordered surprisingly good. While by no means of the standard to which he was used at the Embassy, it was full of body without being sweet. A little fearful of the ordeal ahead, he fortified himself with several glasses, before letting Stephanie persuade him to take the floor.

If Stephanie had hoped to find in him a natural dancer, she was grievously disappointed. Although she danced well herself, and could have controlled a smaller man, Robbie's size and his being so much taller than she was made it very difficult for her to guide him. Moreover, although the quickness of his physical reactions had improved greatly since his boyhood, they were still markedly slower than those of a normal man.

Owing to his inexperience, he was quite unconscious of this, and gave himself up to the pleasure of holding Stephanie's well-made, yielding body against his own, delighting in the scent she had put on for the occasion, and smiling down into her upturned face. When he had seen other young men dancing with pretty girls he had often envied them, although it had never occurred to him to take a course of dancing lessons. Now, for the first time, he realized what a joy it could be and hardly noticed that, from time to time, they collided with other couples. Had it not been for his ear for music, his first attempt must have proved disastrous; but his ability to at least move his body in time to the rhythm enabled Stephanie to get him round the floor a dozen times, before she asked breathlessly to be taken back to their table.

Half an hour later, at his suggestion, they danced again. Afterwards, he asked her cheerfully: 'Well! How am I doing?'

She gave him a rueful smile. 'I'm afraid you are not exactly a born dancer, Robbie. Unfortunately, too, you're too tall for me to see over your shoulder to steer you. And you have got awfully large feet.'

As his face fell, she added quickly: 'Never mind. Perhaps you'll turn out to be a marvellous driver when you try your hand with the car.'

'But . . .' he began. 'I don't——'

'. . . don't mean to learn,' she finished for him, with a laugh. 'But you ought to, Robbie. I'm not trying to shirk my job, but every man ought to know how to drive a car, and there should be plenty of opportunities for me to teach you.'

'Well . . . yes . . . thanks,' he stammered, again a little shaken at the speed with which this laughing, blue-eyed creature, unknown to him thirty-six hours ago, was opening up for him one new vista after another. 'Of course, you're right. I ought to have learned to drive a car ages ago.'

'That's settled then. I take it we shan't be going across the gulf to see the ruins at Pleuron until Monday; so I could give you your first lesson tomorrow morning.'

Her suggestion jerked his thoughts on to a very different track. On Monday he had to be in Patras to see the *Bratislava* dock, and find out all he could about the people who came ashore from her. Then the group that was landed might not remain in Patras, but set off inland. Should they do that, unless he was to fall down on the job he had set himself he must follow them in order to learn where the villa was that they were to occupy while they did their prospecting. After that, events might prevent his returning to Patras, and it would look very queer to Stephanie if, having talked to her so much about his book and stressed his desire to visit the ruins of Pleuron, he should leave Patras without doing so.

After a moment, he said: 'No, I'm afraid tomorrow's no good. You see, I've got to be here to transact some more business on Monday; so tomorrow may be our only chance of going to Calydon and Pleuron.'

'What time do you wish us to start?' she asked.

'That depends on the times the ferry goes; but I should like to leave fairly early, so as not to have to rush things on the other side.'

'In that case,' said Stephanie, seizing on the excuse to escape any more of the arduous dancing she had brought on herself, 'I think we ought to go back to the hotel soon, so that we can get some sleep.'

'Oh not yet! ' he protested. 'It's only just on midnight, and I'm enjoying myself so much.'

'I'm glad.' She gave him a little smile, but added firmly: 'You forget, though, that I have to do the driving, and that the roads over there are certain to be awful.'

Immediately contrite, Robbie began to apologize for his thoughtlessness, but with a flutter of her fingers she checked him and went on: 'I think, too, you would be wise to order a picnic lunch. That is, unless you like goat's meat, sour cream and resinated wine, because there is not usually much else to be had in Greece once you get off the beaten track.'

He grinned at her. 'What a splendid secretary you make. I shall have to raise your wages.'

'I haven't had any yet,' she countered, with a laugh. 'But don't worry. I'm rather enjoying my job of looking after you.'

They finished their second bottle of the Achaia champagne, then the waiter got them a taxi. During the short run back to the hotel, Robbie was sorely tempted to take and squeeze the small, firm hand that he had recently held while dancing. But he did not dare. This new relationship was the sort of thing he had dreamed of, but feared to be far beyond his powers ever to establish. Suddenly, almost overnight, he was experiencing unalloyed delights which, every moment he was in Stephanie's company, made him feel in the seventh heaven. To have taken the risk of doing the slightest thing that might lead to this sweet-scented, glamorous being ceasing to smile upon him would have been sheer madness.

At the hotel, the night porter produced the time-table for the ferry service, and they decided to take one leaving at nine-forty-five. Robbie gave orders for a picnic basket and for the car to be brought round at nine o'clock, then they went up to their rooms.

Next morning, they set off in good time and drove the few miles north to the little harbour of Rion, at the narrow entrance of the great Corinthian gulf. Opposite it, only two kilometres away, lay another small harbour, Andirrion, to which they were going. As it was a Sunday, instead of the odd, dusty lorry and herds of sheep and goats which would normally have made up the ferry's freight, it was empty except for a battered Ford and two cyclists.

On their way over, Robbie pointed out to Stephanie the roofs of a small township about three miles away. 'You Greeks,' he said, 'call that little town Navpaktos, but in the history books of every language it is known at Lepanto. I was telling you on Friday how, at the battle of Salamis, the West was saved from coming under the heel of Persia. In the bay there, some two thousand years later, another great naval battle was fought that again saved the West from becoming enslaved to Asia. A fleet of two hundred Turkish galleys was destroyed there by the combined forces of Venice, Spain, Genoa and the Knights of Malta, under Don John of Austria. If he hadn't won, it's quite on the cards that today we would all be Mohammedans.'

'It didn't save the Greeks from having those horrid Turks on their necks for a long time afterwards, though,' Stephanie remarked.

'No,' Robbie agreed. 'You had to put up a terrific fight before you won your independence. On our way to Pleuron, we shall be going through Missolonghi and, as I expect you know, that was one of the stoutest centres of resistance. Rather than surrender to an army of thirty thousand Turks, who had been besieging it for weeks, the Greek leader, Khristos Kapsalis, blew up the magazine and killed three thousand of his own people. Nine or ten thousand others were captured and sold as slaves, but he got away to the hills.'

Stephanie nodded. 'It's much more famous on account of Lord Byron. For a man of that kind to have roughed it serving with the patriot guerilla bands, until he became so weak from fever that he died, fills me with real admiration.'

After landing, they headed west and, near the township of Krioneri, got out to see the ruins of Calydon. In ancient times it must have been a considerable town, as there were acres of stone foundations, fallen pillar drums and big, up-ended blocks, mostly half overgrown with coarse grass and nettles. Excavations had brought to light part of a temple, but there was little else of interest; so they returned to the town and drove across the moor to Missolonghi.

It differed little from hundreds of other small towns in Greece. There were few modern buildings and much evidence of poverty; but the peasants, dressed in their Sunday best, looked clean and healthy, and waved cheerful greetings. Without stopping in the town, they ran on for another five kilometres, which brought them to Pleuron.

The place had far more to show than Calydon. A great part of its walls were still standing, and many of its thirty-odd towers. There were seven great gateways, a small theatre, a vast cistern and, near the east rampart, a terrace, with ruined shrines along it, over a hundred and fifty yards long. It was there that they decided to eat their picnic lunch. Few travellers visited this remote ruined city, and at that hour not a soul was to be seen in any direction; so few spots could have been pleasanter.

Having gnawed the meat from a wing of chicken and eaten a three-cornered pasty stuffed with liver and rice, Stephanie began to peel an enormous orange and said: 'Come along, Robbie. Tell me what happened here.'

He spat out some of the pips from a big mandarine and admitted: 'I'm sorry, I don't really know. I suppose there were the usual processions and dances and sacrifices.'

'What! No stories of maidens having a thin time of it owing to the attention of winged lions, or of a lady being seduced by a gentleman who had disguised himself as a bunch of grapes?'

'No, I'm afraid not. It's a curious thing but, although Olympus is up in northern Greece, nearly all the adventures of the gods and Heroes seem to have taken place either in the Peloponnesus or overseas. That is, except for the neighbourhood of Athens and, of course, Thebes.'

'Tell me about Thebes, then.'

'I don't want to bore you,' he forced himself, out of politeness, to say. 'After all, I talked to you about the gods and goddesses during nearly the whole of our drive from Athens.'

'I know.' Stephanie was sitting in a moss-covered niche, between two great stones, and now she lay back in it. 'But I'll have to make a start on this book of yours soon, and the more I know about its background the better. If I fall asleep, you can always give me a gentle prod.'

Robbie finished his mandarine, licked his fingers, gave her a rather doubtful glance, and said: 'Very well, then; and it won't really matter if you do drop off. This is another chapter that I haven't written yet, so telling it will help to get my ideas in order.' After another drink of the red wine that had been put in the hamper, he started off:

'Cadmus, who was the founder of Thebes, definitely ranks

as one of the Heroes, although he differs from the others because so many of his descendants also played big parts in Greek history. Unfortunately, though, they nearly all came to sticky ends.

'He was not a Greek, but the son of Agenor, King of Tyre, and he had a very lovely sister. You'll have heard of her because her name was Europa. One day, she was making sand-castles on the beach with a bevy of attendant maidens. From up aloft, old Zeus happened to spot her and, not wanting to scare her, he came mincing along the sands in the form of a beautiful, white bull.'

'You can skip what happened next.'

'Yes; you're right. The little idiot made him a chaplet of flowers and let him lick her neck; then, when he knelt down she climbed on his back and the next thing she knew was that she was clinging to his horns for dear life, while he ploughed through the sea like a speed boat, carrying her off to Crete. When he had got her safe ashore, he told her who he was, and said that if she were willing to give him a good time without making any trouble, he would see to it that a whole continent was called after her. Much flattered by that, she said: "All right; go ahead," and, in due course, she bore him two sons, Minos and Rhadamanthus; both of whom were later made judges in Hades.

'Meanwhile, her father had got himself terribly worked up about her disappearance, and sent his three sons, Cadmus, Phoenix and Cilix, off to search for her. Her mama, Tele-phassa, couldn't sleep at nights for thinking of what might be happening to her ewe lamb, so she decided to go along with the boys.

'Phoenix was the first to get bored, so he pegged out a claim for himself and founded Phoenicia. Cilix threw his hand in next, and started a kingdom called after him, Cilicia. But Cad-mus and his mother kept plodding on, until the old girl gave out and died by the wayside, still urging him not to give up.

'He took ship for Greece, but could hear nothing of Europa, who by then had become quite used to providing bed and breakfast for Zeus in Crete. As a last hope, Cadmus decided to consult the Oracle at Delphi. Apollo, being a decent sort, must have realized that, if he told Cadmus where Europa was, things could only end in Zeus turning him into a praying mantis, or something; so the Oracle gave him no news of his sister. Instead, it told him to follow a cow that was browsing in a nearby field and that, wherever the cow lay down, he should build a city.

'That cow would have won a prize at any cattle show. She crossed a range of mountains, and walked over a hundred kilometres before she decided to have a lie-down. And when you think of the pace of a cow, following her must have driven Cadmus nearly potty.

'They landed up in Boeotia but, unfortunately, the cow had chosen to go to sleep near a grove that was the property of a three-headed dragon. Cadmus sent his servants into the grove to fetch some water from a stream. As they didn't come back he went in after them, and found that they were all as dead as doornails from having been overcome by the dragon's bad breath.

'Being a Hero, Cadmus naturally had to slay the dragon, and, after some pretty lively give and take, he managed to nail one of the dragon's necks to an oak tree with his sword. As is usual with dragons, this one was belching flames and smoke, but it bled so much that it acted as its own fire extinguisher and put itself out.

'Athene, as the patroness of brave men, then put in an appearance and said to him: "Jolly good show." As all his henchmen had been killed off by the dragon, and it was a bit much to expect him to build a city on his own, she showed him how to get a fully grown labour force in no time at all by sowing some of the dragon's teeth. With their help he built Thebes, which henceforth was the capital of the Kingdom of Boeotia.

'As both Apollo and Athene took a good view of Cadmus, they decided to provide him with a very special wife: in fact a young goddess. She was the daughter of Aphrodite and Ares, and her name was Harmonia. I suppose that is why the marriage was such a success, for they lived in harmony for the rest of their lives.'

'Surely it is more likely that the word "harmony" is derived

from her marriage having been so free from quarrels,'
Stephanie suggested.

'Perhaps. Anyhow, all the gods came to the wedding, and
Aphrodite gave Harmonia a beautiful necklace and a wonderful veil. These were known as "the heirlooms", and later
caused a whole packet of trouble; but there was already trouble
brewing, because the dragon Cadmus had slain was a pet of
Ares. The God of War took its death very badly, and put one
of those frightfully unfair Biblical curses on Cadmus. You
know, "unto the third and fourth generation".'

'But if Ares had a "down" on Cadmus, why should he have
given his consent to his marrying his daughter?'

'He wasn't asked. You see, he wasn't Harmonia's legal
father. She was the result of his having had a tumble behind
the bushes with Aphrodite while her husband Hephaestus was
hard at it in his smithy.'

'Even then, to have cursed the progeny of his own daughter
doesn't make sense.'

'He was a big, brutish chap, with very little grey matter.
Anyhow, his curse took effect. Cadmus was dethroned by his
own grandson, Pentheus, and finally the family ended up in
an absolute welter of blood and death.'

'Like the last Act in *Hamlet*.'

'Oh, that is nothing to the goings-on in Thebes. One of
Cadmus's sisters, Ino, drowned herself, because her husband
had, in a fit of madness, killed her sons. Another, Semele, had
an affair with Zeus, and——'

'Did that old rip never stop?'

'Not often, I imagine. Poor Semele came to a very sticky
end. Hera was always terribly jealous of her lord's mistresses,
so she told Semele what a lucky girl she was, and how she
ought to persuade Zeus one night to show himself to her in all
his glory. He didn't like to refuse her, and, as Hera had known
would be the case, the electricity that radiated from him and
the lightning flashing from his head was so powerful that
Semele was roasted like a chicken before she could even get
out of bed.'

'How absolutely frightful.'

'He managed to save the son she was having by him,

though. He plucked it out of her body, and put it in his own thigh till it was ready to be born; then it became the God of Revelry, Dionysus. The parties he thought up for his worshippers must have been quite something. One gathers they always ended with everyone very lit up, and the girls doing a sort of bees' and birds' Paul Jones with Dionysus's Satyrs in the moonlight. Anyway, the ladies of Thebes felt that they had never had it so good, and it was that which put paid to Cadmus's grandson, Pentheus. For those times he must have been a bit strait-laced, because he forbade the women of his household to attend these midnight hops. When they read the notice he had posted up, they held an indignation meeting and became so enraged that, led by his own mother, they ran into his room and tore him to pieces.

'The heir to the throne was a young Princess, named Antiope. She must have been a good-looker, too, as Zeus had already spotted her and given her twins. They were called Amphion and Zethus. But the throne was usurped by a chap called Lycus; so Antiope hurried her boys off up into the hills, to be brought up as herdsmen. Later, she fell into the hands of Dirce, a nasty, spiteful woman, whom Lycus had made his Queen. She gave orders for Antiope to be tied to the horns of a wild bull, so that she would be gored and dragged to death. But it wasn't Dirce's lucky day. The two chaps to whom she had given the orders happened to be Antiope's sons, and they recognized their old Mum. So they tied Dirce instead to the horns of the bull. Then Amphion led a revolution, killed off Lycus, and became King in his place.

'Amphion at least had a pretty good innings before the curse caught up with him. He married Niobe, and she presented him with seven handsome sons and seven beautiful daughters. As they all grew into youths and maidens, their parents can't have had much less than twenty-five years of domestic bliss. But Niobe about takes the cake for stupidity. One day, at the Women's Institute, or somewhere of that kind, she ran into Leto and started to needle her. Putting out her tongue, she said: "Yah! You're not much good. You've had only two children, and I've had fourteen," or words to that effect.

'Leto could have retorted: "You silly old bag, mine were by Zeus and are among the greatest of the Immortals, so they're worth fourteen thousand of anything you could produce." But she didn't. She just went home, feeling a bit hurt, and next time her children came for the week-end she told them about it.

'Apollo and Artemis were not the types to take an insult to their old Mum lying down; so, like a couple of rockets, they took off for Thebes. Apollo shot dead all Niobe's sons, and Artemis put one of her deadly arrows into each of the daughters. Amphion was so upset by seeing all his boys killed that he stabbed himself through the heart, and Niobe was so overcome with grief that sorrow turned her into a stone statue that still continued to weep whenever the sun or moon shone on it.'

Stephanie rolled her blue eyes up to the blue heavens. 'Goodness, what a massacre!'

'We've not half done yet,' Robbie cheerfully assured her. 'Amphion's family having been wiped out, the Boeotians sent for another descendant of Cadmus to be their King. His name was Laius, and that of his wife was Jocasta. Laius was warned by an Oracle that, if he had a son, that son would kill him and be the ruin of his Queen. So, when Jocasta gave birth to a boy, there were no free cakes and ale for all and sundry at the Palace.

'Laius gave the infant to a goat-herd and told him to expose it on Mount Cithaeron, so that it died of cold. But the goat-herd felt a bit squeamish when it came to the point, so he passed on the bundle to a pal of his who was going down to Corinth. At that time, a couple called Polybus and Merope were King and Queen of Corinth, and they had not managed to have any children; so, when this goat-herd turned up with a jolly healthy-looking baby boy, they promptly adopted him and gave him the name of Oedipus.

'He was brought up as a Prince, and everyone might have lived happily ever after if it hadn't been for a rude fellow who chanced to be in the secret that Oedipus was not really the son of the King and Queen. He got stinko one night at a banquet, and taunted Oedipus with being the by-blow of some tart who had left him in the gutter.

'Very perturbed about this, Oedipus went to the King and Queen. They said "not to worry", because they loved him as a son, even though it was true that they were not his real parents. Like an ass, instead of socking the drunk for six, and staying put to inherit the kingdom, Oedipus packed a grip and went off to ask the Delphic Oracle who his parents were. Even the Oracle tried to save him from himself, and said: "Forget it, son. If you ever find out, you will land yourself in one hell of a mess." But the pig-headed clot would not be warned and, instead of going home, set off on a hiking tour, in the hope of finding someone who could tell him the truth about his birth.

'Fate decreed that he should head for Boeotia, and soon after he had entered that country the road became a narrow defile. From the opposite direction a chariot, in which an old gent. was being driven, was approaching, and a slave was running in front of it, shouting a bit breathlessly: "Out of the way! Out of the way for my master! "

'Having been brought up as a Prince, Oedipus wasn't standing for that sort of thing. First, he struck down the runner then, when the old man chucked a javelin at him, he gave him, too, a biff over the head, overturned his chariot and left him dead in the ditch. Only the driver of the chariot got away, and when he reached home he excused his own cowardice by saying that his master had been attacked and killed by a band of robbers. When Oedipus arrived in Thebes, he found the city in mourning for its King, and——'

'Then it was his father that Oedipus had killed,' put in Stephanie.

'You've hit it. But, of course, he didn't know that at the time, nor did anyone else. And their King's death wasn't the only thing the Thebans had to worry about just then. The Sphinx had taken up her residence outside their walls. This creature was said to be the sister of Cerberus, the monstrous hound that guarded the entrance to Hades. She had the body of a lion, the wings of an eagle and the head of a woman, and she was playing merry hell with the standing corn.'

'So, of course, Oedipus went out and slew her.'

'No, it wasn't quite like that. She must have been a queer sort of creature. Before gobbling up people, it was her custom to give them a chance to save themselves by guessing a riddle; with the sporting understanding too that, if they guessed right, she would go off and play ring-a-roses with herself in the cornfields of some other city. Every day for weeks, some bold Theban had gone out and had a shot at answering her riddle, but none of them had returned; so the girls in the place were getting very gloomy about the increasing shortage of dancing partners.

'Creon, Jocasta's brother, had taken over the Government when the news of Laius's death had reached the city, and he had sent out his own son to tackle the Sphinx. But this young hopeful hadn't proved up to it, and Creon was getting really desperate. He had posters put up, announcing that anyone who could answer the riddle of the Sphinx, and rid Thebes of this awful creature, should be rewarded by being made King of Boeotia and, into the bargain, be given Jocasta as his wife.

'By then, Oedipus was so down in the mouth that he hardly cared if he lived or died; so he said he didn't mind having a crack at answering the riddle. Naturally, everyone said: "Jolly good show", and hurried him outside the walls, just on the off-chance that he might have a lucky break. Pretty gloomily, he trudged through the bleached bones of his predecessors, until he came to the huge nest that the Sphinx had made for herself.

'She blinked a bit, then asked him quite civilly: "What creature is it that alone changes the number of its feet? In the morning it goes on four feet, at midday on two and in the evening on three." Rather generously, I think, she gave him a clue, by adding: "When it has the fewest feet, it is really at the top of its form."

'Oedipus just shrugged and replied: "That's kindergarten stuff. The answer is Man. As a babe, he goes on all-fours, at the height of his strength he goes on two feet, and when he gets old, he needs a stick on which to lean."

'The Sphinx was very peeved at having her pet riddle guessed but she honoured her bond, and with a loud squawk, flew off to play "boomps-a-daisy" in somebody else's corn.'

'After that, the Thebans hailed Oedipus as the tops. They made him King and, as Jocasta was still a very good-looking piece of goods, he was delighted to have her for his Queen.'

'I remember the story now,' murmured Stephanie drowsily. 'It's the famous tragedy about the young man who fell in love with his mother, isn't it?'

'That's right,' Robbie nodded. 'It seems he did fall for her, and she for him, although neither knew who was who at the time. They were frightfully happy together, too. Jocasta had four children by him; twin sons named Eteocles and Poly-nices, and two daughters, Antigone and Ismene. Everything went marvellously until the children grew up, but then an awful plague fell on the land; so Oedipus sent his brother-in-law, Creon, to Delphi to ask the Oracle how to get rid of it.

'For once, the Oracle didn't try to make a monkey out of anyone, but said right away: "The plague is a punishment sent because Laius's murder has never been atoned for." The local Scotland Yard was put on the job, but couldn't discover who had done in the late King; so they sent for a famous blind seer, named Tiresias. He was very loath to do his stuff, but eventu-ally he recalled to Oedipus the old boy in the chariot and the prophecy that Laius would be killed by his own son.

'At this, Jocasta began to give a bit at the knees but she rallied sharply and declared that it could not possibly be Laius's son who had killed him, because his only son had been left as a babe to die of exposure on Mount Cithaeron. But up popped the old goat-herd with an account of how a pal of his had taken the babe to Corinth; and then, of course, the fat was properly in the fire.

'On discovering that she had been living with her son for the past twenty years, Jocasta went upstairs to her bedroom, locked herself in and hanged herself with her girdle. When they had broken down the door, Oedipus said death was too good for him; so, with the prong in the buckle of her girdle, he put out both his eyes.

'The next Act concerns their children. Oedipus's daughter, Antigone, was a very good sort of girl, and refused to desert him while he wandered about the world in this parlous state until he died. Meanwhile her twin brothers, Eteocles and Polynices, decided to take turns in ruling Boeotia year and year about; but after a bit Eteocles threw his brother out. Polynices took refuge in Argos. There he made a number of chums among the local bloods and between them they collected an army, to help him get back his kingdom. It was called the War of the Seven against Thebes, and . . .'

Robbie broke off. He had just caught a gentle snore from Stephanie. Looking down, he saw that her eyes were closed, her dark eyelashes making fans upon her cheeks, and that she was clearly sound asleep.

For a while, he continued to think about Thebes. How, eventually, the twin brothers had agreed to settle their quarrel in a duel to the death, and had killed one another. How Creon, who had taken over again, had refused to allow Polynices to be buried, because he had brought war to his mother city. How Antigone had performed the last rites for her brother at dead of night. How Creon had found out and, because she had defied him, had her walled up in a cave to die of starvation. How the people had revolted and forced him to order her release and how, when her lover Haemon broke down the wall, he found that she had strangled herself; so he had drawn his sword, stabbed himself and fallen dead upon her body.

Even that Romeo-and-Juliet-like scene had not been the last act in the Theban tragedy. The Heirlooms—the magnificent necklace and wonderful veil that Aphrodite had given Harmonia as wedding presents—gave rise to endless quarrels. Still thinking vaguely of the welter of blood and death they had caused, Robbie, too, dropped off to sleep.

They woke about an hour later, finished the rest of the wine, spent another hour wandering about the ruins, then started for home. They were back at the Cecil by six o'clock, after a very pleasant day; but it had been a tiring one, so they decided to dine in and go early to bed.

Next morning, they took the car out on the coast road to the east of the city, where the road ran for several miles across flat, low-lying ground and any approaching vehicle could be seen well away in the distance. There, Stephanie gave Robbie his first driving lesson. He was not very quick at picking up the use of the various controls but she found that, once he had got them fixed in his mind, he handled them firmly and she had no need to fear that he would suddenly do something that might land them in trouble. Whenever they were about to pass anything, she made him slow right down and put her hand on the wheel as a precaution; but he was not in the least troubled by nerves, so kept it perfectly steady. Moreover he proved a good pupil, in that he made no attempt to run before he could walk, and obeyed her every instruction. The willingness with which he accepted the limit of thirty miles an hour, to which she restricted him, showed that he was not of the stuff of which racing drivers are made. However, when Stephanie took over to drive them back to the hotel for lunch, she felt that he had done a good bit better than she had expected.

Over lunch, Robbie told her that he would be out during the afternoon and could not say when he was likely to be back. He added that he might not even be back for dinner. Seeing her look of surprise he quickly averted his glance, showing that he did not wish to pursue the subject. But it struck him that, if his enquiries did give him a new lead, it might make it difficult for him to keep up a pretence with her that his business activities were no more than normal ones.

She suggested that, if he did not want to be driven anywhere, she should take the opportunity to start reading his manuscript; so, when he went up to his room, he got it for her. Then he changed into his oldest suit, which he had brought with him for just such an occasion, slipped out of the hotel by a side door and made his way along the water-front. He had purposely left the hotel bare-headed and, when he came to the market, he found a cheap clothing store at which he bought a soft cap with a shiny peak that gave him something of the appearance of a seaman. By then it was nearly three o'clock and, when he reached the far basin, he was only just in time to see the *Bratislava* dock.

As he came nearer, two Customs Officers went aboard her with two other men, the taller of whom he thought was probably Barak; but he could not be certain from that distance. After that, he had to kick his heels for an hour and a half. Several groups of men leaned over the *Bratislava*'s rails, idly looking down on the water-front, occasionally exchanging a remark or spitting over the side; but nothing happened.

At last there was a stir of movement, both on the ship and ashore. The Customs men came off, a crane clanked into action, a gang of dockers came on the scene, the groups of loungers broke up and the *Bratislava* started to unload a part of her cargo. Some twenty big packing cases were lowered to the wharf and wheeled across it into a Customs shed. About half-way through this proceeding the tall man, whom Robbie now definitely identified as Barak, came down the gang-plank, followed by three others, and walked over to the shed. Evidently, they were going to clear the cargo and it would then be taken off somewhere.

Suddenly, it occurred to Robbie that his only means of finding out where the cargo went and of what it consisted was to follow it. Already three lorries had driven up, and Barak had emerged to speak to the leading driver. There was only one car in sight. It had already been parked near the Customs shed when Robbie arrived, and was a powerful-looking black six-seater; so obviously it was not a taxi. At a hurried walk, Robbie set off in the direction of the Citadel, hoping to pick up a taxi there. A quarter of an hour elapsed before he managed to find one and was driven back in it.

As his taxi approached the wharf at which the *Bratislava* was lying, he saw the six-seater begin to move. Another minute and it was running swiftly past him. The face of the man who had all along been sitting at the wheel looked vaguely familiar, but Robbie had only a glimpse of it as his glance moved on to the others in the body of the car. They were Barak and three quite well-dressed men; the same, Robbie thought, as those who had accompanied Barak into the Customs shed.

Robbie told his driver to pass the ship, run on for a hundred yards, then turn round. As the taxi came to a halt, a small, private bus appeared and pulled up opposite the gangway. From beside the driver, a big, middle-aged man scrambled down. Owing to his enormously broad shoulders, thick neck, short legs and porkpie hat, Robbie recognized him at once. He was a Sudetenlander, a German-Czech named Stoll, and had been employed by the Czech Travel Agency to take parties of tourists round Athens. He had been to the office only twice while Robbie was there, and they had never even exchanged greetings; so Robbie thought it unlikely that, if they did come face to face, Stoll would recognize him.

Stoll had no sooner boarded the ship than he left it again followed by eight men, most of whom were wearing sweaters, or shirts without ties, under shapeless jackets. The cheap, fibre suitcases or bulging grips they carried also indicated that they were low-grade technicians or labourers. Stoll led them over to the Customs shed, but they were not inside it long. In less than ten minutes, they emerged and piled into the small bus.

By this time, one of the lorries had been loaded and the others were more than half-full. Robbie was faced with the question—should he wait until all the packing cases had been loaded and follow the lorries, or follow the bus? Deciding for the working party, he told his driver to keep fifty yards behind the bus then pass it when it halted.

The bus did not go far. It pulled up outside a small hotel called the Ionia, the major part of the ground floor of which consisted of a narrow café with a long bar. When Robbie's taxi had carried him some way beyond it, he asked the driver to pull up and paid him off. He was just in time to see the tail end of Stoll's party disappearing into the Ionia, so had no doubt that it was to be their quarters for the night.

It was now close on seven o'clock, and he made up his mind to pay a visit to the Ionia later that evening. If he returned to the Cecil in his old clothes and Stephanie saw him in them, that would call for an explanation which was going to be difficult to think up and, for his foray later, he would need to put them on again. In consequence, he decided to leave her to dine on her own, and have something himself at some little *taverna*.

While walking back towards George I Square, it occurred to him that, if he did succeed in getting a look at the contents of the crates when they were unpacked, the odds were that they would consist of machinery which would mean nothing to him. The obvious answer was to try to photograph it, then send the picture to Luke. But he had no camera and had never owned one.

After traversing several arcades, he found a shop that sold cameras. When he went in to buy one, he was amazed to learn how costly the most expensive kinds can be. He had half a mind to leave his purchase till the next day, when he could draw more money from the local branch of the Bank of Greece; but the man who was serving him very honestly told him that, if he had never used a camera before, he would do better to buy a medium-priced one. So he bought an ordinary Kodak, which the salesman showed him how to operate, and three rolls of film.

At a small restaurant nearby, he dined off *keftedes*—balls of rice crisply fried outside and with a centre of minced meat— followed by a large slab of cake which seemed mainly to consist of assorted preserved fruits and Turkish delight. As it was still early, he followed it with two brews of thick, Turkish coffee, and fortified himself for his coming venture with three goes of a local liqueur made from tangerines.

At nine o'clock he walked back to the Ionia. He thought it almost certain that, even if the Czech workmen had not been forbidden to leave their hotel, they would not have enough money to go out on the town. And he proved right. All eight of them were sitting at two marble-topped tables, obviously eking out two carafes of cheap wine between them.

Only one table was occupied: at it, two Greeks were sitting with two girls. Two more girls were at the bar but, evidently having already discovered that the Czechs could not afford to pay for their attentions, were carrying on an earnest argument together. When Robbie came in, they broke it off and eyed him hopefully; but he was too unused to that sort of thing to smile at them and shake his head. Quickly he looked away, ordered a drink and remained standing at the bar, straining his ears to overhear what the Czechs were saying to one another.

Those at the table nearest to him were arguing quietly about, as far as he could make out, the football results of their favourite teams during the past winter. But at the other table a young fellow with a mop of ginger curls was declaiming loudly against the 'bosses'. It emerged that he hotly resented having been ordered to come on this expedition, because he

had had to leave his girl. Another supported him, but said
he would not so much mind having been separated from his
wife if they were to have the good time in Greece that they had
been led to expect; but here they were, the very first evening,
left without money, and no arrangement made to take them
round the town.

At that, Robbie pricked up his ears. He had ample money
on him and was only too willing to do the honours of Patras
for this little party if he could manage to scrape acquaintance
with it. Nerving himself for the effort, he picked up his glass
and walked with it over to the table at which the red-haired
young man was sitting.

As he approached, the Czechs fell silent and looked up at
him a shade suspiciously; but he managed a smile, greeted
them in Czech and added: 'I could not help hearing the
language you were speaking, and one doesn't often meet Czechs
in Patras.'

The eldest of the party, a man with a scar on his forehead
and grizzled hair, said: 'You are not a Czech, though, are
you?'

'No, oh no,' Robbie hastily admitted. 'But my mother was.
She taught me Czech and told me a lot about her country,
so I always enjoy talking to people who know it.' There
followed an awkward pause, then he said hesitantly: 'Will you
allow me to stand you another carafe of wine?'

His offer met with an instantaneous response from the
grizzled man. 'Why yes, Comrade. That is handsome of you.
Come and sit down and tell us all about yourself.'

The football fans at the next table had been listening, so
they promptly moved their table round to make it one large
party. Robbie ordered two carafes of wine and a chair was
produced for him. The barman drew the wine from a cask
and brought it over. Glasses were filled and Robbie's health
ceremoniously drunk. Like all the cheapest wines in Greece,
resin had been put into it—the theory being that this prevents
the peasants from becoming drunk when, owing to the intense
heat, they drink great quantities of it while working in the
fields—but although harsh, it was not unpleasant.

For a while, Robbie had to cope with a barrage of questions: 'Did he live in Patras?' 'How did he earn his living?' 'What was life like in Greece?' 'Was it true that the Capitalist Imperialist Industrialists lived in great luxury, while the bulk of the people slaved for them on starvation wages?'

As they had assumed him to be a Greek, Robbie did not have to go further into his nationality. He said that he was only on a visit to Patras, and was a professional writer seeking local colour. As far as the Greek people were concerned, he told his hearers that they had only to walk through the streets to see that the great majority was well clothed and well fed, and the amount of goods in the shops was ample evidence that, at all events in the towns, only a small minority could not afford to buy everything in reason that they needed.

A small, wizened man, with a face like a dried apple, insisted that, even if this were true, the workers were still not receiving their proper share from the resources of the State, otherwise there would not be millionaires like the oil king Onassis.

Robbie was about to reply that Mr. Onassis made his money not out of producing oil, but by transporting it in his great fleet of tankers from place to place. Before he had a chance to do so, the young, red-headed man gave a guffaw and declared:

'He does not know what is coming to him. Within a few months we will have many more oil-wells than he has in Greece. We will flood the market, undersell him and put him on the rocks.'

To this statement, Robbie made no reply. Putting aside the men's obvious ignorance of Mr. Onassis's principal activities, it presented a new conundrum. Had the Czechs really discovered, by some new scientific device, that there were great oil resources in Greece, and were about to exploit them? Or was that only the belief of these technicians—a cover plan that they had been sold by their bosses, only a small inner ring of whom were as yet aware of their Government's true intentions?

Robbie was still pondering this when two of his companions suddenly looked towards the street entrance. Three men were standing there. Barak, Stoll and a third man—the man who had been at the wheel of the big six-seater that afternoon. With a horrid, sinking feeling in the pit of his stomach, Robbie recognized him. It was Cepicka.

All three men were staring at him. Cepicka said something in a low voice to Barak. The tall, lean Czech drew a finger along one side of his black, toothbrush moustache. Then, followed by the others, he suddenly strode towards the table.

Robbie's companions had fallen silent. With a sense of rising panic, he half came to his feet. By then, Barak was within three feet of him. The barman, the Greek sailors and the girls had also fallen silent. The movement and voices of the crowd out on the water-front came only as a murmur. In the café one could have heard the plop of a lump of sugar dropped into a glass of *ouzo*.

When Barak spoke, it was neither in Czech nor Greek, but in English, His black eyes boring down into Robbie's, he said:

'Englishman, we know why you are here. You are a spy. You haf before poke your nose in our business. You poke your nose again, ha! If there is next time I gif you no warning.' He swept a hand round to include the ten Czechs now grouped round Robbie. 'These men obey me, no question asked. They beat you so you spend three months in hospital, perhaps more. You get out now. Yes, you also get out of Patras tomorrow first thing. Or I order beating for you that leave no bone un-broken in your body.'

14

Of Hades and a Double Bed

Robbie took a pace back. Coming to his full height he gave a swift glance round. The eyes of every one of the eighteen people in the narrow café were fixed on him. As Barak had spoken in English, it seemed unlikely that any of them, with the possible exception of Stoll and Cepicka, had understood what he had said. Even if they had, there was no reason to suppose, should a fight develop, that the Greek sailors or the barman would come to the assistance of a man who had just been denounced as a spy.

To deny Barak's accusation would have been futile, because Cepicka must obviously have told him about the theft of the briefcase in Athens ten days before. As Cepicka stood there, with his little pig-eyes, pink cheeks and thick lips screwed up into a leer, he looked more than ever like an ex-Gestapo man. The enormously broad-shouldered, barrel-chested Stoll was also grinning at Robbie's evident discomfiture. In addition to these two hefty thugs, Barak had only to say a word in Czech to the eight men from the *Bratislava* and, Robbie had no doubt at all, he would be playing the part of a ball in a football scrum. It was a terribly disappointing end to a situation that had seemed full of promise, but it had to be accepted.

With a shrug, he muttered: 'I don't know what you're talking about,' and moved towards the door.

'Hi!' called out one of the Czechs he had been treating. 'What about paying for the wine?'

'So he was standing you drinks, eh?' said Cepicka. 'In that case, as we know him to be an English capitalist-imperialist he may as well provide you with enough wine to last you the evening.'

The barman came over. He had already sized up the situation, and demanded double the proper price for another half-dozen bottles of *retsina*. As the only alternative to trouble, Robbie had to pay up and, when he walked out, the mocking laughter of the Czechs followed him on to the waterfront.

The humiliation he felt at having had to submit to this blackmail, on top of having been found out, was so great that he could think of nothing else while making his way back to the Cecil. He even forgot about the clothes he was wearing; so, instead of slipping into the side entrance of the hotel, he strode into the front hall.

To one side of it, the wide glass doors of the lounge stood open. Just inside them, Stephanie was sitting at a low table, reading his manuscript. Catching sight of him as he walked towards the lift, she called his name.

Startled, he shuffled to a halt, then turned and reluctantly went in to her. He was still holding his cheap, floppy cap with the shiny peak. Her glance fell on it, then ran disapprovingly over his worn tweed jacket and grey sweater.

'Where have you been?' she demanded. 'And why are you wearing those awful old clothes?'

Their relationship had already reached a point at which he could not possibly have brought himself to reply: 'I do not have to account to my secretary for my actions', or 'what I have been up to is no business of yours'. He went red in the face and, after a moment, blurted out: 'As a matter of fact, I've been down at the docks, er . . . slumming.'

'Wherever you've been, you look as if you need a drink.'

'Good idea,' he agreed, sinking into a chair beside her. Then, beckoning the lounge waiter who was standing just outside in the hall, he ordered himself a double Metexas and ginger ale.

Stephanie gave him time to recover from his evident embarrassment at having been caught unawares, then she asked: 'Does "showing the flag", as you put it, for this oil company you represent entail "slumming", or was this a private venture?'

By then he had decided that, unless he was to be constantly straining his imagination for plausible lies with which to fob her off, he must disclose at least the fact that some of his activities were likely to be unorthodox; so he replied:

'This was business, but not quite the ordinary kind. There is a new foreign company that is trying to muscle in on my company's territory. Exactly what their plans are we don't yet know, but I've been given the job of finding out as much as I can.'

Stephanie's blue eyes widened. 'Does that mean you are really a sort of secret agent?'

'No! Oh no!' He took a quick drink of the brandy and ginger ale that the waiter had just brought him. 'This is commercial rivalry, that's all.'

'Yet you have to dress up for it, and go snooping down at the docks.'

'I had to find out about a ship that arrived here today, and I thought I'd be more likely to get the wharf hands talking if I went down in these old things than in a smart suit.'

'And did you get the information you were after?'

'Well, yes.' He paused for a moment. Then, realizing that he had yet to break it to her that they would be leaving first thing in the morning, he decided to go on. 'But afterwards I had rather a nasty break.'

'I thought you looked rather queer when you came in. What happened?'

'I was standing drinks in a café to a group of Czechs who had landed off the ship, when their boss came in. With him there was a thug that they employ——'

'A thug?'

'Yes; they aren't a very nice lot. I'd had some trouble with this chap in Athens. He recognized me, of course, and denounced me to them as a snooper from U.K.P. There were nearly a dozen of them there altogether, and the long and short of it was that they threatened to beat me up unless I left Patras tomorrow morning.'

'Do you mean to go or stay?' Stephanie enquired bluntly.

'Well.' Robbie gave an uncomfortable wriggle. 'There are a lot of them, and only one of me. I'll be safe enough as long as I stick around the hotel, no doubt, and in the centre of the city; but I wouldn't care to risk going into the dock area again, so there's not much point in my staying here any longer.'

'I see. Does that mean you won't be doing any more of this snooping business?'

'I don't quite know,' Robbie replied non-committally. 'Perhaps I will later.'

'If you do, and you'd like to tell me about it, I might be able to help you.'

'That's awfully sporting of you'—he gave her a grateful smile—'but I couldn't let you get mixed up in this. If any harm came to you, I'd never forgive myself.'

'They say two heads are better than one, so we might talk things over, anyway. That is, unless you are one of those people who think women's minds are not up to weighing the pros and cons on serious matters.'

'Oh no!' he protested. 'As a matter of fact, I should think your brain is a good bit quicker than mine. You may have noticed that at times I'm a bit slow in the uptake. It's not that I'm a fool—at least I hope not. When I was six, I was in an air crash. Both my parents were killed and I got a knock on the head that set me back all through my childhood.'

'Really! How awful for you.' Stephanie's voice was warm with sympathy, so he told her about his never having been to school, and of his unusual upbringing.

When he had done, she said that she would never have guessed that he had not had a proper education, although she found him quite different from any of the other young men she knew and liked him the better for it. As he finished his drink, she asked:

'What time do you want to leave tomorrow?'

'I'd like to get off about nine, if that's all right with you?' She nodded. 'And where shall we be going?'

'I haven't had time to think yet. Let's settle that in the morning,' he replied; and shortly afterwards they went up to their rooms.

As Robbie undressed, he was still feeling very sore at the

humiliation he had suffered in the café and, although he had
temporized with Stephanie, he had never had any intention
of abandoning his mission. On the contrary, Barak's threats
and Cepicka's sneers had only stimulated in him the determination to find out what they were up to. In them, too, he now felt
that he had two tangible enemies, which would make his further endeavours much more exciting than setting such wits as
he had against a nebulous organization.

For the next move he felt he had the advantage, for they
would probably think they had scared him off altogether. In
any case, he knew all the places at which groups were to be
stationed, and they could not possibly guess which group he
might decide to spy on. Corinth and Pirgos were the two
nearest places. For the former, it was a safe bet that a second
group would be landed at Patras, and sent with their machinery
either by road or by motor-caique up the gulf. The *Bratislava*
would then move down to Pirgos and land a third group there
before proceeding to drop others at Kalamai and the islands.
The machinery for the Corinth party would be cleared at
Patras, but that for Pirgos would have to go through the Customs there. From this Robbie reasoned that Barak, who
appeared to be in charge of the whole operation, and probably Cepicka, would go down to Pirgos; so he would stand
less risk of running into them again if he went to Corinth.

As he dropped off to sleep, his last thoughts were of
Stephanie. He still had no intention of telling her the whole
truth about his mission, but she had been sweetly sympathetic
about the handicap from which he had suffered during his unusual childhood, and it was a great comfort to think that he
could now talk to her freely about his unorthodox activities.

By half past nine next morning, they were well clear of
Patras and once more running along the road that followed the
shore of the broad gulf. Across its blue waters, the mountains
rose in a magnificent procession to the heights of Parnassus
towering above Delphi. Even at such a distance their main
features stood out distinctly, owing to the extraordinary clear-
ness of the atmosphere which is peculiar to Greece.

Stephanie had so far made no comment upon Robbie's
manuscript and, after they had covered ten miles, he could

restrain himself no longer from asking her what she thought of it, as far as she had read.

'I like it, Robbie,' she replied; then, after a slight hesitation, she added: 'But it's rather an unusual book, isn't it?'

'In what way?' he asked guardedly.

'It's difficult to explain. It's crammed full of slang expressions that you rarely use except when you are talking about the Immortals. That makes it unlike both the person you seem to be, and an ordinary book, so rather queer to read. Surely, too, in these days authors don't refer to their "gentle reader".'

'I don't see why they shouldn't. I like to think of my readers as though they could be my friends.'

'I'm sure you do, Robbie. That's just the sort of thing which is so nice about you. What puzzled me most, though, is your attitude towards the Olympians. Things you have said to me have given me the impression that you almost think of the gods as divinities still to be venerated; yet you give them awful characters.'

'They had different standards from ours, so one can't blame them for always hopping into bed with one another. Admittedly, they could turn pretty nasty if they felt they had been insulted, but most of the time their decrees were just, and they spent much more time protecting people than harming them. Anyhow, it wouldn't have been right not to tell the truth about the way they behaved.'

'Yes, I agree about that; but they don't seem exactly the sort of people one would choose to worship.'

'Most races have chosen worse. Look at the Babylonians, who worshipped Moloch, and the Aztecs with their frightful gods who were always demanding human sacrifices. Come to that, how about the Christians? They took over Jehovah from the Jews, a harsh, jealous old brute who hated to see people enjoy themselves and had to be constantly pacified by the smell of burnt offerings.'

Stephanie laughed. 'I suppose you are right. But how about your treatment of the Heroes? You always seem to be poking fun at them, and as far as I have read they all appear to have been dead from the neck up.'

A lot of them were. Odysseus was an exception. He was

as cunning as a cartload of monkeys. And Hercules had some pretty bright ideas. But, generally speaking, it's not fair to judge them by their brains. The great thing about them was their chivalry and courage. Most of them were Princes, who could have lived very pleasant lives if they had chosen to stay at home. But instead, they were always game to risk their lives to protect their peasantry from terrible monsters, or to suffer years of discomfort fighting not for themselves but to right a wrong done to one of their friends. The one thing they cared about was their honour, and never giving in before they had done what they set out to do. By that, they set a wonderful example to the whole people of Greece; and if it had not been for that spirit, Greece would never have survived the Persian hordes.'

For a while they were silent, then Stephanie said: 'In your first chapter about the Royal Family of Olympus, you say lots about Zeus and Poseidon and the innumerable *affaires* they had, but practically nothing about the third brother, Pluto. Didn't he care for the girls?'

'The chronicles don't give much information about him. They record only two cases of his being unfaithful to Persephone.'

'In view of the family temperament and the fact that she lived with him for only one-third of each year, that seems somewhat odd.'

'It does,' Robbie agreed thoughtfully, 'but perhaps he was really no better than the others. You see, he possessed a helmet that made him invisible whenever he visited the Upper World; so there is no saying what games he may have got up to without anyone being able to pin them on him.'

'That's certainly a thought. And his own kingdom sounds so gloomy that I should think he liked to get away from it as often as he could.'

'Oh, it couldn't have been so bad if you were the boss of it; at least, not as described by a chap named Er.'

'Who was he?'

'Er was a brave warrior who had a most extraordinary experience. He was killed in battle; so his chums did the usual, and put his body on a nice big bonfire. But it wouldn't burn, and after being cooked for twelve days he suddenly sat up and got off the red-hot ashes as fit as a fiddle. He said he had spent the twelve days in Hades, and had been sent back to tell everyone what it was like down there.

'According to him, it had a great vestibule called the Garden of Persephone, where black poplars and willows grew. Then inside, the Judgment Hall and Throne Room would have made the Palace of Versailles look like a pig-sty by comparison. Their walls, floors and ceilings were covered with wonderful designs in every kind of precious metal and the whole place glittered with precious stones.

'After crossing the Styx, the shades of the dead were brought before the three judges, Aeacus, Minos and Rhadamanthus, and given their deserts. The lucky ones got chits for the Elysian Fields and the bad hats were sent to do time in Tartarus, but the great majority were drafted into great gloomy caverns that were sort of concentration camps in which they stood around for years and years with nothing to do.

'However, Er was able to cheer up his pals by telling them that none of the shades was stuck in these places for ever. While the incoming queue was disposed of, another queue was being passed out up a passage where Heaven and Earth met in the rainbow. A character known as Necessity sat on a throne there with her three daughters, the Fates, who were named Lachesis, Clotho and Atropos.

'Necessity told the outgoing shades that they were about to be born into new bodies. Then she offered them in turn the choice from a big collection of lots, the outsides of which were marked "tinker", "tailor", "soldier", "sailor", and so on. But it was an awful pig-in-a-poke, because all sorts of other things were written inside. Some of the men who had an early choice naturally picked King, or rich merchant, only to find that they would be born blind or have their all taken off them by pirates, and some of the girls who snatched at beauty or S.A. found that their fathers would sell them to brothel keepers to pay the rent. They could change their sex if they liked and, of course, they weren't all unlucky. But really the whole thing was a bit of a hoax, because they all had to work off debts of one kind or another that they had incurred in their past lives, and the Fates had already fixed things so that, in their next lives, they would get, good or bad, what was due to them.

'Finally, Er saw all those people pass on to the treeless plain of Lethe, where there was a broad river beside which they had to doss down for the night. It was so hot there that they all got throats like ash-cans, and had to quench their thirsts at the river. Most of them drank so much of the Lethe water that it caused them to forget they had ever lived before; but there were a few who didn't drink quite so much, and that is why some people are born still retaining vague memories of their past lives. A little before dawn, they were all turned into shoot-ing stars and scattered over the world, to descend invisibly into the bodies of the mothers who had been chosen for them.'

'Then the ancient Greeks believed in Reincarnation,' Stephanie remarked. 'Do you?'

Robbie nodded. 'Certainly I do. I've read books about all sorts of religions, and it is the only belief that makes sense. In nine hundred and ninety-nine cases out of every thousand, to grant eternal bliss or condemn to unending torment accord-ing to what a person has done in a single life would be a travesty of justice. It is impossible to believe in a god who would want any creature of his to roast in hell-fire for ever. But to have to work one's passage through many lives, each based on what has gone before, and gradually learning to control all the brutal, primitive instincts, is very different. Then, when at last a person becomes incapable of a mean or unkind action, he really has earned the right to be promoted to some happier state of being than we know on earth.'

'I've never thought about it much, but it certainly sounds logical that one should be given a chance to make good the evil one has done and learn to become a better person.'

For a while they fell silent, then Stephanie asked: 'Was Er the only mortal who is said to have gone down to Hades and brought back an account of it, or were there others? That is, apart from Hercules when he had to go there to collect that ghastly dog?'

'Yes; Orpheus did, although he wasn't there long. He was the all-time-high pop-singer of those days. When he got back from going with Jason to pinch the Golden Fleece, he fell for a sweetie called Eurydice and made an honest woman of her. But while she was jiving at their wedding feast, she was bitten by a snake and died that night. As you can imagine, Orpheus was absolutely shattered, and when Death carried her away he followed him down to Hades. Charon, of course, refused to ferry him across the Styx, but Orpheus was simply wizard with his lute. First he played to the old boy, then to Cerberus. The ferryman rowed him over the river and the Hell-hound let him through the gate. Having got in, he performed his very best number in front of the King and Queen. Persephone, being a nice girl, begged her lord and master to let Orpheus have his brand-new better-half back. Pluto was a bit reluctant, but he agreed, provided that Orpheus didn't look behind him while Eurydice followed him out. Just before they reached the gates of Hades, Orpheus couldn't resist the temptation to make sure that his poppet was really behind him. She was there all right, but the instant their eyes met, he'd had it. Eurydice's rosy flesh suddenly became transparent, the gates clanged to, and he found himself outside them, having lost her for good.'

'What a terribly sad story.'

'I can tell you a similar one, that had a happier ending. That was about Hercules again. He really was a terrific guy, and didn't give a hoot for either god or man. This affair arose from Apollo having tried to put a fast one over his old pop. Zeus was no Victorian parent, but all the same he was not the kind to stand for any nonsense, and he sentenced Apollo to serve for nine years on earth as a mortal.

'One of Apollo's main interests being cattle, he got himself a job as herdsman to Admetus, King of Thessaly. The King treated him so well that, when his nine years were up, he decided to show his gratitude in a very unusual way. After a little haggling with the Fates, he persuaded them to agree that, when Admetus's time came to die, he should be allowed to live on if he could find anyone who loved him well enough to go to Hades in his place.

'In due course, Death sent a messenger to tip the King off that very shortly he would be coming his way. Admetus fairly rushed round, trying to find somebody willing to stand-in for him, but no one would play. He was just about to go down for the count when his young wife, Alcestis, stepped into the breach. She said she'd rather die herself than live on without her old tickley-whiskers, provided only that he would promise not to marry again, because she couldn't bear the thought of a step-mother who might be unkind to her children.

'Admetus must have been a pretty poor fish. He wept a lot but, nevertheless, accepted her offer and made the promise. Alcestis took a bath, put on her latest Dior creation and fell into a swoon. The funeral rites were duly performed and Death carried her off.

'Shortly afterwards, Hercules turned up. Seeing that the house was in mourning, he said he wouldn't stay and, of course, if he had known that it was Admetus's wife who had just died, he would have flatly refused to inflict himself on the bereaved husband. Knowing that, and being a great stickler for offering hospitality to strangers, Admetus said not to worry, the dead woman was only a friend of the family. Then he did the usual drill of putting a wreath of flowers round Hercules's neck, producing some good bottles and having his dancing girls do their stuff.

'Hercules liked his liquor, so he got a bit lit up and started singing bawdy songs at the top of his voice. An old retainer then tapped him on the shoulder and said: "You ought to be ashamed of yourself, behaving like this when the poor Queen's body has only just been taken out of the house."

'That sobered up our Hero and, seeing how generously his host had treated him, he felt he ought to do something about it. So, instead of going to bed, he made enquiries about which way Death had gone, and hurried off after him. In the morning he came back with a young woman smothered from head to foot in veils and said to Admetus: "Look, old chap. I was terribly sorry to hear that you'd lost your wife; so I've been out and got you a girl to cheer you up. And, believe me, she's a stunner," or words to that effect.

'But Admetus put up a good show then. He replied: "That's awfully decent of you, but no can do. I shall never love anyone but Alcestis, and I've made up my mind never to have a woman in my house again."

'Hercules did his utmost to persuade him to change his

mind, but he wouldn't budge. You can guess the rest. The Hero unveiled the lady and, of course, she was Alcestis, whom he had torn from the very arms of Death.'

'Did they live happily ever after?' Stephanie enquired.

'As far as I know.'

'What a pleasant change. So many of your characters seem to come to a sticky end.'

'Or worse,' Robbie commented with a rueful smile. 'Some were condemned to eternal torment. Even the sufferings of the damned in Dante's Hell can have been no worse than some of the punishments the gods thought up for people they sent to Tartarus.

'There was Tantalus, who had been King of Phrygia. Why, I haven't an idea, but the Immortals did him the extraordinary honour of inviting him to dine on Olympus, and he stole some of their nectar and ambrosia. Not content with that, he asked them back, and just to see if they were clever enough to know what they were eating, he killed his own son, Pelops, cut him up, cooked the bits and served them to his guests for dinner. Of course they rumbled him, and before he knew what had hit him he was down in Tartarus. They put him waist deep in the middle of a lake that had trees all round it bearing the most luscious fruit, but every time he tried to drink the water evaporated, and every time he stretched out a hand to grab a fruit a gust of wind bobbed it out of his reach. There they left him to suffer the torments of hunger and thirst for ever.

'Another bad egg who got it in the neck was the tyrant Ardiaeus. He killed lots of people just for the fun of it, among them his father and his brother; so the gods decreed that he should spend the rest of Time being dragged backwards and forwards through a hedge of enormous thorns. Then there were the Danaides, about as nasty a bunch of girls to go to bed with as any you could imagine.'

'Why, Robbie? Don't spare my blushes. Tell all.'

'Oh, it wasn't anything of that kind. They were the daughters of a chap named Danaus. There were fifty of them, and——'

'Fifty! My hat! He must have kept their mother busy.'

'It's hardly likely that they were all by one wife. Anyhow,

he had a brother named Aegyptus, who had fifty sons. The whole family lived in Egypt, but the brothers quarrelled, so Danaus took his girls off to Greece, where he did in the King of Argos and seized his throne. After a while, Aegyptus's boys began to miss their pretty cousins, so they crossed the Med. to Argos and suggested putting an end to the family quarrel by marrying them. Danaus agreed, but he was still mad with Aegyptus; so he gave each of his girls a dagger, and told her to stick it good and hard into her husband on their wedding night. All except one of these sweetie-pies did as they were told, and turned their bridal couches into a blood bath.'

'How absolutely barbarous! '

'That's what the big boys on Olympus thought. Aphrodite and most of the other big girls were of that opinion, too. They all agreed that, if that sort of thing were allowed to go on, it would discourage chaps from getting into bed with girls, and lead to a lot of young people becoming psychopathic cases through frustration; so an example must be made. The forty-nine Danaides were packed off to Tartarus and condemned to try to catch water in sieves for ever and ever, amen.'

'What punishment did the father receive?'

'I'm sorry to say I don't know. He certainly deserved anything he got. So did a chap called Ixion, who murdered his father-in-law by throwing him into a burning ditch. The ancients were frightfully hot on paying proper respects to one's in-laws; so he would have been for the high jump if Zeus had not granted him sanctuary on Olympus. But while up there, he was ass enough to make a pass at Hera; or rather, at a piece of cloud that Zeus, having tumbled to the way Ixion's mind was working, had made to look like Hera. He let Ixion have his fun with the cloud, too; but afterwards he told him that, for his cheek, he should learn how his father-in-law felt while burning in the ditch. Then he had Ixion tied to a wheel that never stops turning in Tartarus while he roasts over a slow fire.'

Across the water to their left, they could now see a headland that protruded from the Isthmus of Corinth, almost enclosing the waters on the south side of the gulf in the great bay that forms a fine, natural harbour for the city. To their right, vineyard-covered slopes rose gradually to steeper heights crowned by a flattened dome many acres in extent and several hundred feet above sea level. Near its crest and straggling down its sides, several sections of great ruined walls could be seen. Pointing at them, Robbie said:

'Those walls are about all that remains of the original Corinth. Owing to its position up there, overlooking the Isthmus and both gulfs, it was known in very ancient days as "The Watch Tower". Later it rivalled Athens in its splendour, and many of the most flourishing Greek colonies in Sicily and Southern Italy were founded by its merchant princes. I expect you've heard that silly saying: "All good Americans go to Paris when they die". That's how the ancients all over the Eastern Mediterranean felt about Corinth. The temple of Aphrodite up there was served by a thousand glamour-pusses —black, white and brown—brought from all over the known world, and it was their job to see to it that business executives on holiday had proper relaxation.'

Stephanie raised her eyebrows: 'Really, you men! It seems that, apart from making money, few of you ever think of anything else.'

'Oh, I wouldn't say that. Of course, a good supply of willing popsies has always been a major tourist attraction. When Paris began to get a bit strait-laced, Vienna and Budapest took its place, and coming right up-to-date, there is Las Vegas. But lots of the ancient Greeks came here for quite a different reason. It was one of the four places at which the great athletic contests were held. Those at Olympia were the most important, but every Hellenic State sent its champions to take part in the Isthmian Games, as those held here, in honour of Poseidon, were called. Tomorrow morning, we might go and have a look at the Stadium, then walk up to the site of the old city and picnic there.'

'What! Climb that mountain?' Stephanie's mouth took a firm line. 'No thank you, Robbie. I don't mind taking on the extra-secretarial duty of helping you to outwit your oil rivals, but I draw the line at trudging for miles up a slope of one in three.'

'I'm sorry,' he said, with swift contrition. 'I should have realized that it would be too tiring for you. Anyhow, there can't be much to see up there, except the magnificent view. We'll picnic in the new city instead.'

'But . . .' she shot him a puzzled glance, 'surely you can't mean that we should eat our lunch in the streets?'

Robbie roared with laughter. 'No; no. Of course not. There are three Corinths. You are thinking of the modern town where we are going to stay. The one up on the hill is called Acrocorinth. It was sacked and destroyed by the Romans somewhere about one hundred and fifty B.C. Then Julius Caesar came along about a hundred years later and built what is called the new city. You can't see it from here, because its ruins are hidden by villas and vineyards, but it's on the lower slopes and only about ten minutes' drive from the town.'

There are no large hotels in Corinth and, when they drove up to the one they had selected from the guide-book, they found no one in its small entrance hall. But there was a bell-push on the desk and, after Robbie had pressed it three times, a middle-aged woman, who said she was the manageress, appeared from the back premises. Robbie told her they might be staying several nights, and asked for the best rooms available. She summoned a waiter to carry their bags and led the way upstairs to the first floor.

Evidently Robbie's Greek had let him down on this occasion, for the manageress ushered them both into a pleasant room with a fine view over the bay, but only one large double bed in it.

Robbie turned scarlet, and for a long moment was entirely bereft of words. Turning, he saw that Stephanie had put a hand up that only half concealed a smile of amusement at his embarrassment. Hastily, he stammered to the manageress that she had misunderstood him; they were not married and wanted separate rooms. Leaving Stephanie there, he swiftly retreated to the corridor and was duly taken to a smaller chamber on the upper floor.

Ten minutes later, they were refreshing themselves under a vine-covered pergola with large tumblers of iced orange juice. After a short stroll along the waterfront, they returned there for lunch and, just as they were finishing the meal, Robbie said:

'Presently, I shall be going out on the job again; but I don't expect to be away long.'

Stephanie raised her eyebrows. 'You might have told me that you meant to go looking for more trouble here.'

'I hope I won't get into any,' he smiled. 'But this happens to be one of a dozen places at which the Czech firm is going to try to muscle in on us; so I ought not to miss the opportunity of making a few enquiries.'

'All right then,' she smiled back. 'I'll resign myself to spending a lonely afternoon on that lovely double bed. I'll be thinking of you.'

When she had left him, Robbie sat staring into his empty coffee cup. Could she possibly have meant . . . ? But no, she was not that kind of girl. He positively must not allow himself to imagine such things.

15

The Villa Dione

A T A L I T T L E before four o'clock Robbie hunted out the manageress and asked her about the estate agents in the town. She said there were three or four, but that one of them handled nearly all the most important business, and gave him the firm's address. He then walked round to their office, presented one of the cards of the United Kingdom Petroleum Company, and asked to see the senior partner.

He was shown in at once to their Mr. Vassilios, a dapper little man who bowed him to a chair, offered him a cigarette and smilingly asked his business.

Now accustomed to 'telling lies in the service of his country', Robbie said that his firm was contemplating setting up an oil installation in the neighbourhood of Corinth, and that he would like to have particulars of any suitable properties that were available.

Scenting big business, Mr. Vassilios was instantly galvanized into enthusiastic activity. He produced a list of building sites and estates that were for sale, and offered there and then to take Robbie in his car to see any that appealed to him.

Having looked through them, Robbie remarked that only two of the properties had access to the shore, and that was essential in order that a wharf could be built off which the Company's tankers could lie. He then added casually: 'I take it that if my Company decided to buy either of these the mineral rights would go with them?'

Mr. Vassilios's dark eyes gave a sudden flicker. 'You

spoke, Mr. Grenn, of an installation. I naturally assumed you had in mind a refinery with storage tanks. Do you mean that your Company intends to bore for oil?'

'We might,' Robbie admitted guardedly.

'Then it is true!' exclaimed Vassilios excitedly. 'I thought another client of ours quite mad some weeks ago when he bought a property here to prospect for oil. But if your Company also believes that there is oil in the neighbourhood of Corinth, it must be so. This is most wonderful news, both for all of us in this city and for Greece.'

Robbie smiled a little dubiously. 'I wouldn't count on that, Mr. Vassilios; not until those other people or my firm have struck a gusher.'

The little man sighed. 'Alas, Mr. Grenn, I regret to disappoint you. It will not be your firm. These first-comers—they are a Czech company—have already spiked your guns. They have secured a concession from the Greek Government for the sole right to prospect for oil. If you acquire one of these properties you could build anything you wish on it, but you would not be permitted to drill.'

Making an appropriately glum face, Robbie said: 'Then I fear I have had my journey from Athens for nothing, and I'll have a very unwelcome report to take back. Without prospecting rights, my Company would not buy; so I am afraid there is no point in my going with you to see either of these properties.'

'I am indeed sorry.' Mr. Vassilios sighed again at this abrupt end to his prospects of handling a very profitable deal.

As Robbie stood up to go, he said: 'If you've no objection, I'd like to know the site these other people have chosen for their operations.'

'None at all.' A large map hung on the wall behind Mr. Vassilios' desk. He pointed to a tiny black square near the shore, just to the west of the town. 'That is it; the Villa Dione. It is a property of about four hectares, mostly orchard and vineyards.'

Having thanked him, Robbie was politely bowed out, very pleased with himself at having hit first go on the agent who had acted for the Czechs, and secured the information he required.

As Corinth is quite a small town and the villa was only just outside it, he decided to walk there right away. Twenty minutes later he halted on the coast road to have a good look at it. The building was large, square and looked to be about a hundred years old. Evidently it had long remained unoccupied, for the short drive, seen through rusty iron gates, was overgrown with weeds, and the yellow paint was peeling from the outside walls. The house and about an acre of ground behind it were enclosed by six-foot walls. Along that nearest to Robbie ran a cart-track, so he walked a little way up it to get a look at the back of the house. When he had gone about sixty yards he came upon a postern gate in the wall and, on his trying it, he found that it opened.

Slipping inside, he took a quick look round. The garden, which was mainly an orchard of orange, lemon and apricot trees, and the back of the house appeared to be deserted. As he turned to close the door behind him, he noticed that there was a key in the lock. On trying it, he found that it worked easily, which implied that it was locked at night. Taking out the key, he slipped it into his pocket.

He had hardly done so when an unshaven man, dressed like a peasant, emerged from a nearby outbuilding, stared at him for a moment, touched his cap and said:

'Good evening, sir. I suppose you are one of these Czech gentlemen who have taken the villa. But I wasn't expecting any of you till tomorrow.'

Obviously the man was the caretaker, and for a moment Robbie was at a loss for a reply. Then an excuse came to him and he said with a smile: 'I didn't know the villa had been let. I am looking for a place to rent for the summer months. Seeing the house was empty, I just looked in. Sorry to have bothered you.'

'That's all right, sir,' the man replied amiably. 'Have a look round if you like.'

Robbie thanked him, accepted his offer and spent the next twenty minutes making a tour of the house. It was furnished, but only very sparsely. There were damp stains on the walls and, no attempt having yet been made to clean it up, a layer of dust over everything. From his inspection he learned nothing of the Czechs' intentions but, in the circumstances, he had not expected that he would.

Afterwards, knowing how sensitive Greek peasants are about accepting money, and wanting to give the caretaker a tip, he asked if he might buy a few of the big, ripe oranges. To that the man readily consented, and found him a paper bag in which to carry the fruit back to the hotel.

At one of the dozen tables outside it, Stephanie was sitting. As he approached, she gave him a bright smile; then, as he took a chair opposite her, she said that she had been so anxious about him that she had even forgotten to order herself a drink. He promptly rectified her omission and, still glowing with his success at having so quickly located the site at which the Czechs intended to start work, told her how he had spent the past two hours, concealing from her now only his belief that the Czechs were using the cover of oil prospecting for some nefarious activity, and that his story to her that he was the representative of an oil company was untrue.

When he had done she congratulated him on his astuteness with the estate agent, but expressed her misgivings about the future. Then she asked what he meant to do with the key he had stolen.

'Having taken it will prevent them from locking the door,' he laughed. 'Tomorrow night, or maybe one night later on when they've had a chance to settle down, I'll go in and have a good look round. With luck I'll even get a peep at the type of machinery they are bringing with them.'

'But, Robbie,' she protested, 'there will be a lot of them and only one one of you. If they catch you they may do you a serious injury.'

'This will be a different party from the bunch who threatened me in Patras; so if I get caught the odds are all against their knowing who I am. I hadn't thought of it at the time, but as an excuse for being in the garden I could say that I'd come to buy some more oranges from the caretaker. Still, as I don't intend to go in till after dark, I think it very unlikely that I'll get caught.'

Stephanie shook her chestnut curls. 'I don't like it. There is always the chance that there will be someone there from Patras who will recognize you. Business men aren't normally expected to take these sort of risks for their firms, so why should you? Please be sensible. Telephone your firm tomorrow morning. Tell them that these Czechs have threatened to give you a beating up; then, if your people have any decency at all, they will tell you that you are not to pursue your enquiries any further.'

'No, I can't do that.' Robbie paused for a moment, seeking a reason, then he added: 'You see, I want to pull this off, because it would lead to my promotion.'

'I don't believe you,' she retorted angrily. 'It's simply that you have a bee in your bonnet about the Heroes of antiquity. You admit that they were a stupid lot, yet you want to be like them. That's why you refuse to throw in your hand.'

That evening they dined in the little hotel and, as there was nowhere to go afterwards, went early to bed. During the night it rained, but by nine o'clock next morning the pavements were drying up and it promised to be another lovely sunny day; so they had a picnic basket made up. On a flat stretch of road to the west of the town Stephanie gave Robbie his second driving lesson, then she drove them up to the 'new' city.

The Greco-Roman ruins covered a huge area and, in addition, there was a quite large museum, containing many fine sculptures that had been excavated at various periods. Unlike Pleuron, there were several coach-loads of tourists being conducted by guides, who addressed them loudly in different languages; but the site was so extensive that it was possible to keep a fair distance from them most of the time.

For the better part of two hours Robbie and Stephanie wandered through the maze of streets, now and then turning off to explore Apollo's temple, rows of roofless shops, the Odeon of Herodes Atticus, the theatre and the beautiful sunken baths with the famous fountain of Glauce.

By half-past-one the tourists had re-entered their coaches, and had been carried off to lunch; so the two picnickers collected their basket from the car and, selecting a shady spot, opened it up.

When they had eaten their fill Stephanie remarked: 'I haven't come across anything about Corinth yet in your book.

Did none of the Heroes perform his deeds of deering-do in these parts?'

Robbie shook his head. 'I've yet to do Corinth, and there's not much to tell; only about Sisyphus and Bellerophon.'

'What did they get up to?'

'It was Sisyphus who founded Corinth. He was a very nasty piece of work, and about as cunning as they make 'em. He split to Asopus, the River God, that it was Zeus who had carried off his daughter Aegina. Zeus felt pretty sore about that, so he sent Death to him; but Sisyphus was such a slippery customer that he tripped Death and tied him up. Ares had to be sent to free him, so Death got Sisyphus after all; but not for long. Before he passed out, he told his wife to bury him without any of the usual funeral honours. Then, when he got down to Hades, he complained most bitterly to Pluto about the scurvy way she had treated his corpse. The ancients set a great store by that sort of thing, so Pluto was very shocked and allowed him to go back to earth to administer chastisement to his better half. When Zeus heard how Sisyphus had made a monkey out of him, he became properly steamed up. While Sisyphus was still telling himself what a clever fellow he was, something seized him by the seat of his pants and pitched him straight down to Tartarus. By Zeus's decree, he was set to rolling a huge boulder up a hill then, every time he got it to the top, it slipped out of his grip and rolled down to the bottom; so that he had to go down and start rolling it up again.'

'And what about Bellerophon?'

'He was Sisyphus's grandson, and his story is rather on the lines of Joseph and Potiphar's wife. He killed a chap here by accident but, all the same, he had to flee the country, and he took refuge with Proetus, King of Argos. Proetus had a lovely wife named Antea. She took a fancy to Bellerophon and, being pretty hot stuff, invited him to come and play tiddley-winks with her in her bedroom. As Proetus had treated him very handsomely, Bellerophon did the decent thing and refused to play.

'You know the old one about "a woman scorned". That was Antea's angle on this set-up, and she behaved like a lousy little bitch. She told her husband that Bellerophon had been showing her filthy postcards, or something of that kind, and making naughty suggestions to her. Proetus was very upset, because he had thought Bellerophon a good scout; yet his own honour demanded that he agree to his wife's request that her would-be seducer should be taken for a ride.

'After a little thought, Proetus so much disliked the idea of handing Bellerophon over to a firing squad himself that he decided to get someone else to do the job. He sent Bellerophon on a visit to his son-in-law, Iobates, King of Lycia, with a sealed packet with a note inside which said: 'This fellow is a bad egg. Please oblige me by doing him in.''

'Iobates put out the red carpet for his handsome young guest, and for nine nights had his Court make whoopee for his entertainment. At the end of them, everyone agreed that Bellerophon was a great charmer, and the King had come to regard him as quite a special pal. In consequence, on the tenth day, when Iobates opened the packet and read the message from his pa-in-law, he was terribly put out.

'He didn't like the idea, any more than Proetus had, of personally giving the order for Bellerophon to be written off. So he, too, did a big think; and, as he was in honour bound to do something, he hit on the idea of getting him killed by a monster. A fire-breathing beast called the Chimaera was then behaving very unpleasantly in those parts, and that night he told Bellerophon about it.

'Bellerophon, being a Hero, naturally sprang to his feet and cried: "Lead me to it." So they buckled his armour on to him, gave him a packet of sandwiches and, a bit tearfully, wished him luck.

'Before he had gone far, he came upon a winged horse called Pegasus, and it occurred to him that this single-seater aircraft would enable him to zoom down on the Chimaera and give it the works without much risk to himself. But, try as he would, he couldn't persuade this splendid beast to let him mount it; so, tired out, he lay down and went to sleep.

'It was, of course, the gods who, feeling that he was being done dirt, had put Pegasus in his way. While he slept, Athene appeared to him in a dream and laid beside him a golden bridle. When he awoke, sure enough there it was. Pegasus submitted like a lamb to the bit being slipped between his teeth, and the rest was easy. Bellerophon settled the Chimaera's business with half a dozen arrows, then made a perfect landing, cut off the beast's head and tail, and flew back in triumph with them to Iobates.

'The King was delighted at these proofs that the Chimaera's goose was cooked, but more put out than ever about how to deal with his guest. Still feeling that he ought not to let down Proetus, he sent Bellerophon on two more missions: first to perform a "High Noon" act as the lone sheriff against a small army of cattle rustlers, then against the Amazons. But, looping the loop on Pegasus, Bellerophon played merry hell with both these menaces to the gracious life.

'After that, Iobates took the view that his pa-in-law must have been one over the odds when he wrote the letter, because no one could have done what Bellerophon had done unless he was beloved by the gods; so he called it a day and gave him his daughter in marriage.

'Unfortunately, that is not quite the end of the story. Bellerophon became so Johnny-head-in-air about his exploits that he forgot that the Chimaera would probably have made Toast Melba out of him with its breath, if it hadn't been for Athene's lending him Pegasus. He decided that he was entitled to the *entrée* into Olympus and he attempted to gatecrash without having been put up for the Club. As the oldest member present, Zeus called a committee meeting and they sent a gadfly to sting Pegasus on his plump behind. Naturally he bucked like billy-oh, Bellerophon was tossed off and hit the ground with a thump that left him lame for the rest of his life.'

'I suppose,' Stephanie smiled, 'that's where we get our expression "Pride comes before a fall".'

As they walked back towards the car along the stone-paved streets, Stephanie remarked on one of them being buckled into a hump that rose several feet above the normal level, and asked what could have caused it.

'An earthquake,' Robbie replied at once. 'The crust of the earth must be very thin right along the Gulf of Corinth, and in several other parts of Greece. As you must know, Greece has suffered a lot from earthquakes all through her history, and hardly a year goes by without some village or other being destroyed by one.'

As they drove back through the vineyards of tall-staked vines that produce the currants which have made Corinth famous, he said: 'I think after dinner I'll walk down to the Villa Dione. It will be too early for me to find out what type of machinery the Czechs intend to use, but I'd like to take just a peep through that postern gate I told you about and make certain that they have arrived.'

At the hotel they had a belated siesta, so they did not meet again until shortly before dinner. Over the meal Stephanie endeavoured to persuade him to give up his intention; but he was so keyed up at the prospect of it that he would not listen to her.

About half-past-nine, after they had whiled away an hour with coffee and liqueurs, he smiled good-bye to her and set off on the fifteen-minute walk to the seashore to the west of the town.

As he approached the villa, he saw that there were lights in several of the windows, and, by the light of the moon, which was just rising, that a large caique lay at anchor off the villa's private beach.

Having secured ample evidence that the Czechs were in occupation, he was in half a mind to turn back; but the temptation to sneak into the garden and find out, if he could, where the Czechs had stored their machinery proved too much for him. Walking swiftly to the door in the wall, he pushed it open and stepped inside.

He had taken no more than a couple of paces when, with a loud shout, a figure leapt at him from out of the darkness. A blow on the side of his face sent him reeling. Next moment there came a chorus of excited cries and a little crowd of shadowy figures came tumbling out through a pair of french windows at the back of the villa.

Recovering his balance, he struck out at his assailant. It was a lucky blow. With a gasp, the man went over backward into the thick undergrowth. Spinning round, Robbie sprang back through the still open doorway and took to his heels. But the pack was after him in full cry.

Sprinting for all he was worth, he kept his lead until he was among the buildings on the outskirts of the town. Praying that he might be seen by a policeman, who would come to his rescue, he raced on. But there is no night-life in Corinth, and the side streets were deserted.

His breath was coming painfully, and with every bound he took he was conscious that his pursuers were gaining on him. They were silent now, but the rhythm of their swift footfalls on the pavement held for him a terrible menace. He knew that if they caught him he would be in for a most brutal handling.

Suddenly an outstretched hand fell on his shoulder. Swerving, he jerked it off. But he realized now that at any moment, unless he turned to fight, he might be slugged on the head. He had reached a gap between two houses of the kind often seen in Greek towns. Above a low balustrade there ran an iron railing. Beyond it was a wide pit shrouded in darkness. Down it there would be a few pillars and big slabs of stone half submerged in weeds and tall grass—the remains of some temple or small theatre that was of little importance and not worth excavating further, but was a protected site on which, by an Act of the Greek Government, it was forbidden to build.

Backing up against the parapet, he hit out at the nearest figure to him. Again it was a lucky blow. With a curse, the man went down. But there were half a dozen others and they closed in, raining blows on him. He was taller than any of them and managed to protect his face, but he was struck a dozen times about his arms and body.

Vaguely, by the moonlight, he saw another figure come panting up behind the rest, and heard a shout: 'Leave him to me, boys. I'll soon settle him.' As the others drew back, he found himself face to face with the enormously broad-shouldered figure of Stoll. With a grunt, the barrel-chested Sudetenlander hurled himself at Robbie. Before he had a chance to hit out, Stoll had flung his long arms round him and seized him in a gorilla-like embrace. Desperately, Robbie strove to break free. His breath was coming in gasps. He felt himself being crushed in that terrible grip. His utmost efforts to break Stoll's hold were of no avail. For a minute or more, they staggered backward and forward, then Stoll forced Robbie back against the parapet. Its brickwork hit him behind the knees and the iron railing bit into his back.

Suddenly, the rusty railing gave. Robbie went backward, carrying Stoll with him. As they plunged the eight feet into the thick grass below, still clasping one another in a fierce embrace, they turned threequarters of a somersault. The Sudetenlander landed on his back with Robbie on top of him. He gave a long, agonized groan and his arms fell away from Robbie. For a moment, Robbie lay panting on his gross body, then he lurched to his feet.

Stoll's companions now lined the parapet, exclaiming excitedly together. But there was no way down into the little ruin and none of them was brave enough to face the drop. Robbie staggered away in the opposite direction. Twice he collided with large blocks of stone half hidden in the grass, and once fell with hands outstretched into a patch of stinging nettles. Oblivious of the pain, he blundered on until he reached the far side of the ruin. Beyond it, there was another street that bordered it on a lower level. Still a prey to terror that he would be caught, he somehow managed to scale the five-foot wall and climb over the parapet. Fear lending him new strength, he began to run again, and broke into a walk only when he was within a hundred yards of his hotel.

It had a small courtyard with stables which had been converted into garages. Still panting, he came to a halt midway across the entrance to the yard, arrested by the lights of a car that was just being driven out. His head was above the level of the car lamps, so he could see clearly the couple in it. As it pulled up to avoid running him down, he saw that it was the Ford, and that Stephanie was at the wheel. A second later, he recognized the man beside her. It was Václav Barak.

16

The Biter Bit

R OBBIE stood rooted to the spot. The sight of Barak sitting beside Stephanie in the car left him utterly confounded. How did they come to be together? Could that be accounted for by some strange coincidence, or were they old acquaintances? And where could they have been going? But perhaps she was not driving him of her own free will. Perhaps he had come to the hotel and threatened her in some way.

Next moment there came confirmation of this last idea. The door of the car was flung open and Barak jumped out. To Robbie the inference was clear. Whatever his enemy's plan might have been, his own unexpected arrival on the scene had nipped it in the bud.

For the first time in his life Robbie saw red. Barak had threatened him with a beating up. Stoll and those other thugs at the Villa Dione were under his orders. It must have been he who arranged for them to lie in wait there. No doubt he had counted on their victim being by now half-dead in a ditch. But that was far from being his worst offence. Somehow he had got hold of Stephanie and had threatened or lied to her. He had been caught in the very act of forcing her to drive off with him. Why, remained a mystery. But it could only be that he had some evil design in mind. The thought that he had meant to harm her drove Robbie berserk. As Barak slammed the door of the car, Robbie leapt at him.

Sudden fear showed in Barak's eyes. Spinning round, he dashed back towards the yard. Robbie raced after him, thinking he meant to head for the side-door of the hotel in the hope of securing protection from some of the staff who might be in the kitchen quarters. But the Czech was swift in wit as well as action. As he came level with the rear of the Ford, he dodged behind it and put out his foot. Robbie tripped over it, flung out his arms and measured his length on the ground.

His hands were badly scraped on the cobbles and the breath half driven from his body. With a gasp, he pulled himself to his knees, then to his feet. By the time he was up, Barak had darted round the far side of the car and was out in the street. Sobbing now, not with pain but with rage, Robbie gave chase.

Barak had gained a fifty-yard start and was running hard along the waterfront. There were few people about for, although it was not late, the April night was chilly; so the patrons of the few small cafés were drinking inside them. Only a young couple, arm in arm, and a solitary fisherman turned to stare as Robbie pounded past them in full pursuit of his enemy.

After covering a hundred and fifty yards, Barak swerved round a corner up a street that led into the centre of the town. But it was a side-street and deserted, except for one old woman. The Czech's legs were long, but Robbie's were longer. When he turned the corner, he had decreased his enemy's lead by half. As the crash of Robbie's flying footsteps grew louder in Barak's ears, he cast a swift glance over his shoulder, ran on another twenty paces, then dived into an alley. Fearing that, if the alley led into several others, he might lose his enemy in the darkness, Robbie forced himself into an extra spurt. Next moment, he was in the entrance to the alley. The narrow passage was shrouded in gloom. The starlight was sufficient for him to see that it was about sixty feet in length and ended in a high wall. But it was empty.

No lights showed in the buildings on either side. Unless a door had been open, Barak could hardly have had time to gain admittance to one of the houses, or to a yard. That meant there must be a turning at the end of the alley. Drawing his breath in gasps, Robbie raced on. When he had covered another thirty feet, the shadows ahead dissolved. He was right. The alley took a right-angle turn to the left, back towards the waterfront. Brushing the wall at the corner with his shoulder, he swerved round it. His heart gave a bound. The turning was a cul-de-sac, only twenty feet long, and Barak stood there, trapped in it.

Without pausing to draw breath, Robbie sprang at him and struck out at his face. Barak dodged the blow and clinched with him. Seizing Barak by the arms, he broke his grip, then flung him with all his force against the wall. For a moment, the tall Czech stood spread-eagled against it, half-dazed by the shock. Robbie hit out at his head again, but again he dodged the blow. Lurching forward, he tried to kick Robbie in the groin. Swerving sideways, Robbie took the kick on his thigh, then he stepped back and, with a murderous grin, took a swift survey of his enemy.

This was his second fight. He had learned by now that windmill blows were rarely effective, and that much better results could be achieved by thinking first at what part of one's opponent to strike. He realized, too, that this time it was not he who was trying to escape; so time was on his side and, as he was much more powerful than Barak, he had him at his mercy.

Suddenly Barak dived sideways, but he was so close-pressed against the wall that with one swift step Robbie had crowded him back again. Robbie then went in to the attack. Feinting with his left at Barak's stomach, he drove his right into his face. The blow took him full in the eye. With a wail, he threw up his open hands to fend off further blows and cried:

'Have mercy! Not my face! Please, not my face.'

'Mercy, you rat!' Robbie snarled. 'You'll be lucky if I don't kill you! And you're vain of your face, eh? Then I'll do to it what you threatened to do to my body.'

For three good minutes he let his fury have full play. Cornered and confronted with Robbie's superior strength and furious rage, Barak had already gone to pieces. Fear robbed him of the power to make more than a feeble attempt to protect himself and, when he started to shout for help, Robbie silenced him by a blow in the mouth that loosened several of his teeth. Three times he slid moaning to the ground. Three times Robbie hauled him upright again by his collar for further punishment. When Robbie at last let him drop, he was still conscious; but his face was covered with blood, both eyes were blacked, his mouth was badly cut and his nose broken.

Staring down at him, Robbie muttered: 'That will teach you to set your thugs on me. And if I ever catch you trying anything on Miss Stephanopoulos again, I'll kill you.'

Turning away, he set off back to the hotel. It was only about five minutes' walk and, as he had done the outward journey at a headlong pace, when he got there he had been away from it not much more than ten. Even so, he was surprised to see the Ford standing outside it, and Stephanie still sitting at the wheel.

When he was within a few paces of the car she caught sight of him, leaned over and threw open the door. The car was not immediately in front of the lit porch of the hotel, so the light inside it was too dim for him to see her face distinctly. But her voice held a mixture of relief and anxiety as she exclaimed:

'Oh, Robbie! Thank God you're safe. Whatever has been happening? I've been terribly worried. I still am.'

'You've no need to be now,' he replied. 'But why are you still out here, sitting in the car?'

'I was waiting to . . . I thought you might want to get away in a hurry.'

'Then it was sporting of you to stand by. But I don't; so run back into the garage and we'll go into the hotel.'

'No.' She shook her head. 'I want to hear what has been going on. There are some people sitting reading in the lounge, and it's such a small one that we can't possibly talk there. Out here we can't be overheard.'

'All right.' He scrambled in beside her, and shut the door. Then he said: 'There's not much to tell. I was ambushed down at the villa and had to run for it. They caught up with me and there was a fight, but I had the luck to get away. What about you, though? How did you come to be in the car with that swine Barak?'

'Is that his name?'

'Yes. Didn't you know?'

'How could I? He didn't introduce himself, and I hadn't

been talking to him for more than a few minutes before you came on the scene.'

'Well, that is his name, and he is my enemy No. 1. He is a Czech, and the top man in this rival oil set-up.'

'Good gracious! I thought he was simply a friendly Greek.'

'Friendly!' Robbie turned to stare at her. 'You can't . . . you can't mean that he had just scraped acquaintance with you and asked you to drive him somewhere?'

'Of course not.' Stephanie's tone was indignant. 'Even if this were my car, is it likely that I would take a strange man for a drive in it at this time of night?'

'I know, I know. But you say he was friendly. Then he hadn't threatened you; he wasn't forcing you to go off with him against your will. If that is so, what the devil was he doing in the car with you?'

'He was going to show me the way to the hospital.'

'What in the world for?' After a moment's pause, Robbie added with quick concern: 'You're not feeling ill or anything, are you?'

'Not unless you count frayed nerves. No; he was taking me to the hospital to see you.'

'Me! But I wasn't there. I don't even know where it is.'

'Neither did I. That's why I asked him to show me the way to it.'

Robbie groaned. 'I don't understand. Please start from the beginning.'

'Very well. About twenty minutes ago, I was sitting in that stuffy little lounge reading. Then this Mr. Barrat came in——'

'Barak; Václav Barak.'

'All right, Mr. Barak. He came over to me and said in a low voice: "Please come outside for a moment, I have a message for you from your husband." Assuming he could only mean you, I went out with him to the hall. Then he said: "I'm afraid it's not a message, but bad news. Your husband has been knocked down by a car and badly hurt. I was among those who picked him up. I chanced to see you lunching together here today and——" '

'But we didn't lunch here,' Robbie interrupted. 'We picnicked among the ruins of the new city.'

'Yes, of course we did. Being so worried about you has driven out of my mind exactly what he said. Perhaps it was yesterday he saw us lunching at one of the tables outside, or having drinks there earlier this evening. What does it matter? Anyhow, he recognized you at once when they were picking you up, because you are such a big man. Then, as he was passing here on his way home, it occurred to him that, as you were unconscious, you might be at the hospital all night, while I worried myself silly wondering where you had got to; so it would be a kindness to come in and let me know what had happened.'

Robbie considered this for a moment, then he said: 'By the time he did his friendly act with you, he obviously counted on his thugs having done their stuff on me. But what I don't understand is why he should have gone out of his way to bring you to my bedside.'

'Surely that was part of a plan to cover up the attack on you?' Stephanie suggested. 'Evidently it was intended that, after knocking you out, the thugs should dump you at the hospital and say that they had seen you run over by a hit-and-run driver. When you recovered consciousness, you would have said that you had been beaten up; but the fact that I had been brought to your bedside by someone who had witnessed the accident would have led the authorities to believe that you were imagining things—that your brain had been slightly affected—then the police would probably not have bothered to start an investigation that might have led to Barak's people.'

'That certainly sounds plausible,' Robbie agreed. 'Anyway, I'm fortunate not to be lying in the hospital now with a broken head and ribs.' He went on to give Stephanie a full account of his visit to the Villa Dione, and how a lucky break had enabled him to escape from his attackers. Then he said:

'I'm puzzled, though, about how they got on to me. Of course, it may have been pure chance that one of them happened to be standing just inside the postern gate; but the fact that all the others were in a downstairs room at the back of the house, ready to dash out at a moment's notice, seems to make that unlikely. I'm pretty sure they were lying in wait for me.'

'It could have been the gardener,' Stephanie suggested. 'He must have missed the key that you made off with and, in mentioning that to the tenants, he probably told them about your visit to the villa yesterday evening. You say that this Sudetenlander, Stoll, already knew you; so he could have recognized you from the gardener's description. Stoll would have jumped to it then that it was you who had stolen the key, and that you meant to pay the villa another visit.'

'By jove, you're right! ' Robbie gave her a glance of admiration. 'That never occurred to me, but it's odds-on that it explains the ambush I ran into.'

There was a moment's silence, then Stephanie said in a low voice: 'You haven't told me yet what happened when you ran off after Barak. Did he get away?'

'No,' Robbie replied grimly. 'I caught up with him in a cul-de-sac and he won't worry us again.'

She stiffened suddenly and gave a cry of apprehension. 'Good God! You didn't kill him, did you?'

'Good Lord, no! I'm much too fond of my own life to risk being charged with murder. I just gave him a darn' good pasting and left him to crawl home.'

Again they fell silent for a minute or more, until Stephanie gave a slight shiver and said: 'Well, now we know where we are. But it's getting awfully cold; let's go in.'

'Let's,' Robbie agreed, 'I could do with a drink.'

She backed the car round into the garage and they walked back to the front entrance of the hotel. As they were about to go in, her glance fell on his right hand. It was dark red with congealed blood. Her eyes distended, she grasped his arm, pulled him to a halt and cried:

'Look at your hand. What have you done? I believe you did kill him.'

'I didn't,' he assured her. 'Most of that is from the broken skin of my knuckles. I admit, though, that I lammed into him quite a bit. Something came over me, a sort of vicious feeling. I've never felt like that about anyone before, but I couldn't stop myself. I kept on hitting him until I'd made a horrid mess of his face.'

'You . . . you. Oh well, I suppose he deserved it. But Robbie,' she drew a sharp breath before going on, 'he was a very good-looking man and . . . and I should think rather vain. If you have permanently spoiled his face he'll never forgive you. And he has all those thugs under his orders. It's certain he'll do his utmost to be revenged on you. We mustn't stay here. If we do you'll be in real danger. I'm sure of it. Please let's get away from Corinth.'

Robbie nodded. 'I think you're right again. In any case, I wouldn't risk another visit to the Villa Dione; so there is not much point in staying on here. But Barak won't be up to planning any further mischief tonight. It will be time enough if we leave in the morning.'

Stuffing his bloody hands into his trouser pockets, Robbie followed Stephanie into the hotel. She ordered drinks for them and went into the lounge, while he went up to his room and cleaned himself up. When he came down and joined her he found that the couple she said had been reading there had gone up to bed, so they had the room to themselves.

She asked him where he intended that they should go on leaving Corinth, and he replied: 'I haven't had time to think yet. I reckon that I've rendered Barak *hors de combat* for the best part of a week, and after his fall Stoll must be in pretty bad shape, too. Of their three top chaps, that leaves only Cepicka, and all the odds are that he is either at Pirgos or has gone down to Kalamai to superintend the arrangements for other groups of Czechs who are to land at those ports. If so, that would leave me a free field at Patras, and by this time the group there must be getting busy; so we might go back there and I could try to find out what they are up to.'

'No, Robbie; no.' Stephanie gave a quick shake of her chestnut curls. 'You seem to have forgotten that you stood drinks to the whole party there and that you were denounced as a spy in front of them. One or more of them would be certain to recognize you.'

'That's true, but I had forgotten it. Although I got the best of things, I've been through a rather rough time this evening, and I'm afraid all the excitement has put my mind a bit out of gear for making new plans. But I'll be all right in the morning. Let's leave it till then.'

Leaning forward, she laid a hand gently on his knee. 'Robbie, let's face it. You've got lots of splendid qualities, but you weren't cut out to be either a spy or a planner. Why your firm should ever have picked you for this job, I can't think. Won't you please telephone them tomorrow; tell them that tonight you narrowly escaped having to spend three months in hospital, and that a man you have beaten up may try to revenge himself on you at any time? Then ask them to release you from this dangerous work. They can't possibly refuse.'

He shook his head. 'No, I don't want to do that.'

'Why not? If you have to take me back to Athens, I'll manage somehow. But you've earned a holiday for the risks you have already taken. Why not claim it? Then we could go on in the car to other interesting places. You would be able to concentrate entirely on your book, and in between driving from place to place, I would type it for you.'

Robbie smiled. 'That would be lovely. I can't think of anything I'd like more. Perhaps after I have found out what these chaps are up to, we might do that; but not until I have.'

'But you do know what they are up to,' she said with a puzzled frown. 'They are establishing a chain of depots in opposition to your firm. At least, that's what you gave me to understand.'

'Well, yes. That, more or less, describes what I believe them to be doing. But I want to find out details: particularly about the type of machinery they mean to employ. And until I've done that, I can't do as you wish. Really I can't.'

Finishing her drink, she stood up. 'All right, then, since you insist on being pig-headed. But you'll have only yourself to blame if that man Barak sticks a knife into you, or something frightful. I'm going up to bed.'

Overnight, Robbie's mind had been so full of his adventure that he had given little thought to its physical consequences, but in the morning they were brought home to him in no uncertain manner. His fall, although broken by Stoll's body, and the many blows he had received on his own, resulted in his waking stiff and aching. As he turned from side to side in bed, the pain from his bruises caused him to take fresh stock of the situation. Those pains, he reflected, might easily have been instead the real agony of broken bones and torn ligaments. There was much to be said for Stephanie's gloomy forebodings that, if he courted the further attentions of the Czechs, they might be luckier next time and give him real cause to regret it. Moreover, her view that Barak would seek revenge for his smashed-in face could not be lightly disregarded.

Barak might be out of the game temporarily, but it was certain that he would regard his English bugbear as still in it; so it seemed highly probable that he would send a detailed description of Robbie to all his groups, with orders to watch out for him. That meant that a certain degree of risk would now be entailed by snooping in the vicinity of any of them.

The very fact that the Czechs had reacted so forcibly to Robbie's initial snooping could be taken as definite confirmation that they were not, against all probability, prospecting for oil, but had some nefarious design to hide. Realizing that, nothing could now have dissuaded Robbie from continuing his investigations. But the more he thought of the matter, the more convinced he became that his future activities ought to be conducted with extreme caution.

It occurred to him then that he might fox the enemy by giving them the impression that he had come out of last night's encounters far worse than he had; and by going to earth for a while lead them to suppose that he had thrown in his hand.

This idea greatly tickled his sense of humour and, again temporarily forgetting his bruises, he spent the time until the chambermaid brought his breakfast planning this new move. When the woman arrived with his tray, he told her that the previous night he had had a bit too much to drink and had become involved in a quarrel in which he had got the worst of it. He then asked her to send out for some healing ointment, bandages, a packet of large safety pins and a stout walking stick, and to take a note from him down to Miss Stephanopoulos. In the note he had written in English the single line: *Don't show surprise at my appearance.*

Three-quarters of an hour later the chambermaid came to

collect his tray, and brought him the things for which he had asked. Getting up, he went along the corridor and had a bath, but he did not shave; and in the mirror he was pleased to see that the blow which he had received on the cheek had coloured up into a fine red bruise with a purple edge near the outer corner of his left eye. Returning to his room, he treated his bruises with the ointment then, with some difficulty, bandaged his head, but left the bruise on his cheek exposed. After packing his suitcase, he made another bandage into a sling for his left arm and, taking the stout stick, hobbled downstairs.

Stephanie, with her suitcase beside her, was waiting for him in the narrow hall. At the sight of his unshaven face and bandaged head, her dark eyebrows lifted and her mouth opened slightly. But she swiftly controlled her features, stood up and asked him how he was feeling.

'Not too good,' he replied. 'I behaved very stupidly last night, and I've had enough of it.' Then he hobbled over to the desk behind which the manageress was sitting, paid the bill and said: 'If any letters should come for me, please direct them care of the British Embassy, Athens.' Five minutes later their bags had been carried out to the car and Stephanie was driving it out of the garage yard.

'What is all this?' she asked with sharp displeasure. 'If you meant to play some trick why couldn't you have told me? And what road am I to take? Do you really mean that we should go back to Athens?'

He gave a low chuckle. 'This is an idea I had this morning for fooling the enemy. Turn into the main road, King Constantine Avenue, and keep going over the level crossings. It's pretty certain that Barak will send his pals to enquire at the hotel about us. I'm hoping that he'll assume from what the manageress tells them that I've thrown in my hand and have gone back to Athens. But you were right last night that they will be on the look-out for me, so I've decided that our best plan will be to lie doggo for a while. If I don't show up for a week or so they'll probably think that they have got rid of me for good. Then, when their suspicions have been lulled, I intend to have another crack at them. In the meantime, I think it would be a good idea for us to go down to Navplion. We'll be hundreds of miles from any of the places where they are putting groups to work, and within easy reach of the ruins of Mycenae and Tiryns which are probably the most interesting anywhere in Greece.'

'Thank goodness you've shown some sense,' she replied. 'But get out the map and tell me which way to go.'

After studying the map for a few moments, he said: 'It's not far: only about sixty kilometres. Most of it is through the mountains, but even so, it shouldn't be much more than an hour and a half's run. About half-way we'll pass through the village of Nemea. It was round about there that Hercules performed his first labour of slaying the terrible Nemean Lion. Mycenae lies on the foothills at the far side of the pass, then we'll come down into the plain of Argos.'

As soon as they were outside the town, he got rid of his arm sling and removed the bandage from round his head, then settled down to enjoy the drive. For some miles they climbed steadily along the twisting way between the two-thousand-foot-high crests of the Onia and Palukoraki mountains, then round bend after bend along a road cut out of the steep hillsides, until at about eleven o'clock they emerged, still several hundred feet above sea level, to see a marvellous prospect below them. It was the fertile plain of Argos, and beyond it the forty-mile-long gulf surrounded, for all but a tenth of its circumference, by mountains.

Robbie leaned forward eagerly and exclaimed: 'Look, look! For years I've longed to set eyes on this. In all history there is no more romantic spot. It was from the bay below us that the Argonauts set sail to seize the Golden Fleece.' Pointing to their left front, he went on: 'And down there on that hillock is Mycenae. It was there, a few years later, after Helen had run away with Paris, that Agamemnon vowed he would get her back and organized a muster of the thousand ships that carried the Greeks to the siege of Troy.'

With an indulgent smile, Stephanie remarked: 'I suppose it is the world's greatest romance. There certainly is no other story in which a whole country went to war for ten years to get back a runaway wife. But, after all, we've only Homer's account of it, so I don't suppose it really happened.'

'How can you think that?' Robbie stared at her in amazement. 'Of course, all the bits Homer put in about the gods and
goddesses having taken sides and helped or hindered the
Heroes is poetic licence. But the siege of Troy is an historic
fact. Schliemann proved that beyond question.'

'Schliemann?' she repeated doubtfully.

'Yes; surely you've heard of him?'

'Was he the German archaeologist who discovered
Mycenae?'

'That's right. He was a most extraordinary chap, and his
own story was the all-time-high of poor boy making good.
From his earliest childhood, he was fascinated by stories of
the ancient Greeks; but for years he had to work on a pittance
as a grocer's errand boy, a cabin boy and a junior clerk. At
night, though, by candle-light in an attic, he taught himself
half a dozen languages. At last, he got a job with the great bank-
ing firm of Schröder and they recognized his abilities. They
sent him to St. Petersburg as their representative, and while
there he managed to save enough to set up in business on his
own as an indigo merchant. From then on, everything he
touched turned to gold. As a contractor, he made a fortune
out of the Crimean War; then he went to America, got in on
the Californian gold rush and made another fortune. After
travelling the world for a while, he came to Greece and in the
seventies settled down to his life-long ambition of becoming an
archaeologist. He had been disappointed in his early love, so
he had never married. However, by then he was getting on for
fifty, and he decided he would like to marry; so he wrote to his
friend the Archbishop of Athens and asked him to find him a
suitable wife.'

'What an extraordinary thing to do.'

'Yes. Still, it turned out all right. She was only eighteen and
a lovely girl, but she became devoted to him and was an enormous help in all his undertakings. His first great success was
the rediscovery of Troy. As you must know, it is on the other
side of the Aegean, in Turkey, not far from the Asiatic side of
the Dardanelles; but he disagreed with the professional archaeologists about the actual site. He received a concession from
the Turks to dig and put scores of men to work for months,

driving a great trench right through a lofty hill. They found the remains of nine cities buried one on top of another, and it turned out that Homer's Troy was the third one down. It was later definitely identified by the remains of great gates and palaces that Homer had described. But Schliemann couldn't find any treasure and everyone was still saying that he was wasting his time, so he decided to throw in his hand. Then, on the very last day, his luck turned. Near what was called the Scaean Gate, he came upon a gold pin; so he sent all his workmen away and that night he and his wife went back there. They unearthed a marvellous treasure—diadems, bracelets, necklaces and over eight thousand rings, all of solid gold.'

'Eight thousand!'

'Yes. But he was in a spot, because to get his concession to dig he had agreed to hand over to the Turkish Government the bulk of any treasure he found. The stuff he had found was absolutely priceless; and it wasn't that he needed the money, but he felt sure that the Turks would melt it down just for its value in gold. As luck would have it, in those days women wore enormous skirts; so his wife was able to smuggle the whole lot out of Turkey and back to Greece under her petticoats.'

'When the Turks heard about that they must have been furious.'

'They were. They brought a case against him, and imposed a heavy fine. But he sent them five times the amount of the fine, in order to win back their goodwill; so they allowed him to return to Troy the next year and continue his digging. In the meantime, though, while the law-suit was going on, he had started to excavate Mycenae.'

Stephanie glanced towards their left where, about two miles away, a lofty foothill rose, commanding the entrance to the valley from which they had just emerged. Upon its crest, some ruins could be seen and further down the slope below it several tourist coaches were parked. 'And that,' she murmured, 'is Mycenae.'

'That's it,' he agreed, 'and I'm longing to see it. But the horde of tourists now being conducted round it would spoil it for us. We'll be staying at Navplion for several days, anyway; so we'll drive out early one morning, then we'll have the place to ourselves.' After a moment, he added: 'Still, we might stop for a bit to take in this wonderful view. Let's drive up to the Tourist Pavilion and have a drink there.'

Stephanie turned left into a side road, and a few minutes later they were enjoying big tumblers of iced fresh orange juice on the Pavilion's stoop. For a while they sat in silence, looking out at the blue, sunlit gulf embraced by its long chains of green and brown mountains etched against the pale azure sky; then she said:

'I think Schliemann's story is fascinating. What did he do with his treasure after he had saved it from the Turks?'

Robbie raised his eyebrows. 'Why, he gave it to the museum in Athens. Surely you must have seen it there?'

'Yes, I suppose I have. But there are such cases and cases of gold ornaments and, knowing nothing about archaeology, I'm afraid I didn't take in which came from where. I remember those lovely gold drinking cups, though, and all those flat gold masks with such curious features. Did they come from Troy?'

'No, they came from here. Excavating Mycenae was Schliemann's greatest triumph. He hit on the Royal burial ground and opened up five or six shaft graves. They contained sixteen corpses and he claimed that one of them was actually that of Agamemnon. Of course, there was nothing to prove it, and it is now believed that they were of people who had lived about three hundred years before the siege of Troy. But out of the graves he got an immense treasure of gold, silver, ivory and precious stones; in fact, by far the greatest treasure that has ever been discovered anywhere in the world. And the ornamentation on these things showed that, in some ways, the artists of the Mycenaean age were superior to those of Athens.'

'A change of fashion could account for that,' Stephanie suggested. 'People always tend to despise the sort of furniture and art their grandparents admired.'

For the third time that morning Robbie stared at her in amazement, then he said: 'But the two civilizations were entirely different. There was a gap of at least four hundred years between the end of one and the beginning of the other. Surely you knew that?'

She frowned and gave a little shrug. 'No. Why should I? When I took on the job of being your secretary, I made no claim to being an authority on ancient history.'

'Of course not. But you are a Greek and every Greek I've met so far is incredibly proud of the achievements of his ancestors, so he——'

'And so am I,' she broke in swiftly. 'But somehow, Robbie, I don't think you have known many Greek girls. And girls of any nationality are much more interested in living people than what happened in the past.'

'Then . . . then,' his face showed sudden distress, 'I must have been boring you terribly.'

'No, no; I didn't mean that. You are a living person and I'm interested in you. Besides, anyone who talks about a subject that fills him with enthusiasm makes it interesting. Only it's silly to be surprised that I don't remember everything I learnt at school. Who does? Naturally, when you tell me these stories, lots of them come back to me; but it's years since I've given a thought to the gods and Heroes and what went on thousands of years ago.'

'I see. Yes. I ought to have realized that.'

'I don't see why you should. Lots of Greek girls probably know nearly as much about these things as you do. It just happens that I have been interested in other subjects. But that doesn't prevent my enjoying hearing from you now about the ancients.'

'Do you really mean that?'

'Of course I do. Counting out the dragons and fire-breathing serpents, you make the Immortals sound wonderfully like real people; and I do want to help you with your book. Tell me now why the civilization here at Mycenae was so different from that of Athens.'

'Well, that means going back to Crete. Before Schliemann's discoveries and those of Sir Arthur Evans, it was thought that no civilization at all had arisen in this part of the Mediterranean until the Athenians started theirs about seven or eight hundred B.C. But actually, round about three thousand B.C. the Minoans in Crete were as far advanced as Egypt and Assyria. After some hundreds of years a series of great earthquakes set them back for a long time, but about two thousand B.C. the Minoans got their second wind. They became a great naval power, with an empire extending all over the north-eastern Med. from which they drew tribute.

'Mycenae must have been one of their principal colonies, as from sixteen hundred B.C. a great civilization began to flourish here, too, with very similar art and culture. Some two hundred years later, another series of earthquakes seems to have knocked out the Minoans altogether, and the Mycenaeans took over. Anyhow, round about twelve hundred B.C. this was the capital of an empire that is believed to have extended all over Greece, Crete, Rhodes, Cyprus, and traded as far west as Sicily. That is why Agamemnon was able to get together such a great Armada and a hundred thousand troops for the siege of Troy.

'But shortly after the Trojan War, a terrible calamity overtook all the cities in the eastern Med. It was one of the great movements of barbarians from the east, like that of Atilla's Huns and Genghis Khan's hordes hundreds of years later. A race called the Dorians came down from the north and looted, burned and murdered wherever they went. The Mycenaean civilization was entirely wiped out; so was that of the Hittites in Cappadocia, and Greece and Asia Minor were plunged right back into a Dark Age.

'This Dark Age went on for four hundred years, then the Hellenes gradually began to evolve a new civilization right from the beginning. It blossomed in the fifth and fourth centuries B.C. into the great age of Pericles and the philosophers, but it owed nothing to what had gone before. The extraordinary thing is that the Athenians did not even know about the Empires of the Mycenaeans and the Minoans that had preceded them, and looked on the ruins they had left behind as the buildings of a prehistoric race of giants. In fact, nobody knew about these ancient Empires until less than one hundred years ago, when Schliemann rediscovered Troy, Mycenae and Tiryns; and it wasn't until the beginning of this century that Sir Arthur Evans revealed to the world that Crete had been a powerful and cultured nation as long before Athens flourished as we are now from the birth of Christ.

'So you see, until comparatively recently, everyone believed that the works of Homer were only fairy tales, and that Heroditus's history was mainly imagination. But every year, now, with the deciphering of tablets that are being dug up, they are coming more and more into their own as the chroniclers of real events. The accounts of the gods and heroes were passed on from generation to generation by word of mouth, of course, so the bards embellished them with every sort of exaggeration and fantasy; but there can no longer be any doubt that long ago these characters were living chieftains and champions.

'As sure as we are sitting here, about three thousand two hundred years ago one of the most beautiful women the world has ever known did elope with her handsome, unscrupulous lover, and it was from down in the bay there that Agamemnon sailed to take command of the hundred thousand men, the majority of whom died before the walls of Troy in the ten years' war that was waged simply to bring her back to Greece.'

Stephanie smiled at him. 'How could you think, Robbie, that I don't enjoy listening to you when you find your tongue like that and make things sound so glamorous?'

A few minutes later they were on their way again, down into the plain. The road now ran between orchards of orange and lemon trees, and fields of ancient olive trees, or planted with ripening corn. Passing through the dusty, ramshackle town of Argos, they saw no signs of its ancient glory; but a few miles further on the road ran within a few hundred yards of the great fortress palace of Tiryns, perched on a hill from which rose its cyclopean walls. By twelve o'clock they were entering the pleasant little town of Navplion. Driving right through it, they pulled up at the Hotel Amphitryon.

The hotel had been built only a few years before, and was very different from that in which they had stayed in Corinth. It was constructed so that all its rooms faced the sea, and in its central block it had an eighty-foot-long lounge, the whole of the outer wall of which was of glass, giving a splendid panoramic view over the bay. All the first-floor bedrooms opened on to a wide terrace, furnished with garden furniture, so that visitors could have their breakfast out in the sunshine in dressing gowns or bathing things before going down to the swimming pool that lay across the road between the hotel and the beach.

After lunch they rested for a while, then Stephanie took Robbie out for another driving lesson on the flat stretch of road that curved round the segment of the bay between Navplion and Tiryns. There was little traffic but, when a lorry or a coach did pass them, it churned up clouds of dust, so they were glad of a bath before dinner. They had been given adjacent rooms, and when Stephanie had had her bath she called to Robbie to come out on the terrace to see the sunset. Each room enjoyed a strip of terrace divided from its neighbour by a low, wire fence. Separated only by this, they walked side by side to the far rail.

From Navplion, which is situated on the inner side of a cape, the narrow outlet of the gulf to the sea cannot be seen; so from where they stood, facing west, it looked like a great, placid lake ringed by mountains. The air was so clear that, although the range beyond the opposite shore lay many miles away, it gave the illusion that it was almost within pistol shot. Immediately in front of them, and about three-quarters of a mile distant, there rose from the waters of the gulf a small island. The whole of it was occupied by a little castle, with sheer walls rising from the rocks and a central tower. It added a touch of romance to the scene.

Stephanie had come out in a dressing gown and mules. As she stood now beside Robbie without her high heels, the top of her curls only just came up to his shoulder, and she seemed to him more desirable than ever. For ten minutes, they watched the salmon-and-gold glory of the sunset outlining the long range of peaks as though beyond them the whole country was on fire. Slipping her arm through his, she said:

'Oh, Robbie, if only you would give up this dangerous business of yours, and if this were not just an interlude, how happy we could be here.'

For a moment he was almost tempted to say that he would. But the shadows were falling, and somewhere up in the cliff that rose steeply behind the hotel an owl hooted. The owl was Athene's bird, and sacred to her. Its cry was both a warning and a reminder of his pledge.

The past week that he had spent with Stephanie had made him into a different man from the lonely young fellow so lacking in self-confidence who had given that pledge. Now, he would have given a great deal never to have stood on the Acropolis asking Athene's guidance. But he had, and he knew that he would never again have a quiet mind unless he obeyed her injunction to go through with his self-imposed mission.

17

Of Troy and a Submarine

ALTHOUGH the hoot of Athene's owl had prevented Robbie from wavering in his resolution, he did his utmost during the next few days to put from him all thoughts of the Czechs and the mystery of their tobacco-oil deal. On their first morning in Navplion, he and Stephanie took things easy. First they explored the little town and, although it was early in the year for bathing, bought swimsuits. Then they walked back beyond the hotel and along the narrow track that ran round the promontory. On its far side they came upon a path that separated the headland from a far higher cliff on the top of which was perched the ancient Acropolis and, by scrambling along it, got back to the town.

Late that afternoon, they drove the few kilometres to Tiryns. The usual coachloads of tourists had gone, so they had it almost to themselves and spent an hour rambling about its ruins. In ancient days the sea had come up to the walls and it had been the port of Mycenae, but now the shore lay nearly two miles distant. The most impressive thing about it was the enormous size of the stones with which the walls were built. There were thousands of them, and many weighed eight to ten tons; so the labour entailed in dragging them up the hill, then lifting them, without mechanical aid, to fit neatly in layer after layer on one another, must have been immense. It was no wonder that the Greeks of the classic age, knowing nothing of the Mycenaean civilization, called such walls 'cyclopean' and believed that they had been built by a race of giants.

Next morning, as the swimming pool had not yet been filled, they braved the sea. Swimming was one of the few things that Nanny Fisher had taught Robbie. She had rightly believed that it would improve the reactions of his muscles, so she had taken him regularly to the baths in Cheltenham, and now that he was fully grown he was a powerful swimmer. The water was on the chilly side, but there was no wind and, as they had left their dip until eleven o'clock, the sun was strong enough to warm them up within a few minutes of leaving the water. During the previous summer, Robbie had been too shy to speak to anyone when bathing on his own from one of the beaches near Athens, and only on three occasions had he been asked to go in a party; so to have a lovely girl for his sole companion was a new delight to him.

On the previous day, they had learned that the little castle on the rock out in the gulf was called Burzi and that, owing to the Greeks' hatred of state executioners, it had once been used as a retreat for those who had retired; but it was now an hotel. A motor-boat was always available to take visitors out there, so they decided to lunch at it. They found it an intriguing place, as the dome-roofed, white-walled bedrooms on the lower floor had, in the old days, been cells; but each had a window looking out on the sea, which gave them a resemblance to comfortable cabins in a stationary ship. The proprietor was his own chef, and cooked them an excellent meal of freshly caught red mullet.

That afternoon, Robbie decided to go up the great headland that rises in an almost perpendicular cliff behind Navplion to see the remains of the fort that, in ancient times and in later times when the Venetians held that part of Greece, guarded the entrance to the gulf. It was seven hundred feet high, and could be reached only by a flight of eight hundred and fifty-seven steps and several tunnels cut in the face of the rock; so Stephanie smilingly declined to accompany him. As they were going to Mycenae the following day she said that, while he was puffing and blowing his way to the summit, he could think of her sitting in a comfortable chair in the lounge reading his chapter on the Trojan War. Half an hour later she started it, and it read as follows:

People blame Helen for the Trojan War but that isn't fair, because it was really Zeus who started the whole trouble by refusing to give a judgment and foisting his job off on to a mortal.

Among the Heroes who sailed to get the Golden Fleece there was a chap named Peleus. Owing to a slight misunderstanding about who had been to bed with whom, his first wife had hanged herself and he was looking for another. His eye fell on a Naiad named Thetis; and she must have been quite a girl, as both Zeus and Poseidon had wanted to marry her. But both had hauled off pretty quickly, because Aunty Themis gave them the lowdown that she would produce a son far more powerful than her husband. In view of this, Zeus decided to put a stiff handicap on her by palming her off on to a mortal; so when Peleus came along, the Father of the Gods said: 'O.K., boy. You can have her.'

Thetis was far from pleased, as she considered herself much too good for a mere King of Thessaly, and she tried all sorts of dodges to get out of this mésalliance. But, as Zeus was backing Peleus, they didn't work. King Peleus was asked up to Olympus and the couple were given a splendid wedding.

However, the social secretary up there blotted it pretty badly by forgetting to send an invitation to the goddess Eris. She was a very unpleasant type and, as her special province was presiding over Strife, she soon thought up a plan for teaching the other Immortals not to ignore her. Arriving unannounced at the party, she threw a golden apple into the midst of those present with a tag on it that read: 'Here's a prize for the best-looking goddess among you.'

The stately Queen of Heaven smiled and said: 'How kind of Eris to make me such a lovely gift.' Athene of the classic features snapped: 'Be your age, Hera, she obviously meant it for me.' Aphrodite simply gave a little wriggle of her hips and said: 'Don't be silly, girls. Ask any of the chaps here and he'll tell you who that golden apple is for.'

By then the gentle reader may bet that Zeus was tiptoeing

away towards the bar. But they called him back and demanded that he judge between them. He shook his head and said: 'Nothing doing. I've trouble enough without setting two of you by the ears. Only last week I had to tie a couple of anvils to Hera's feet to prevent her following me when I was just popping down to earth to see how an old friend's wife was getting along; so she doesn't deserve such a pretty toy. And if I awarded it to either of you others, she would make my life hell for the next six months.'

'All right, then,' they said. 'You must appoint someone to judge for you.'

It was this that triggered off the whole awful business. Zeus probably had a date with one of Thetis's bridesmaids behind the nearest peak. Anyhow, he wanted to be done with the matter quickly; so, without much thought, he said: 'On Mount Ida you will find a handsome young herdsman named Paris. He is just the age to have no doubts about "what it takes" most among women. Go and ask him.'

At that, the three goddesses took off like Sabre Jets for Mount Ida. But now I must tell you something about this chap Paris.

The Trojan race sprang from Dardanus and the daughter of a shepherd King named Teucer. Their great-grandson was Ilus, and he built the city of Ilion, which was another name for Troy and of the 'topless towers' of which my gentle reader must have heard. His son, Laomedon, was a heel. After Poseidon and Apollo had helped Hera to try to put Zeus in the bin and they had bungled the job, both of them had been condemned to put in a spell of servitude on earth. Poseidon got himself taken on by Laomedon as a builder, and it was he who built the impregnable walls of Troy. But when he had done, Laomedon refused him his promised reward.

Poseidon never forgave the Trojans and soon inflicted pain and grief on them. The upshot of this was that Laomedon's daughter, Hesione, had to be put on the slab and offered up as an appeasing sacrifice. She was rescued in the nick of time by Hercules; but Laomedon did him down, too, so a few years later Hercules returned, did in the King and gave Hesione as a birthday present to one of his pals. However, she managed to wheedle Hercules into sparing her favourite brother, Priam, and letting him succeed his father as King of Troy.

Priam and his Queen, Hecuba, had lots of children, the noblest among them being Hector and the handsomest Paris. But before she had Paris, Hecuba dreamed that she would give birth to a fire-brand. The soothsayer who was called in said that meant the child she was about to have would put paid to Troy; so the usual drill was followed. A slave was sent off with the newborn babe to leave it to die up on the mountain. But, of course, it didn't. These Kings never did swipe the kitty when playing games of one-upmanship against the Fates.

In the case of Paris, it was a lady bear who came along and suckled him, until he was found by some herdsmen and brought up by them. He made quite a name for himself, pinning back the ears of cattle thieves, and got hitched up to Oenone, the highly desirable nymph of the mountain; so he might have continued to live a quiet and very happy life, if only the Immortals had left him alone.

But no. One fine day, Hermes came zooming down out of the bright blue sky with the three goddesses in tow. Handing the golden apple to the flabbergasted Paris, he said: 'Look, feller, the Big Chief sent me to give you this, and tell you to pass it on to whichever of these—er—ladies that you think would make the best selling picture on the cover of a glossy magazine,' or words to that effect.

Of course, all three of the claimants simpered at him like mad. Then they introduced themselves and each of them tried to bribe him. Hera said: 'I am the Queen of Heaven. Give me the apple and I'll make you a great King with lots and lots of lolly.' Athene said: 'Fame brings more happiness than money. Give the apple to me, and you shall be acclaimed the wisest guy on earth.' Aphrodite said nothing. She just took off her clothes.

Paris shut his eyes, swallowed hard, then looked again. Handing Aphrodite the apple, he said: 'The fruit's yours, ma'am.'

She dished him out one of her sweetest smiles and said: 'You're a nice lad and if these other—er—ladies weren't present I'd have found it a pleasure to—er—help you with your education. But not to worry. I'll fix things so that the most beautiful girl in the world will fall in love with you, and you can have her for keeps.' Then the four Immortals all winged it back to Olympus.

As the reader will, I am sure, agree, such an experience would prove somewhat unsettling for any young man. For some days Oenone must have wondered what had got into her handsome husband. Then he put on his best goatskin coat and, for the first time in his life, went down to the city.

It happened that his papa was about to hold some public games. Naturally he went in for them and, naturally, he won all the prizes. This created quite a stir, and one of his sisters, named Cassandra, went up and had a word with him. This wench had the gift of second sight, and at once declared him to be the infant sent out to die on Mount Ida. King Priam and his Queen were so delighted to find that they had such a splendid son that they seem to have forgotten all about the prophecy that he would prove the ruin of Troy. Paris was naturally as pleased as Punch to learn that he was really a royal Prince, and took to the life like a duck to water.

The thoughtful reader will not have forgotten that, when Hercules had given King Laomedon the works, he had more or less white-slaved Priam's sister Hesione. Somewhat belatedly, Priam appears to have remembered her. As Paris had, in no time, made the grade as a general in the Trojan Army, his papa mustered a great fleet and sent him off to Greece to rescue his aunt.

Unfortunately for all concerned, instead of getting on with the job he had been given Paris turned aside to say 'hello' to Menelaus, the King of Sparta. Helen was the King's wife and, as Aphrodite thought her the most beautiful girl in the world, the moment her husband introduced Paris to her the fat was in the fire.

That Helen really was a sort of mortal edition of Aphrodite there can't be much doubt. Of course, she had very exceptional parents. As most people know, Zeus thought Leda so beautiful that to have a few minutes' conversation with her he turned himself into a swan. That night she had the same sort of conversation with her husband, King Tyndareus, and all this chat resulted in her giving birth to two babies and two eggs. The babies were Castor and Clytemnestra, and out of the eggs came Pollux and Helen.

But quite apart from Helen being out of the very top drawer, she was already such a poppet when only ten years old that the hero Theseus could not resist the temptation to abduct her from her parents. Her brothers, Castor and Pollux, hurried after him and got her back, but naturally this titbit of gossip went all round Greece. The result was that chaps from all over the place came to Tyndareus's palace out of curiosity, just to take a look at this budding Venus. The moment they set eyes on her, they all agreed that they could think of far better ways for her to spend her time than studying to pass her Eleven-Plus.

In fact, so many princes went absolutely potty over her that her step-father, old Tyndareus, saw that, unless he did something about it, she was going to be the cause of a whole packet of trouble. He did his best to solve the problem by getting all these young Lotharios together and saying to them:

'Listen, boys. I want my little Helen to have a happy marriage and enjoy her life; but she won't stand an earthly as long as you are set on cutting one another's throats to get her. Whoever I give her to will find a ticket for Hades under his pillow before the honeymoon is over, and before he is a fortnight older the chap who carries her off will be done in by another of you. To be hauled willy-nilly into a whole succession of beds is no life for a girl. What is more, the papas of those of you who get bumped off are certain to take it badly; so, before we know where we are, there will be half a dozen wars ravaging Greece to avenge the "goners".

'Now, to prevent such a slaughter, what I suggest is that when I have decided to which of you I will give Helen, the rest of you should take a solemn oath not only to refrain from any attempt to take her away from the lucky guy but also, should anyone do so, to combine in a war against him until you have got her back for her husband.'

The Princes saw the sense in this; so when Menelaus was chosen as the lucky lad, they all swore to get together and come down like a ton of bricks on any Dirty Dick who tried to take Helen from him. That is why, when she ran away with Paris, pretty well every warrior in Greece started yelling for his field-boots and feathered hat and went chasing after them.

But I've got a bit ahead of my story. When Paris stopped off at Sparta, Menelaus put out the red carpet for him and for a week or two a good time was had by all. Then, as Paris showed no sign of packing his grip and Menelaus had a job to do up-country, he rashly left his wife to entertain their guest. By this time they were batty about one another, so Paris found no reason at all to complain to the management. Since Aphrodite had decreed that Helen should fall for Paris, I don't feel that she was to blame; but he behaved like a most frightful cad. When Menelaus got home, he found that not only had his guest run away with his wife but that he and his Trojans had looted the palace and made off with the whole vast treasure of Sparta.

Menelaus's elder brother was Agamemnon, King of Argos, and he had married Helen's half-sister, Clytemnestra. Moreover, Agamemnon was then top King in Greece and all the others owed allegiance to him. So Menelaus jumped into his fastest chariot and drove hell for leather to Mycenae where he told his tale of woe to Big Brother.

Agamemnon promptly called on all the chaps who had wanted to marry Helen to fulfil their oath, and in addition on all his vassals to bring ships and men to show Paris where he got off. The majority of them—including the giant Ajax, wise old Nestor and brave Diomede—came fairly spoiling for the fray, but two of the best bets in a free-for-all tried to wriggle out.

Odysseus, King of the island of Ithaca, was a most cunning man. Feeling a preference for remaining with his wife, Penelope, and his infant son, Telemachus, rather than join in a war that he thought might prove a long one, he pretended to be mad. However, his bluff was called by a chap named Palamedes, who had been sent to fetch him; so he had to go along.

Once Odysseus had joined the outfit, he proved invaluable. It was he who roped in the other shirker, Achilles. The gentle reader will recall the prophecy that stalled off Zeus and Poseidon from marrying the goddess Thetis—that she would bear a son greater than his father. She did, to the mortal Peleus; and it was Achilles she had by him. Knowing that the Trojan War would be a bloody business, she concealed her son in girl's clothes among the daughters of the King of Scyros. But Odysseus paid them a visit and showed them a really natty line in swords and javelins. Achilles, being a born fighter, seized on them with enthusiasm, so gave his sex away. But his goddess-mama had taken the precaution to dip him in the Styx, which made him invulnerable to any wound, except in the one heel by which she had had to hang on to him.

It was from Mycenae that all these heralds went galloping off, and it was there that the plans were made for a great Armada to sail to Troy; but Agamemnon still hoped that they might get back Helen without a war; so he sent a diplomatic mission, consisting of Odysseus, Palamedes and Menelaus, to say to King Priam: 'Look, your son Paris has put up a shocking black, but we don't want trouble, so if he'll cough up the loot and return the lovely, we won't ask any compensation for his having borrowed her,' or words to that effect.

But their account of Paris's goings-on left his old pop speechless, because Paris hadn't even sent him a postcard. He and Helen were still having a high old time on a year-long honeymoon round the eastern Med., renting the biggest villas wherever they stopped off and entertaining the locals to champagne and caviare on the cash that they'd pinched from the Sparta treasury. Knowing nothing of this, Priam told the Ambassadors that he must wait till his boy got home to hear his side of the story; so they returned to Greece empty-handed.

When Paris did get back, there was no end of a rumpus. Lots of the Trojan big-wigs said he could go and boil his head if he thought they were going to war just so that he could keep his girl friend. But Helen had brought along a handpicked beauty chorus to brush her hair and help her into her two-way stretch. This bunch of cuties got busy playing cat's cradle with the top brass of the Trojan Army, and Paris, still being lousy with Menelaus's money, paid off the mortgages on their houses for them and that sort of thing; so, what with the cash and the cuties, these chaps were all for Helen staying put.

Cassandra came into the picture with one of her doleful

prophecies that, if Helen were not put on the doorstep, Troy
would be destroyed. However, Apollo had a 'thing' against
Cassandra, so he had ordained that nothing she predicted
would ever be believed. Finally, Paris's mum, Hecuba, had a
heart-to-heart with Helen and asked her had Paris taken her
by force? She said: 'No, I was batty about him and I still am.'
So, as Paris was Hecuba's favourite son, she persuaded Priam
to defy the Greeks.

The war being on, Agamemnon sailed from the Gulf of
Argos and ordered all the other ships to rendezvous with him
at Aulis, the most handy port in western Greece for an assault
on Asia Minor. Getting them together took months and
months, so he killed time by going ashore and doing a bit of
hunting. Unfortunately, just before D-Day, he killed a hind
sacred to Artemis. She was so put out that she decreed a calm
that prevented the Armada from sailing. After the calm had
lasted for some weeks, everyone got very fed up, so they consulted a seer named Calchas. He said there would be no wind
until Agamemnon had pacified the angry goddess by sacrificing his eldest daughter, Iphigenia, to her.

Agamemnon was naturally against this idea, but all the
others said he must not let a little thing like the life of one girl
stand in the way of their great enterprise, etc., so eventually
they nagged him into writing to his wife, Clytemnestra, to bring
Iphigenia down from Mycenae to Aulis. But, in his letter, he
gave as his reason that he'd fixed up for her to marry Achilles.

Delighted at the thought of this fine match for her girl,
Clytemnestra duly arrived and got busy on the trousseau. When
she learned the truth, there was hell to pay. Then Achilles
found out that he had been used as a lure for this horrid business and he, too, blew his top. What is more, the moment he
set eyes on Iphigenia he fell for her in a big way, and threatened
to let the daylight into anyone who laid a hand on her.

But Iphigenia turned out to be the whitest girl they ever
knew. She said she was quite willing to die for the honour of
Greece; so they tied Achilles up, put her on the slab and prepared to cut her throat. Seeing that she had put up such a jolly
good show, Artemis's heart was touched. She whisked the girl
off up into the clouds and dumped a faun on the altar to be

sacrificed instead. That stopped everyone wailing except Clytemnestra, who was livid at having her daughter taken from her. But a fine wind sprang up, so she was left screaming curses while all the chaps ran to their ships, shouting to the girls: 'We'll be back by Christmas,' and off they sailed for Troy.

The landing was made between the rivers Simois and Scamander. There the Greeks hauled all their thousand ships up the beach and used them to form streets, squares and wooden walls, enclosing a vast camp for their hundred thousand men. But, of course, the Trojans had had loads of time to prepare a hot reception for them. Paris's brother, Hector, had been made C.-in-C., and as his Second in Command he had his brother-in-law, Aeneas, the Prince of the Dardanians. This Aeneas was no mean ally, as he was the result of one of Aphrodite's nights out down on earth, and when Priam asked for his help he brought a large army to the support of Troy.

The Heroes on both sides could hardly wait to get at one another, so out came the chariots, the archers, the javelin throwers and the rest, and before long the whole place was littered with corpses. But neither side could get the better of the other; so the battle was renewed week after week, month after month, with truces now and again only for them to lick their wounds and make a bonfire of the dead.

One would have thought that after a while they would have got bored with this senseless slaughter. But not a bit of it. For years on end, they shouted rude things about their enemies' mothers, got blipped on the head for their pains or stuck the other fellow in the gizzard. The Greeks had a much bigger army, but the Trojans had the advantage of the impregnable walls that Poseidon had built round their city. When they felt like a battle they could sally out, and whenever things got too hot for them they could scamper back inside and cock a snook at the Greeks from their battlements.

As both armies had to be fed, the war spread for miles over the countryside between parties sent out to get supplies, and one of the raids made by the Greeks led to the father of all upsets. With the plunder they brought in some girls. One very pretty one, named Chryseis, was the daughter of a priest of Apollo. Agamemnon liked the look of her, so he sent her to his tent and said: 'See you later, ducks.' Another nice little number, named Briseis, he gave to Achilles. Then up came Chryseis's papa and offered to ransom her. Agamemnon said nothing doing; so the priest called on Apollo for help, and the god sent a plague from which the Greeks started to die off like flies. After nine days they were in a fine dither and they consulted old Calchas, their seer. He told them: 'The plague won't let up until the Big Shot returns Chryseis to her clergyman father.'

Evidently this young woman had a lot of what it takes, for Agamemnon was very loath to give her up. As all the others were anxious to die by sword thrusts and not by germs, they eventually badgered him into agreeing; but he was mean enough to stipulate that Achilles must give up Briseis to him to fill Chryseis's place.

Now Achilles had found Briseis the absolute tops at darning his socks—or something—so he became positively berserk with rage. He was just about to yank out his sword and nail the King to his own tent pole when Athene appeared and lugged him back by the hair, although it seems that the others present didn't see her. I should explain here that the Greeks had taken an oath not to cut their hair until they got Helen back, so he had plenty of hair for her to hang on to. She whispered to him: 'Steady, lad. Hand Briseis over and I'll see you right in some other way'; so he did. But he said he would take no further part in the war. Then, with his very special pal Patroclus and his Myrmidons, as his host of followers were called, he went off to sulk in his tent.

However, that night he was so maddened by the thought that Briseis was now darning Agamemnon's socks—or doing whatever she had done when with him—that he appealed to his goddess-mama to persuade Zeus to show the Greeks how much they had lost by letting their scurvy King drive their best champion from their ranks.

Thetis said Zeus had just gone off on a hol. to preside at a twelve-day feast down in Ethiopia, but when he got back she would do her best. She did, by clasping him round the legs, and, being partial to cuddlesome females, he agreed to oblige. Afterwards he was a bit sorry, because Hera was so strongly pro-Greek that he felt sure she would make trouble for him if he openly helped the Trojans. Hoping to fox her he lay doggo, but sent Agamemnon a false dream to the effect that if he had another crack at Troy he would, at last, take the city.

Agamemnon then made a complete fool of himself. To test the will to victory of his men before sending them to attack, he assembled them and said: 'Look, chaps. We've had nine years of this, and I reckon that's about enough. How about throwing in the sponge and going home?' To his consternation, they all cried: 'Bully for you, Ag!' then cheered him to the echo and ran hell for leather to launch their rotting ships.

That would have been the end of the war had Hera not happened to be looking on. She had never forgiven Paris for giving the golden apple to Aphrodite and was determined that Troy should fall. Summoning Athene, she sent her down to undo the result of Agamemnon's idiotic blunder. With the help of Odysseus, the goddess changed the minds of the Greeks and soon afterwards they were all drawn up outside the city in battle array.

However, there was no battle that day because Paris came out and challenged any Greek to meet him in single combat. Menelaus fairly jumped at the chance, so a truce was called and it was agreed the war should be settled by this duel between Helen's two husbands. When actually faced with Menelaus's long-bottled-up fury, Paris got cold feet and backed away towards his pals, but they shouted nasty things like: 'Don't drop your lipstick' and 'You ought to be washing the baby's nappies,' and Hector gave him a kick in the pants; so he had to pluck up the courage to fight.

He bungled the first throw with his javelin, whereas Menelaus got home with his, splitting his enemy's breastplate. He then set about him with his sword, but it snapped off short. Undismayed, Menelaus ran in, seized him by the crest of his helmet and started to drag him off to the Greek end of the pitch. But Paris was saved by the gong, the gong in this case being Aphrodite. After all, he had given her the apple, so she caused his chinstrap to snap. The helmet came away in Menelaus's hand and he sat down with a bump on his backside. He was up again in a flash and chucked another javelin at Paris, but Aphrodite felt that it was not her champion's day; so she descended in a cloud, picked him up and dumped him on his bed in the palace.

Helen, of course, had been watching all this from the walls, and Paris having put up such a poor show made her feel that perhaps her legal husband was the better man after all. Still, she went along and bound up Paris's wounds, although one suspects that she may have put a drop more iodine on them than was strictly necessary.

The Greeks naturally went off to celebrate their victory and knocked off all the best bottles they had put by for such an occasion, while Menelaus told them again and again just what he would have done to Paris had not Aphrodite interfered. But while he was gradually becoming incoherent, a big pow-wow was taking place up on Olympus.

Zeus had called a Council of the Gods. He wanted to stop the war and said the time had now come when they should do it by making the Trojans hand over Helen to the Greeks. Most of the others agreed with him, but Hera dug in her toes. She was determined that Troy should fall; so she arranged that Pandarus, one of the Trojans' crack snipers, should put an arrow into Menelaus. It only wounded him but, of course, it broke the truce; so the war was on again.

A terrific battle then took place, with many of the Immortals lending a hand to those they favoured. Hera, Poseidon, Athene, Hermes and Hephaestus were for the Greeks; Apollo, Aphrodite, Ares and Artemis for the Trojans; while Zeus watched the conflict most unhappily and would have brought it to an end had he not feared the trouble Hera would make for him if he robbed her of her vengeance on Paris.

Athene healed Diomede of a mortal wound, so that he could hurl a stone twice his own weight that would have done in Aeneas; but Aphrodite screened the Trojan with her veil. Diomede was so peeved by this that he told the lovely goddess to her face that she was a whore, and threw a dart at her. Wounded by it, Aphrodite took off for Olympus and sobbed on Zeus's shoulder that she had never been so ill-treated in all her life. He patted her on the head and said: 'Sweetie, you were never meant to go to war. Just you forget it and find some strong-limbed young fellow to hop into bed with.'

Hera was too shrewd to get hurt herself. She took the form of Stentor, the Greek who could shout louder than any other, and stood in the background yelling: 'Go on, chaps! Give 'em hell. No quarter. Hit 'em for six and jump on their faces!' The brutal, stupid Ares did not come out of it at all well. Athene, wearing her helmet of invisibility, acted as Diomede's charioteer, and the Hero wounded the God of War so severely that he made off howling to Olympus.

On going back into the city to collect reinforcements, Hector felt pretty sick at finding Paris with his feet up nattering away to Helen. He gave his brother a piece of his mind and Helen backed him up; so Paris reluctantly put on his tin hat again and returned to the fray. Hector came out with him and challenged any of the Greeks to single combat. They drew lots and it fell to the giant Ajax to meet him. While everyone else looked on, they went for one another hammer and tongs, but darkness came down before either of them was seriously injured; so the duel was declared a draw.

Next day it became clear that the Trojans were on the up and up, so the Greek General Staff got to work on the C.-in-C. They told him that the only thing for it was for him to eat humble pie and persuade Achilles to lead the troops again. Finding himself right up against it, Agamemnon agreed, and one must give it to him that he did the generous thing. He sent three of his staff to offer Achilles not only Briseis back but also seven cuties to serve as side-lines, one of his own daughters in marriage when they got back to Greece and about his own weight in gold and ornaments. Achilles stood his visitors a jolly good blow-out but refused to budge.

When the news was received at G.H.Q. everyone was very down in the mouth, and next day the Greeks again got the worst of it in battle. They might have been scuppered for good had not the Immortals once more taken a hand. Hera pinched Aphrodite's girdle, knowing that no male could resist anyone who wore it. Then she sidled up to her husband. Somewhat later, Zeus felt so tired that he fell asleep and, as Hera had intended, missed what was happening down below. Poseidon, meanwhile, had taken the form of Calchas and had put new heart into the Greeks. The terrible Hector was temporarily knocked out, the Trojans took to their heels, and Poseidon, yelling: 'Up, Guards, and at 'em,' led the Greeks in pursuit. But Zeus woke up just in time, realized that Hera had made a monkey out of him, gave her a smack in the puss, ordered Poseidon back into the sea, then sent Apollo to revive Hector and restore the situation.

With Apollo's aid, the Trojans drove the Greeks right back to their ships and began to set fire to them. Achilles and his pal Patroclus were looking on from a distance, and at last Patroclus could bear the sight no longer. Achilles still refused to lift a finger, but he reluctantly agreed that Patroclus should lead out the Myrmidons, if only to prevent the ships, without which the Greeks could not get home, being burnt to cinders. Being much attached to Patroclus, Achilles lent him his own custom-made suit of armour and his Mark IX chariot to do the job in. In consequence, when Patroclus came charging out with the Myrmidons behind him, everyone thought he was Achilles.

At the sight of him the Trojans panicked and the Greeks chivvied them right up to the walls of the city. They might even have got in if Apollo hadn't given Patroclus a biff that half stunned him. Hector, being on hand, took advantage of this to slay the Greek and strip him of his armour. It was only after a desperate fight that the Greeks managed to rescue his body and carry it back to Achilles.

At the sight of his dead friend, Achilles nearly burst himself with grief and rage. He wept all night and even Briseis, whom Agamemnon had sent back to him, could not stop him crying. But his mama turned up and cheered him a trifle by telling him that she had got Hephaestus to make a new suit of absolutely super armour for him in which to avenge his buddy.

In the morning he put it on, went along to G.H.Q., buried the hatchet with Agamemnon and demanded instant battle. Led by him again the Greeks attacked and hour after hour made mincemeat of the Trojans. There were so many dead that the river Scamander was choked with their corpses and overflowed with blood. Achilles gave scores of them the works. Aeneas and Hector were only saved from his fury by Poseidon's temporarily changing sides and sending a mist to hide them. Athene heaved a rock the size of a house that sent Ares sprawling over an acre of ground, then as Aphrodite tried to help him up Athene gave her a black eye. Hera pulled Artemis's hair until she screamed. The Trojans knew they had had it and ran like rabbits for the shelter of their walls. Apollo held the gate for them and only Hector, still game to fight, remained outside.

But he wasn't all that game. As Achilles leapt at him he took to his heels. Three times the Greek chased him right round the city. Tough as those boys were, one imagines that after that they must have been a bit breathless. Pulling up, Hector tried to make a last-minute pact that whichever of them survived should see the other decently buried; but Achilles swore he'd feed Hector's carcase to the dogs, then he killed and stripped him. Not content with that he bored holes through his feet, tied them with leather thongs to the boot of his chariot and dragged the naked body bouncing up and down full-tilt round the walls of Troy, while Hector's parents looked on, yelling: 'Have a heart, you cad!' and lugged their hair out by the handful.

Even Hector's death did not end the war. Old Priam sent out an S O S for help to everyone he knew. The Amazon Queen, Penthesilea, responded by bringing an army of her tough babies down from the north. Achilles jabbed his spear right through her; but afterwards, when he wrenched off her helmet and saw what a good-looker she was, he was sorry for what he had done. Priam's nephew, Memnon, then arrived on the scene with a useful contingent from Egypt, but Achilles also cut short this young Pharaoh's career.

At last it became Achilles's turn. The Trojans had apparently got hold of a few of the arrows left by Hercules that had been dipped in the Hydra's poisonous blood. Paris fitted one of them to his bow and, with Apollo guiding his aim, managed to land it in Achilles's vulnerable heel, so he died ingloriously and had a very uncomfortable death. Unfortunately, too, by one of those silly wills, he had left his armour to 'the bravest' of his pals. Naturally half a dozen champs said at once: 'Of course, poor old Achie meant it for me.' To prevent bloodshed, Agamemnon called in the Trojan prisoners and asked their opinion. They voted Odysseus Champ No. 1, upon which Ajax became so jealous that in a fit of apoplectic rage he committed hara-kiri.

The loss of two of their best fire-eating types was such a bad set-back for the Greeks that most of them declared that they had reached the limit and meant to beat it for home, but Odysseus persuaded them to stick around for just a bit longer to try out a brainwave he had had. This was the famous hollow horse on wheels about which every schoolboy knows. It was made of wood and large enough to hold twelve men in its belly. When it was finished, Odysseus, Diomede, Pyrrhus and nine others shut themselves up inside and some of the troops dragged it up to within a stone's throw of the city gates. Then the Greeks got their ships afloat and sailed away bag and baggage.

Naturally the Trojans were all terrifically cock-a-hoop. They came streaming out, the poorer types to scrounge round the site of the Greek camp for any tins of bully beef that might have been left behind and the better-off to crowd round the Wooden Horse, airing their views about it. If Odysseus and his buddies could hear the suggestions made they must have been jolly sorry that they had ever put on this Commando act. Some of the Trojans wanted to burn the Horse, and others to push it over a high cliff. They were just about to break it open when a cry went up that a Greek who'd missed his boat had been found hiding in the bushes.

This was a young fellow named Sinon. He said that, while Agamemnon had been packing for home, the seer, Calchas, had told him that, if he wanted a favourable voyage, just as Iphigenia had been sacrificed before the outward trip so someone else must be sacrificed before the homeward one, and they had picked on him, Sinon; but he had managed to do a bunk. Now, of course, he was equally in a dither that, having been caught by the Trojans, he would be done in by them.

But the Trojans were in such good heart that they said not to worry, gave him a snorter to steady him up a bit and asked

K

him about the Wooden Horse. He said that was another of
old Calchas's ideas. The seer had had them make the Horse
in honour of Athene, because she had told him that if it were
left outside the walls of Troy she would fight on their side
when they returned to have another crack at the city next year.
He added that the reason it had been made too large to go
through the gate was so that the Trojans could not take it inside to her temple, which would have caused her to give
her favour to them.

Taking all this for gospel, the idiot Trojans started to
knock part of their wall down so that they could draw the Horse
into the city; but an old buffer named Laocoön, who was a
priest of Apollo, ran out crying: 'Hi! Stop that. Even the gifts
of the Greeks are poison.'

They put out their tongues at him and told him he was
talking through his hat; so he ran back, collected his two sons
and got busy doing a bit of protective magic. I suppose in his
excitement he recited the wrong spell, or something, because
two great serpents emerged from the sea, came streaking across
the plain and made a beeline through the city to his temple. In
a trice they had coiled round him and his boys and crushed
them to death.

After that, one can hardly blame the Trojans for saying
that he hadn't known what he was talking about and dragging
the Wooden Horse through the breach they had made in
their wall. It is understandable, too, that when night fell they
should get down to celebrating the departure of the Greeks.
By midnight most of them were as tight as ticks, each telling the others that for years he had made a habit of going
out and killing a Greek every morning as soon as he had
finished his cornflakes.

Young Sinon, meanwhile, was doing a job that Bulldog
Drummond, the Saint and Lemmy Caution would have hesitated to tackle between them. He climbed the topmost tower and
stood there waving a flaring torch. The Greek Fleet had gone
only as far as the island of Tenedos and was lying in hiding
behind it. At his signal that he had got the Trojans where he
wanted them, it sailed back. By the time the Greeks were landing on the beach he had run down the stairs three at a time,

got into the temple to which the Wooden Horse had been dragged and let Odysseus and Co. out of their stuffy prison. It was then, apparently, just a piece of cake to open the gates and give the 'Big Hello!' to Agamemnon and his boys as they came pouring in.

The Greeks didn't have it all their own way. Aeneas and some of the Trojan bloods fought like tigers, but they hadn't an earthly. For hours on end it was blue murder, with the Greeks butchering men, women and children, then looting and burning the houses. Pyrrhus broke into the palace, slaughtered Priam's youngest son before the King's eyes, then slew the old boy on his own altar. Helen was sitting in a corner of the same room feeling a bit off-colour at the thought of what they might do to her, and with some reason. Pyrrhus spotted her and aimed a swipe at her with his sword that should have cut her lovely head off, but just in time Aphrodite gave a flick of her nightdress and turned the blade aside.

By morning everyone was decidedly part-worn, so the Greeks let up with the killing and roped in the surviving Trojans to be shared out as slaves. One is glad to be able to record that brave Aeneas managed to get away and later married a lady named Lavinia, the daughter of an Italian King, with whose help he founded another Troy on the banks of the Tiber. Paris, too, escaped to Mount Ida, and there had the undeserved good luck to be taken back by his wife the Nymph Oenone.

Even after Helen had spent ten years in Troy she was probably still under thirty, so all the odds are that the sight of her would still have made plenty of chaps trip over their own feet in anxiety to make way for her on the pavement. Anyhow, Menelaus took one look at her and said: 'How about forgetting all this nonsense and coming home with me?'

Paris hadn't put up anything like such a good show during the siege as Menelaus had, and I think that sort of thing counts quite a lot with women. They like to be proud of their men. Helen, no doubt, just fluttered those long curved eyelashes of hers and replied: 'You know, Mene dear, I can't think what came over me. I always loved you best.' And that was that.

*   *   *   *   *

When Stephanie had finished reading she sat for a while wondering whether Robbie's book would ever be published. His interpolations had given her a few laughs and, in a strange way, the characters of some of the Immortals and Heroes came through; but it was utterly unlike any other book, fiction or non-fiction, that she had ever read, and it was hopelessly amateurish.

Her own English was far from perfect but, even so, she felt that she might be able to improve the punctuation a little and, if he would let her, cut out a lot of the slang expressions with which he peppered his writing. Yet, if he agreed to that, what would be left? A dull and colourless repetition of stories that had been told a hundred times before.

It occurred to her then that she was wasting her time concerning herself about it—at all events, for the present. Unless she could persuade Robbie to abandon his investigation, all the odds were that he would run into serious trouble long before he could finish his book or she have the opportunity of typing more than the first few chapters.

Another hour went by before Robbie joined her. He was bent almost double and, as he collapsed into a chair, he declared that, after climbing and descending the eight hundred-odd steps to the Acropolis, the last twenty stairs from the hall of the hotel up to the lounge had almost finished him. But he insisted that the view from the stronghold had been out of this world, and well worth it.

As the tourist season was now getting under way the hotel was already half full, and among the guests there was a number of Americans. After dinner that evening, Robbie secured a table in the lounge while Stephanie went to her room to get a book. An elderly American with horn-rimmed spectacles paused beside his table and, giving him a friendly but rather worried smile, said in a rich, Southern voice:

'Bad business this about our submarine, isn't it?'

Robbie smiled back, but shook his head. 'I haven't seen a paper for some days, so I'm afraid I don't know anything about it.'

'Don't you now!' The American raised a pair of bushy eyebrows in surprise. 'Well, one of our latest atomic subs has got herself cornered under the ice in a bay up on the Arctic coast of Russia, somewhere near Murmansk.'

'Really; what bad luck,' Robbie commented.

'It certainly is. The Russians are accusing us of sending her up there on a spying mission. They've named their price for letting her out—that we should surrender her and her crew.'

'What, with all your latest nuclear stuff in her?'

'That's it,' the American nodded glumly. 'And I don't see the President agreeing to that. This looks pretty bad to me. Maybe it's just one more threat to peace that will come to nothing; but if things do blow up I don't want to be caught here. If the news isn't better tomorrow morning, I think I'll telephone Athens to fix me a seat on the next plane home.'

18

The Amateur Photographer

John Foster Dulles's ostrich-like mentality had forced the West into playing the dangerous game of Brinkmanship instead of attempting to bring about world disarmament in the days when the United States's superiority in nuclear weapons might well have induced the Russians to listen to reason. This had resulted, ever since Robbie's early teens, in periodic crises that had threatened to usher in a Third World War. Therefore, Robbie took no serious notice of the elderly American's fears that this new cause for friction between the Soviet Union and the United States might develop into the blotting-out of all the major cities of Europe. In fact, on the following morning, while he was dressing to set off with Stephanie for an early visit to Mycenae, he never gave it a thought.

By arrangement, they picked up a private guide outside the Tourist Office at the end of the town and soon covered the twenty-odd kilometres up the slope to the prehistoric capital of Greece. It had once covered a considerable area, but the visible remains were concentrated in three places not very far apart: the Acropolis on the crown of the hill, which contained the palace; the royal burial ground with its adjacent courts some way down the slope and, still lower down, the famous beehive tombs.

As they arrived there by a quarter to nine, they had the place to themselves with little likelihood of coachloads of people on conducted tours arriving for over an hour and a half; so they took their time going round the Acropolis. There was no Temple there with standing pillars so Stephanie found it disappointing, and Robbie was soon irritated by their little guide reeling off facts and figures in parrot fashion. Although he had never before been to Mycenae, he knew so much about the place that he felt he could have done the job better himself.

On the lower level, the famous Lion Gate and the cyclopean walls, similar to those at Tiryns, forming courts and narrow passages, were impressive. It was intriguing to think of the vast fortune that had remained undiscovered for so many centuries in the oblong graves which pitted the stone-flanked circular enclosure that had formed the burial ground. But it was several hundred yards away down the slope that the most remarkable survival of Mycenaean building was to be seen.

This consisted of a great underground chamber, known as the Treasury of Atreus. It is a perfectly symmetrical hollow cone, over forty-five feet in diameter at its base and gradually narrowing in a graceful curve up to a small circular slab over forty feet above floor level. The inner surface of every stone in its walls is curved, and their courses are graduated from big blocks at the bottom to small ones at the top. Between there is no cement, yet there is not enough space to put the blade of a knife. The chamber is reached by a broad, deep corridor, having cyclopean walls, and the lintel stone above the seventeen-foot-high doorway is said to weigh one hundred and twenty tons.

Their guide said that no one knew how, with only human labour, it could ever have been got into position. Robbie could have told him. It had been dragged up a ramp, then rocked into place, in the same way as the Egyptians had built the Pyramids; but that did not detract from his admiration for the wonderful craftsmanship of those ancient people.

Just below the steep entrance to the Acropolis, there was a similar, though smaller, underground chamber called the Tomb of Clytemnestra and, as they walked back to their car, Stephanie asked why it was that Agamemnon should have been buried in the Royal Cemetery but his Queen outside it.

'She was a bad woman,' the guide replied. 'She murdered her husband; so, when she died, the people would not agree to her being buried in the Acropolis.'

As they had breakfasted early, they had brought biscuits, fruit and drinks with them. Leaving the guide by the car, they found a comfortable bank nearby and sat down to their 'elevenses'. When Stephanie had unpacked the basket, she said:

'What rotten luck for Agamemnon that, having survived ten years of fighting outside Troy, he should have been murdered.'

Robbie nodded. 'Yes; and when he got back, he didn't enjoy even one night in his old home. His cousin, Aegisthus, was the nigger in the woodpile, although Clytemnestra played the part of a Lady Macbeth. She never forgave Agamemnon for being the cause of her losing her eldest daughter, Iphigenia, and no sooner had he sailed for Troy than she took Aegisthus for what old-fashioned authors call her "paramour".

'After a while, they gave out that they'd had news from Troy and that Agamemnon had copped it; so they could live together openly as man and wife, and they ruled the kingdom between them. The ten years went by, then they had secret intelligence that Troy had fallen and that Agamemnon was on his way home.

'Some of the Heroes never got home, and others had very rough trips. Odysseus took years and years, because Poseidon had a grudge against him and kept on wrecking his ship in places where he had all sorts of terrifying adventures; but that's another story. Agamemnon was not delayed for very long, and as his wife had arranged for a chain of beacons to be lit as soon as his ship was sighted she had ample warning of his coming.

'His people were delighted when they learned that he wasn't dead after all, and the two younger children he had had by Clytemnestra, a girl named Electra and a boy named Orestes, gave him a terrific welcome. Clytemnestra, too, pretended to be overjoyed to see him; but Cassandra, Priam's daughter, whom Agamemnon had brought with him, threw a fit. You may remember that she had the gift of foreseeing the future, and she implored him not to go into the palace. But Apollo had decreed that no one should ever believe her prophecies, so Agamemnon ignored her warning.

'Everyone was bustling about preparing a huge banquet, and Agamemnon said that he would first like a bath. As soon as he was in it, Clytemnestra came into the bathroom with a big openwork woollen blanket made like a net. She chucked it over his head, and when he tried to push it off his hands got entangled in it. Then out popped her boy friend Aegisthus from behind a curtain. He was armed with a battle-axe and he sliced poor old Agamemnon to pieces with it, so that the water in the big silver bath turned scarlet with his blood.'

'What a horrible business. Did the people rise up and kill them?'

'No, they got away with it; at least, for some years. But Agamemnon's children avenged his death later on. Apparently Clytemnestra hated her younger daughter, Electra, and made her into a sort of Cinderella; but she was a good girl and very attached to her brother Orestes, who was only about twelve at the time. She found out that Aegisthus was planning to do a "Princes in the Tower" act on Orestes——'

'Who were the Princes in the Tower?' Stephanie interrupted to ask.

Robbie smiled. 'I forgot you might not know. They were two young English Princes who were believed to have been murdered by their wicked uncle. Anyhow, when Electra learned that Aegisthus intended to do Orestes in, so that he could not grow up and claim the throne, she managed to have him smuggled out and away to Phocis, where King Strophius gave him a home.

'Orestes and King Strophius's son, Pylades, became terrific buddies and when they reached "man's estate", as the saying is, they decided to take a trip to Mycenae. Of course, they went in disguise and with them they took an urn containing wood ash. On their arrival they went to pay their respects at Agamemnon's grave, and there they found Electra putting flowers on it.

'She didn't recognize Orestes; so he told her that they had

come from Phocis, that Orestes was dead and that they had brought his ashes to be buried in the family vault. She was frightfully upset; so Orestes then told her the truth, and when she had dried her tears she took the two chaps into the palace.

'Producing the urn, Orestes told the same yarn to Clytemnestra and Aegisthus. They were so pleased to hear that they no longer need fear Orestes turning up one fine morning with an army at his back, that they got up from the cellar a special bottle for their guests. No sooner was the butler out of the way than Pylades pulled a knife out of his stocking and stuck it into Aegisthus's middle and Orestes, only pausing to tell his mama who he was, did the same to her.'

Stephanie frowned. 'Whatever she had done, it was a terrible thing to kill his own mother.'

'Yes; that's just what his people thought. They were glad to be rid of Aegisthus and Clytemnestra, but scared stiff that the gods would show what they, too, thought of Orestes' deed, by putting a curse on the country. None of them would even sit down to a cut off the joint with him. In fact, some of them actually suggested stoning him to death; but their priests said the gods would not take it out of them provided they drove him out of the country.

'By then the thought of what he had done was giving him awful nightmares and daily fits of the staggers; so, seeing that he was in such poor shape, his sister and his faithful friend went into exile with him. Apollo then appeared to him in a dream and told him that he must dree his weird for a year in the forests of Arcadia.'

'What is one's "weird" and how does one dree it?' Stephanie asked.

'I gather it means traipsing around with everyone hating you on sight, and being haunted by every sort of bugaboo. Anyhow that's what happened to Orestes, and Electra and Pylades didn't fare much better. They got married; but they couldn't have had much of a honeymoon, living like gipsies in the woods and watching Orestes gradually going crackers. The Furies made the poor chap's life such hell that he seriously considered doing himself in, but before taking the plunge he thought he would try begging Apollo to let up and call off his tormentors.

'Apollo told him that if he could get back a statue of Artemis that had been carried off by a barbarous people called the Taurians, who lived up in the Crimea, the gods would call a Council to consider his case and perhaps give him a new deal. So he and Pylades got hold of a galley manned by fifty oarsmen from somewhere and set out for the Black Sea.

'Barbarous people are always scared that strange gods may do them a mischief if they are not polite to them, and to keep Artemis in a good humour the Taurians had built a little temple to house her statue. This temple was not far from the shore, so when Orestes and Pylades reached Tauris and landed to have a snoop round they soon came upon it. But their luck was out that night. They were caught by the guards and lugged before the priestess, whose job it was to sacrifice any foreigner turning up in those parts.

'Now you may remember that when Iphigenia was about to be sacrificed, Artemis had relented at the last moment and whipped her up to the heavens. But instead of keeping her there, as everyone had believed to be the case, she had promptly dumped her down in Tauris to act as priestess to the stolen statue.

'Of course, Iphigenia didn't much care for her job of slitting castaways' throats, and was longing to get back to her family in Greece. When the two young prisoners told her they were Greeks she was particularly put out at the thought of having to kill them, so she said:

"Look, chaps, the horrid hairy man who is King here is not altogether a bad sort. When there are several shipwrecked mariners for me to do my stuff on, he sometimes lets me beg a few of them off. But it's sure as that Zeus made little apples that he won't agree to let both of you beat the rap. Of course Artemis loathes these human sacrifices, but the King can't get it out of his head that unless I spill some blood on her altar now and again she may come after him one night with a carving knife. So I can save one of you, but not both. Now, which is it to be?"

'Being frightfully loyal types the friends naturally said to one another: "My dear old boy, what a splendid break. I'm so glad for you. As for me, not to worry. I've always wanted to die by having my throat slit. In fact, I've been hoping that would happen to me for years."

'Hearing all this, Iphigenia got the idea that neither of them was telling the truth but just putting on the sort of act that two Englishmen would have done when dressed in boiled shirts and threatened by cannibals in the jungles of darkest Africa.'

'Wouldn't that have been a bit after Iphigenia's time?' Stephanie remarked.

Robbie grinned. 'Yes, I suppose it would. But you know the sort of thing I mean. And being the "whitest girl that any-one ever knew", Iphigenia felt that these chaps were just up her street; so she became more than ever reluctant to do either of them in.

'To put off the evil hour she asked them about themselves, and it then emerged that Orestes was the kid brother that she hadn't seen since he was two years old. She didn't let on for the moment who she was but pretended to be very tough and had them thrown into a dungeon to await slaughter.

'That evening she went to see the hairy King, and said to him: "Sire, I find myself in a bit of a fix. A couple of young Greeks have been cast ashore and I couldn't be more anxious to give them the works, but my goddess has tipped me off that they are criminals of the deepest dye. Unless they are purified first they will pollute her altar and she would be so annoyed that she might even cause your beard to drop out."

'The King clutched his face fungus and asked: "What's the drill then? You'll be for the high jump yourself unless you can get me out of this."

' "I can sort it for you," Iphigenia reassured him. "Both these thugs and the statue of the goddess must be dipped in the sea. That will wash their sins away; then I'll be able to stick a knife in their gullets without fear of any unpleasant after-effects."

' "Go to it, then," said the King, "and good luck to you."

'But he must have been a very trusting type, as later that night Iphigenia was allowed to lead both the prisoners from their cell with only a dog leash attached to their wrists and no escort. What is more, they took the wooden statue of Artemis with them.

'Orestes had left his galley with its fifty oarsmen hidden behind a headland, so all they had to do was to go aboard her and get the crew to row like hell for Greece. The King's coast-guards told him what was doing, so he sent his fleet after them; but Artemis was very pleased with her own people, so she got her brother Apollo to put up the sun an hour or so early that day and it blinded the pursuers.

'When they got the statue back to Greece it was set up in Athens so that it could be duly honoured by Artemis's worshippers. Then, the year being up, a Council of the Gods was called to assemble on the Areopagus there and judge Orestes. It is rather interesting that they should have used white stones and black stones in their ballot, just as a committee do when voting whether to receive or reject a candidate who has been put up for membership of a modern club; although in their case it had to be a majority of black balls to exclude. At the count the whites and the blacks came out even, but suddenly Athene winged her way down to the meeting and threw a white ball into the urn.

'That saved Orestes and gave him a new lease of life. He returned to Mycenae and, suddenly, everybody there became frightfully pleased to see him. Then he married Hermione, the beautiful daughter of Helen and Menelaus, that Helen had borne before skipping off with Paris to Troy. So Orestes and Hermione and Pylades and Electra lived happily ever after.'

Stephanie sighed. 'How pleasant it is to think that at least a few of the ancients escaped from some frightful fate decreed for them by the gods.'

They were back at Navplion in time for a bathe before lunch and slept in the afternoon. In the early evening Stephanie gave Robbie another driving lesson. At dinner that night he noticed at a table on the other side of the room the elderly American who had spoken to him the previous evening of getting an air-passage home. As he had not, after all, left for Athens that morning, Robbie assumed that the situation with regard to the trapped submarine had not deteriorated. Then he again forgot all about it.

The next four days went all too quickly. On two occasions, Stephanie half-heartedly suggested that she ought to make a start on typing Robbie's manuscript; but he knew that if she did, he would have to leave her to it, and he took such delight in her company that he assured her that there would be plenty of time later for typing it.

Besides, there seemed so many things to do. One day, they drove the twenty miles across the isthmus to Epidauros. It had been the Greek equivalent of Bath, and the Greeks of classical times had gone there in their thousands for treatment by the priests of the healer-god, Asclepius. There were no cyclopean walls, but the ruins of the great temple to the god, of the rotunda and of other buildings still standing were sufficient to give a good idea of what this famous spa of a later age must have looked like. Above all, there was its theatre. It was the best-preserved of any in the ancient world and so cleverly constructed that no modern auditorium could equal the perfection of its acoustics.

During part of another day, they explored the much less interesting remains of ancient Argos. That city, too, had had its theatre. It had once seated twenty thousand spectators and was the largest in Greece, but the greater part of it had since fallen into ruin. Then there were their daily bathe, long naps in the afternoons and a driving lesson for Robbie every evening. It was, therefore, with the greatest reluctance that, while they were at lunch on the Thursday, he said:

'It's a week today since we arrived here, so our hol. is pretty well over. We must hit the trail again tomorrow morning.'

'Oh no!' Stephanie exclaimed. 'Do let's stay on here a few days longer.'

He shook his head. He had never even hinted to her that he had pledged himself to Athene; so he had, naturally, made no mention of the owl that had hooted on the evening of their arrival and checked his impulse to give in to her plea that he should abandon his mission. But the owl evidently had its nest somewhere up on the cliff behind the hotel. Every evening since, after dusk had fallen, he had heard it hooting. These hoots had been a nightly reminder to him that he must not linger at Navplion for longer than might serve to make the

Czechs believe that they had no more to fear from him. Now he said firmly:

'No; and please don't try again to persuade me to throw in my hand. My mind is made up. We are leaving tomorrow morning, so you had better pack tonight.'

There was a quiet authority in his voice that would have been quite foreign to it ten days earlier; so, instead of attempting to argue with him, she asked: 'Where are we going?'

'To Olympia,' he replied. 'It is about two hundred kilometres. That may not sound very much for a day's drive, but the hall porter tells me that four-fifths of the way lies through the mountains, so we ought to allow at least five hours. I hope you won't find it too tiring. If we start at ten o'clock, we should be at Tripolis by twelve. That is the only town of any size through which we pass, so we could take a two-hour break for lunch there and do the longer stretch in the afternoon.'

She shrugged. 'That suits me all right. But why Olympia? I thought all those groups of Czechs you are interested in were taking up their quarters near the sea.'

'They are, and the group that I have decided to try and get a good look at will be somewhere near Pirgos. I have chosen that lot because it must be ten days since they landed there, so by now they will have had plenty of time to get to work. But I decided against staying in the city, because there is just a chance that Barak, or some of the others who saw me either in Patras or Corinth, might be there. If I happened to run into one of them, it would put them on their guard. Pirgos is only a little over twenty kilometres from Olympia, so I can easily work from there. Also, by staying at Olympia, I can keep going, for what it's worth, my cover that I'm writing a book about ancient Greece.'

The first ten miles of their journey the following morning were easy, as the road was almost flat. It ran in a great semicircle, through Argos right round the head of the gulf. On the far side they passed through the little town of Miloi, on the site of the ancient Lerna, near which Hercules had slain the Hydra; and thereabouts the country was very pretty. There were many plantations of oranges and lemons and, in several places, the road was lined with pepper and mimosa trees. The latter, as Robbie had noticed in several other low-lying parts of the country, had much larger blossoms than the varieties imported into England, but that was more than offset by the fact that they had no scent.

Soon after leaving Miloi, the road began to rise in a series of sharp curves, and in a quarter of an hour they had climbed over a thousand feet. As the road zigzagged to and fro round sharp spurs of the mountain, they frequently drove back in the direction from which they had come, only on a higher level; so time and again they got an increasingly bird's-eye view of the great gulf that they were leaving behind them, with the little castle of Burzi in its centre and Navplion on its further shore.

For a stretch of over fifteen miles the road was cut out of the mountain side and, even on the most dangerous curves, it had no parapet or row of posts which might have prevented a recklessly driven car from going over. There was not much traffic, and during the first hour they met only two tourist coaches, three private cars and half a dozen lorries. Stephanie drove at a fair pace, but carefully, and Robbie was relieved to see that she showed no trace of nerves when passing other vehicles. For that he gave her full marks, as he found his own muscles tensing slightly every time they approached a blind corner, from dread that a long coach would appear just as they were about to go round it.

By eleven o'clock they were up to two thousand five hundred feet and wisps of cloud, coming down from the peaks on either side that were shrouded in it, drifted across the road. But by that time they had reached the pass and for a few miles there were only gentle gradients. Then once more the way became a succession of hairpin bends, now sloping downward and seeming even more dangerous; for, had the car brakes failed when approaching any of the corners, nothing could have stopped them from going straight over the edge of a precipice.

A little before midday they entered Tripolis, the largest town in the interior of the Peloponnesus and almost in its centre. Like most Greek country towns, the streets were crowded with donkey carts, ageing motor vehicles of all descriptions and shouting peasants trying to keep their herds of goats together. Most of the buildings looked shoddy and there were few of more than two stories; but there was a pleasant, arcaded square in the centre of the town and at a restaurant there they had quite a passable lunch.

They still had two-thirds of the journey before them, and Stephanie was in favour of pushing on; so at about half past one they drove out of the town. After a few miles the road began to twist and mount again and, at a height of over three thousand feet, it took them round bend after bend, through a great area of steep slopes covered with firs. At times the road spiralled downward for some distance until the drop over the edge was reduced to a mere hundred feet, but only to snake up again to still loftier heights.

Up there in the mountains the villages were few, small and very far apart. Occasionally, at the bottom of the valleys, there were patches of olive trees, and small strips of vines or corn, but by far the greater part of the land was wild scrub, upon which only goats could browse, rising to vast masses of barren rock. The scenery was magnificent but, as this was a fair sample of two-thirds of Greece, it could not be wondered at that its people were so poor. The great ranges of barren mountains, shutting off the fertile valleys from one another, explained too why in ancient times there had been so many Kings in Greece. Most of them had, in fact, been no more than petty chieftains, submitting only for comparatively short periods to the over-lordship of aggressive monarchs such as Agamemnon and, later, the powerful City States of Athens and Sparta.

Between half-past-two and half-past-three, they passed between peaks rising to six thousand feet on either side of them, and in places the drop from the road to the valley was close on four thousand. The bends seemed to grow still sharper and at scores of them it needed only a small error of judgment on Stephanie's part to send them both hurtling to their deaths. She kept her eyes fixed steadily on the road ahead, but Robbie was free to look about him. From time to time he could not resist the temptation to glance over the unprotected edge of the road down into the valley three-quarters of a mile below, but each time he swiftly looked away again and tried to comfort himself with the thought that coaches, lorries and cars made this journey safely every day and night; so there was really no reason to fear that they, too, would not do so.

Soon after four o'clock, at a place where there was one of the most precipitous drops from the road, they came upon a small township. Why such a spot should ever have been chosen, and how its houses had been built into the almost perpendicular mountainside above the road were mysteries. But it had a café with a few tables outside; so they pulled up there to give Stephanie a rest and to have a drink. Opposite the café there were only the road, a strip of pavement and a railing. When they had finished their drinks, they walked across and looked over. There were more houses perched precariously below, and beyond them nothing. A running jump from the front door of any of them would have taken the jumper well over a thousand feet to land in the bottom of the valley.

'What a place to live!' Robbie muttered, turning away with a shudder. 'I've no head for heights and within a week I bet I would have thrown myself over.'

'Fortunately, I don't mind them,' Stephanie replied. 'But, all the same, I'd hate to live here, especially if I had children. I should be worried out of my wits. But I suppose the mothers in these places get used to it and the children soon become as sure-footed as goats.'

The township, as they saw from the map, was called Tropaia, and soon after leaving it they began the long descent. For the better part of another hour they again slewed round bend after bend, occasionally slowing down to pass another vehicle, until they reached the fertile plane through which runs the river Alfios. The last lap was through charming woodland country, and it was just on five o'clock when they drove up a slope to the Spap Hotel.

Its main block, with a fine entrance hall and broad staircase, gave it something of the atmosphere of a big, private villa; but it had recently been built on to, and was now one of the few de-luxe hotels in Greece, outside Athens. From the rooms they were given they could see, about a mile away, a part of the famous ruins and beyond them the curve of the broad river, but most of the ruins were hidden by tall Scotch pines which grew among them.

Their day had been a tiring one, so after resting they dined early with a view to getting in a long night. But before they went to bed, Robbie told Stephanie that he wanted her to drive him into Pirgos in the morning.

She expressed surprise that he was not anxious to see the temples; but he said that, as the next day was Saturday, if he did not make a start with his business in the morning he would have to waste the whole week-end.

As it was quite a short run, they reached the port by ten o'clock. It was nowhere near as large as Patras, but a little bigger than Tripolis, and most of the buildings were of the same shoddy variety. A few sites were occupied only by cracked walls and heaps of rubble, as the town had suffered from a long series of earthquakes.

They parked the car and Stephanie went off to have a 'hair-do' while Robbie set about locating the Czech group by the same means he had used in Corinth. In this somewhat larger town it took him longer, and he had to announce himself as a representative of United Kingdom Petroleum at three estate agents before he had any luck. Eventually, he learnt from a Mr. Levantis that the Czechs had bought a small factory some three kilometres to the south of the port. The factory had been partially destroyed by the last earthquake and then abandoned.

At half-past-twelve he rejoined Stephanie and asked her to drive him out of the town along the coast road until they were in sight of the factory. The solitary chimney had broken off about twenty feet up and some of the walls were jagged, with big gaps in them. But a small house to one side of it, in which the owner or manager had probably lived, still appeared intact, and several of the smaller buildings had their roofs on. After Robbie had studied the place for some minutes, Stephanie turned the car round and they drove back to Olympia in time for a late lunch.

Later in the afternoon they paid their first visit to the ruins, set so attractively among the sprinkling of tall pine trees. But Robbie seemed unable to get up much interest in them because his mind was now once more fully occupied with the Czechs.

On the Sunday morning he suggested to Stephanie that they

should have a swim in the river; so they collected their bathing things and strolled down to it. The Alfios was several hundred yards wide there, but at that season the greater part of its bed consisted of dry, stony patches, between which the main stream and a few smaller ones meandered. However, after walking some way along the bank, they came upon a good-sized pool about five feet deep where water had collected from a little stream that flowed through it. They changed behind some bushes and on going in found the water delightfully warm, so they spent most of the morning either in it or sunbathing on the sandy bank.

It was not until they were seated at lunch that Robbie announced that he wanted to be driven into Pirgos again that afternoon. He then went on to say that he thought it fairly certain that the Czechs, like other people, would take Sunday off; so the odds were that most, if not all, of the group would have gone into the town, and that would give him a better chance than at any other time during the week to take some photographs without being caught.

Stephanie made no demur and by three o'clock she brought the car to a halt behind a group of tamarisks about two hundred yards from the factory. Instead of making for it, Robbie walked down to the beach, then sauntered slowly along it as though he were looking for pretty shells or brightly coloured stones. One wall round the half-ruined building merged into a stone jetty that ran out into the sea and barred his further progress along the beach. Turning inland, he followed the wall until he reached the first gap in it. He saw at once that it had recently been rendered impassable by a score of strands of barbed wire stretched at intervals of nine inches or less across it. But he had chosen his hour well. It was the middle of the siesta period and, on peering through the wire, he saw that, even if all the Czechs had not gone into the town, none of them was about.

The gap in the wall gave on to a spacious yard. Near the middle there stood a tall, steel tripod with very stout legs, the upper part of which he had already seen from a distance over the top of the wall. Near it, there was a small crane and a bulky piece of machinery, which he took to be some form of powerful motor or electric engine, under a shelter that had been rigged up to protect it from rain. The barbed wire was no impediment to his taking photographs so, resting his camera on one of the strands, he took two shots.

He then moved along the wall to another gap. That, too, was sealed off with barbed wire, and the view through it was the same from a slightly different angle; but it did include a better sight of a big pile of spiral screws, each about six feet long and one foot in diameter, so he took two more shots from there. Lastly, through a third gap round the corner of the wall, he got two photographs of a line of trolleys on rails that were evidently being used for running the earth churned out by the drills down to the jetty and from there into the sea. He then made his way back to the beach, sauntered along it again and so returned to the car.

'Did you get what you wanted?' Stephanie asked.

He nodded. 'Yes; and they are drilling after all.'

'Drilling?' she repeated interrogatively.

'Perhaps I didn't tell you; but the information my firm secured was that this Czech company meant to drill for oil. We couldn't believe it because there are not supposed to be sufficient oil deposits in Greece to make it worth while. We thought they might be up to something else. I mean . . .' he added hastily, 'establishing depots with storage tanks, and that sort of thing.'

'But you are satisfied now that what you were told is right?'

'Yes. There's no doubt they are drilling. I've got photographs of the plant and the tip-trucks they're using to run the churned-out earth down into the sea. One can only suppose that by some new radar process, or something, they have been able to detect oil deposits that no one else believed to exist.'

Stephanie gave a sigh of relief. 'Thank God for that, then. Now you have done your job you won't have to take any further risks of being beaten up. We can forget all this and concentrate on your book. That is if your firm will give you a few weeks' leave, and they jolly well ought to.'

Robbie smiled. 'Oh, I can fix that, all right. I must get these photographs developed as soon as possible and send them in. Then, so far as I am concerned, that will be the end of the matter.'

She drove the car back through Pirgos then, when they were a little way out of the town, let him take the wheel. The road back to Olympia was on low ground, so if he had run off it there would have been no great danger of a fatal accident; and by this time she felt that he was driving quite well enough to apply for a provisional licence as soon as they were again in a town where one could be obtained.

That evening, while he was lying in his bath before dinner, he took stock of the situation and found his feelings very mixed. For his self-imposed mission to be over was a great relief. On the other hand, it was annoying to think that for the past month he had been scheming and exerting himself to no purpose. His belief that there was some sinister design behind the Czech tobacco-oil deal had turned out to be only a figment of his imagination. That meant, too, that he would not now enjoy the triumph of having pulled off a fine coup as a secret agent and so gain the astonished respect of his uncle.

Then, as he thought further about it, he began to wonder if he really had got to the bottom of the matter. That the Czechs were definitely drilling indicated that he had, but the fact remained that Luke Beecham had assured him both that no one believed there was oil in Greece and, that if some new scientific device for discovering it had been invented, he would have heard about it. Could it be then that the Czechs were drilling for some other purpose—perhaps to sink concrete pylons on which rocket launchers could be based? That idea certainly gave much food for thought, and perhaps the photographs he had taken would provide the answer to it. Luke would know if the machinery in them was of a type used for sinking oil wells and, if not, he might be able to deduce from them what the Czechs were up to.

First thing next morning, Robbie walked down to the pharmacy in the village. Handing his camera to the man behind the counter, he asked him to take the spool out because, not being used to a camera, he was not quite certain how to do it. Then he asked that the film should be developed as quickly as possible.

After a glance at the camera, the man said: 'You have used only six of the eight films on the spool. Don't you wish to take something with the other two?'

'No,' Robbie told him. 'I'm in a great hurry for the six I've taken. How soon can you let me have two sets of prints? If possible I'd like to get one off to Athens by the evening post.'

The man wound up the unused part of the film, removed the spool, handed the camera back to Robbie, and said:

'Usually we ask people to call the following morning, but if it is all that urgent, I'll oblige you. Come back at half past four this afternoon and I'll have them ready.'

Returning to the hotel, Robbie collected Stephanie and they paid a visit to the little museum on the slope below it. The museum contained a number of fine Roman as well as Greek statues, but the outstanding exhibits were the world-famous Hermes of Praxiteles and the Victory of Paeonios. The former occupied a central position at the far end of the main hall, and its base was raised on a square, deep bed of sand that extended for some way all round it. On Stephanie's asking the reason for this, an attendant standing nearby told her that it was a precaution against earthquakes. Should one cause the masterpiece to be toppled over, the sand would save it from being damaged.

Going round the museum took them only three-quarters of an hour, so they had ample time for a bathe in the pool they had discovered. Then, after lunch, they went to their rooms for their usual read and nap. Soon after four, Robbie set off down to the village, eager to see the results of his first efforts as a photographer.

As he entered the pharmacy, the man behind the counter looked up and said: 'I'm sorry about your photographs, but the whole lot has been ruined.'

'Ruined!' exclaimed Robbie. For once there was anger in his voice.

'Oh, not by me,' the man retorted with asperity. 'You said you were not used to handling a camera, and you must have opened the back of it to have a look inside. If you remember, you hadn't used the whole of the film; so, until I wound it off to take out, it would have been loose. It was the light getting in that spoiled your pictures. The tops and bottoms are quite gone, and whichever way I held them up I couldn't make anything out of the middles. It would have been a waste of time and paper to print them.'

19

A Bolt from the Blue

Robbie had the man put a new film in his camera, then left the shop, angry and puzzled. He had certainly not opened the camera and he could not recall having dropped or knocked it—which the man had also suggested might account for light having filtered in.

When he joined Stephanie for tea on the broad terrace of the hotel his expression was so woebegone that she asked with quick concern what was the matter. On his telling her, she said:

'What rotten luck. But, of course, that is liable to happen at times with inexpensive cameras. Since you can't remember giving it a knock yourself that would have sprung its back, someone else must have. Perhaps when the chambermaid was in your room last night, turning down your bed, she moved and dropped it; or perhaps the man at the pharmacy made a mess of developing the film and told you this story to cover up his clumsiness.'

'Ah! Now I believe you've hit on it!' Robbie exclaimed. 'He seemed a bit on the defensive when he told me about it. That was probably because he had a guilty conscience. How infuriating—the results of the lucky break I had yesterday simply chucked away.'

'Do the photographs really matter?' Stephanie asked gently. 'After all, you have found out that these people are drilling for oil. Surely your firm will take your word for that.'

'Yes, I . . . I suppose so,' he replied, a shade hesitantly. He had never even hinted to her his original belief that the

313

Czechs might be up to something sinister, and was averse to mentioning that possibility now; so he added after a moment: 'All the same, I would like to have sent to Athens some photographs of the plant that is being used. I think I'll go to Pirgos again and take another lot.'

'Oh, Robbie!' she protested. 'You said yesterday that you were definitely finished with this dangerous business.'

He shrugged. 'Then, the photographs I took hadn't been ruined. But I won't risk going in while they are likely to be working on the site; so you've no need to worry about me. We'll think no more about it for the next few days.'

Next morning, after their swim, Robbie hired a guide to take them on a proper tour of the ruins. They lay between Mount Kronion and the river, on level ground covering an area of a quarter of a square mile. The whole of it was thick with the remains of temples, porticoes, baths, treasuries and other edifices, so that in its heyday it must have formed a great town consisting entirely of beautiful public buildings. Even in ruin, its broad flights of steps, huge, fluted pillars and still-standing arches were immensely impressive in the dappled shade of the tall Scotch pines that grew among them.

They visited in turn the Philippeion, the Heraion, the terrace with the twelve Treasuries, the great temple of Zeus, the house that had been built for the Emperor Nero, the Beuleuterion and the Leonidaion. This last had been a building as big as many modern hotels, in which distinguished guests lived while attending the Games. In its interior there had been small grass courts and round the outside a quadruple row of pillars supporting a shady colonnade, which must have made it very beautiful. Further on lay the workshop in which Phidias had carved his greatest masterpiece—the forty-foot-high ivory-and-gold statue of Zeus. Beyond it lay the gymnasia in which the athletes had practised under the eyes of their trainers before competing in the Games.

Crossing the area of ruins again, they left the sacred precincts by a tunnelled way and entered the Stadium where the Games had been held. From the first Olympiad in 776 B.C.— which had afterwards been taken by the Greeks of classical times as the starting date of their history—the Games had been

held there every fifth year, with very few breaks, right up to
the fifth century A.D. For over a thousand years the most per-
fectly-formed young men from all over the country, proudly
displaying the beauty of their naked bodies, had competed
there in running, jumping, wrestling, throwing the javelin and
the discus, and in other sports. The victors of the contests won
not only honour and life-long security from want for themselves, but also renown for the cities which had bred them.

Yet the Games brought to Greece a benefit far exceeding
the pleasure and excitement of following a great athletic contest. When their date was announced, any wars that were being
waged in the country automatically ceased. Kings and
Democracies alike declared a truce for the period of the Olympiad. Not only that, but every State sent its great men as
Ambassadors to the Games, with valuable gifts to be laid in
the Treasuries of the gods. Then, meeting to witness the
Games provided the perfect opportunity for discussing terms of
peace in an atmosphere of goodwill; so many a bitter conflict
between States was temporarily stopped by an Olympiad and
was never resumed after it, to the relief and benefit of their
peoples.

It was next day, after they had enjoyed a swim and were
sitting sunning themselves on the sand beside their pool, that
Stephanie asked:

'About your book, Robbie. Will there be much more of it
than the parts you have already written and those you have
told me about?'

'No,' he replied after a moment. 'Not much more. The only
long piece would be about Odysseus and his return from the
Trojan War, and I'm in two minds whether to include that or
leave it out.'

'Why?'

'Well, owing to Poseidon's having a grudge against him, he
was ten years on the way, and his adventures nearly all have to
do with overcoming giants and monsters; so, apart from tricks
he played to get away from people who were trying to hold
him up, it would read rather like a repetition of the deeds of
Perseus and Hercules. Also, unlike the Iliad, which tells of

the siege of Troy, the Odyssey seems to have very little in it based on real history.'

'Oh, come!' Stephanie laughed. 'Surely that applies also to lots of other matters you have written about. For instance, the war of the gods and giants in which they heaved mountains at one another.'

'But that was historical; or, at least, a race memory of an historical event. So was the account of Phaethon's terrible end.'

'He had something to do with the sun, hadn't he?'

'Yes. He was the son of Apollo by Clymene. When he grew up, she told him that his father was a god and he became so bumptious about it that all his school friends said he was only boasting. That made him so wild that he went to his father and demanded to be publicly recognized. As he had grown up into a real maiden's dream, Apollo felt quite proud of him and promised him any proof he liked to ask.

'To show his friends what a fine fellow he was, Phaethon asked to be allowed for one day to drive the Chariot of the Sun. Apollo was frightfully against letting him, but he had sworn by the Styx to grant his son's wish; and as that oath was to the gods like having sworn on the Bible, he couldn't refuse.

'The chariot was drawn by a team of tremendously power-ful steeds and, in spite of Apollo's advice about how to hang on to them and prevent them from charging into one of the constellations, a stripling like Phaethon hadn't got a hope. In no time at all, he lost control and the chariot was zigzagging all over the heavens. It came swooping down over the earth, drying up rivers and burning up forests with its heat as it passed. Whole cities went up in flames and vast tracts of fertile land were scorched into barren desert. Great rifts appeared in the land, the earth trembled and the volcanoes erupted. It was on that day, so it is said, that what remained of the negro races were burnt black.

'Naturally, everyone who had escaped death from heat-stroke sent up frantic prayers to Zeus to do something about it, and that woke the old boy from his noonday nap. What-ever one may think about his morals, he was a good man in an emergency. He grabbed one of his thunderbolts and heaved it at Phaethon. That not only settled the young man's hash but freed the horses from his futile jerking on their reins; so they galloped back to their stalls beneath the eastern horizon and on earth it became night at midday.'

Stephanie smiled, but shook her head. 'How can you possibly say that has anything to do with history?'

'But it has,' Robbie insisted. 'It has been scientifically proved that all the other planets revolve with their axes at ninety degrees to the sun. Earth is the only exception and our axis is tilted to an angle of twenty-three degrees. The only possible explanation for that is that at one time a big comet came so near that it threw the earth off balance. And it is easy to imagine the sort of thing that would have happened while the comet was passing. Its pull would have brought about tidal waves, earthquakes and volcanic eruptions. Whole peoples would have been annihilated, the courses of rivers would have changed and the sun would have appeared to have gone haywire in the sky. Here and there groups of people would have survived, of course, just as in remote places some people would survive an all-out atomic war. Those who did handed down their memories of the cataclysm, and gradually the powers of Nature came to be attributed to the gods; so the accounts took the form of Phaethon's losing control of the chariot of the sun, and the Immortals waging a ten-year war in which whole mountains were thrown about.'

'Yes, I see,' murmured Stephanie. 'There certainly seems something to that.'

'The Deluge is another example,' Robbie told her. 'At the time of the Flood there was not just one Noah but several. They lived in different countries, some as far apart as Babylonia and Mexico; but all of them, by forethought or luck, managed to save their families and some of their domestic animals, and their descendants re-populated their parts of the world.

'The Greek Noah was named Deucalion. He was one of the first race of men created by Prometheus, who tipped him off that the Flood was coming and told him to build an Ark. He did, and shut himself up in it with his wife, Pyrrha, a daughter of Pandora. They floated round for nine days and nights, then the Ark beached itself on Mount Parnassus. When the water had gone down a bit, they hiked it to Delphi and begged the gods to create another human race. As usual, the reply that they got was pretty obscure. They were told to veil their heads and cast behind them the bones of their first ancestor. That foxed them for a bit, but they worked it out that Gaea, the Earth-Mother, was the beginning of all things; so they went about throwing stones over their shoulders, and the stones turned into men and women.

'Of course, no one takes the stone-throwing part of the story literally, but that's not to say that Deucalion and Pyrrha were not real people who lived at the time of the Flood. No one who has read Sir James Frazer's *Golden Bough* can doubt that the Flood happened, because there are memories of it in the folklore of scores of different races on both sides of the Atlantic. It wasn't world-wide, but it affected the whole of Central America, Western Europe and the Mediterranean countries, and such a terrific cataclysm can only be accounted for by the same great comet, or perhaps another one, having nearly collided with the Earth.'

For a few minutes they sat silent, then Stephanie picked up a small stone and threw it so that it made a loud plop in the pool. Robbie had been looking at her as she raised her arm, and her right breast was forced outward by the action. She was wearing only a bikini. It was of white satin and showed up her golden skin to perfection. For the hundredth time his eyes drank in her loveliness, and he toyed with the thought of attempting to take the role that Zeus had so often played with beautiful mortal maidens in this sunny land of Greece.

He had only to stretch out his arms, seize her in an overpowering embrace and smother her with kisses. Yet he dared not do it. He felt certain that, instead of responding, she would do her utmost to fight him off. Then, whether he succeeded in having his way with her or not, everything between them would be finished. She had come to mean so much to him that the thought of losing her was unbearable. It would have sent him mad with grief.

Again and again since he had met her he had cursed his upbringing and his total lack of experience with young women. During their youth other men all seemed to have gradually acquired the ability to attract girls by semi-serious chaff and clever little compliments, leading up to declarations of their feelings; but he simply did not know how to begin on such a normal type of courtship. In the three weeks they had been together his self-confidence in handling all other situations had enormously increased and, with her, he had for the first time really found his tongue. He could talk, laugh or sit silent with her more naturally than with anyone he had ever met. Yet the one thing that still froze him with shyness and embarrassment was the thought of saying anything which would reveal that his feelings for her were more than those of a friend.

While his thoughts were still racing, she threw another stone into the pool and said: 'What else are you going to put in your book? Aren't there some love stories that would counterbalance a bit those full of horrors?'

Her mention of 'love' brought him back with a start. It was a golden opportunity for him to begin talking of love, not as between the ancient Greeks but living people, then reveal how much he had come to care for her. But, even before he thought of taking it, he found himself replying:

'Oh yes; there are several. Pyramus and Thisbe, Pygmalion and Galatea, Hero and Leander. Then there's Cupid and Psyche.'

'Tell me some of them.'

By that time he felt he had lost his chance so, after a moment, he started off. 'Pyramus and Thisbe lived in Babylon, and theirs was the original case of "the girl next door". As children, they planned to marry. By the time they were well into their 'teens, their love had developed into a grand passion; but their fathers hated each other's guts, and were so dead against their getting hitched-up that they forbade them to see one another. A high wall separated the gardens of the two houses, but it was built only of mud and straw; so they made a hole in it just large enough to whisper sweet nothings through when no one was looking.

'At last they became so fed-up with not being able to get together that they decided to elope. Thisbe was to slip out of her home at midnight and make for a place in the woods outside the city, known as "The Tomb of Ninus", and Pyramus was to be there to meet her. But she was so impatient to have Pyramus cuddling her that she set off too early. With a white veil wrapped round her head, she scurried through the dark streets and into the wood, only to find when she reached their dating place that her boy friend was not there.

'She knew that she hadn't mistaken the place because a big tree with white mulberries grew beside the tomb.'

'White mulberries?'

'Yes, I'm coming to that. When she had stood round for a bit, she heard a rustling in the bushes, and ran forward to get Pyramus in a clinch. But instead of Pyramus she found herself face to face with a lion slobbering blood from a prey that it had just devoured. Letting out a yell, she threw her veil at the lion and sprinted off down the track for dear life. However, the lion had had his supper; so he just mauled her veil about a bit, then went off on other business.

'Ten minutes later Pyramus turned up. He recognized her veil, saw that it was all bloody and concluded that a lion must have killed his sweetie-pie, then dragged her body off into the bushes. Frantic with grief, he drew his good and trusty and killed himself.'

'How awful!'

'Wasn't it? But worse is to follow. Thisbe, meanwhile, finding the lion was not after her, had pulled up; then, half an hour later, she plucked up the courage to creep back to the tomb. There she found Pyramus lying on his side, apparently asleep. With a yodel of joy, she threw herself upon him, only to find herself clutching a corpse. Snatching up his sword, she stuck it into herself and fell dead upon his body.'

'Oh dear,' sighed Stephanie. 'I think that must have been the original from which Shakespeare got Romeo and Juliet. But what about the mulberries?'

'The blood of the two lovers soaked into the roots of the tree and that is why the fruit of most mulberry trees afterwards became dark purple.'

'Now tell me about Hero and Leander.'

'Leander was a handsome Trojan and he lived at Abydos on the Asiatic side of the Dardanelles, or the Hellespont as the ancients called it. Hero was a priestess who served in Aphrodite's temple at Sestos on the European side, and all Aphrodite's mortal stand-ins had plenty of what it takes. These two fell for one another in a big way, but they were separated by about three or four miles of water.

'As Leander was a strong-limbed chap, he didn't let that deter him from get-togethers with his honey-bunch. Every night she came down to the shore with a lamp and he swam over to her. For them every night of the spring and summer was a night of gladness, and he swam back in time to get to the office, or whatever he did, every morning.

'But autumn came, then winter, and the Hellespont got colder and rougher. Still drawn like a magnet by what was waiting for him on the other side, Leander continued to take the nightly plunge; then one night there was a terrible storm. The wind blew out the lamp Hero was holding. In the pitch darkness and swirled about by the strong current, Leander could no longer tell in which direction the shore lay. Lost, and with the icy water numbing his limbs, he swam round until he was exhausted, then he went under once, twice, thrice. By the time dawn came, Hero was right off her rocker, because by then she felt pretty sure he must have had it. Gazing desperately round, she suddenly caught sight of his body washed up on some rocks; so she rushed into the water and was drowned, too.'

Stephanie pulled a face. 'What a gloomy ending.'

'Never mind,' Robbie smiled. 'I'll cheer you up with the story of Pygmalion and Galatea. He was a king of Cyprus and immensely rich. But he didn't care about power or lolly or the things it could buy. He was interested only in his art, and he was the all-time-high sculptor of his day. Girls left him cold, because he said he had never seen one half as well made as the beauties he could carve himself, and at length he made a life-size ivory statue of one that was an absolute smasher.

'He called the statue Galatea, and the more time he spent looking at it the more it got him under the fifth rib, until he was hopelessly in love with it. His statue was so life-like that he almost thought he could hear it breathing, and he fondled it and kissed it madly, hoping that it would come to life; but, of course, it didn't. The only warmth it had was from his embraces, otherwise it remained just cold ivory.

'Then the feast of Aphrodite came round. Being a pious type, Pygmalion took a whole lot of rich gifts to her temple, and although he knew that it was a silly thing to ask, because statues don't come alive, he begged the goddess to take pity on him and give life to Galatea. The altar fire flared up three times, which was usually taken as a sign that the supplicant's prayer was to be granted. He simply couldn't believe it; but, all the same, he ran all the way home. When he entered the studio, Galatea smiled at him, stepped down from her throne and melted into his outstretched arms.'

'That's much nicer,' Stephanie commented. 'Now let's have Cupid and Psyche.'

Robbie smiled at her. 'All right. I think we'll just have time for that before we have to get dressed and go up to lunch. Psyche was one of three Princesses. They were all good-lookers, but she was something out of this world. The other two hooked husbands, but she was so devastatingly lovely that no one could pluck up the courage to ask her to name the day, and so dumb that she hadn't the know-how to bring any of the chaps up to scratch. But no one was interested in her mind, and people thought her such an eyeful that they even deserted the shrines of Aphrodite to come and strew flowers under Psyche's feet when she went out shopping.

'Aphrodite got to hear of this and became frightfully steamed up. She sent for her son Cupid, or Eros as the Greeks called him, and packed him off on a special mission. Her orders were that he was to shoot Psyche with one of his arrows, so that she should go absolutely goofy about the most horrid, mean, brutal man he could find, who would beat her and make her life a misery. Eros located Psyche, but he made a mess of things. The very sight of her beauty made him gasp, and he dropped the arrow on his own foot; so, of course, from that moment he was head-over-heels in love with her himself.

'Just about this time, Psyche's father got a bit tired of having an unmarried daughter on his hands; so he went and consulted the Oracle at Delphi on what to do about her. The answer was to fit her up with a first-class trousseau, then take her up to the top of a high mountain and leave her there. Her parents were very upset about this, but they were afraid that if they disobeyed the Oracle they would get it in the neck. Poor Psyche—who, you can bet, was jolly upset too—was decked out as a bride, accompanied by all and sundry up to the mountain top, kissed her good-bye and left, as she and everyone else supposed, to be devoured by some horrible monster.

'But things didn't pan out like that at all, and although the chronicles don't say so, it's pretty clear that Eros must have fixed with Apollo what his Oracle should decree. As dusk fell, Zephyr arrived and whisked Psyche, complete with trousseau, on a light breeze to what the estate agents would describe as a very desirable property. She was set down in a lovely garden outside the most enchanting small palace that ever you did see. Having smelt a few of the flowers, she took a peep inside the mansion then, as nobody was about, had a good look round. She found that it had all mod. cons., and that by comparison the furnishings made those in her old home palace look as if they had come out of a junk shop. She was just thinking that the curtains in the dining room must have cost about twenty times as much as her papa gave her as a dress allowance each year when a voice said in her ear: "I expect you must be pretty peckish. Please ask for anything you fancy and it will be here in a jiffy."

'That must have shaken her a bit, because there was still no one to be seen. But she plucked up her courage and opted for a boiled egg, to keep her figure down, to be followed by lashings of strawberries and cream and a stick of nougat to round it off with.'

'Really, Robbie!' Stephanie interjected. 'I'm sure that's not in the chronicles.'

'Well, no,' he admitted. 'But I imagine that's the sort of meal a sylph-like young girl without much brain might have asked for; and putting in little touches like that makes me see the characters in these stories better. Anyhow, in the flicker of an eyelid, there was her supper on the table, with gold spoons and forks to eat it with and a milk-shake to wash it down.

'When she had finished licking her fingers after the

nougat, she felt a bit drowsy; so she tripped lightly up the marble staircase to the best bedroom. A look in some of the cupboards showed her that, while she had been having supper, someone had unpacked for her. All her trousseau had been put neatly away, and to it had been added a full-length chinchilla coat. She put it on and was just preening herself a bit before the cheval glass when she got another shock. A voice said: "Not for now, dearie," then invisible hands removed the coat and started to undress her.

'As this voice had been a female one, she let herself be stripped, then led into the next room and popped into a silver bath full of scented asses' milk. When the hands had helped her dry herself, she was taken back to the bedroom where she lay down on a bed of rose petals. That bit really is in the chronicle.'

Stephanie laughed. 'What does it matter? You would have made up something just as suitable. But what happened then?'

'All the lights went out, plunging the whole place into complete darkness.'

'I think I really would have been scared by that.'

'Psyche didn't have time. There was a stir in the rose-leaves beside her, and a charming male voice said: "You may never see me, but you can hear and touch me, and I've been absolutely crackers about you from the moment I set eyes on you. This palace and everything in it is yours. The servants will remain unseen, but they will obey your every wish. I am the husband that the gods chose for you, and I shall come to you like this every night. Now, in about ten seconds, I'm going to start kissing and caressing you all over. I promise you there is nothing to be frightened of. You are going to enjoy this."

'The voice was that of Eros, of course, who had taken the form of an athletic young man. Before the first crack of dawn he left her; and he had been dead right. She had enjoyed it; in fact so much that she could hardly wait for night to fall so that he would come back and do whatever he had done to her all over again.

'Well, for a month or two everything went splendidly. Psyche was perfectly content to stooge round her lovely palace and garden during the day, wondering what new kissing game her invisible husband would teach her that night. But, very understandably, the time came when, with not a soul to talk to day after day, she became lonely; so she begged him to stay on for lunch just now and again.

'He said: "There's nothing I'd like better, sweetie; but it's just not on. If you ever set eyes on me our lovely romance would go right up the spout. I'll send you some copies of *Woman's Own* so that you can amuse yourself with some knitting." But Psyche said she wasn't a knitting sort of girl, and begged him to let her pay a short visit to her family, or to have them to stay for the week-end. He was dead against that, too; but she became so unhappy that at length he did agree that she should have her sisters up for the day.

'When her two sisters arrived their eyes fairly popped on seeing the luxury in which Psyche was living. At first, when she told them that invisible hands brushed her hair and painted her toenails, they wouldn't believe her; but when they asked for Lobster Newberg and Crêpe Suzette for lunch and these items instantly appeared on golden platters on the dinner table they simply had to.

'On their asking about her husband, she confessed that she had never seen him either. At that the sisters, having become green with jealousy, began to work on the poor girl. They told her that very soon she would be paying for that chinchilla coat in no uncertain manner. It was all very well for her to say that her chap felt like a beautiful young man, but demons could assume any form they liked. At any time he might turn into a terrible monster and tear her limb from limb. To escape such an awful fate, there was only one thing for her to do. As he was afraid of her seeing him, it was evident that when asleep he resumed his true, hideous form, and when looked on would lose much of his power. They advised her to put an oil lamp under her bed and, when her husband had dropped off to sleep, to get it out and light it. They added that she must also conceal one of the kitchen knives somewhere handy; so that when she set eyes on the horror that had been making love to her, she could plunge the knife into him before he could do her any harm.

'As I have said, Psyche was no great brain; so she believed all her envious sisters said, and acted accordingly. As soon as her husband was sound asleep that night, she got out the carving knife and lit the lamp. The gullible little idiot got such a surprise that she dropped her knife. Instead of a three-headed baboon, or something of that kind, on the crushed rose petals, snoring slightly, lay the sort of boy friend that Helen of Troy, Cleopatra and the Queen of Sheba, had they been around at that time, might have fought to get their hands on.

'Eros's bow and arrows lay on the floor beside the bed. Psyche was so knocked all of a heap by her luck that she hardly knew if it was Easter or Christmas. Still in a swoon, she picked up one of the arrows and tried it on her finger. The point drew a bead of blood, and instantly the yen she felt to cuddle up alongside the slightly snoring young man redoubled. But wounding herself with the arrow caused her to jerk the oil lamp and a drop of the hot oil fell on Eros's shoulder.

'He started awake, yelling: "Murder! Fire! Thieves! Rape! " Then he realized that his little nitwit had ignored the warnings that he had been at such great pains to instil into her. Sadly he told her that she had bitched the whole shooting match, and that now they must part for ever. His wings sprouted from his shoulders and he took off. At the same instant the enchanted palace vanished, lock, stock and barrel, and Psyche found herself back on the barren mountain top.

'After a bit she began to scramble down. Coming to a river, and being by then cuckoo with despair, she chucked herself into it. But she was washed ashore further down, and I suppose someone took her in, gave her some clothes and sent her on her way. Her sisters handed her the frozen mitt. Instead of condoling with her, they both hurried up to the mountain top, hoping that Eros would take a good view of them; but a mist came down, so they walked over a precipice and broke their necks. That served them right, but it didn't do Psyche any good; and for quite a time she wandered all over the place, distractedly seeking a way to make contact with Eros.

'He had winged it like smoke back to Olympus, yelling blue murder about his tiny little burn; but perhaps he had a very delicate skin. At all events he tearfully begged his beautiful mama to nurse him well again, although he refused to tell her how he had come by his burn.

'Aphrodite then put her Intelligence Service on the job, and a little bird brought her a report of her son's affair with Psyche. The goddess was absolutely furious; largely, I suppose, because it was Psyche at whom people had deserted her temples to go and stare. All the same, I think she behaved very unreasonably in being beastly to her son just because he had had fun with a mortal, when she was practically on the Dilly herself.'

'What does "on the Dilly" mean?'

Robbie smiled. 'Oh, it's an old-fashioned expression I happened to see in a book, for the girls who used to saunter up and down Piccadilly on the look-out for chaps they could persuade to come home with them for the night as paying guests; although, of course, Aphrodite never took money for that sort of thing. Generally, she was a very kind and easy-going goddess, but evidently in this case she felt that her supremacy as the Queen of Beauty was being challenged; so she pursued Psyche like a she-wolf after a ewe lamb.

'She persuaded Zeus to send Hermes down to proclaim that anyone who took Psyche in would suffer the wrath of the gods, and offered seven kisses from her own lips to anyone who would give up her mortal rival. As you can imagine, down on earth poor Psyche was having a very thin time; so thin, in fact, that after a while she decided to hand in her checks.

'That didn't do her any good at all. No sooner had she given herself up at one of Aphrodite's temples than she was hauled before the goddess by her golden hair, beaten, made into a slave and given all sorts of impossible tasks to perform.

'First Aphrodite mixed up a great heap of wheat, barley, millet, peas and beans, told Psyche to sort them out by evening, then went off in her latest creation to a wedding feast. Of course, Psyche hadn't a hope; but a kind little ant came on the scene, then brought all his pals to help; so when Aphrodite came back, trying to smother occasional burps from the amount of champagne she had drunk, she found that the job had been done.

'Next morning the goddess took her hated daughter-in-law to the bottom of a rocky hill and pointed out to her a thicket at its top, in which was feeding a flock of sheep with golden fleeces. She told Psyche that they were as fierce as lions, but she must go and get her a good handful of their golden wool. Again Psyche knew that she just was not up to it, so she decided to make an end of herself by taking a header into a deep pool that lay close by. But the nymph who was the tenant of the pool popped up just in time and said:

' "Hi, you! I don't want your body going rotten and making a nasty smell in my water. Have some sense and the job you've been given will be easy. While those vicious rams are playing tag with the sheep among the bushes, you have a nap down here. By afternoon they will be tired out and want a nap, too. Then you can go up the hill without their seeing you, and pick off the golden wool they have left on the thorns."

'Naturally Psyche took this advice; but even the lapful of golden wool she brought Aphrodite did not appease the goddess. She gave the wretched girl other impossible tasks to do, but one way or another Psyche was always helped out with them.

'Then at last Eros felt well enough to come downstairs, and he discovered that Psyche was sleeping under the scullery sink or some place like that. When he heard of all she had suffered on his account he loved her more than ever, and rushed off to beg Zeus to make his mother stop being so beastly to his beloved.

'Zeus, never having seen anything against a god uniting with a mortal, lent a sympathetic ear and summoned a Council of the Gods, ordering Aphrodite to bring Psyche with her. His Address from the Throne amounted to: "You all know that I've never been altogether sold on true love myself, but I admire it in others; so it is my intention to bless the banns of these two young people. What is more, since we can't have outsiders as members of the Club, I'm going to make the bride an Immortal." Then he beckoned to Psyche and, holding out a beaker of nectar to her, added: "Come here, my dear. Take a sup of this, and it will do the trick."

'When Psyche got her breath back everyone was queueing up to kiss her; and when Aphrodite saw how deliriously happy Eros looked, her mother's heart softened and she promised to love Psyche, too. Then they held the biggest-ever wedding feast. Hephaestus cooked fabulous dishes, Dionysus got up the best bottles from the cellar, the Seasons produced wonderful flowers, the Muses sang their sweetest songs, Ganymede went round filling all their goblets with nectar——'

'I thought Hebe was the Cupbearer of the Gods,' Stephanie put in.

Robbie hesitated a second. 'Well, she was at one time, but she lost her job. As I think I've told you, the Immortals were distinctly prudish when they were in company. I suppose the truth is that Hebe had been lifting the elbow herself too frequently. Anyhow, one night when they were feasting, she tripped up, and she can't have been wearing much in the way of undies because, as she fell, everyone saw all there was to see. Apparently they were so shocked by this that Zeus gave her the sack and brought in handsome young Ganymede to do butler instead.'

'I see. And did Eros and Psyche live happily ever after?'

'Yes. They never seem to have become tired of one another, and they had a beautiful daughter whom they named Joy.'

'Well, I am glad about that,' Stephanie said, getting up. 'And now it really is time for us to dress and go up for lunch.'

Late in the afternoon they had a ramble on their own round the ruins and it was on their return from it that they heard more about the submarine. During their stay at Navplion the weather had been good, so they had spent nearly the whole of every day out of doors. In consequence, they had not exchanged more than a few words with any of their fellow guests. Here, too, at Olympia, they had kept themselves very much to themselves; but there was one English couple who had the next table to theirs in the dining room, and with them they had become on casual conversation terms. The name of the couple was Jackson. He was middle-aged and a partner in a well-known firm of London auctioneers; his wife, a smart and pretty woman, was some years younger.

As Robbie and Stephanie came into the lounge, the Jacksons were sitting near the door. Glancing up from a newspaper, Mr. Jackson said: 'Things don't look too good, do they?'

Stephanie caught sight of the banner headline of the copy of the *New York Herald Tribune* that he had just lowered and, pausing at their table, said: 'I suppose you mean about the submarine?'

'Why, yes,' Mr. Jackson replied with a somewhat hesitant smile. 'I don't know of any other international headache at the moment; but this seems a really nasty one.'

'To tell the truth,' Robbie admitted, 'I've hardly given it a thought. We heard about it last week in Navplion, but English papers are not easy to come by in these places, and I haven't seen one for days; so I got the impression that the trouble had blown over.'

'It will,' declared Mrs. Jackson optimistically. 'Come and sit down and join us for a drink. Frank here has been indulging in such a fit of the blues since he got that paper that I badly need cheering up.'

Chairs were pulled round from another table, a waiter summoned and the order given; then Robbie said: 'I must confess that I don't even know how the trouble started.'

'Well, there are two versions about that,' Frank Jackson told him. 'The Americans say their sub. was making an under-ice cruise for scientific purposes. She left Honolulu in mid-March, came up through the Bering Straits, went west well inside the edge of the Arctic Circle, cruising some way north of Russia, and should have come down south of Greenland to New York. But, when passing between Franz Joseph Land and Novaya Zemblya, something went wrong with her steering apparatus; so her course was deflected too far south and she found herself in very shallow water, which turned out to be off the Russian coast near Murmansk.'

'I know nothing about such things,' Robbie remarked, 'and my geography is not too good. But it seems extraordinary that, with all those wonderful scientific gadgets they have now, she should have got so far off her course.'

'That's just the point. Both Franz Joseph Land and Novaya Zemblya are Soviet territory, and the captain of the sub. states that in the ice-free passage between them there was a number of Soviet warships. In the coded radio report he made, extracts from which have since been published by the American Government, he puts up the theory that the Russians have some new scientific device by which the ships of theirs that he passed, and which followed him down, were able to throw his compass out by several degrees. In fact, that they deliberately drove him on to their coast; and that, on learning where he was, he took refuge under the nearest ice.'

'And what do the Soviets say?' Stephanie asked.

'Oh, they naturally deny that. They say that, following normal procedure, they tracked the sub. down from Novaya Zemblya to see that it did not enter their territorial waters. But it did, and began to snoop round the defences in the neighbourhood of Murmansk. It was only then that they took action and sent out everything they had to head it into the bay, where it is now lying virtually captive.'

'I gathered from an American I met at Navplion,' Robbie said, 'that the Russians had demanded that it should come out and that its captain should surrender the ship and her crew to them.'

'That's right. Of course, the Americans firmly denied that it had been sent on a spying mission and refused. The Russians then did the correct thing and put the question to the United Nations. That eased the tension, as most people thought that, after a lot of talk, some solution would be arrived at. There was plenty of talk all right and yesterday the United Nations gave its verdict. Most of the Afro-Asian countries ganged up against the West, and that gave the Soviet bloc a majority. They say that there is no evidence to show that the sub. was forced into Soviet waters, but the fact is that it is there, and got there under its own power. Therefore, the Russians are in the right in demanding that it should be handed over.'

'Looked at fairly,' Stephanie remarked, 'I don't see how they could have come to any other decision.'

Mrs. Jackson nodded. 'That's just what I say. But Frank

gets all worked up and says that is absolutely out of the question.'

'Of course it is, Ursula,' her husband took her up a trifle shortly. 'That submarine must contain the fruit of years of nuclear research by the Americans, and by British and Canadian scientists, too. In addition, it almost certainly has in it all sorts of other secret devices for under-water navigation, air-conditioning, guiding missiles to their targets, and so on. To surrender her would be to hand the Russians on a plate the key to all our latest methods of defence. The West would be left naked in the breeze.'

Robbie fully agreed with him, but the two women stuck to their opinion that the Americans had once again asked for trouble which, whether it was or was not true, was neither here nor there; so, over further drinks, they argued round the subject until it was time to freshen up for dinner.

Next morning, while Robbie was having his coffee, rolls, Hymettus honey and the little, sweet buns that were always sent up in Greek hotels on the breakfast trays, he again thought over the question of the trapped submarine. He still could not believe that it would lead to war; but there could be no doubt that the two Great Power blocs were still giving the highest possible priority to every activity which might put either one ahead of its enemy, if things did blow up.

That led his thoughts again to the Czechs and the conclusion to which he had come just on a month ago—that if there were no oil in Greece, their operations could only be a cover for some other project that boded no good to the N.A.T.O. countries. In view of the crisis that was now developing, he began to wonder if he had been justified in wasting the past few days. The site near Pirgos having been completely deserted on the previous Sunday had led him, on learning that the photographs he had taken had been ruined, to decide to wait until the coming Sunday before going there again to take another set. Had he attempted to do so earlier, it seemed certain that some of the Czechs would be about, and, mindful of his escape from serious injury in Corinth, he had naturally been averse to risking another encounter with them. But now, in view of a possible emergency, to find out quickly what they were up to assumed a new importance. By the time he had had his bath, he had decided that, when he went down for a bathe with Stephanie that morning, he would tell her the full truth about his self-imposed mission; so that, if anything happened to him, she could let Luke Beecham know. Then he would tell her that he meant to try to take another set of photographs at Pirgos during the siesta hours that afternoon.

Half an hour later, carrying his bathing things, he was on his way to the lounge to wait for her. As he passed the office, the porter held out a letter to him and said: 'This is for Miss Stephanopoulos, sir. Perhaps you will give it to her?'

As he took the letter, Robbie wondered how anyone could have found out that she was staying at the Spap Hotel, Olympia. Then he remembered that, on their last night in Navplion, she had written and posted a letter that she had told him was to her closest girl friend, asking her to let her mother know, without disclosing her whereabouts, that she was well and happy. In the letter she had evidently said that she was going on to Olympia and this was a reply.

Glancing at the letter, as he turned into the lounge, he saw that it had an Athens postmark, and was addressed in a bold, vigorous hand. The writing did not look like that of a girl, and it struck him that there was something familiar about it. Sitting down, he turned it over, striving to remember where he had seen that heavy, rather old-fashioned writing before.

Suddenly he seemed to go cold all over and his big hands began to tremble. He had seen the writing a score of times. It was that of Marak Krajcir, the manager of the Czech Travel Agency.

20

No Holds Barred

For a full minute Robbie sat stunned, holding the letter in his hand and staring at it. During the whole of the time they had been together, Stephanie had made no reference to any Czech except when they had been talking of his own investigation. She had never mentioned Czechoslovakia or any wish to travel. Then what possible explanation could there be for her receiving a letter from Krajcir?

Having asked himself that question, Robbie's brain temporarily stuck. Then the awful thought that had come to him when he had first recognized the writing on the envelope returned with renewed force. Could it be . . . No, that was utterly unthinkable. And yet . . . how else could one possibly account for her being in communication with his enemies?

His heart seemed to turn over inside him, and he suddenly felt sick. It simply could not be true that Stephanie was betraying him. Why should she? What had she to gain? She was not a Czech, but was half Greek and half English. Money apparently meant little to her for, on several occasions when he had tried to press a generous wage upon her, she had refused to accept more than one or two hundred-drachma notes. She always said that the holiday she was having amply repaid her for driving him and that it would be time enough to give her more money when she had done some work on his book. Besides, while he did not regard it as remotely possible that she had, in secret, the same feelings for him as he had for her, she had shown great concern for him when he had gone into danger, and had treated him with a warmth of friendship that could almost be said to be affection.

And yet . . . ?

After another long minute of soul-shaking agitation, he decided that he must find out for certain. He had never spied on other people, let alone opened a letter addressed to someone else. But unless he resolved this horrible doubt once and for all, how could they possibly go on together? Their lovely companionship, their carefree laughter, those long talks about his beloved Immortals in whom she seemed to share his interest, their planning of things to do that would fill other happy days, those delightful dinners during which he could gaze his fill at her every night across the table—how could they be resumed as long as suspicion of her motives never ceased to nag at his mind?

Had he been a professional secret agent, he would have gone to the kitchen and given the chef a handsome tip to let him steam open the letter over the spout of a kettle. Then, if his worst suspicions had been realized, he would have re-sealed the letter, given it to her and beaten her at her own game by acting a part while she remained ignorant that he knew the truth about her. But by nature he was far too straight-forward to adopt such finesse, even had he thought himself capable of carrying it off. As it was, the idea never occurred to him, or how he should try to excuse himself if he opened Stephanie's letter, found some innocent explanation for it, and had to give it to her afterwards. Unable to bear remaining in ignorance of its contents another moment, he ripped it open.

The letter it contained had neither opening nor signature. It was typed on a single sheet of thin paper and was in Czech. At the sight of the language, Robbie shut his eyes. Sickly, warm saliva ran in his mouth. With an effort he swallowed it, opened his eyes and read:

N. is pleased with you. Since there was no way in which you could prevent him from taking the photographs, it was an excellent idea to render the film useless by opening the back of the camera. Had you stolen and destroyed the film, that would

*have revealed that we have him under observation, and he
might even have suspected you. As he remains in ignorance of
the fact that his visit to Pirgos is known to us, it seems likely
that he will make a second attempt to get photographs of our
plant there. Now that he is showing a greater inclination to
confide in you, it should be easier for you to find out his plans
in advance, and it is of the utmost importance that we should
be informed if and when he decides to go to Pirgos again, so
that we may be ready for him. N. says that as he shows such
persistence, we now have no alternative to putting him out of
the way for good, and another visit by him to Pirgos would
provide an excellent opportunity. As soon as you have anything to report, ring Pirgos 8721. A day and night service has
been installed, so at any hour there will be someone there to
receive your call.*

Robbie's eyes misted over. It was really true then. She was
working for the Czechs. She might even be one herself. As the
letter was in Czech, she must know that language; so the odds
were that she was. If so, that would explain a lot of things: for
one, her ignorance about Greek mythology; for another, her
blue eyes and the fact that her colouring was much lighter than
that of the great majority of Greek women—although he had
put that down to her story that her mother was English. Then
there was the curious accent with which she spoke Greek. He
had attributed that, too, to her associations with England,
although it was sufficiently marked for him, a foreigner, to
have noticed, and it should not have been if she had spent all
but her early childhood in Greece. He thought it probable now
that her accent was much more noticeable to the Greeks than
to himself, and that it was unlikely that she had ever been in
England. To tell him that she had been brought to Greece when
still a child had been a clever precaution, enabling her to say,
should he attempt to check up on her, that her memories of
England were only very vague ones.

But how cleverly she had deceived him from the very
beginning. He closed his eyes again and winced as he thought
of the way in which he had taken as gospel truth her story that

she, a woman of twenty-four, was being forced into a repugnant marriage and that, if he did not take pity on her, she could see no alternative to becoming a hostess in a Piraeus night club. In this day and age, it was so highly improbable that only a simpleton like himself would have believed it.

As he opened his eyes again, he caught sight of her passing some remark to the page boy, who was holding the door of the lounge open for her. Stuffing the letter into the pocket of his jacket, Robbie stood up. Next moment she was coming towards him, smiling her usual morning greeting.

Somehow he found his voice and, to his surprise, it sounded quite normal as he automatically made his usual response—hoping that she had had a good night and was looking forward to their swim.

As he picked up his swimsuit and towel, she remarked how lucky they were that the weather still remained so lovely; then, side by side, they left the lounge and walked down the broad staircase out into the sunshine.

Robbie's brain was still racing. He knew now why it was that the Czechs had been waiting for him in Corinth and why, after he had escaped from them, he had found her about to drive off with Barak. He knew, too, why she had constantly pressed him to confide in her. Should he blurt out his discovery here and now, and charge her with her perfidy? No; there were other guests from the hotel about, making their way down to the ruins. It would not do to start a blood-row within their hearing. Better to wait until they reached the river. They passed the little museum and descended the slope to a bridge that spanned one of the tributaries of the river. As they walked along she chatted away lightly, first about a group of Germans who were a little way ahead of them, then about the Jacksons. She said that on the previous night, before going to bed, she had returned to the lounge to get a magazine, and had run into Ursula Jackson, who had asked her how long she had known Robbie, and several other vaguely leading questions. She added with a laugh that she was sure that charming lady had not accepted Robbie's statement that he was a business man and herself his chauffeuse-secretary, but believed them to be lovers enjoying an unofficial honeymoon.

Had Stephanie made such a remark the day before, Robbie just might have plucked up the courage to break the ice by saying: 'How I wish we were.' But now he could think only of the horrible deception she was practising upon him. The letter, which seemed to be burning a hole in his pocket, proved beyond any shadow of doubt that she was only waiting for the chance to betray him into the hands of his enemies. He thought of Jael, who had driven a tent-peg through Sisera's head only an hour or two after she had slept with him; of Delilah who had cut off Samson's hair and so sent him to be slaughtered. That sweetly smiling, gentle-seeming creatures could calmly carry out such acts of treachery upon men who loved them seemed unbelievable; yet history provided scores of examples of such betrayals, and there seemed no escaping the fact that Stephanie was just one more of that hideous breed.

When they had covered another few hundred yards, she glanced at him and said: 'Why are you so silent this morning, Robbie? Aren't you feeling well?'

'I'm all right,' he managed to reply. 'I had rather a bad night, but I'll feel better when I've had a swim.'

Reassured about him, she went on to suggest that next day they should cut out their bathe and run down to Phygalia and Theatron where, she had learned from a folder in the hotel, there were some interesting ruins.

He said he thought that was a good idea, and they would talk about it over lunch. But it brought home to him more sharply than ever that there could be no such next day. Those runs in the car and jolly picnics while he told her stories of the ancient Greeks were over for ever. The sweet companionship with her that he had enjoyed more than anything in his whole life was a thing of the past, and only bitter loneliness lay ahead.

His thoughts then turned to another case of woman's treachery that was for him nearer home. The city of Megara had once been besieged by Minos, King of Crete. The siege was long; so Scylla, the daughter of Megara's King, Nisus, often saw from the battlements Minos in his shining armour and fell in love with him. Her father had one lock of purple hair, and he had confided to her that an Oracle had predicted that the city would never be taken unless he was shorn of this lock.

Scylla's passion for Minos became so great that one night she crept into her father's chamber and cut off the lock. Then she secretly left the city, made her way to Minos's tent and offered him the strand of purple hair, with her undying love.

Minos, being a chivalrous King, refused to take it, gave King Nisus honourable terms and spurned Scylla, telling her that he would not demean himself by having anything to do with a woman capable of betraying her country.

For a moment, Robbie imagined himself in the place of Minos. He thought of the satisfaction he would derive from having Stephanie clinging to his knees and beseeching him to make love to her, then breaking her evil heart by haughtily thrusting her from him.

But the cases were not parallel. Stephanie did not love him. She had exerted all her charm and woman's guile on him only to lead him to confide in her; so that she could pass on his intentions to unscrupulous men who, it seemed, were now prepared to go even to the length of killing him. Far, far from loving him, she probably despised him for not even having had the courage to make a pass at her, when for these past weeks she had been in such a situation that, if she were to keep her job with her employers, she would have been put in a spot had she shown her resentment at his attentions.

It then struck Robbie that Minos had behaved like a fool. It was said that Scylla had been a very beautiful girl. Why, before throwing her out, had he not had the sense to enjoy himself with her? The humiliation earned her by her treachery would afterwards have been all the greater.

Robbie took a swift, sideways glance at Stephanie. There she was, in height barely up to his shoulder. But a fine, strong, square-shouldered little figure with a beautiful bust and broad hips that curved gracefully away under the thin skirt she was was wearing to legs having perfect proportions.

'Why not?' he thought. 'Why not? It would give her something to remember me by. It would teach her a lesson for life; that even poor simple devils like myself are not to be trifled with.'

By that time they had reached their pool. With a smile over

her shoulder, Stephanie disappeared into the clump of bushes behind which she always changed into her bathing things. Robbie went behind another clump some ten yards distant. His mind in a ferment, he tore off his clothes, but did not put on his swimming trunks. For a few minutes he stood there with his heart throbbing wildly. He could feel it beating like a hammer under his ribs. From experience gained during their previous bathes he knew how long Stephanie took to get undressed. Imbued with inflexible purpose, he suddenly strode towards the other clump of bushes.

At a glance, he saw that he had timed things perfectly. Stephanie had fastened on her white satin top but was only in the act of stepping into her bathing skirt.

The sound of his approaching footsteps crunching twigs and dead leaves caused her to look up. As she saw him advancing on her, she uttered a low cry, tripped on the garment into which she had put one foot, and staggered sideways. Next moment he was upon her.

With one hand he ripped the bikini-top from her breasts; the other hand he flung round her waist. Her blue eyes, distended by shock and fright, stared into his. Jerking herself backward, she attempted to break away from him, but his grip on her waist was firm. With a sudden movement, he drew her to him, forcing her body against his. Then his head came downward and his mouth fastened greedily upon hers. She wrenched her face sideways, but his devouring lips fastened on her neck below the chin. Another moment, and one of his legs had curled round hers. Under the pressure, her knees gave and she fell backward. Robbie came down on top of her, temporarily driving the breath from her body.

'No, Robbie, no!' she managed to gasp. 'Not like this!' Then she suddenly relaxed, gave a little moan, and offered no further resistance.

In less than a minute it was all over. At one moment he had been smothering her face with kisses, the next he had thrust himself away from her and was up on his knees. Sobbing for breath, he lurched to his feet and staggered away towards the bushes where he had left his clothes.

As he collapsed beside them, he was conscious of bitter

disappointment. Apart from the softness of her lips under that first, snatched kiss and the delicious feeling of her warm, satin-like skin against his, seizing her like that had given him no pleasure.

Then, within a few moments, a reaction set in to the urge he had felt. Because she had turned out to be a secret agent that was no justification for treating her as though she were a whore. She was unmarried and had never given him the least reason to suppose that she was unchaste. However much she had lied to him had still given him no right to punish her by abusing her physically. It had been a swinish thing to do, and the very antithesis of the conduct of the paladins of chivalry, whom he had for so long admired.

Yet what was done was done. There could be no going back and seeking explanations. That, at least, he knew would have been futile, for there was no possible explanation by which she could have put herself right with him. She had been proved up to the hilt to be a whited sepulchre; fair-seeming without, but rotten as carrion within. There had had to be an end between them, and that it should have been in this fierce, vengeful way was, perhaps, the will of the ancient gods.

Some minutes later he heard a rustling of the bushes and, opening his eyes, saw Stephanie looking down on him. She was again fully dressed. Her face looked drawn and almost ugly, as tears had caused the mascara to run down from her eyelashes on to her cheeks.

'Why . . . ?' she asked in a hoarse whisper. 'Why did you do that to me, Robbie?'

Rolling over, he got the letter from the pocket of his jacket and, without a word, threw it towards her.

Picking it up, she ran her eye swiftly over it, nodded slowly, gave a sudden sob and murmured: 'I see. Yes: now I understand.' Turning away she left him, and with stricken heart he listened until the sound of her footsteps had faded away in the distance.

He continued to lie there for what seemed an eternity, tortured by thoughts that went round and round: the humiliation of having been so completely fooled by her; remorse for having behaved so brutally to her; agony at the thought that those happy days he had spent with her were gone for ever; then again anger at the way she had led him to look on her as the most wonderful person in the world.

At last he dressed and, still in a daze, walked back to the hotel, to find that it was long past lunchtime. He assumed that Stephanie would be leaving as soon as she could make arrangements to do so: perhaps that afternoon, but possibly not till next morning. In the latter case she would still be there for dinner, and for them to sit down to another meal together was out of the question. He was most reluctant to see her again and he could have left a message for her, saying that he intended to dine out at one of the smaller hotels down in the village, but conscience urged him to face the unpleasant task of apologizing for the way he had treated her; so he walked along the corridor to her room.

He found the door ajar. He knocked, but there was no reply; so he went in. It was empty and the only sign that Stephanie had ever been there was some soiled face tissues on the dressing-table. Obviously she had already packed and gone. Walking over to the dressing table, he gently fingered the face tissues. A suggestion of her scent still lingered in the air, but the empty room struck him with a terrible air of finality. Tears welled up into his eyes but, with a curse, he suddenly swung about, marched out of the room and slammed the door behind him.

Going into his own room next door, he had a wash to freshen himself up. As he came out of the bathroom, his glance fell on the bedside table. Something was missing from it. Next moment, he realized what it was. He always kept his manuscript there, and it was gone. Only Stephanie could have taken it. Digging his nails into the palms of his hands, he slumped down on the bed. If anything could have added to his misery it was the loss of that bundle of papers which represented so many weeks of arduous work. She would have known that, and could have thought of no better way of revenging herself.

Yet, greatly as its loss infuriated him, it had one salutary effect. It enabled him to adjust his feelings towards her. In a

way, the theft of the manuscript had evened up the score
between them. It made him feel less guilty towards her, and
enabled him to see her in a better perspective. He felt that he
could now divorce in his mind the Stephanie in whose company he had enoyed so much happiness from the real woman
who had tricked and robbed him. Given a little time, he would
be able to remember the one with pleasure; but he would not
be tormented by hopeless longings for her, because she had
revealed herself as the other.

Suddenly, it occurred to him that the manuscript might not
be the only thing she had taken. She might have made off with
his passport and money and perhaps the car. Pulling out from
under the bed the suitcase in which he kept his papers, he was
relieved to find it still locked. On unlocking it, he found that
his papers were intact. Leaving the room, he hurried downstairs and round to the garage, to find his fears again groundless. The Ford was out on the wash and one of the garage hands
was hosing it down. He gave Robbie a friendly grin and said:

'When I got back from running your young lady into
Pirgos I thought I'd better give the car a going-over.'

That solved for Robbie the question of how and where
Stephanie had gone; but he thought it unlikely that Pirgos was
her destination. From the little station at Olympia, the trains
were slow and infrequent, and to get to Athens she would have
had to change at both Tripolis and Argos. On the other hand,
by going to Pirgos, she would be able to take a fast train up
the coast and round the gulf of Corinth direct to the capital.

For a few moments he speculated grimly on whether, when
she made her final report to Krajcir, the Czech would realize
that it was his writing that had given her away. Anyhow the
'N' of the letter, who was most probably the First Secretary,
Nejedly, was going to be far from pleased when he learned that
she had been winkled out of her job.

As Robbie walked back into the hotel, he suddenly remembered that he had intended to go into Pirgos himself that afternoon to try and take another set of photographs. It was too late
to do so now; so it would have to be the next day, unless he
reverted to his original intention, put it off for two more days

and lessened the risk by making his attempt on Sunday. But would that now lessen the risk? No; on the contrary, Stephanie still thought that he had meant to wait the week out, and she would certainly let them know what she believed to be his intentions. Possibly, realizing that, they would think it unlikely that he would stick to his plan; but, just in case he did, they would certainly not leave the place unguarded on Sunday, so it looked as though his chances would now be better during the siesta hours on any other day.

There was also the fact that the dispute over the submarine might just possibly lead to war. As Stephanie had been congratulated, in Krajcir's letter, on spoiling the photographs, that was a clear indication that the Czechs had something to hide. What could that something be if not a warlike preparation? Therefore, he felt more strongly than ever that his impulse first thing that morning, to get the photographs with a minimum of delay, had been a sound one.

Having decided that he would make the attempt next day, he went into the lounge and found a Greek newspaper. It was full of the Soviet-American crisis, but as yet the Russians had made no further move. Putting it down, he reverted to considering his own situation. He was in half a mind to dine down in the village, so as to escape having to give some explanation to the Jacksons of Stephanie's abrupt departure. But if he was to get those photographs, it would mean his staying in the hotel for at least another twenty-four hours. During that time he was certain to run into them; so it seemed better to face up to that rather than put himself to considerable inconvenience by taking all his main meals out.

When he met them at dinner, he announced at once that an unexpected call from Athens had necessitated his sending Stephanie off there to deal with an urgent business matter. He added that, in any case, he did not expect her back until after the week-end and that, if she proved unable to handle the affair for him, he would himself have to leave either the next night or on Saturday.

The Jacksons then insisted that he join them at their table. Much as he would have preferred to remain at his own, it was not in his nature to hurt the feelings of people who made kindly gestures towards him, and afterwards he was glad that he had accepted their invitation. Frank Jackson was a loquacious man; soignée Ursula Jackson also liked to air her views and Robbie had long been accustomed to the role of patient listener. In order to be able to make an occasional suitable comment, he had to take in what they were saying, and that kept his mind from the gloomy thoughts which would otherwise have occupied it. After dinner they continued their conversation over coffee and liqueurs in the lounge; so he went to bed much less harassed by memories, regrets and frustration than he would otherwise have been.

On the Friday morning, the very thought of going to the pool sent a wave of sickness through him, but he had somehow to get through the hours until the afternoon; so he decided to take the Ford out for a run. He had at first intended to hire one of the garage hands to drive him into Pirgos and back, but on second thoughts he did not see why he should not drive himself. There were no high cliffs with dangerous bends on the way and, as the town was not a big one, he felt confident that he would be able to get through the traffic safely. The only snag was that he had no licence. As long as Stephanie had been with him while he was driving they could, he thought, have got away with it, had a policeman pulled them up, by saying that he had taken the wheel only for a short lesson. Should he be challenged while alone in charge of the car, he would find himself in trouble; but he decided to chance that.

His morning's spin on his own considerably increased his confidence, and after an early lunch he set out for Pirgos. At that hour the traffic in the town was at its lowest ebb; so he got through it without any difficulty, and by ten past two he halted the car at the side of the road alongside the group of tamarisks where, on his previous visit, Stephanie had waited for him. He then followed the same procedure of going down to the beach and walking slowly along it, stopping now and then as though he were collecting shells.

When he reached the wall of the ruined factory, he stood for a couple of minutes listening intently. No sound came to him, other than the gentle breaking of the surf on the shore; so it seemed that no work was at present in progress and that, as he had hoped, the Czechs had adopted the Greek custom of knocking off during the hottest hours of the day.

With high hopes now of succeeding in his intent, he walked quietly but quickly to the nearest gap in the wall. From some yards away, he saw that the barbed wire had been removed and the opening was in the process of being bricked up. A low wall about three feet high already filled the lower portion of the gap, and an unfinished row of bricks with still-fresh mortar below them showed that somebody had been working on it that morning.

Partially concealed by standing close up to the jagged edge of the original wall at one side of the gap, he cautiously peered round it. As he had supposed, all the machinery was at a standstill and, to his delight, no one was about. By stepping over the new low piece of wall, he had only to turn from side to side, so that his camera covered different sections of the yard, to take pictures that would show the whole of it. Taking out his camera, he took care not to knock the freshly laid top course of bricks, and stepped over into the yard. His camera clicked twice, then a whistle blew.

Next moment, men came running at him from all directions: from the little house, from sheds and from behind the big machine that had been installed near the derrick in the middle of the yard. Swivelling round, he dived for the gap in the wall. In his stride he put his foot down on the side of a square board on which there was a small mound of hardening mortar. His camera flew from his hand, and he fell across the length of newly made wall, dislodging half a dozen of the last-laid bricks.

Desperately he heaved himself upright, but only to find that two men had either been lying hidden in the long grass outside the wall, or had just dashed round there from some other opening. As he faced them, one of them sprang at him, aiming a blow at his head with a stout length of wood. He raised his arm to parry the blow, but the men in the yard had now come up behind him. They seized him by the shoulders and swung him round. He found himself face to face with Barak. The face of the tall, good-looking Czech still carried a symbol of the pasting Robbie had given it. The bruises had disappeared, but his nose had been broken and was now slightly crooked. While two other men hung on to Robbie's arms, Barak hit him again and again under the jaw until he slumped down unconscious.

21

Twelve Hours to Live

Robbie came to with a shock. A bucket of cold water had been dashed into his face to bring him round. His first sensation was only of a terrible pain in his chin and neck, as though the one had been broken and the other dislocated. Then, as his eyes focused, he saw Barak's face still in front of, but now above, his. He realized then that he was sitting on a stout wooden chair and that his arms and legs were bound to it. As he painfully turned his head from side to side, he became aware that he was being regarded with cold curiosity or casual amusement by a number of men on both sides of Barak. He saw, too, that he was in a shed, facing its half-open door, but there was plenty of light because the sun was streaming down on him through a great hole in the roof.

When his eyes had been open for a few moments, Barak grabbed a handful of his shirt and tie and shook him, so that excruciating pains ran through his neck and head. But he heard him snarl in Czech: 'Wake up! Wake up! I am impatient to talk to you.'

'Stop!' Robbie croaked. 'For God's sake stop, and I'll listen.'

Barak released him, then spoke sharply to the other men, ordering them out of the shed. All but one of them trooped out, and the exception was standing a yard or so away from Robbie's left shoulder. Screwing his head round, Robbie got a quick glimpse of him. First he saw a fat little paunch, then the pink face and pig's features of Cepicka.

'Now, Mr. Grenn,' Barak began in a harsh voice. 'This meeting with you gives me very special pleasure. You have caused us a considerable amount of trouble, and we are determined that you shall cause us no more. I warned you in Patras to keep your nose out of our affairs. You chose to ignore my warning, but I should have thought your narrow escape from having to spend some months in hospital in Corinth would have made you see sense. Had you a grain of intelligence in that thick head of yours, nothing would have induced you to come here again after learning yesterday that the lady you knew as Miss Stephanopoulos is a Czech agent. But that is just why you must be regarded as dangerous. By your amateurish blunderings, you may learn much more about our secrets than the N.A.T.O. professionals who are paid to do the job. Therefore, Mr. Grenn, now that you have so stupidly thrown yourself into our arms, we should be lacking in our duty to our country if we failed to take this opportunity to eliminate you.'

'Do you mean . . . that you intend to kill me?' Robbie asked hoarsely.

'Exactly,' Barak nodded and drew a finger along one side of his little tooth-brush moustache, 'and I cannot say that I am in the least sorry that your folly has landed you in this situation where your death has become necessary to protect the interests of my country. In fact, Mr. Cepicka and I spent most of last night in a train coming from Athens, on the off-chance that, within the next few days, you would pay this place another visit. You see, I wished to be, as I think you say in England, "in at the kill".'

'You bloody swine,' Robbie muttered.

Barak gave a slightly twisted smile, then shook a warning finger in front of Robbie's nose. 'Do not become abusive, Mr. Grenn, otherwise I might forget myself. Or, rather, recall too vividly that I have a personal score to settle with you. Nothing would give me greater pleasure than to smash your face to pulp; but we have to remember that we are in a foreign country. Therefore your body, should it be washed up, must show no marks of violence in excess of such buffets it might receive through being thrown about by the waves.'

'So . . . so . . . you're going to drown me?'

'Yes. Presently I shall send one of my people into the town to buy the largest size in men's swimming trunks for you. At the quietest hour—shall we say three o'clock in the morning—Mr. Cepicka and I will come to you here. We shall take off your clothes and put you into the swimming trunks, then we shall take you down to the motor-boat we have here in our little harbour, run you out to sea and drop you overboard.'

Robbie's heart lightened a little. He thought it unlikely that they would take him out more than four or five miles and, unless there was a very strong current against him, he felt sure he could swim that distance back.

Next moment his hopes were dashed. With another slightly twisted smile, Barak went on: 'Miss Stephanopoulos tells me that you are a very powerful swimmer; so naturally we shall take precautions against any chance of your swimming ashore. In that, too, we must be careful not to leave tell-tale marks on your body. A loop of hose under your armpits, with its end stoutly wired so that you cannot undo it with your fingers, will serve. By it we shall troll you behind the boat, just as one trolls a hooked fish. Now and again we shall haul you in, to find out how you are standing up to the treatment. It will be interesting to see how long you take to drown. When we are quite satisfied that there is no longer life in your body we shall cut the wires at the neck of the loop of hose and cast you off.'

As Robbie listened his eyes were lowered and, when Barak spoke of trolling him in a noose of hosepipe, he noticed that his wrists were secured to the elbows of the chair in which he was sitting by short lengths of smooth, rubber hose. That ensured that, however much he wriggled his wrists, the skin would not become broken and cut as it would have against rope or cord. In consequence, when he was thrown out of the motor-boat, the only mark on his body would be a bruising where Barak had hit him under the chin and that, when he was washed up, would be taken as one of the bruises that a body normally receives through being tossed by the waves on to a beach. All this made it obvious to him that the manner of his death had been carefully planned in advance and, as he thought how idiotically foolhardy he had been to come to Pirgos again after Stephanie had returned to her employers, Barak gave him the final details of their arrangements.

'Of course,' he said, 'we shall collect your car and drive it a few miles further down the coast. Then we shall leave your clothes and an unmarked towel on a quiet stretch of beach. When your body is washed up and identified, the authorities can take their choice. Either that fine swimmer, Mr. Grenn, became bored with bathing in a pool of the river Alfios, so decided to run down to the sea for a real swim and had the misfortune to swim too far out; or that Mr. Grenn had been desperately in love with his pretty secretary, and her desertion had disturbed the balance of his mind, so he had chosen this way of putting an end to his life.'

This mocking reference to Stephanie turned the knife in Robbie's mental wound, and he was about to hurl curses at Barak when Cepicka, who had so far remained silent, gave a titter and added: 'How such a high-spirited girl survived three weeks of boredom with this fool, I cannot imagine. I congratulate you, Comrade Barak, on her fine sense of duty in not leaving him before she had to.'

So that, thought Robbie, was the impression of him that Stephanie had given these friends of hers. He could have wept with rage and humiliation, but managed to control himself by the thought that, if he showed how deeply he was hurt, they would only bait him further.

Barak gave an abrupt laugh and said to Cepicka: 'Come along, we will leave him now.' Then, when they had stepped out through the doorway, he glanced at his wrist-watch, turned and said to Robbie:

'It is now a little past three o'clock, Mr. Grenn, so you have just about twelve hours to live.'

A minute later, the door was shut and padlocked, and Robbie was left to his bitter thoughts, fears and self-reproaches. He realized now that he had been mad to pay another visit to Pirgos. He should have left Olympia and gone down to Kalamai, or across to Crete, where other groups of Czechs would not have been expecting him.

Thinking it over, he decided that the shock of finding out

that Stephanie was betraying him, and all that followed, must
have robbed him temporarily of all sense in handling the affair.
Evidently, though, she had counted on his being fool enough to
come there again, otherwise they would not have been waiting
in ambush for him. How they could have found out that he
intended to pay a second visit to the factory that afternoon
remained a mystery. He could only suppose that their secret was
of such importance to them that they had decided to lie in wait
between one o'clock and four every day, in the hope of cap-
turing him.

The fact that they had succeeded had, at first, dismayed
but not particularly frightened him. But as Barak had given
particulars of their programme for the coming night, it had
become more and more clear that the Czech was not simply
trying to scare him and that, in the end, he would get off with
a very nasty beating up. By the time they had left the shed, he no
longer had any doubts that they really meant to murder him.
As his mind grasped the fact, real fear caused the sweat to
break out on his palms and forehead.

As soon as he had regained consciousness, he had automatically attempted to free himself, only to find that he could
move neither his wrists nor ankles more than half an inch. In
addition, the chair to which he was bound appeared also to be
made fast to a stout wooden crosspiece, immediately behind it,
that formed part of the framework of the shed; for he could
jiggle the chair about, but not stand up with it still tied to his
back.

A more careful examination of his bonds showed that
through each length of hose there ran a wire, the protruding
ends of which were twisted together a dozen times below the
elbows of the chair and a good six inches beyond the reach
of his finger tips, however hard he stretched them. His ankles,
secured to the chair legs, were even more impossible to get at.
For five or six minutes he jerked the chair back and forth,
hoping that he might loosen it from the wooden strut, but at
the end of that time it was as firmly fixed as ever.

By squinting upward, he could see the big rent in the cor-
rugated iron roof of the shed. Evidently several sheets had
been brought down in the earthquake, and the roof had never

been repaired; but as long as he remained bound to the chair it was futile to think of getting out that way. Apart from a heap of sand in one corner and a few old wooden boxes, the shed was empty; so, even if he could have moved his chair, there was no sharp metal angle in it against which, by rubbing his bonds, he might have worn them through.

In less than a quarter of an hour, he had examined and exhausted every possibility for regaining his freedom. At last he sat quiet, endeavouring to resign himself to the fate in store for him. Although Barak had said he intended to drown him, and he knew that the Czech meant that, his brain still refused to accept as a fact that in a few hours his lifeless body would be drifting about in the sea, and that he, Robbie Grenn, would be finished and gone from this world for ever.

Hour after hour through the long afternoon he sat there, his mind forming an endless series of pictures with thoughts appropriate to each: Stephanie laughing with him across a dinner table; his uncle's anger on hearing that he had got a job with the Czechs; the wan face of his beloved Aunt Emily as she lay in bed during her last illness; Stephanie naked and bending forward with one foot raised and the other through the leg of her bathing skirt just before he had seized her; the square head and pale blue eyes behind the pince-nez of the tutor whom Aunt Emily had engaged to help teach him German; the back of Nejedly's bald head and Barak's face beyond it, as they had sat lunching together that fatal day at Toyrcolimano; Stephanie wearing an absurd piece of blue veiling on her chestnut curls as he had first seen her; the sacred olive tree up on the Acropolis; old Nanny Fisher peeling an apple for his breakfast; and so on, and so on, until, in spite of the threat that hung over him, he dropped off to sleep.

For how long he slept he had no idea, but when he awoke night had fallen, and his limbs felt very stiff. As the realization of his position flooded back to him, he panicked and made frantic efforts to break free; but his bonds were unbreakable. After a few minutes of futile struggling, he slumped back exhausted and, from fear of what might now happen to him at any moment, began to weep.

Gradually his tears ceased, and another series of mental

M

pictures, similar to those of the afternoon, began to drift through his mind. From time to time, he now began to feel rather hungry and distinctly thirsty. It must, he reckoned, be at least eight hours, perhaps more, since he had finished lunch, and evidently his captors did not think it worth while to bring food and drink to a man they had condemned to death. Had they come to tell him that he could have anything he chose for his last meal, he felt sure that he could not possibly have done justice to a lavish dinner; but to try and keep his mind off what it would be like to find oneself choking and gasping without hope in the sea, he began to think of all his favourite dishes.

It was not completely dark in the shed, as faint starlight came through the open portion of the roof, yet it was sufficiently dark for him to notice instantly a pale line of light that appeared about four feet up, where the double doors of the shed met. Next second he heard the key turn in the padlock. His heart gave a thump. The door was pulled open and his eyes were dazzled by the glare of a torch that was directed full on him. Sweat again broke out on his forehead. At the thought that his murderers had come for him, he began to shake with terror.

The beam of the torch swung away from him. By its diffused light he saw the outline of its bearer, who had turned at that moment to close the door. In was neither Barak nor Cepicka, but Stephanie.

Instantly hope flamed in his mind. She could have come only to rescue him. He strove for words to cry out to her his gladness and relief, but his mouth had become so dry that, for a moment, his tongue seemed to rasp in it. Before he could speak, she said in a hard voice:

'I take it you don't like the idea of dying.'

Her tone and words abruptly quashed his hope. He now felt certain that she had come there only to taunt him: to tell him what a fool she had always thought him; to say how perfectly he had demonstrated that belief to her friends by so readily blundering into this trap; to compensate herself for the way in which he had humiliated her by enjoying the sight of his fear. She hoped, perhaps, to hear him scream for mercy as Barak and Cepicka stripped him and dragged him down to the motor-boat.

He swore to himself that he would not give her that satisfaction, then replied in a surly tone: 'Of course I don't want to die. Who would?'

'Well'—her voice still held no touch of warmth—'if I save you—if I release you—will you give me your signature on a document?'

His heart bounded again. She meant, after all, to give him his life—provided he was prepared to ransom it. But what did having to pay up matter? Anything, even ruin, was preferable to being dragged at the end of a hosepipe from a motor-boat until one drowned. He gave an abrupt, unnatural laugh, and said:

'I'm ready to do a business deal. It's no good asking for a sum beyond my ability to pay, but you must know that I'm pretty well off. Ask anything in reason, and if it's within my means I'll sign on the dotted line.' Then, in his bitterness, even though he might pay for it with his life, he could not resist adding: 'That you should be one ahead of your pals in this is hardly surprising. Double-crossing people comes so naturally to you.'

'Yes,' she replied sharply. 'I am double-crossing them, and at considerable risk to myself. But only because I don't like the idea of being a party to murder. From the very beginning I did my utmost to persuade you to stop running into danger, but you wouldn't listen. I'm not out to rob you of your dirty, unearned, capitalist money, either. The paper you are going to sign—that is, if you still wish to be alive tomorrow morning—has to do with this absurd amateur spying of yours. Here; read it.'

Thrusting a paper under Robbie's nose, she held her torch so that the light fell on it. The document was in her own writing, in Czech, and read:

I, Robert Grenn, hereby take oath and swear by everything I hold sacred that, as from midnight on Friday, the 18th of April, I will cease from the investigation into Czech affairs on which I have been engaged for the past month. I further

*undertake to return forthwith to Athens, to leave Greece within
forty-eight hours and not to return to that country during the
next six months.*

Well, Robbie thought, there it is. The only person I've ever
been committed to is Pallas Athene, and she can hardly expect
me to throw away my life. When she spoke to me of carrying
things through to the bitter end, she must have meant the bitterness in which my association with Stephanie has ended. At
least, when I pass through Athens, I can see Luke, tell him
what has happened to me, and impress upon him that the
Czechs being prepared to commit murder in order to guard
their secret is proof enough that it must be something worth his
getting our professionals to investigate. To Stephanie he said:

'Very well. I know when I'm licked. Undo me, and I
promise not to lay a finger on you. Then I'll sign this thing,
and carry out its stipulations.'

Moving away, she put two of the empty boxes one on top
of the other, and on the rough table so formed laid the paper
and her torch. She then produced a pair of wire cutters from
the pocket of her skirt and, after something of a struggle, cut
the wires that ran through the short lengths of rubber pipe
that kept his wrists and ankles in place.

At his first attempt to lift his arms, pains shot through
them, causing him to give a low moan and quickly lower them
again. He found that he was so stiff from sitting for so many
hours in one position that he could hardly move. But she
showed little compassion.

Stepping up to him, she said: 'Come on. We haven't all
night, and I don't want to be caught here. If we are, it will be
curtains for you; so this is no time to sit pulling faces just
because you have pins and needles.' Then, seizing his arms,
she began to pinch and pummel them vigorously.

For a few minutes, her rough ministrations caused him
agony; but he managed to get to his feet, upon which she thrust
a Biro pen into his hand and he signed the document.

Instead of picking it up, she left it there on the top of the
box, produced a letter from her pocket, which she laid beside
it, and said: 'When they find those, I'm hoping they'll be satis-

fied, and not come after us. One can't guarantee that, because after what you did to Barak in Corinth he is thirsting for your blood; but I'm hoping that Cepicka will persuade him that my having spiked your guns in my way, it would be pointless to take any further action. Now follow me, and for God's sake keep those big feet of yours from making more noise than you can help.'

Having switched out her torch, she led the way from the shed and, keeping in the shadow of other buildings alongside it, led him to a corner of the big yard where there was a double gate. A quick glance round had shown him that there were no lights in the little house or in any other part of the ruined factory. The gate was not locked and, after they had stepped through it, he closed it carefully behind them. Beyond the gate lay the flat, stony surface of what had once been an outer yard. Two lorries and three cars were parked there. Stephanie led the way over to one of the cars, and he recognized the Ford Zephyr. As she got in, she said in a low voice:

'If you really believe in your Immortals, now is the time to pray to them. Barak and the others went early to bed, to get some sleep before having to get up in the small hours to settle your business. If the noise of the engine wakes them, we'll be in trouble. That big Mercedes of his would overhaul us before we had gone five miles.'

'What time is it?' Robbie asked in a whisper.

'It's not yet quite twelve. I had to wait until they were well asleep before risking coming out to you. But I wanted to get as much leeway as I could before they are due to wake. If the engine doesn't rouse them, we'll have a good three hours' start. That should give us lead enough if Barak does decide to come after us.'

The engine purred and she let it run for a moment then slipped in the clutch, turned the car and headed it through a gap in the wall, down a rough track. Robbie twisted round to stare anxiously out of the back window; but no lights came on in the upper part of the house, which was all that he could see over the two walls.

When they reached the highway, Stephanie put on speed

and, as the road was an open one, they were soon doing seventy miles an hour in the direction of Pirgos.

'Where do you intend to drop me?' Robbie asked.

'Athens,' she replied laconically.

'Athens!' he repeated in surprise. 'That means then that you don't trust me to go there under my own steam?'

'I don't see why I should trust you in anything.'

'No,' he agreed, as a guilty memory of their last encounter rushed back to his mind. 'I suppose not. But we can't possibly make Athens in a night. We'll have to stop off at various places, so I could easily give you the slip.'

'I don't advise you to try it. You would have cause to regret it if you did.'

'Apart from having broken my pledge, I don't see why. That is, unless you are toting a gun, with which you mean to shoot me if I run off into the bushes.'

'Yes; I have got a gun with me; and I would have shot you if you had set on me after I released you. But you had better not try to get hold of it. Yesterday you took me completely by surprise; otherwise things would have gone very differently. I've told you that I'm against murder, but I wouldn't hesitate to put a bullet through your leg; so I advise you not to attempt any monkey tricks.'

By then they had reached Pirgos. There were still people sitting drinking in the cafés, but the streets were almost deserted, and, reducing her speed only to forty, Stephanie drove through the town. When they had come out on the road to Olympia, she continued:

'I may as well tell you, though, that making sure that you don't feel tempted to go back on your word is not the only reason that I am taking you to Athens. For one thing, although you succeeded in driving the car twenty-odd miles this afternoon, you couldn't have hoped to get very far with it in the dark without an accident; and if you had a smash, the odds are that Barak would have caught you. Having risked my own skin to get you out, I'd naturally have felt pretty sick if I found afterwards that I had done so to no purpose.'

'Risked your skin!' Robbie turned to stare at her. 'Do you mean they would have killed you?'

'Oh no; they wouldn't do that. But Barak can be a real devil when he is angry. When he learned that I had enabled you to escape, he would have beaten hell out of me and might quite well have marked me for life.'

'But he is bound to find out . . . That letter you left.'

'Of course, and that's why I left it. If I hadn't, they would anyhow have assumed that it was I who freed you. Who else would have? You couldn't possibly have got away without help. Barak would have believed that, having spent three weeks driving you round Greece, I had fallen for you. He would then have every reason to do his utmost to recapture you. And when he got back, with or without you, he would have put me through the hoop.'

She paused for a moment, then went on: 'By leaving your pledge and my letter, I hope to show that, although I freed you, I am still doing the right thing by my own people. In the letter, I've said that I am taking you to Athens myself, to keep you, one way or the other, to your promise, and that on the 20th I intend to see you aboard a plane that will take you out of Greece. To put an end to your poking your nose into our business is the only thing that really matters and no one but Barak is going to be disappointed at being deprived of the pleasure of watching you drown.'

'I see,' said Robbie thoughtfully. 'But won't he try to take it out on you later on, when he sees you again?'

'By then, I'll be among friends at our Legation. Besides, he will have had time to calm down. That was one of my reasons for deciding that if I did mean to free you I had better accompany you to Athens. Of course, when I do come face to face with him, there will be a fine old dust-up. But that's not your worry.'

Robbie fell silent and remained so for some while. Then he remarked: 'Your room at the Spap was still unoccupied when I left, so——'

'So what!' she cut him short. 'Surely you don't suppose that I mean to spend the night at Olympia? I hope to get to Argos.'

At the thought of the road by which they had come to

Olympia, Robbie exclaimed: 'What! You mean to drive through those awful mountains in the dark?'

'Why not?' she shrugged. 'Plenty of lorries and other cars make the trip by night. If I find it too much for me, we'll have to stop at Tripolis; but in case Barak does come after us, I want to keep as big a lead as I can. Argos is well over half-way to Athens—the worst half, too—but with luck we'll reach there in about six or seven hours. We'll sleep through the morning, and do the remaining hundred and twenty kilometres to Athens in the afternoon.'

The idea of skirting those terrifying precipices for hour after hour with only their headlights to keep them on the road did not seem to intimidate Stephanie and, although it appalled Robbie, he realized he was in her hands. Since she had the courage to face it, he must too, and without showing his fears. After a minute, he said:

'Well, you're doing the driving. All I ask is that, when you do feel tired, you won't press on at the risk of breaking both our necks. We could always pull off the road at some level spot and you could sleep for an hour in the car. I give you my solemn promise that I won't try to sneak off while you were sleeping. Anyhow, you'll get a first quarter of an hour's easy at the Spap while I pay my bill and throw my clothes into my suitcases.'

Stephanie gave an unpleasant little laugh. 'I always thought you were a little off the beam; now I know that you're right round the bend. You have just had a very narrow escape from death, yet you suggest risking your life again for the sake of collecting a few clothes.'

'If they did hear us drive off, Barak would have caught up with us by now; if they didn't, he won't even be getting dressed for another two and a half hours,' Robbie argued, 'so what do fifteen minutes matter?'

'They matter because I mean to keep every minute of lead I've got.'

Robbie made a face. 'All right, then. But I was hoping to get a drink at the hotel. It's over twelve hours since I had one, and I'm absolutely parched.'

'Put a hand over the back of the seat,' she told him. 'If

you feel round, you'll find a basket with some biscuits and a Thermos that has milk in it. I'd have liked to have made some coffee to warm us up when we are in the mountains, but I didn't dare. One of them might have come down and found me in the kitchen with my suitcase beside me, and that would not have been at all easy to explain.'

After Robbie had found the Thermos and gratefully drunk some of the milk, he said: 'You had two suitcases and, from what you say, it sounds as if getting away with one was as much as you could manage. I hope you put my manuscript in it.'

'No,' she replied promptly. 'I didn't.'

'What . . . what have you done with it?' he asked, striving to keep out of his voice the acute anxiety he felt.

'It will serve a most useful purpose.' She paused for a moment, then went on with malicious amusement: 'In that little house there were fourteen of us, and they were running short of toilet paper; so I left it in the lavatory.'

'Oh God! You didn't!' The cry came from Robbie's heart.

For a good two minutes she let him remain a prey to utter misery, then she said quietly: 'No; as a matter of fact, I didn't, though it would have served you right if I had. The truth is that I took it in to Pirgos this evening and sent it *poste restante* to the G.P.O., Athens. Knowing how much you value your book, I did that as a much sounder precaution than carrying a gun against your being tempted to double-cross me. If you behave like a good little boy, I'll arrange for it to be handed back to you at the airport on your way out of Greece.'

He gave a great sigh of relief, and was just about to thank her for her promise to return it to him, when she exclaimed: 'What on earth's the matter with the car? What have you been doing to it?'

'I—nothing,' he protested. 'I took it out for about two hours this morning, to practise along flattish roads on my own; then, after lunch, I drove it out to the factory. It went perfectly and I had no trouble at all.'

Stephanie's question had been caused by a cloud of steam which had suddenly issued from the bonnet. Looking quickly down at the dashboard, she saw that only a few inches of the chain working the radiator blind was hanging from its V. Turning on to Robbie, she stormed: 'You imbecile! You've been running her with the radiator blind nearly full up. Now she's blown a core plug and if I keep her running the engine will seize up.'

She drove the car into the side of the road. They both got out and, having confirmed the cause of the trouble, she said angrily: 'I don't suppose Nisio will be able to make us another core plug under four or five hours at the least.'

'Who is Nisio?' Robbie enquired.

'He is the mechanic at the Spap; and, thank goodness, it can't be much more than a mile away. It was Nisio who drove me into Pirgos yesterday. I bribed him, too, to telephone me if you either took out the car or hired one. That's how it was that Barak was all ready to receive you this afternoon. Nisio also telephoned about your taking out the car this morning, but we felt sure that you wouldn't try anything until the siesta hour.'

'Well,' Robbie shrugged, 'since we are stuck for the night, at least we are lucky to have broken down so near the Spap. As it can't yet be half past twelve, I expect it will still be open; although your friend Nisio is pretty certain to be in bed.'

'Then we must get him out,' Stephanie declared. 'If Barak does come after us later in the night and notice the Zephyr abandoned by the roadside, he'll guess at once that we are at the Spap and lie in wait for you when we leave tomorrow morning.'

Robbie got Stephanie's case out of the boot and, leaving the car lights on, they set out for the hotel. When they reached it, there were still lights on in a few of the windows. Up in the lounge, a yawning waiter was watching four guests playing a final rubber of bridge. Nisio was roused and appeared with an overcoat over his pyjamas. He agreed to go out and tow in the Ford, but jibbed at Stephanie's suggestion that he should work on it during the night.

When Nisio had gone off to get it and the tired waiter had produced brandies and ginger ales, Robbie said to her: 'I know you want to get me to Athens and out of the country as quickly as you can; but, if we don't leave here until after lunch tomorrow, we'll stand much less risk of running into Barak at Tripolis or somewhere further along the road where, if he has chased us, he may have pulled up.'

She nodded wearily. 'Perhaps you are right. If he does by-pass us, the longer lead he has the better. In fact, in the long run, our breakdown may have turned out all to the good.' Then, finishing their drinks, they went to bed.

In the morning, Robbie was woken by a sharp knocking on the door of his room. Tumbling out of bed, he pulled on his dressing gown and opened the door, to find Stephanie standing outside. She was fully dressed, but had no make-up on and her hair had not been done.

'I got up early,' she said, 'to find out about the car. Nisio says that, with servicing the cars of the other guests, there's not a hope of getting ours done till three o'clock, and it may even be four or five before he's through.'

Robbie blinked at her sleepily. 'Except that we'll have to do the last part of the mountain road to Argos after dark, I don't see that that matters much. If Barak did give chase, he's missed us, although he can't know that. He must be in Tripolis or even further off by this time.' As he spoke he was gingerly feeling his chin, where Barak had hit him, for on his waking it had begun to throb painfully.

'You are probably right,' she agreed thoughtfully. 'But Barak is no fool. As soon as it became daylight, he would start enquiring at the villages through which they passed for some-one who had seen the Zephyr go through. When he has drawn several blanks, he'll guess that we are not ahead of him after all. Then he'll think one of two things: either that we took the other road, in which case he will drive on to Athens; or that we deliberately put up here for the night, hoping to fox him. If he does think that he's by-passed us, he won't need to stop somewhere to sleep, because it is certain that he will have Cepicka with him, and they'll be driving turn and turn about. They'll turn round and come back, hoping to meet us on the road this morning. They won't, of course, but, when they get as far as this without meeting us, they are sure to stop here to make enquiries.'

'Well, what if they do learn we're here? They daren't come

busting into this place as though it were a saloon in a Western, and shoot me dead. Even if they got away with it for the moment, there would be a hue and cry after them in no time. All the odds are that they would be caught, and there would be lots of people to identify them as my killers.'

'That's true. But if they do find out that we are here, they might hang round outside on the chance of getting a shot at you. For example, if they spotted you having another look round the ruins, and there was no one about. That's what I came to say to you. I've told them at the office that you've got a tummy upset, so will be staying in bed most of the day. Your meals will be brought along to you but, of course, only something light.'

'Oh dear!' Robbie exclaimed ruefully, 'and after yesterday I am as hungry as a hunter.'

'You are very lucky to be alive,' she said sharply, 'and, if you want to make sure of remaining alive, you had better do as you are told. After lunch, pack your things and be ready to leave at three o'clock. As soon as the car is ready, I'll come up for you.'

Robbie turned in again, but he spent a miserable morning. The previous night, after the twelve hours of acute strain he had passed through, he had been too exhausted to think much about his defeat; but now the knowledge that he had failed so lamentably greatly depressed him.

He was, too, most unhappy about his new relationship with Stephanie. By a miracle, as it seemed to him, after he had accepted that she had passed out of his life for good, she had returned to it. But she was not the Stephanie he had known. She was as lovely as ever in his eyes; but no longer his gay, sweet-tempered companion. He was well aware that he owed his life to her, yet could not believe that she had lifted a finger from any personal feeling for him. He felt sure that her action had been inspired by a reluctance to have it on her conscience that a man who had fallen into a trap she had laid had been murdered, and that she would have taken nearly as much risk to save a dog. Moreover, the fact remained that it was through her lies and treachery that the only undertaking he had ever ventured upon of his own accord, and one that was to make him in his own eyes and the eyes of others a man who could hold his head high in any company, had come to an ignominious end.

After he had eaten a disappointingly meagre lunch, brought to him on a tray, he got up, packed and dressed; then he sat down to wait for Stephanie. Three o'clock came; then four and half past, the time dragging by wearily. At last, at about ten to five, a bang on his door brought him quickly to it, to find her there with a luggage porter behind her. With a frown she said:

'These country mechanics are hopeless. Nisio ought to have been able to make a new core plug in five hours; but of course he wouldn't forgo his siesta, and it's taken nearly ten.' Thrusting a paper into Robbie's hand, she went on: 'I had your bill made up and looked through it. As far as I can judge it's correct; so pay it on your way out, and we'll get off as quickly as we can.'

Without argument he did as she had told him, and five minutes later they were in the Ford, running down on to the main road. When they reached it, she said: 'You know, last night I would have bet any money that Barak would come after us as soon as he found out that you'd escaped. But I think now I was scaring myself unnecessarily. Either that, or he thought it more likely that we had taken the road via Patras round the Gulf. I had an early lunch and spent the whole afternoon watching the main road. If the Mercedes had come back along it, I couldn't have failed to see her; and, if they had pulled up where the road is hidden by the trees and one of them had walked the last half mile here to make enquiries, I should have been bound to see him, the hotel being perched up on a cliff as it is.'

Robbie nodded: 'If they did go as far as Tripolis, then turned back hoping to meet us, they would have passed here hours ago. Anyhow, knowing nothing of our breakdown, they wouldn't expect us to spend the day at Olympia. Whether they ever left Pirgos or stayed put, they must be assuming that, by this time, we can't be far from Athens.'

For the first three-quarters of an hour the road ran through comparatively flat country, although rising all the time. Then it gradually became steeper and its curves more frequent until, by six o'clock, they were up to two thousand feet and still mounting by a long succession of hairpin bends. At times they could see the road ahead, snaking away higher and higher, a thin, yellow line etched in the precipitous sides of the mountain chain; at others the view ahead closed rapidly from a quarter of a mile to a matter of twenty feet as they approached some tall cliff of solid rock that formed a sharp corner, completely cutting off all sight of what lay beyond it.

Soon after six they passed through the little town of Tropaia, that clung so precariously to the mountain-side; but they did not pull up there as they had done on their outward journey, because Stephanie wanted to make the most of the light. For another twenty minutes or so they ran on along the narrow shelf of road, beyond the edge of which lay seemingly bottomless gorges with, on their far side, range after range of rugged heights rising to peaks, many of which were capped with cloud.

It was then that Robbie at last plucked up the courage to say something that he had been contemplating saying for an hour or more. Unlike their journeys in the past, during which he had told Stephanie stories of the Immortals, or they had laughed together over all sorts of trivialities, they had exchanged hardly a word since leaving Olympia. Now he stammered out:

'On Thursday, after . . . after what happened down by the pool, I stayed there a long time. When at last I did get back to the hotel, I went along to your room.'

'And found me gone,' she volunteered. 'I packed at once. It didn't seem to me that there was much point in my remaining there till you put in an appearance just for us to have a slanging match.'

'I suppose not. To have found out about you was a shock . . . a most frightful shock. But, all the same, I wanted to apologize. I felt absolutely terrible.'

'I'm glad to hear it,' she said slowly. 'You know, for some girls an experience like that might spoil their whole lives—give them a hatred of men and warp their natures. It was very clear that, in spite of your age, you are still completely ignorant about that sort of thing. But that wouldn't have made it any the less terrifying for a girl who was as ignorant as your-self; so I hope you will never let yourself go like that again. As far as I am concerned, it was a beastly way in which to try and take your revenge. Fortunately, though, it did me no harm. It's quite a long time since I left my mother's apron strings, and I've seen enough of the world to make allowances for you.'

Robbie threw a quick glance sideways. Stephanie's eyes were fixed steadily on the road ahead. She had spoken without the least embarrassment and her face showed no trace of heightened colour. Yet what she had said amounted to a con-fession entirely out of keeping with the picture he had built up of her.

'D'you mean . . .' he stammered, 'do you really mean that . . . that you've often made love . . . well, not quite like that . . . but . . . but . . . ?'

'I didn't say that,' she replied. 'But, since you've found me out, hasn't it occurred to you that, as I am twenty-four, I might quite well be married?'

'Married! No! Are you?'

'Yes. My real name is Madame Václav Barak.'

'Good God!'

'What is there surprising in that? You must at least have realized that the story with which I took you in, about having a father who was forcing me into marriage with a rich cement manufacturer, was all nonsense; and that I'm not a Greek but a Czech. You seem to have known all along, too, that it is Barak who is responsible for establishing the groups of Czechs on special missions. When he learnt that you were spying on them, what could be more natural than that he should use his English-speaking wife to keep an eye on you?'

'It wouldn't seem natural to me,' Robbie commented. 'After all, before you came into the game, he can have known very little about me. I might have been much more attractive to women than I am, and a Don Juan by nature. To send you off round Greece with a man who might have turned out like that seems to me an extraordinary thing for a husband to have done.'

Stephanie gave a mirthless laugh. 'Oh, that side of the

matter wouldn't have worried him. He was quite mad about me once, but he isn't any more. And I've long since lost the admiration I had for him in my teens, when we married. As I told you last night, he's quite capable of beating me when he's really angry, and that sort of thing is not calculated to turn schoolgirl hero-worship into love.'

'Why do you stick to him, then?' Robbie asked.

'Because it suits me to. And I don't think he would like to lose me, either. I'm a very useful wife to him in a lot of ways, and I've helped him quite a bit in his career. Until now, I've never actively gone against him in anything that is important. How he'll take it, I don't yet know; but I'm quite prepared to stand up to him because, provided you do as you have promised and leave Greece, no one can say I've let down my country. There is no sense in committing murder when it can be avoided, and I feel certain that all the Comrades at the Legation will back me up in what I've done.'

'That's all very well,' said Robbie gloomily. 'But, as he is your husband, you'll have to face up to him when they are not there. I . . . well, it seems silly to talk hot air about wanting to be your champion, but all the same I wish to God that when you do meet him I could be there to protect you.'

'How nice of you, Robbie.' Her voice was softer and it was the first time she had used his Christian name since the affair at the pool. 'But,' she added, 'I don't think you need worry. I mean to keep away from him for the next few days, and by then several other people will have talked to him about all this, and his anger will have died down.'

For the past few minutes, they had been approaching one of the great cliffs of rock jutting out from the mountain-side and making a blind corner. The bend was a sharp one, so Stephanie took it slowly. As they rounded the mass of rock, they saw the black Mercedes parked behind it, only fifty feet away. Barak was in it and Cepicka was at the wheel. Its motor whirred and the big car slid forward, blocking the way.

22

Wanted for Murder

STEPHANIE was forced to pull up. With the long Mercedes drawn across the road, it was impossible for her to pass it either on the near side or the off. In the one case, she would have jammed the Ford between the rock face and the boot of the big black car, in the other gone over the edge of the precipice.

As she braked the car to a halt, she cried: 'Get out, Robbie! Get out! No stupid chivalry! Run for your life! Leave this to me!'

Even as her cry echoed down the mountain valley, Barak and Cepicka were both getting out of the Mercedes. Cepicka, who had been at the wheel of the car, was the nearer. As he jumped out on to the road, he drew an automatic from an armpit holster. Robbie knew then that Stephanie was right. This was no time for heroics. Although he was completely ignorant about weapons, he would have given a lot to have been armed and to stand beside Stephanie. But he knew that, however unsatisfactory her relations with her husband might be, she was in no danger of losing her life; whereas his own clearly hung by a thread.

Flinging open the door of the Ford, he scrambled out, stepping on to the road at the same moment as Cepicka drew his gun. There was not much more than thirty feet between them, but by the time Cepicka had swung round and aimed with his weapon there were fifty. Even then Robbie might have been shot down; but one of his flying feet hit a stone,

causing him to stumble sideways. At that second, the Czech's
pistol cracked, then it cracked again, but the bullets sang past
Robbie.

At the sound of the shots, he threw a swift glance over his
shoulder. He saw that Stephanie and Barak were now also out
of the cars and standing in the road facing one another. Next
moment, he was round the corner of the cliff. In front of him
lay a long, down-sloping gradient, several hundred yards in
length, before the road passed out of sight round another bend.
With a gasp of fear he realized that, running down that open
stretch with two gunmen pursuing him, he would not stand a
hope. They would wing him for certain and, as he fell wounded
in the road, race up to finish him off.

Desperately, he looked right and left for a chance of salva-
tion. To his left lay the precipice, an almost sheer drop of some
three thousand feet. Even if it had jutting rocks and scrub on
it that would have provided tenuous hand-holds, Cepicka
would be upon him and put a bullet into him before he could
scramble down his own length. He would lose his hold and,
with arms and legs whirling, hurtle into the chasm. To the
right rose the twenty-foot-high cliff of rock. For most of
its frontage it presented a flat, smooth surface; but in one
place, round the corner from the cars, it had a chimney in it—
a three-foot-deep gulley, broken here and there with small
bushes and tufts of coarse grass growing out from the crevices
in it. The chimney was narrow at the bottom, but grew deeper
towards the top. It offered the only alternative to being
slaughtered on the open road, and Robbie took it.

Hurling himself into the fissure, he seized on stunted bushes
of myrtle and clumps of wild thyme and began to haul himself
up. Half the plants he grasped broke off or came away under
the pull of his weight; but fear lent him such speed that, almost
as the twigs of one bush snapped, he thrust up his arm and
grasped another. Meanwhile his feet scrabbled wildly on tufts
of grass and little ledges of rock, forcing him further upward.

He had nearly reached the top when he heard shouts and
screams below him. As he had just secured a firm handhold, he
paused to look down. Cepicka stood below him at the foot
of the gulley and had just raised his gun to shoot. A few feet

away Stephanie, the butt of a small automatic clutched in her right hand, was wrestling with Barak. At that moment Barak wrenched the pistol from her, but she broke free and launched herself at Cepicka. She caught him sideways on, throwing him off balance just as he fired. He swore and hit out at her. She fell in the roadway and Barak lugged her to her feet.

By then, Robbie had reached the summit of the rock. When he again looked down, Barak and Stephanie had disappeared, but their voices could still be heard as they continued to shout abuse at one another round the corner of the cliff. Cepicka, with his pistol thrust back into its armpit holster, had begun to scale the chimney and was coming grimly up, hand over hand.

Robbie stared wildly about him. The top of the rock formed a small, natural citadel about forty feet in width. Round the semi-circle that overhung the road, a ragged line of rounded humps rose up from three to five feet above the level of the uneven floor on which he stood. Behind him rose another tangle of great boulders, spreading up the slope for half a mile. In some places, there were dark gaps between them large enough to squeeze through; in others they were partially overgrown with wild vegetation.

Frantically, he cast about for big stones or a small chunk of rock that he could grab up and throw down on Cepicka. One hit on his head or face should be sufficient to dislodge him from his precarious hold in the chimney and send him crashing back on to the road. But there were no loose stones. Nothing larger than pebbles was to be seen anywhere within easy reach of where Robbie was standing.

He was left with a choice, either of which might prove fatal. He could run for cover between the great boulders thirty yards away, which meant risking Cepicka's getting to the top of the chimney and shooting him before he reached them; or he could wait where he was until Cepicka appeared, then bank on rushing him before he had a chance to take proper aim.

Deciding on the latter course, Robbie crouched down behind the big stone hump beside which the chimney emerged. As he did so he could hear Cepicka's heavy breathing as he hoisted himself up, only a few feet away. Suddenly an idea came to Robbie. If he could tackle Cepicka while the Czech still needed both his hands to clamber out of the top of the chimney, and had not one free to draw his gun again, he would be caught at a serious disadvantage.

Throwing caution to the winds, Robbie came to his feet and stepped round the buttress of rock just as Cepicka's head appeared above its level. He already had one knee on the ground at the top of the chimney. For an instant, they stared at one another. Cepicka's hand leaped to his gun, but Robbie stooped and seized the weapon before the Czech could aim it. In striving to wrench the pistol from Cepicka's grasp, Robbie stepped backwards, dragging Cepicka after him, up over the edge of the cliff. As the Czech found his feet, he struck out at Robbie with his left fist, catching him a blow on the right ear that made him dizzy. But Robbie had shifted his grip to Cepicka's wrist and gave it such a violent twist that he was forced to drop his pistol. Next moment they had seized one another in a bear-like clinch, and were staggering to and fro across the platform of rock.

In spite of his little paunch and pasty face, Cepicka was very strong and he knew all the tricks. Suddenly he thrust his leg between Robbie's so that his right heel was behind Robbie's left heel, then threw forward the full weight of his powerful shoulders. Robbie staggered, lost his balance and went over backwards. As he fell, he lost his hold. The Czech came down on top of him. Now that Cepicka's hands were free, he used the left to seize Robbie by the throat and raised the right to smash into his face. Just in time, Robbie jerked his head aside. The clenched fist came down with terrific force on the bare rock. Cepicka let out a yell and his whole body twitched with the agony he had caused himself. Robbie seized his opportunity. With a violent upward jerk of his thighs, he threw off his enemy. They both scrambled to their feet simultaneously. Panting as though they had run a mile, they stood a few feet apart, facing one another, poised like wrestlers seeking an opening for a crippling hold.

Blood was dripping from Cepicka's right hand, where he had smashed the side of it on the rock; but, in spite of this handicap, he showed no sign of retreating. His small, pale eyes glared murder into Robbie's. Suddenly he took a pace forward, feinted with his right foot as though to kick, but came down on it and shot out his left. Robbie had acted almost at the same second. His right fist had been aimed at Cepicka's jaw but the Czech threw his head up, and his own movement caused the blow to land on his left shoulder. He was already off balance, so his kick missed Robbie's shin and the force of the blow swung him round. For a moment he swayed, striving to regain his balance, sideways on to Robbie and unable to use his uninjured fist to protect himself. Rushing in, Robbie grabbed him with one hand by the back of the collar, and with the other by the seat of the pants. Exerting all his great strength, Robbie gave one terrific heave, lifting Cepicka as though he were a sack of potatoes. For a moment, he held his enemy high above his head, then threw him over the low battlement of boulders down into the road.

For twenty or thirty seconds Robbie stood, legs splayed, gasping for breath; then he stumbled to the boulders and looked over. Twenty feet below, Cepicka lay sprawled, his limbs twisted at unnatural angles.

From where Robbie stood, Barak and Stephanie could not be seen. Straightening himself, he ran the few paces across the curve of the rocky platform and crouched again over the boulders there, to look down into the road round the corner. Stephanie was standing near the bonnet of the Ford. Her back was to the precipice and she was only a few feet from its edge. Barak stood facing her and was shaking his fist in her face. Robbie heard him shout:

'How dare you upset my plans? How dare you? You shall be disciplined for this. I'll teach you to sneak off with your boy friend. Cepicka will deal with him within the next few minutes, then we'll take you back and I'll deal with you.'

His mind whirling, Robbie wondered how he could possibly get the better of Barak. To scramble down the chimney to the road would have been suicidal. He would have had a bullet in him before he could get within yards of his enemy. From where he stood, up on the shoulder of the mountain, he could see the road winding away for a considerable distance in both directions, and it was empty. During the two hours or more since he and Stephanie had set out from Olympia, they had met only one coachload of tourists, three lorries and one private car, and the traffic going in their direction could be assumed to be no more frequent. The odds were, therefore, against Barak's being forced to abandon his hold-up through a vehicle arriving on the scene in the next ten minutes or quarter of an hour.

As Robbie's glance swept the distant road, he suddenly caught sight of a solitary figure some way to his left and about half a mile away on the slope above it. The man was evidently a goat-herd and from up there he must have had a clear view of Robbie's struggle with Cepicka, but he was too far off to be called on for immediate assistance. Swinging round again, Robbie once more stared down at Stephanie and her husband.

Her voice, shrill with anger, came up to him clearly: 'You murderous brute! I'll stay with you no longer! I'm sick to death of you and the Party and all its filthy work. But don't think you can get me sent back to Czechoslovakia. I know too much about you. If you refuse me my freedom or fake a lying report about me, I'll give Janos chapter and verse about the bribes you've taken. Then it's you who'll be sent back, and you'll find yourself in the uranium mines.'

For the space of a minute they stood glaring at one another, and there was complete silence on the mountainside. Then Barak took a pace forward. Suddenly his hand shot out. It landed on Stephanie's chest. She staggered back. Robbie saw the earth on the edge of the precipice crumble under her heel. Her eyes instantly became round with terror. Her mouth opened wide and she gave a piercing shriek. Then, as though a trap-door had opened under her, and with her hands wildly clutching empty air, she shot downwards into the abyss.

Barak stepped back and passed a hand over his eyes. Robbie, twenty feet above him, remained for some seconds paralysed by horror at the awful scene he had witnessed. Then he found his voice and shouted:

'You fiend! You fiend! I'll kill you for this. I'll kill you! I'll kill you! I swear I will!'

Swinging round, Barak stared up at him. His hand went to his shoulder holster and he jerked out a gun. It was not the small pistol he had wrested from Stephanie, but a big blue-barrelled automatic. As he raised it, Robbie ducked down behind the boulder. Realizing that Robbie was well under cover, Barak did not fire, but Robbie heard his footsteps as he walked quickly round the corner of the cliff to the gully. A loud exclamation told Robbie that he had just come upon Cepicka's body.

Robbie wondered if his enemy would come up the chimney. On all fours he wriggled over to the boulder nearest to it, to be ready for him; but after he had crouched behind it for a minute, the footsteps moved away. For what seemed an age he continued to crouch there, then he heard the engine of a car start up. Crawling quickly back to the other side of the bastion, he risked a quick look over.

Barak was seated at the wheel of the Mercedes. He had run it back as far as it would go. As Robbie watched him, he let in the clutch and sent the big car forward, so that it hit the bonnet of the Ford sideways on with a loud metallic clang. According to the rule of the road in Greece, a vehicle going towards Olympia on that route would have had the right to the inner side; so, had the Mercedes not blocked the way, Stephanie would have passed it on the outer. In consequence, the Ford had been halted alongside the precipice and only some four feet from it. On the Mercedes charging it, the front wheels slithered another two feet nearer the edge. Backing the Mercedes, Barak charged the Ford again. This time one of its wheels went over and it tilted sharply, retaining a precarious balance only owing to its weight. For the third time, Barak launched the Mercedes at it. Churning up a cloud of small stones and dust, its whole body lifted, showing for a moment its underside, then it disappeared without a sound into the gorge far below.

Robbie had no doubts about Barak's reason for forcing the Ford over the precipice. He meant to account for Stephanie's death by an accident. The battered buffers of his own car could be produced as evidence that there had been one, and Stephanie might easily have tried to jump out, or have been thrown clear, as the Ford went over.

As Robbie was thinking that he must get to the police as

soon as he possibly could, a motor horn sounded. Unnoticed by him, a lorry coming from the direction of Olympia had approached to within a few hundred yards. Standing up, he waved and shouted to the driver; but the man had his eyes fixed on the road ahead and a moment later, had he glanced up, the roof of the cab would have prevented him from seeing Robbie.

Neither, to Robbie's surprise, did the driver notice Cepicka's body and pull up. Then, on looking over, he saw that it was no longer there. Evidently, on finding it, Barak had removed it, and either pushed it over the precipice or carried it to his car. Meanwhile, on hearing the long hoot, he had backed the Mercedes alongside the rock face and, rounding the corner, the lorry ran past him on its way, the driver still in ignorance that his arrival there five minutes earlier might have prevented a ghastly tragedy.

When the lorry had passed, Barak ran the Mercedes to and fro again several times, until he had turned it round; then, at a slow pace, he drove off towards Tripolis. As he did so, Robbie could see, through the back window of the car, a pink cropped head lolling forward and rolling limply from side to side. This confirmed his idea that Barak might have carried Cepicka's body to the car and hoisted it into the back seat. But Barak drove no more than three hundred yards, then he pulled up and got out.

The cliff on which Robbie stood was not continuous. The edge sloped down to the level of the road further on, and it was just at that point that Barak had halted the Mercedes. By taking this longer way round, instead of struggling up the chimney, he had only to walk up the slope to reach Robbie's redoubt. Although Robbie's brain was still half-bemused by Stephanie's terrible death, he realized his enemy's intention. In his hands lay Barak's life. As long as he remained alive, he could charge Barak with murder; therefore, to be safe, Barak dare not leave him unaccounted for. He was coming up the slope to hunt out and kill him.

Robbie knew that his enemy was carrying two pistols—his own and Stephanie's—and neither of them had been fired. They must contain anything from a dozen to eighteen bullets.

To attempt, weaponless, to face Barak would, Robbie felt certain, be to throw away his life. The only alternative was to take to his heels while there were still several hundred yards between them. As he turned to run, a sudden thought struck him. While he had been struggling with Cepicka, the Czech had dropped his pistol. Stephanie's murder, so soon after, had put it right out of his mind. Now he swerved, dashed for the place where they had fought, and began frantically to hunt for it.

The pistol was nowhere on the barren platform of stone, so it must have fallen among the long grass and scrub growing at the head of the chimney. Going down on his knees, Robbie thrust his fingers agitatedly in among the greenery, unheeding the tears in his hands made by the long thorns of a low bush that had little yellow flowers on it. The knowledge that Barak was coming up the slope behind him made him half choke with fear. At any moment, his enemy might breast the rise and put a bullet through his back. Turning this way and that, he scrabbled in the undergrowth like a maniac, but to no avail. The automatic must have fallen further off, and to give more time to searching would prove fatal.

As he jumped to his feet, he cursed the thought that had led him to giving precious time hunting for Cepicka's gun. By so doing, he had greatly lessened his chances of remaining alive. Had he run for it directly he saw Barak leave the road, he would have had a good lead, well out of pistol-shot, and might have got away. Now he would be easily in range when Barak appeared over the crest, and could have little hope of escaping some of the many shots with which Barak would attempt to maim, then kill, him.

His eyes staring, his mouth hanging open, he jerked his head from side to side. For a moment he even thought of jumping over the parapet of low boulders, but he knew that there could be little hope of surviving the twenty-foot drop. He would either break his neck, like Cepicka, or break both his legs, fracture a dozen other bones and die soon after from an internal haemorrhage. It was then that his eye lit on the tangle of great boulders only thirty yards away, separated here and there by gaps. Without losing another second, he dashed up the slope and threw himself headlong into a narrow opening between two of them.

Most of the tumbled rocks were no more than six feet high; so the places where they were not actually touching were narrow tunnels, rather than caves, and these formed a small, irregular maze. Some were impassable, others partly obstructed by scrub, and most of them could have been looked down into by anyone patient enough to clamber over the top of the whole area.

Robbie wriggled in for about eight feet, then found that the cleft he was in led to a small open space, where there grew a fine crop of stinging nettles; so, panting heavily, he stayed where he was. He could only pray that Barak had not seen him dive in among the rocks, but he thought it unlikely that he had. They would not have been in view until Barak had breasted the rise and, had he caught sight of Robbie, it seemed certain that he would have taken a pot shot at him.

When Robbie's breathing eased he lay very still, listening intently. After a few minutes he heard the sound of footsteps brushing through scrub, then, to his amazement, voices. Barak's came quite clearly; he was speaking in Greek and said: 'He can't be far away. He must be in among these rocks somewhere.'

The voice that replied also spoke in Greek, but it was rough and so near a *patois* that Robbie had difficulty in understanding it. After a moment, it flashed upon him that the speaker must be the goat-herd whom he had seen in the distance just after he had thrown Cepicka down into the road. Evidently, during the past quarter of an hour, he had made his way down the mountain-side to find out what was going on.

As far as Robbie could understand, he was saying that, had he had his dog, it would have been easy to flush out the man they were after; but he had left his dog to look after the goats. By the time he had been up to fetch him, it would be sundown. There was some further discussion; but Robbie did not catch it as the two men moved away, presumably to skirt the tangle of rocks and see if they could find any traces of him.

It occurred to him then that, now Barak was no longer alone, it would be safe to come out, as his enemy would not dare to shoot him in front of the goat-herd. But, on second thoughts, he decided that to be a rash assumption. Only by killing him could Barak save himself from being charged with Stephanie's murder. To escape that he might well be prepared, after shooting Robbie, to shoot the goat-herd, too. Afterwards, he would have only to carry their two bodies into the middle of the tangle of rocks, wedge them into two of the narrow tunnels and block up the entrances; then, in that incredibly desolate country, the odds would be a hundred to one against anyone finding them until they had long since become unidentifiable skeletons. Restrained by this grim possibility, Robbie remained where he was for the next ten minutes.

When he did crawl to the entrance of his tunnel and peep out, he could not see Barak; but on emerging a little further, he caught sight of him and the goat-herd going over the crest of the rise in the direction of the Mercedes. Having given them another few minutes, Robbie crawled through the scrub on his hands and knees until he could see over the crest. By that time, the two men had nearly reached the car; then, much to Robbie's surprise, the goat-herd got into it with Barak and it drove off in the direction of Tripolis.

At last, Robbie was freed from the fear that he was fated to die out there on that lonesome mountain-side, riddled with bullets. But, mentally, he was still in a state of distress that defied description. Although Cepicka had been gunning for him and he had acted in self-defence, the fact that he had actually killed a fellow human being had, as he had stared down on the twisted body in the road, appalled him. Yet even that had faded into insignificance beside the tragedy that had followed so swiftly upon it. He felt that his dreams would for months be harrowed by that terrible scene in which he had been powerless to intervene, and that to his dying day he would be unable to blot out from his mind the terror on Stephanie's face as the earth gave way beneath her and she slid down the side of the precipice. That he was marooned there without transport, miles from anywhere and with night coming on, seemed by comparison of no consequence.

Instead of risking a slip and fall by going down the chimney, he walked down the slope, the way Barak had gone, and, on reaching the road, turned back along it till he came to the place where the Ford had gone over. The sideways marks the front wheels had made in the dust as the car had been forced towards the precipice were quite clear, but he did not think they would provide evidence that Barak had rammed it three times. The marks might just as well have been made had it been a genuine accident and he had crashed into the Ford when taking the corner at a fair speed.

Kneeling down, Robbie nerved himself to look over the edge. From it, evidently as part of the road's construction, there was a slope, about ten feet wide, at an angle of forty-five degrees. Below that, the cliff dropped sheer for some two hundred feet, then the ground sloped again, but very steeply; so the car would have bounced on the lower slope, probably several times, before it was finally dashed to pieces in the distant bottom of the ravine.

To the west, the sun was now setting in a glory of gold, rose and crimson; so the bottom of the valley was already in deep shadow. Even in full daylight it might have been difficult to spot the wreckage of the car at that distance; but Robbie thought he could detect a smear of smoke lingering down there from its having been burnt out.

Looking down had already given him a touch of vertigo, and he was about to draw back. Then his heart missed a beat. Twenty feet to his right, and about six feet down, protruding round the corner of the cliff, there was something white. It looked . . . it was . . . it could only be an outflung hand and forearm.

Leaping to his feet, he ran to the corner, knelt again and peered over. Stephanie was lying there, near the bottom of the short slope. She was on her side, supported only by one elbow which had caught in the V of a tough root. Her head was thrown back and her eyes were closed. It looked as if she had been knocked unconscious by hitting her head on a rock, or had fainted.

'Stephanie!' he called to her. 'Stephanie! Oh, thank God you didn't go over.'

At the sound of his voice, her eyes opened. They stared up at him transfixed by terror. As he stared back, his relief at finding her still alive was suddenly submerged by a wave of apprehension. Her body was more than half-way down the slope. How could he possibly get her up? He had no head for heights. His only asset was his strength, and he had no rope or anything of that kind he could throw to her.

He drew back, stood up and looked round, his eyes searching feverishly for something which might enable him to rescue her. The long stretch of road to either side of the cliff was empty: there were no tough creepers that he might have twisted into a rope; no long, stout branch broken from a tree, one end of which he could have lowered for her to cling to. As his glance darted this way and that, an anguished cry floated up from her.

'Don't leave me! For God's sake, don't leave me!'

The inference that he might even contemplate abandoning her angered him; yet at the same time it fixed upon him more firmly than ever the obligation to drag her up to safety, and he trembled at the thought of having to set about it. Kneeling down again, he stretched out his hands and legs until he was lying at full length, with his head and arms protruding over the edge, then he called to her.

'Don't worry. Don't worry. Everything will be all right. I'll get you up somehow.' Yet even as he sought to reassure her, he felt that he could not possibly do it. His arms, when thrust downward to their fullest extent, did not bring his finger-tips within two feet of her and, each time his glance left her face for a second, it took in the yawning gulf that lay beyond her head and shoulders. From where he lay, he could not actually see down into the chasm, but the fact that no more than eighteen inches beyond Stephanie's feet the slope abruptly ended, with nothing between it and the now shadowy far side of the valley, made him feel sick and giddy.

An inch at a time he edged forward, his chest gradually protruding further over until the weight of his hips and legs, still lying on the flat, was no longer sufficient to anchor the upper part of his body. His hands were now within a few inches of hers. He was already having to dig his fingers into the soft earth to prevent himself slipping further down the slope. Had he attempted to take her weight, they must inevitably both have gone over.

For a few moments he remained in that position, knowing that to attempt to haul her up must prove fatal, yet his mind in revolt at the thought of beating a retreat. As he stared downward, he imagined what must follow if his hands suddenly lost their grip on the earth.

He would slither head first down the slope, cannon into her, tearing her from her precarious hold, and the two of them would shoot out into space. There would be the sensation of rushing downwards more swiftly than in the swiftest lift. The plunge into the abyss would not rob them of consciousness, and time was an illusion. Everyone knew that hours spent in school dragged on leaden feet, while those spent at a jolly party sped on silver wings. It might take only seconds by the clock for them to hurtle downward the first two hundred feet with the uprush of air whistling through their hair but, in their terror-stricken minds, it would seem long minutes of waiting to be smashed to pieces. With luck, when they hit the lower slope, they would break their necks, but the odds were against their striking the mountain-side head first. It was more likely that their bodies, twisted grotesquely out of shape and tortured by splintered bones, would bounce and bound onward, accumulating still further injuries while they continued to remain conscious for several minutes longer.

As these nightmare thoughts raced through Robbie's mind, the sight of the razor edge beyond which death lay began to have a terrible influence upon him. It seemed to be exerting a physical pull on his shoulders. He was seized with the impulse to kick out with his legs and throw himself over. A wave of nausea swept over him. He closed his eyes and somehow fought it down. But when he opened them again he knew that if he remained where he was, even a few minutes longer, he would be overcome by vertigo and that that would be the end of him. Meeting Stephanie's eyes again, he whispered hoarsely:

'I can't make it. I'm sorry. There will be a lorry or car along soon. You must hang on till help comes.'

Her face was chalk-white. For the past few minutes, while he had been edging himself down towards her, she had remained silent and unmoving, courageously conserving her strength for the effort that would be needed to take as much of her own weight as possible, while he hauled her to safety.

At his admission of defeat, terror showed in her eyes again, and she gasped: 'No! No! The earth under me may give at any moment.'

Then, rendered desperate by her fears, she shifted her position and made an upward grab at one of Robbie's hands. She missed it by inches; and worse. Her sudden movement snapped off one prong of the V of root that had been supporting her. With a piercing scream, she slithered down another two feet. Now on her stomach, she clawed frantically at the earth. Her fingers dug into it, getting a dubious hold, but, before she managed to check her slide, her feet and legs up to the knees were dangling over the precipice.

'Hang on!' yelled Robbie. 'Hang on! Hang on!' But there could now be no question of waiting for help to arrive. Had she not moved, there would have been a good chance that the root would have supported her until a vehicle had come on the scene with the means to rescue her. Now she was clinging to the steep slope only with her bare hands. In a matter of minutes, her muscles must tire, her hold relax and with one last scream she would disappear into the abyss.

Impelled by instinct rather than conscious courage, Robbie accepted the challenge that this crisis had forced upon him. He slithered forward until only the toes of his shoes still retained a purchase on the edge of the road above him. He could now have grasped one of Stephanie's hands but, as she was supporting herself by them, he dared not. Instead, he seized her by the hair.

As she felt the pull on it, she only gritted her teeth and, now that he was holding her from slipping backwards, threw her hands upward, clawed at the earth again, then drew her legs in from over the yawning gulf.

For a full minute they remained like that, while the sweat poured off Robbie's face and he could hear her breath coming in short, harsh gasps. He had saved her from going over; but for him to wriggle up the slope backwards, much less draw her after him, he knew to be impossible. It seemed that they were now stuck there, until she croaked:

'Let go my hair and dig both your hands into the earth. If you can support yourself like that, I think I can clamber up alongside you.'

He did as she said, striving to embrace the earth with his whole body; then he closed his eyes to check another wave of nausea. To him, the next few minutes seemed an age. He could feel her beside him and now and then she laid a hand lightly on him while steadying herself in her upward climb. Once she slipped and bore heavily upon him to save herself. His heart missed a beat, but his grip on the surface of the slope held.

'I'm up!' she shouted suddenly. 'I'm safe. But stay where you are. Don't move for a moment.'

A minute later, he felt her grasp on his right ankle. Both her hands were round it, and she was pulling on it. 'Now!' she cried. 'Wriggle yourself backwards.'

Again he did as she told him. As he levered himself up, hand over hand, she knelt above him, hauling with all her might on his leg. The support that gave him enabled him to thrust himself back up the steep gradient. After three minutes of frantic exertion, he rolled over beside her on the edge of the road.

Both of them were so exhausted that for several minutes they lay quite still; then he slowly sat up and muttered: 'That was a near one for both of us.'

Stephanie propped herself on an elbow, looked at him and replied, 'It came to that. But you didn't have to come down for me, Robbie. I owe my life to you. I . . . I'm terribly grateful.'

He gave her a faint smile. 'I owe my life to you. If you hadn't got me out last night, by now I'd be feeding the fishes. That makes us quits. But it was a piece of luck for both of us that I was still alive and kicking to come down and get you. Up there on that cliff above us, first Cepicka did his best to murder me, then that charming husband of yours came after me with a gun.'

'Tell me what happened after . . . after Václav pushed me over.'

'I had already dealt with Cepicka. I threw him down into the road and he broke his neck. Barak didn't know that, because it happened round the corner from where you and he were standing. About a minute later, I was looking down here and saw you having a row with him, then he gave you a shove and over you went. I yelled something and he turned. I suppose he thought that Cepicka would have made a corpse of me by that time. Anyhow, when he realized that I'd seen him murder you—or that's what we both thought then—he pulled a gun to take a pot at me. But I dived down behind the boulders. When next I looked, he was ramming the Ford with the Mercedes, and he kept on until he had sent it over the precipice. I suppose he means to say that there has been an accident and you went over in it. When he had put an end to the Ford, he came up to put an end to me; knowing, of course, that as I had seen him do you in, unless he killed me it was a sure thing that I'd get him for murder.

'I took cover again in a sort of outsize rabbit warren of great, tumbled rocks. Thank God, he failed to find me. But, by that time, another character had come on the scene—a goat-herd whom I had noticed half a mile away up on the mountain-side just after I had pitched Cepicka down into the road. Barak and the goat-herd sniffed round for a bit, then they went off together. Shortly after you ceased to play an active part in matters, and while I was under cover, Barak must have carried Cepicka's body to his car. I saw it later, rolling about on the back seat, and it was still in the car when Barak finally drove off towards Tripolis, taking the goat-herd with him.'

After a moment, Robbie added: 'As you are still alive, for which thank God, I can't get him for murder now; but we can get him for attempted murder.'

'Where was the goat-herd at that time?' Stephanie asked. 'Did he see everything that happened?'

'Oh no. He was up on the mountain-side. He must have seen me throw Cepicka over the cliff, because up there our figures would have stood out clearly. But he couldn't have seen you and Barak quarrelling down here, or Barak when he used the Mercedes to push the Ford over, because the cliff would have masked this section of road from his view.'

'Then I'm afraid you wouldn't get anywhere by accusing Václav of attempted murder,' Stephanie said thoughtfully. 'It would only be your word against his, and my testimony

N

wouldn't be worth much because it would be believed that I was lying to help you defend yourself by bringing a counter-charge.'

'A counter-charge?' Robbie echoed. 'Why should I be charged with anything?'

Stephanie shook her head unhappily. 'How Václav will handle it I don't quite know; but he's very clever. I've an idea, though, that he will soon be telling the police something like this. You took me away from him. He came after us with his friend Cepicka. They first missed us, then ran into us on this bend. I was driving and tried to pass them. There was an accident. The Zephyr went over with me in it. Remember he believes me to be dead. You managed to jump out. Naturally, you were half off your head with rage. Cepicka had been driving the Mercedes and you held him responsible for my death. He got out. There was a violent quarrel and you threatened to kill him. In an endeavour to escape you, he shinned up that gully. You went after him, seized him, threw him down into the road and broke his neck.'

Having paused for a moment, Stephanie went on: 'You see, Robbie, that is all the goat-herd can actually have seen; so that is all the evidence he can give, and he will be an independent witness. That, I'm sure, is why Václav took him with him into Tripolis. It is a wicked twist of Fate . . . wicked. But we must face it. Within a few hours, the police will be hunting for you, and it is you who will be wanted for murder.'

23

On the Run

R o b b i e could not deny the logic of Stephanie's reasoning. 'I suppose you're right,' he admitted. 'But, damn it all, I was acting in self-defence. If I hadn't killed Cepicka he would have killed me.'

'I know.' Stephanie sat up and began to brush some of the dirt off her clothes. 'You can't prove, though, that it was Cepicka who chased you up that chimney, and not you who chased him. Nor can you prove that Barak forced the Zephyr over the precipice or that he did his best to kill me. And no one is going to believe what I say. After all, would you? It will be said that we ran away from Athens together and that for three weeks my husband lost all trace of me. Then he learned that we were at Olympia, and persuaded me to return to him. But, after one night, you turned up at Pirgos and carried me off again. He and his friend Cepicka gave chase; then comes his version of what happened.'

'There is one thing that won't fit. According to the story you suggest he will tell, the cars met by accident head on and you went over in the Ford. Only I managed to jump out. Yet you are still alive.'

'Seeing the crash coming, I might have opened the car door and tumbled on to the slope where you found me, without any of you realizing that I hadn't gone over with the car.'

'What about the shots Cepicka fired at me? It's so still up here that the goat-herd must have heard them.'

Stephanie gave a mirthless laugh. 'Oh, Robbie, be your

age. Is it likely that Václav will admit that they were fired by
Cepicka? He'll say that it was you who fired them, and that
it was terror of you that led Cepicka to dash round the corner
of the cliff and try to get away from you by shinning up that
gulley. The fact that you haven't got a gun will cut no ice,
because you could have thrown it away.'

'I'm in the very devil of a fix, then. But if the police once
start hunting for me, they are certain to get me in the end;
so I suppose the best thing I can do is to go to them with my
side of the story and pray to God that the truth will prevail.'

'I wish I thought it would, but I'm afraid that our having
spent three weeks together, and the independent testimony of
that goat-herd, are going to weigh the scales against you. And,
once you give yourself up, you'll have no further opportunity
of securing proof that you were justified in killing Cepicka.'

Robbie turned to stare at her. 'I don't get you. How could
I possibly secure proof of that?'

'You might, if you continued your snooping. If you could
get proof that Václav and the others are up to something contrary to the interests of Greece and you have been trying to
find out what it was, that would provide a motive for their
attempting to kill you. Your plea of self-defence would then be
credible. What is more, you would have earned the gratitude
of the Greek Government and have it on your side.'

'But . . . but what about that document you made me sign?
I promised——'

'Forget it;' Stephanie shook her head impatiently. 'When
you signed it my husband hadn't tried to murder me. Anyhow,
you signed it at my request; so I can absolve you from it, and
I do.'

Over the mountains to the west, the last rays of the sunset were fading, and it was now almost dark. As Robbie
glanced at the lingering flush on the peaks, he suddenly spotted
on the road below them the lights of an approaching vehicle.
Jumping to his feet, he said: 'There's a car or lorry coming.
We must get it to give us a lift.'

'Yes; we can't stay here all night,' Stephanie agreed, as she
stood up beside him. 'But what are you going to do: give your-

self up to the police when we get to Tripolis, or take a chance on eluding them, anyway for a time?'

'I don't know. I've not had time to think, but there's a lot in what you have just said. We'll talk about it later.'

'That won't be much good, unless you cover your tracks from the beginning,' she said hastily. 'You had better take a new identity right away. You speak German, don't you?'

'Yes.'

'So do I. We had better pass ourselves off as German hikers. We've lost our kit in an accident. Let me do the talking.'

By then, they could see that the approaching vehicle was a car. Robbie ran out into the middle of the road and held up his arms. The car slowed down to take the corner, but hooted angrily for him to get out of the way. He stood his ground and, with evident reluctance, the driver brought the car to a halt only a few yards from him.

It was a four-seater, and there were two men in it. As Stephanie stepped up to the window beside the driver she saw that they were well dressed and, from the clothes and horn-rimmed spectacles they were wearing, she judged them to be Americans. In halting English, she asked if either of them spoke German.

The driver replied that he spoke a little, upon which she launched out on a piece of fiction that recalled to Robbie, a trifle grimly, the story-telling ability she had displayed when he had given her lunch at Floca's.

She said that they had set out from Tropaia that morning with the intention of sleeping at Vitina that night and they had had a map showing the goatpaths over the mountains by which they meant to go. At midday they had selected a place to picnic, with a beautiful view. Oh, such a beautiful view. Then tragedy. It was above a sandy cliff that had a rabbit warren in it. There were hundreds of rabbit holes; yes, hundreds. Walking about up there must have disturbed the earth. Suddenly there came a landslide. They were carried down nearly forty feet and buried up to their waists. Their picnic basket, their rucksacks, everything had been lost and they were lucky to have escaped alive. Their map, of course, had been buried too; so for hours they had been lost in the mountains and only a quarter of an hour ago had sighted the main road. Would the well-born gentlemen please give them a lift?

Had it been full daylight, it might have occurred to the occupants of the car that the clothes and footwear of the two unfortunates did not at all tally with the story that they were hikers; but in the near darkness they passed unnoticed. Evidently relieved that they had not been forced to pull up by tramps or other undesirables, the Americans expressed their sympathy to Stephanie and willingly agreed to take her and her boy-friend on their way. Coats and bundles in the back of the car were re-stacked, they climbed in and within a few minutes had left behind the spot where they had so nearly lost their lives.

The Americans, with the friendly communicativeness usual in their countrymen, gave their names and said they were professors on their sabbatical vacation from a Mid-Western university. They had toured England, France, Italy and, the previous Thursday, had left their wives to amuse themselves in Athens while they made a five-day tour of the outstanding antiquities in Greece. They had done Delphi and Olympia and were on their way to Navplion from which they would do Tiryns, Mycenae and Epidauros, then do Corinth on their way back to the capital.

Robbie's natural instinct was to tell them of things they must not miss in the places to which they had not yet been; but Stephanie kicked him into silence, fearing that he might give too much away about his real self. She had already given her name as Greta Heine and Robbie's as Willi Muller, and she went on to say they were from Heidelberg University, that they had flown out with a party of students for ten days, at a special rate during the Easter vacation, but that they preferred hiking and seeing the country to being rushed from place to place in a coach.

Neither of the Americans spoke very good German; so, after a while, the conversation lapsed, and within a quarter of an hour they reached Vitina, with its little summer resort nearly four thousand feet up in the mountains. Their driver drew up to set them down there; but Stephanie quickly said that, as they had lost all their kit, they must now go on to a town at which they could buy more.

Soon after nine o'clock, they arrived at Tripolis, where the Americans said they planned to break their journey for dinner at the Arkadia Hotel. Robbie by now had a ravenous appetite and would have given a lot to be able to dine there, too. But he knew that to have a meal at an expensive hotel would not be in keeping with his new role; so he began to thank them for the lift, preparatory to saying good-bye.

Stephanie, however, had other plans. She was most averse to Robbie's spending the night in Tripolis, in case Barak had already put the police there on to him; so she cut in to say that, if the well-born gentlemen would be so good as to take them on to Argos, it would be a great kindness, as they would then be able to see Mycenae from there next day. The professors agreed and dropped them in the arcaded square of the town, with the understanding that they would pick them up from the same corner at ten o'clock sharp.

On the corner where they had been set down, there was a small café-restaurant. As they were about to go into it, Stephanie said in a low voice: 'During the war and occupation, nearly all the Greeks in the towns picked up a little German or English; so not a word of Greek. Remember we are Germans. If need be, we'll use a few words of English to help out.'

Inside the place was fairly full, but they got a table to themselves and, with the help of an elderly waiter who had worked for some years in the United States, they ordered a meal. When they had given their order, Stephanie told the man in broken English that they had sent their suitcases on ahead by train from Argos, then cadged a lift from a lorry; but on going to the station, they had found that their luggage had not arrived. As the shops were now shut, this had put them in a nasty fix. She then asked if there was any way he could suggest by which they could buy two bags or knapsacks and things for the night.

The waiter could and would. Like all Greeks of his class, he was both obliging and ready to go to some trouble to earn a small commission. He had a friend who had a friend, etc. Two small children were despatched on missions. A quarter of an hour later, several men and women with bronzed faces and gleaming white teeth arrived. One had some inexpensive fibre suitcases to sell; another cotton pyjamas, nightdresses and dressing gowns; a third sponges, scent, soaps and certain rubber goods that, turning his back to Stephanie, he displayed to Robbie with a whispered recommendation as to their reliability.

Robbie waved him away but, at Stephanie's urging, made as swift a selection as possible from the other items, so as to get rid of a crowd that was quickly collecting and which might have aroused the interest of a policeman. In the half hour that remained to them, Robbie managed to dispose of two *taske-baps* on skewers, a *splinantero* of fried intestines, a dish of French fried, which are good anywhere in Greece, and a hunk of white Féta cheese. Stephanie contented herself with a so-called omelette that had chunks of highly-spiced sausage in it, and a compôte of prunes and figs. After washing down these items with two large carafes of the local *retsina*, they both felt considerably better for their meal.

With their purchases packed inside their small, cheap suitcases, they were picked up by the Americans promptly at ten o'clock and were driven off into the darkness.

On their way to Tripolis, Robbie's mind had been so fully occupied by the harrowing events in which he had recently been involved, and in anxious speculation about the future, that he had remained oblivious of the road they were travelling. But now, soon after they left the chief market town of Arkadia, he again became highly conscious of the perils of the road.

They met no coaches or private cars; but it seemed that, owing perhaps to come commercial arrangement, a whole fleet of lorries was taking this road into the interior by night. Sometimes they could see the approaching lights snaking along the curves of the mountain-side a mile or more ahead; at others they came upon them round a blind corner, with only the briefest warning, and it seemed that they now came head-on to one about every five minutes.

Knowing that, when passing any other vehicle, the outer wheels of the car were usually no more than three feet from the edge of a precipice, such encounters caused Robbie to shut his eyes and hold his breath. To add to his fears, the Americans were none too happy about it, either, for the lorries never used their horns when coming round a corner. The driver's only warning of their approach was the beam that their headlamps cast on the road ahead. Moreover, when they did come rushing forward, like huge, fiery-eyed monsters, it was their custom to keep their dazzling lights still on until within fifty feet of the vehicle they were about to pass, then black them out completely. To get by in total darkness, without a scraping of the sides which might have proved fatal, or giving too wide a berth, which would have proved equally so, called for good nerves and fine judgment.

Fortunately, their driver displayed both, and at last the long, long road, with its innumerable bends, from the mountains down to the west side of the gulf of Navplia, had been safely negotiated. Less than a quarter of an hour later, the kindly Americans set them down in the irregular central square in Argos and wished them luck.

There were cafés there, with lights still burning and people in them; so, carrying their fibre suitcases, they made enquiries at one of them for rooms. A waiter gave one glance at their dirty and dishevelled state, then directed them further down the street to a café that was also an hotel. It was a shoddy-looking place, and Robbie demurred about going into it; but Stephanie told him that it was just the sort of cheap rooming house in which no one would look for anyone like himself. Still posing as German students, they went in, and were met by a scruffy-looking landlord in an open-necked shirt. He spoke a few words of German and took them up to two sparsely furnished rooms with thin mattresses on iron beds.

Robbie then told Stephanie that he was very anxious to have a talk with her, and asked if she was too tired to go downstairs for a drink before they turned in. She replied that she was not feeling too bad, as she had managed to sleep for an hour in the car on the way from Tripolis. At that he marvelled, as he had thought the only reason they had all kept silent for most of that perilous drive was from fear of distracting the driver.

In a dimly lit room downstairs, with a small bar at one end

of it, they sat down at a bare wooden table. Several of the others were still littered with dirty glasses, but the people who had used them had gone home. Robbie asked the landlord for *ouzo* and he brought a bottle, two thick glasses and a carafe of water. He then dumped on the table the usual saucers of black olives, gherkins and some kind of stringy vegetable soaked in oil, and left them.

When the landlord had gone and Robbie had poured the drinks, he said:

'Just before the Americans came along and gave us a lift, you were suggesting that I should continue trying to find out what Barak and Co. are doing, and you released me from my promise not to do so. Having thought things over, it seems to me that my case will be little worse if the police pick me up in a week or two than if I give myself up tomorrow morning. I also think that you're right in your idea that I'd be in a much stronger position if, in the meantime, I could secure definite evidence that Barak is up to no good. But what I am not clear about yet is your attitude. Before Barak pushed you over the cliff, I heard you shout that you were sick to death of him and the Party and all its filthy works; and now you are suggesting that I should continue to spy on your own people. Am I to take it that you really mean to break with them for good?'

She drew heavily on the cigarette she was smoking, then nodded: 'Yes. I couldn't go back now, even if I wanted to. Since you heard me quarrelling with Václav, you probably also heard me threaten that I'd report him to a man named Janos for taking bribes. Janos's official job is butler at the Legation; but he is the real boss, and even Havelka goes in fear of him. He could have Václav expelled from the Party, sent home and given a prison sentence. But that wouldn't do me any good now. Cepicka will have been the only person other than Václav to see the document you signed and the letter I left behind at Pirgos; and he is dead. Václav believes me dead too, but the moment I turn up alive he will destroy both the document and my letter—if he hasn't done so already. They were my let-out that I was acting in good faith with the Party. Without them, it will be taken for granted that, in helping you to escape, I deliberately betrayed the Party because you were my lover. That will be the version of the affair that Václav will be reporting to Janos tomorrow; so whatever I might say about Václav now, whether it's believed or not, I'd be finished and better dead myself.'

'I see. Yes,' Robbie murmured. 'You had told me before, of course, that for a long time your husband hadn't meant anything to you. But how about the Party? Up till this afternoon, you were definitely playing for their side. When you shouted out about their filthy works, were you really fed up with the way the Communists ran their show or were you referring only to Barak having planned to murder me?'

Stephanie hesitated a moment, then she said: 'All this having happened only this afternoon, I haven't quite got my bearings yet. You see, my father was a Communist and I was brought up as one. I have accepted Communist principles all my life, and I still believe that, if the ideal State on Communist lines could be established, it would better the lot of the great majority of people. But the trouble is that it never works in practice. It results only in dispossessing the old ruling class and putting another in its place. If the new lot were all idealists and prepared to work for the benefit of the masses, that might be all right. But they are not. Nine out of ten of them are out only for themselves and are quite unscrupulous; so it's a case of "dog eat dog" and every smaller dog goes in constant terror of being eaten by a bigger one. None of them dares to take any action because he believes it to be right. Instead, they spend their time spying on one another and either betraying their superiors or covering up their blunders, whichever suits their own book the better. In the meantime, they grab all the perks and privileges there are to grab and leave the masses they are supposed to represent to struggle along as best they can. Greece is a poor country, but the people here are far better off than they are in Czechoslovakia. In some of the slum areas and villages there, the poverty is appalling; yet the Party never does anything about it.'

To Robbie, it was evident that she was now pouring out thoughts which she had long kept pent-up; so he made no comment when she paused to take a drink.

'There is the Police State side of it, too,' she went on. 'It's nothing like so bad as it used to be and, of course, it doesn't affect any great number of people. Most of them have learned by now that if they do their jobs without complaining about hours, or conditions, or food shortages, and refrain from having anything to do with the occasional firebrands who want to start making trouble, they won't be interfered with. But the fact remains that Communism has to be imposed by force. All the Iron Curtain countries would blow up, like the Hungarians did, if their peoples weren't convinced that Big Brother in Moscow would send in his tanks. And, of course, everyone who holds a position of any importance does have to be very careful what he does and says. Anyone who is fool enough to include in a speech a few sentences implying that perhaps, after all, life was a bit jollier under the old Austro-Hungarian Monarchy, or gets so tight that he allows himself to make a dirty crack at one of the Party bosses, is still liable to disappear quietly from his home overnight. And we all know where he's gone. He's been sent to work in the uranium mines. That is equivalent to a sentence of death by easy stages. I gather that few of the workers in them last more than two years, and, personally, I would infinitely rather be shot.'

'From what you say,' Robbie commented, 'it seems as if quite some time ago you had come to the conclusion that the old way in which the capitalist countries muddle along means a better life for most people than they would have if they lived in a totalitarian State.'

'Yes, I suppose I had. I've never actually admitted it before, even to myself. But I must have recognized it subconsciously It is the reason why I have remained with Václav for the past four years. I had nearly made up my mind to break with him, then I heard he had been nominated as our Security Chief in Greece. Although I was a dyed-in-the-wool Communist, and fully believed that in the capitalist-imperialist countries the bloated rich actually treated the poor as slaves, I wanted to see for myself what went on; so I decided to stick to him for a bit longer. The diplomatic staffs of Iron Curtain countries are not allowed to mix freely with the people in whose countries they are stationed; so it was quite a time before I realized that the Greek lower classes were really a good bit better off than most Czechs and that nobody here need fear being imprisoned, whatever he may say about the Government. But, meanwhile, I was becoming accustomed to the good food, the pretty clothes, the hair-dos, the really worth-while cinema shows, the glossy magazines and all the other things I'd never had in my own country. To have broken with Václav would have meant being sent home. I suppose it was weak of me, but rather than have that happen I put up with his infidelities and the way he treated me, and did whatever he told me to, without argument.'

'Given the same circumstances, I think most people would have done as you did,' Robbie smiled. 'But where do you mean to go from here? Up till now, you have been doing your bit to help the Communists reach the goal they have set themselves of imposing their ideology on the whole world. But, willy-nilly, you have burnt your boats with them through helping me to escape. What is more, you now admit that Communist domination brings with it misery to all classes. As you know, I've been trying to defeat what I believe to be one move in that direction. Did you suggest that I should carry on with that only because you like me enough not to wish to see me condemned to death for killing Cepicka, or are you prepared to give me your help?'

Stephanie took another drink, then sat silent for a little, while Robbie anxiously awaited her answer. At length, she said: 'The more I think about life in Greece compared with life at home, the more certain I feel that the spread of Communism ought to be checked and, if possible, rolled back.'

'Then you will help me?' he asked eagerly. 'Even though you would be working against your own country?'

She shook her head sadly. 'I haven't got a country, although perhaps I may have one again one day. Czechoslovakia is now just a part of the Soviet Bloc. Besides, as far as blood goes, I'm half and half. I told you all sorts of lies, but I was telling the truth about my mother having been English.'

'Really! '

'Yes. I haven't a drop of Greek blood in me. But, like you, I'm good at languages and three and a half years in Athens have enabled me to speak Greek very fluently. I've still got quite an accent, though, and all along I was a bit scared that we would meet a Greek who would insist to you that I must be a foreigner.'

Robbie smiled. 'I noticed your accent myself, but I put it down to your having spent your early years in England and always talking English with your mother.'

'I was born in England, but I didn't remain there for long. My father was a Czech, and a technical expert in the manufacture of pottery. The pay for such work was much higher in England than it was in Czechoslovakia and, early in the thirties, through a friend, he got a job with a firm in Staffordshire. He had always been a Communist and, although my mother wasn't one then, she was an extreme Left-wing Socialist. Incidentally she was a school-teacher, and I owe it to her that I had a really good education. They were married in thirty-five, but I wasn't born until thirty-eight. Then, at the time of the Munich crisis, the Czech Government called up its Army reserves. Father was naturally madly anti-Nazi, so he went back to serve and took mother and me with him.'

'You were there all through the war, then?'

'Yes. I don't remember much about it, except that we were all half-starved and miserable. During the German occupation, father was in the Resistance and, as he managed to survive, he was given an administrative job when the Russians drove the Germans out. From then on, things improved for us and I was sent to a good school. Owing to the private teaching I had had from mother, I found lessons easy. Then, when the Government was taken over by the Communists, father became quite a big shot, and I was made a Youth Leader in the Young Communist Organization. I was just seventeen when I met Václav at a Party rally. He fell for me and I was flattered, because, in his way, he is a fine-looking man and he was already regarded as quite a shining light among the younger officials of the Party. On that account my mother and father encouraged the match, and that was that.'

Again she took a drink. 'There's no point in going into details about what followed. Within a year, it became a marriage of convenience. I was still young enough to console myself with the status that being his wife gave me, and meeting important people. He amused himself with other women, but was careful not to drive me too far, from fear that he would lose my father's influence in helping him with his career. Then, when we came to Greece, I liked it too much here to face being sent home, and he found he could make valuable use of me. You see, there are no other wives of the Legation staff who can speak as many languages as I can and . . . why shouldn't I say it?—are smart and attractive. One way and another, I was able to pick up a lot of useful information for him; and, of course, as I am half English, I was the obvious choice when your advertisement for a chauffeur-secretary appeared and it was decided to put a woman on to you.'

'And now?'

'I thought I'd made it plain. I daren't let myself be sent home. About a year ago, my father died; so there's no one there now who would protect me. I've decided to put the past behind me and come in with you.'

'Thank God for that.' Robbie refilled her glass and his own, then lifted his, saying: 'Here's to us,' and they drank to one another. When he had set his glass down, he said:

'Your decision may be the means of your saving my life for the second time—now that there is no need for us to keep any secrets from each other. For my part, I have no connection with any oil company. I came into this thing only because I speak Czech and happened, one morning out at Toyrcolimano, to overhear Barak and Nejedly discussing the oil-prospecting concession they had got from the Greeks in exchange for taking the Greek tobacco crop. When I learnt that there was no oil in Greece, I became curious and suspected that it might be cover for installing some scientific device— something that, in the event of war, could be used against the N.A.T.O forces. I told my uncle, the Ambassador, what I thought but he pooh-poohed my ideas, so I made a start on my own. I expect you already know all about the week I spent as a stooge in the Czech Travel Agency, and how I burgled the place and got away with some of Krajcir's secret papers. Anyhow, I have no official backing and you are the only person who knows how I've been spending my time since we left

Athens. Now it's your turn. You have only to tell me what Barak and Co. are up to. Then, even if the police pick me up before I can secure proof of it, I'll be able to get them to start enquiries that should lead to justifying me for having killed Cepicka.'

Stephanie shook her head. 'I'm sorry, Robbie. I wish I could tell you, but I don't know. That is the truth. I swear it. Of course, you are right about the prospecting for oil being only a cover plan. That much Václav didn't attempt to conceal from me. But, on these sort of jobs, no one is ever told anything that is not strictly necessary for him to know in order to carry out his work. They may be making launching sites for rockets, or perhaps a chain of radar stations to assist the Communist submarine fleet that is based on the Albanian ports. Those are just shots in the dark. Honestly, I haven't a clue.'

'Oh, dear!' Robbie pulled down the corners of his mouth. 'That's very disappointing. Still, I quite see that they wouldn't have let out their secret further than they had to, and your job was confined to keeping an eye on me. We must start again from the beginning, then. But your mind is much more fertile in ideas than mine. What do you suggest should be our next move?'

'To cover up your disappearance further by every possible means we can,' she replied without hesitation. 'We've had a lucky break to start with, by being picked up by two Americans. They can't read the Greek papers, so all the chances are against any account of this evening's affair coming to their notice. Even if it does, I shall be reported as dead and the police will be looking for an Englishman on his own; so our American friends are most unlikely to think that one of the German hikers to whom they gave a lift might have been you. Again, the people in the café in Tripolis and the landlord here will have no reason to connect a German couple with the wanted Englishman. So, so far, so good; but we must not let the grass grow under our feet. The sooner you can get out of Greece, the better.'

'Out of Greece!' echoed Robbie. 'But I'd be caught when I showed my passport. Besides, if we are going to try——'

'You don't need to show your passport when going to any of the Greek islands,' she interrupted, 'and surely the least risky place to try to find out what Václav's groups are up to is on one of them.'

'You're right,' he agreed. 'Which do you favour?'

She considered a moment. 'I think it should be either Crete or Rhodes, because many more people go there than to the others. In any of the smaller ones, more notice would be taken of you as a visitor; so when your photograph is put into the papers, there would be a bigger risk of someone identifying you.'

'That's one thing we needn't worry about.' Robbie gave a little laugh. 'I haven't had a photograph taken since I was a small boy, except for my passport, and they won't get hold of that because I've got it on me.'

'Well, that's a blessing. But I still favour Crete or Rhodes. There's an air service to both, so we could get to either of them quickly. And time matters, because it's not on our side— or won't be, once the police start an all-out search for you.'

'If we are to go by plane, we'll have to return to Athens. Since so many people know me there, that will mean my running a big risk.'

'Not if we keep to the poor parts of the city, and eat in the sort of places to which people we know never go. There is certain to be a train from here tomorrow morning and we'd better go by it. Lorry drivers and drivers of cars who give lifts would be much more likely to remember our faces than would other travellers in a third-class railway compartment. There is one thing, though. We shall need money and as soon as the police learn that you are carrying a Letter of Credit, they will notify the banks to hold you should you attempt to draw any money. It is bound to be two or three days before they get round to that; but, all the same, I suggest that you go to the bank here first thing in the morning and draw out as big a sum as they will let you have.'

Robbie gave her a glance of admiration. 'You think of everything, don't you? Without you, I wouldn't last twelve hours.'

She smiled back at him. 'You saved my life this evening,

Robbie. And, knowing that you can't face heights, I can guess what coming down that slope to get me must have meant to you. For what my mind is worth, every bit of it is yours. Can you draw enough money to keep us going for a week or two?'

'Yes. When we left Athens, I had no idea how long we should be away; so the Letter of Credit I'm carrying is still good for quite a large——' Suddenly he stopped in mid-sentence, then continued with a frown: 'But I've just remembered. Tomorrow is Sunday.'

'So it is. I'd forgotten that, too. Then you'll have to draw the money in Athens on Monday. That is a pity as it will give away the fact that you have been there. Still we should be out of the capital again before your bank learns that the police are after you.'

They talked for another ten minutes or so, making further plans. There was always the odd chance that the Americans might learn that a car smash and murder had taken place just before their arrival at the spot where they had picked up the two young Germans. If so, and they informed the police, it was certain that the police would endeavour to trace the hikers, in order to find out if they had seen Robbie or could give any information about the affair; so they decided that, on reaching Athens, they would change their identities again and pass themselves off as French. They also decided that they would go to Rhodes. By then it was getting on for half-past-twelve, and the scruffy landlord came in to say that he was shutting up for the night.

In spite of the hardness of the beds, they were both so tired that they slept well. In the morning, a slatternly woman brought them unappetizing breakfasts of bad coffee and sweet buns. The geyser in the only bathroom did not work, and the lavatory stank to high heaven but at least the bill amazed Robbie by its modesty. Having never before stayed in any but expensive hotels, he had had no idea that it was possible to get a night's lodging so cheaply.

The train for Athens left at eleven o'clock. It consisted of only four coaches: three thirds and one first. Robbie had travelled on a Greek train some months before, out to Marathon, so he knew that going first class was much more pleasant than travelling first on British Railways. A third of the coach consisted of a kitchen, and between each pair of broad, stuffed seats there was a wide table on which at any hour one could have a well-cooked meal of one's own choice from an enormous menu.

But Stephanie insisted that they would draw less attention to themselves if they travelled third, and the third-class coaches were very different. They had wooden seats and were packed to capacity. As it was a Sunday, the travellers were mostly dressed in their best and no live-stock accompanied them. Even so the smell was considerable, and the strong sun grilling down on the roof of the carriage soon set everyone perspiring freely.

The little train puffed its way past Mycenae and up into the mountains, then round bend after bend through them and so down to Corinth. From there it crossed the canal and, ascending again to several hundred feet above sea level, followed the north shore of the Gulf of Athens as far as Eleusis. When it stopped there, Robbie drew Stephanie's attention to the name of the station and sighed with relief. They had already been cooped up in considerable discomfort for over four hours, and he judged that another quarter of an hour should see them at their journey's end. But he was counting his chickens. Instead of following the coast further, the train turned inland and, stopping frequently, made an hour-long detour right round the capital; so it was after five o'clock before they arrived in Athens.

While in the train, they had pretended to know no Greek and had spoken German to one another. Now, carrying their light suitcases, they went into the station buffet, talking loudly in French. Robbie, pretending to know only a few words of Greek, then ordered drinks for them and, in halting sentences, asked the woman behind the counter if she could give them the name of a small hotel that was both cheap and clean. The woman consulted her colleague, who called a waiter who spoke some French. A heated argument between the three ensued then, with many smiles, the Hotel Theodori in Paleologou Street was recommended, and the waiter gave Robbie the number of a bus that would take them there.

They found the hotel drab but adequate, and registered there as Monsieur Jules Colbert and Mademoiselle Louise Hachette. Until half past seven they rested in their rooms, then met again downstairs and went out for a meal at a nearby tavern. Over the meal they held another conference.

Now that Robbie was in Athens his Letter of Credit was redundant, as he had only to walk along to his own bank to draw money. But to do so would mean that the police would soon know that he either had been or still was in Athens. Stephanie suggested that he should make out a cheque, bearing a date a week old, which she should take to his bank and cash for him. He still had on him about fifty pounds in Greek money; but he felt that he ought to obtain at least another two hundred while he had the chance as, apart from the few items he had bought in Tripolis, they had only the things they stood up in. The question was, would the bank cash such a large cheque, made out simply to 'bearer', without requiring evidence of the identity of the young woman who presented it?

For Stephanie to produce such evidence would, in due course, lead to the police learning that she had not been burnt up in the Ford, but was still alive. She was greatly averse to that because, as long as they believed her to be dead, they would be hunting for Robbie as a man on his own, not one accompanied by a woman.

In this connection he said to her: 'It's a pity that we can't pose as brother and sister, but we are so unlike that we would never get away with that. It would only make people more suspicious of us.'

After a moment, she said thoughtfully: 'The best cover of all for you would be for us to travel as husband and wife. But we would have to share a room then. Of course, that need mean no more than when a man and a girl share a bathing tent and take it in turns to change in it. You could get up an hour earlier than me in the mornings, have your bath and go downstairs, and at night I would go up to bed half an hour before you. I'm not standing for any repetition of that business by the pool, though; and the question is, can I trust you?'

'You can,' Robbie gave a solemn nod. 'It's terribly good of you, Stephanie, to go that far to give me a better chance of keeping out of the hands of the police until I can pin something on Barak. If I let you down in this I'd never again be able to look at my own face in a mirror.'

She smiled. 'I believe you, Robbie. We'll do that, then. The next question is: when we get to Rhodes, are we going to stay poor or live medium rich?'

'Normally, I'd be all for staying at the Hotel des Roses. I've heard that it's one of the best in Greece. But won't it be in that sort of place that the police will look for me?'

'I don't think so. By playing poor in Argos and here in Athens, we should have put them off your track and, naturally, they will assume that you have gone to earth in some cheap hotel somewhere in the Peloponnesus. The last place they are likely to look for you would be sunning yourself on the beach of the Hotel des Roses with—if I may say so—a rather pretty wife.'

'Oh, come on!' he exclaimed spontaneously. 'Don't be so modest. You know jolly well that you are lovely.'

Her eyebrows went up and she gave a sudden laugh. 'D'you know that's the first compliment you have ever paid me? It's nice that you should think so. Still, I hope you are not going to let that give you ideas, otherwise I'll have to call off our sharing a bedroom.'

He had gone red at finding that, without thinking, he had said the sort of thing he had wanted to say to her for a long time past. But he quickly shook his head. 'Don't worry. I've given you my word.'

Stubbing out her cigarette, she said: 'There are several advantages to staying in a big hotel. It is not so likely to be noticed if we never go up to bed at the same time, or come down together in the morning; and if we want to hire a car, there will be no nosey landlady to wonder how we can afford such an extravagance.'

'Right, then. The des Roses it shall be, providing we can get hold of enough money.'

That question was solved by an idea that came to Robbie while he was still lying in bed the following morning. Luke Beecham could get a cheque cashed for him without any questions being asked, and Stephanie could collect the money without having to give away her identity. As soon as he got downstairs, he wrote a note to Luke on a plain sheet of paper. Not wishing to embroil his friend, he made no reference to the events which had led to his present situation. The note ran:

I am still on the war path, and am certain now that the people I am interested in are up to something pretty nasty. But, for the time being, it is essential that I keep under cover, and I need money. Would you be good enough to cash the enclosed cheque right away through your bank and hand the proceeds to the bearer of this, who wishes to remain anonymous but is entirely reliable?

As soon as Stephanie came downstairs, they went out and had an early coffee. Over the table he gave her the note and the cheque, telling her the address of Luke Beecham's office. It was then agreed that if Luke were there and she got the money, she should go to the Olympus Airways office and try to get two seats on the next morning's plane to Rhodes. Then she was to buy herself a better suitcase and some clothes which would pass muster for a stay at the Hotel des Roses.

At her suggestion it was agreed that he should go meanwhile to a barber and have a crew-cut, and also buy himself a pair of dark glasses. When she had set off, with considerable reluctance he had the back and sides of his head shaved, so that he felt he looked like a convict; then, with some of the money he had on him, he bought himself two shirts, another pair of shoes, some socks and four ties.

When they met again for lunch, he learned to his relief that Stephanie's mission had been successful. Luke had asked no questions; she had the money and a note from him, which said:

I was getting quite worried at hearing nothing from you. Things are looking far from good, so anything you can get hold of in the immediate future may prove of exceptional value. I take it the 'bearer' is the 'chauffeuse-secretary' you told me about. No wonder you refused to take my advice, and preferred to risk blackmail or having to cough up alimony. What a dark

horse you've turned out to be. Anyhow lots of luck to you,
and let's hope that we are still all alive this time next week.

Robbie and Stephanie had been so completely absorbed in
their own affairs for the past three days that they had not
given a thought to the international crisis. Now he got hold of a
paper. The headline read: 'Soviet Threat. Unless U.S. accepts
terms, Russia will consider issuing Ultimatum.'

They read the leader, and a long article which amounted
to little more than a recapitulation of what everyone already
knew. The American submarine was sitting on the bottom
under the ice in a bay on the Arctic coast of Russia. She was
hemmed in by Soviet surface ships, and Moscow, asserting that
she had been on a spying mission, demanded her surrender.
As a gesture, the Russians had offered to release and return
her crew, but they insisted on the ship being handed over un-
damaged and complete with all her secrets. The Americans
continued to refuse.

Since there was nothing that Robbie and Stephanie—or the
many millions of other people whose lives hung upon the issue
—could do about it, they returned to their own affairs, and
Stephanie searched through the paper to see if there was any
mention of themselves. But, as they had supposed, it was too
early for the police to have issued any statement to the Press.

Stephanie had also secured their air tickets. She said that
she had taken them in the names of Monsieur and Madame
Max Thévanaz and had given their nationality as Swiss, as a
precaution against their being forced into contact with either
German or French people at the des Roses. In the first case,
their imperfect accents would be accounted for by the belief
that they were French Swiss and, in the second, German Swiss.

Later in the afternoon Robbie bought himself, now that he
no longer had to be so careful about what he spent, a dark
blue suit for evening wear, a raincoat and a soft hat. Then
they went to the G.P.O.; and, to his considerable relief, he
saw his precious manuscript handed over to Stephanie. He
straightway re-addressed it to himself, to await collection, care
of Luke Beecham, then posted it off again.

On the Tuesday morning they were up early, because they

had to be at the Air Terminal in Constitution Square by half
past seven. There Robbie wrote labels in the name of 'Max
Thévanaz' and tied them on to their luggage. The bus then took
them out to Phaleron, where they spent an anxious half hour
going through the formalities. But Robbie was wearing his
dark spectacles and carrying his hat in his hand, so that his
semi-shaved head might mislead anyone who thought he recognized him. He was given no cause for anxiety and, soon after
eight-thirty, they were airborne on their way to Rhodes.

In less than ten minutes, they had crossed the Sounion
Peninsula and were heading out over the blue Aegean, glitter-
ing in the sun and starred with its many rocky islands. The big
islands of Ándros, Kéa and Kithnos could all be seen clearly
from the aircraft. It passed right over Siros and, when half an
hour out from Athens, over Delos.

Once up in the air, Robbie had felt a sudden relief from the
tension under which he had been for several days. In Rhodes
he would still be liable to be picked up by the Greek police and
charged with Cepicka's murder, but the psychological effect of
having got safely away from the mainland acted on him like
a tonic. For the first time in nearly a week his mind ceased
to be occupied with his personal anxieties, and he craned eagerly
forward to see as much as he could of the sacred island on
which the mighty twins, Apollo and Artemis, had been born.

Looking down on Delos made him think of his book and,
in his new mood of optimism, he allowed himself to assume
that somehow he would get out of the mess he was in and, in
due course, finish the book. The islands below them brought to
his mind Ithaca, of which Odysseus had been Prince, although
that lay far away on the other side of Greece. He wondered
again if he should include a chapter on the Odyssey and, as
he had already done one on Homer's other immortal epic, the
Iliad, with its tale of Troy, felt that perhaps he should.

That Odysseus had taken ten years to get home from the
siege of Troy had been due to his incurring the wrath of Poseidon, because he had blinded one of the Sea God's sons, the
Cyclopes, Polyphemus, by driving a pointed stake through the
giant's solitary eye. Thinking of that, Robbie suddenly wondered if all his recent troubles had been brought on him owing

to Athene's anger at his having signed that promise at Pirgos
to abandon his mission. If so he could only pray that, now he
had resumed it, she would forgive him.

Poseidon never let up on the unfortunate Odysseus and he
was unlucky from the start. He lost some of his men on the
island of the Lotus-Eaters and others were eaten by Polyphemus. Then, after the King of the Winds had tied up all the
winds in a bag for him, except one which very nearly brought
him home, his inquisitive sailors opened the bag and his ships
were driven to the land of the fierce Laestrygonians, who
murdered the crews of all the vessels except his own.

The survivors next came to the island of the lovely enchan-
tress, Circe, who turned a number of them into swine. Odysseus
saved himself and rescued them only through the god Hermes
giving him a more potent drug than that used by the witch.
He became her lover and stayed there a year, until his homesick men became mutinous. Circe let them go but said they
would never reach home unless they consulted the ghost of the
blind seer Tiresias. Under Circe's directions they reached the
land of perpetual night, and there dug a great hole into which
they poured the blood of sacrificed oxen, while Odysseus called
on the shade of Tiresias to appear. The smell of the blood
brought the ghosts crowding up from Hades to lap at it and so
enjoy a brief return to life. Among them was his mother,
whom he had not known to be dead, Agamemnon, Achilles,
Ajax and others of his companions at the siege of Troy. At last
old Tiresias appeared and prophesied that, although Poseidon's malice would continue to give them a rough passage, they
might get safely home provided that, should they come to
the coast of Trinacria, they did no harm to the Sun god's cattle
pastured there.

On their return to Circe's isle, she gave Odysseus further
good counsel, for they next had to sail through the waters of
the Sea Sirens, whose beautiful voices lured sailors to their
death. She told him to stop the ears of his crew with wax and
have himself lashed to the mast. Circe's advice saved them
but they then had to pass between Scylla and Charybdis, a
narrow passage of grim rocks made trebly dangerous on the
one side by great waterspouts belched out by a daughter of

Poseidon, and on the other by a six-headed monster that plucked six of Odysseus's best men from the vessel as it passed.

They came then to Trinacria and went ashore. Contrary winds kept them there for a month and they exhausted all their provisions. Odysseus's lieutenant, Eurylochus, incited the starving sailors to revolt and, despite the warning of Tiresias, they slew the Sun god's cattle. After a week of feasting, a favourable wind sprang up; but no sooner were they out of sight of land than vengeance fell upon them. A tempest arose, the vessel was sunk and all hands lost, except Odysseus. He succeeded in clinging to some wreckage and, after nine days and nights, was washed ashore on the island of Ogygia, on which lived Atlas's divinely beautiful daughter, Calypso.

He lived with her for seven years, but at last became homesick again; so Zeus decreed that Calypso must release him. He built himself a raft but, on his seventeenth day at sea, Poseidon learned what had happened and sent a storm that wrecked it. A sea nymph saved him by throwing him her veil and, three days later, he was washed up naked on the shores of the rich kingdom of Phaeacia.

At last his luck changed. The King's daughter, Nausicaa, found and clothed him. Her father received him kindly and, on learning that he was Odysseus, renowned for his exploits before Troy, but believed dead long since, did him great honour, then lent him one of his ships. When they reached Ithaca, Odysseus was still asleep. The sailors carried him ashore on his bed, leaving many rich gifts beside him on the beach, and when he awoke he found himself in his own land again at last.

It was twenty years since he had left it. Telemachus, his son, whom he had left an infant, was now grown up. His wife, Penelope, had remained faithful to him, although he had been reported dead, and a number of nobles were endeavouring to force her to marry one of them. Believing him to be still alive, she had resisted their pressure by saying that she would choose a new husband only when she had finished weaving a beautiful shroud for old Laertes, Odysseus's father. Each night she undid most of the work she had done on it during the day.

Odysseus might have been murdered by his wife's suitors

had he gone straight to his house alone and unarmed; but his natural caution led him first to appear as a castaway, so that he could find out what had been taking place during his absence. In turn, he revealed himself to his old shepherd, his father and his son, then he went to his own house as a beggar. No one there recognized him, except his old dog, who crept off a dung-heap to welcome him, then died at his feet. The place was filled with the suitors, who had taken it over and were wasting his substance in riotous living. While they were drinking at a banquet, Odysseus and Telemachus hid all their arms, then rallied their own faithful servants and exacted vengeance, slaying the leading interlopers with their arrows and driving the rest from the house.

As this bare outline of the greatest adventure story ever written ran through Robbie's mind, he decided that he could not leave it out. By then, the aircraft had passed over the southern tip of Kos. To the right lay the marvellous prospect of the coast of Turkey, with its mile upon mile of mountains outlined against the blue sky. Before them, only a few miles off, lay the great island of Rhodes.

Sheltered by the Turkish mountains from the east, and further south than the mainland of Greece, it was, Robbie knew, one of the most favoured spots in the world. It was said not to have been there when Zeus had taken land as his Kingdom and had given Poseidon dominion over water, but to have been thrown up later by a volcanic eruption. Apollo had asked Zeus for it and it had been given to him. It was his own tiny province and he had made it a land of sunshine and roses.

The aircraft landed and the passengers walked across the tarmac to the small airport building. Then ensued the usual wait while the baggage was being unloaded. Robbie and Stephanie sat down at a table and had cups of coffee. While they were drinking it, one of the airport men came through carrying a big bundle of the morning's newspapers which had just come off the plane. He was carrying one loose copy in his hand. Whistling cheerfully as he passed, he threw this copy on the bar counter. It did not land squarely and slipped off near Robbie's feet. He picked it up and, as there was no one behind the bar at that moment to whom to hand it, he unfolded it.

The headline in heavy type on the front page was a cheerful one:

'SOVIET AND U.S. ACCEPT INDIA'S OFFER TO MEDIATE'

Then, further down the page, another headline in smaller type caught his eye. It ran: 'Police anxious to trace British Ambassador's nephew.'

24

The Persistent American

THE muscles round Robbie's mouth tightened and he swiftly read the paragraph, which ran:

'On Saturday evening last a fatal accident occurred on the Olympia-Tripolis road some miles west of Vitina. A Mercedes driven by Mr. Carl Cepicka, an official of the Czechoslovak Legation, ran into another car, sending it over the precipice. The second car is believed to have contained Mr. Robert Grenn, the nephew of the British Ambassador, and Mrs. Václav Barak, the wife of another official of the Czechoslovak Legation, who are known to have left Athens together on March 28th.

Mrs. Barak went over with the car, which was later found burnt out, and Mr. Cepicka is reported to have died shortly after the accident. Mr. Grenn, however, is said to have jumped from the car before it went over; but he has since disappeared, and the police are anxious to get in touch with him.'

Stephanie had leant over and also read the paragraph. Robbie re-folded the paper and put it behind him on the bar, then she said in a low voice: 'We had to expect they would put something in, and it might be worse. Evidently the police have not yet let on to the Press about the way Cepicka met his death. They may think, too, that making it look as though they want to question you only about the accident will induce

you to give yourself up. Anyway, this won't start a public
hue and cry after you.'

Seeing the paragraph had brought Robbie sadly down to
earth; but he took such comfort as he could from her comment, and soon afterward recovered his spirits sufficiently to
take an interest in the pretty country through which a taxi
they had secured was taking them. The Airport lay inland, but
the road from it led to the north-west coast, then ran right
round the northern end of the island to the city of Rhodes,
which faced east from its tip. The run gave them no sight of
the city as the Hotel des Roses lay at its northern extremity,
a palatial block surrounded by its own gardens and overlooking its private bathing beach.

They were there soon after eleven o'clock. Robbie duly
signed the register for them as Monsieur and Madame Max
Thévanaz of Basle and they were shown up to a comfortable
room with twin beds, windows looking out on the sea and a
private bathroom.

For the first time in his life Robbie was about to share a
room with a girl, and the thought suddenly made him feel
terribly self-conscious. To hide his embarrassment, he quickly
pretended to be absorbed in the wonderful prospect of the deep
blue sea and the Turkish coast, with its chain of snow-capped
mountains. But Stephanie, being used to sharing a hotel room
with her husband, took matters in her stride. As soon as the
porter had brought up their luggage, she began to allot the
ample cupboard and drawer space between Robbie and herself,
then, humming a little tune, started to unpack.

Before lunch, they explored the amenities downstairs—a
seemingly endless succession of spacious lounges, terraces, bars,
a ballroom and two restaurants. But, for the size of the place,
there were comparatively few people about, and when they
went to the office to get a map of the town, an assistant manager told them gloomily that the war-scare had led to many
cancelled bookings.

Immediately after they had lunched, they set off for the
town and, in a half hour's walk, were amazed by its contrasts.
Rhodes and the other islands of the Dodecanese had been
liberated from the Turks in 1912 and occupied by the French

n 1915 with a promise that, after an Allied victory, they would be restored to Greece, but by the Treaty of Sèvres they had been awarded to Italy. The Italians had then occupied them for over a quarter of a century, until expelled after the Second World War.

Whatever views one might hold about Mussolini, it was evident that Rhodes owed him a great debt. Between the des Roses and the 'new' town stood half a dozen splendid buildings of golden-yellow stone, erected by the Italians to house their Administration of the Dodecanese, and one for the Municipality of Rhodes with an arcade modelled on that of the Palace of the Doges in Venice.

The new town, too, had no resemblance to Tripolis or Argos. Instead of a maze of alleys for a market and streets of ramshackle buildings, its market stalls were housed in the long sides of one building that formed a hexagon, having a big open space and a bandstand in the middle. In the well-kept streets that surrounded the market, there were scores of modern shops.

Seaward of the new town lay the harbour of Mandrakhi, with the old castle of St. Nicholas at the end of its mole, and two statues of antlered deer gracing the pylons at either side of its entrance. Somewhere there, Robbie told Stephanie, had once stood the Colossus of Rhodes, which the ancients had accounted one of the Seven Wonders of the World. It had been a bronze statue of Apollo, over a hundred feet in height and with thumbs so large that only a big man could make his hands meet when embracing one in his arms. But it had been the pride of Rhodes—then a great sea-power—for only fifty-six years. In 224 B.C. it had been overthrown by an earthquake and all traces of it had long since vanished.

South of the new town lay the old city. It was entirely encircled by vast walls built by the Crusaders and dominated by their huge castle in the north-west corner. To seaward of it lay the commercial harbour and it was there that the *Bratislava* must have discharged the cargo that she had for Rhodes. After a few enquiries, Robbie located the Port Authority and learned that she had docked on April 7th, sailing again the following evening. He also secured from the clerk who gave him this information the name and address of the shipping agent who had acted for the ship's owners.

He was a Mr. Pilavachi and, when they found the street in which he had his office, Stephanie left Robbie on the corner. She then went on to the office and, presenting herself as Mrs. Sebesta, of the Czechoslovakian Travel Agency, enquired for Mr. Pilavachi. It transpired, as she had expected, that he had never heard of Mrs. Sebesta, but he had corresponded with Krajcir and had actually met Barak when he had flown to Rhodes to meet the Czech group landing from the ship.

Having established these mutual acquaintances, Stephanie said that she believed one of the engineers in the group was an old friend of hers, named Zdenek, and, as she was on a few days' visit to the island, she would very much like to renew her acquaintance with him. Upon this, the Greek shipping agent made no difficulty about telling her that the Czech group was prospecting for oil in the bay of Monolithos, which lay on the south-west coast of the island, some eighty-odd kilometres distant.

When she rejoined Robbie, they walked along to a pleasant café on the water-front, with Venetian arches surrounding a square terrace, and over a drink there discusssed future plans. Both of them were only too well aware that, now the police were looking for Robbie, time was an all-important factor; so there could be no question of putting off until Sunday an attempt to find out what was going on at Monolithos.

As they thought it almost certain that Barak would believe Robbie either to be lying low in one of the small towns in the Peloponnesus, or in one of its ports endeavouring to get himself smuggled out of the country, it seemed very unlikely that the Czech group in Rhodes would have been specially alerted to keep a look-out for him. Even so, the chances of his being able to secure photographs of the site during a week-day seemed slender.

In consequence, Stephanie put forward the idea that she should go openly to the site and enquire for her mythical friend, the engineer Zdenek. Presenting herself as a Czech should allay the suspicions of whoever she talked to there and, although she would not be able to take any photographs of the site, she would be able to carry away in her mind a very full picture of it.

Robbie was naturally greatly averse to her exposing herself to danger, but the odds against Barak's being there, or anyone else who knew her, were so long that he had to admit that the risk of her running into trouble was very small. As he could think of no other plan, he reluctantly agreed to hers.

That evening they made up for their past three days of privation by an excellent dinner, washed down with a bottle of the local red wine, Chevalier de Rhodes, which they found quite palatable. They followed it with two glasses apiece of another local product, the rich, sweet wine of Kamiros, which they thought really excellent.

There was dancing in the ballroom, but Stephanie evaded further contact with Robbie's large feet by saying that, having got up so early that morning, she was tired out. Shortly before ten o'clock, she went up to bed.

He gave her the stipulated half hour, then followed. Although he had every intention of keeping his promise, he could not prevent his thoughts from running riot as he went up in the lift; but on entering their room he saw that she was lying in bed with a woolly bedjacket over her shoulders, reading a book, and she did not even give him a glance. He undressed in the bathroom then, while she continued to ignore him, slipped off his dressing gown and got into bed. For some ten minutes he lay there, not daring to look at her, then she yawned, put down her book, said: 'Good night, Robbie. Let's pray that we have good luck tomorrow,' and switched off the light. For a time he lay awake; but he, too, was tired from his long day and, while still vaguely thinking of her as so near and yet so far, he dropped off to sleep.

He had already informed the office that he was one of those eccentric people who preferred to get up and have his breakfast sitting at a table downstairs; so when they were called at eight o'clock, he dressed himself in the bathroom, then left her in bed to enjoy her coffee, rose-petal jam and rolls.

They had decided that, as Monolithos lay some distance from any of the main roads in the island, they might have some

o

difficulty in finding it if they hired a car for Stephanie to drive; so Robbie had booked one with a chauffeur.

At half past nine, with a picnic lunch on board, they set off, and they had not gone a mile before they found that their driver, Tino, spoke quite good English. As a Swiss couple of the educated class, it would have been absurd for them to pretend that they did not also speak English, and there was no escaping his determination to act as their guide.

Some thirty kilometres from Rhodes he insisted on pulling up and taking them round the partially overgrown ruins of Kamiros, which had once been the capital of one of the three City-States of the island; but later they were amazed to find that, although he had not a good word for the Italians, the only decent buildings in the squalid little townships through which they passed had been Fascist Headquarters.

Believing them to be tourists, which they were in no position to deny, he took them on a long detour up to the Prophet Elias mountain, from which the whole island, set in its deep blue sea, could be seen. Half an hour later they left the main road, snaked inland through the Ataviros Mountains until, still at over two thousand feet above sea level, they passed through the village of Monolithos, turned into a rough track and, a few miles further on, came out of the woods to a flat piece of ground that was evidently a roughly-made car park. There Tino pulled up and, pointing to a ruined castle perched on a mound a hundred feet or more above them, announced: 'We are arrived.'

When engaging him, Robbie had not realized that Monolithos, although off the ordinary tourist beat, was considered one of the beauty spots of the island, but naturally Tino imagined that to be the reason why he had been hired to bring them there. In the circumstances, and as they still had no idea in which direction from that spot lay the site at which the Czech group was operating, there seemed nothing for it but to accept the situation. By a steep, twisting path between stunted pines they climbed the hill and when, panting, they reached the ruin, they felt that their effort had been well worth it.

The view from the crumbling walls of this long-deserted stronghold was superb, but to them it awarded something

more. To the left of the headland, near the shore on the long
bay that curved away southward, they could see some scattered buildings. Near them rose a pylon that, from that distance, looked like a child's piece of Meccano, and beyond the
tiny line of creaming surf several boats were anchored. These
indications made them confident that it was the place they
were seeking.

Returning to the car, Robbie gave Tino his instructions.
During the next twenty minutes, going slowly over devious
stony ways, he brought them down to within a hundred yards
of the buildings. There Stephanie got out and went forward on
her own.

For some ten minutes Robbie remained in the car, a prey
to considerable anxiety, until he saw Stephanie emerge from
the largest of the cluster of buildings with a squat, broad-
shouldered man beside her. When they reached the car
Stephanie, now speaking Czech, introduced her companion as
Comrade Rybáček, the engineer in charge of the group, and
Robbie to him as Comrade Witold, a Polish travel agent who
was making an exploratory tour of Rhodes with her.

Comrade Rybáček said that he and his two senior assistants had been just about to sit down to their midday meal,
and he would be delighted if Comrades Sebesta and Witold
would join them. It then emerged that the mythical Comrade
Zdenek, for whom Stephanie had enquired, was not one of the
group and that Comrade Rybáček did not recall his name as
that of one of the hundred-odd passengers who had sailed in
the *Bratislava* but, no doubt, he was in one of the other
islands.

Stephanie, having introduced Robbie as a Pole, protected
him from discovery, through his accent, that he was not a
Czech. He readily accepted Comrade Rybáček's invitation and
they spent the next hour very pleasantly with the three Czech
engineers in a little house which for many generations had been
occupied by a Greek family of modest means.

During the meal, Stephanie kept up her role as Krajcir's
principal assistant by mentioning Havelka, Nejedly and Barak
with the respect due to Party bosses, but implying that she was

well acquainted with them. She then asked innocently how the work was going.

It was Rybáček who replied: 'As well as can be expected, Comrade, since we are working with an entirely new type of machinery. But, no doubt, our scientists know what they are up to and we shall strike oil in due course.'

From his answer it was impossible to guess if he really believed that his group was prospecting for oil by some new process, or if he was in the confidence of his superiors and blandly maintaining their cover plan. However, both on their way into the house and out of it, Robbie and Stephanie had ample opportunity for a good look round.

The plant being used was exactly similar to that at Pirgos: a single, hollow pylon formed of steel struts, inside it the big screw piercing the earth, nearby a crane for hoisting the weighty sections of screw into position and a powerful engine for driving down the screw; a light railway with tip trucks to run the excavated earth into the sea, and a pile of fifty or more as yet unused screw sections. At these Robbie was able to get a closer look than at those at Pirgos and he saw that, instead of being solid screws, they were more like drainpipes with spirals on their outside. The six-foot lengths were about a foot in diameter, and of that foot eight inches were hollow.

Having said good-bye to their hosts, they saw, as they walked back to their car, that another car had drawn up behind it and that a young man was talking to Tino. In that lonely spot, so difficult of access except by sea, they naturally supposed that he belonged to the Czech group working there; but as they approached, he hailed them cheerfully in English, with a strong American accent.

'Hullo, folks! What goes on around here?'

Robbie, who had constantly to remind himself that he was supposed to be a Swiss, tried to make his voice as guttural as he could, and replied: 'I understand they prospect for oil.'

'Is that so, now,' the American smiled. He looked about thirty, was tallish, loose-limbed and had crew-cut fair hair. Extending a muscular hand, he added: 'Let me introduce myself. My name is Mahogany Brown—Henry Mahogany Brown.'

As he caught the flicker of surprise in Robbie's eyes, his

smile broadened to a grin and he went on: 'Funny name, Mahogany, isn't it? Just a quirk of humour on the part of my old Dad. I've two brothers and he called them Elliot Walnut Brown and James Satinwood Brown. I got Mahogany, but I'm Henry to my friends.'

Robbie shook the outstretched hand, gave his name as Max Thévanaz and introduced Stephanie as his wife. Mr. Mahogany Brown jerked a thumb in the direction of the castle far above them and asked: 'Been up to the top?'

'Yes,' Stephanie replied. 'The view is marvellous, isn't it? And all this wild, unspoilt country is absolutely beautiful.'

'It certainly is,' he agreed, 'and, if I may be allowed to say so, Mr. Thévanaz, it's made just that bit more beautiful by the presence of your lady.'

That was just the sort of compliment Robbie was always wanting to pay Stephanie, yet never managed to, and it annoyed him that a complete stranger should get away with it so glibly. But he hid his feelings with a smile as the American went on: 'It's all the more pity that these vandals here should be allowed to spoil the bay with their pylon, though it doesn't look to me the sort of gear that's used for drilling for oil.'

'They are using, I think, a new process,' Robbie informed him.

For some minutes they continued talking. Apparently Mr. Mahogany Brown had seen the Czech working site from the ruined castle, and idle curiosity had brought him down to find out what was going on. It then transpired that he, too, was staying at the Hotel des Roses; so when he left them to go back to his car, he gave a cheery wave and cried: 'I'll be seeing you.'

Slowly the two cars made their way back up the narrow, stony track, then the American put on speed and left the other car behind. Tino, still determined to show his passengers as much of his lovely country as he could, drove them back by a different route, via Petaloudes, so that they might see the famous Valley of Butterflies. It was a delightful glen with several waterfalls and, as they walked through it, there rose a pinkish-grey cloud, formed by the myriads of butterflies that breed there year after year.

Soon after they got back to the hotel Robbie wrote to Luke,

describing as exactly as possible all that he had seen on the Czech site. He then added a final paragraph:

By this time, you will have seen from the papers that the police are looking for me. Although they have not so far disclosed it, I have good reason to believe that, if they catch me, they may bring a very serious charge against me. For this reason, I am staying here under the name of Max Thévanaz. The fact is that I have landed myself in a very dangerous situation and about my only hope of getting out of it is if it can be proved that the Czechs' activities are some form of preparation for a war against the West. There are two ways in which you can help me in this. The first is that, should the particulars I have listed above give you any idea what the Czechs may be doing, you let me know immediately as I will then do my best to check up on it. It is in the hope that you will have some idea that I can work on that I mean to keep my freedom as long as possible. The other thing is that you should pass on such information as I have secured to the police and persuade them to start an investigation. With this threat of war, there is every possible justification for their doing so; and if they do find out that the Czechs are up to no good, that would let me out. I really am in a bad spot and shall be eternally grateful for anything you can do to help.

In his letter he purposely refrained from telling Luke what had actually happened, so that it could not be said later that he had known both that Robbie was wanted by the police for having killed Cepicka and Robbie's whereabouts, yet had failed to inform the police. Stephanie knew how much Robbie wanted to pour out the whole story to his friend but, on reading through the letter, she agreed that it would not be right to compromise him. Having sealed the letter and marked it 'Private', Robbie took it down to the Post Office himself, to make certain that it would catch the air mail for Athens next morning and, when it reached the capital, go by express delivery.

That evening after dinner Mr. Mahogany Brown, dressed in a smart tuxedo, came up to their table, asked Stephanie if she would like to dance and, on her replying that she would, suggested that they all move into the ballroom. The two hours that followed were miserable ones for Robbie. The American danced with practised ease and Stephanie obviously enjoyed partnering him. Robbie knew only too well that he could not compete. He felt, too, that it was one thing to flounder cheerfully round a little night-club in Patras, and quite another to make an exhibition of himself in a ballroom, with several score of sophisticated people looking on. Even when, having danced twice with the slim, loose-limbed Mr. Brown, Stephanie asked him if he wouldn't like to dance, he said that he preferred to watch. Yet he could not altogether dislike their new acquaintance and when Stephanie, to get herself half an hour to undress, suggested that the two men have a last drink together, he found that the American had a seemingly endless repertoire of funny stories.

Next morning, when the papers came in from the daily aircraft, the news was still good. Delegations of United States and Soviet statesmen were on their way to Delhi to submit their respective cases to the mediation of the Indian Prime Minister. Hastily Robbie and Stephanie scanned the other sheets, then went through them carefully, but they held no mention of their own affair.

They were already in bathing things, which they had bought the afternoon of their arrival; so they went out to the beach. As they emerged from their first swim Robbie was far from pleased, but not surprised, to see Mr. Mahogany Brown appear. With an affability too polite to be resented, he settled himself beside them and began to talk amusingly of other pleasure resorts at which he had stayed. As they were posing as a married couple but in fact had never before been to a famous holiday beach together, they had to conduct their side of the conversation with considerable care, but the American did not appear to think it strange that they had never been to any of the places he mentioned.

Just before lunch they went in for their second swim, and Robbie at least had the satisfaction of showing that, although he was no good on a dance floor, he was much the better man in the water. As they came out Mr. Brown, who by then was

calling Robbie Max and Stephanie by the name she had given
herself, Julie, asked them if they had yet been along to the old
city. On their replying that they had not, he declared:

'But it's a "must"! The place those old Crusaders built
there is real history, and the greatest sight in the whole
Aegean. I've hired a car for my stay here, and I'll run you
down there this afternoon.'

To have refused would have been not only churlish but
stupid, so by three o'clock they were on their way there with
him. Although they had already seen the castle and the walls
of the old city from a distance, they found the third of a
square mile within those walls both fascinating and astounding.

Part of the fascination lay in the narrow streets and alleys
in the lower part of the city, adjacent to the harbour, where
for four hundred years the Greek population had lived under
Turkish rule. Coppersmiths, leather workers, cobblers and
tailors still plied their trades there, as they had done for a
thousand years, in small, windowless shops. There could have
been no greater contrast to the new town erected by the
Italians outside the walls.

But the upper part of the city held far greater interest. There
lay the great stone palaces in which the Crusaders had lived.
After being driven from the Holy Land early in the fourteenth
century, the Knights of St. John of Jerusalem had made Rhodes
the bastion of Christianity against the Infidel and, although
within sight of Turkey, they had held the island for over two
hundred years. In 1480, the Sultan Suliman I had brought an
army of two hundred thousand men against it, yet had been
forced to abandon the siege after losing nearly half his troops.
It had not been until forty years later that the Knights had
abandoned Rhodes, and then upon honourable terms.

The Knights had been of several nationalities, among them
French, English, Italian, Portuguese and Spanish. Each group
had been termed a 'Tongue' and had lived in their respective
'Inns' as the stone palaces in the Street of Knights were called,
while their Grand Master had lived in state in the enormous
castle. A great part of the castle had been allowed to fall into
ruin before the arrival of the Italians, but their Governor, de
Vesci, had made it his life-work to restore it. Mussolini had

provided him with many millions of lire to carry out this task; so the battlements again towered up in all their pristine glory against a background of bright blue sky.

The most staggering thing about this fortress city was its walls. They extended for three miles, completely encircling the city and being strengthened by more than a dozen great protruding bastions. In most places, they were a hundred feet in height and over forty feet broad at the top; so that along their now grassy surface four or five cars could have been driven abreast.

While Robbie, Stephanie and Mahogany Brown were making the tour of the city and the vast ramparts, they naturally talked in English about the extraordinary achievements of its mediaeval builders. Stephanie expressed herself well but, being Czech, had a marked accent. Robbie, however, having temporarily forgotten that he was supposed to be a Swiss, lapsed into his normal speech. As they came down from the wall to the broad quay outside it enclosing the harbour, the American suddenly turned to him and said:

'For a foreigner, Max, you speak remarkably good English.'

Robbie was completely nonplussed, but Stephanie stepped into the breach and said quickly: 'That is not surprising. He was at school in England.'

That evening after dinner, Robbie again had to watch Mr. Mahogany Brown—now 'Henry' to them—and Stephanie obviously enjoying themselves as they danced together. He would have given a great deal to break the association but, short of being deliberately rude and probably also upsetting Stephanie, he could think of no way of doing so. And before they parted for the night, it had been agreed that next day Henry should take them in his car to Lindos.

On the Friday morning the paper reported that the statesmen from East and West had met in Delhi and that, at the opening of the proceedings, the heads of both delegations had made conciliatory speeches. Everyone was much cheered by this; guests at the hotel who had been talking of curtailing their holidays, to get home in case of trouble, decided to stay on, and the management was receiving numerous cables from people who had cancelled, renewing their bookings.

There was, however, a disturbing paragraph on an inside page of the paper headed 'British Ambassador's nephew wanted in connection with death of Czech official'. The letter-press beneath it read:

'In a police statement, it has now been disclosed that Mr. Cepicka, an official of the Czechoslovak Legation, did not meet his death as a result of the car collision which occurred some miles from Vitina on the evening of Saturday last, but that he subsequently died from other causes. Mr. Robert Grenn, the nephew of Sir Finsterhorn Grenn, C.M.G., is known to have been present at the time of Mr. Cepicka's death, but has not been seen since, and the police are anxious to take a statement from him.

It was earlier reported that Mrs. Václav Barak, the wife of another official at the Czechoslovakian Legation, who was travelling with Mr. Grenn, had gone over the precipice in their car; but no human remains have been found in the burnt-out body of the car. It is possible, however, that Mrs. Barak's body was thrown clear and is lying still undiscovered among rocks or scrub somewhere on the mountain-side. The search for her body continues.'

It was in order to see the morning paper that Robbie had stipulated that they should not start for Lindos before half past eleven. But now they settled themselves in Henry's car, Stephanie beside him and Robbie, with a well-stocked picnic basket, in the back, and set off.

The ancient town lay less than sixty kilometres away, down the east coast of the island; so they reached it by half past twelve. The town itself, lying in a bay behind the shelter of a great headland, was small but picturesque. It had a number of mediaeval houses, in some of which the many-generations-old craft of tile painting by hand was still carried on, but the streets were so steep and narrow that they had to leave the car down in the square.

Up on the headland, dominating the scene for miles round, stood the well-preserved ruins of another vast Crusaders' castle. After twenty minutes' muscle-testing walk up paths with a gradient of one in four, they passed through the huge portico. Mounting still higher, they made the round of this impregnable fortress which rose, on its far side, from cliffs that dropped sheer nearly four hundred feet to the sea below. It was unique also in that, nearly two thousand years before the Crusaders built their castle, the site had been that of a splendid temple, the remains of which still stood in the centre of the castle. On its highest platform of rock, a broad flight of steps led up to a row of Doric columns, clear-cut against the brilliant blue of the sky.

Half an hour later they selected a place to picnic, just off the road near the headland on the opposite side of the bay. Thinking again of the paragraph in the morning paper, Robbie was far from happy but, as there was nothing further he could do until he received a reply from Luke, he felt that it was just as well that his mind had been occupied by Henry taking them on this expedition. After their meal they chatted, then dozed for some while. It was nearly five o'clock when they got back to the des Roses.

As Robbie passed the hall porter's desk, the porter on duty gave him a letter with his key. It was from Luke. Robbie had not expected a reply until the following day. Evidently, Luke had received his letter the previous afternoon and had got off a reply at once, so that it had come in on the morning plane. Swiftly, Robbie opened it and read:

I am most deeply distressed to learn from your letter that your efforts have landed you in such grievous trouble, more especially as among the well-informed here all sorts of rumours are flying round. It is being said that you took Mrs. Barak away from her husband; that he was with Cepicka in the car which ran into yours and that, after your car had gone over the precipice, you had a blood row with the two of them, during which you killed Cepicka. I only pray to God that these rumours are untrue.

It is also said that, as no human remains have been found in your burnt-out car, Mrs. Barak may still be alive. This naturally leads me to speculate upon the identity of the charming young lady who brought me your cheque to cash. But the less

*I know from you about the business, the better; and I am grate-
ful to you for not having compromised me in any way by admis-
sions about what you may have done.*

*With regard to the Czechs, the machinery described by you
bears no resemblance to the machinery normally used when
drilling for oil; but, alas, I am at a complete loss to suggest
to you any further line of investigation. From what you say,
there are no indications whatever that they are erecting some
form of radar station, and their sites cannot be designed as
bases from which to launch missiles. For that it would be
necessary to drill a number of holes, perhaps some twenty or
thirty feet in depth, into which to sink pylons to support a
heavy concrete platform, or to excavate a large chamber having
a concrete platform underground; but for such a purpose one
very deep hole would be completely useless.*

*About passing on the information you have so far secured.
Soon after you left Athens, I mentioned to a friend of mine in
the N.A.T.O. set-up the possibility that the Greco-Czech
tobacco/oil deal might be well worth investigating. But I am
afraid that it would be quite useless for me to pass on to the
police your description of the apparatus the Czechs are using.
There is little prospect that any action would be taken. You
must remember that the Czechs hold a concession from the
Greek Government to prospect for oil, and that we can offer no
proof that it is not what they are doing, with a new type of
machinery.*

*Further to this, I am the last person who could expect a
sympathetic hearing from the Greek authorities on such a
matter. It is certain that they would jump to the conclusion
that, as the chief executive in Greece of one of the biggest
oil companies in the world, I was simply endeavouring to hold
up the Czech activities and queer their pitch, as a means of
protecting my own company from future competition.*

*To end, Robbie, I can only say how sorry I am that for
the present I can see no way to help you. But of one thing
I am certain. Whatever you may have done has been brought
about through your honest desire to serve your country. And
whatever may befall you, you may rest assured of my continued
friendship.*

Up in their room, Robbie showed the letter to Stephanie. She read it through, handed it back to him with a shake of her head and said: 'It's terribly disappointing, Robbie. I feel sure Mr. Beecham would help you if he could but I do understand how he is placed, and there is nothing more we can do here. What do you intend to do now: give yourself up and trust that the truth will prevail?'

He shook his head. 'No, I won't do that. At least Luke says that he put the N.A.T.O. people on to this thing. If they have taken it seriously, they are far more likely to get to the bottom of it than I ever could. For all we know, they are on the job in half a dozen places—Patras, Kalamai, Crete, Milos, here, Chios and the rest. Even if they are investigating only one of the groups, there is still a sporting chance that they will find the answer to the riddle before the police get me. So I mean to keep out of their clutches as long as I possibly can.'

After dinner that evening they followed the same routine of sharing a table in the ballroom with the lively, talkative, somewhat inquisitive Mr. Mahogany Brown. Robbie found it beyond his powers to hide the depression into which Luke's letter had plunged him. It seemed that there was now no more that he could do, and that for him the outcome of the affair was almost certain to be disastrous. His gloom was such that the American kept on enquiring if he felt unwell, and Stephanie, having vainly tried to cheer him up, sent him off early to bed.

He went with reluctance and, having got up to his room, regretted that he had allowed himself to be got rid of. As he lay in bed, he began to be tortured by ideas that, by this time, Stephanie and Henry were out on one of the dimly lit terraces, or perhaps on the beach, and that she was letting him make love to her.

Suddenly he decided that, although he was not her husband in fact, he was in name, and that he would no longer put up with playing second fiddle to this American interloper. He would take him aside the following morning and tell him in no uncertain terms that he, Max Thévanaz, found Mr. Mahogany Brown's attentions to Madame Thévanaz unwelcome. If Mr. Mahogany Brown wanted a lady to flirt with, he must seek one elsewhere, otherwise Monsieur Thévanaz would find himself under the regrettable necessity of pushing in Mr. Mahogany Brown's face.

However, on the Saturday morning, the Fates decreed that Robbie should be deprived of any opportunity of playing the role of an exasperated husband. Soon after eleven o'clock, clad in his bathing robe, he was anxiously waiting in the main hall for the papers to come in. A taxi from the airport drove up and a couple got out. As they entered the hall, Robbie gave one look at them and his blood seemed to freeze. They were the English couple that he and Stephanie had met at Olympia, the Jacksons. At the same moment, they recognized him and Frank Jackson exclaimed:

'Why, if it isn't Mr. Grenn!'

25

A Trap is Set

'W H Y , so it is! ' added Ursula Jackson, as she and her husband came up to Robbie. 'For a moment, I didn't recognize you with those dark glasses and your hair cut like an American student. Is that charming Miss Stephanopoulos still with you?'

'Yes . . . Oh yes,' Robbie managed to reply. 'How . . . how nice to see you again.' Meanwhile, he was in agony that the reception clerk behind the desk near which he was standing might have heard him addressed as Mr. Grenn.

'We returned to Athens the day after you left Olympia,' Frank Jackson went on. 'Things looked so bad we had made up our minds to go home; but we could not get a seat in an aircraft for love nor money, and every sleeper on the trains had been booked for a week ahead. While we were still wondering what to do, the good news came through about both sides accepting the Indian offer to mediate. That was a sure sign that neither side really meant to fight so we decided not to curtail our holiday after all, and to put in a week here as we'd originally planned. At first sight, this place reminds me of the Hotel Excelsior on the Lido at Venice. Is it as good as it looks?'

'It's fine,' Robbie assured him. 'Lovely bathing, good food and the town—the old city—is fascinating.' Swiftly, he stole a look behind him at the desk. The reception clerk had not been there, but was just coming out from the office behind it. Hastily he said to the Jacksons: 'You'll be wanting to register. Julie—Stephanie, I mean—is waiting for me to go out and bathe, so I must run now. I'll be seeing you later.'

As soon as he was clear of the hall, he dashed upstairs.
Stephanie had been manicuring her nails in their room, while
waiting for him to bring up the morning papers. Breathlessly,
he said to her: 'We're sunk! The Jacksons have just come in
on the plane! They greeted me as "Mr. Grenn", and asked
after you as Miss Stephanopoulos.'

'Oh dear!' she exclaimed, her blue eyes widening. 'What
damnable luck. Still, if they did no more than that, they can't
know that you are wanted by the police.'

'No; it was obvious that they didn't. It's very unlikely that
any mention of our business would get into the English papers
until I'm actually charged with murder. But my name would
be sure to ring a bell with some of the Greek management
here, and there's that damned American who is always shooting questions at us. He speaks Greek and I expect he'll have
read about us in the paper. You can bet that he will be
hanging on to us all day, as usual, and we can't possibly avoid
the Jacksons. Naturally, they will go on calling me "Grenn"
and, before the day is out, that is certain to be noticed by a
waiter or someone. The management will telephone the police
and they'll be coming here to collect me.'

'Then we must leave—leave at once.'

'Yes, but how can we—leave the island, I mean? The daily
plane for Athens left over an hour ago.'

'We could move to some place in the town—get lodgings
there.'

'That's no good. Rhodes is much too small for us to stand
any chance of going to earth. The police would trace us within
a matter of hours. And once they are on to me, if they don't
pick us up tonight, they'll have men at the airport to stop us
getting away tomorrow.'

For a few minutes they stood facing one another in dismayed silence, then Robbie snapped his fingers. 'I've got it!
Today is Saturday. It's the one day in the week that there's a
flight from here to Crete, and I remember when I looked at
the time-table wondering why it didn't leave till afternoon.
If only we can get seats on it.'

As Robbie spoke, he stepped over to the bedside telephone,

snatched up the receiver and asked to be put through to the office of Olympic Airways. In agonized suspense he waited until the booking clerk replied to his enquiry. Now they had good reason to bless the war scare. It had so thinned out tourist traffic that the aircraft was almost empty. He was told that he could pick up the tickets at the office at two o'clock. The flight left at ten past three.

They started to pack at once, so as to get out of the hotel as soon as possible. Robbie had some anxious moments while paying the bill downstairs, but neither Mahogany Brown nor the Jacksons appeared in the hall. By half-past-twelve they were on their way to the town in a taxi and, after lunching there in a back-street café, caught the airport bus. Soon after three, they were on their way to Crete.

On this flight the only land they saw was the northern tip of Karpathos, and Robbie's mind was much too occupied with his own problems for it to drift to the gods and Heroes. His elation at getting away from Rhodes, too, was marred by one unavoidable circumstance. When telephoning for their air tickets, he had realized that the call would be booked to him as Monsieur Thévanaz and, as the hotel telephone operator could hear what he said, he had not liked to risk arousing unwelcome interest in their abrupt departure from the des Roses by giving a different name. In consequence, the booking had left a clear trail behind them and they had no option but to land in Crete as Monsieur and Madame Thévanaz.

He made up his mind that, somehow, he must get the labels off their suitcases when they arrived at the Crete airport so that, when they registered at an hotel in Heraklion, they could do so under yet another identity; but in this he was defeated by the informal procedure at the little airport. There was no bus there; only two taxis, into one of which the four passengers from the plane were crammed, while all their luggage was loaded into the other. When they arrived at the Town Terminal and Robbie had pointed out their bags, a porter asked him at which hotel they intended to stay. He had thought that they would stand a better chance of escaping any enquiry from Rhodes if they went on to a small place, but he had had no chance to get the name of one.

On his replying that he had not yet booked anywhere, the porter pointed to the des Roses labels which had been stuck on the bags, gave a toothless grin and said: 'Hotel Astir for you. New and very good. Just across the road. You follow me.'

Then he picked up their suitcases, and five minutes later Robbie was at the hotel desk, forced to continue the fiction that he and Stephanie were Monsieur and Madame Thévanaz.

The Astir was not very large, but was bright and pleasant, and they were given a good room on the first floor, with a private bath. However, when they had had a wash and came downstairs, they were greatly surprised to learn that it had no restaurant; neither, as the hall porter told them, had any other hotel in Heraklion. The custom was for him to give guests a 'chit' on which they could eat out, and the amount they spent was then charged on their hotel bill.

As it was by then nearly eight o'clock and they had had only a light lunch, they decided to go out straight away. The porter recommended a restaurant that rejoiced in the curious name of the Glass House, and gave them the number of a bus that stopped on the corner opposite the hotel. He said the bus would take them to the restaurant in ten minutes.

The bus ride confirmed the impression they had formed when coming into the city from the airport that, unlike Rhodes, Heraklion had neither beauty nor glamour. There were ugly gaps between half-ruined buildings, even the main street was full of potholes and, as the bus turned from it along the water-front, it was still light enough for them to see that for a quarter of a mile the inland side of the road consisted almost entirely of great heaps of rubble. As they soon learned, Heraklion had suffered terribly in the war. First the Germans had bombed it, then, for many months, the British and Americans. Hundreds of buildings, in fact one-third of the city, had been destroyed and, although twenty years had elapsed, the Greeks had been unable, through lack of financial resources, to rebuild more than a small percentage of their properties.

The Glass House proved to be the only building on the sea-ward side of the road. It occupied a promontory at the end of the water-front and justified its name for, except for that part of the building in which the kitchens were housed, its walls consisted entirely of small, rather dirty panes of glass. It was a big place with perhaps eighty tables in it and a three-man band. Not more than a dozen of the tables were occupied; so they chose one well away from other people and, over a meal of fresh fried mullet, settled down to discuss their situation.

They felt that, had they remained at the des Roses, the discovery that Max Thévanaz was Robbie Grenn would have proved inevitable; but, now that they had left it, there was no great reason to fear that fact would emerge. It was certain that Mahogany Brown would ask at the office what had happened to his friends the Thévanaz, and the Jacksons might enquire there for Mr. Grenn. However, with the large managerial staff at the des Roses, those enquiries might not be made of the same person and, even if they were, might not be linked up. Yet if these enquiries did start anything, the search would be for a married couple who had flown to Crete using the name of Thévanaz. For this reason, Stephanie said she thought they ought both to abandon that name and separate as soon as possible.

Robbie gloomily agreed with her, then began to speculate on their chances, if they could locate the Czech group in Crete, of penetrating the secret that lay behind the group's activities. But he had little hope in that direction as it seemed almost certain that a view of the site where they were working would disclose no more than had those at Pirgos and Monolithos. It was then that Stephanie remarked:

'You had your chance to get right to the bottom of things when we were in Corinth. It's a thousand pities you didn't take it.'

He gave her a puzzled look. 'I'm afraid I don't get you.'

'I mean when you had Václav at your mercy in that cul-de-sac. You could have screwed it out of him then, by just keeping on gently making more and more of a mess of his face until he had told you all you wanted to know.'

'But that would have been using torture on him,' Robbie said in a shocked voice.

Stephanie shrugged and finished the glass of Malvoisie wine

she was drinking. 'Considering that you kept on hitting him until you spoiled his looks, isn't it rather straining at a gnat and swallowing a camel to imply that it would have been a bad thing to get something out of him while you were at it? Given the same circumstances, he would certainly have tortured you without hesitation. And, you know, seeing how much may hang on this thing, it might even be argued that if he would use torture, and you wouldn't, he's the better man as far as serving his country is concerned.'

'I suppose there is something in that,' Robbie agreed reluctantly. 'But what's the good of talking about what I might have done over three weeks ago?'

'Because I wanted to see how you felt about it. If you are too squeamish, an idea I've had would be of no use.'

He refilled her glass. 'Well, anyway, let's hear it.'

'It is that I should try to get Václav to come to Crete. The fact that he came after us from Pirgos shows how obsessed he is with the desire to pay you out for what you did to him. By offering to betray you to him, I believe I could lure him here. In spite of the fact that he did his best to kill me, I'm not thirsting for revenge. It is simply that I would rather that he had his ears torn off than that you should be convicted of having murdered Cepicka.'

Robbie gave her a wry smile and said: 'Horrible as this idea sounds, I give you full marks for being realistic. I certainly count my life of more value than your husband's ears, and if I felt faint-hearted when I came to tackle the job, as you've pointed out, I could gin myself up with the patriotic motive. But how would you set about it?'

'I could write and offer to make a bargain with him.'

'Say he accepted and came here, what could we do then? It is not enough to lure him to Heraklion. You would have to persuade him to come to some place where I could beat the daylights out of him, without anyone hearing his shouts for help. How could you possibly manage to do that?'

Stephanie lit a cigarette and pulled hard at it. 'I think the answer lies in these new arrangements we have to make. Instead of your moving to a small hotel, it should be possible for you to rent a little house or, better still, a cottage just outside the city. Then, if I could bring him there, you would be able to tackle him without anyone being the wiser.'

Robbie considered that for a good minute, then he said: 'If you write to him you'll have to tell him how he can contact you. Isn't there a big risk that, instead of coming here himself, he'll simply put the police on to you, knowing that you will lead them to me and so he'll get his revenge that way, without lifting a finger?'

She shook her head. 'I don't think so. I know Václav and the way his mind works. He thinks that justice in the capitalistic countries is just as corrupt as it is behind the Iron Curtain. By charging you with Cepicka's murder, he knows that he will be putting you in a nasty spot; but I would bet any money that he doesn't believe that, if you are caught, that will be the end of you. Given the same set-up at home the bosses would get you off, and I haven't a doubt that Václav thinks that here your uncle and the N.A.T.O. people have quite enough influence to secure your acquittal. That is why I feel pretty certain that he would come to Crete if I offered him the chance of quietly putting a bullet into you.'

Again Robbie gave a wry grin. 'Well, I suppose he might, unless we handle this jolly carefully.'

'Yes,' she agreed soberly. 'Václav is no fool and if he does come it will be with the intention of killing you. That is a very nasty risk. The question is, are you prepared to take it, for the chance of being able to blow sky-high the whole of this secret Communist operation?'

Robbie nodded. 'As far as I am concerned it's the last card in the pack, so let's play it.'

When they got back to the Astir, Stephanie sat down in the lounge to write to her husband and, after two rough drafts, she produced the following:

By now the failure of the police to find my dead body will probably have led you to guess that I am still alive. That is no fault of yours, but luckily for me my elbow caught in the fork of a tough root protruding from the steep slope just above the precipice. Grenn found me there and, at the risk of his own life, pulled me up on to the road.

I do not propose to go into my past or present relations with Grenn. It is sufficient to say that, whereas you deliberately pushed me over the precipice, he saved my life. For that, any woman would be grateful. So, when I realized that you would try to pin Cepicka's death on him, I gave him all the help I could to evade arrest.

However, now that a week has elapsed, I have had time to consider my own position. For a long time, you and I have remained together only because it has suited our individual interests. Your attempt last Saturday to murder me is proof enough that the time was very much overdue for us to part company and, even if you were prepared to take me back, I would not agree to return to you. But I must take such steps as I can to secure my future.

You will, no doubt, have reported to Janos that I betrayed the Party by enabling Grenn to escape from Pirgos, and by later endeavouring to protect him when you intercepted us on the road. That means that, once it is known that I am still alive, I shall be expelled from the Party and, perhaps, black-listed for 'special treatment'. Even should certain people not catch up with me, it would mean spending the rest of my life as an outcast. As you well know, I am a Communist born and bred. I could never reconcile myself to living among our enemies. I am prepared to make any sacrifice in order to be accepted again by our own people—even, if need be, to make a confession and submit to being disciplined. But only you are in a position to arrange this.

Knowing your feelings towards Grenn, I offer him to you as the price of my rehabilitation. We are here in Crete and, although we are not living together, I am in touch with him. He has gone into hiding in a place where it would be difficult for the police to find him and, from the time you receive this letter, I shall not go near him; so it would be futile for you to suggest to the police that they should try to trace him through me. But, if you will come over, I can take you to his hide-out, where you could surprise him on his own and do what you like with him.

For obvious reasons I am not giving my address, so send a reply to this addressed to Madame Polacek, c/o G.P.O. Heraklion. If you agree to my terms and give me the date and number of your flight from Athens, I will be at the airport with a car to meet you.

When she had finished, she gave Robbie the letter to read through. He said that he thought it a little masterpiece, for Barak could not show it to the police without incriminating himself for attempted murder. Even if he informed them only that he had good reason to believe that the man they wanted was in Crete, they would still, from the way Stephanie had put things, have to look for a needle in a hay-stack.

'All the same,' he added glumly, 'this means that after Monday I won't even be able to see you until you come to tip me off if Barak takes the bait, and I'm going to miss you desperately.'

She smiled at him. 'Things won't be so bad. We'll have to live apart, of course, but that bit was put in only to give Václav the impression that there is very little chance of catching up with you unless he comes over to do the job himself. If he does go to the police, which I think very unlikely, the only way they could pick me up is by lying in wait for me to go to the G.P.O. to collect his reply. But there is no charge upon which they can arrest me and, naturally, I should say I hadn't the faintest idea where you had got to. So, until that happens—if it ever does—there is no reason why we shouldn't continue to spend most of our days together, provided we are not seen too much in the town.'

By then it was past ten o'clock, but posting the letter that night would ensure its getting on the morning flight to Athens. Robbie got a stamp from the hall porter and went out to post it at the G.P.O., while Stephanie went upstairs and undressed.

On the Sunday Robbie woke early; but the window curtains were of very flimsy material, so light was already flooding the room. In the other bed, barely a yard from him, Stephanie was still sleeping peacefully, her face turned towards him. Her chestnut curls made a halo for her head against the white back-

ground of her pillow, her eyelashes made little fans upon her
pink cheeks and her full red lips were slightly parted.

He had kept faith with her only by forcing himself to think
of something else every time the fact that they were together
in the same bedroom consciously entered his mind. Now, he
wondered if he had been a fool to be so scrupulous. He had
heard it said that women who extracted from men promises to
behave themselves never expected those promises to be kept,
and rarely wanted them to be. Stephanie had never again
referred to the episode by the pool and, from her attitude
during the past week, had shown that she harboured no resentment against him on account of it. That she liked him was
beyond all doubt. Indeed, the lengths to which she had gone
for his protection showed that, apart from being grateful to
him for having saved her life, she had come to regard him
with real affection. Yet she had given him no shadow of en-
couragement to break his word and attempt again to make
love to her.

This, he knew, was his last chance. From now on, they
would no longer be sleeping in the same room, and even their
separate rooms would be in different hotels. For five nights he
had exerted all his willpower to exclude the nearness of her
presence from his senses; in another hour or two the opportunity would be gone of feeling his arms again round her strong-
limbed yet deliciously soft-skinned little body and, so far as he
could possibly foresee, it would have gone for ever.

He got out of bed and stood staring down at her, his heart
pounding in his chest so hard that it hurt and made him breathless. Then, with sudden resolution, he turned away, choked
back a sob and tiptoed swiftly out of the room to the bathroom
next door. He had undressed there the previous night; so he
shaved, bathed and dressed himself. When, three-quarters of
an hour later, he returned to the bedroom to collect his wallet,
he found Stephanie awake.

Normally, whenever he was in the room, she kept the bed-
clothes up to her chin; but this morning she was sitting up
against her pillows with her plump bare arms, shoulders and
neck freely displayed. As he came in, she said in surprise:

'I thought you were only having a bath. Why have you dressed so early?'

'It's nearly half-past-eight, so not all that early,' he replied. 'And I thought I'd walk down to the harbour. Barak may ignore your letter. Even if he doesn't, while we are waiting to hear from him I can't just sit about doing nothing. I mean to find out when the *Bratislava* docked here and, if possible, whereabouts the group she landed is operating. There is at least a chance that I might be able to get in touch with them, as I did with that first party at Patras, and maybe I could pick up something.'

'But this is Sunday,' she protested. 'There will be nobody at the harbour office, anyhow not at this hour.'

'Oh, by nine o'clock there will be plenty of longshoremen about, and probably a few Customs officers off duty. Not many ships call at a small port like this, and a Czechoslovakian ship must be quite an exception. I've no doubt plenty of people who frequent the docks will remember her.'

Stephanie gave a little moue. 'As there is no restaurant downstairs for you to breakfast in, and this being our last morning together, I had thought that we might both have had our breakfast on trays in bed, while we talked over what we mean to do later in the day. But since you have dressed and are going out, it doesn't matter.'

Turning over, she gave her pillow a thump, thrust herself down in the bed, pulled the sheets up round her shoulders and shut her eyes again. Robbie cast an unhappy look at her, as he wondered if that idea of hers had been due to the trust she now placed in him or if, with feminine unpredictability, she had suddenly been seized with an impulse to make an overture to him. But he thought the latter unlikely and her attitude made it plain that, now he had dressed, she certainly did not expect him to undress and get into bed again.

Downstairs, he found that he could get coffee and rolls in the bar. Twenty minutes later, he walked down the depressing main street to the harbour. At the extremity of the mole it had a castle very similar to that of St. Nicholas at Rhodes, and on the inland side of the port there were still to be seen the outlines of large, vaulted berths. These forerunners of the modern submarine pens had housed the Venetian galleys during the four-hundred-and-fifty-year-long occupation of Crete by the Serene Republic—from the thirteenth to the seventeenth century—until the Turks, after a siege lasting twenty-four years, had wrested the island from that great seafaring nation.

There were plenty of people about: women and old men hawking fruit, Turkish delight, roast nuts and hot rings of dough sprinkled with sugar, and the usual collection of loungers to be found in any small port. For an hour Robbie moved about, entering into conversation, on one excuse or another, with more than a score of them; but not one could tell him anything about a Czechoslovakian ship that had berthed there early in the month. A number of them assured him that, had the *Bratislava* called there, they could not possibly have missed her. Much puzzled, but convinced at last that she could not have put in at Heraklion, Robbie returned to the Astir about half-past-ten.

He found Stephanie dressed and packing. She had already telephoned down to the hall porter and found out about bus services. There was one to Khania, the principal town at the western end of the island, that left from the main square of the town at twelve o'clock. The bus would get them to Khania about five o'clock, so she had said they would take it.

It would have been easier to have covered their trail by having themselves dropped at a railway station; but there were no railways in Crete, so they would have to manage as best they could at the place where the long-distance buses picked up their passengers. As this was only a few hundred yards up the street, the head porter urged them to walk and would have sent one of his underlings with them to carry their bags. But Robbie insisted on having a taxi. By doing so, they freed themselves of the underling who would have waited to put their bags on the bus, and prevented his telling the hall porter later that they had not, after all, gone to Khania.

After the taxi had dropped them with their suitcases, they waited a few minutes, then separated. As soon as another taxi came along, Stephanie took it to a small hotel called the Ken-

rikon, where she registered as Fräulein Anna Schmidt. Five
minutes later, Robbie was on his way to an equally unpreten-
ious hostelry called The Palladium, at which he registered as
Signor Giacomo Lombardi. An hour later, they met by arrangement for lunch at a little restaurant named the Ariadne.

During the afternoon, they walked round the town. Except
for the Venetian Morosini Fountain in the main square, there
was nothing beautiful in it. By comparison, for its size, it had
suffered far more from bombing than had London, and practically nothing had been done to restore it. Even the pavements
in the principal streets were, in many places, still cracked and
uneven. There were no fine shops and the now-deserted market
was a maze of small streets resembling an Oriental bazaar
which, indeed, for over two hundred years it had been.

Unlike the Venetians, the Moors, and the other great coloni-
zing powers of Portugal, Spain, Britain, France and Italy which
came after them, the Turks had done nothing for the peoples
over whom they ruled during the long centuries of their Empire.
They had taxed the populations of the Balkan countries to the
limit, persecuted them on religious grounds, administered the
laws through corrupt officials, and had given nothing in
return. They had left behind them no fine buildings, no beautiful gardens, no hospitals or schools and not a single great work
of art; only a legacy of incompetence, laziness, disease and
dirt. Here, in Crete, the lamentable results of their rule could
be seen even beneath the devastation caused by the bombing;
for the Cretans, in spite of many gallant attempts to throw off
the Turkish yoke, had not gained their freedom until 1898.
Then had followed two world wars and Crete had not had the
time to emerge from the dire poverty in which the Turks had
left her.

Their walk led them eventually down to the sea wall at
the western end of the city. Turning back along it, they skirted
a small bay littered with refuse and, on reaching its further
promontory, found themselves again at the Glass House. Now
that, within a few days, it would be May, the afternoon sun was
very hot; so they went in and spent half an hour refreshing
themselves with iced orange juice. They then resumed their
walk in the direction of the harbour.

To their left lay the sea, to their right the many acres of desolation they had noticed from the bus the night before. Adjacent to the road, only one complete building was still standing. It looked like a huge barn. There were some stacks of timber alongside it and a glance between its loosely padlocked double doors showed it to be a saw-mill. Some way behind it, among the crumbling walls and heaps of rubble, stood a little house. The chimney pots were gone and the upper windows broken, but otherwise it appeared to be intact. Stephanie drew Robbie's attention to it and said:

'That would be a perfect place for you to go to earth in and for me to bring Václav to, if he does come to Crete. Let's go over and look at it.'

On one side of the saw-mill there was a track made by lorries. This brought them to within sixty yards of the house; for the rest of the way they scrambled over the rubble alongside a low wall which ended against one side of it. The building had only two stories and looked as if it contained two or three rooms on the ground floor with, probably, four small bedrooms above. The downstairs windows were cracked and covered with cobwebs; the door stood a few inches ajar. The damp had warped it and it was stuck, but it flew open at a thrust from Robbie's powerful shoulders.

'You stay here,' he told her. 'As it's been abandoned, it is probably dangerous and may fall down.' But she ignored his warning and followed him into a narrow hall, half of which was taken up by a steep flight of stairs. A door on the right stood open. Through it, they could see lumps of plaster on the floor and peeling wallpaper, which suggested that it had been the sitting room. Robbie forced open a door on the left and they saw then why the house had been left uninhabited. A small, old-fashioned, now rusty, iron range showed that the room had been the kitchen, but beyond it there was no wall. From the road it had not been noticeable, but the whole of the wall on that side of the house had fallen out.

Robbie insisted that Stephanie should remain below, then went gingerly up the stairs. He returned to report that two small bedrooms on the sitting-room side of the house were habitable; although virtually they were now one, because the

laster partition between them had collapsed, leaving only the
wo upright posts that had strengthened it.

'Do you think it would be safe to live in?' Stephanie asked.

'I don't see why not,' he replied. 'If the good half of it has
tood up like this for twenty years, I don't see why it should
all down in another week.'

'It will be horribly uncomfortable; no electric light or gas
or cooking, no water, and outside sanitation. But, at this time
of year, it won't be damp or cold. And, if the police do start
a hunt for you in Heraklion, they will check up on every
oreigner in even the smallest lodging houses, whereas they
are very unlikely to look for you among these ruins.'

'The men who work at the saw-mill are bound to see me
come and go.'

'Not necessarily. There's certain to be a back entrance to
this place, and you could use that in the daytime. Let's go
and see what it's like round there.'

Twenty yards behind the house a tall wall, with gaping
windows, which had formed part of a much bigger building,
was still standing. It screened the back entrance from being
overlooked by houses a few hundred yards further inland which
were inhabited, and just beyond it lay what had once been a
narrow street but now blocked by rubble, was the end of a
cul-de-sac.

'You're right,' Robbie declared. 'I should be able to lie
doggo here for quite a time before anyone tumbles to it that
I've moved in. And we could hardly find a better place to which
you can bring Barak. I'll have to go without a bath, but I can
get a shave at a different barber's every morning. I must have
something to sleep on, though.'

'Of course you must. The only difficulty is to get a few
things here for you without being seen. But I know what we'll
do. Tomorrow I'll hire a car and in the afternoon we'll buy
what you require and take it with us; after dark I'll drive it
here as near as I can get and we will carry in the things.'

That night, they had dinner at another small restaurant,
then, after arranging where to meet next morning, parted to
sleep at their respective hotels. At eleven o'clock, Robbie stood

waiting for Stephanie at the far end of King Constanti—
Avenue. A few minutes later, she drove up in a car she ha
hired. When they had exchanged information about the sort
night they had had, he got in and she drove on through Liber—
Place out of the city.

'Where are we off to?' he asked.

'To Knossos,' she replied. 'I'm already sick of the sight
this dreary town, and the less we are seen about togeth—
in it the better. Besides, I felt sure you would be longing
see the ruins of the palace.'

'I suppose I ought to be,' he said with a sigh, 'but the trut
is that these days I can think of nothing but what may l
ahead of us.'

'Oh, come! You musn't let yourself get depressed,' sh
chided him. 'I know you were very disappointed yesterday t
find that no Czech group had landed here; so you couldn't eve
check up on whether they appeared to be doing the same so—
of job as the others. But, with any luck, my letter will brin
Václav here in a few days' time, and you ought to be able t
get a far more worthwhile dividend out of him.'

'Perhaps; but I'm not looking forward to the way in whic
I shall have to get it.'

'No decent man would. Still, it will be your one big chanc
to save yourself and, if that is not enough inducement, yo
must think of the much greater things that are at stake. D
you know, I heard a rumour at my hotel this morning that th
conference in Delhi has broken down.'

'Yes, I heard the same thing, while I was being shaved at
barber's. It's said that last night the Russians walked out.
suppose something has come through on the wireless. All th
same, neither side can be quite so crazy as to go to war. If the
did they would blow one another to pieces, and they know it.

While the car ran on past the back lots and dusty building
in the suburbs, they fell silent. Soon they reached more ope
country and, some twenty minutes' drive from the city, ra
down a hill to the valley in which Knossos is situated. Th
palace occupied the whole of a low, extensive hill in th
valley. There was no fine view in any direction and it wa

ome distance from the sea; although it was believed that, at ne time, the sea had come up to it and its site had been chosen or that reason. However, the contours of the country had nce been radically changed by violent earthquakes.

A first palace had been in existence there in two thousand .C., as the centre of a brilliant civilization which had lasted wo or three hundred years. It had then been destroyed by an arthquake. From the sixteenth century B.C., a second great ivilization had arisen, and Crete, under the Minoan Kings, had ecome a sea power of the first rank, trading with distant lands nd drawing tribute from many coast towns in the Eastern Mediterranean. But again, towards fourteen hundred, another errible earthquake had destroyed Knossos and the other prinipal buildings throughout the island. The Minoans had never ecovered from this second, devastating blow.

It was believed that the palace originally had five stories; ut the ruins of only the two lower ones remained, and these ad lain undiscovered until the colossal labours undertaken by ir Arthur Evans in the early nineteen hundreds. No photo-raphs could give an adequate impression of the vastness of he ruin, because there were no lines of tall pillars or lofty rchways. It was simply a huge, man-made mound, riddled vith passages, staircases and chambers. Owing to the pre-alence of earth tremors the rooms were small, but there vere said to have been no fewer than one thousand three hun-dred of them.

Sir Arthur Evans had done far more than simply excavate he ruins. He had spent a large part of his great fortune in estoring many of the most interesting chambers. The original rescoes had been moved for preservation to the Museum in Heraklion; but artists had painted exact copies of them on the valls where they had formerly been, and they consisted of olourful representations of birds, beasts, fish and flowers, ren-lered with a technique far more modern in conception than he art of any other people of the ancient world.

That the Minoan nobility had lived in a state of luxury com-arable to modern standards was also evident. Some of the rescoes showed women who had lived nearly four thousand years ago, yet their elaborate coiffeurs, jewels and the richness

of their brocade dresses could have rivalled those of twe
tieth-century Parisians. The Queen's private bathroom cou
still be seen and had been better equipped than that of Mar
Antoinette at Versailles. By a skilfully devised system of pip
for sewage and steam, the inmates of the palace had enjoy
both modern sanitation and central heating.

For the better part of two hours, Robbie and Stephan
wandered about the endless succession of rooms and staircase
then they lunched at the Tourist Pavilion. Afterwards, th
walked right round the ruin to see the theatre and the lon
solidly-built sunken road which connected the great palace
a smaller one a quarter of a mile off, on the far side of t
highway. By then the sun was blazing down, so they found
shady place in which to sit and Stephanie said:

'I suppose the famous Labyrinth, in which young men ai
maidens were sacrificed to the Minotaur each year, lies som
where below the ruins of the palace. But the Minotaur couldr
really have been half man, half bull, could it?'

'It is impossible to say,' Robbie replied. 'Modern opinic
is that these young captives were just trained as bull-fighte
and put into a bull-ring to amuse the Minoans. But there a
well-authenticated accounts of some pretty queer creatur
that women have given birth to in quite recent times. Accor
ing to the ancient chronicles, King Minos angered Poseido
so the god inflicted Minos's Queen, Pasiphae, with a monstro
passion for a bull. In order to gratify it, she had the great i
ventor, Daedalus, make for her an imitation cow that she cou
get inside, and the result of his efforts was so lifelike that t
bull took it for a real cow and acted accordingly. The resu
was that she gave birth to the Minotaur.'

'It must have been jolly uncomfortable for her,' Stephan
remarked; then she added hastily: 'Anyhow, one must gi
Daedalus full marks for having made a cow good enough
deceive the bull.'

'Oh, he was a genius. When he got into trouble with Min
and was imprisoned here, he is said to have invented wings t
which he and his son, Icarus, escaped. Unfortunately, Icaru
flew too high; so the sun melted the wax by which the wing
were attached to his shoulders, and he fell in the sea and wa

drowned. But Daedalus got away safely and later invented all sorts of wonderful things for a new patron, King Cocalus, who reigned over a large part of Sicily. It was through the Minotaur that Daedalus got on the wrong side of King Minos; because it was he who had the bright idea of providing Theseus with the ball of thread that enabled him to find his way out of the Labyrinth after he had killed the monster.'

They were silent for a moment, then Stephanie said: 'Tell me about Theseus, Robbie.'

'Oh, I don't know.' He gave a shrug. 'Somehow, I find it difficult to think about that sort of thing any more.'

'But you should,' she urged him. 'You mustn't let yourself brood about the trouble you are in, and awful things in the future which may never happen.'

He smiled at her and, after a moment, admitted: 'I suppose you're right. Very well, then. Theseus was one of the greatest of the Heroes and came of the royal line of Athens. They were a pretty tough lot and, to start from the beginning, the city was founded by a chap called Cecrops. His grandson, Pandion, had two daughters, Procne and Philomela. In those early days, the Athenians still had great difficulty in preventing barbarian invaders from ravaging their country; so Pandion called in a fierce King of Thrace, called Tereus, to give him a hand. When Tereus's tribesmen had done their stuff, Pandion said he could have whichever he liked of his daughters as a reward.

'Tereus chose the elder, Procne, married her and took her off to Thrace, where she had a son by him called Itys. But, as the years passed, Procne grew lonely; so she asked her lord and master to let her go on a visit to her old home. He wouldn't hear of it but, after a while, he agreed to go down to Athens himself and bring back Philomela, so that the sisters could have a few weeks' get-together.

'When he collected Philomela he found that, since he had last seen her, she had blossomed out quite a bit. That gave him wicked ideas. In the ship on the way back, he did his best to make a good impression on her by fetching her cushions to sit on, admiring her hair-dos and feeding her lots of Turkish delight. Naturally, she took all this simply as proof of what a charming brother-in-law she had. But, once they got ashore, as the story books say "the villain revealed himself".

' "Be mine," he said, "and I will make you my Queen in your sister's place." "No, no!" she cried. " 'Twould be a crime in the eyes of gods and men." "I care not a fig for either," he stormed. "You shall lie with me, girl, or else——" "Unhand me, wretch," she sobbed. "I'd rather die first—and anyway, I don't like men with beards," or words to that effect.'

Stephanie laughed. 'That's better, Robbie. Now you are getting into your old form.'

'Well, there it was. She was set on death rather than dishonour, and he seems to have got cold feet. He didn't like to kill her but he became scared that when he got her back to his palace, she would spill the beans to her sister about the pass he had made, and Procne was the sort of wife who might have hit him over the head with a rolling pin. To prevent Philomela telling on him, he did an awful thing. He cut out the poor girl's tongue.'

'Oh, Robbie, how ghastly!'

'Yes, wasn't it? And not really very clever, either; because he couldn't take her home with him after that, so he imprisoned her in a house in the woods and gave out that she had died en route. But Philomela still had a kick left in her. After she had been behind bars for some while, she secured permission to pass away the time by doing a bit of tatting. Her gaoler got her some white and purple wool. With that, she wove a tapestry illustrating Tereus's ungentlemanly behaviour and persuaded her gaoler to take it to the Queen.

'As soon as old Tereus had gone off to look at the rabbit snares, or whatever he did in the mornings, Procne bustled off into the woods, released Philomela from her prison and took her along to the palace. It so happened that, just as they were crossing the courtyard, Procne's son, Itys, came along whistling a bit out of tune and swinging his lesson books. It chanced, too, that this unlucky youngster had grown up the "spit 'n' image" of his father. The sight of this likeness sent Procne right off her rocker. She snatched up a bread knife and jabbed it into her own son's throat.'

Stephanie closed her eyes. 'Really, the things these people did.'

'Oh, that wasn't all. These two beauties fell on the boy, tore him limb from limb between them and put the bits in a pot. Then, when Tereus came home, his wife served him up their son for lunch. Procne stood by while Tereus had a great "tuck-in". After he had belched a bit, he asked her: "Was that delicious dish, grouse en casserole or partridge Strogonoff done with truffles?"

' "No," she told him. "It was a hash of Itys." Then, just so that he should not think that she was joking, Philomela popped out at that moment from behind a curtain and threw his son's head on the table.

'Tereus had a very soft spot for his only son; so, naturally, he took umbrage at having been led into eating a good part of him. Snatching up his trusty blade, he chivvied the two women out of the house and into the woods. But evidently the gods felt that he was most to blame for having started the trouble; so they saved Procne and Philomela by turning them into a swallow and a nightingale.'

'What a revolting story. And, anyway, what has all this to do with Theseus?'

'Only that these two charming ladies were his aunts, which goes to show that even the girls in the family he came from were not the type to take things lying down. His father, King Aegeus, didn't behave exactly according to "Cocker" either. He had been married twice, but he'd had no luck in getting a son by either wife. However, he evidently believed in the old Robert the Bruce stuff of "If at first you don't succeed . . ."

'When on a visit to Pittheus, King of Troezen, his roving eye settled on the King's daughter, Aethra, who was then a pretty little piece of fifteen. That night, he gumshoed along to her room and told her about the facts of life. He concluded the lesson by saying: "Now, my dear, there's just a chance that you may have a beautiful little baby all of your own. If it's a girl you can have her for keeps, and if it's a weedy, sickly boy I don't want to be bothered about him either. But, just on the chance that he is worthy to bear my name, I'm going to bury my sword and sandals tomorrow under a heavy rock. If, when he is sixteen, he is strong enough to lift it and bring them to me in Athens, I'll make him my heir." Then he patted her on the head and told her not to let on to anyone that kind 'uncle' Aegeus had been along to see her and given up most of his night's sleep to tell her all those interesting things.

'Aethra must have been quite a smart kid because, when people began to notice that her dresses were becoming a bit tight round the middle, she said that Poseidon had been to see her in a dream. Maybe he had, since with his helmet of invisibility he could get up to all sorts of larks without the bother that Zeus had to go to of turning himself into a bull or swan or something. Anyhow, when her baby was born, Poseidon behaved like a good sport and acted as Theseus's protector all through his life.

'Theseus, of course, turned out to be a boy wonder and modelled himself on Hercules, who was a friend of the family and came to stay. As a child, Theseus even attacked with his toy sword the skin of the Nemean lion, believing it to be a live animal. Hercules usually wore it, but on this occasion had left it lying about in the garden. Then, when Theseus was sixteen, his mother came clean with him about his birth; so he heaved up the rock, recovered the sword and sandals his father had left there, and went off with them to Athens.

'On the way, he spoilt the fun of all sorts of people. First he killed Periphetes, a terrible bandit who wielded a club as large as himself. Next he met a character called Sinis, who invented the game that the pirates of the Spanish Main used to play hundreds of years later. It was to bend two pine saplings inward, tie the ankles of a captive to their tops; then, having made a book on which tree would tear off the biggest piece of the victim, let them spring back. Theseus, of course, treated Sinis to his own medicine.

'A giant named Sceiron was the next unlucky person to fall in with our Hero. He kept an enormous turtle and, instead of buying food for it at the local pet shop, he used to force travellers to wash his feet then, when they knelt down in front of him, he kicked them over a cliff so that they fell into the turtle's pool. The day he met Theseus, the turtle got an extra large dinner.

'Soon afterwards, Theseus came upon another giant, one Procrustes, who had a rather warped sense of humour. He invited anyone who came along to spend the night. In his guest room there were two beds, one very long and one very short. If the guest chose the long bed, Procrustes tied his wrists and ankles to cords, then used a rack to stretch him to fit it; if he chose the short one, he cut off the bits that overlapped. Theseus, of course, put paid to him too, then gaily went on his way, killing off all sorts of monsters, until at last he reached Athens.

'There he found things in a pretty pickle. King Aegeus had gone a bit soft in the head; so he was being pushed around by his two nephews, the Pallantids. Still worse, he had taken as his wife the witch Medea. You'll remember she was the sweetie-pie that Jason brought back with the Golden Fleece, but who had left him after boiling his uncle in a cauldron under the pretext of giving him a beauty treatment.

'Being gifted with psychic powers, Medea tumbled to it at once that Theseus was the heir to the throne and would do her no good; so she spun her old man a yarn that her familiar spirit had told her this brash young stranger meant to do him in. Aegeus, being under her thumb, fell for this and agreed that she should give Theseus a cup of poisoned wine. But, just at the moment she was saying to Theseus: "Here you are, Big Boy, knock this back and I'll get you another," he produced his father's sword from out of his hiker's pack. Recognizing it at once, his papa knocked the drink out of his hand and, as usual in such cases, a dog which was handy lapped it up, then threw seven fits and went rigid. Seeing the game was up, Medea gnashed her false teeth in rage, snatched up her broom and flew off out of the window.

'Theseus sorted out his uppish cousins, the Pallantids, in no time at all and, as his old Pop was more or less gaga, virtually took over the kingdom. But, after a year or two, the Minoan tribute became due. Twenty-nine years earlier King Minos's son, Androgeos, had been bumped off by some Athenian athletes who were jealous because he had won so many prizes at their Games. Minos then arrived on the scene with his two-Power Navy to avenge his son, and had consented to spare the city only if every nine years the Athenians antied up their seven most likely lads and their seven most come-hither virgins for his Minotaur to chase round the Labyrinth. For the third time, the Minoan galleys turned up to carry this nice little cargo off to Crete.

'One must hand it to Theseus that he had bags of courage, for he volunteered at once to go as one of the lads. However, no one could say he was a particularly modest type, as he also declared that, after five minutes with him, the Minotaur would wish his mother had never set eyes on a bull. His old Pop implored him to stay put, but he said: "Not to worry, Dad. You go and do a spot of fishing off Sounion Head. You'll get first sight of my ship from there on her way back, and I'll hoist a white sail instead of a black to let you know that I'm O.K.'

'When he reached Crete, he continued to throw his weight about and boast that the Minotaur wouldn't stand an earthly against him because he was a son of Poseidon. King Minos took him up on that, threw a gold ring into the harbour and said: "If the god's your father, in you go boy. Ask him to hand that back to you." Theseus stripped off his clothes, did a jack-knife dive and came up not only with the ring but also a diamond tiara straight out of Cartier's. This, with a graceful bow, he handed to the King's daughter, Ariadne, who happened to be looking on.

'Having had a good look at Theseus while he was still dripping wet, Ariadne felt her heart go pitter-pat; so she sought out Daedalus in his back room and said: "Look, you dear old egg-head. That Athenian diving champ has made me go all groggy at the knees. Please think of a way to save him for me so that he can restore my equilibrium." Upon this, Daedalus gave her a magic sword and a ball of twine, so that Theseus couldn't help killing the Minotaur with the one and, by un-rolling the other as he went into the Labyrinth, find his way out again by it.

'That evening, she passed on these useful accessories to her new boy friend. He gave her a pat on the behind and promised her the full treatment later; then went off to do his stuff. She didn't let the grass grow under her feet, either. She spent the night boring holes with a gimlet in the bottoms of all the ships in her papa's fleet, so that they sank to the mud of the harbour and could not be used for pursuit. Round about dawn, Theseus kept his date with her at his own ship and, just as a make-weight, brought along her pretty little sister, Phaedra.

'Theseus's ship reached the island of Naxos, but accounts differ about what happened there. According to one version, poor Ariadne was so seasick that she had to be put ashore for a bit; then a terrible storm sprang up and drove the ship away from the island before Theseus had a chance of picking her up. In the Aegean, that could easily happen. The other version is that all the Athenians landed and spent several days holding a decidedly hectic party to celebrate their escape from an awful fate in the Labyrinth. That seems the more likely story. It goes on to say that Ariadne, being a daughter of Pasiphae, proved too much for Theseus. He simply could not take it, so he deliberately ditched her.'

'What a very sad end to the story,' said Stephanie.

'Oh, that's not the end. There's yards more of it. Theseus's abandoning of Ariadne turned out to be a stroke of luck for her. Dionysus happened to come along and found her weeping on the beach. Being a god he knew just how to console her, and they found that they were so well suited to one another that they got married.

Theseus, on the other hand, after he'd been a few days at sea, seems to have regretted giving her the brush-off. Anyhow, his thoughts are said to have been so full of her that he forgot to pull down the black sail of his ship and hoist a white one. Poor old Aegeus, up on Sounion Head, naturally took it that his son was a goner; so he threw himself over the cliff to feed the fishes that he had been killing time trying to catch.

'However, having inherited the kingdom didn't stop Theseus from taking time off now and then to go adventuring. He went with Hercules on an expedition to beat up the Amazons, captured their Queen, Antiope, and married her. But he soon got tired of her, kicked her out of bed, and installed Ariadne's sister, Phaedra, as his wife instead. Then, after several years during which he slew many more monsters, he went with a pal of his named Peirithous to Sparta and they abducted that precocious little ten-year-old poppet Helen.

When they drew lots for who should have her, Theseus won and, judging by his form with the girls generally, maybe she wasn't quite as innocent as she looked when she got home again.

'Peirithous must have been as mad as a March hare. He conceived the fantastic idea of consoling himself for not having got Helen by going down to Hades and carrying Persephone off from Pluto. Theseus could not do less than lend a hand; so off they went and landed themselves literally in the Hell of a mess. Peirithous got stuck there for keeps, and Theseus got away only because the doyen of all the Heroes, tough old Hercules, came down and pulled him out by the coat-tails.

'When he got back to Athens, he found his palace in an uproar. Helen's brothers, Castor and Pollux, had turned up and were threatening blue murder unless he gave her back to them. Being pretty part-worn from his Hades adventure, he agreed; but he was faced with worse trouble between his wife and Hippolytus, a son he had had by the Amazon Queen, Antiope.

'Hippolytus had grown up into a good-looking teenager, and Phaedra felt that he was just the lad for her to talk to about this and that by the fireside on the long winter evenings, while his father was away killing dragons or teaching young girls like Helen how one and one can make three. But Hippolytus was a religious type and he had dedicated himself to Artemis; so he said to his stepmother: 'Thanks awfully, but I've taken a vow never to do that sort of thing.''

'If Phaedra had been a decent sort, she would have said: "You silly young mutt; you don't know what you are missing. Forget what I suggested and keep your mouth shut. That beefy Captain of the Guard is always asking me to go and hear his long-playing records; so I'll brighten up a few of my evenings with him until your pa cames home." Instead, she got mad with the youngster and, when Theseus did get back, she complained to him that his son had tried to rape her.

'That fairly put the cat among the pigeons. Theseus flung Hippolytus out on his ear and called down Poseidon's wrath upon him. The Sea god obliged by sending a sea-monster to scare the horses of Hippolytus's chariot, which resulted in it overturning and the unfortunate youth being crushed to death beneath it.

'Later, Theseus felt that perhaps he had acted a trifle hastily and that, by and large, he hadn't made a great success of his life; so he left Athens and went into retirement as the guest of Lycomedes, the King of Scyros. Unfortunately, he could not keep himself from boasting about his exploits; and Lycomedes got so bored with hearing about them, over and over again, that he had Theseus thrown into the sea so that he was drowned.'

As Robbie fell silent, Stephanie said: 'Then it was a sad ending, after all.'

'Well, yes,' Robbie agreed, 'but Theseus had a wonderfully full life, you know. And, in between his expeditions, he did a lot for Athens. He was its first great King, and by his laws he laid the foundations for what it afterwards became.'

By half past four they were back in Heraklion. Stephanie dropped Robbie in Liberty Square, so that he had only to walk across it to the Museum of Antiquities, where it had been decided that he should spend a couple of hours while she bought the things he would need in his new quarters.

At seven o'clock they met again at a small restaurant outside which she had parked the car. The boot and back now contained a folding camp bed, mattress, sleeping bag and pillow, a folding chair, a primus stove with a supply of methylated spirit and paraffin, about twenty yards of dark stuff to serve as black-out material, a hammer and tacks, two torches, a packet of candles, a tin bucket, a broom, two jerry cans to hold water, two towels, a saucepan, an enamel mug, three bottles of wine, coffee, sugar, oranges and biscuits.

When she had given him a list of her purchases, she added: 'With the other things you have in your suitcase, you should be all right. We can fill the jerry cans at one of the public fountains; with the water from one, you can wash in the bucket, and with some from the other boil yourself up a mug of coffee on the primus in the mornings.'

Robbie smiled across at her. 'You really are a marvel. You think of everything.'

She smiled back at him. 'I think I told you when you took

me on in Athens that I rather prided myself on looking after people; but I never expected to have to do this sort of thing. I only hope now that Václav falls for the bait I offered him in my letter.'

After they had eaten, they sat on over coffee and liqueurs until it was fully dark. At the Morosini Fountain Robbie filled the jerry cans, then Stephanie drove him to within a hundred yards of his hotel. A quarter of an hour later, he had paid his bill and rejoined her with his suitcase. They had some difficulty in finding the cul-de-sac behind the little house; but at length they identified it, pulled up and switched off the car lights. There was by then sufficient star-light for them to find their way over the rubble and, in half a dozen journeys, they transported all the things they had brought.

On exploring the house further, they found the upper floor much clearer of fallen plaster and debris than the lower. There was the point too, that, should children play among the rubble and chance to enter the house, they were less likely to go upstairs than just look into the sitting room; so it was decided that Robbie should occupy the bedroom. While he swept the floor, Stephanie nailed the black-out material along the tops of the windows so that it would hang down over them at night, but could be rolled up so as not to show through the broken panes in the daytime.

When they had fixed everything, they agreed to meet next day at ten o'clock at the same place as they had met that morning. Since Stephanie could not expect to hear from Barak until the following evening at the earliest, she was anxious to keep Robbie's thoughts occupied; so she proposed that they should fill in the day by an expedition across the island to Phaestos, the other great centre of Minoan civilization, near the south coast. As it was advisable for Robbie to be seen as little as possible about the town, in case the police in Rhodes had asked their colleagues to try and trace Max Thévanaz, he agreed that her suggestion was a sound one. They then parted for the night.

Next morning they drove right round the outside of the great Venetian ramparts which still surrounded the city, to get on to the road leading west along the coast. After a few kilometres it turned south, inland, and ran through a valley rich n vineyards with, between the vines, such masses of oxalis that heir flowers formed a bright yellow carpet. Gradually the road nounted, in a series of zigzags, until in front they had an excel-ent view of Mount Ida.

It was in Crete that Zeus had been brought up in secret o save him from his father, Cronos, and it was said that, as a nemorial to this, he had reshaped the mountain as a portrait of himself. Seen from the south, its outline certainly looked like he profile of an enormous head of splendid proportions lying on a pillow, with brow, nose and chin all sharply defined.

By half-past-eleven they had come down through the pass ınd reached the village of Ayioi Dheka, in the vicinity of which lad lain Gortyne, the capital of the island during the centuries of occupation by the Romans. According to a pamphlet which Stephanie had acquired, there were a number of interesting ıemains there on both sides of the road; so, on seeing a ruin hrough the trees on their left, they pulled up, got out of the car and went over to inspect it.

The country there consisted mainly of small orchards, separated by low, crumbling walls largely composed of blocks of hewn stone, obviously from ancient buildings. Sightseers were so infrequent that there were no sign-boards or even tracks, and the foliage of the fruit trees made it difficult to see far in any direction. The ruin they had seen proved to be only a fifteen-foot-high section of a thick, brick wall but, during twenty minutes of scrambling about, they found the foundations of what must have been an enormous temple, and the ruins of the Roman Governor's palace. The remains of an Egyptian temple were also said to be there, but they could not locate them; so they returned to the car and drove on for a quarter of a mile, till they came to a large ruin on the right of the road.

This, they learned from the pamphlet, was the oldest Christian church in Crete, and had been built by St. Titus. Beyond it lay a Greek theatre, in which St. Paul had preached, and a wall inscribed with the 'Law of Gortyne' which was of special interest because it was the first Code of Laws formula-ted in Europe, and the work of Greeks living in the second century B.C.

Having walked round the church, they followed a path to

the other ruins. The theatre was quite small, with only abou
twenty-five semi-circular rows of seats, in good preservatio
and quite charming. Unlike the other ruins they had jus
visited, it was not entirely deserted. Two men were sittin
smoking cigarettes on the edge of the slightly raised stage fron
which St. Paul had preached. They exchanged nods and smile
with Robbie and Stephanie who, the moment they had passe
them, gave one another a swift glance. The two men were talk
ing in Czech and one of them had said:

'It went more quickly than one would have expected; bu
I'm glad the job is finished and we'll soon be home.'

Robbie could hardly control himself for excitement. Czecl
visitors were so rare in Crete that he felt it highly probable tha
these were some of Barak's people. What the man had saic
tended to confirm that. It suggested that the *Bratislava* had
after all, landed a group in Crete.

Stephanie had jumped to the same conclusion. In order tc
overhear more of the conversation, she halted to examine ar
inscription carved on the back of one of the seats in the fron
row. They heard the other man reply:

'I don't agree. I'm glad to have had the chance to see some
of these old places. I only wish we had longer, so that I could
visit more of them.'

For once, Robbie took the lead. To have remained where
they were would have looked as if they were deliberately listening to the Czechs' conversation. But, instead of walking on,
he took Stephanie's elbow and guided her up the steep staircase made by the rows of seats. When they reached the top
they appeared to be out of earshot but, owing to the admirable
acoustics in Greek theatres, they could still hear perfectly
every word spoken by the two men sitting on the stage.

As they were making their way up, the first speaker had
said: 'It's all very well for you, Frantisek; you are a bachelor.'

'What of it?' the second replied. 'I'd have thought you'd
be glad of the chance to get away for a bit from your wife and
kids.'

Their conversation then continued:

'Well, it's a change; but I prefer ordinary jobs and the sort
of food I'm used to. I resent having my life upset by the Bosses.'

'My dear Viliam, I hope you will not be fool enough to show it. Far better pretend that, like myself, you are glad to have been one of those selected to be sent here for this work.'

'Anyhow, they can have no complaints. We have made a good job of it.'

'True. All the same, I wonder if all the labour and material we have expended could not have been saved.'

'How would you have done that?'

'By making use of the place we went to yesterday. That grotto where they say Zeus was hidden as a child.'

'What! Drop one down there, instead of having bored our shaft?'

'Yes; why not? The pit there is said to be bottomless. Of course, it's not. But, all the same, it's probably quite deep enough to have served the same purpose.'

'It might, but it's a long way from the N.A.T.O. air base.'

'I don't think that has any special bearing on the operation.'

'Perhaps not. But you couldn't possibly control the drop of a five-foot-long cylinder down a wide hole in the rock, and with jagged sides, too. It would smash itself to pieces before it got to the bottom.'

'It could be lowered carefully. Still, perhaps you're right. Anyhow, it was only an idea. Let's get back to the car.'

As the two Czechs stubbed out their cigarettes, stood up and walked away, Robbie whispered excitedly to Stephanie: 'They are two of Barak's people. They must be, and we're really on to something now. They haven't been boring for anything; only holes down which they mean to drop something. Atom bombs, perhaps.'

'What good could that do—unless the bombs explode under something that matters? And one of them said he didn't think it had anything to do with the N.A.T.O. air base. Anyhow, we know that the sites in Pirgos, Corinth and Rhodes were nowhere near any military objective.'

'I don't get it,' Robbie agreed, 'but come on. We must follow them. With luck, they may lead us to the site where they've been working.'

Keeping the two Czechs in view, they walked back along

the path. As they approached the road they saw now that, just round the bend, a hundred yards ahead of where they had left their car, there was another with a driver sitting at the wheel. The Czechs got in and were driven off towards Phaestos. Robbie and Stephanie got to their car as quickly as they could and, keeping about a quarter of a mile behind, followed.

After about twelve kilometres, they could see the ruins of Phaestos perched up on a hill ahead and, to the left, a well-made-up side road that led off up to them. But the Czechs had not taken it. For another few kilometres, Stephanie kept on their tail along the rutty, dusty, little-used main road to the south coast. Having breasted a rise, she suddenly applied the brakes and brought the car to a standstill. At the bottom of the slope in front of them, the other car had pulled up. The Czechs got out and one of them paid off the driver. He ran his car to and fro until he had turned it round, then started to drive it back up the slope. Stephanie took off her brakes, ran down the hill past the other driver and pulled up at the spot where the Czechs had paid him off.

'You stay here,' said Robbie quickly, jumping out.

'Take care of yourself,' she called after him, but he had already disappeared into the bushes on the left of the road, along a footpath that the Czechs had obviously taken. Five minutes later, he caught sight of them. The belt of trees and bushes ended abruptly along a line of greyish pebbles that formed a river bed. Some distance away, a sluggish stream flowed roughly in the middle of its course. One of the Czechs was standing on the far side of the water, the other was in the act of crossing it on a donkey guided by a peasant. Beyond the river lay a steep hill.

When the Czechs had set off up the hill, Robbie went forward. The peasant had brought the donkey back to the near bank. Pointing towards the hill, he called out: 'Ayia Triada. Ayia Triada.'

At this, Robbie was greatly relieved. He knew that Ayia Triada had been a Royal Villa used by the Lords of Phaestos in the summer months because it had a view of the sea. Evidently, the Czechs were about to pay it a visit. If they now glanced round and saw him it would not matter, because they would assume that he was simply coming up to have a look at the ruin.

He clambered on to the donkey, grasped the worn saddle and let the poor, scruffy beast splash its way with him across the shallow stream. On the far side, he paid the peasant and hurried after his quarry who, by then, had nearly reached the top of the hill. As he made his way up it by a winding track, he could not help noticing that the wild flowers there were more profuse and varied than any he had seen in Crete. Almost breathless, he reached the top of the rise and gave a quick look round.

There, only a little below the level on which he stood, lay the ruins of Ayia Triada. They were all roofless, but the small palace had had many outbuildings; so the area covered by chambers and walls was considerable. From its south-west front, the palace had looked out over the bay of Mesara. The bay was some miles away and the view magnificent. But the Czechs were nowhere to be seen.

From where Robbie stood, the ruins sloped slightly upward; so he hurried along one side of them until he reached higher ground, then pressed on through low scrub up a still steeper slope. When he halted and looked towards the bay again, he caught sight of the Czechs. They were walking in Indian file down a narrow path that led to a farmhouse about half a mile away. To one side of the house stood a steel pylon but, although it was mid-week, no men were working there and he could see no pile of six-foot lengths of giant screw. That confirmed what he had overheard while the two Czechs were talking. The job there had been completed.

Fearing again that one of the Czechs might turn round and see that he was spying on them, he got to his knees, then lay flat, peering out between two wild sage bushes. In the far distance, he could see the great N.A.T.O. air base that, while at the Embassy, he had heard mentioned as having recently been completed by the Americans. A mile or more from it, there was a little township on the sea shore that had a small harbour. That explained why the *Bratislava* had never called in at Heraklion. She must have anchored off the south of the island and landed a group with all its gear by lighter.

Robbie was still studying the scene spread out below him when in his rear a quiet voice said in English:

'I've got you covered, Mr. Grenn. Stay where you are and put your hands above your ears.'

His heart missed a beat. Still lying flat, he put his hands up as he had been told, but screwed his head round so that he could look over his shoulder. Lying a few feet behind him, and pointing an automatic at him, was Mr. Mahogany Brown.

26

The Show-down

ROBBIE drew in a quick breath. He knew now that the game was up and that he had lost it. There would be no chance of trapping Barak. That last hope of learning the Czech's secret and getting himself cleared of Cepicka's death on a plea of self-defence was gone. They had been too clever for him. He had been caught again and it seemed too much to hope that he would escape with his life a second time.

The American's presence at Ayia Triada explained why he had so persistently forced himself on them in Rhodes. It was not that he had been attracted by Stephanie; he had kept them company from morning to night to ensure that they would have no opportunity of going off on their own and finding out anything further.

It was at Monolithos, just outside the Czech working site, that they had first met him. As he had addressed them in English, they had naturally jumped to the conclusion that he was another tourist who, by coincidence, happened to be visiting that lonely spot at the same time as themselves. But, of course, he had been a Czech security agent, attached to the group, just returning from a run inland, perhaps to Rhodes, to buy something that was required. It seemed certain now that he was not an American at all, but a Czech who had either been brought up there or, like Stephanie, was of mixed parentage. Barak, Robbie felt sure, would have circulated his description to all the groups. The two engineers at Monolithos who had given them lunch had been deceived by his crew-cut and dark glasses, and by Stephanie's story that they were travel agents. But the so-called Mr. Mahogany Brown must have spotted him at once, and probably also identified Stephanie as the missing Mrs. Barak. They had given their name to him as Thévanaz and, on his learning that they were staying at the des Roses, he had said that he was staying there too. But he had driven off ahead of them and, as they had made a detour on their return to see the Valley of the Butterflies, he could easily have bought a few things in the town and checked in at the hotel before they got back.

It was now obvious that he had been on to them from that very first meeting. When they had failed to appear on the bathing beach on the Saturday morning, he would have enquired about them at the office and learned soon afterwards that they had flown to Crete. As there was only the once-weekly air service from Rhodes, he would have had to take the Sunday plane to Athens to follow them, then the Monday flight down to Heraklion. He must have arrived the previous evening. No doubt, he would have been to the Astir and learned that Monsieur and Madame Thévanaz had spent Saturday night there, then left. An enquiry at the Olympic Airways office would have satisfied him that no couple answering their description had since left Crete by air. He would have concluded that they had gone to earth somewhere on the island and that, by then, they would probably have found out the location at which the Czech group was working. To have hunted for them would have been looking for a needle in a haystack; but it was a good bet that they would come to Ayia Triada and try to find out what was going on there, just as they had done at Monolithos. That must be why he had come out there that morning. He had probably been prepared to lie in wait for them there for several days. As things had turned out he had been lucky, and had not had to wait long.

In a few tense moments, those thoughts ran through Robbie's agitated mind. With them alternated others. Should he attempted to run for it? If he did, he would be shot in the back before he had covered a couple of yards. Should he squirm round, wriggle to his knees and pray that, by launching himself forward, in one swift move, he would be able to grab the gun?

No. That would be equally suicidal. He could not possibly reach it before his enemy pressed the trigger and a bullet smashed into his heart or skull. If he surrendered, what would become of him?

In this lonely spot, it was quite possible that 'Mahogany Brown' might decide to put an end to him there and then, and hide his body in one of the many deep ditches that scored the scrub. The only person near enough to be certain to hear the shot was the peasant with the donkey down at the ford. But they were hidden from him by the rise of the hill; so he would probably think that one of the Czechs on the opposite side was out after small game.

On the other hand, there seemed a chance that his captor would march him down to the farmhouse and keep him a prisoner there during the day, with the intention of putting an end to him, as Barak had meant to, by taking him out to sea and drowning him that night. In the latter case, Stephanie would become anxious when he failed to rejoin her and, with ten or twelve hours to work in, might, perhaps, bring help to save him before he was taken down to the beach.

But she would have no idea where he had got to. Even if, when searching the hills, she came upon the Czech site and guessed he was being held a prisoner there, she would still be many miles from any police station. It was certain, too, that there would be delays before anyone high-up enough could be induced to give an order for a raid. So, even if she did find out some time during the afternoon what had happened to him, only if given great good luck would she be able to bring help to him.

At length, those silent moments that had seemed years to Robbie ended by his gasping out: 'What . . . what do you mean to do with me?'

'Do? Why, nothing.' The fair eyebrows behind the levelled automatic were raised in surprise. 'All I want is to get you talking.'

'Talking!' Robbie repeated. Then it struck him that his enemy would naturally want to get out of him how much he knew and might already have passed on, before putting him out of the way for good.

But Mahogany Brown had lowered the point of his pistol and was going on: 'I caught you napping and sure put the wind up you, didn't I? You were such a sitting pigeon I thought I'd get a laugh out of announcing myself. Come on. Let's crawl back out of sight of those lousy Czechs, so that if one of them happens to look this way he won't spot us.'

As he spoke, he put his gun back in a shoulder holster, turned round and began to scramble away through the scrub.

Robbie was left speechless. He was overwhelmed with relief at the extraordinary turn affairs had taken but utterly at a loss to understand it. After a moment, he began to wriggle after the American until they were over the brow of the hill and again within a hundred yards of the ruins of Ayia Triada. Getting to their feet, they walked the rest of the way, then Mahogany Brown sat himself down on a low wall, took out his cigarette case, offered it to Robbie who shook his head, lit a cigarette and said:

'Now, stop acting like a clam and tell all you know.'

'I . . . I don't understand,' Robbie muttered.

'Then it's quite time you did. You damned Limeys are too cagey by half. I'm C.I.A. and in Rhodes I indicated that to you clearly enough, but you wouldn't take a hint. You are British M.I., and Standing Orders are that, when the occasion arises, we should work together.'

Robbie shook his head. 'No, I'm not M.I. I assure you I'm not.'

'Oh, cut it out. You're the nephew of the British Ambassador, aren't you? It's no good telling me that he let you go into this thing without putting you in touch with your own Secret Service.'

'My uncle knows nothing about this. He hasn't the faintest idea what I have been doing these past few weeks.'

'Do you really mean to tell me that you're a "lone wolf" and have been risking your neck snooping on the Czechs for the fun of the thing?'

'Well, not exactly for the fun of it. More because I am convinced that they are up to something that will do neither your country nor mine any good.'

'At least, then, you'll see the sense of our working together.'

'Yes,' Robbie agreed heartily. 'I certainly do. But how did you get on to me?'

'About the end of March, someone in Athens suggested to my Chief at N.A.T.O. that we ought to look into the Greco-Czech tobacco-oil deal. It was hinted at the time that a Britisher had already left the city to investigate some of the sites, but, as there were so many of them, it would be a good thing if our people took an interest too. My Chief put two of us on the job. I've been in Lesbos, Chios, Kos and Samos. The day I got to Rhodes, I saw a piece in the Press about a car smash up in the mountains. Your name was mentioned and that of a Mrs. Barak. We had known for some time that Barak was in charge of this so-called oil prospecting, so it looked to me that you might be the British agent we'd heard talk of. I got through to Athens on the blower from our H.Q. in Rhodes. They had had it directly from the police that you had bumped off a Czech strong-arm man named Cepicka; so odds-on I was right.'

The American paused to stub out his cigarette, then he went on: 'Of course, I was only out for information. I didn't expect to run into you, but it was just on the cards that I might; and so happen I did. I went out to Monolithos to see if the site there was any different from those I'd seen in the other islands further north; and there you were. Hoping you'd had better luck than I had, I hooked on to you, but that was as far as I got. Every time I tried to get you to open, you stone-walled me.'

Robbie frowned. 'You certainly asked us any number of direct questions, but you said nothing to let me know that you were a Central Intelligence Agency man. Why didn't you tell me straight out?'

'Because I believed you to be British M.I. If you had been, you'd have got the cue quickly enough. As you didn't respond, I couldn't be certain that my guess about you had been right. Your having left Athens with Mrs. Barak and still having her in tow seemed a mighty queer set-up. I couldn't figure it out at all. But it was just on the cards that you might be playing along with the Czechs and naturally I wasn't taking any chances by showing my hand—not with her around.'

'How did you find out for certain, then, that I was playing the same game as yourself?'

'Your suddenly quitting Rhodes for Crete gave me the idea that you might have got on to something here; so I followed. I got in yesterday evening, but I couldn't trace you; so I came out here this morning. I had a hunch that if I sat around for a while, you might show up. You did, and when I saw you stalking those two Czechs, that told me for sure that you were not on their side but on mine.'

'Well, where do we go from here?' Robbie asked.

'We've got to have a long talk: compare notes. Two heads are always better than one in this game. If we argue round all the possible theories we can think of, we may get somewhere. That is, unless you've already solved this riddle?'

'No; I wish to God I had.'

'I take it, er . . . well, to call a rose by any other name, Julie Thévanaz is still with you?'

'Yes, she's in a car we've hired, down on the road about a mile away, waiting for me.'

The American sat silent for a few moments, then he said: 'Look, friend. I've no wish to butt in on your private life, and I've no doubt you trust her. But that's no reason why I should. I've no intention of discussing this business in front of her, and before we go any further I want your word that you won't let on to her that I'm anything but an American playboy.'

Robbie shook his head. 'I'm afraid I can't give it. Not if we are going to work together. That would mean my leaving her for hours, or perhaps days, and I wouldn't do that without giving her a proper explanation. You see, she's been absolutely marvellous as far as I am concerned. You are right about my having killed Cepicka and being wanted by the police. Without her help, I doubt if I could have kept out of their clutches for twenty-four hours, so——'

'Since you admit to having killed that guy,' Mahogany Brown cut in, 'as I see it, there is only one way you can beat the rap. That is by helping me get the better of the Czechs. If we can pin the goods on them, it is they who will be up before the Judge; then, whatever actually occurred between you and Cepicka, you can plead that it was all part of the job, and put yourself in the clear by pleading self-defence.'

His proposal had exactly the same object as that by which

Stephanie had urged Robbie ten days before at Argos to try to save himself, and which they now hoped to achieve by luring Barak to Crete. But Barak might not take the bait, and here was a second life-line. Robbie was desperately tempted to snatch at it but he felt that, after all Stephanie had done for him and with all she had come to mean to him, he could not possibly deceive her in this way. He was about to say so when the American, who had been watching the struggle plainly to be seen on his features, said:

'It's no good making promises unless you mean to keep them, and it's clear that this woman's got right under your skin. But say, now, could you honestly agree to this? Tell her that I'm C.I.A., and that we're going to work together; but don't disclose to her any information I may give you and keep her absolutely in the dark about any action that we may decide to take.'

'Yes,' said Robbie, 'that's fair enough. I'll agree to that.'

'Right, then, let's get moving. Since she's waiting for you, we'll have to put off our talk, because it's got to be a long one. I take it you are staying in Heraklion?' As the American asked the question, they headed for the track that led down the far side of the hill.

'Yes,' Robbie replied.

'Where about?'

'That's my business.'

Mahogany Brown grinned. 'Afraid I'd make an unwelcome third in your love nest, eh? You needn't worry. It's you I'm interested in at the moment; not Julie, or whatever you care to call her. When I've left you, tell her that we are going to work together and that you are going to have dinner with me this evening at the Heraklion Club, so as to swop information. It's in King Constantine Avenue, so you'll have no difficulty in finding it. The premises and the cooking are not exactly à la Ritz, but they give you an edible meal there, and at the Candia Palace, where I'm staying, guests have to eat out. Be there at seven thirty and I'll be setting up the drinks.'

'How did you get out here?' Robbie asked.

'I hired a motor bike. It's down there among the bushes, just off the road.'

They came to the stream and crossed it in turn on the donkey. As they were walking along the path on its far side, the American said: 'Remember, as far as Julie is concerned, we've met again by chance. I don't want any talk of this and that while she is round. I'll just say that, after leaving Rhodes, I decided to fly down from Athens for a few days in Crete and came out this morning to take a look at Ayia Triada. Later, when you have her alone, you can tell her I'm C.I.A. That way she'll have no chance to ask me any questions to which I'd be put to the bother of thinking up lies for answers. Have you made any plans for lunch?'

'We meant to lunch at the Tourist Pavilion at Phaestos, but I spotted those two Czechs at Gortyne and followed them here.'

Mahogany Brown glanced at his wrist-watch. 'It's only just half after one, and Phaestos is less than six kilometres from here. There's nowhere else within miles where we'd get anything better than a slice of tough goat, olives and sour cheese, so we'd better make for there. I'm told it's worth seeing, too.'

Two minutes later, they came out on the road. Stephanie was still sitting patiently at the wheel of the car. The moment Mahogany Brown came within sight of her, his personality changed back to that of the irrepressibly cheerful young man they had known in Rhodes. Raising his hand, he gave a loud cry.

'Hello! Hello! What d'you know! Just fancy seeing you again. Say, Julie, you're prettier than ever. What a bit of luck for me running into old Max here, while I was giving the once-over to those ruins. I've got a motor bike somewhere round in these bushes. Soon as I can find the darn thing we're all going on to Phaestos, and lunch there is on me.'

Stephanie had enjoyed dancing with him in Rhodes and had encouraged him, not with any view to making Robbie jealous but because his gay, inconsequential chatter helped to keep both her mind and Robbie's off the serious developments that might arise at any time through the police learning Robbie's real identity. Now she was far from pleased that he should have turned up again, since he might prove very difficult to throw off, and their situation in Crete was very different from what it had been in Rhodes. Nevertheless, she returned his greeting with a smile and called out: 'Why, Henry, what a lovely surprise to find you here.'

Henry found his motor cycle. Stephanie turned the car round and ten minutes later they were winding their way up the hill on which stood the ruins of Phaestos.

The situation of the Palace had been greatly superior to that of Knossos, as the hill that it crowned lay between two ranges of mountains, and it had been built in a series of terraces looking out on the long valley between them. The Tourist Pavilion was above the highest of these terraces; so while they ate a pleasant lunch on the shady verandah, they had the ruins just below them and could admire the splendid twenty-mile-long vista.

Over the meal, they talked of the international situation. The American said that he had found Athens almost empty of foreigners. The tourist season, which meant so much to Greece and which should now be in full swing, had been ruined, the Stock Markets had taken another plunge after the break-down of the Delhi Conference, and many rich Greeks were leaving the capital, either for places in the country or the islands in the Aegean, because they thought that would give them a better chance of survival in the event of war. But he was still of the opinion that there would not be war.

The crew of the submarine was reported to be in good shape. Modern scientific devices in the ship would enable them to remain so for several weeks to come, without being compelled to surface for air. The United States had long since made a declaration that she would never be the first to launch a nuclear conflict, and the Russians would be mad to do so. There was still plenty of time for further negotiations and, in some way or other, a compromise would be reached. 'Any-how,' the optimistic Mr. Mahogany Brown concluded, 'if the Russians do go crackers and start the big party, we couldn't be better situated than we are right now. No one's going to waste an I.C.B.M. on Crete.'

When they had finished lunch, they spent an hour wandering about the great open courts, broad imposing stairways and small rooms of the Palace. It was not so large as Knossos but, with its many terraces, must have been much more beautiful. It had been destroyed in the same great earthquake that had devastated the island from end to end somewhere about 1400 B.C.

A little before four o'clock, they set off back to Heraklion. As Mahogany Brown started up his motor bike, he gave a casual wave, shouted 'I'll be seeing you', then roared away.

Stephanie let in the clutch of the car and, as it sped down the hill, said to Robbie: 'Fancy running into him again. How unlike him, though, not to have suggested our doing something together this evening. He didn't even ask where we were staying. Or did you fob him off by giving him a false address when you were up there with him at Ayia Triada?'

'No. But he gave me the fright of my life.' Robbie then told her how Mahogany Brown had held him up, and of their conversation afterwards.

She made no comment until he had finished, then she said: 'It was very loyal of you, Robbie, to have refused to co-operate with him without telling me. I take it you didn't deny that I was Mrs. Barak?'

'No. I saw no point in doing so. During the few days between your reported death and his coming upon us at Mono-lithos, the odds against my having found another woman who more or less answered your description and was willing to pose as my wife would be fantastic.'

'That's true; and, knowing me to be Václav's wife, it's perfectly understandable that he should be unwilling to trust me.'

'I didn't give him any particulars about what happened, but gave him simply to understand that you were on our side and that it was only by your help that I had so far kept out of the hands of the police.'

'He would put that down to the belief that we ran away from Athens together as lovers; but that doesn't make me any the less a Czech. You were absolutely right, though, to accept the compromise he suggested. Václav may not take the bait I offered, and this gives you another chance to justify your having killed Cepicka. That's the all-important thing. How about our

an, though? If Václav does come to Heraklion, do yo
let Henry know?'

'No, I don't think there's anything to be gained by
at. Quite apart from getting all I can out of Barak, I've
personal score to settle with him and I don't want any int
rence.'

It was half-past-six by the time they were back in Heraklion.
arking the car in Morosini Square, they went over to a café
have a drink. They noticed then that little groups of people
ere standing about, either moodily or arguing excitedly to-
ether. As they gave their order to a waiter, they learnt the
eason. At midday Russia had issued an ultimatum to the
nited States. Either the submarine must be surrendered intact
ithin seven days or mines would be exploded in the ice under
hich she lay, to drive her out.

That was grim news. Actually to attack the submarine
ould almost certainly lead to war. The Americans were a
roud and courageous people. In every country, there was
lways a 'peace at any price' party, but the majority would
ot submit to the humiliation of allowing their warship to be
estroyed without retaliating. The Russians must realize that
o, had they really wanted a 'showdown', surely, instead of
suing an ultimatum, they could have blown New York off
he map without warning. Even so, things had now reached a
oint where an impatient finger on a trigger might cause that
o happen at any moment.

When Stephanie and Robbie had talked over this latest
ews and finished their drink, it was time for him to walk up
he street to the Heraklion Club. Next day, there might be a
etter for Stephanie from Barak; so it was agreed that, after
he had called at the G.P.O., she should come in the car to their
sual meeting place at ten o'clock. If there were no letter, and
Mahogany Brown had not asked Robbie to give him his help
n some way, they would spend the day motoring to the east
long the northern coast of Crete, to see other remains of the
Minoan Age and the bay of Malea with its scores of windmills.

Robbie found the entrance to the Club without difficulty
nd a lift took him up to the premises, which proved to be airy
ut bleak. Mahogany Brown was waiting for him at the cloak-

...unter and led him straight down a long passage, pa...
...in which some men were playing billiards, to the resta...
It was a large, lofty room that had only about twen...
...es in it, although it could easily have held double th...
...mber. There was a bar in one corner and, beside one end...
..., a serving door to the kitchen, which stood open, revealing...
chef and three women all talking at the tops of their voice...
Apart from them and a solitary waiter the place was empt...
as it was well before the hour at which the Greeks usual...
dine.

The waiter served them drinks and they carried them ov...
to a table in a far corner of the room, then got down...
exchanging information. It soon transpired that all the group...
which either of them had investigated were carrying out exact...
similar operations, the drilling of a single, deep hole about...
foot in diameter, with long screws having in their centre...
hollow eight or more inches across. It was not until Robb...
gave an account of the conversation he had overheard...
Gortyne that morning between the two Czechs that Mahogan...
Brown showed sudden interest.

'So he wanted to drop one down the Zeus Grotto, eh?' h...
said. 'Well, anyway, that confirms my guess that they mean t...
put something down those holes. But what? Have you any so...
of idea?'

'Atom bombs,' replied Robbie promptly. 'Or rather,...
suppose, by this time they've got cobalt bombs.'

'I thought of that. But there'd be no sense in it. Even th...
site we saw today on the bay of Mesara is several miles from...
our big, new air base, and none of the others are anywhere nea...
important military installations. What would be the point o...
blowing great holes in the Greek coastline and several of th...
islands?'

'At one time, I thought they might be installing some form...
of radar gadget which would, in some way, assist Russian sub...
marines,' Robbie remarked.

'That would make more sense, but why the holes?'

'I don't know a thing about science, so I couldn't even mak...
a guess. From tonight's news, though, it looks as if we ma...

soon be given the answer in a way we won't like. Or are you still of the opinion you expressed at lunch?'

Mahogany Brown shook his fair, crew-cut head. 'What I said at lunch was all hooey, except for one thing. That was that, if the big bang is coming, we're as well placed here to survive as anywhere, except the outspots like darkest Africa or Peru.'

'You think it really looks like war, then?'

'I wouldn't wager more than evens that it won't come to that. We've been at maximum alert since midday, and whatever declarations may have been made from the White House, I wouldn't put it past one of our top brass in the Pentagon letting off the fireworks rather than risk letting the Russians have first crack at us.'

'If we are as near the edge as that, why in God's name don't your people go right into these sites and stop the Czechs doing whatever they are at?' Robbie asked.

'Because the Greeks won't let us.' Mahogany Brown beckoned the waiter over to replenish their drinks, then he went on: 'That's the big handicap the West has been up against all the time. Moscow has only to say the word to get done in any of the Iron Curtain countries anything the Kremlin boys want —and done at once. But N.A.T.O. has to say "Please may we?" to the Governments of each separate sovereign State in the Alliance when she wants some action taken in that State's territory. To get a reply usually takes months and, when it does come, often as not it's "No".'

'Yes, I realize that. But surely, in a case like this, you could have got the Greek Government to send their own people in to inspect these sites and find out what the Czechs are up to?'

'That's what my Chief tried to do. But the Greeks wouldn't wear it. The trouble is that West and East have played at Brinkmanship for so long that most people simply won't believe that it will now ever come to a hot war. Stockholders get the jitters, but they do that anyway every year or two when there's a threat of depression, or it looks as if a disarmament agreement is at last going to put half the world's heavy industry out of business; tourists get out in a hurry because, rather than face even a remote possibility of being cut off in a foreign country,

folk naturally incline to beat it for their homes. But Govern
ments don't scare all that easy. The Greeks are getting wha
they regard as a lot of money for nothing out of this tobacco
oil deal and, so far, they've had only a ten per cent payment o
signing of contract so, naturally, they don't want to upset th
Czechs before they get the rest.'

'One couldn't blame them for that if the Czechs really wer
prospecting for oil. But we know they are not. They are no
using the right kind of apparatus. If your Chief made that clea
to the Greek Government——'

'He has, but it's cut no ice. The Czech story is that the
are using an entirely new process, and it is their secret. That'
why, when it was tentatively suggested to them that they shoul
allow an inspection, their refusal sounded quite reasonable t
the Greeks. And Greece is a poor country, remember. Thin
what it would mean to the Greeks if the Czechs really did strik
oil. Looked at from their point of view, one can't expect then
to risk busting their chances of a bonanza just because a
American sub. has got herself stuck in Soviet waters and ther
is one more of those recurrent crises that we've had durin
most of our lives.'

They went out to the kitchen, where the fat, cheerful che
produced in a ladle for their inspection various bits and piece
from his row of big, bubbling pots. Mahogany Brown chos
one of those mysterious stews. Robbie hesitated over chicken
but as, owing to lack of corn, the hens in Greece were alway
so small and skinny he settled for fried meat balls.

By then, half a dozen men had come into the dining room
but none of them was near enough to the table that Mahogany
Brown had chosen to overhear their conversation; so, whe
they were settled at it again, Robbie asked:

'If the Russians do bore through the ice to depth-charg
the submarine, what will happen? She must have a dozen o
more missiles on board, so could fire them off. Won't the
Russians be afraid that she may, and might blot out Moscow?'

'No, she couldn't do that. If she were clear of the ice and a
sea, she could. But the several feet of ice on top of her would b
certain to deflect the aim of the missiles. I don't know enough
about it to speak for sure, but I think the chances are tha

itting the solid ice would cause them to go off prematurely.
n that case, the back blast would blow her to bits. Of course,
 would put paid to any part of the Soviet Fleet that was
ithin miles. But the Russians regard ships and men as expend-
ble; so they wouldn't lose much sleep over the sinking of a
ew mine-laying vessels and, perhaps, a couple of cruisers.'

'Say the worst happens,' Robbie enquired. 'How do you
hink things will go?'

Mahogany Brown poured some more vinegar over the stew
e was eating, and shrugged. 'Your picture is probably as good
s mine. Even if the Russians do strike first and blot out New
'ork, Chicago, Detroit, London, Paris and various other big
entres of production, we'll flatten Moscow, Leningrad, Kiev,
harkhov, Warsaw, Prague and so on. But the earth is one hell
f a big place and there's a limit to the damage that the
.C.B.M.s can do, even allowing for fall-out. After a few days
he missiles will have been used up, then what's known as the
'broken back" war will begin.'

Having tossed back half a glass of the Cretan red wine they
ere drinking, he went on: 'As I see it, the big problem is
oing to be getting rid of the millions of dead before a plague
ets in. But, providing an epidemic doesn't kill off those of us
ho are left, the survivors in the fighting services on both
ides will gradually get themselves organized and set about
aving old-fashioned battles.'

'If they do, they will be pretty well back to bows and
rrows.'

'Oh no; not necessarily. When I said old-fashioned, I meant
ort of 1914–18, or maybe even 1939–45. There should be
uite a few ships, aircraft and tanks left around, and the
inner is going to be the side that's got the oil to run
hem. That's why, strategically speaking, the Aegean is so
mportant. Nine-tenths of Russia's oil is concentrated in the
'aucasus and Rumania. The nearer our subs can get to those
ields, the more accurate the aim of their missiles will be. They
aren't go through the Bosphorus into the Black Sea. That
ould be too risky. But you can be sure we have a number
f them sitting on the bottom of the Aegean right now, ready to
last off at the word "go"; so as to make certain of putting

the Soviet oil wells out of business even before the "broke
back" war gets going.'

They finished off their meal with slices of an incredib[l]
sweet cake that consisted mainly of crystallized fruit, then ha[d]
Turkish coffee and Greek brandy. As they were about to leav[e]
the table, Mahogany Brown said: 'I shall get on to my Chi[ef]
tonight, to let him know that bit you picked up today abo[ut]
dropping things down grottoes, and urge that he have anoth[er]
crack at the Greeks to go in and find out what it is the Czech[s]
mean to drop. For the moment, I don't see what else we ca[n]
do. But I'd like you to keep in touch, because a lone wolf lik[e]
you can sometimes do things that I'm barred from doing unle[ss]
I go against Standing Orders and risk blotting my copy-boo[k.]
Look in at the Candia Palace, just along the street here, roun[d]
midday tomorrow, will you?'

Robbie promised to do so, then the American said: 'Ju[st]
one other thing. I'm holding you to your word not to mentio[n]
to Madame Barak anything we've discussed. How she save[d]
her pretty neck after she was supposed to have gone over th[e]
precipice in your car I wouldn't know, and I'm not askin[g.]
But one thing I am certain about. It is that the Czechs fixe[d]
it that you should take her with you when you left Athens, s[o]
that she could report back to them how much you were findin[g]
out. Maybe that's news to you. If so, I'm sorry to have spoile[d]
any illusions you may have about her having gone with you a[t]
for love. But there it is. She started out on the other side, an[d]
maybe is so still. So, for the sake of the Europe that yo[u]
evidently like, not to mention the old U.S. that means a lot t[o]
me, you've really got to watch your step with her.'

With a rueful grin, Robbie replied: 'Since you know s[o]
much I'll admit that, to begin with, she was acting under he[r]
husband's orders. But after we met Barak on the mountai[n]
road, he pushed her over the precipice and I had the luck t[o]
save her. As a result of that, she is completely through wit[h]
him and has come over to us.'

'Maybe she is through with him as a person. If they ha[d]
still been turtle-doves, it's odds-on he would have found som[e]
other cutie to lead you up the garden path. But, in my experi[-]
ence, once a Communist always a Communist, with onl[y]

remarkably rare exceptions; so keep on loving her plenty if you wish, but do it with your mouth shut.'

After spending another far from comfortable night in his draughty hide-out, Robbie went to a barber's, had himself shaved, then met Stephanie on the corner of Liberty Square. As soon as he was in the car, she said with an excitement which she could not altogether conceal: 'At the G.P.O. I picked up a letter from Václav. He is arriving by the evening's plane and, as I suggested, has asked me to meet him.'

'Thank God for that!' Robbie exclaimed. 'I can't say that I am looking forward to taking him to pieces, but the way things are developing, it has become terribly urgent to force him to talk. I've just got to put any scruples about fair play behind me.'

'How did you get on last night with Henry?' she asked.

'Very well, although he's still no wiser than we are about the so-called oil prospecting. I told him that your husband had tried to do you in, and that you had since come over to us. But he wouldn't take my word for that. I have to meet him at the Candia Palace at midday.'

'Then that knocks on the head a trip down to Malea to see the windmills. We couldn't possibly get back in time. How would you like to fill in the morning?'

'We might run out to Knossos and spend an hour there. I'm sure there are lots of it that we haven't yet seen.'

Without comment she accepted his suggestion and, twenty minutes later, they left the car in the parking place, took tickets and again made their way across to the vast pile of ruins.

After exploring the treasury and store-rooms on the eastern side of the slope and admiring the giant oil jars which—shades of Ali Baba and the Forty Thieves—could each have held four men, they made their way up again to the reconstructed parts with their curious red pillars, broader at the top than at the base, and gaily painted walls. For the second time they strolled through the room of the Double Axes, the room of the Dolphin frescoes and the Throne Room, in which the throne—a leaf-back stone chair with a hollowed seat, and the oldest throne in the world—still stood.

In all the principal rooms, to one side or in a corner, steps led down to a sunken area several feet below the level of the floor. On their first visit, a guide had told them that these pits had been filled with sacred water, because the Minoans were so superstitious that they were constantly feeling the need to purify themselves by total immersion.

Looking down into one of the pits, Stephanie remarked: 'You know, I can't believe that a people so civilized as the Minoans were so obsessed by their religion that, every time they ate or kissed or told a naughty story, they felt such a compulsion to cleanse themselves by jumping into holy water that they couldn't wait but had to have a bath of it in every room.'

Robbie smiled. 'No, I'm sure the guide was wrong about that. The Minoans were so far advanced as architects, with their drainage and that sort of thing, I should think it certain that these pits in every room have something to do with minimizing the effects of the earth tremors. That ties up with the established fact that the Minoans held all their public ceremonies in the great open courtyards, and built only small rooms indoors; so that they would stand up better against earthquakes.'

As Robbie said this last word, his mouth remained open on the last syllable and his eyes suddenly grew wide.

'Whatever is the matter?' Stephanie asked, giving him an anxious look.

'Earthquakes,' he repeated. 'Earthquakes; earthquakes. My God, I've got it! That's the answer.'

After a quick look round to make sure that no guides or visitors to the ruins were within earshot, he hurried on: 'Don't you see? Every site to which we've been has suffered from a series of earthquakes. All the Aegean islands are subject to them. Many were thrown up by them, even, according to the ancient chronicles, the great island of Rhodes. Barak and Co. mean to drop H-bombs down those holes and, when the time comes, explode them underground. Explosions in a confined space have many times the power that the same amount of explosives would have in the open. These won't only rend vast holes in the earth; the shock will operate downwards, too. The crust of the earth is thin here and violent fires are always raging beneath it. The shock of each explosion will link up with that of the next in the chain. Rents scores of miles long will be torn in the land and under the water. The sea will boil, whole mountains will come sliding down. It will be just like another war of the gods and titans. The bomb at Corinth will destroy the isthmus so that the Peloponnesus will become an island. All round Greece, and right up to the Dardanelles, the whole coastline will be changed.'

Taking Stephanie by the arm, he added: 'Come along. I mustn't lose a moment in letting Henry know about this.'

As they hurried back to the car, she said: 'I can't believe that even a dozen H-bombs would have quite such terrible results. But say you are right; what is the object of destroying great chunks of Greece? What have the Soviets to gain by churning the Aegean into a raging lake, just for a day or two?'

'It will be far more than that. Parts of it would become impassable, owing to the vast quantities of molten lava and mud thrown up. That would take months to settle. In the meantime, the levels of its bottom would have altered so much that all navigational charts would be rendered useless. Every ship in it would be wrecked, and that's what they are gunning for. They are planning to bring about this cataclysm in order to knock out at one stroke every U.S. submarine in the north-eastern Med.'

Sixteen minutes later, Stephanie pulled the car up outside the Candia Palace Hotel. As Robbie was about to jump out, she said quickly: 'Shall I wait for you or shall we meet somewhere?'

Stepping on to the pavement, he replied: 'I may be some time. Better go to some small restaurant and wait for me. I know; go to that little place where we lunched on Sunday. It was called the Ariadne. We'll lunch there again.'

It was only twenty to twelve, so he was early for his appointment. At the desk, he learned that Mahogany Brown was up in his room; so he rang through, said he wanted to see him urgently and asked if he might come up. Two minutes later he was shown into a bedroom where the American was sitting with his coat off, working at some papers at a small table by the window.

After one look at Robbie's face, he grinned and asked:

'What's cooking? Have you just heard that the police are on to you at last?'

Robbie gave a quick shake of his head and launched straight into his theory. Hardly pausing to draw breath, he spoke for three minutes. As Mahogany Brown listened, his expression changed gradually from mild scepticism to wondering dismay. Having heard Robbie out, he exclaimed:

'Hell's bells! I believe you've hit it. And if you're right about all these places being so susceptible to earthquakes, this could lose us the war.'

'There is no question about the situation of the earthquake belt,' Robbie assured him. 'It runs from Naples in the north and Sicily in the south, right across Greece and the Aegean to Turkey. Any geologist will confirm that. They may be playing some game similar to this in Italian territory; but I doubt it. You were saying last night that the nearer your submarines could get to Rumania and the Balkan wells, the better their aim would be. From that it follows that they wouldn't be stationed off Italy, but in the Gulf of Corinth and the Aegean. The only thing which might make nonsense of my theory is if a dozen nuclear bombs with intervals of so many miles between them would be insufficient to do the trick.'

Mahogany Brown considered for a moment, then he said: 'One of those Czechs you overheard talking at Gortyne spoke of dropping cylinders five feet long. Given an eight-inch diameter, now that the mechanism to explode such bombs has been so much reduced in size, they could contain as much fissionable material as would go into the warhead of an I.C.B.M. and, of course, they could be exploded by remote control. The Russians are believed to have about fifty I.C.B.M.s, and with those they reckon they could flatten most of the principal cities in the West. Things have gone a long way since Hiroshima. It's calculated now that the bomb used there was only about the power of old-fashioned T.N.T., compared with the power of the stuff we have now. One megaton of it would render a thousand square miles of territory uninhabitable. That should give you the picture.'

Robbie drew a sharp breath. 'Then I'm right. Even if those cylinders contain only a quarter of the load in the war-head of an I.C.B.M., a dozen of them would set earthquakes going that would destroy the islands and tear southern Greece into pieces. As for your subs. in the Aegean, they would be thrown about like matchsticks and smashed to bits.'

'You've said it, friend.' The American grabbed his coat. 'I'm off to my local H.Q., to get on the "blower" to my Chief in Athens. I'm telling him that he's got to act fast and, whether the Greeks like it or not, bust this Czech oil-prospecting wide open. If you're wrong, I'll be out on my ear; but if you're right, I'll get the Congressional Medal and be the No. 1 hero in the United States.'

As they went down together in the lift, he said to Robbie: 'I gather that this big think came to you while you were out at Knossos this morning. Was your girl friend with you?'

'Yes. That car you saw us in yesterday is one we've hired for the week in her name, and whenever we go anywhere she still does the driving.'

'Did you tell her this theory of yours?'

'I saw no reason why I shouldn't. It has nothing to do with any arrangements between you and me; so my telling her didn't infringe our pact.'

'Sure, sure. I'm not complaining. You'll be seeing her again shortly, I take it?'

'Yes, we're lunching together.'

'Well, she's certain to want to know what I thought of your idea and I'd be glad if you said that I didn't consider it practical. We can't be too careful. Where will you be lunching, in case I want to get in touch with you?'

'At a little place called the Ariadne.'

'Good. I don't suppose I'll be bothering you but, as you're so cagey about giving me your address, you'd best look in here again this evening, round seven o'clock, to see if I've left a message for you.'

By this time, they had reached the entrance to the hotel. They parted on the pavement outside, Mahogany Brown to get on his motor cycle and Robbie to walk down to the Ariadne.

Stephanie was having a drink at one of the tables on the

narrow pavement. As Robbie sat down beside her, she said eagerly: 'Well?'

He grinned at her. 'Henry is still afraid that you are in secret communication with your husband; so he didn't want me to tell you. But I made no promise that I wouldn't. He thinks I'm right, and by this time he will be in communication with his Chief in Athens. He means to push him into having all the sites raided, and hopes to get the Congressional Medal for having spiked the great Communist plot.'

'What cheek!' Stephanie exclaimed indignantly. 'He hasn't discovered a thing. All the credit for this ought to go to you.'

Robbie shrugged. 'I don't give a damn who gets the credit. What matters is preventing the possibility of this part of the Med. being blown up, and the destruction of the U.S. subs.'

'Anyway, you are safe now. Once the sites have been raided and the plot uncovered, no one is going to hold it against you that you killed Cepicka while trying to prevent Greece being blown off the map. I think we ought to celebrate. Instead of lunching in this shoddy little place, let's go down to the Glass House.'

'I told Henry I'd be lunching here, in case he wanted to get hold of me,' Robbie demurred. 'Still, he said that was unlikely, and I promised to look in at the Candia Palace about seven, to pick up any message he might have left during the afternoon. So let's leave it at that.'

At the Glass House, a quarter of an hour later, they found that the chef had just had in some live crayfish; so they selected a fine hen and, while it was being boiled, they ordered the rest of their meal at a table at the far end of the restaurant. When the waiter had taken their order, Stephanie said: 'What shall we do about Václav?'

'You mean, what is the best way to secure him when you have brought him along to me?'

'No.' She shook her head. 'I wasn't thinking of that. I was wondering if you still wish me to meet him. After your wonderful hunch this morning, and now that Henry is acting on it, we could let sleeping dogs lie. You never have liked the idea of taking him to pieces. Now, apart from the fact that you hate him on account of what he did to me, there's no reason why you should.'

After a moment, Robbie replied thoughtfully: 'I think you're wrong there. I feel pretty certain my guess is the right one, but there's a chance that it might not be. There's a chance, too, that Henry's Chief may refuse to believe him and do nothing, anyhow for the present. Your getting Barak here will give us the opportunity of making certain, and I don't think we ought to throw it away.'

'Very well, then. His plane is due in at the airport at ten to five. That means that I should be able to deliver him over to your tender mercies at about half past. Unless, of course, he wants to register at an hotel first and drop his bag. In that case, it will be nearer six. But you'll be careful how you tackle him, won't you? Remember, it is you he is coming to get, and it's certain that he'll be carrying a gun.'

'You bet I'll be careful,' Robbie smiled. 'I should look pretty silly if this boomeranged on me.'

'You wouldn't have a chance to look anything,' Stephanie told him grimly. 'Once I've led him into the ambush there must be no mistakes. When we've finished lunch, we'll go over to your hide-out and work everything out very carefully.'

About half-past-two, Stephanie drove the car back to its garage, while Robbie made his way to the half-ruined house among the rubble. Half an hour later, she joined him. Their problem was to think of a way by which Robbie could stun Barak, by hitting him over the head with a sandbag, before he realized that he had fallen into a trap and drew his gun. Their difficulty was that there was no place in the house in which Robbie could lie concealed and that, being empty, even taking a few steps on tiptoe from one room to another meant boards creaking so loudly that they would give away a stealthy approach.

After much discussion it was decided that Barak must be ambushed outside the house and, as this required darkness to prevent anyone seeing from a distance the assault on him, the following plan was adopted: Stephanie was to tell him that Robbie had gone over to Phaestos to see what he could find

out about the site there, and he would not be back until eight
o'clock. When he returned he would go straight to his hide-out
for a meal, since he avoided as far as possible being seen in
the town from fear of the police. She would take Barak to
the hide-out about half-past-seven, and he could lie in wait
for Robbie there. That was the sort of set-up that Stephanie
had suggested in her letter, and it would still be daylight when
she brought Barak to the house; so there would be no reason
for him to suspect that she was leading him into a trap.

Actually, however, a little before the time that Barak was
due to arrive at the house Robbie would conceal himself
behind the low wall outside it. Having brought Barak there,
Stephanie would leave him. The half hour would pass and
twilight would be falling. Barak, believing Robbie's return to
have been delayed by some unforeseen circumstance, would
continue to wait for another hour, perhaps two, or it might
even be three. But it was certain that by midnight, at the latest,
he would become so weary of standing in the darkness that he
would throw in his hand and decide to go to his hotel. As he
passed along the low wall, Robbie would then rise up, slog
him on the back of the head and drag him into the house. The
plan might mean a long vigil for Robbie, but it reduced to a
minimum the risk that he might be shot by Barak before he
could overcome him.

At four o'clock, Stephanie left to collect the car and drive
out to the airport. Robbie also went out and bought some stout
cord with which to tie up Barak. On his return to the house, he
tore an old shirt into strips, suitable for gagging his enemy,
and put them in his pocket, then filled a sock about a third
full of finely crumbled plaster. These preparations completed,
he had a meal from one of the tins and some of the fruit
Stephanie had bought for him and washed it down with half
a bottle of the red wine.

By that time it was half-past-five. As there was just a chance
that Barak, believing him to be absent at Phaestos, might
demand to be driven straight to the hide-out so that he could
reconnoitre it in daylight before returning later to lie in wait
there, Robbie decided to play for safety and leave the house.
Putting a slab of chocolate, some biscuits and a paper-back

thriller' in his pockets, he went out and selected his hiding-place.

The wall ran from the side of the house down to the great barn that was used as a sawmill and faced on to the road along the sea front. From the road a track led up along the side of the barn to the beginning of the wall, and up to the end of that track Stephanie would bring Barak in the car; after that they would have to walk. The wall was broken and crumbling in places, so Robbie had no difficulty in finding a spot only about thirty feet from the house where he could force out a few bricks and so make himself a spy hole which would command the approach to the building. Having got over the wall he settled down with his back to it, on a pillow which he had brought out with him, then endeavoured to concentrate on his 'thriller'.

For a variety of reasons he found it far from easy to do so. He still disliked intensely the idea of tying up any man—even the husband who had been cruel to Stephanie and had attempted to murder her—and torturing him. The thought that Stephanie was again with her husband filled him with uneasiness. To carry out their plan, she would have to spend at least two and a half hours with him and, excellent actress though he was, should she make a slip during that long session in her husband's company, not only would their plan be brought to naught but she would then be in great danger. There was also the chance that the plan might somehow go wrong. Robbie could think of no reason why it should but, all the same, the thought that if it did he would probably pay for it with his life was distinctly unnerving.

For the next two hours, in fits and starts, he read a few pages of his book then, each time realizing that he had not taken in a word of what he had been reading, he turned back and went over most of the passage again. By half-past-seven the light began to fail; so he put the book in his pocket and, knowing that if Stephanie had succeeded with her part of the plan she should soon be bringing Barak to the house, he began to listen intently.

About ten minutes later he caught the sound of a car approaching, and it pulled up not very far away. Then came

footsteps. But they puzzled him, for it sounded as though mor
than two pairs of feet, and one of them a woman's, wer
crunching the rubble. Anxiously, he peered through the spy
hole he had made. He suppressed a gasp of dismay and hi
heart began to hammer heavily. Stephanie was leading, bu
there were two men behind her. Barak must have brought on
of his thugs to help him exact vengeance on the man who ha
ruined his looks.

The party of three went on into the house. Robbie sat dow
again and endeavoured to rally his wits to cope with this un
foreseen complication. Stephanie must have received the sam
shock as he had, on finding that Barak had brought one o
his men with him; but, having met him, she had evidentl
found herself unable to think of any excuse for not taking then
both to Robbie's hide-out. According to plan, having led Baral
there, she should now come out of the house leaving hin
behind. But his companion would remain with him. If, later
they left together, Robbie could have no possible hope o
knocking out both of them. Even if Barak came out alone
leaving his underling to remain on watch, Robbie would no
be able to sandbag him without the other man hearing the
scuffling on the rubble and appearing on the scene to find ou
what was going on.

Clearly the whole plan had broken down. The only thing to
do now was to wait till Stephanie came out, follow her to the
car and go off with her to some place where they could talk
over the situation, devise some new plan to trap Barak or, i
that seemed beyond them, agree to abandon their idea o
forcing him to disclose his secret.

Anxiously, Robbie waited for the sound of Stephanie's
light footfalls as she walked from the house; but they did no
come. After a while he decided that Barak must be keeping
her there, to ensure that she should not give way to a last-
minute change of heart and waylay Robbie to warn him tha
she had betrayed him. They had envisaged such a possibility
but had agreed that Stephanie's being with Barak when Robbie
knocked him out would have no adverse effect on their plan.
The only thing Stephanie had stipulated was that she should
not be present afterwards for, although she had not an atom of

love left for her husband, she was still averse to standing by and watching while he was maltreated.

For over an hour, that seemed like an eternity, Robbie sat behind the low wall, straining his ears. Darkness had fallen and, being so near the house, he could see tiny chinks of light round the edges of the black-out curtains in the upper room. Now and again a low, indistinct murmur, which he knew must be muffled voices, came to him, but that gave no indication of what was going on up there. He had been due to return at eight, and a glance at the luminous dial of his wrist-watch showed him that it was a quarter to nine. Barak, he felt, must by now be becoming impatient.

Ten minutes later, he had evidence of it. The murmur coming from above suddenly became louder and faintly there came to him what sounded like cries of protest. There was a brief interval of silence, then the sounds of a scuffle, followed by a wail of pain. The blood drained from Robbie's face. Those sounds could mean only that, on his failure to appear, Barak had become suspicious that Stephanie had deliberately misled him, and was now trying to drag out of her the truth about where Robbie might be found.

The thought of the extent to which their plan to trap Barak had now miscarried appalled him. Standing up, he stared with agonized gaze at the blacked-out windows. His imagination ran riot as he visualized the scene now taking place behind them. Stephanie bound and with the end of a lighted cigarette pressed against her skin, or her arm being twisted to near-breaking point behind her back, or Barak's fingers clutching her throat, so that she could get her breath only in gasps at intervals when the pressure was relaxed.

But what could he do? To dash into the house and attempt to rescue her from two armed men would be hopeless. He would be riddled with bullets before he could even strike a blow. In desperation, he looked about him. He could run to the road and back along the quarter of a mile of deserted sea-wall to the harbour, then up into the town until he met a policeman. But when he did, would one policeman be willing to return with him, and go into the house, knowing that there were two men in it who, rather than allow themselves to be arrested, might shoot him?

Robbie's glance suddenly came to rest on lights sixty yards away. They were those of the car at the end of the track. As twilight had been falling when Stephanie drove up, she had switched them on before leaving the car. He had not driven a car since he had taken the Ford Zephyr into Pirgos, but he knew that most cars were much alike; so he should be able to get this one started and drive it to the police station. The explanations he would have to give there would necessitate his giving himself up but, in the circumstances, he felt that was a small price to pay for help.

He started off towards the car. Before he had taken two paces that muffled, agonized wail came again. The sound brought him to a halt. He had no idea where the police station was. Even if he met with no hitch in starting the car, a quarter of an hour or more must elapse while he enquired the whereabouts of the station, then found it. To rush in, shouting that a woman was being tortured, would not be enough. He would have to give particulars, perhaps to some slow-witted junior who might insist on taking them down, then repeat them to someone higher up before any action was taken. Even after that further time would be needed for the return journey. Given the best of luck, it would be twenty-five minutes before he could bring a squad of police to the house, and it might well be forty.

Meantime, what would be happening to Stephanie? In the space of half an hour, she could be made to suffer terribly. Far worse, having wrung all he could out of her, Barak might kill her. He had failed when he pushed her over the precipice, but here there was no one per cent chance of her possible survival should he decide to rid himself of her for good, and no attempt could be made to stop him. In a matter of minutes, he could strangle her and, with the help of his man, in a further ten carry out her body and bury it under a pile of rubble. If Robbie went for the police, it could easily be all over by the time he came back with them; Stephanie dead: her body hidden, Barak and his thug gone and only Robbie's word for it that they had ever been there.

Driven frantic with fear that Stephanie might be murdered before he could get help, he decided to go in. Whatever Stephanie had said to Barak, he would hardly ignore the possibility that Robbie might return to the house. Therefore it seemed certain that, while he held her prisoner upstairs, he would have left his companion downstairs; so that he could hold up Robbie the moment he entered the front door. If that were so, Robbie felt that he had at least a sporting chance, because he could enter the house from the side where the wall had collapsed. With luck, he might take the man on guard by surprise, overcome him and get his weapon. Then the odds between Barak and himself would be even.

Quickly, but as quietly as possible, Robbie moved round to the side of the house. He was armed only with the plaster-filled sock and, while that would be as good a weapon as any for knocking out an unsuspecting man from behind, he might have to tackle his opponent from the front. Fortunately, amongst the rubble of the kitchen wall, there were a number of pieces of broken wood. He knew roughly where they lay and the star-light was now sufficient for him to find them without difficulty. Hastily he rummaged amongst them, discarded two or three, and chose a tapering piece about three feet long, with a thick end, that would make a good club.

Stepping over what was left of the side wall of the kitchen, he tiptoed across it. As he did so, the fallen plaster crunched under his feet. Actually the sound it made was faint, but to him, in his state of acute tension, it seemed so loud that his enemies could not fail to hear it. At the doorway to the hall, he paused for a moment. Down its side showed a two-inch-wide streak of faint light. When he had first taken up his quarters in the house he had tried to shut this door, but the wood had swollen and it had jammed like that. The question that now faced him was—should he attempt to ease it open on the chance that he would not be heard, or should he wrench it wide and go bald-headed for Barak's watch-dog, if he were standing on the other side?

As Robbie stood there, he clearly heard a moan that came from upstairs. Spurred to action by this confirmation of his belief that Stephanie was being tortured, he pulled the door open. There was no one in the hall but next moment a dark figure showed up in the faint light, emerging from what had been the sitting room. Robbie raised his club high and rushed at it. The figure side-stepped so that the club, instead of striking it on the head, came down on the shoulder. At the same moment, a pistol flashed. The bullet struck Robbie in the upper part of his right arm, partially swinging him round. The club dropped from his nerveless fingers. He heard a clatter of feet on the stairs and realized that Barak was plunging down them. As he turned his head to look up at Barak the man who had shot him hit him hard under the chin, knocking his head back violently against the door post. The double blow made his head sing. The bitter thought that he had failed, and failed dismally, entered Robbie's mind then his knees gave, he slumped to the floor and passed out.

He was not out for long. When he came to, Barak and the other man were dragging him up the steep stairs. By the time they threw him down on the bedroom floor, his eyes were wide open and taking in everything round him; but his right arm was hanging limp, he had lost his club and he was miserably aware that Barak had him at his mercy.

As he sat up, his glance met Stephanie's. She was sitting in the folding canvas-backed chair she had bought for him. The cord he had bought only that afternoon, with the optimistic intention of using it to bind Barak, now bound her. Its ends secured her wrists to the two flat pieces of wood that served as the arms of the chair. Her hair was dishevelled, her blouse torn open, tears were streaming down her cheeks and a towel was over her mouth. Its two ends dangled behind her, so that it could be pulled tight to muffle her cries.

Suddenly, to his horror, Robbie saw that the two middle fingers of her right hand were bent back unnaturally. It was obvious that, while her wrist was tied, the finger tips had been raised and gradually turned over backwards, until the joints at her palm had broken, enabling the useless fingers to lie at an acute angle to the back of her hand, which was now dripping blood.

If Robbie had had the power, he would have killed Barak there and then; but, still half stunned and with his right arm useless, he could do no more than curse him. Barak only smiled at him with cynical satisfaction, then he said to his man:

'Keep him covered, Alexej. If he tries any tricks, put a bullet through his other arm. But don't kill him. I want to arrange his death myself.' Then he went round behind Stephanie, began to undo the cord that bound her, and added: 'We shall need this to tie him up.'

Owing to the collapse of the plaster partition at the time the house had been bombed, the back and front bedrooms on that side of it had become one. Only two stout, wooden posts which had given strength to the partition, and a heap of plaster on the floor, remained to show where it had been. When Barak had freed Stephanie, he said to Alexej: 'Get him up now. I want to tie him to one of those posts.'

Alexej gave Robbie a sharp kick and he stumbled to his feet. For a moment he contemplated striking out with his left fist, but he was still feeling very groggy and realized how futile it would be. Under the threat of Alexej's gun, jabbed against his left shoulder, he backed up against the post. Barak went round behind him and lashed him to it. When he was firmly secured, the Czech came round to the front, fingered his little hair-line moustache and said to him:

'I don't know exactly how you two turtle doves planned to get the better of me, because my wife is still reluctant to talk about it. But I guessed that you must be somewhere round and that by letting her open her mouth a little, while giving her the treatment, I should bring you running to the rescue. Anyhow, now you're both in the bag.'

He paused for a moment, then went on: 'This is a nice little hide-out you have here, Mr. Grenn. You could stay here for months without anyone being the wiser, couldn't you? And that is exactly what you are going to do. Presently, we will tear your towels and a few other things into strips and use them to tie my wife firmly to this other post. Then you can stand looking at one another until your eyes begin to pop and your swollen tongues stick out of your mouths from thirst. I'm told it takes quite a time to die that way, and it's very unpleasant. But before——'

'You . . . you! My God, if I could only get my hands on

you!' Robbie burst out, beside himself with mingled anger and terror. What Barak had said was so terribly true. Not a soul, other than those then in the room, knew about the hide-out; so, if Barak left them tied up there, before anyone found them they might have become skeletons hanging from posts in loose bundles of clothes. Their only chance, Robbie realized, lay in his being able to shout loud enough to be heard perhaps by a passer-by on the water-front. He opened his mouth to yell for help. But Alexej was too quick for him. Guessing his intention, the thug hit him a sharp blow in the stomach.

As Robbie gasped for breath, Barak nodded. 'Good work, Alexej. I doubt if anyone would hear him, but we'll take no chances so you'd better gag him.'

Seeing that one of Robbie's side-pockets was bulging with something soft, Alexej put his hand into it and pulled out the very strips of stuff that Robbie had prepared for the purpose of gagging Barak. Before he could get his wind back, Alexej had forced one of them into his mouth and tied its ends behind his head.

'Now,' said Barak. 'As I was about to say when you so rudely interrupted me, I owe you something extra for this.' He gingerly fingered his broken nose. 'Before we leave you, I mean to do some carving on your face.'

Producing a long flick-knife from his pocket, he opened it and took a step towards Robbie. Stephanie had so far remained silent, her face a picture of pain and despair. Suddenly she jumped up from the chair, seized Barak's arm with her un-injured hand, and cried:

'No; no! Not that. We've lost! I know you mean to kill us. But at least have the mercy to do it quickly.'

Snatching away his arm, Barak turned and gave her a violent push that sent her reeling back into the chair. Then he said to Alexej: 'Get behind her. Hold her down by the shoulders if she tries to interfere again. When I've finished with him we'll tie her up to the post, then we'll go and have some supper.'

As he advanced again, Robbie began to struggle violently. The cord that bound him to the post was too strong and too tightly tied for him to have any hope of freeing himself; but the post was loose, both where it entered the floorboards and about two feet above his head, where it joined the rooftree that formed the apex of the ceiling.

Barak stood for a good minute, watching his futile struggle with amusement, then he said: 'I think your nose first. We'll see what you look like when I've slit it.'

At that moment, there was a sharp knocking on the front door of the house and a voice cried in Greek: 'Open up! We know you're there. We can see chinks of light round the windows.'

Alexej was standing behind Stephanie. She opened her mouth to shout. But, as he had been with Robbie, he was too quick for her. His hands shot out, gripped her round the neck and strangled her cry.

Barak said to him in a whisper: 'Quick. Go down. Find out who it is. Get rid of them somehow—anyhow. I'll look after her.'

With a swift, cat-like tread, Alexej ran across the room and down the stairs. Barak put away his flick-knife and took a pace towards Stephanie. Then all three of them up in the bedroom strained their ears to catch further sounds from below.

They heard Alexej wrench open the front door, then the Greek voice came loud and clear: 'We are police officers. Mr. Robert Grenn, alias Monsieur Thévanaz, I have a warrant for your arrest in connection with the murder of Mr. Carl Cepicka.'

Robbie's mind took in the words as though they had been printed in poster-size letters and held in front of his eyes. The police had succeeded in tracing him after all. The trail had been clearly laid from Rhodes to Crete, yet how they could have succeeded in discovering his hide-out he could not imagine. But what did that matter? Their arrival at this moment could have been decreed only by a Divine Providence.

Then an awful thought struck him. They had taken Alexej for the man they were after. Barak had told his underling to get rid of whoever it was, 'somehow—anyhow'. The police probably had only a rough description of the wanted man and, in the uncertain light of torches down in the hall, would not get a very clear view of Alexej's features. What if he let them believe for the moment that he was Grenn—alias Max Thévanaz

—and allowed the police to march him off? Stephanie and he would again be left to Barak's mercy.

The same thought had rushed into Stephanie's mind. Again she made a move to cry out. Alexej had gone from behind her chair, but it was no more than three feet from Barak. His left hand shot out and grasped her throat in time to prevent her uttering a sound. With his right, he took her injured hand and crushed it in a sudden, fierce grip. What would have been a scream of pain passed his stranglehold on her windpipe only as an agonized gurgle. Her eyes rolled up and she slumped back in a dead faint.

Being gagged, Robbie could not cry out, but already he had resumed his desperate struggle to free himself from the post. Planting his feet firmly, he tensed all the muscles in his strong back and strained on it. Under the tug of his body, the top of the post was now attached to the rooftree by only a single nail. Compelled to witness Barak's fiendish treatment of Stephanie, Robbie was seized with a frenzy of rage. He redoubled his efforts. Barak, evidently fearing that the groaning of the post against the floorboards would catch the attention of the police below, again pulled out his knife. Flicking it open, he stepped up to Robbie and said in a fierce whisper:

'Keep still, you swine! Keep still, or I'll stick six inches of this into your stomach.'

Robbie ignored the threat. He gave another mighty heave. The old post came away at the top. Still tied to it and with his feet still planted on the floor, he suddenly fell forward. Before Barak had time to jump out of the way, the top of the post hit him on the head. He went over backwards. Robbie came down on top of him. But Robbie's last effort proved a minor repetition of Samson bringing down the pillars of the Temple. As the two men crashed to the floor, there came a rending round. The beam of the rooftree suddenly sagged. Great lumps of plaster began to fall, the room was filled with noise and dust. One of the lumps struck Robbie on the side of the head. Darkness descended on him, in which he saw flashing stars and whirling circles. Then he passed into oblivion.

*   *   *   *   *

When he came to, he was lying in bed and a nurse was bending over him. His wounded arm was strapped to his chest and his head ached abominably. For a few moments, he had no idea where he was or what had happened to him; so he asked the nurse in English. When she shook her head and murmured a few soothing words in Greek, memory flooded back to him. He was still very muzzy, but his thoughts flew to Stephanie and he stammered out an anxious enquiry.

The nurse had only a vague idea how her patient had received his injuries but she was positive that a girl had been brought in with him, suffering from nothing worse than shock and one hand with broken fingers, and that she was now in the women's ward. Unutterably relieved, Robbie drank the sedative that the nurse gave him and soon afterwards fell into a deep sleep.

He was woken by the sound of cheering outside the hospital, and wondered what could be going on. It was daylight now and his thoughts turned quickly to the events of the previous night. But he had little time to ponder them, for shortly afterwards another nurse and a doctor arrived to dress his wounded arm.

The doctor told him that the cheering had been due to the news having just come through that the war crisis was over. On the orders of the President of the United States, the trapped submarine had attempted a break-out during the night. It had succeeded and the blockading Soviet warships had not endeavoured to sink her. It had been a terrible risk to take because, if the Russians had attacked her, presumably the Americans would have retaliated by launching their rockets and strategic bomber force. Once the submarine was free of ice she might, too, have sent her missiles hurtling towards Moscow before she could be sunk. Evidently, when the Russian bluff had been called, they had had the good sense to refrain from an act which could have plunged half the world into chaos.

Robbie's arm, the doctor told him, would probably never regain its full former strength, because muscles and ligaments in it had been badly torn; but he had been lucky that the bullet had not shattered the bone, as he might then have had to have his arm amputated. He had sustained no permanent injury but the wound was inflamed, so he must remain where he was for several days.

He sent a message to Stephanie and asked for news of her. Then he was given another draught and slept again.

It was late afternoon when he was roused by the nurse looking into his cubicle. 'He's awake,' she said to someone behind her, 'but don't stay too long.' She stepped aside and Mahogany Brown came in. With a grin he sat down beside Robbie's bed, asked how he was, then said:

'Well, we fixed them. The boys went in with the Greek security people last night and caught every group cold. You were right about their intending to put nuclear bombs down those deep holes and start a chain reaction of earthquakes. What a night and day it's been. First scotching this Czech racket in the small hours, then the good news coming in that our sub. is out again in neutral waters and heading for home.'

Robbie said how pleased he was, then asked if the police had got Barak.

'He's dead,' came the prompt reply. 'The beam you were tied to hit him on the temple. His buddy got a broken jaw as a result of resisting the police and, like you, was brought to the prison hospital. He's only a few cubicles away.'

'So I'm in prison,' Robbie said.

'Why, yes. What did you expect? The police here are holding you for Cepicka's murder. But not to worry. I've already had a word with my Chief about how I met up with you, and found you were on a private venture gunning for the Czechs. When you are taken back to Athens, that will all be sorted out and you'll be given a clean bill for having killed Cepicka during your endeavours to prevent Greece being blown off the map.'

'It's good of you to have spoken to your Chief,' Robbie said gratefully. 'And I've certainly no right to complain about being under arrest. If the police hadn't come along to pick me up, I'd probably be dead by now. I wonder, though, how they managed to trace me. Do you happen to know?'

Mahogany Brown grinned broadly. 'Sure. I put them on to you.'

'You what?' exclaimed Robbie indignantly, pushing himself up with his good elbow. With an 'ouch' of pain, he quickly sank back again as the American replied:

'If you'd lunched at the Ariadne, as you told me you were going to, you'd have still more to thank me for. You'd have escaped getting a bullet through the arm and what I gather must have been a pretty sticky time while Barak had you cornered. I tipped off the police to pick you up at the Ariadne. As you weren't there and didn't come into the Candia Palace at seven o'clock, they alerted all stations to keep a look-out for you. They might not have found you for days, but for a lucky break. Your girl friend left her car with the lights on in the middle of a quarter of a mile of rubble. A patrolman went over to investigate, checked the car number with the one I'd given when I filed your description, and jumped to it that the pair of you must be somewhere in the offing. He telephoned his H.Q., and they sent out a search party. They spotted chinks of light coming from your hide-out and that was that.'

'But why?' Robbie asked in a puzzled voice. 'What conceivable reason had you for turning me in?'

'It wasn't you I was worried about. It was Mrs. B. who had to be put out of circulation. You admitted to me that you'd told her about your earthquake theory, and I wasn't trusting you not to tell her that I had fallen for it. Knowing that, she might have managed to get a message through to her pals, alerting the whole set-up that we were on to them. If a tip-off had got through, they could have dumped their bombs in the sea before our people had the chance to get them with the goods.'

'You're talking nonsense,' Robbie protested. 'She was on our side and doing her utmost to help me.'

The American gave a disbelieving shrug. 'She was Barak's wife and we knew that she was being used to keep tabs on you.'

'She was to begin with; but, as I told you, Barak tried to kill her. Naturally, that altered everything. After that——'

'It altered nothing. Communists, like other people, may change their sex relationships, but they don't stop being Communists. She was still selling you down the river.'

'She was not! I swear she wasn't!' Robbie cried indignantly.

'She was. We have proof of that. On Barak's body the police found a letter. It was from her, admitting that she'd slipped up, but asking to be taken back into the good books of the Party. As the price of her pardon, she offered to sell you out to him.'

'But . . . but,' Robbie stammered, 'she wrote that with my knowledge. We'd planned to lure Barak here and get the truth out of him, but he turned the tables on us. That's how it was that our car happened to be left outside for so long with the lights on. He prevented her from coming out and driving off in it.'

'Where were you at that time?'

'Hiding just outside. Our plan was that she should tell Barak that I'd be back in half an hour, and then leave him there. We hadn't counted on his bringing another man with him. We thought that, after he had waited there for a couple of hours and I hadn't shown up, he'd get sick of waiting and come out on his own. Then I meant to sand-bag him from behind.'

'Very nice. But it didn't work, eh? And I don't have to be a crystal-gazer to tell you what happened. Instead of coming out, she stayed there chatting with him about this and that for a while. Then he told her to open her pretty mouth and let out a yodel or two, so that you'd hear and think he was beating her up. You fell for it and came bursting in to rescue her. Isn't that just what you did?'

'Yes. That's why I went in. But you are utterly wrong about her. She didn't lure me into an ambush. The cries I heard were because she was being tortured.'

'So you say.'

After thinking hard for a moment, Robbie exclaimed triumphantly: 'Her hand is the proof of it. That fiend Barak had broken two of her fingers. When they lugged me up into that room, her hand was all out of shape and bleeding. You have only to go over to the women's ward to check on that. When I came to in the night and asked about her, the nurse told me that Stephanie had suffered no other injury but, as I feared, some fingers on one of her hands were broken.'

Mahogany Brown stood up. 'I've a lot to do, so I must get

along now. But listen, pal. You say the nurse told you about this hand. Well, it could easily have been crushed by a falling brick, and there's only your word for it that she got her injury any other way. I know you're nuts about this dame, and you're not the first guy who's been prepared to swear black is white in the hope of getting his sweetie out of trouble. But it's just no good. She's in this up to the neck.'

Robbie was appalled at the thought that Stephanie was believed to have aided her husband and that there might be no way in which her innocence could be proved. 'What . . . what d'you mean to do with her?' he asked hoarsely.

The American's reply was shattering. 'Why, she'll be shipped back to Athens with the other saboteurs we've caught in Crete. Maybe she'll get a prison sentence, maybe the Greeks will be satisfied by ordering that she's to be repatriated to her own country. Anyhow, except in a Court of Justice, you won't be seeing her again, so the sooner you forget her, the better.'

Epilogue

I T W A S a week later, the 7th of May. Robbie had been back in Athens for two days. On his second day in hospital in Crete, a senior police official had taken a long statement from him. The following morning the British Consul had come to see him, with a message from his uncle that his case would be put in good hands and that he was not to worry. The Consul had then offered his services, if there was anything he could do. Robbie had asked him to find out about Stephanie, and had later received a note informing him that she was being flown back to Athens under escort that evening, with the other Czech prisoners.

His wound was clean and mending well. On the Sunday he had been pronounced fit to travel and, also under escort, had followed her that afternoon. At the Athens airport he had been met by his uncle's P.A., and it then transpired that Sir Finsterhorn had entered into recognizance for him. His escort handed him over and he found himself a free man or, at least, in the position of one on bail.

Six weeks earlier, the knowledge that he would have to give an account of himself to his uncle would have made him sweat with fear, but the Robbie Grenn who had left Athens towards the end of March was an utterly different person from the one who returned there early in May. During those few weeks he had changed from a shy, overgrown adolescent to a self-confident, mature young man.

He had accepted his uncle's message as a normal expression of *esprit de corps*, to be expected from an older relative when a member of his family was in trouble in a foreign country. However, he took it for granted that Sir Finsterhorn would

ent most strongly his having got himself into a situation
ere he had killed a man and been hunted by the police.
hogany Brown had, he imagined, taken all the credit for
ving the riddle of the oil-prospecting by the Czechs, so he
l no expectation of receiving praise for that; but at least he
l the satisfaction of knowing that, however angry his uncle
ght be with him, he would now be able to face a dressing-
wn with complete indifference.

In consequence, when he reached the Embassy he was all
more surprised by his reception. Lady Grenn had returned
m England. She greeted him like a long-lost son, saying
w worried she had been about him, and showing great con-
n over his wound. Sir Finsterhorn stood beside her, patted
n twice on his unwounded arm and said: 'We haven't had
full story yet, Robbie, but we've heard enough to be very
ud of you.'

That evening, suppressing only the episode with Stephanie
the pool, he had given them an account of all that had hap-
ned to him since he had started on his self-imposed mission.
then learned that Mahogany Brown had not taken all the
dit, but had reported that they had been working together
l had given him a share of it. Sir Finsterhorn had been told
t by Luke Beecham, who in turn had had it from Mahogany
own's Chief. Before they went up to bed, Robbie had begged
uncle to help him save Stephanie from the terrible situation
which she was placed, and the Ambassador had promised
do everything that lay within his power.

On the Monday, accompanied by the lawyer who acted for
British Embassy, Robbie went to the Ministry of Justice.
ey had a long interview with a high official who was in
arge of the prosecution against the Czechs. The upshot of it
s that, as it had been Barak who had brought the charge
ainst Robbie of murdering Cepicka, and Barak was now
ad, it was probable that the charge would be dropped; but, if
Czechs insisted on a trial, one would have to be held. How-
er, in the circumstances, that was most unlikely and, should
happen, a plea of self-defence would certainly be accepted.
bbie anxiously asked about Stephanie's prospects; but the

official would say no more than that she would be brought
trial with her compatriots, and it was not for him to foreca
the sentence she would receive.

That evening Robbie dined with his good friend Luk
thanked him for taking the steps that had set Mahogany Brov
on the warpath, and again recounted his adventures. But whe
it came to Stephanie's prospects, Luke proved far from hopefu
He had heard on the side that the Czech Travel Bureau ha
been raided and among the papers seized had been Stephanie
reports of Robbie's activities in Patras, Corinth and Pirgos. I
the face of those and her last letter to her husband, Luke fe
than any plea that Robbie might make for her would be di
regarded, in the belief that he had become so enamoured o
her as a mistress that he would go to any lengths to get he
off; so, in spite of all he could say, she would be sent to prison

On Tuesday Robbie could settle to nothing. All day h
thoughts were never far from Stephanie, alternating betwee
desperate depression at the thought of the fate that might l
in store for her, and hope that his uncle might succeed in ge
ting her released after an interview that he was to have wit
the Minister for Home Affairs the following morning.

And now it was just before lunch on Wednesday. Sir Fir
sterhorn had come in from his interview and was facing Robbi
in his study. In reply to Robbie's almost breathless enquir
he replied:

'Well; I have good news for you. In the first place the Gree
Government wish to give you a decoration—and a good one
too.'

'What!' Robbie's eyes opened wide. 'A decoration
For me!'

'Yes, my boy.' Sir Finsterhorn patted him on his good arm
'A decoration for gallantry. From now on, whenever you hav
to attend a full-dress function, you'll be able to hold up you
head with the best of them. Of course, I must get permissio
from our people for you to accept it, but there will be n
trouble about that. I'd have recommended you for a Britis
decoration myself, if I'd thought there was any chance of you
getting it. But now that we live in the era of the Welfare State

corations are more or less reserved for fellows who can boost
r export market, do things for charity or have sat behind a
sk for thirty years without blotting their copy books.'

'Thanks, Uncle,' Robbie said quickly. 'But what about
ephanie?'

'Good news there, too. They are fully convinced of her
ilt, of course; but, as a gesture of goodwill to me—and to
u—they've agreed not to prosecute. They will only inform
r Legation that she is *persona non grata* and must be sent
ck to Czechoslovakia.'

'But . . . but,' Robbie stammered, 'that's worse . . . worse
an her being in prison here. Her own people know she
uble-crossed them. They'll send her to the uranium mines.
e'll die a lingering death from radio-activity. It's condemn-
g her for two years to a living hell.'

*   *   *   *   *

That afternoon, Robbie again took a taxi to the parking
ace below the Acropolis. Slowly, he climbed the steep slope
the Propylaea, mounted its great, broken steps and came out
to the lofty plateau. Now that it was May, it was baking hot
there. The sun blazed down relentlessly, making the stones
t to the touch and dazzling to the eyes. Owing to the great
at, no conducted tours were scheduled to be taken round
in the early hours of the afternoon; so only a few perspiring
urists and people inured to tropical sunshine were strolling
out the ruins.

Robbie made his way over to Athene's olive tree. Casting
quick look round, to make sure that he was not observed, he
ok a small medicine bottle from his pocket. It contained
other ration of his uncle's port, to which he had helped him-
lf after lunch was over. Pouring the wine as a libation at the
ot of the tree, he bowed his head and said in his thoughts:

'Great Goddess, you told me that, for the sake of my
untry and for yours, I must go on to the bitter end. Well, with
ephanie's help I've done that. But must the end be so bitter?'

A light breeze rustled the leaves of the little olive tree, a a golden voice replied: 'Strange mortal, who in this mod age still has faith in the great ones of Olympus. One by the cruel gods who demanded human sacrifices have di Now, those who have for so long demanded sacrifice of self a dreary life of humility, poverty, fasting, chastity and s denial, are also dying. But we, who are no more than the el brothers and sisters of men and women, created by the Ma of All Things with the same weaknesses and strengths, given greater powers; we, whose only wish is to see each hun derive the maximum of joy from life, are the true Immort We shall live on for ever, and never lack the power to grant prayers of those who believe in us.'

Then the great goddess Pallas Athene told Robbie Gra exactly what to do.

*   *   *   *   *

The following morning, Robbie secured a special permi visit Stephanie in prison. The Deputy-Governor received h and handed him over to the head wardress, with instructi that he should be allowed to talk to the prisoner for half hour, on the same footing as if he were her lawyer.

In consequence, he was taken to a waiting room in wh there was no barrier between prisoner and visitor, but sim a wooden table and a few chairs. Stephanie was brought th and the wardress who escorted her took a chair in the corri outside.

Stephanie's hand was still bandaged and her face v drawn; but she raised a faint smile as she entered the roc and said: 'It's nice of you to come, Robbie. I hadn't expec to see you again.'

He cleared his throat and asked: 'You know what th intend to do with you?'

She nodded. 'Yes. They told me this morning. I'm not be charged with the others. I'm to be handed over to my Le tion to be repatriated.'

'And we both know what that means.'

'Don't, Robbie, please. I . . . I'd rather not talk about it.'

'But I must. I want to know if you think there is any chance their letting you off.'

She shook her head. 'No. They'll add it to my other crimes t I was responsible for bringing about Václav's death. For t, they would never forgive me. If only they'd kill me and ve done. But they won't. They . . . they'll send me to the nium mines. But please, please——'

Seeing her intense distress, Robbie cut her short and said: e come here to suggest a way out for you.'

'There isn't one,' she said pessimistically. 'I know you'd p me if you could, Robbie. But there's nothing you can do.'

'Yes, there is,' he blurted out. 'I can marry you. If you are rried to me, you'll become a British citizen. No one will able to send you back to Czechoslovakia then.'

Her blue eyes wide open to their fullest extent, she stood ring at him as he hurried on: 'Of course, I know you don't e me; so I'm not suggesting that it should be a real marriage, hough it would have to be a legal one. We . . . we'd live gether only as we did in Rhodes. I'd take you to England h me. Then, after a few months, I'd let you divorce me. t you'd be safe there. And, later on, perhaps you'd meet ne nice chap that you liked . . . and . . . and——'

Tears suddenly welled out of Stephanie's eyes and began run down her cheeks. She laid her sound hand on his good n and choked out:

'Of course I'll marry you. Even if you were the most revolt- man on earth, any woman in my position would be crazy refuse such an offer. But . . . but tell me something. Down the pool at Olympia. Did you . . . did you do what you did t because you wished to humiliate me . . . to be avenged? because you wanted to? I mean, had wanted to for some e?'

'Well, I was angry with you,' Robbie admitted. 'It was t which gave me the courage. But I'd been having to struggle h myself for days, not to seize hold of you and kiss you as ugh I'd never stop.'

A radiant smile suddenly broke through Stephanie's tears,

and she whispered: 'Then need we . . . need we think abo‑
divorce? Oh, Robbie, you're so different from any other r
I've ever known. So kind, so gentle, so brave. Everythir
woman could ever want. I think I've loved you from the v
moment I met you.'

DENNIS WHEATLEY

OTHER BEST-SELLING *Arrow* TITLES

DUKE DE RICHLEAU

Strange Conflict

The Forbidden Territory

The Golden Spaniard

The Prisoner in the Mask

The Second Seal

Codeword—Golden Fleece

Three Inquisitive People

Vendetta in Spain

The Devil Rides Out

DENNIS WHEATLEY

OTHER BEST-SELLING *Arrow* TITLES

GREGORY SALLUST

Black August

Contraband

The Scarlet Impostor

Faked Passports

The Black Baroness

V for Vengeance

Come into My Parlour

Traitors' Gate

The Island where Time Stands Still
